MW01297156

THUNDER AND STORM:
THE HAVERFIELD INCIDENT

A NOVEL

BY
RICK AINSWORTH

This book is a work of fiction. All names, characters, places and incidents portrayed in this novel are the product of the author's imagination or are used fictitiously. Any resemblance to actual events, locales, or persons, living or dead, is coincidental.

Published by VRA Publishing of Las Vegas
www.vrapublishing.com

Thunder & Storm: The Haverfield Incident. Copyright © 2005 by Rick Ainsworth. All rights reserved. Printed in the United States of America. No part of this book may be used or reproduced in any manner whatsoever without written permission except in the case of brief quotations embodied in critical articles and reviews. For information, address VRA Publishing, 965 Aspen Valley Ave, Las Vegas, NV 89123.

Cover design and formatting by Matt Mitchell (mattmitchelldesign.com)

Original Cover artwork by Therese Van Rijn

Edited by Debbie Hall (hallwayprod@yahoo.com)

ISBN: 0-9770376-0-6
       978-0-9770376-0-5

Library of Congress control number: 2005905878

The trademark JACK DANIEL'S appears courtesy of Jack Daniel's Properties, Inc. JACK DANIEL'S is a registered trademark of Jack Daniel's Properties, Inc.

The trademark COORS appears courtesy of Coors Global Properties. COORS is a registered trademark of Coors Global Properties.

The trademark PEPSI appears courtesy of Pepsico, Inc. PEPSI is a registered trademark of Pepsico, Inc.

The trademark ZIPPO appears courtesy of Zippo Manufacturing Company. ZIPPO is a registered trademark of Zippo Manufacturing Company.

The trademark PABST BLUE RIBBON appears courtesy of Pabst Brewing Company. PABST BLUE RIBBON is a registered trademark of Pabst Brewing Company.

The trademark BRASSO appears courtesy of Reckitt-Benckiser, Inc. BRASSO is a registered trademark of Reckitt-Benckiser, Inc.

The trademark SAN MIGUEL BEER appears courtesy of San Miguel Corporation. SAN MIGUEL BEER is a registered trademark of San Miguel Corporation.

FOR THERESE:
My partner,
My best friend,
My wonderful wife.

AND FOR IRENE M. DAVIS AND ROBERT H. DAVIS:
May the good Lord bless their souls,
and hold them forever in the hollow of his hand.

ALONE

From childhood's hour I have not been
As others were - I have not seen
As others saw - I could not bring
My passions from a common spring.
From the same source I have not taken
My sorrow - I could not awaken
My heart to joy at the same tone -
And all I loved - I loved alone.

Then - in my childhood - in the dawn
Of a most stormy life-was drawn
From every depth of good and ill
The mystery which binds me still -
From the torrent, or the fountain -
From the red cliff of the mountain -
From the sun that 'round me roll'd
In its autumn tint of gold -
From the lightning in the sky
As it passed me flying by -
From the thunder, and the storm -
And the cloud that took the form
(When the rest of heaven was blue)
Of a demon in my view.

—Edgar Allan Poe
1829

PROLOGUE

Newport Beach, California
January, 2003

The letter arrived just before lunch. It was in a plain white envelope and had no return address. R.J. had been glancing through the morning mail impatiently to distract him from his real problem. His computer had been freezing up and he couldn't run the daily interest rates. To make matters worse, the damn IT guy was stuck in traffic on the Santa Ana Freeway and couldn't get there until early afternoon! When he saw the envelope he stopped rifling through the mail. There was something unusual about this particular envelope. It was written in a sloppy hand, obviously addressed in a hurry. R.J. looked at the postmark, Selma, Alabama, and wondered who in hell would be writing him from Alabama. It appeared to be personal in nature, but had been delivered to his office with the business mail. Impatient to get to his lunch date, R.J. slit open the envelope with his letter opener and sat for a moment, staring blankly at the short, terrifying note. Suddenly, his head was swimming with a tangled stream of memories from many years ago. He sat staring at the note for what seemed like an eternity before his secretary stuck her head in the door.

"Hey, boss, you going to lunch, or you going to sit here day-dreaming?" Pamela Brown asked, arching her eyebrows, a sly smile on her face. She pushed her glasses up over her forehead, and they disappeared into her soft, brown hair. Her left hand was on her hip and she held an ever-present file folder in her other hand.

R.J. didn't answer. He just scowled. Pamela took the hint and quietly walked back to her desk. R.J. got up from his desk, put on his suit jacket, carefully folded the letter back into its envelope and slid it into his inside jacket pocket. Frowning, he put on his sunglasses, picked up the keys to his Cadillac CTS and walked out the front door of the mortgage office, waving idly to the receptionist who started to say something, but he was out the door.

He slid behind the wheel of the Cadillac and started it up. The purr of the engine gave him a comfortable, secure feeling as it came alive, and he felt confident and in control like he always did when driving the Caddy. It was a magnificent machine. Then he remembered the letter. *After all these years someone was dredging up the past.* A chilly fear rippled through his stomach and he knew he should get something to eat, or the acid would begin its burning march. He wheeled the Caddy onto the southbound 405 freeway and headed for the Split Rock Tavern in Laguna Hills. He concentrated on maneuvering the car through the traffic, pushing any other thoughts from his mind. He exited the freeway at El Toro Road, turned down Valencia Ave and pulled into the parking lot of the "Rock." It was just past noon. He made a quick call to the office and told Pamela to cancel his lunch appointment. He wasn't in the mood to eat or conduct business. *The Raven was back.*

Trent the bartender saw him coming and had R.J.'s Jack Daniel's and rocks sitting on the bar. "Mr. *DAVIS* is in the house," he announced cheerfully to the four customers seated at the bar. R.J. picked up his drink, nodded to Trent and motioned with his head toward the back of the bar. Trent bowed low, smiled and wiped his hands on a bar towel. R.J. sat in the back booth, sipping his drink, trying to get up the courage to read the letter again. The envelope felt like it was burning a hole through his suit jacket. His mind wandered back over forty years, stretching, reaching into the past, seeking to blow away the almost opaque mist that shrouded his memory. He felt the dark specter of the Raven casting its shadow over him, pushing him deep into sorrow and depression, all too familiar feelings he had fought all his life. The Raven sat in the deep dark corner of his imagination, always staring, never blinking, never speaking, just sitting and staring. Gulping down half his drink, he took the letter out of his jacket pocket and unfolded it on the table. He read it again. It was short and simple:

> *My name is Rafer Sample, Jr. and I believe you were in the Navy with my daddy. Do you remember August 1964 and what happened on that ship? My daddy told me that something very bad happened on that ship, and my uncle Andy won't talk about it. Daddy told me to look you up and get the story from you. He said you would tell me the truth because you had an honest heart. Daddy died last month and on his deathbed he asked me to pray for him because of what happened. He took the secret to his grave. I need to talk to you.*
> *Rafer Sample Jr.*
> *770-555-3520*

R.J. hadn't thought about the Haverfield incident for a long time. He had pushed it down deep into his subconscious, to reside there quietly among the unhappy memories of his youth in Denver. He had assumed everyone else had forgotten the incident too. At times he almost believed it had never happened. But it did...almost forty years ago.

PART ONE:

ARRIVAL

ONE

Apra Harbor, Guam
March 6, 1963
2300 Hours

R.J. Davis, RMSA, got out of the Navy gray pickup truck and slammed the door shut. He took a breath of heavy, humid tropical air, which felt like a wet wool mattress thrown over his face, and pulled his seabag out of the bed of the truck, dropping it in a heap at his feet. He stood on the dock looking at his new duty station; his first ship, the U.S.S. Haverfield DER-393. She was moored starboard side about halfway down the long concrete pier, a hundred yards forward of her sister ship, the U.S.S. Brister DER-327. He was exhausted after the long flight from Honolulu on the crowded MATS jet. He felt dirty in his dress blues, in need of a shower, and the humidity of Guam, where everyone was wearing whites, seemed to paste his wool uniform to his body. *If it's this hot late at night*, he thought, *what was it like during the day?* His excitement at finally getting a chance for sea duty was dampened by the appearance of his new duty station, and it depressed him. *Figures*, he thought, sighing and looking at the ship, *they're gonna keep on punishing me.*

The Haverfield sat low in the water, the tide out, and at first look was not an impressive vessel. A canvas awning was erected to cover her fantail, and on every level and every bulkhead R.J. could see red lead anti-rust paint covering sanded down patches, awaiting the final painting of the ever present Navy gray. Her hull number was obscured by more red lead in anticipation of new paint, but he could make out the numerals, 393. Hoses of all types and sizes originated on the pier and snaked along her scuffed and travel-worn decks, disappearing down through several deck hatches into her bowels below. Forward on the yardarm the signal lanyards hung limp in the damp night air, and the radar mast amidships seem to strain as it hefted on its beam the custom made, round black radar antennae for which the radar picket ship was named. She looked badly in need of repairs. *I hope that's what's going on*, he thought. She reminded him of descriptions of the ship in *The Caine Mutiny*, a novel he had read in radio school. R.J. sighed. IIis first ship did not look likc it bclongcd in the United States Navy, at least not in the Navy he had heard so proudly described by his father and his uncles. All three of them had served in the 'old' Navy during World War II, and had regaled him with stories as he was growing up. This ship looked more like it belonged in the Guamanian Navy. *Does Guam even have a Navy?*

The ship's truck driver, Billy Lopez, a handsome, dark-haired sailor from Los Angeles with a charming smile, gunned the engine of the pickup and swung it around in a big arc. "Go on aboard and give your orders to the OOD," he called. "Tell him I'm parking the limo and I'll be right back." He waved, smiled that charming smile, and popped the clutch of the old truck so it leaped forward. R.J. watched as Charming Billy gunned the pick-up truck, grinding the gears toward a Quonset hut perched back from the dock. R.J. smiled at Billy and the old, beat up pickup. *Just like the cars me and my friends drove as we cruised up and down Main Street in Longmont, Colorado,* R.J. thought. He smiled at the memory. Up and down Main Street, daylight and dark, regardless of weather, from South Johnson's Corner to North Johnson's Corner. Cruising all day and all night, drinking 3.2 Coors, honking at each other, honking at the girls, drag racing and ducking the cops. To think all that happened just a little over a year ago. Longmont, Colorado seemed a long way away from where he was now standing. A very long way, indeed.

"Hey boot-camp," the OOD bellowed from the quarterdeck, "Y'all comin' aboard or you waitin' for an escort?"

R.J. snapped out of it and his memories evaporated into the thick night air. He hefted his seabag onto his shoulder and looked up at the quarterdeck. *Oh well,* he thought, *back to reality.* He sighed and strode up the brow to the quarterdeck. Stopping at the top, he saluted aft and then saluted the OOD. "Davis, R.J. reporting for duty, sir," he said as he handed over his orders.

The Officer Of the Deck was not actually an officer. Officers being in short supply in the 'Coconut Navy,' the OOD on duty was a second class electrician's mate named Crawford. A tall, thin good ol' boy from Mississippi with an easy grin and a lazy slouch, he took the envelope from R.J. and looked him over, up and down, slowly appraising the fresh-faced nineteen-year-old. "Damn, boy, you look like you about fourteen," he scoffed good-naturedly. "You run away from reform school or somethin'?"

R.J. nodded. "Something like that, sir."

"Sir?" Crawford bellowed, aghast. "Why you callin' me sir? See this whitehat?" Crawford pointed to his head. "I ain't no officer, boy. My parents were married. You only say sir to officers. And let me tell you somethin' else, boot-boy, why you salutin' the fantail? You only salute the fantail when there's a flag flyin' there, and we don't fly no flag at night. Shit," Crawford walked to the water side of the ship and spat into the harbor, slowly shaking his head in disgust. "Don't they teach you kids nothin' in boot camp?" The entire time Crawford was talking he was also recording R.J.'s information into the ship's log. "OK, kid," Crawford smiled to show he was only giving the new guy a hard time, "sign this here log and you are officially a Havernaut." His brow furrowed as if he were trying hard to think. It appeared to be difficult for him. "Of course, you ain't really a Havernaut," he cautioned, "till you been to your Thunder Party."

R.J. looked puzzled. "Thunder party?" he asked, signing the log.

The messenger of the watch returned from his hourly rounds checking the ship's duty section and heard the last of the conversation. "New meat, huh?" he asked, nodding and looking R.J. over. "Better tell the 'Nauts to get ready to thunder." He laughed and slapped Crawford on the back.

"This here's Tanner," Crawford said, as if describing a misbehaving child. He hooked a thumb toward the messenger. "He from Philly, so he ain't too bright." Crawford grinned good-naturedly. "But he'll find you a rack to sleep in for the night until you're assigned one permanent."

Tanner leaned on the quarterdeck desk and smiled. He was short, stocky and had a casual air of confidence in his bright blue eyes. He took off his whitehat and ran his hand through his dark, straight hair, replaced the whitehat and carefully straightened it on his head. The hat had been worked and kneaded into the perfect shape and Tanner was proud of the way it fit, cocked forward just a bit, its starched sides creased into perfectly shaped wings. To R.J., Tanner looked like the quintessential Navy sailor. His white uniform was starched and pressed, and his shoes gleamed with a carefully-applied spit shine. Tanner reached over and offered his hand. "P.T. Tanner," he announced. "Happy to meet you."

R.J. shook Tanner's hand. "R.J. Davis," he said, smiling wearily. "What's the P.T. stand for?"

"What's the R.J. stand for?" Tanner countered.

"Ruben James," R.J. said. "But don't tell nobody."

"OK," Tanner laughed, "but everyone already knows what the P.T. stands for." He grinned mischievously at R.J.

"So, what does it stand for?" R.J. was curious.

"Well, it was 'cause of my Dad, see. He worked in a circus when he was a young kid and he heard all the old stories about P.T. Barnum while he was sitting around the fire with the other roustabouts. He became a fan. So he vowed to name his first son after the great P.T. Barnum, and I am his first son." Tanner slowly chewed his lip, thinking. "His only son, actually," he decided.

"That's it?" R.J. asked. "P.T. just stands for P.T.?"

"Phineas Taylor," Tanner replied, shrugging his shoulders with his hands out, palms up. "What can I tell you? Most guys just call me Tanner."

"OK, Tanner," R.J. grinned. "What's the chances of getting a shower?"

"Real good," Tanner replied. "You're lucky we're in port, so we have fresh water." He looked R.J. over and grinned. "Looks like you could use a shower," he said.

R.J. pulled his jumper away from his damp skin. "You only have fresh water when you're in port?" he asked, squirming in the hot blue uniform.

"When we're steaming, the evaps don't always work and we don't get enough fresh water," Tanner explained. "Know how we shower then?"

"Use salt water?" R.J. ventured.

"Naw, that ain't healthy. We just head for the nearest rain squall and everybody gets up on deck and douches off." He chuckled and motioned for R.J. to follow him aft.

R.J. didn't buy Tanner's yarn at all. He knew when his leg was being pulled, but he was having a little trouble keeping up as Tanner led him down a hatch to the after crew's compartment. Tanner moved down hatches and through passageways effortlessly, wasting no motion getting to where he was going. He obviously knew the ship well.

Sailors were asleep in their racks everywhere, separated by only a few inches side-to-side and by about a foot top-to-bottom. The compartment felt more oppressive than topside, and smelled of sweat, paint, diesel fuel and some other odors R.J. didn't want to think about.

"Grab that top rack there," Tanner pointed to the top of a three-tier bunk, with the bottom two occupied by snoring, smelly sailors. "Stow away your gear and I'll show you where the showers are." He watched the new guy curiously as R.J. folded his clothes and neatly stowed everything in a metal locker built into the bottom of the three-tier bunks. Tanner smiled at R.J.'s neatness and thought, *the new guy still folds and stores his gear according to regulations.* Tanner figured R.J. would be a slob like the rest of them in about two months. He grinned and nodded approval when R.J. was done, then led him up an interior ladder to the after crew's head, which housed the showers. "I got to get back on watch," Tanner said. "You can find your way back, can't you?" Without waiting for an answer, Tanner disappeared down through a hatch and headed back to the quarterdeck. Crawford would have the cribbage board set up, ready to play, probably ready to cheat to win. Tanner was determined to 'skunk' the redneck old bastard before the off-duty crew returned from their nightly rowdiness up at the Mocombo Club.

R.J. stood in the shower and let the hot water pour down on his head for what seemed like a heavenly eternity. The eighteen-hour trip on a crowded, cramped MATS jet from San Francisco to Honolulu and then to Guam had tired him to the bone, and he was really feeling it now that his body began slowly to relax. As he turned off the shower and started toweling down, he heard a ruckus in the passageway that passed through the after crew's head. Four figures in Navy whites, their hats askew on their heads, obviously inebriated, strolled through the head singing a rendition of the Moonglows' "*Sincerely.*" It was a sour, off-key rendition and R.J. had to smile.

As the four approached the shower area of the head, they noticed an unfamiliar figure there toweling down. All four stopped short, which caused a chain reaction as they ran into the backs of each other, and watched as R.J. dried himself, then tied the towel around his waist. He looked at the four men and smiled. "Hi," he called.

"Up yers, Wog," spat the tallest, a lean and mean-looking boatswains mate third class. He thought for a moment, concentrating, head down. He looked up again and said, "Fuck you, Wog."

The other three nodded solemnly, as if they had thought it through and found themselves in total concurrence with Tall-Guy. "Wait a minute, Lester," one of the others offered. "Maybe he ain't a Wog." Number two squinted drunkenly at R.J. "Maybe he been across," he speculated, squinting harder, trying to focus.

"Bullshit," Lester retorted. "This Wog's as white as my little sister's ass. He ain't been nowhere yet."

"Let's ask him," number three suggested, proud he could contribute.

"OK," number two said. "Hey boy," he challenged, squinting at R.J. "You ever been across the line?"

R.J. admitted he hadn't, since he didn't know what the 'line' was.

"Fuck you, Wog," Lester said. The four left the head laughing and sourly singing as they faded down the passageway.

Later in his rack, weary but intrigued, R.J. stared blankly at the overhead, snaked full of pipes and wires, going to and coming from God-knows-where, and wondered if he would ever get any sleep. The long trip had worn him out, to the point of exhaustion, yet he was wide-awake and staring at the overhead.

Two minutes later he fell into a sound sleep, while trying to fathom what in the hell's a "Wog." One thing was certain: Wog wasn't a compliment.

TWO

Next morning R.J. awoke at 05:30, a half-hour before reveille, and was one of only three sailors in the after crew's head, shaving, brushing teeth and combing hair. R.J. finished quickly and returned to the compartment quietly, so as not to wake the others, and put on his dungarees and white-hat. He then set off to find his way topside.

Up on deck, the morning air was still quite heavy with humidity but not yet as oppressive as it would be later in the day. It smelled fresh and clean to R.J., especially after a night in the after crew's compartment. R.J. didn't think he would ever adjust to living so close to other men. The harbor before him was peaceful and calm, the water like blown glass, glowing with a colorful light reflecting the warm tropical sunrise. *It's breathtaking, really*, R.J. thought, watching the soft, white round clouds gathering high atop that mountain to the northeast. *What was that mountain called?* The golden glowing warmth spread across the sky like paint spilled on the deck, growing brighter, stronger, more brilliant in concert with the rising morning sun.

"The ship might not be much to look at," R.J. mumbled, "but this is sure a hell of a view." He slowly drank it all in, the deep green colors of the vegetation contrasted against the cobalt blue waves of the Pacific churning out past the breakwater. He sighed, resting his head back, face to the dawn, basking in the soft brush of the sunlight as it gently painted his face. The water in the harbor splashed quietly against the ship. He breathed in the fresh morning air in large gulps and exhaled each breath slowly, savoring the sweet freshness. He smiled at the inner glow he felt, and while he didn't realize it, he was establishing a ritual he would repeat each and every morning the Haverfield was in port, for as long as he was a member of her crew. This morning he felt peacefully happy with the world. He knew he could put his past troubles in the past. He looked around, smiling at the glorious new morning, full of hope and the promise of a new day, and saw the hope and promise of a new start for himself. He was stationed a long way out of the mainstream of the Navy, exiled to an isolated and lonely outpost, but he felt he had a chance in this God-forsaken place for a new beginning, a new start, a second chance. He felt a little like the Beau Geste of the Navy. He would begin his Navy career anew, forget the past, overcome the bad start. *Yes*, he thought, *my problems are behind me.*

In that moment, he could not have known how wrong he was.

"Hey, man!" Tanner came up behind R.J. as he was gazing at the harbor scene. "You ain't gonna jump in, are you?"

R.J. turned and smiled. "I was thinking of a morning swim," he replied.

"Naw, you don't want to jump in this water," Tanner explained. "This water is full of garbage and a lot of crap from the ships and the gooks who work here. There's some nasty shit floating in this harbor."

"How often does this ship go out to sea?" R.J. asked.

"Whenever we get orders to patrol," Tanner answered. "We hit maybe two islands a day for about three weeks, then back here to lay low and do repairs. This old tub ain't as young as she used to be. She's like any old broad. Needs lots of tender loving care." He chuckled at a private memory.

"We patrol islands?"

"Yeah. We land on 'em and make sure the native people are OK, and we keep the Japs from fishing around the islands. This whole area belongs to the United States. Don't want nobody fuckin' with it," Tanner explained. "See ya later." He waved and started to leave.

"Hey Tanner," R.J. stopped him. "Last night I met a few of the crew and they called me a Wog. What's a Wog?"

Tanner grinned wide and nodded at R.J. "Yep, you a Wog alright," he laughed.

"OK, but what's a Wog?" R.J. persisted.

Before Tanner could answer, a short, pleasant looking radioman 3rd class came walking aft toward them. "You must be Davis, the new radioman," he said, offering his hand, which R.J. took. "I'm Riley and I'm supposed to show you around this here Haverbucket. You hungry?"

"Not really," R.J. replied, "I'm still trying to get my bearings. That was a long flight from San Francisco." R.J. related how the enlisted men on the flight had been assigned to help dependents, mostly wives and kids joining their husbands serving on Guam. R.J. had drawn a chubby little moon-faced brunette with slightly crossed eyes and two moon-faced children who whined incessantly at their mother, who whined incessantly back.

"I wanted to ask her if she would like me to slap the shit out of those kids for her, but I figured it was a waste of time." R.J. shook his head. "I didn't get any sleep on that flight."

Riley sighed and put his hand over his heart. "San Francisco? You flew out of San Francisco? Ah, San Francisco, City by the Sea, Baghdad by the Bay. The promised land. I left my heart there, you know?" He smiled and stared off into space for a few moments. Shaking his head, he motioned for R.J. to follow him. "Yeah, San Francisco is my city. I fell in love with a little chink in Frisco but she dumped me because her chink family didn't want her running with a round-eye." He shook his head sadly. "She was fucking beautiful, you know? Cutest little butt you ever saw." Riley stopped and pointed a finger at R.J. "See, the main difference between chink girls and jap girls is the butt. The japs have dumpy asses," he explained, "but Chinese women maintain a tight ass up into their fifties. Trust me, I've made an exhaustive study of the subject." He shook his head in admiration. "Man, she had the cutest little butt." Riley drifted off again, remembering fondly, then quickly snapped out of it. "C'mon, I'll show you the radio shack. That's where you're gonna spend most of your time."

"Hey Riley," R.J. said. "What's a Wog?"

Riley started to answer, but stopped when he spotted a burly chief petty officer coming toward them in the passageway. "Shit, here comes Twitchell," he swore. "Duck in here." He led R.J. into a small compartment filled with paperwork, filing cabinets, a beat up Olivetti typewriter and a tiny desk. "This is the yeoman's office," he explained. "As you can see, it's a one-man job. We'll wait here until Twitchell is gone."

"Who's Twitchell?" R.J. asked.

Riley held up a finger, signaling *wait*. He looked out the hatch down the passageway and turned back to R.J. "Twitchell? He's the meanest sono-fabitch in the seventh fleet. He hates everybody, especially boots like you. My advice? Keep clear of that asshole. He gets on your ass, he won't quit till you're in the brig."

Riley led the way up a ladder to the 02 level and into the radio shack. The bulkheads were crammed with electronic equipment, and three work-stations were scattered around the small compartment. Each had a Morse code key and a head set. One of the stations had a speed key. *Must be the top guy's key,* R.J. thought. A regular Morse code key was operated by tap-ping it down to make the electronic connection which made the tone that became the dits and dahs of the code. A speed key was operated from side to side, making the connection on each side, enabling the sender to send extremely fast. Of course you had to be good at the code to use a speed key properly. He sat down and played with the key, sending quick little exercise words like 'Tennessee' which sounded like, *dah dit dah-dit dah-dit dit dit-dit-dit dit-dit-dit dit dit.*

"Hey, that's pretty good," Riley smiled. "Tennessee, right? Sounds musi-cal. You must be pretty good at code."

R.J. nodded. "It's a beautiful language if you know how to use it. It's a secret language between radiomen. Others don't understand it."

"Signalmen understand Morse code," Riley reminded him.

"Flashing light?" R.J. asked. "That's a whole different thing. That's visu-al, they can't hear the music of the code. Besides, how many signalmen do you know who can send and receive code at 60 words a minute?"

"Hell, boy," Riley laughed, "I can't read code that fast. Only one in this shack that fast is Murray, and he's an RM1."

As if on cue, Radioman First Class Paul Murray stepped into the radio shack. He was small, thin and wore a sardonic look on his face. He held a cup of coffee in his right hand. The cup was custom made in Japan and was painted with a first class radioman's insignia, with lightning bolts in the center, the emblem of radiomen, and below the insignia it said *MURRAY, RM-1*. He looked at R.J. and Riley disapprovingly and noticed R.J. was sit-ting at the speed key station.

"You Davis?" Murray challenged.

"That's me, RM1." R.J. smiled and held out his hand. Murray ignored it and brushed past Riley.

"Get the fuck off my speed-key, boot," Murray snapped.

Riley interjected, "Hey Mur, this guy is good with code. He sends as fast as you."

Murray set down his coffee cup and stared at Riley and R.J. "Yeah?" he asked. "Well tough shit, because this here boot ain't gonna be in this shack for long." He tested his speed-key and inspected it closely, trying to determine if anything was wrong with it. Without looking up he said, "The exec wants to see you, Davis. He heard you were aboard and he wants to have a little chat with you."

"A little chat?" R.J. asked. "What kind of chat?"

"Why don't you find out for yourself," Murray said, still not looking at him. "But I'll tell you this much." He turned and glared at R.J. "Don't even *think* of wearing your fucking suspenders aboard this vessel."

A cold fear swept over R.J. *Oh, shit,* he thought. *There goes my second chance. How far do I have to go to get away from that crap?* Guam isn't far enough?

Murray turned to Riley. "Take this Wog to the exec's office. He's waiting and he ain't a patient man."

Riley nodded. "That's for sure." He motioned to R.J. "Come on Davis."

Riley led R.J. up to the exec's office, which doubled as his cabin. "Knock on the door and wait," Riley instructed. "He'll say come in, and you go in. Don't forget to remove your cover." He pointed to R.J.'s whitehat.

"Why do I get the feeling I'm not going to like this?" R. J. asked.

Riley stuck out his hand. "It's been nice knowing you, boy," he said, and disappeared down the passageway. R.J. knocked softly on the door.

"Enter," the exec barked.

R.J. took off his whitehat, opened the door, and stepped into the exec's office.

THREE

The Haverfield's executive officer, Lieutenant Chester Carlysle 'C.C.' Edgars, known to the crew as "Complete Control Edgars," sat at his desk, a personnel file opened in front of him. He did not look up. R.J. stood at attention and announced, "Davis, R.J. reporting as ordered, sir." He handed over his orders and the exec snatched them out of his hand without looking up. He tossed them on the desk and returned to studying the personnel file. R.J. gritted his teeth. The guy just threw his orders away in disdain. This wasn't going to be a pleasant meeting.

R.J. stood at attention and studied the exec as the exec studied the personnel file. The lieutenant was a typical officer in R.J.'s eyes. *Tight assed big shot,* R.J. thought contemptuously. *The Navy's full of big shots. A little authority and they go all...*

Mr. Edgars slowly closed the file and looked up at R.J. with an expression of disgust on his face, as if he were observing something loathsome. He swiveled his chair around so that he could stare directly up into R.J.'s face, and he slowly drummed his fingers on the closed file. R.J. could see that it was his own personnel file, and again he felt uncomfortable and on edge. He knew that was exactly the way the exec wanted him to feel. *Typical prick,* R.J. thought.

"I've been reading all about you, Davis," the exec sneered, still drumming his fingers on the file, "and I'm here to tell you I don't like what I've learned about you." He stood and folded his arms across his chest. He was as tall as R.J. and was dressed in a khaki uniform that was laundered and ironed neatly, the creases of his shirt and trousers sharp and straight, the brass of his lieutenant's insignia bright and polished. His face was tanned and showed the weathering effects of the tropical climate. His dark eyes, almost black, were completely devoid of any emotion, like the eyes of a shark. He stared hard at R.J. in an obvious attempt at intimidation. It was working. R.J. squirmed uncomfortably.

C.C. Edgars picked up the file, holding it in front of R.J.'s face. "Your reputation precedes you, lad," he said, staring directly into R.J.'s eyes. "And your reputation is that of disrespect for the Navy and the uniform. You a lone wolf, Davis? You know better than the Navy how things are done?" He spoke with the calm confidence of someone who was in complete control of his environment, and R.J. gritted his teeth again.

"No, sir," he said quietly. He could feel the rush of anger, and he bit his lip to keep from letting it show. His face was beginning to redden.

"You're going to find out that around here the tail don't wag the dog, Davis," the exec said, "and your first lesson is today." He turned and tossed the personnel file on the desk. "I'm going to make an example out of you," he said firmly. "You can forget that RMSA stuff. Your designation as a radioman is forfeit and your security clearance has been revoked. You won't see the inside of our radio shack as long as I'm the executive officer on this ship. You are being transferred to the deck force, where the real work is done, and I'm going to keep a very close eye on you." The exec snatched his sound-powered phone from its cradle on the wall and cranked the handle on the side of the cradle, sending a shrill, siren-like *whoooooop* through the air. He barked into the mouthpiece, "Send the messenger of the watch to my cabin," and hung up the phone.

R.J. stood silently, his face burning red with anger. He was stunned by the exec's words. He wanted to protest, to say something. He just stood there, feeling helpless and angry, his hands clenching at his side.

"You are in the Fleet now, Davis," the exec continued. "This may not be the Navy you imagined when you joined. This may be a tired, beat up old WWII DE stationed in the butt-hole of the world, but this is the fleet nonetheless. You are going to learn to be a real sailor if it kills you, and you're going to learn it in the deck force."

Someone knocked softly on the door. *Good, the messenger's here,* R.J. thought. *Get me outta here!*

"One moment!" The exec barked at the door. He looked back into R.J.'s eyes and R.J. once again felt helpless and intimidated. "That crap you and that street gang of yours pulled in San Diego isn't going to be tolerated on this ship. What was it you called yourselves, the Straps?" He spit out the word in disgust.

"Yes sir," R.J. answered. He was getting tired of this prick. "But we weren't a street gang." He said it defiantly, insolently. *Who was this asshole to pull his RM designation and security clearance?* R.J. had worked hard through six months of radio school to earn them, and this self-appointed big shot was pissing away all that work.

The exec pointed a finger in R.J.'s face and exploded, "Shut the fuck up, sailor! I don't want to hear any of your smart ass back-talk, you got that?" He was angry now, his neat composure was gone and his face was full of rage. "You got that?" he repeated louder.

"Yes sir," R.J. said, feeling the anger surge once again. He gritted his teeth. He had to force himself to keep his mouth shut.

The exec turned to the door. "Get in here!" he shouted.

The messenger of the watch, a freckle-faced kid no older than R.J. stepped cautiously into the cabin and said softly, "Yes sir?"

"Take this man down to Chief Whipple and tell the chief this is the newest addition to First Division," he ordered.

"Yes sir," the messenger replied, and stepped out of the hatch, holding it open for R.J. to follow. R.J. followed. The messenger closed the door and looked at R.J. questioningly, his eyebrows arched.

"You just set a new record, pal," he said. "You pissed off the exec quicker than anybody I ever seen. You better watch your ass."

"That's what I'm good at," R.J. answered, pulling his whitehat down on his head.

"Which? Pissing people off or watching your ass?"

"Both." R.J. looked back at the door to the exec's cabin. "He always in that good a mood?" he asked.

The messenger chuckled and offered his hand. "I'm Peacock," he said, "but they just call me Pea."

"R.J. Davis," R.J. said. He took the hand and shook it. Pea was short, about five foot five, and slim. R.J. doubted if he weighed over one twenty. He had a baby face and a broad, toothy grin.

"Yeah, I know," Pea said, motioning for R.J. to follow him. "Everybody on this ship has heard of you. Snively, that's the ship's yeoman, reads everybody's file before they get here, and he told us all about you." He stopped and cocked his head at R.J. "You guys had some secret club in San Diego?" he asked.

"It's a long story," R.J. replied.

"You really beat up a guy and rolled him and left him naked in the base commander's garden?" Pea asked.

"It's a long story," R.J. said impatiently.

"Well, you got eighteen months aboard this tub, so you got plenty of time to tell it. C'mon, let's get your gear and go see the Whip."

* * * * *

Chief Boatswains Mate Tom Whipple sat in the rear booth of the mess decks drinking coffee and working on the crossword puzzle in the Stars and Stripes, the military newspaper. His khaki uniform was wrinkled and worn, and his chief's hat sat on the table next to him, the brass insignia caked green with Pacific Ocean salt. The chief was proud of his hat. It had taken him a year to season it, and it marked him as a true "old salt." He had served at sea for over twenty years, having joined the Navy on December 8, 1941 as an eighteen-year-old from Elkhart, Indiana. Tom Whipple was the chief of the boat, as they called the senior boatswains mate aboard, and he was proud of his status. Next to the captain and executive officer, he was the most influential man aboard. His bright blue eyes twinkled in a leathery, wrinkled face turned brown by constant exposure to the sun. He studied the crossword puzzle with a frown on his face, occasionally running his hand over his closely cropped sandy hair. He chewed constantly on the end of a well-worn stub, which looked like it might have been a pencil in a previous life.

Pea led R.J. into the mess decks and toward the chief of the boat. R.J. couldn't help a feeling of looming dread as he played over in his mind the meeting with the exec. It was obvious the exec was going to make things tough for him, but when he saw Whipple at the rear of the mess decks, he instinctively knew that this man could make his life far more miserable than the exec could. *Wolf Larson*, R.J. thought, *this is how I pictured Wolf Larson!*

"S'cuse me, Chief," Pea said as they approached Whipple's table.

"Huh?" The chief grunted, still studying his puzzle.

"We got a new man for First Division," Pea explained. "This here's Davis and the exec assigned him to the deck force."

The chief continued studying his puzzle and nibbling on the stub. "What's a six-letter word for mythical that starts with an F?" he asked, frowning down at the puzzle.

Pea shrugged. "I don't know, Chief."

R.J. cleared his throat. "Fabled?" he offered. R.J. felt somehow more comfortable with a man like Whipple than he had with the exec. This was a man he could respect. Not a tight-assed officer with a silver spoon in his mouth, Chief Whipple was a man who had earned his position on performance. This man represented the real Navy.

Whipple slowly removed the stubby pencil from his mouth and counted the spaces in the crossword puzzle, then filled in the answer. "Fabled...that makes 29 down...lorry, English truck." He laid the chewed-up stub on top of the puzzle, frowning slightly, and looked up at R.J. for the first time. Despite his rough exterior, the chief had a kindly, fatherly look in his eyes as he appraised the young newcomer.

Without taking his eyes off R.J., he said quietly, "You can go, Pea."

Pea nodded and left the mess decks, waving slightly at R.J.

"Sit down, Davis," the chief ordered, nodding to the seat opposite him. R.J. sat and folded his hands on top of the table.

The chief took a breath, let it out slowly and began the speech he gave every newcomer to First Division. "Two years ago I was one of three chief boatswains mates on the cruiser Long Beach. The chief of the boat was an asshole who hated me because I was better at the job than him. One night in Yokosuka a couple of buddies and me were raising hell in a bar in The Alley when this chief of the boat comes in all liquored up and looking for trouble. He found it with me. I had enough of his bullshit and we went at it, a fair fight, and neither of us came out the winner, but next morning he went to the exec and I found myself transferred to this ship...on Guam." He sipped his coffee and made a face. "Christ, I hate piss-warm coffee," he grimaced, sliding the cup away.

R.J. sat patiently watching the older man, wondering if he were going to get to the point.

As if he had read R.J.'s mind the chief explained, "See, Davis, just about everyone here on this ship pulled some stupid stunt to get transferred here. We got an officer on board, I won't say who, got kicked out of nuclear power school and sent here for porking another officer's wife. She was married to one of his instructors at the school. We got guys who been busted for various things all over the fleet. It seems they send all the fuck-ups to the Haverfield. Reason I'm telling you this is because I don't give a shit what you done to get sent here. All I care about is making sure this bucket runs smooth and we get from here to there without too much sweat." He lit a cigarette, blew the smoke out of the side of his mouth and went on. "I'm hoping you're not just another fuck-up." The chief knocked his ashes off into the butt-kit and looked directly into R.J.'s eyes. "With me you get the same even chance everybody else gets," he said, "but you fuck up with me and you'll be choppin' boonies in the Marine brig, you understand?"

R.J. nodded, though he really didn't understand what the chief meant.

"The only thing a real sailor cares about, next to his woman," the chief explained, "is his ship. The Haverfield ain't pretty. She's old and tired 'cause she's been around a long time." The chief stubbed out his cigarette in the butt-kit on the bulkhead and continued. "She patrolled the Atlantic convoy lanes in the early days of World War II searching for German U-boats, and she actually sank one of those bastards in forty-four." The chief smiled. "See, as chief of the boat it's my job to know everything about the vessel I'm on, so let me tell you about this one." He lit another cigarette, blowing the smoke out of the side of his mouth. "This ship's been to Casablanca, the Canary Islands, through the Panama Canal and patrolled the waters from Saipan to Okinawa. She's been to China and San Diego, Florida to Philadelphia where she was reclassified as a Radar Picket Ship. Then she went to Seattle and Pearl Harbor and then here to Guam where she's been responsible for patrolling the U.S. Trust Territory. Last year we patrolled the Formosa Strait, visited Japan, Taiwan and Hong Kong." Chief Whipple smiled and nodded to himself. "Last November a typhoon, Karen was its name, practically destroyed all of Guam. Haverfield provided medical supplies, food and electricity to the island until power was restored."

R.J. was entranced at this history lesson. He could tell the chief was proud of his knowledge of the ship, and R.J. listened politely and attentively, soaking up the information and trying to imagine what it must have been like to hunt and destroy a German U-Boat. Listening to Chief Whipple was like listening to the Navy stories from his dad and uncles. R.J. relaxed. He liked the chief of the boat.

"One of these days," Whipple went on, "they're gonna retire this old tub and make razor blades out of her. But until they do, we're gonna take good care of her. We got a new captain been aboard only a couple of months, and he's an academy guy. He's the type that's gonna want this ship squared away and Navy-like, so if she rusts, we're gonna paint her. If she gets sea salt in her face, we're gonna wash her and scrub down her decks. We're gonna polish her and make her shine like a new nickel. And we're gonna treat her like a lady, even if she is a tired old broad. You understand?"

R.J. understood. This man loved his ship. "Yes sir," he replied, quietly.

"And don't call me sir," Whipple said impatiently, "I ain't no officer. You only call officers sir." Then almost to himself he muttered, "Not that some of 'em fucking deserve it."

"OK Chief."

"Go down to First Division's compartment and tell Queen to get you settled. Then I want you to lay up to the quarterdeck for line handling duty."

"Which one's Queen?" R.J. asked, standing up and picking up his whitehat.

Chief Whipple managed to look amused without losing his frown. R.J. doubted the man ever smiled. "He looks like Edward G. Robinson, only bigger." The chief wrapped his hands around his stomach to illustrate. "And uglier." He chuckled, still frowning, and waved R.J. away. When R.J. left the mess decks Whipple continued to study his crossword puzzle and chew on his pencil stub.

It wasn't hard to spot Alfred Queen, Boatswain's Mate First Class. He was big and ugly, his fat face round and huge beneath his whitehat, which seemed way too small for his head. And he did look a lot like Edward G. Robinson, but he had a jovial nature, kidding everyone around him and laughing in a large, mocking way. He was over six feet and probably weighed more than 250, but he had a certain grace and charm, like a big Dracula without his tuxedo. He smiled easily and he seemed not to quite comprehend his unattractive appearance. When R.J. entered First Division's compartment, Queen was standing between two rows of triced-up bunks, one foot resting on top of a metal locker, eating ice cream from a small bowl. He refused to share it with anyone, though everyone in the compartment ribbed him about it.

"C'mon, Queenie," Pea exhorted him. "Hawkins gave you ice cream and you won't share it." Pea pointed a finger at him. "Shame on you!"

Queen looked down at Pea and smiled mischievously. The effect was not pretty. He spit into the ice cream and offered it to Pea. "Here you go, deck ape," he laughed, "you want ice cream, you can have some of my own special recipe." He laughed again, and his laugh sounded like the plaintive bellowing of a wounded buffalo. "Here you go, Pea," Queen challenged, "you want ice cream or not?" Again that rumbling, horrible-sounding laugh erupted from Queen's ample belly. R.J. couldn't blame Pea for declining the offer.

Queen snorted at Pea. "You still got the watch, right? Get your freckled butt back to the quarterdeck, moron." He smiled and let the ice cream dribble between the big gaps in his teeth. R.J. had never seen such big teeth.

Suddenly the compartment grew silent as the sailors gathered there noticed R.J.'s presence. Then the tall boatswain's mate from the shower scene the previous night spoke up.

"Well, lookey here," Lester sneered. "We got a gen-yoo-wine boot here." He motioned to R.J. and several sailors gathered around as Lester approached him.

"We hear tell you a regular rebel, kid," Lester continued to sneer. "Got yourself a reputation for being a real bad-ass. That right, boy?" Lester leaned into R.J., making him draw back. "Maybe you like to try yourself out with a real-life fleet sailor." Lester gestured to himself with his thumb. "How 'bout it, Wog," he challenged, "feel froggy?"

R.J. looked into Lester's eyes and recognized the stupidity. He had grown up with morons like Lester. "Not today, Lester," he replied, "I got enough trouble and I only been aboard this ship one day."

"Trouble?" Lester asked. "Let me tell you something, Wog, you ain't seen trouble yet." He played to the other sailors in the compartment, watching their reactions out of the corner of his eye. "But you gonna see trouble." He grinned and nodded slowly. "You gonna see a lot of trouble. See, around here I'm the lawn mower and your ass is grass."

Everyone laughed loudly.

"That why your teeth are stained green, Lester?" Tanner had walked into the compartment. "Hell, I figured it was because you never brush 'em." Tanner was smiling, but R.J. knew the look. Tanner didn't much like Lester, and enjoyed toying with him.

"Fuck you, Tanner," Lester countered. "Fuck you."

"If you ever did you'd give up screwing chickens," Tanner countered.

Queen stepped between them. "Let's turn to, sailors. Time to get some work done. Let's go!" he barked. "Knock off the grab-ass and get up on deck!"

The sailors filed quietly out of the compartment, many glancing back curiously at R.J. As Lester left the compartment he looked back at R.J. and made a fist, shaking it at him, still sneering.

"Don't let him bother you, kid," Queen said, shoveling ice cream into his ugly mouth. "Gomer's just a pain in the ass, if you know what I mean."

"Gomer?" R.J asked, amused.

"Yeah," Queen explained. "His last name is Lester, but his first name's Gomer." He scraped the last of the ice cream from the cup and it disappeared into his mouth. "Guess he never forgave his momma for that." Queen broke into that wounded buffalo sound that passed for laughter. He looked hard at R.J. "So what's the skinny on you, boot-camp?" he asked, a curious look on his ugly face.

"Me?" R.J. answered, "I'm just trying to get along."

"Well, boy," Queen considered R.J. carefully. "Then you on the wrong ship." He looked thoughtfully at the younger man. "But long as you're here, stow your shit in that there locker, and get your young, stateside ass up on deck!"

When R.J. reached the quarterdeck he noticed that Pea was getting chewed out by a burly chief petty officer who had his back turned and was gesturing at Pea with fat, stubby hands. "...I don't give a flying fart about your excuses, Pea-brain," he shouted, his stubby arms gesturing wildly, like those of a man in the deep end of the pool who couldn't swim. "When I'm the OOD and you're the fucking messenger you do things like I tell you or you get stomped. Understand, Pea-brain?"

"Sorry, Chief," Pea responded weakly.

"Sorry don't milk the fucking cow, ass-wipe," the chief continued. "When I tell you to round up the fucking line-handling party I don't mean you can go below and play slap-and-tickle with your buddies. You been gone fifteen minutes, Pea-brain, and I'm still short one body!"

Pea gulped and looked past the OOD's shoulder, spotting R.J. approaching. "Here he comes, Chief." He motioned meekly to R.J.

When the OOD turned around R.J. stopped abruptly in his tracks. The chief was short and squat with a face like a pig. His squinted eyes were yellow in the morning sun and his nose looked like the snout on a hog. His lip was curled in an ugly sneer and he looked at R.J. with unconcealed disgust. It was Chief Twitchell.

The chief clasped his stubby hands behind his back and waddled toward R.J. "Well, well," he almost whispered, "the New Shit-Head has arrived." He looked R.J. over carefully and shouted, "Where the hell you been, New Shit-Head?"

R.J. was startled by the outburst and jumped nervously. "Getting squared away downstairs, Chief," R.J. explained. The other sailors on the quarterdeck snickered.

"Downstairs?" Twitchell repeated, *"Downstairs?* You mean you was *below,* New Shit-Head? Ain't no downstairs aboard a ship." He walked back to the quarterdeck and motioned for R.J. to follow. "You think you're home with your Mommy? Let me explain something to you, New Shit-Head." Twitchell was enjoying himself. He pointed toward the forecastle. "That's forward, and that's aft," he gestured toward the fantail. "That's above," he pointed up in the air, "and that's below," pointing downward. "You would do well to remember that, New Shit-Head." His hands were on his hips and he was inches away from R.J.'s face. "Questions?" he breathed.

"No sir, I... I mean Chief." The other line-handlers snickered again.

Twitchell snorted and pointed to the other line handlers. "Fall in with those idiots over there," he instructed. He walked over and put his hand on the shoulder of onc of the line-handlers, Jefferson, who winced at the touch. "You men get your asses down on the pier and Lopez will bring the truck around to take you to the munitions dock." He squeezed Jefferson's shoulder and Jefferson winced again. "And this here nee-gro's in charge," he spat.

The four line-handlers filed down the brow quickly as a smiling Billy Lopez brought the truck to a screeching halt in front of them. The line handlers piled into the truck and Billy gunned the engine, popped the clutch and shot down the pier as the sailors in the back held on for dear life.

One of the line-handlers, a young Mexican from Arizona named Cortez, looked over at Jefferson who was sitting with his back to the pickup's cab, a pissed-off look on his face. "Why do you let that asshole talk to you like that, Jefferson?" Cortez asked. "That man's a bigot and he treats you like shit."

"Mind y'own bidness, Pancho," Jefferson replied.

"You don't have to take that crap, man," Pancho continued, "put that asshole on report. You got the right under the Uniform Code of Military Justice." Cortez fancied himself an expert on Navy Regs. "I'll show you in the book," he offered.

Jefferson chewed his lip. "One these days I'm gonna pop that muh-fuh in the mouf," he said angrily. "Ain't gonna be no re-port." He nodded slowly, his eyes glaring at Cortez. "Wait, Pancho. One these days..."

R.J. took it all in, wondering what kind of duty station he had gotten himself into. He had been aboard less than twenty-four hours and he had been chewed out twice, had his security clearance pulled, transferred to the deck force and physically threatened by that creep Lester. *Things are going to get worse before they get better,* he thought.

He was right.

FOUR

Lieutenant Commander C.C. Edgars sat in the officers' wardroom, sipping coffee and reviewing the engineering report on the power plant repairs. The Haverfield's power plant consisted of four geared-diesel engines, capable of twenty-one knots when all four were on line and running smoothly, which was very rare. Edgars looked up when the captain stepped into the wardroom.

"Morning, Captain," the exec said, half rising to his feet.

Captain D. Paul Oliver was a tall, handsome lieutenant commander with an easy smile and a friendly manner. He was an Annapolis graduate and wore the ring proudly. C.C. Edgars was a reserve officer, and the sight of the captain's class ring annoyed the exec. It also annoyed the exec that the captain was already popular among the crew. Edgars knew that he himself was despised by the same crew.

"Good morning Chet," the captain replied, motioning for the exec to remain seated. "How're the repairs coming?"

"Well," the exec began, assuming a concerned look and frowning down at the report in his hand, "we've got two and four running pretty smooth, but one and three are going to need some parts. Chief Risk tells me he's located the parts to fix them."

The captain raised his eyebrows at the exec. "Located?" he asked. "The parts are in inventory?" Captain Oliver knew that in the so-called "Coconut

Navy" parts were hard to come by and were usually obtained by barter or other methods he chose not to think about.

"We should have number one up and running by the time we go out on the next survey, but three is going to take a while," the exec explained.

Captain Oliver nodded. He knew he could patrol with only three engines. Hell, the ship had patrolled with only two engines many times over the years. "Well, let's hope we don't have to exceed fifteen knots and we'll be fine," he decided. "What about the evaps?"

"The evaporators are a different story, I'm afraid," the exec said, slowly shaking his head. "Risk and Twitchell have gunny-decked the hell out of them, and they'll last as long as they last." He slid the repair report across the desk.

The captain sat down with a cup of coffee and looked at the report. Fresh water evaporators were critical to the operation of the ship, not to mention the comfort of the crew. The evaps were always going out, and fresh water for cooking, cleaning and showering was always at a shortage when the Haverfield was at sea. New parts for the evaps were non-existent and Chief Machinists Mate Twitchell, a wizard at keeping machinery operating, struggled daily with the fresh-water problem while the ship was at sea.

Captain Oliver slid the report back across the table. "By the way, Chet," he said, lighting his pipe with a kitchen match. "I won't be aboard for dinner tonight." He shook out the match and blew blue smoke at the overhead. "The new admiral has arrived, and he's throwing a wing-ding at the Officer's Club. Dress whites." Captain Oliver was a clothes horse, and loved dressing up. He was also an eligible bachelor, which made him a necessity on all naval social functions' guest lists. Lieutenant Commander D. Paul Oliver was what is commonly referred to as a smooth operator. He was at ease in any social situation, an excellent public speaker, and always charming and gracious, especially to the young ladies who seemed to flock to him when he entered a room.

Edgars took back the repair report and tucked it away into his leather-bound folder. "Something else, Captain," he said, retrieving another file from his folder. On the front of the folder he had printed neatly, "DAVIS, R.J." in black letters. He slid the file across the table and the captain picked it up.

"Davis?" the captain asked. "New man aboard?"

"Problem child," the exec replied. "I took away his security clearance and assigned him to First Division." Edgars gestured to the file in the captain's hand. "It's all in there, Captain."

Captain Oliver opened the file and began reading, slowly sipping his coffee. *Why do I get all the renegades*? he thought as he leafed through the file. He frowned, looked up questioningly and said, "Straps? What the hell were these men thinking?" He began flipping pages in the file. "Why did they call themselves the Straps?" he murmured to himself.

FIVE

San Diego, California
October 19, 1962

As usual, Frank Findlay was the last man to leave the Naval Training Center and arrive at the locker club across Rosecrans Street. He was short, only about five-seven, and he had a shock of curly hair that often caused him problems during personnel inspection. His ever-grinning baby face was covered with freckles, his bright brown eyes twinkled constantly with mis-.chief and he was always in motion. He could easily pass for a teenager of fifteen. It was difficult for Frankie to sit still even for a minute. He bounced into the locker room, snapping his fingers and bobbing his head to some imaginary beat.

R.J. and two other radio school students were already changing into their civilian clothes when R.J. spotted Frankie coming through the door, heading toward his locker. Radio school students often rented lockers off-base to store their civilian clothes, something frowned on by the school's instructors.

"Frankie," R.J. called, "It's about time, boy. Where the hell you been? We're gonna miss the first Pony!"

"That'll be the fuckin' day," Frankie sang back, doing his best Buddy Holly impression. "I'll pony your ass off and all you other boot-campers, too!" He indicated the other two men, who laughed and flipped him the finger.

Radio school wasn't like being in the real Navy, although the students could see Navy ships in the harbor and were allowed to visit them. Radio school was more like an extension of high school since everyone attending was very young. In radio school there was the absence of girls and the required daily marching in formation to and from class in uniform, but it still had that 'high school' atmosphere and the mentality to go with it.

Since the other three were already dressed in civvies, Frankie quickly got dressed, putting on his ruffled-front shirt, slipping his "taste" of a tie under his collar, stepping into his tight, peg-leg slacks and fastening his suspenders into the buttons on the front and back of his trousers. He turned and grinned mischievously, his eyes twinkling. "Got my straps on," he sang, hooking his thumbs under the suspenders and snapping them against his shirt. "Got to dance. Got to find a little chickie and jam down!"

R.J. laughed. "You better put your shoes on, stupid," he pointed at Frankie's feet. "You can't dance without your shoes!"

Frankie slipped his feet into Italian boots with half-inch leather heels. The heels made a distinctive clicking sound when he walked or danced. Frankie was proud of his shoes. He stood up and instantly looked taller. Then he started clicking his heels on the floor and snapping his fingers. "It's Pony time," he shouted, "Get up! Boogedy-boogedy-shoot!"

The four Straps folded their suit jackets across their forearms and began dancing the Pony out of the locker club and down the street, their heels clicking on the sidewalk in time with the imaginary music. They were headed to the bus stop to catch the afternoon bus. Their destination was the Y.M.C.A. on Broadway in downtown San Diego for the Friday night U.S.O. dance. They were cool and they knew it. The civilian clothes had transformed them, and they felt a lot more like civilians than military, which was, of course, the point.

The city bus dropped off R.J. and the others on Broadway a block and a half south of the Y.M.C.A. As they approached the huge granite-stoned building that housed the "Y" several other Navy men were filing up the concrete steps into the double doors. Some were in uniform but most wore civilian clothes. A sign above the doors announced, "U.S.O. Dance To-Nite." Inside were tables of coffee and donuts, magazines and board games handed out by the U.S.O. volunteers, many of whom were high-school girls. Other girls who had volunteered to attend the dances stood around in groups, waiting to be asked out on the floor.

Once inside R.J. and Frankie broke off and headed across the scarred wooden dance floor to the front of the stage, where a large group of young men and women was assembled. The guys were all dressed like R.J. and Frankie, complete with various types and colors of suspenders. Thick maroon-colored theatre curtains bracketed the large stage and in the center was a table with a record player on it where a disc jockey sat playing 45 RPM records. At each end of the stage was an electronic sign that flashed "Tag Dance" whenever the deejay pushed a button. This meant that anyone could tap on the shoulder of someone dancing with a girl and cut in. Only the slow songs were designated "Tag Dances."

As R.J. and Frankie approached the group they began to strut and chant, "Strap time, strap time..." The guys in front of the stage picked up the chant, "Strap time, strap time, strap time!"

The disc jockey on stage recognized the chant and put a 45 RPM record on the turntable, playing *Do You Love Me?* by the Contours.

> *"You broke my heart 'cause I couldn't dance,*
> *You didn't even want me around..."*

This was the Straps' theme song and they smiled at each other in recognition and began moving out on the floor, bobbing their heads and snapping their fingers.

> *"But now I'm back, to let you know,*
> *I can really shake 'em down."*

The song broke into a strong rock and roll beat and the group began dancing the pony in a line of two abreast, circling the dance floor and clicking their leather heels on the wooden slats.

> *"Do you love me? I can really move.*
> *Do you love me? I'm in the groove.*
> *Do you love me? Do you love me,*
> *Now that I can dance?"*

Many kept their jackets folded neatly across their forearms as they danced. Other dancers soon joined the line and followed the Straps around and around the dance floor until the strains of the song faded out. The group broke ranks and milled about in front of the stage, pairing off with the girls and talking about the music, the dancing and comparing their suspenders.

Big Lenny Andrews, unofficial leader of the Straps, leaned against the stage with his arm around his girlfriend, and grinned widely as the disc jockey put on another record and *"The Man Who Shot Liberty Valance"* by Gene Pitney began playing. Lenny's fire-red hair and freckles gave him a boyish look, but he was very tall, about six foot four, and had the body of a wrestler, which was what he had been in high school before joining the Navy.

"Can't dance to that stupid song," Lenny announced, still grinning. "Hey R.J.," he called, "Did you do the cowpoke shuffle to songs like that in Denver?"

"Damn right," R.J. replied, "where do you think the Pony was invented?"

"Shit, boy," Lenny said, "I invented the Pony, don't you know that?"

The disc jockey put on *"Let's Dance"* by Chris Montez and the Straps broke apart and moved out onto the floor, dancing the Watusi and various versions of the Twist. They danced most of the evening until the U.S.O. closed at 10:00 P.M. The last song was always Jesse Belvin's *"Goodnight My Love,"* and the crowd began to wander out onto Broadway as the song faded into the night. The Straps gathered in front of the USO building, smoking cigarettes and needling each other. The evening air was crisp and damp in October this close to the harbor, and they loitered for awhile until Lenny stepped forward, his finger in the air motioning in a circle for the Straps to muster up.

"A little more than an hour and a half before we turn into pumpkins," he announced. "Papa Joe's!" He pointed up the street and the Straps began strutting up Broadway to their favorite pizza joint, singing and laughing, the girls holding onto their arms. Others on the street turned to watch as the procession made its way toward the pizza joint. R.J. and the Straps strutted with pride. They knew they were the "in crowd" and there were only two types of guys on that street: those who were Straps and those who wished they were Straps. They half-danced, half-strutted along proudly, feeling cocky, self-sure, in charge of their environment.

Just before they reached their destination a shore patrol jeep pulled up to the curb and squealed to a stop. Two shore patrol petty officers, one a tall boatswain's mate first class and the other a sonarman second class, got slowly out of the jeep and motioned Big Lenny over. As he approached the shore patrol the Straps gathered around the jeep, surrounding it and inspecting it as if they were shopping for a used car.

"Whatcha got under the hood?" Frankie asked.

"This thing got power steering?" Carl Foretti asked. He smiled coldly at the Shore Patrol. Carl was a stocky guy with big muscular arms pushing through his shirtsleeves.

The tall shore patrolman cocked his head at Big Lenny and asked in a southern drawl, "Y'all in charge of this here rabble?" He motioned to the guys around the jeep. "What y'all think, y'all in West Side Story and you the Jets?" The short one laughed, a quick snort of a laugh that brought snickers from the Straps.

Big Lenny grinned. "Just going to get some pizza, Boats," he explained, motioning toward Papa Joe's with his thumb.

The short sonarman rested his hand on the handle of his nightstick and gestured toward the Straps with a sweep of his other hand. "Get these fuckers away from my jeep or I'm going to start pulling I.D. cards," he warned. The Straps began backing away, moving up on the sidewalk, taking a "stand by" posture. Pulling their I.D. cards meant they had to return to the base with a chit issued for a violation of liberty regulations. The violation chit meant certain restriction to the base for at least a week.

The tall boatswain's mate looked the Straps over, shaking his head. "You people in the Navy or what?" he asked. "Reason Ah ask is on account of y'all look like you goin' to the prom or somethin'. Why ain't y'all in uniform? Don't like the uniform?" he drawled, "or you just like struttin' around my town wearin' those faggoty suspenders?"

Big Lenny grinned, but his eyes were cold and resentful. "Just having fun at the dance, Boats," he explained slowly.

"Let's see some liberty cards," ordered the short sonarman. "I hope you all got one."

The Straps went into their pockets and pulled out their liberty cards, holding them up, showing them to Shorty, who inspected each one carefully before giving it back. "You people got Cinderella liberty and it's going on 2300 hours, so why don't you head back to the base now?" he snorted. "Here comes the Rosecrans bus." He pointed to a city bus making its way down Broadway toward the harbor. "We'll just wait here till you are all on board safely," he announced, snorting.

The Straps looked to Lenny, who peeked at his watch and said pleasantly, "It ain't even ten-thirty, man."

Shorty drew himself up to his maximum height. He stepped close to Lenny and curled his lip in a sneer. "Get your asses on that bus!" he yelled.

Lenny looked down at the short sonarman. The little SP was about half his size, and Lenny grinned down at him, eyes cold and angry. Without taking his eyes off Shorty, Lenny motioned for the Straps to climb aboard the bus, leaving the girls on the sidewalk waving good-bye. Lenny climbed on, the doors closed, and the bus belched black smoke as it pulled away from the curb.

The two shore patrolmen leaned against their jeep and watched the bus chug down Broadway on its way to the base. They looked at each other and Shorty snorted, "If those punks are the new Navy, we are in a world of hurt."

On board the bus, the festive feeling of the evening evaporated into the air, replaced with the knowledge that they were not free to do as they pleased. The Straps were quiet and subdued on the ride back to the base. They arrived at the locker club, and slowly walked to their individual lockers where everyone quietly hung up his civvies and got back into uniform. R.J. looked around him. Everyone had a hang-dog look, depressed and deflated as they climbed slowly back into their dress blues.

Just as quietly the group filed through the Rosecrans Street gate, holding up their liberty cards for the shore patrol manning the gate. It was well before midnight. The Cinderellas were in under the wire. No pumpkins tonight.

R.J. lay in his bunk and thought of the dance and the little blonde, Tonya, he had been flirting with the entire evening. *Sweet little Tonya with the big boobs and the tiny waist,* he thought wistfully. She gave him her phone number and he promised to call, or at least see her the next evening at the Saturday night U.S.O. dance. He smiled, remembering the look of promise in her eyes, and couldn't wait to see her again. What he didn't know was that events were taking place a continent away that would restrict him and his buddies to the base for the next week. It was October 19, 1962 and in Washington D.C. the President of the United States and his closest advisers were huddled together, deciding how they would react to Soviet nuclear missiles and their launchers recently discovered ninety miles from the Florida coast, in Castro's Cuba.

PART TWO:

THUNDER

SIX

Apra Harbor, Guam
March 7, 1963

Charming Billy Lopez enjoyed being the Haverfield's duty driver. He loved driving the old pickup truck up and down the concrete piers of Apra Harbor, grinding the gears and exceeding the speed limit...by a lot. The old truck wasn't particularly fast, but Billy drove it as fast as he could get it to go. He imagined himself drag racing down Pico Boulevard in West Los Angeles, squealing his tires, gunning his engine and impressing his friends. As he approached the munitions pier with his truck bed loaded with line-handlers he called out the window, "Hold on, boys!" and screeched to a stop, sliding sideways in front of the arrival point. A big AE was due to dock there and take on munitions, and the line-handlers were responsible for getting her moored to the pier.

As the line-handlers crawled out of the bed of the truck, Pancho came over to the driver's side window and pointed at Billy. "Loco, hombre," he laughed, "You are mui mas loco!"

Billy smiled his charming smile and shrugged his shoulders. "How come you talk Mexican to me, Pancho?" he asked. "You know I don't habla. I'm from L.A., man, not Mexico." He spun the truck around and gunned the engine, popped the clutch and fish-tailed down the pier, tires squealing. He stuck his head out the window and shouted, "I'll be back to pick you up," and ground all three gears as he sped away.

The line-handlers stood in a group, shaking their heads and smiling at the slowly disappearing truck. "That foo's gonna kill sumbody sumday," Jefferson complained. "Dumb fuck."

R.J. looked around the pier. It was getting hotter and more humid as the morning sun continued its ascent in the tropical sky, and he was beginning to sweat through both his tee shirt and dungaree shirt. The other line-handlers seemed pretty comfortable, and he wondered if he would eventually become acclimated to the heavy heat. Looking across the harbor, he spotted the Haverfield directly opposite from them, and realized they had driven around to the other side of the harbor. The Haverfield rode higher as the tide came in, and from this distance looked more like a real Navy vessel.

The other three line-handlers sat on the edge of the pier, their feet dangling over the side, smoking cigarettes. R.J. sat down with them cautiously and asked, "What now?"

Jefferson and Cortez ignored him, but the third man, a tall, thin sailor from Oklahoma named Sonny Metzner spat into the harbor and answered, "We wait." He had a long, skinny neck with a bulging Adam's apple that bobbed up and down when he talked. R.J. thought he looked like Ichabod Crane.

They sat there for what seemed to R.J. like hours until Sonny pointed to the mouth of the harbor and called, "Here she comes!"

R.J. could see the masts of the AE making its way past the breakwater and into the harbor. The big ammunition ship sailed slowly toward them and a tug-boat merged with her to help her to the munitions pier. As if on cue, three large trucks, painted Navy gray, came slowly down the pier toward the line-handlers. Each truck flew red flags from its bumpers, the *Bravo* flag, indicating the trucks were carrying explosives.

"Time ta turn to," Jefferson announced, tossing his cigarette into the water. "The smokin' lamp be out." The others followed suit, throwing their smokes into the harbor and standing, ready to greet the ship and the trucks.

R.J. thought he understood. "So we help load the ammo onto the ship?" he asked.

"No, foo," Jefferson said, smirking, "we tie the ship up to the pier and then we wait for that dumb shit Billy to come back and pick our sorry asses up." He shook his head at R.J. "Stupid Wog. They gots cranes and shit aboard the AE that loads the ammo. We just here to handle the lines." Pancho and Sonny nodded agreement.

R.J. was getting a little aggravated. "Everyone I meet calls me a Wog. Just what the hell is a Wog, anyway?"

"A Wog," Jefferson explained, moving closer to R.J., "is a boot-camp muh-fuh who need to keep his mouf shut." He stood close to R.J., breathing on him, trying to intimidate him.

R.J. decided he wasn't going to be intimidated. "Back off, Jefferson," he snapped, "you're in my face and I don't like it."

Jefferson and R.J. stared at each other, neither blinking, until Sonny broke the spell, laughing. "Yeah, Jefferson," he said, "you breathin' on the guy and your breath could knock a vulture off a road kill."

Cortez broke up, laughing. Then R.J. and Jefferson started laughing and the confrontation was over. "Man," Cortez laughed, shaking his head at Sonny, "you are the funniest dude I ever met."

"Sonny," Jefferson called, pointing to the closely approaching bow of the AE, "you and boot-camp go forward. Pancho and me'll go aft."

R.J. had no clue as to what was expected of him, nor did he know anything about line handling, but he figured he would just follow Sonny's lead.

"Come with me, Boot," Sonny said, walking toward the bow of the ship. "See that guy up on the focsul? The one with the coil of line in his hand?" Sonny pointed to a sailor high on the forecastle of the AE, hefting a coil of line in his hand and joking with his buddies. R.J. nodded.

"That guy's gonna throw that line to you. When the weight on the end of the line hits the pier, you grab that line and start pulling it in." Sonny demonstrated with his hands and arms. "That line's tied to the big line. We pull the big line in and put the loop over that cleat." He indicated a large, cast iron cleat welded to the pier. "Then the ship does the rest."

A shrill whistle came from the forecastle of the AE. R.J. and Sonny turned to see the sailor with the line waving to them, indicating he was ready to throw. They waved back and the sailor swung the coiled line behind him and then stepped into the throw, swinging the coil in a wide arc, releasing it in a smooth motion at the height of the arc. The line began to slowly uncoil as it sailed through the air toward the pier. R.J. stood and watched in admiration as the lead weight on the front of the line thudded onto the dock.

"Go get it!" Sonny yelled, and R.J. sprang on the line and began hauling it in. Sonny joined him as the ship's big mooring line came inching across the water. This big line was much harder to reel in and Sonny and R.J. were sweating heavily by the time they looped it over the cleat.

Jefferson and Pancho were finished doubling up the lines aft, and moved forward to help double up those lines. From there all four line handlers doubled up the two sets of lines amidships and then took a much needed break, sitting on the edge of the pier, far away from the ammo trucks, feet dangling over the water, smoking and relaxing. The breeze felt good on their sweating faces and they began to cool off.

Jefferson looked over at R.J. "Y'know what, boot-camp?" he asked.

R.J. shook his head. *Here it comes*, he thought.

"You done okay for y'first time," Jefferson smiled. "Man you was pullin' that line in like you knew what you was doin'." Jefferson started pumping his arms, imitating R.J. pulling in the line hand over hand. He had the others laughing and pumping their arms and pointing at R.J. He was the butt of their jokes, but he didn't care. He wanted to be a member of this crew, a Havernaut, whatever that was, and he wanted to go to sea. He yearned to go to sea. That's why he had joined the Navy in the first place.

For the first time he was beginning to relax a little around these men. They, too, seemed to be relaxing a bit around him, and he was gaining an understanding of what it would take to be a member of this crew. He figured their acceptance of him would be based on one thing only and that was his ability to do the work. As long as he could keep up, he would be accepted as one of them. He knew the men he worked with were the men he needed to impress. He was determined to learn as much as he could about seamanship and sailing.

R.J. looked over at Jefferson. "So what's a Wog?" he asked.

Jefferson looked at Sonny and Pancho, who shrugged. "Wog is short for Pollywog," Jefferson explained. "If you ain't been across the equator, you a Pollywog." Jefferson smiled. "But we goin' across in July, and you gonna get to go through the initiation." All three smiled at R.J., nodding and winking at each other.

"So what am I after I cross the equator?" R.J. asked.

"*And* go through the initiation," Sonny cautioned, raising his index finger in the air.

"And go through the initiation," R.J. agreed. "Then what am I?"

The screeching gears of the old pickup truck announced the return of Charming Billy. The four line-handlers got up and moved up the pier to meet him.

"After you been across, you become a Shellback," Pancho explained. "Like us!" he added proudly, indicating himself, Sonny and Jefferson.

"But the best thing about it," Sonny added, smiling fiendishly, "is that the Shellbacks get to initiate the Pollywogs." R.J. didn't like the way he said *initiate*, and was going to press for more details when Billy Lopez squealed to a stop in front of them and waved out the window. "Your limousine is here, my friends," he called. "And I bring cold water!"

The line handlers cheered and jumped into the pickup's bed. A large cooler filled with water and ice sat propped up against the cab. Billy had even remembered paper cups. All four drank their fill of cool water and leaned back against the sides of the bed, talking about the big AE and how hard it was to handle those big lines. And how about that throw the guy made from the forecastle? That was sweet. All the time they were chattering they were careful to hold on tightly as the truck bounced and swerved, speeding in the general direction of the Haverfield. Billy was cruising Pico Boulevard again, smiling charmingly.

SEVEN

It was just before 1200 hours when the line-handlers returned to the Haverfield and went below to clean up for noon chow. The morning watch had been relieved by the noon watch, but Chief Twitchell was still hanging around the quarterdeck, complaining to his relief, Chief Risk, about a number of subjects including Guam, the Haverfield, the captain, the crew and anything else he could think of. Chief Risk, tall, handsome and even-tempered, listened patiently to Twitchell with an amused expression. He had heard it all before. He and Twitchell were the only chief engineer's mates on board. They worked together and were billeted together in the chief's quarters with the other three chief petty officers. There was Whipple, chief of the boat, Belame, chief gunners mate and Lyons, chief quartermaster. While the other chiefs didn't like Twitchell and didn't hide the fact, Chief Risk had befriended the pig-faced, overweight machinist mate and considered himself Twitchell's only friend. He did this mainly because he thought everyone should have at least one friend, even someone like Twitchell, and he truly believed there was good in all men, if you only scratched deeply enough. Today, he was smiling to himself because he had scratched very deeply into Twitchell and had discovered absolutely no good in him...yet. Chief Risk was a patient man, and he would keep trying.

"Why don't you get some chow, Chief?" Risk asked. "After chow I was hoping I could talk you into going up to the base machine shop and picking up that parts order for me while I've got the watch."

Twitchell beamed. Risk was the only person on board he wanted to please, and he was eager to do so. "Hell," he snapped, "I'll go get the parts now and eat when I get back." He turned to the messenger of the watch. "Go get that idiot Lopez and tell him to start up his truck."

"I think he's at chow, Chief," the messenger said.

Twitchell's pig-face got red and angry. "I don't give a shit if he's rolling around in his rack with his five-fingered girlfriend!" he snapped. "Get his ass up here!" The messenger ran below. Chief Risk smiled patiently. Twitchell paced and fumed.

The messenger returned shortly with charming Billy, who was still chewing his lunch. He was not smiling. "You wanna go somewhere,

Chief?" Billy asked, hesitantly.

"Why the hell else would I call you up here?" Chief Twitchell spat. "Go get the truck. We got some parts to pick up."

Billy hurried down the brow to the pier and ran to where he kept the truck parked next to a tin-covered Quonset hut. He jumped in, rolled down the windows to force, in a breeze and dispel some of the sauna-like hot air, and started up the truck. Chief Twitchell was waiting on the pier, at the bottom of the brow, staring impatiently at Billy.

With Twitchell in the cab of the truck with him, Billy gently urged the truck forward, shifting the gears very carefully so as not to grind them. He proceeded down the pier in strict observance of the speed limit. He still was not smiling.

Up on the bridge, Tanner sat with three other crewmen, playing pinochle on the quartermaster's chart table. He stood up as the sound of the pickup truck passed by and looked out the hatch of the flying bridge. "Billy's got Twitchell in the truck with him," he laughed. "I never saw him drive so careful!"

Chief Risk, standing on the quarterdeck with arms folded across his chest, watched as the pickup truck faded down the pier. He smiled to himself as he thought of Chief Twitchell and his tirade on the quarterdeck. Chief Risk knew he could get Twitchell off the ship on that errand if he played it right. Now, the quarterdeck was peaceful again without all that unnecessary stress, and by the time Twitchell returned he would be relatively calm...for Twitchell. Chief Risk was particularly amused by the careful way Billy Lopez was driving. Shaking his head at the disappearing truck he muttered to himself, "I've never seen him drive that carefully."

R.J. sat with the other line-handlers in the messdecks, eating noon chow and talking. The messdecks had booths, like at a diner, lining each side and secured to the deck and bulkheads. Each booth could accommodate four men during chow. Sailors came, ate and left. The messdecks were almost empty when Lester came sauntering in. He folded his whitehat and stuffed it into the back pocket of his dungarees, and spotted the line handlers eating at their booth. He picked up a metal tray, some silverware and moved down the chow line, inspecting the selections.

"Hawkins!" Lester yelled. "Where the hell are you, old dude?"

Hawkins, first class ship's serviceman and head cook, shuffled slowly into the galley from the dry goods locker. His large black hands carried a twenty-pound bag of flour in front of him. He walked like an old, pregnant woman. Hawkins never did anything quickly, except make pancakes, and he glared at Lester with unconcealed contempt. "What you want, Lester?" he drawled. ·

"Some better food!" Lester replied loudly, looking around to make certain he had an audience. "Something other than what you got here. Shit, ·man, there ain't nothin' left to eat." He gestured toward the mostly-empty steam trays.

"Then you shoulda got your skinny ass down here a little quicker," Hawkins replied slowly, dumping the flour on the deck and heading back into the locker. Hawkins didn't like criticism, and he didn't like clutter. His galley had to shine, not just be clean but shine. As soon as any meal was over, Hawkins stood over his charges and personally saw to it that everything was cleaned, swabbed, disinfected and shined. He often bragged that he had the cleanest galley in the seventh fleet. The crew of the Haverfield thought it was probably true.

Lester scowled and filled his tray with leftovers, mumbling, "Most of this stuff looks like it was already eaten once." Then he turned and sauntered toward the line-handlers.

Oh, shit, R.J. thought.

Lester tossed his metal tray on the table across from the line handlers and slid into the booth, his back to the bulkhead so he was facing them. He stared at R.J. as he shoveled food into his mouth with a soupspoon. Lester didn't seem to like forks, or maybe he was unsure how to operate one.

"Thunder Party tonight, boys," Lester said, his mouth full of food, his jaw working as he chewed. He pointed to R.J. with his spoon. "And you the guest of honor, boot-camp." He shoveled the rest of his lunch into his mouth and seemed to swallow it whole, throwing the spoon on the tray where it made a loud clang. He slid out of the booth and stood in front of the line-handlers.

"By the way, boot-camp," Lester said, "you got the mid-watch on the focsul tonight since you the new guy aboard." He smiled but it didn't improve his looks any. "New guys always got the duty first night aboard," he declared. He wiped his mouth on his shirt sleeve and headed toward the scullery where he deposited his tray and spoon for washing. He turned and pointed a finger at R.J., then made a fist with the middle finger knuckle sticking up. He smiled again and shook the fist at R.J., then left the messdecks and headed topside.

Sonny shook his head and said to R.J., "Looks like y'all got a new best friend."

"So what was that all about?" R.J. asked.

Jefferson explained, "Every new guy comes aboard, he has to be initiated twice before he's a Havernaut. First is the Thunder Party and then the equator crossing. Then you a Havernaut."

R.J. thought for a moment. "Is that like an Argonaut?" he asked.

Pancho laughed. "Hey, you ain't as dumb as you look, boot," he said, slapping R.J. on the back. "You know about the Argonauts?"

"Yeah," R.J. replied. "I like to read a lot."

"Well here on this ship," Pancho explained, tapping his index finger on the table, "we got MacDonald and the Havernauts." He smiled at Sonny and Jefferson who smiled back in agreement.

"OK," R.J. sighed. "I'll bite. What's MacDonald and the Havernauts?"

"Cain't tell you that, boy," Sonny said. "But after you been thundered you get all your questions answered."

R.J. thought he might as well resign himself to the initiation if he were ever going to become a member of this crew. All these guys went through it, and if they could do it, he damned sure could!

"Don' worry, boy," Sonny said, smiling. "It only takes about five minutes to get thundered."

"I can probably stand anything for five minutes," R.J. said, smiling.

The other three broke out laughing. "Don't be too sure of that, *amigo*," Pancho warned, his eyes narrowing. "Don't be too sure." He reached across the table and pressed his index finger into R.J.'s chest, in the center of the breastbone just above the solar plexus. "Know what this spot is?" he asked, grinning.

"What?" R.J. asked, looking down at the finger in his chest.

"That's where the knot on your neckerchief goes when you're in dress blues." He laughed loudly and Jefferson and Sonny laughed, too. *Obviously a private joke.* R.J. didn't get it.

The four sailors left the messdecks and headed aft toward First Division's compartment. They had fifteen minutes before "Turn To" would be announced, and R.J. wanted to get his gear organized and stowed. They met Chief Whipple coming down the passageway.

"Davis," he called when he spotted R.J. Whipple motioned for R.J. to join him as he walked. "I want you to go up on the bridge and tell Tanner it's time to knock off the pinochle game and turn to," he instructed. "Tell him I said you are to work with his crew today, understand?"

R.J. nodded. "Yes sir," he said.

"Knock it off with the sir shit, lad," Whipple snapped. "I told you I ain't no officer. You call me that again and I'll have you scraping out the bilges. You got me, sailor?"

"Yes, Chief," R.J. replied, although he didn't know what "scraping the bilges" meant. It didn't sound like much fun, though. *Damn,* he thought, *I gotta stop talking like a boot!* He turned to apologize but Chief Whipple was gone, purposely striding aft toward the fantail, blowing cigarette smoke out of the side of his mouth. *More troops to get moving. More work to get done. The old lady wasn't going to get the rust off with the crew just sitting around on their asses.*

R.J. turned, looked forward and up toward the 03 level where the bridge was located. *OK,* he thought, *now how do I get to the bridge?*

"I know, I know," Tanner protested as R.J. finally found his way to the bridge. First he traveled up this ladder, down this passageway, up another ladder, around the signal bag to the wing-bridge and into the pilot house, where Tanner and three others were still huddled over their pinochle game. "Whip sent you up here to break up our game, didn't he?" Tanner asked, smiling pleasantly. R.J. recognized Riley, but didn't know the other two card players.

"He told me to work with you and your crew," R.J. explained.

"C'mon, Tanner," one of the players complained. He waved his cards in the air. "The bid's to you at sixty-five," he said. "Let's get this hand in."

"Sorry, Chuck," Tanner threw his hand in, face up. "Time to turn to."

"Shit!" Chuck yelled, throwing his cards into the air. "I had a thousand fucking aces!" He pulled away from the chart table and headed out to the wing-bridge. "Gotta go see if Risk got my generator parts," he said. He slipped out the hatch and was gone.

Riley returned to the radio shack and Tanner introduced R.J. to the fourth card player, a young, white-haired deckhand with skin so pale he almost looked albino. The hair on his head and arms was white and fine, but his blue eyes sparkled with color. "This is Chris Haynes," Tanner said, "but we all call him Cotton." He grinned at R.J. "Guess why?"

R.J. shook Cotton's white hand. "Don't you get sunburned easy?" he asked.

Cotton shook his head. "Don't know why, but I never burn and I never tan." A wooden toothpick dangled from his mouth. "But I think the sun's bleaching my hair whiter." He looked up as if trying to see his hair.

"He's a surfer dude from California," Tanner explained. "I can't believe the sun never burns that white skin."

R.J. marveled at Cotton. His own skin, dotted with freckles, was sensitive to the sun and he could already feel his face, neck and arms getting hotter, signaling a developing sunburn from the line-handling adventure. Right now, he was quite comfortable standing in the pilot house, in among the operational tools of a Navy ship; the helm and lee-helm, the chart table, the radar scope set over in a corner with a large plastic cone-shaped viewing scope mounted around the screen. The scope allowed a clear radar picture during the daylight hours. At night, the ship was practically blacked out and there was no light interference, so the scope was not necessary. Communications equipment inhabited the bulkheads and was mounted on the overhead. R.J. took it all in. He had enlisted over a year ago, and right now, at this moment, he was beginning to feel like he *was* a sailor in the U.S. Navy. He couldn't wait to get to sea.

Cotton broke out a can of Brasso brass cleaner and an old tee shirt and headed down to the quarterdeck. "Time to polish up the ship's bell," he called as he left the bridge.

Tanner gathered up the pinochle cards and secured them with a large rubber band before putting them in the drawer under the chart table. "You play pinochle?" he asked R.J.

"Nope. My grandparents played it when I was a kid, but I never picked it up."

"Well, here on the Haverfield we are a bunch of pinochle playin' fools," Tanner explained. "You'll pick it up. It's a good game to pass the time, especially at sea when you're off duty." He closed the drawer and motioned for R.J. to follow him into the chart room aft of the bridge. "The Whip always wants the new guys to know about the Haverfield," he explained. "So let me show you who Mr. Haverfield was."

R.J. followed Tanner into the chart room where a large brass plaque was mounted on the bulkhead. It was a bust of the namesake of the ship, James Wallace Haverfield. Below his sculptured likeness a legend described how James Wallace Haverfield joined the Navy in 1940, accepted an appointment as a midshipman and was commissioned an ensign in 1941. He was assigned to the U.S.S. Arizona, home-ported in Hawaii, in the summer of that year, and during the Japanese attack on Pearl Harbor in December,

Ensign James Wallace Haverfield was one of 46 officers and 1057 enlisted men who went down with the famous battleship when it sank in the harbor.

R.J. stood staring at the plaque, trying to imagine the Japanese surprise attack, the sinking of the Arizona and the deaths of so many sailors. His mind drifted back to the story of the sneak attack on Pearl Harbor he had heard so often growing up in Denver. At that moment he felt he had a better understanding of why his own father and two of his uncles had joined the Navy right after the Pearl Harbor attack. He read the legend several times standing in front of the plaque, and vowed he would always remember Ensign Haverfield as a hero of his father's war. All his life he had heard the stories, from his father and uncles, about the United States Navy and its heroic performance in the Pacific. But they were only stories, and he had always had a hard time relating to them. Here, in the presence of this tribute to one who lost his life in that war, R.J. felt some of that pride. *This is what the Navy is all about,* he thought, *and I'm part of it.*

"Kinda gets to you, don't it?" Tanner broke into R.J.'s trance.

"Yeah." R.J. nodded.

"You seem like a pretty good guy," Tanner went on. "But the fellas on board this ship think you're a troublemaker, a renegade."

"How come? They don't even know me."

"We heard all about that bullshit in San Diego," Tanner said. "You boys had a good time sticking it to the Navy, huh?"

"It's a long story," R.J. replied.

"Yeah, it always is," Tanner nodded. "But I'll tell you one thing." He led R.J. out of the chart room and back into the pilothouse. "Being on board a ship is totally different from being stationed on a base. You can fuck around all you want on base, but aboard ship, at sea, everybody's got to do his job, you know what I mean?" He looked directly at R.J. with a very serious expression on his face. "You fuck up at sea and you put other guys' lives in danger. One little fuck up, and somebody can get hurt or killed."

R.J. got the point. "I always wanted to go to sea," he said quietly. "And I'll work as hard as I have to. I don't want to get in any more trouble."

"Good," Tanner slapped R.J. on the back. "I'll try to remember that when I'm thundering your ass." He smiled good-naturedly and waved R.J. out onto the wing-bridge. "Meantime, let me show you around a little."

Tanner gave R.J. the tour of the 03 level which included the port and starboard wing-bridges, the pilot house and the flying bridge, which was just forward of the pilot house and ran the length of the 03 level. The flying bridge was where the captain and other officers directed the ship when at sea. The captain's chair was secured to a stanchion on the starboard side of the flying bridge. From that vantage point the captain could view everything ahead of the ship through the plexi-glass windows that covered the front of the flying bridge from port to starboard. Portholes were installed in the pilothouse behind the flying bridge so the captain or officer of the deck could communicate with the helmsman, the lee-helmsman and the radar operator.

What intrigued R.J. the most was the signal bridge, tucked behind the pilothouse. On each side of the signal bridge stood a large metal box that held the multi-colored signal flags, arranged neatly in their designated slots, a brass hook-clip sticking up so that the signalmen could attach flag to flag as he raised the required flag hoist. A typical flag hoist was the ship's call sign, always beginning with the letter 'N' as in November in the Pacific theater, and the letter 'W' as in Whiskey in the Atlantic theatre. The call sign was not displayed in port, only when the ship was at sea. The Haverfield's call sign was November Kilo Kilo Bravo, or NKKB.

Signal lights used to send Morse code were attached to the railings on both sides of the ship. They were placed on swivels so they could be pointed in any direction for communications. R.J. tested the handle of the port signal light and watched as the louvers opened and closed. The louvers, when closed, shut off the light, and could be manipulated by the handle to send the appropriate coded messages. R.J. fiddled with the handle, trying to form letters in Morse code, but it was quite different from the radioman's signal key, and he fumbled with it.

"I hear you're pretty good at Morse code," Tanner said, watching R.J. fiddle with the signal light. "Riley told us."

"I can read and send it on a radio key, but I don't know about this flashing light thing," R.J. replied, working the handle and trying to get the rhythm of the thing. The handle made a loud clacking sound every time he worked it, and no matter how hard he tried, he couldn't manipulate the handle without making noise.

"Who the hell is slamming my signal light?" John Anselmi, signalman second class had come up the ladder to the signal bridge and was eyeing R.J. and Tanner suspiciously.

"How you doin', Salami?" Tanner asked, greeting the signalman by his Haverfield-appointed nickname. Anselmi nodded, frowning at Tanner and R.J. His thin, almost bony face expressed skepticism and suspicion. Taller than R.J., he was all elbows and knees. He ambled more than walked, taking large strides with his long, thin legs. A Navy man for twelve years, he had mastered the slouch of the veteran salt.

Anselmi looked from Tanner to R.J. "This is the new guy, huh?" he asked, motioning to R.J. with his head.

"Yeah, I'm giving him the tour."

"Did he see Mr. Haverfield?" Anselmi asked.

"Yeah, he saw him."

"Then the tour's done. Get the hell off my signal bridge." Anselmi was smiling but R.J. had a feeling he wasn't joking. He and Tanner left the 03 level and Tanner led him down to the forecastle to continue the tour.

"This here's the focsul," Tanner explained, "and this is the capstain." He pointed to the large, round cylinder-shaped mechanism that pulled up the anchor chain electrically. Around its smooth sides, sailors would loop the mooring line after it had been attached to a cleat on the pier by line-handlers, and the capstain would turn and pull the ship closer to the dock. Tanner explained its operation, pointing to the two large chains leading to the port and starboard anchors.

"Yeah," R.J. nodded. "I saw that big AE do that this morning."

"Below this deck," Tanner went on, "is the bosun's locker where we store a lot of line, tackle blocks, turnbuckles and bosun's tools." He chuckled at R.J. "But you'll get to see the bosun's locker later tonight." He winked mysteriously.

Tanner led R.J. to various places on the ship, pointing out how different duties contributed to the running of the Haverfield. It was obvious to R.J. that Tanner knew his stuff when it came to seamanship. It was also obvious the other sailors respected him as one of the top hands aboard. Time passed very quickly during his tour, and before R.J. knew it, it was 1600 and time to knock off work. He and Tanner headed down to First Division's compartment. R.J. wanted to get his stuff organized.

Queen was at his usual post, standing between two tiers of bunks, arms extended and resting on opposite sides, directing activities and chiding the men as they filed into the compartment.

"C'mon, girls," he sang in his deep gravelly voice. "Get this compartment squared away and ready for inspection."

Groans came from the men. "Inspection?" Pea wailed. "We got inspection?"

Queen smiled, and his big ugly teeth protruded from his mouth. "No Sis," he said to Pea. "I said get it *ready* for inspection. Don't mean we're gonna *have* one. I want to see this compartment ship-shape and squared away." He stepped closer to Pea and looked at him suspiciously.

"You still a virgin, ain't you, Pea?" he asked, laughing his big ugly laugh.

This was a signal to the rest of the men that Pea was the target du jour and they all chimed in.

"No he ain't," Sonny said. "Just ask his right hand." More laughter.

"Well," Cotton chimed in, "when you think about it, who in her right mind would screw Pea?"

"Bend him over," Lester volunteered. "I'll break his cherry!"

"Yeah," Charming Billy said, "bend him over and I'll drive him home!"

"Not the way you drive!" Pea protested.

The crew laughed and joked their way good-naturedly through the compartment clean-up, hurling insults at each other, pushing each other playfully and generally having a good time.

When they were done, Queen walked slowly through the compartment, making a big show of inspecting every rack. He ran his finger across every surface and checked for dust, nodding and smiling as he went.

"You boys are lookin' good," he announced. "You get a four-oh. Let's go get chow!"

The members of First Division scrambled up the ladder to the messdecks, playfully jostling each other and continuing with the insults. As R.J. came up the ladder he realized that no one in the compartment had said a thing to him. In fact, no one had even acknowledged his presence, not even Lester. R.J. wondered if something was up. He had heard these guys liked to party, liked to take liberty as soon as they knocked off work, but no one was getting dressed in whites and no one was leaving the ship. *Maybe they're getting ready to initiate me? When will I find out?*

He didn't have to wait long.

After evening chow R.J. went back down to First Division's compartment, finally getting the chance to store his gear and get squared away. He knew he had the mid-watch on the focsul so he got out his shaving kit and shower shoes so that he could shower and get some sleep before his watch. Before he could get his dungarees off, Pea came up to him.

"Come with me, Davis," Pea beckoned. "Tanner said you have to tour the bosun's locker."

R.J. thought, *this is it,* and followed Pea forward through the messdecks and the operations division compartment and through a hatch leading to the bosun's locker. Here the passageway narrowed as they approached the bow of the ship, and as Pea stopped to sip water from a scuttlebutt, he glanced back surreptitiously as if he wanted to make sure the others were following.

R.J. had enough street smarts to know he was being set up, and he had a sudden impulse to slam Pea's head into the scuttlebutt and try to escape, but he didn't know how to get out of there. Besides, he liked Pea, and he was anxious to get this whole thing over with. So after Pea got his drink of water R.J. followed him dutifully and they proceeded forward.

R.J. ducked and stepped through the hatch into the small forward compartment used as the bosun's locker. On the bulkheads hung several loops of line, both manila hemp and nylon, of various sizes. Tackle blocks and turnbuckles along with brooms, shovels, grappling hooks, wire brushes and paint scrapers were stored in several boxes on the deck. The locker was shaped like a triangle, wider at the entryway hatch and narrower, almost coming to a point, where the ship formed the peak of the bow.

R.J. looked around and took everything in. Suddenly, the overhead hatch wheel spun around and opened. Several First Division sailors came dropping down the ladder into the locker and several more came through the entryway hatch. Some of the men R.J. had met, and some were strangers. They gathered around him in a circle, and Tanner stepped forward, taking command.

"OK, Wog," he said, "we can do this the easy way or we can do it the hard way." He cocked his head at R.J. "Which way you wanna do it?" The others stood around smiling and punching their fists into their palms.

"What's the easy way?" R.J. asked.

"You lay down and take it easy. We thunder you and then you go topside and kiss the Union Jack for luck," Tanner explained.

"And the hard way?" R.J. asked, not really wanting to do this the hard way.

Lester stepped through the crowd and got into R.J.'s face. "You fight and we throw you down on the deck, thunder you twice and then toss your sorry ass in the drink," Lester sneered nastily. "Personally, I hope you go for the hard way."

R.J. stared directly into Lester's sneering face. "You'd like that, wouldn't you, Gomer?" he challenged. This brought laughter from the crew.

Lester just sneered and nodded. "I'm gonna pay you back for that Gomer shit."

R.J. sat down on the deck and lay back. Immediately several men grabbed his arms and legs and pinned them to the deck. Tanner bent down and ripped open R.J.'s dungaree shirt and pressed his finger into the center of R.J.'s chest, just above the solar plexus. "Know what this spot is?" he asked, smiling pleasantly.

R.J. remembered the conversation in the messdecks. "Yeah, that's where the knot of my neckerchief goes," he answered.

"Correct," Tanner replied. He removed his finger from the spot on R.J.'s chest and raised his fist about three feet into the air, the knuckle of his middle finger protruding from his fist. He brought the knuckle down hard, like a jackhammer on R.J.'s chest three times, chanting, "Welcome to the HAV-*bam*-ER-*bam*-FIELD-*bam*!"

"Ow! Shit that hurts!" R.J. howled.

"Next!" Tanner yelled, and one by one the men thundered R.J. with their middle knuckles, repeating the Haverfield welcome while R.J. writhed on the deck, hollering in pain.

Cotton, Sonny and Pea were a little gentler, as were Pancho and Billy, but when it was Lester's turn he pounded R.J. very hard, not three times, but four.

"Hey," Pea shouted at Lester, "three times, man! Not four!"

"Fuck off, Pea," Lester said calmly, looking down at R.J. "This boot-camp muddafucka needs to know he ain't in San Diego no more!"

"Take it easy, Gomer," Tanner hissed, pushing Lester back. Lester didn't like being called by his first name, but he wasn't about to challenge Tanner, and he backed off.

The thundering continued until the last man was done. With every blow R.J.'s chest became more swollen and painful. He thought it would never end, and he felt the tears welling up in his eyes but he wasn't about to cry in front of these men. Just when he thought he couldn't take any more, they were through. Slowly, they backed away and some made their way up the ladder through the overhead hatch. Others filed out through the entryway hatch. Only R.J., Tanner, Lester, Sonny and Cotton remained. R.J. felt as if they had been pounding on him for hours, but looking at his watch, he realized it had only been about ten minutes. He got up and pulled the front of his shirt closed. The middle of his chest was red, swollen and hurt like hell. He was going to have one hell of a bruise.

"Get your cover," Tanner said, pointing to R.J.'s whitehat on the deck. "Now you gotta go topside and kiss the Union Jack."

"Then it's over?" R.J. asked weakly.

Tanner nodded. "Then it's over."

R.J. climbed the ladder to the overhead hatch and pushed himself through to the deck of the forecastle. Several members of the Thunder Party were gathered there, waiting for him.

"Where's the Union Jack?" R.J. asked no one in particular.

"Right there," Sonny pointed to the flag flying at the bow of the ship. It had fifty white stars on a field of dark blue, like the stars on the American flag.

"And I got to kiss it?" R.J. asked.

The Union Jack was fluttering gently in the evening breeze. "That's right," Tanner said. "Just step up there, gather it in and kiss it."

R.J. felt his chest, touching it gingerly. It was very sore and hurt like hell. He went to the bow of the ship and reached up for the Union Jack. He got a handful of it, brought it in and kissed it. When he turned back, five men grabbed him, lifted him up over the lifeline and threw him over the side into the harbor.

R.J. smacked into the water head-first and sank about twenty feet before scrambling to the surface. When he broke the water's surface, he was sputtering and coughing, choking on a mixture of diesel fuel, salt water and God-knows-what-else floating in the harbor. The men on the focsul were cheering and laughing, pointing down to where R.J. treaded water.

"Man overboard, port side!" Sonny laughed. He looked down at the pitiful picture of R.J. flailing away in the water. "He looks like a drownded rat!" The men on the focsul only laughed harder.

"Throw him a Mae West!" Cotton yelled.

"Throw him an anchor!" Lester called.

"We ain't supposed to dump garbage in the harbor!" Pea yelled at R.J.

Tanner leaned over the sideline and called to R.J. "Swim over to the dock and pull yourself up on the beams," he instructed.

R.J. swam to the dock and dragged himself up on the lowest wooden beam. He was tired, beat-up, coughing, sputtering and half drowned. From there on the lower beam he could climb up, beam to beam until he was standing on the pier. His whitehat was floating in the harbor.

Tanner pointed to a spot aft where the ship's deck was lowest and closest to the pier. R.J. stepped up on the pier, wincing in pain and climbed over the sideline to the ship's deck. He was wet, tired, in pain and more than a little pissed-off, but relieved that the ceremony was over.

"Welcome to the Haverfield," Tanner said, smiling and extending his hand which R.J. shook wetly. "You can't be called a 'boot' anymore."

Billy Lopez was next to shake R.J.'s hand. "Welcome aboard," he smiled charmingly.

One by one the men of First Division shook R.J.'s hand and welcomed him to the Haverfield. The last in line was Lester who grudgingly took his hand and shook it.

"You *still* a fuckin' Wog!" he sneered.

* * * * *

Lieutenant Francis MacDonald stood on the port side of the flying bridge, watching as R.J. was hoisted up and thrown over the side. Mr. MacDonald did not approve of Thunder Parties, but he didn't interfere partly because the tradition preceded his service aboard the Haverfield, and partly because he thought the initiation helped to bond the men.

MacDonald had been on board only six months when Captain Oliver took over command, and he shared the captain's disgust with the appearance of the ship and the attitude of the crew. MacDonald had already begun to develop and implement training programs for the men in First Division. At first they resisted, as most men do when their routine is changed. But recently the lieutenant felt that perhaps they were beginning to jell, if only a little. It was, as he was fond of telling them, a matter of establishing good habits and then repeating them until they became automatic. That's how a good deck force operates: *Automatically.*

This new man, Davis, was somehow different from most of the men under his command in First Division, though the lieutenant couldn't quite say why. *Instinct?* He chuckled. Yes, instinctively, MacDonald felt there was much more to R.J. than was recorded in his service file. He had read the file, courtesy of the exec, and he knew R.J. was going to be assigned to First Division as soon as he reported on board. He observed the new man from afar, not approaching him, but watching as he interacted with the crew. Earlier, he had quizzed Chief Whipple and P.T. Tanner extensively about their interaction with R.J. and their impressions. Davis seemed to be easy to get along with, at least as far as Chief Whipple and Tanner were concerned. MacDonald was aware of the animosity Lester held for the man, but that was just Lester. Lieutenant MacDonald prided himself in his ability to read a man, and this one seemed on the surface to be pretty much like all the others when they first came aboard the Haverfield. Still, MacDonald had that feeling about Davis. He was trying to find the words to explain the new man. *Would I call Davis different? Maybe he is different in some way I can't quite fathom.* The First Division lieutenant couldn't shake the feeling that there was some depth there not yet revealed. Also, there was that unfortunate incident in San Diego. *What the hell,* MacDonald thought, *we are all shadowed by the past in some way. That's why we're here and not in the fleet.* He chuckled again. *Or nuclear power school!*

Lieutenant MacDonald was determined to forge an efficient, well-trained deck crew, a crew that would operate as a real team, working together and depending upon each other like a good team does. He wanted a team that could handle any situation at sea with speed, professionalism and pride. And yes, he *wanted* that white 'E' for deck-crew excellence to be painted on the ship's stack. Then everyone would recognize the Haverfield as having an outstanding deck force. That was very important to him, although he rarely mentioned it to anyone other than Whipple, and he knew the ship's chief bosun shared his desire for the white 'E.' What Mr. MacDonald needed were a few more men who could rise to leadership and inspire the rest of the crew. Men like P.T. Tanner and Sonny Metzner. *Perhaps this new man Davis would be one of them. Davis exhibited the signs. Perhaps. Or maybe the exec was right and this man was just another fuck-up.* Mr. Mac would keep a close eye on his progress.

R.J. returned below to First Division's compartment and began peeling off his wet dungarees. His boondockers, the leather deck boots worn by all the crew, squished when he walked and often he slipped and slid on the deck as he got out of his clothes.

Big Queen stood leaning against a bulkhead, sucking his teeth and watching with amusement as R.J. sat on the deck and pulled off his boondockers.

"Put those things up on the 04 level for about an hour," Queen instructed, pointing to the boots and smiling that ugly smile. "They'll be dry and then you can spend a little time putting a spit shine on them. You know how to spit shine boots, don't you, R.J.?" He smiled his kindliest smile as pleasantly as he could. The effect on his face was scary.

It was the first time Queen had addressed him in that manner and it made R.J. smile wanly. Hopefully, it was a sign of acceptance by the big man. "That I can do, Boats," he replied. *But not tonight,* he thought.

As R.J. pulled off his dungaree shirt, Queen let out a whistle. "Boy, you gonna have *some* bruise," he observed. "That soft, white, state-side skin of yours ain't used to that kind of abuse." He chuckled, a deep rumbling sound that came from somewhere down in his big gut. "And you gettin' sunburned, too," he chuckled, pressing an index finger into R.J.'s reddening neck. "Guess you had a pretty rough first day, huh, kid?"

"Yeah, pretty rough." R.J. acknowledged. *And it ain't over yet,* he thought to himself. *Still got to stand that mid-watch.*

Queen watched R.J. closely as he undressed and got ready to hit the shower. "Tell you what you do," the big man said. "After you shower, put some of this on the sunburn." He tossed a small bottle of witch hazel to R.J. "Then go to the galley and get some ice for your chest. Keep the ice on there as long as you can. That bruise'll be gone in a week or so." He chuckled again as R.J. started out of the compartment.

"I want that witch hazel back!" Queen called after him. The big boatswain's mate watched as R.J. passed through the hatch and headed to the shower. He stroked his big ugly chin thoughtfully and murmured to himself, "Where the hell does the Navy get these little weak-assed sisters anyway?" Queen sighed and returned to pacing up and down the compartment, looking for infractions such as a sock lying on the deck, or a rack not made up properly.

R.J. showered slowly, reflecting on the events of the day. It had been a pretty eventful day. First, he got chewed out by the exec and delegated to the deck force. Then he had had his session with Chief Whipple, his introduction to the men of First Division, the line-handling party, the tour of the ship by Tanner, and finally he had endured his Thunder Party and a soaking in the harbor. *I can't wait to see what tomorrow brings,* R.J. thought acidly. He toweled off, put the witch hazel on his sunburn (ouch) and made his way back down to the compartment to dress in clean dungarees.

The compartment was empty, except for Jefferson who had the duty as messenger of the evening watch, beginning at 2000 hours. Most everyone who didn't have the duty had caught the liberty bus to the Mocombo Club. Jefferson was donning the duty belt and nightstick of the messenger of the watch and grinned widely as R.J. began to dress in clean clothes.

42

"Hey, man, dat was fun, huh?" Jefferson asked. "Bet you won't forget where the knot on yo' neckerchief goes."

R.J. just smiled and buttoned up his shirt.

"I remember my Thunder Party," Jefferson reminisced. "Shit, I almost drownded when they deep-sixed me!" He shook his head, grinning at the memory. "But you get over it. The good news is that you get to thunder the next new guy come aboard." He squared his whitehat on his head, checked to make sure his neckerchief was knotted at the right spot and threw R.J. a smart salute. "Goin' topside, m'man. See you later." He started out the hatch, but turned back to R.J. and said, "Movie call in fifteen minutes. No sense you trying to sleep. I gotta wake yo ass in less than fo' hours."

"Do we have movies every night?" R.J. asked hopefully.

"Yeah, but mostly they a bunch of shit," Jefferson explained. "We never get good movies until they been out a couple years. Remember, man, we in the foreign legion out here." He laughed and set out to relieve the watch.

R.J. finished dressing and went up the aft ladder which led from First Division's compartment to the awning-covered fantail. There the movies were shown on a large, stretched white sheet. Men who had the duty or just didn't take liberty were sitting around on the deck and on the torpedo tubes waiting for the movie to start. As R.J. came up on deck, a scattering of applause broke out among the moviegoers when they spotted him. Apparently, everyone aboard ship knew about his Thunder Party.

Pea waved him over to one of the torpedo tubes and offered him a seat. R.J. accepted and pulled himself up onto the tube, wincing in pain. "Damn," he exclaimed, massaging his chest. "That hurts like hell."

"Put some ice on it," Pea said. "That helps a little."

R.J. had forgotten to get ice for his swollen chest. He started to hop off the torpedo tube when Billy Lopez came over and handed him a paper cup full of ice chips. "Hold this on it," he offered, smiling charmingly. R.J. remembered that Billy was one of the guys who didn't pound too hard on him, and he took the cup thankfully. As he looked around at the men watching him with smiles on their faces, he realized he had passed an important test today, one more small step toward being accepted by the crew. They all had their Thunder Parties when they first came aboard, and they remembered how it felt. Although he was sore and very tired, R.J. relaxed on the torpedo tube a little happier and even a little content, though he wasn't quite sure why.

Snively, the ship's yeoman, was tinkering with the film projector and getting the reel ready to thread when the announcement came over the 1MC, the ship's loudspeaker. "Movie Call! Movie Call on the fantail!"

The crowd began to murmur as Snively hit the switch and the film began to feed through the projector. After a bit of flickering on the screen, the sound started and the film's title came on: *"Beau Brummel"* the big letters said as the music began to rise.

The men on the fantail started howling and complaining. R.J. looked around puzzled. "What's wrong?" he asked Pea.

"Oh, shit," Pea said. "We done seen this fucker six or seven times already. Hey Snively!" he yelled at the yeoman, "can't you find no other movies up at the supply office?" A loud chorus of boos coming from the moviegoers indicated they all agreed with Pea.

Snively became defensive. "You want 'Splendor in the Grass' again?' You want 'Stagecoach' again? All the movies they got up there we seen about fifty times!"

"What about that James Bond movie?" Billy Lopez asked. "They made a movie out of that book, what's it called...Dr. NO?"

"Yeah, the base Officer's Club has that checked out for the next week," Snively replied. "And then every ship in port gets to see it, then it goes back to the Officer's Club and maybe we get it in six months."

As the complaining became louder and eventually simmered down, Snively switched off the projector and looked around. "You wanna see this, or not?" he challenged.

Everyone quieted down and sat resignedly as Snively turned on the projector and for the fifth time in two months, the crew sat back to watch 'Beau Brummel'.

R.J. leaned over to Billy. "How come we can't get better movies?" he asked.

"Cause Twitchell pissed off the supply people on the base, and to get even they put us on the bottom of the list...for everything."

"Yeah," Pea agreed. "They always short us on rations, too. When we at sea for two weeks or longer, we run out of everything. The Cap'n tried to fix it, and the supply officer up there said he would take care of it, but nothin's changed."

R.J. sat back and watched the movie. *Twitchell again. What an asshole*, he thought, shaking his head.

EIGHT

A duty driver from the 'Hill,' as the Officer's Club at the Guam Naval base was affectionately known, picked up Captain Oliver at 1900 hours. Reception and cocktails at 1930 and dinner at 2000, the invitation had said. Captain Oliver looked sharp in his dress whites. The high, stiff collar accentuated his perfect military posture. He looked like a Naval officer from a recruiting poster.

The car pulled up to the officers' club and the driver opened the door for Captain Oliver. It was cooler up there on the hill, with a strong, smooth breeze, and tropical flora and fauna scented the air with pungent aromas. D. Paul Oliver stepped out of the car and put his hat on, nodding thanks to the driver. As he mounted the dozen steps up to the club he could hear an orchestra playing a Tommy Dorsey tune...or was it Jimmy Dorsey? Well, the new admiral is pushing fifty, so swing would be his preferred music. Though Captain Oliver had yet to meet the new admiral, he had met enough older officers to know what to expect. He would spend the evening sitting between the admiral and his frumpish but gracious wife and he'd listen politely to her social gossip with one ear and to the admiral's World War Two stories with the other ear. He had heard that the new admiral had married very well. *Some rich matron named Von Dulm from Miami. The Miami Von Dulms,* he mused. He hoped it wouldn't be a long, boring evening. *Perhaps there would be an interesting woman there tonight, one he could charm, one he could talk to.* He shook his head. *Too much to ask.*

Checking his hat and putting the claim check in his pocket, Captain Oliver stood inside the entryway and scanned the room. There was a receiving line to the right with several officers and their ladies ready to meet the new admiral. It was considered polite to greet the host and hostess before one went to the bar, and Captain Oliver was nothing if not polite. He joined the line and looked toward the front, trying to get a look at the new admiral. People were moving in and out of his line of sight, and he thought he caught a glimpse, but someone moved in front of him again. Then someone else moved away, and at that moment D. Paul Oliver, smooth operator and eligible bachelor, first laid eyes on the woman who would wrench his heart and torture his thoughts for a long, long time to come.

She disappeared again. *Damn! Where did all these people come from and why was this line moving so damn slow?* Captain Oliver craned his neck toward the front, bobbing and weaving his head, trying to get another look at that beautiful creature. *Was she the admiral's daughter? Some other officer's wife? Just my luck she'll be married,* he thought.

At last the line evaporated and D. Paul Oliver's name was announced to the new admiral.

"Hello, Paul." Rear Admiral Quentin Prescott shook Paul's hand warmly. "It's great to meet you." He nodded toward the beauty at his side. "Allow me to present my wife, Lorelei," he beamed.

Wife? Captain Oliver smiled and took the proffered hand. "A pleasure, ma'am," he heard his voice say. "Welcome to Guam." *Welcome to Guam? That sounded stupid!*

Lorelei Von Dulm Prescott was a remarkably beautiful woman. Her dark hair framed her lovely face and fell below her shoulders. She wore a white, off the shoulder dress with a full skirt that swung when she moved and the only jewelry she wore was a single strand of pearls around her neck. *Besides, of course, that wedding ring!* Paul stood there and stared into those lovely, violet eyes.

"It's a pleasure to meet you too, Captain Oliver," she cooed, smiling sweetly. "May I have my hand back, please?"

Paul looked down. He was still holding her hand! He snatched his hand back quickly, which brought another smile from Lorelei. "My goodness, Captain, did I burn your hand?"

"I...I'm going to get a drink. May I bring you something?"

"Not right now," she smiled sweetly. "But I'll take a raincheck."

Paul nodded dumbly and wandered off toward the bar. Lorelei and the admiral continued greeting the guests in line. At the bar Paul ordered a vodka tonic and busied himself with rearranging the ice in his glass with the plastic stir-stick provided by the bartender. When dinner was announced, he gulped down the drink and walked to the dining room. The big ballroom was furnished with enough large, round tables to seat almost a hundred people, but only five were set for dinner. Counting the admiral, his staff and guests including ship's captains, plus their wives or dates, there were only forty of them. Paul found his nametag on a table near the front of the room, and was pleased to see from the other name tags that this was the admiral's table. Admiral Prescott and Lorelei would be sitting directly across from him.

Paul Oliver couldn't take his eyes off her. She was the most beautiful woman he had ever seen, and forbidden thoughts were creeping into his mind. Every once in a while during the dinner their eyes would meet and she would smile that sweet smile at him. His heart jumped each time her violet eyes met his, and he thought he sensed something in her manner, the way her eyes danced when she smiled at him, the look that lingered a little longer than it should have, that suggested she shared the attraction. But then he would force himself to be realistic. The admiral's wife! He knew he shouldn't be thinking what he was thinking, and he forced himself to pretend he was participating in the conversations on both sides of him. His eyes would always return to her, and when she caught him looking at her she would smile that beautiful smile and send his heart jumping. Paul wanted the dinner to end so he could return to his ship and stop mooning like a schoolboy.

At last the meal was over. Plates and silverware were picked up by white-jacketed ship's servicemen. The admiral stood and conversations dwindled and stopped. "I believe this would be the appropriate time for brandy and cigars, gentlemen," he announced. "If you will join me in the next room, please."

"Yes, please do go, gentlemen," Lorelei agreed, standing. "We women can't very well talk about you when you're in the room." A smattering of laughter ensued. Paul stood and graciously pulled back the chair of the woman sitting next to him. As she stood and thanked him, he looked at Lorelei. She was smiling at him! Not a pleasant dinner smile, but a warm, affectionate smile that lit up her face. His heart thumped again, and it irritated him. He didn't want to be smitten with the admiral's wife, or anyone else's wife for that matter. He prided himself on being in control of his emotions, and he didn't like this feeling, as though his emotions were running amok. He avoided her eyes as he joined the admiral and other officers in the club's sitting room.

The admiral sat in one of the overstuffed leather chairs and gratefully accepted a small glass of brandy offered to him by one of the stewards. A box of cigars was passed around. Paul declined the cigar, preferring his pipe, but accepted the brandy and sat on the leather couch with two other officers. The admiral lit his cigar and blew out the smoke slowly, savoring the tobacco. "Ah, that's good," he said, looking at the cigar appreciatively.

The officers sat and smoked in silence, sipping their brandy and waiting for the admiral to initiate the evening's conversation. Admiral Prescott set his brandy glass down on the end table next to his chair and leaned forward. The other officers took this as a sign and the room grew quiet.

"What do you gentlemen think of the situation in Southeast Asia?" he asked, looking around the room at the officers. "I'm speaking primarily of Viet Nam."

"As far as the South Vietnamese are concerned, I think their president, Diem, is a fascist." Captain Bill Pollock, Admiral Prescott's chief of staff, threw the comment out to encourage discussion. "He's stomping all over the people's civil rights, jailing anyone he thinks might be a communist. Hell, he isn't even a Buddhist. He's Catholic, and a lot of people think the communists are gaining popularity because Diem is so unpopular."

The admiral smiled and looked around at the other officers. *Good old Bill. He could always be depended on to spur the debate.*

Paul Oliver cleared his throat and set his brandy glass on the coffee table. "He's got a big job," he offered. "The communists in the north are bound and determined to take over the entire country. If they do it there, they'll do it in Cambodia, Laos and Thailand."

"So what are you saying, Paul?" the admiral asked, leaning forward and smiling. The conversation was becoming lively.

"I think we need to help them all we can, but President Kennedy is playing it pretty cozy. He's all for shipping supplies and arms to Diem, but the only troops he's sending are a handful of advisors, whatever that means."

"I agree with Paul," Lieutenant Commander Lee Piper, captain of the Haverfield's sister ship, the U.S.S. Brister said, blowing cigar smoke. "We have to fight communism wherever it rears its ugly-ass head."

"Like Korea?" Captain Pollock urged. The Naval officers all nodded solemnly. Korea was a sore subject in the military, and the Navy was no exception. "We went to war in Korea and lost thousands of men," the captain continued. "The north is still communist."

"But not the south," Paul countered. "And with all due respect for Truman and Eisenhower, if we had committed to that war with the same force and purpose we did against Germany and Japan, that communist regime in North Korea wouldn't exist." Paul looked around the room. Most of the officers were nodding agreement. Captain Pollock sat and smiled, enjoying the debate he had instigated.

"We certainly lost a lot of men over there," the admiral agreed. "And I don't like the thought of fighting for a draw, but the Chinese had a lot to say about how we conducted the war. Their entry into it changed the whole complexion of the thing."

"With respects, Admiral." Lee Piper leaned forward in his seat, his elbows resting on his knees. "The rules of engagement in Korea were an embarrassment to our military. We didn't approach Korea as a war, we looked at it as a police action. Our forces were not allowed to cross a certain latitude, and our flyers couldn't chase communist planes if they flew into Chinese air space. Meanwhile, the Chicoms were killing Americans right and left." He sat back and spread his hands. "We fought a stupid war in Korea, and if it comes to it in Viet Nam, well, we'd better be prepared to fight a war this time, not a police action."

"I don't think that's going to be a problem," Admiral Prescott replied. "We learned our lesson in Korea. If Viet Nam gets out of hand, and mind you, I don't think it will because Diem is a strong anti-communist, we will prosecute that war properly, with overwhelming force." He sipped at his brandy thoughtfully. "I agree with you about communism, Paul," he said. "We have to stop the stain of communism wherever we encounter it."

"Maybe we should build a wall between the north and south," Captain Pollock said, grinning. He was obviously referring to the wall the communists had built to shut off the flow of East Germans to the west. "You could say we stopped communism in Germany, too."

"Except in the Soviet-controlled part of Germany," the admiral said. "We've stalemated them in Germany and Korea. Perhaps that's the best policy. Contain the spread of communism and hope the world wakes up to the threat." The admiral didn't really believe that was the ideal approach, but he was enjoying the conversation and wanted to encourage more debate. He was overruled by Lorelei who appeared suddenly in the doorway.

"My goodness," she exclaimed. "There's so much smoke in here I thought the building was on fire." She walked over to the admiral, waving her hands in front of her, trying to shoo away the smoke. "You've got an early staff meeting in the morning, darling," she said, taking the admiral's arm as he stood. "I think it's time we bid our guests a gracious good-night."

Her voice was musical, Paul decided as he watched her walk by. And she didn't walk so much as glide, seeming as if her feet didn't touch the ground.

The admiral put out his cigar and nodded to his wife. "All right, dear. You heard the boss, gentlemen. Our little stag party has come to an early end. Duty calls."

The officers and their ladies lined up at the front door to say goodnight to their hosts. Paul stood back, determined to be the last to leave, and watched Lorelei thanking her guests for coming, shaking hands, and offering little pecks to the cheeks of the women She was very beautiful standing there, smiling and chatting. Finally it was Paul's turn to say goodnight.

"Great to have you here, Paul," the admiral said, taking Paul's hand and shaking it warmly. "I've seen good reports on you, which is why they gave you the Haverfield. First command, right, Captain?"

"Yes sir," Paul replied. "It's a good ship, but tired. We have some work to do. I'd consider it an honor if you paid us a visit."

"Well, if anybody can bring her around, you can. And I'd love to come aboard the Haverfield. Why don't you set up a little dinner, just the commanding officers of the ships ported here and their ladies?"

"I'll do that, sir. We're going out on patrol soon, but when we return I'll host a dinner party."

"Excellent," the admiral said. "I'll look forward to it."

Lorelei offered her hand. "Thank you for coming, Captain," she said sweetly. Her violet eyes were lovely and glowed in the soft light of the club's porch. She squeezed his hand gently and let it go. "We hope to see you again soon," she said.

"A pleasure, ma'am," Paul replied. He stood there for an awkward moment, trying to think of something else to say, then turned silently and walked down the front steps to wait for his ride back to the ship. When he reached the bottom of the stairs he looked back. The admiral was disappearing inside the club. Lorelei was still standing at the top of the stairs, watching Paul, her small hands folded in front of her. She smiled sweetly again when he looked back, then she turned and followed the admiral inside.

Paul stood at the bottom of the stairs staring at the spot where Lorelei had said goodnight. He was glad the evening was over. It was difficult for him to think in her presence and Paul didn't like feeling like a school boy with a crush on the teacher. His thoughts were interrupted by Lee Piper who came up beside him.

"Let's share a car to the harbor, Paul," he suggested. "We're berthed close to each other. No sense in taking two cars."

Paul nodded agreement. Lee Piper was the only other bachelor among the dinner guests, and he was right. No sense in taking two cars.

They sat in the backseat of the gray Navy sedan, staring out the side windows in silence. Finally Lee Piper broke the quiet. "The admiral seems like a pretty good guy," he offered. "A lot more personable than Admiral Smith was. He was kind of a tight ass."

Paul nodded agreement.

"And the admiral's wife is quite a dish," Piper said appreciatively. "She's gotta be the most beautiful Navy wife on this island."

Paul again nodded agreement. *She's the most beautiful woman I've ever seen*, he thought to himself.

Then aloud to Piper he said, "I think I'll hold a dinner reception for Admiral Prescott aboard the Haverfield. Just officers and wives to welcome him to Guam."

"Good idea," Piper replied. "I'll look forward to it." He thought for a moment, then added, "If I'm invited, that is."

Paul laughed. "Of course you're invited. I'm going to invite all the ships' captains and their ladies. You'll have to be my date, though."

Piper grinned. "Just so you don't try to feel me up," he laughed.

Paul sat back and thought of Lorelei. It would be great to have her aboard his ship. He could show off his command and impress her with his ability to plan a social event like a sit-down dinner. There was a lot of work to be done to the ship first, though. Paul Oliver wasn't about to bring the admiral and his wife aboard before he got the ship in shape. He stared out the side window. As hard as he tried, he couldn't bring her face into his memory. He couldn't picture that lovely face in his mind. Why was that?

They drove in silence for awhile, each deep in his own thoughts. Finally Lee Piper said, "That name, Lorelei. That's a pretty name."

"Yes, it is," Paul mumbled, trying hard to picture her face.

"Lorelei was a siren in German legend, right?" Piper mused.

"Yes, she was," Paul replied. "She sat on a rock in the Rhine River and sang to sailors. They say her siren song lured sailors to shipwreck on the rocks."

"Well, I hope she doesn't shipwreck the admiral," Piper laughed.

I hope she doesn't shipwreck me, Paul thought.

NINE

The movie ended with Beau Brummel dying, much to the glee of the moviegoers, so R.J., Pea and Billy went up to the forecastle to shoot the breeze with Cotton, who had the evening watch there.

When they reached the forecastle, R.J. heard several voices talking excitedly. There with Cotton were Crawford and Queen, laughing and jumping around on the deck.

"Get 'im!" Crawford yelled. "Step on 'im, or kick 'im or somethin'!"

Queen had the watch's nightstick and was hammering at something on the deck. When R.J. and the others reached the bow, R.J. noticed something silver was shimmering and wriggling under Queen's feet. It was a long, thin silver fish with big black eyes and sharp razor-like teeth.

"What the hell is that?" he asked.

Pea and Billy laughed. "Barracuda," Pea gasped. "Queen and Crawford catch 'em almost every night up here."

"What for?" R.J. asked.

"The gooks love 'em," Pea explained. "They give Queen fifty cents each for 'em. They make stew out of 'em and eat 'em. Even the eyeballs!" He laughed as R.J. made a disgusted face.

Billy grinned and said, "The barracuda know when it's movie time. They start feeding as soon as they hear 'Movie Call' and these guys usually catch about a dozen or so every night." He walked over to a big bucket set on the capstain head and looked in. "Looks like you got your limit," he said to Crawford.

"Yeah, we about to knock off," Crawford replied. "Gonna gut 'em and put 'em in the freezer till tomorrow. Sablan'll take 'em home." He referred to Ship's Serviceman Freddy Sablan, a native Guamanian who had joined the U.S. Navy.

R.J. got a kick out of the scene. Big ugly Queen and the redneck Crawford up on deck every night catching barracuda to sell to the Guamanians. It must be better than watching 'Beau Brummel' for the fifth time.

"Tatoo!" barked the 1MC from the quarterdeck. R.J. looked at Pea and Billy, confused by the announcement.

Billy saw his confusion. "That means five minutes to Taps," he explained. "Guess I'll hit the rack. I got the focsul for the morning watch. I'll see you then," he called to R.J. as he sauntered aft toward First Division's compartment. Pea waved and followed Billy aft.

R.J. stayed to talk with Cotton.

"So, what does the focsul watch do, anyway?" he asked.

"Nothin'," Cotton replied. "Just stand up here and make sure no Commies shinny up the mooring lines and take over the ship."

R.J. laughed. "And if one tries to get up here I hit him with that nightstick?"

"Naw, this ain't for Commies," Cotton replied, holding the nightstick in the air. "This here's for bonkin' the barracuda on the head when they pull 'em out of the water." He smiled at the nightstick. "You might say that's your primary duty as focsul watch," he explained. "Hey," Cotton pointed across the harbor where the big AE was moored. A red signal light was flashing from her bridge toward the Haverfield. "Can you read that?"

R.J. squinted at the light, trying to pick up the characters of the Morse code. He could catch a letter now and then, but couldn't quite put the words together. Seeing the code and hearing the code were very different, and R.J. stared at the light, trying to concentrate. A light on the Haverfield's signal bridge began to blink in response as Anselmi answered the AE.

"I'll see you around midnight, Cotton," R.J. said, "I'm going up there." He indicated the signal bridge.

"Quarter TO," Cotton called after him. "Be here at a quarter TO midnight."

R.J. climbed the necessary ladders to reach the signal bridge and stood quietly some ten feet behind Anselmi as he worked the signal light. The light had a red filter on it for signaling at night. He was sending code pretty fast, and as he manipulated the handle of the light, it made almost no sound. His movements were practiced and smooth, and R.J. marveled that he wasn't making the clackety-clackety sound he himself had made earlier with the light's handle.

Anselmi finished sending and signed off. He shut off the light, turned around, and spotted R.J. watching him. "I hear you know code," he said.

"I went through radio school and I could read it pretty fast," R.J. replied. "But I can only pick up a little bit of it visually." He stepped forward and inspected the light. "How come you got a red filter on it?" he asked.

"So I don't blind everyone in the harbor. This is a very bright light, and at night it will definitely blind you. We use a red filter for port and a green one for starboard," Anselmi explained. "Same as our running lights. You can always tell which way a ship is facing by her running lights. Red for port and green for starboard. But don't touch the light, cause it gets pretty hot after it's been on a while."

R.J. could feel the heat coming off the light. "What kind of messages were you sending?" he asked Anselmi.

"Messages?" Anselmi chuckled. "We were just shootin' the shit," he said.

"It's okay to do that?" R.J. asked, aware that radiomen could be put on report for sending anything but official traffic.

"Yeah, every signalman in the fleet does it. Especially late at night when we got the watch and nothin' to do. We talk to each other for hours by flashing light. Where you from, what's your girl's name. Stuff like that.

It's kinda like talkin' on the phone, you know?"

"Keeps you in practice, huh?"

"You might say that," Anselmi said, looking R.J. up and down. An idea began to take root in his mind. He seemed like a pretty good guy, so Anselmi made him an offer.

"You get to where you can read the code and I'll let you come up here and practice if you want," Anselmi offered. "But only after 'Movie Call' when no one is around, okay?"

"How about Becker?" R.J. asked, thinking of Signalman First Class Andy Becker, who never seemed to be around.

"Becker has his wife and kids here," Anselmi explained. "Spends all his time at home with them when we're in port." He smiled to himself and said, "In fact, at sea he's always so sea-sick he can't get out of his rack." Anselmi started laughing at Becker's malady. "He hasn't stood an under-way watch in years. He gets violently ill when we're only doing four knots in the harbor."

"That's kinda inconvenient for a Navy sailor," R.J. observed.

"This is his first ship. The man has been in the Navy for twelve years and spent all his time ashore at the signal tower in Dago, and instructing at the Signalman's school in Key West." Anselmi frowned and shook his head slowly. "I only miss him when we're underway. I have to stand all the signal watches 'cause he's in his rack the entire time. Doesn't eat anything, and hardly ever goes topside." Anselmi looked sideways at R.J. "I could use a striker up here. Maybe if you get to where you can read the code...anyway, be sure he's gone before you fire up the light."

"Cool," R.J. answered. "Thanks, Anselmi."

"Call me Salami. Everyone else does."

"Ok, Salami," R.J. stuck out his hand and Salami shook it. "Thanks."

"No problem," Salami said. "I'm gonna hit the sack. It's almost 2300."

R.J. stood on the signal bridge and looked out at the harbor. The view was good from there. Lights from small buildings and a few scattered ships twinkled in the warm, wet air and reflected shimmering ghosts across the water. *This is a good spot*, R.J. thought of his vantage point on the signal bridge. *I could get used to this.*

After a few minutes, R.J. decided to take his own tour of the ship's decks and went down the ladder to the 02 level. He walked around the deck, looking at the equipment, the davits holding the motor whaleboat in its place on the deck, and the various vents protruding from the deck here and there. Hoses seemed to be splayed everywhere across the deck, coming from the pier and back. He went back down on the fantail, deserted now, and inspected the torpedo tubes and three-inch gun turret. The Haverfield had an identical three-inch turret on the forecastle, the two guns making up pretty much the extent of the Haverfield's firepower. Toward the stern of the ship sat the depth charge rack, complete with large drum-like depth charges, poised to be dropped on enemy submarines, should the ship encounter one. At the very back of the stern, a large, hollow oil drum had been welded to the deck, pointing downward toward the water. This,

R.J. knew, was the garbage chute used for emptying trash and garbage at sea. He looked around and sighed. He had always imagined himself on an aircraft carrier or a battleship. He hadn't seen himself on a small, tired radar picket ship patrolling islands and rusting in the harsh tropical environment of the West Pacific. This wasn't Pearl Harbor, that was for sure. He stood leaning on the lifeline and staring at the harbor, lost in thought. His reverie was broken rudely by the rasping voice of Chief Twitchell who had come up behind him.

"Get off that fucking lifeline, shitbird!"

R.J. straightened and turned to face the angry chief. "Sorry, chief," he said. "Didn't know I wasn't supposed to do that."

"Sorry don't milk the cow," Twitchell barked. "And there's a lot of shit you *don't* know." He moved within an inch of R.J.'s face and R.J. could smell the alcoholic stink of his breath. "I don't like you, shitbird," the chief growled. "I didn't like you the first time I saw you. You fuck up on this ship and I'm gonna be on you like pimples on a whore's ass, you got me, shitbird?"

R.J. ground his teeth. Maybe it was instinct, or maybe it was his contempt for authority, but he truly did not like this fat chief. "If it makes you feel any better," R.J. replied insolently, "I didn't like you the first time I saw you either." He grinned big, real big, knowing it only enraged the chief more. R.J. didn't give a shit. He was fed up, tired and a little cranky. He had been screamed at, cussed at, beaten up and thrown in the filthy harbor. He got stuck with the mid-watch and had to sit through "Beau Brummel."

"You smilin' at me, boy?" the chief demanded. "You like me? You want to screw me?"

R.J. bit the inside of his cheek to keep from laughing at this ludicrous little man. "No to both, Chief," he replied. *This chief wasn't anything like Whipple. The chief of the boat was someone to respect. This asshole...*

"You don't like me?" Twitchell demanded, breathing heavily into R.J.'s face. "You don't think I'm good-looking enough to screw?"

R.J. couldn't help making a wisecrack. Sometimes it just came out and he had no control over it. "I haven't been on Guam that long," he snickered.

The chief exploded. "Wise-ass-shitbird," he hissed. "I'm gonna make your wise ass miserable, you little punk. Stay the fuck outta my way, boy. You see me comin' you move aside, got that?"

"Gotcha, chief," R.J. said, grinning widely and giving the chief the 'thumbs up' sign.

Chief Twitchell stared bleary-eyed and menacingly at R.J. for some thirty seconds, then turned on his heel and stalked off through the port hatch that led to the engineering division's compartment. He fumed as he made his way through the compartment to the chief's quarters. He was going to make that little punk feel the heat every time he saw him. He had seen his kind before...a wise ass. There was no place in the Navy for wise asses and Twitchell was going to ride him until he drove him right into the brig. Chief Twitchell had a new purpose for living, and his name was R.J. Davis.

Jefferson came around the corner from the quarterdeck as Chief Twitchell went through the port hatch. "What the hell he so pissed off 'bout?" he asked R.J.

"I was leaning on the lifeline," R.J. explained, shrugging. "Guess it made him mad."

"Well, don't make 'im mad, okay, man? He take it out on the rest of us." He checked to make sure Twitchell was out of earshot before he added, "Pig-face mudda-fucka."

"He's something else, huh?" R.J. observed.

"He the worst," Jefferson replied. "He ain't got a happy bone in his body. He wanna make everybody as miserable as he is." Jefferson spat over the side into the harbor. "Fat-ass-pig-face mudda-*fucka!*"

R.J. decided he would try to stay out of Twitchell's way, and not give him any reason to blow up. That wasn't going to be easy, but R.J. didn't want or need any more trouble with the Navy. He had learned his lesson, and if he were going to spend eighteen months on board the Haverfield, he was determined to make that time as pleasant as possible.

Jefferson looked at his watch. "Time to roust the mid watch," he said. "I'm gonna go down to the compartment and wake up they sorry asses. G'ahead and relieve Cotton on the focsul. I'll tell the OOD you got the watch."

"Okay," R.J. agreed.

Jefferson stopped and turned back to R.J. "Give you some advice, m'man," he said. "You ain't no boot no mo, so when someone give you an order, you say 'Aye.' Got it?"

R.J. came to attention and saluted. "Aye, aye, cap'n."

Jefferson laughed and headed below to wake the relief. "Stay away from him!" he called as he went down the aft ladder.

R.J. returned to the forecastle.

"You're a little early," Cotton said when R.J. reached the bow. "But that's okay with me." He shed the duty belt and handed it and the nightstick over. "You got the watch, and I'm relieved," he said.

"Aye," R.J. nodded. "I got the watch." He grinned at Cotton. "And I'm relieved that you're relieved."

"Well, I'm relieved to hear that," Cotton shot back, and headed aft.

R.J. buckled the duty belt around his waist and hefted the nightstick. It was heavier than it looked. He began twirling it and swinging it, trying to do it the way the beat cops did in downtown Denver, but he couldn't get it right and it fell to the deck, making a loud rattling sound. *Practice,* he thought, *practice makes perfect.*

The evening had cooled a bit, and a soft breeze blew across the forecastle. The ship and the harbor were eerily quiet and peaceful and R.J. thought the midwatch wasn't so bad. At least it would be calm and quiet and he could relax with his thoughts. But then the liberty bus pulled up on the pier and several returning sailors, full of drink and song, piled off the bus noisily and headed toward the ship, singing and laughing, jostling each other around and peppering each other with good-natured insults. Lester was at the head of the column, making the most noise. He looked up at the fore-castle and spotted R.J.

"Hey, the fucking Wog's on watch," he called to the others.

Oh, great, R.J. thought. *I hope he doesn't come up here.*

"Let's go up to the focsul!" Lester called, and staggered toward the brow, three other sailors in tow.

* * * * *

Chief Quartermaster Tom Lyons was a man of habit and routine. He didn't feel comfortable without a set procedure for doing things. Each morning he arose at precisely 0530 and took a brisk walk along the pier before showering and shaving. His khaki uniform was always clean, starched and pressed so that the creases formed a sharp, defined edge. He did not smoke or drink, and he retired each night at exactly 2000, unless he had the watch.

On a night like this night, when Chief Lyons had duty as the OOD, he followed another routine. After relieving the watch at 2345 he took a tour of the ship, ensuring that everything was in its proper place, and that the other members of the watch were on duty and alert. He began his tour on the fantail and ended it on the forecastle, checking on the watch up there and letting everyone know that he would be touring the ship at various times during the four hours they were on duty. He toured the engine room, the radio shack and all decks of the ship. Chief Lyons did not like sloppiness in any way, and the men on duty with him were expected to look and act in a sharp military manner. When Chief Lyons was the OOD, the men standing watch were ever vigilant. No one wanted to be caught goofing off, or worse, sleeping on watch.

Another thing Chief Lyons would not tolerate was obnoxious behavior, especially when the obnoxious behavior was fueled by alcohol. While he understood the need for sailors to let off a little steam, he had no respect for anyone who would allow himself to become drunk and disorderly, or to behave in an unseemly, non-military manner.

As Chief Lyons conducted his tour of the ship for the mid-watch, he happened to be in the radio shack when the liberty bus arrived on the pier and deposited its passengers at the Haverfield brow. By the time Lester and his mates found their way to the forecastle, Chief Lyons was on his way up there as well to instruct R.J. on the proper way to stand the forecastle watch. Unfortunately for Lester, he did not see Chief Lyons until it was too late.

"Hey Wog," Lester called, staggering up the deck toward the bow, his whitehat set back on his head and his neckerchief knotted high on his jumper in 'old salt' fashion. "How about another swim?" Three other sailors stumbled behind the tipsy Lester to the forecastle.

Lester made a grab at R.J.'s nightstick and they wrestled for it, stagger-ing over the anchor chain, R.J. cussing and Lester giggling. The other three sailors spotted Chief Lyons coming up the starboard side, and being less drunk and more in control than Lester, they faded down the port side and scurried toward First Division's compartment.

"What are you doing, sailor?" Chief Lyons asked, coming up behind Lester, surprising him.

Lester spun around and froze. He quickly stopped wrestling with R.J. and squared his whitehat properly on his head. "Nothin' Chief," he replied, shrugging his shoulders. "Just havin' a little fun." Lester giggled and Chief Lyons could smell the alcohol on him. R.J. slipped the nightstick back into its scabbard and stood by self-consciously. Chief Lyons looked from Lester to R.J., taking in the entire scene. He didn't care for Lester. The man was undisciplined and sloppy. He was a loud-mouthed bully who didn't know when to quit. Chief Lyons decided the man needed to be taught a lesson.

"It looks to me as if you were trying to take the nightstick away from the focsul watch, is that correct?" Chief Lyons asked calmly, staring into Lester's bleary eyes.

"Uh, no, Chief," Lester stammered. He looked around and shrugged helplessly.

"Interfering with a man on duty is a serious offense," the chief observed, walking around Lester and looking him over. "In fact, it's a Captain's Mast offense, don't you agree?"

Lester gulped and stammered, "Uh, I was just foolin' around, Chief. Sorry."

"Or was it because you wanted to stand this watch in his place?" the chief asked, indicating R.J. with a nod of his head.

"Uh, no...I mean..." Lester fell silent. He looked down, staring at his shoes.

"Well, Lester," the chief considered, "If you weren't trying to take over the watch, then you were interfering with the watch. Which is it?"

Lester remained silent, his head down.

"It's very simple, Lester," the chief went on. "You either want to stand this watch or I put you on report for interfering with the watch." He pointed a finger into Lester's chest. "You decide."

"I don't wanna go on report," Lester answered finally. "But E-4's don't stand focsul watches, Chief." He indicated the BM-3 'Crow' on his sleeve.

Chief Lyons looked over at R.J. "Davis, isn't it?" he asked.

"Aye, Chief," R.J. replied, shuffling his feet, embarrassed by the situation. Lester fidgeted.

"Give your duty belt over to Lester," the chief instructed. "You are relieved. Go below and hit the rack. This man will stand your watch."

Lester's face fell, and he looked at R.J. desperately.

R.J. shrugged his shoulders at Lester and handed over the duty belt.

"Put it on." Chief Lyons ordered.

Lester complied, buckling the duty belt around his waist and looking helplessly at R.J. who ignored him.

"Good night," the chief said to R.J., indicating it was time for him to leave the forecastle. Then to Lester he said, "I'll be up here every half hour to check on you, Lester. You better not be asleep or goofing off, or you go on the pad. Understand?"

"Yes, Chief," Lester said miserably.

R.J. made his way down to the compartment where he was met by the other three liberty sailors, one of whom was Sonny Metzner. "What happened?" Sonny asked. R.J. told them, expecting to be blamed and further ostracized. Instead, all three began laughing and hooting hysterically, which woke up most of the crew in the compartment. When they learned that Lester was forced to stand R.J.'s watch, they all had a good laugh before climbing back into their racks. As they lay in the dark waiting to fall asleep, one of them would begin snickering, and soon the whole compartment was laughing and hooting again. Lester would not soon live this down.

R.J. lay back and stared at the pipe-encrusted overhead above his rack. *Boy, it sure has been an interesting first day*, he thought just before falling asleep.

* * * * *

Next morning R.J. was up and dressed before reveille and stood on the fantail, watching the dawn creep carefully and colorfully up and over that mountain to the northeast. (What *was* the name of that mountain?) R.J. stood at the lifeline and gazed at the calm, green water in the harbor as it began to accept the dawn's morning light. The harbor water winked and twinkled, changing hues as the creeping morning sun spread down the mountain and into Apra Harbor. R.J. touched the bruise on his chest gingerly. Damn, it hurt more than it did yesterday, and it was swollen up the size of a grapefruit. Even his dungaree shirt rubbing against the bruise was painful.

"Reveille! Reveille!" the 1MC barked. "All hands heave out and trice up! The smoking lamp is lit in all authorized spaces! Now, reveille!" And then a few moments later, "Messdecks! Messdecks!" the pre-chow announcement for chief petty officers and men on the morning watch to lay up to the messdecks and eat early chow before the crew filed in.

"Sweepers, sweepers, man your brooms!" The 1MC continued yelling at the crew. "Sweep the ship fore and aft, sweep all compartments! Sweepers!"

R.J smoked and watched the morning arrive. It sure was a beautiful place to experience a sunrise. Early morning on Guam was the best part of the day. The Guamanians say that Guam is where the new day begins for America. Being west of the international dateline, Guam was a day ahead of the United States, or to be precise, twenty-nine hours ahead of Los Angeles, thirty-two hours ahead of New York, and thirty hours ahead of Longmont, Colorado.

R.J. thought of Longmont and tried to imagine what it was like at eleven A.M. this morning. Actually, *yesterday* morning. It would be cold, maybe snow still on the ground, and Renee would be on her way to work. Renee was the only girl he really cared about. Tonya in San Diego was more an afterthought, a challenge. Janice in Denver was more of a habit than a relationship. They had gone together, off and on, since they were in junior high. Neither she nor Tonya had the sweet nature Renee possessed. But Tonya did have those lovely boobs. He had been careful not to mention

Renee or Janice to Tonya.

His mind played around with the memories for several minutes, and he felt a strong desire to get back home as fast as possible. He would love to be running around with his buddies, staying up late, with no worries or problems to plague him.

"Hey, Wog!"

R.J. turned to face Lester coming across the fantail. *Oh, well. Back to reality.* "Morning, Les," R.J. said pleasantly. He watched Lester's face carefully, expecting an angry tirade, and braced himself for it.

Lester strode up to R.J. sneering. He looked tired. He obviously didn't get a lot of rest after his mid-watch. His eyes were puffy and his face marked with lines from sleeping face-down on a wrinkled sheet.

"You owe me one mid-watch, you sonofabitch!" Lester sneered.

"Hey, that wasn't my fault, Lester," R.J. protested.

"Yeah? Whose fault was it, then?" Lester sneered again, getting in R.J.'s face.

"Yours," R.J. answered, matter-of-factly.

Lester poked his finger in R.J.'s swollen chest. It hurt and R.J. slapped his hand away. Lester pushed him and R.J. pushed back. Both men cocked their fists and began the slow, circling fistfight dance, each daring the other to throw the first punch.

"You clowns discussing the morning weather?" Big Queen had come up on deck and stepped between Lester and R.J. He looked from one to the other menacingly, grinning his big-teeth grin. It was not a pleasant sight.

Lester backed off and his body relaxed. R.J. stepped back and dropped his hands.

Queen quietly appraised the situation, looking back and forth between the two men and showing his big teeth. "You shitbirds lookin' for a fight?" he growled. "'Cause if you are, I'll be happy to accommodate you. Both of you." His lip curled up and he stepped toward them. "Both of you at once," he threatened.

"No problem, Boats," Lester said, shaking his head.

"You?" Queen gestured at R.J. with his huge head.

"No problem," R.J. said quietly.

"Then get your lily-white asses to chow," he grumbled. "We got quarters in less than an hour." Queen waited until R.J. and Lester left the fantail, R.J. through the port side hatch and Lester down the ladder to First Division's compartment.

Queen stood on the fantail watching thoughtfully as the two combatants left. He took a small cigar out of his shirt pocket, bit off the tip, spit it into the harbor, then lit the cigar with a large chrome-plated Zippo lighter. He let the smoke swirl around his face and decided not to report the incident to Chief Whipple. Lester was a hothead, and this new kid was a wiseass, but Queen knew how to handle them. He was certain there would be no more problems with those two.

TEN

Lieutenant Commander D. Paul Oliver stepped into the wardroom where his officers were already gathered for their morning meeting. Today's meeting would be a little different. He was about to lay out his plan for the rehabilitation of the Haverfield and the training of its crew.

"Attention on deck!"

"Be seated, gentlemen," the captain began. "I've been the commanding officer of this ship for the past three months, and I have to tell you, I'm not pleased." He looked around the room. The officers fidgeted and exchanged veiled looks with each other.

"This ship is in poor shape, gentlemen. And I'm not just talking about the rust on the decks and bulkheads or the outdated engines or the unreliable evaporators. This crew has a sloppy attitude, born from going about their jobs in a slip-shod, casual manner unbefitting American sailors, and today, this is going to stop."

The officers shifted around in their seats, stealing sideway glances at each other. MacDonald sat forward in his chair, leaning his forearms on the wardroom table.

"Something you want to say, Mac?" the captain asked.

"Yes, sir." MacDonald cleared his throat. "I think we all agree with you, Captain. It's a matter of training. I've put together some programs for First Division to cover everything from ship handling to knot tying. We've developed a ten-day plan to get rid of all the rust and repaint the ship from bow to stern, and the men are getting enthusiastic about it."

"That's good," the captain nodded. "It's a perfect place to start." He looked around the room. Notepads and pens were appearing from the officers' pockets. "I want every department on this ship to formulate step-by-step training programs. I want these programs to cover even the most basic fundamentals, including military bearing and conduct, physical hygiene and common courtesy. When these men start looking and acting like sailors, they will perform like sailors." He stopped and leaned back in his chair. "I'm going to pass out a list of items I want corrected on board this ship." He began passing out mimeographed sheets, stapled together. "Painting and cleaning up the deck areas are important for appearance," he continued. "But we must clean up below, in the engine room, the sick bay, the ship's office and all compartments and work areas. Teach your people how to do things right and have them teach others. We will instill a sense of pride in these men if we do this right. I want there to be unanimous concurrence in this wardroom." He looked around again at the officers, who were much more alert than when he first began speaking. "Anybody have any objections to turning this ship into a Navy vessel?"

No one protested, and Mr. MacDonald winked at Ens. P.J. Jones, who grinned back stupidly. Mr. MacDonald's second in command was not the sharpest knife in the drawer, but if Mr. MacDonald was pleased, Mr. Jones was pleased, even if he didn't quite understand why.

"Good." The captain stood and all the officers jumped to their feet. "I'll expect to see training programs from every department by..." he picked up his calendar and ran his finger over the month of March. "...the fifteenth. That's a week from today. Next Friday." He closed his notebook and opened the wardroom door, preparing to leave. He turned back to the room and looked around once more at his officers. "I'm serious about this, gentlemen. Make it happen." The door closed and he was gone, with the exec close behind.

The officers looked around at each other, no one knowing what to say. MacDonald slapped his hands on the table and stood. "I liked the old Skipper, but Captain Oliver is a regular Navy man. I for one am damned glad he's aboard. Now we can get this ship squared away and back into the fleet!"

"But we aren't part of the fleet, Mac," said Pedro Almogordo, the engineering officer. "We don't do fleet duty. We just hop from island to island, scaring off the Jap fishermen and trying to keep the machinery operating."" He rubbed his eyes with the heels of his hands. "I doubt my engines are going to be much infected with this new enthusiasm."

"Think positive, Pedro," countered Lieutenant Barkman, the operations officer. "Don't you realize what the power of positive thinking can do for your life?" He stared at the engineering officer, eyes wide and eyebrows arched. "Don't you think I sound like Norman Vincent Peale?" he asked. Then he started laughing and Mr. Almogordo started laughing and soon the entire wardroom was whooping it up. The meeting broke up and the officers headed enthusiastically to their respective departments for morning quarters.

Captain Oliver was joined in his stateroom by the exec. Lieutenant Edgars sat on the captain's bunk while the captain sat in his swivel chair and lit his pipe with a wooden kitchen match.

"I think it's a waste of time, Captain," the exec began. "It's a matter of too little, too late if you ask me."

"How so, Chet?" Captain Oliver had inherited his executive officer, and was not entirely happy with him. Chester Edgars was caustic and rude to the crew, traits the captain disapproved of in an officer.

"Sloppiness and laziness are ingrained in this crew." Edgars leaned forward, resting his elbows on his knees. "Even if you could create a little spark in them, it wouldn't do any good. You've seen the way they amble around the decks, like zombies in slow motion."

"That's the tropics for you, Chet," the captain said. "If you let it happen, the tropics can turn you to mush. There's a lot more cases of clinical depression in the tropics than you might think. It's a muggy, oppressive environment not conducive to hard labor, but we are in the U.S. Navy. We will operate like a fleet Navy vessel. There is no alternative." The captain looked the exec straight in the eye. "I expect your full compliance on this, Chet."

C.C. Edgars nodded and stood, putting out his hand, which the captain took. "Of course, Skipper," the exec said solemnly. "I'm with you all the way."

"Good," nodded the captain. "I'm going to depend on you." He puffed his pipe thoughtfully, then added, "Knock off ship's work at 1200, Chet. Give the crew the day off. Come Monday we're going to start turning them into sailors."

"Aye, aye, sir." The exec didn't like giving the crew any time off, considering their lousy appearance and work habits, but he deferred to the captain.

The exec left and Captain Oliver turned in his swivel chair toward the desk. He opened his journal and began to record the morning's events, describing the wardroom meeting and Lieutenant MacDonald's input which was, unknown to the other officers, rehearsed and staged. He made notes about the exec, too. If he had his choice, he'd find another executive officer; an academy man. As he sat re-reading what he had written, the announcement came over the 1MC:

"Quarters! Quarters! All hands stand by for morning colors!"

At exactly 0800 the call 'attention on deck!' and 'hand salute!' brought the crew to attention, facing the fantail where the colors were being raised. No bugle sounded, since the Haverfield didn't have a bugler. No music blared, since the Haverfield didn't have a band. The men stood at attention, saluting the flag for about one full minute before Queen bellowed, "To!" and the men dropped their salute.

"First Division!" Queen bellowed. "Dismissed from quarters!"

"Turn to!" the ship's loudspeaker blared. "Commence ship's work!"

* * * *

R.J. spent the rest of Friday with Tanner, learning more about the operation of the ship. He was amazed at the knowledge Tanner possessed. The man knew everything about seamanship. R.J. constantly asked questions, eager to learn and absorb as much as possible in as short a time as possible.

"Whoa," Tanner told him after R.J. had grilled him about the anchor mechanism on the forecastle. "Take your time, man. You don't have to know everything at once!"

"I'm after your job, Boats," R.J. replied, winking at Tanner.

"Well, Wog," Tanner replied jokingly, "that's gonna take you a while."

"Hey Tanner!" Cotton came walking up the forecastle from the starboard hatch, Pancho close behind. "Guess what?" Cotton teased.

"Whaa?" Tanner asked, annoyed at the interruption.

"The word is being passed to all departments." Cotton beamed.

"What the fuck are you talking about, Cotton?" Tanner demanded, becoming more annoyed.

"We're knocking off ship's work at noon," Cotton said, beaming. "Cap'n givin' us the afternoon off!"

Tanner frowned. *The crew had never had a Friday afternoon off. Must be something going on.* He bit his lip in thought, trying to fathom what it could be and how it would affect him.

"Let's take R.J. to the Mocombo Club for his welcoming ceremony," Cotton said.

"Another initiation?" R.J. asked, gingerly touching the bruise on his chest. This was getting ridiculous.

"This one's based on pleasure," Cotton explained, "not pain."

"Pleasure?" R.J. asked. "That would be a nice change."

"Okay, boys," Tanner agreed. "Let's break his cherry." He pointed at R.J. "Put yourself in our hands, m'boy. We promise not to hurt you...much."

* * * * *

Tanner didn't want to wait for the liberty bus to appear on the pier, so he took up a collection from Cotton, Pea, Pancho and Sonny and called a taxi from the quarterdeck phone. The cab arrived and R.J. piled into it along with the others. "Mocombo Club!" Tanner announced. The cabbie smiled, nodded and hit the gas.

The six sailors sang loudly as the cab ground its way up the hill to the Mocombo Club.

"Roll me over, in the clover, roll me over, lay me down and do it again!"

The cab reached the top of the hill and slid to a dusty, squealing stop at the club's double front doors. R.J. got out of the cab and looked around. The Mocombo Club was an old Quonset hut with palm trees framing its entrance, and gravel covering its parking lot. The metal skin of the club was rusting in places, and the double doors were dented and pockmarked by years of sailors bursting through them, coming and going. R.J. pushed through the doors and found himself in a large ballroom. Plastic tables and chairs littered the deck and surrounded the dance floor. At one end of the hall was a bandstand, an old, beat-up set of drums perched at the rear. At the other end of the hall stood a long bar, spanning the length of the wall and manned by off-duty first class and chief petty officers.

The group staked out a table along the wall next to the bandstand and tilted the chairs up, leaning them against the table. This would signal to other arriving sailors that this table was taken.

Sonny pulled R.J. aside. "Now, Wog, you get to drink with the Havernauts!" He put his arm around R.J.'s shoulder and explained. "We buy your first drink," he said. "And the first drink is always a double tequila. It's traditional." The others nodded, smiling at him. "Here's a buck. Fifty cents a shot. Get a double," Sonny instructed. R.J. headed for the bar.

Pea watched him go and turned to the others. "Bet he passes out but don't puke," he said.

"How many times we pull this, Pea?" Sonny asked.

"I don't know," Pea admitted. "Maybe a hundred."

"You ever know a guy who don't get sick and puke when the sun hits him after a coupla double shots of tequila?" Sonny asked.

"Man, I remember my tequila ceremony," Pancho laughed. "You get that stuff in your blood and walk outside, the sun drops you to your knees!" He leaned across the table, grinning. "Besides, my people got hot blood to begin with."

"This is gonna be good," Cotton said, watching R.J. approach the bar, dollar bill in hand.

R.J. stepped up to the bar and a grizzled, off-duty Navy veteran greeted him. "What'll ya have, kid?" he growled.

R.J. resisted the impulse to answer, 'Pabst Blue Ribbon.' "Gimme a double shot of tequila," R.J. ordered, slapping the dollar bill on the bar.

The bartender looked at R.J.'s baby face and freckles. He cocked his head at R.J. and scowled. "Boy, why don't you just have a beer?" He put a can of beer under the opener and punched holes in it. "Fifty cents," he said, and slid the beer to R.J. with a look on his face that dissuaded R.J. from arguing with him.

R.J. returned to the table with the beer and the change. He sat down and sipped the beer, looking around at the others who were staring at him menacingly.

"Where's the tequila?" Sonny asked.

"He wouldn't sell me any," R.J. replied, gesturing at the bartender. "Guess he thought I was too young."

"Shit!" Pancho exclaimed. "That ruins it!"

"Ruins what?" R.J. asked.

Tanner smiled at the others and began chuckling. "Every new guy comes aboard, we bring him up here, get a coupla tequilas in him and take him outside. The heat hits him with all that tequila in him and he pukes or passes out or both." Tanner shook his head slowly. "First time I can remember it didn't work."

"It's that baby-face he got!" Pancho yelled, pinching R.J. on the cheek. "Saved his ass!" He started giggling and the table erupted in laughter.

"You skated, Wog!" Tanner said, sucking down a big gulp of beer. "But now you gotta buy a round for the table."

"No problem," R.J. said, standing and grinning. "But you guys better be happy with beer."

ELEVEN

For the next three weeks, R.J. spent his time chipping, sanding and painting the many rust spots on the decks and bulkheads of the ship. The captain's orders had come down: the Haverfield was to be transformed into a spit-and-polish Navy warship. When they weren't scraping and painting, R.J. and the other members of First Division were cleaning. They swabbed and scrubbed the compartment, the after crew's head and all passageways leading to and from their quarters. Slowly, the ship's appearance began to improve, and so did the appearance of the men. Under Queen's watchful eye, the Havernauts kept their dungarees clean and pressed and their boondockers shined. Their military bearing improved and as a group, they seemed to enjoy the changes. The improvement was thanks in large part to Mr. MacDonald's guidance, Chief Whipple's insistence and Queen's threats of bodily harm. R.J. found he was enjoying himself. He had not been part of the crew that lapsed into sloppiness, so the new orders didn't bother him. He was happy to do his part, making certain he stayed out of Twitchell's way. He doubted, though, that he could find a way to get along with Lester, who took every opportunity to insult him.

One Thursday afternoon R.J. was assigned to another line-handling party, and he actually enjoyed it this time, having known what to expect. He and three other 'deck apes' tied up the U.S.S. Brister, the Haverfield's sister ship returning from patrol. It was the Brister's turn to relax in port and make repairs. The Haverfield was due to go on patrol the next week, Friday, April fifth.

After quarters on Friday morning, the twenty-ninth, the announcement came over the 1MC: "Turn to! Commence ship's work. A four-man working party will muster on the quarterdeck!"

Working parties were not accepted happily by the men assigned to them. A working party could be for almost anything, but was usually for loading supplies aboard ship. Carrying heavy boxes and milk cans in the stifling humidity wore down a man to the point where he wanted to jump into the harbor. Everyone tried to avoid the call to a working party, and the departments usually sent their most junior crew member as their contribution. R.J., finding himself most junior, was instructed by Queen to lay up to the quarterdeck and report for the working party.

"He had line handling yesterday, Boats," Pea protested.

Queen slowly shifted his gaze from R.J. to Pea. "That right?" he asked crossly, frowning from the brow down. "You his momma?"

"Jus lettin' you know. You know?" Pea said, grinning.

"Well thank you, Pea," Queen rumbled. "Since you're so worried about the young man, you can go with him to keep an eye on him."

Pea's grin faded. "But...ah..."

"No buts, no ifs, no maybes," Queen replied, smiling his ugly smile. "Go with Davis to the quarterdeck and inform the OOD that he now has a five-man working party."

Pea stood motionless, his face a mask of pain and disappointment.

"Now!" Queen bellowed, and Pea and R.J. scrambled out of the compartment and up the ladder to the fantail.

"Goddammit!" Pea yelled as they reached the quarterdeck and joined three other crewmembers from various departments. "Now I gotta fuck around hauling big fuckin' boxes of heavy fuckin' supplies. That Queen's always screwin' around with me."

"I think he likes to screw with people," R.J. said.

"That's for sure," Pea replied. "He's on everybody's ass. Big ugly water buffalo!"

R.J. started laughing. "That's exactly what he looks like, Pea! A fuckin' water buffalo!"

Charming Billy brought the pickup screeching to a stop at the foot of the brow, and the working party scooted down to the pier and climbed into the bed of the truck.

"Hold on, fellas!" Billy yelled out the driver's side window.

"He ain't kidding!" R.J. yelled as Billy popped the clutch and lurched forward down the pier, gaining speed and grinding the truck's gears. The members of the working party held on for dear life, bouncing around in the bed as Billy pointed the truck toward the supply depot and floored it.

"See? I tol' you so!" Pea yelled over the sound of the wind and the roar of the truck's engine. "We goin' to the supply depot. Means we gotta load the truck with a bunch of heavy shit and haul it back." He frowned and chewed on his thumbnail. "Then we gotta *unload* it," he said sadly.

R.J. sat back against the side of the truck and removed his whitehat, turning his face up to the sun. His chest was almost healed, and he felt pretty good, all things considered. The hot wind blew strongly over his face as the truck sped toward the supply depot, and R.J. closed his eyes and thought of Tonya. Sweet, pretty little Tonya with the big boobs and tiny waist.

She had occasionally let him play with those boobs, but almost never inside her bra, and only when he brought her flowers. He smiled as he remembered trying to get into her pants, using every charm and ploy he knew. He told her in all sincerity how he might never come home, that something terrible could happen, like the Russians attacking his ship, and he wouldn't survive. How would she feel then? Tonya had replied that she would feel just terrible, then pulled his hand from where he was trying to slip it down the front of her jeans. R.J. smiled at the memory as the warm sun splashed on his face.

The old truck came to a squealing stop, jarring the working party and jolting R.J. out of his fantasy. *Oh, well,* he thought. *Back to reality.* He jumped off the tailgate and lighted on the ground easily, his knees absorbing the shock of the landing. "Ta da!" he sang, striking a pose like a ballet dancer.

"C'mon, R.J." Pea coaxed him. "Quit actin' like a fag. We gotta load all that shit!" He was pointing to a large stack of wooden and cardboard boxes arranged alongside the truck cargo bay at the rear of the supply warehouse. A large hand-lettered sign sat in front of the stack, saying 'DER-393.'

Billy came around to the back of the truck with a clipboard in his hand. He looked at the stack of supplies and looked at the clipboard. "Uh oh," he mumbled. "Mr. Winters ain't gonna like this."

"What?" R.J. asked, looking down at the clipboard.

"See that stack of stuff we're here to pick up?" He motioned toward the boxes. "That's about three-fourths of what we're supposed to get." He shook his head and threw the clipboard into the bed of the truck where it banged and bounced around, sliding to a stop.

"It's that fuckin' Twitchell!" Pea exclaimed. "He pissed off Bobby Gamboa at the Mocombo club that night, remember?" Pea was tapping Billy on the arm for emphasis.

"Bobby Gamboa?" R.J. asked, brightening. "Is he..."

"I know it, Pea!" Billy snapped. "I was there. I seen Twitchell screaming at him and Bobby left all embarrassed."

"Bobby Gamboa?" R.J. asked again. "Hey, I know a..."

"Never mind, R.J.," Billy said quietly. "We're gonna run out of shit again next patrol. Shit!"

Pea and Billy stood there at the entrance to the truck bay and looked around helplessly. "Let's talk to him," Pea urged. "It ain't our fault Twitchell is such an asshole."

"I know a Bobby Gamboa," R.J. interjected before Pea and Billy could protest. "I was in boot camp with a Bobby Gamboa. He still owes me a carton of smokes. Wonder if it's the same guy?"

Billy looked at R.J., staring at him intently. Slowly the idea began to dawn on him. "Probably not the same guy..." He turned and looked toward the door to the supply office. "Still, let's go talk to him," he decided. "Pea, stay here and keep an eye on the truck."

"Aw, shit, Billy," Pea protested. "Why can't I come with you?"

"'Cause you're pissed off and I wanna try and smooth-talk the guy. You know, diplomatically. You'll yell at him and call him names. That's why."

"I ain't gonna say nothin' to the stupid dick-headed gook," Pea whined. "Not my fault his momma married a water buffalo!"

R.J. laughed and patted Pea on the back. "That's being very diplomatic, Pea," he said.

"Fuckin'ay," Pea agreed. "You should hear me when I get nasty." Pea returned to the truck where he found the other two members of the working party asleep in the cab. He reached in through the driver's window and leaned on the horn. The two sleeping sailors jumped awake, startled.

"Reveille, shit heads!" Pea yelled, cackling and honking the horn. "Let's get this shit loaded on the truck!"

Billy turned back to the truck and put a finger to his mouth. "Shhhh," he hushed. "You wanna piss off the supply people even more?"

R.J. and Billy pushed open the door to the supply office and stepped in. R.J. stopped and held his arms out to his sides, head back, smiling. "Ah, air conditioning!" he sighed, breathing deeply. "Man that feels good!"

"Hey! I oughta charge your dumb ass for sucking up my air conditioning!" Bobby Gamboa came out of the storeroom and spotted R.J., his old buddy from boot camp, luxuriating in the supply room's air conditioning.

R.J. didn't open his eyes or lower his arms. "You owe me a carton of smokes, Bobby G," he said quietly.

Bobby Gamboa smiled broadly at R.J. "Hey, if I knew you were coming I woulda baked a cake!" He pushed through the swinging, waist-high door and came around the front of the counter. "Besides, I think you cheated on that last hand," he said.

R.J. opened his eyes and looked appraisingly at Bobby Gamboa. He had put on a little weight, but on his big frame he could carry it. His hair was longer, no more boot camp burr-cut, and he had developed a deep tan, but other than that, it was Bobby G. Same bright, intelligent eyes, same flat nose and high cheekbones, same teeth stained brown from chewing on betelnut.

"E-four!" R.J. yelled, spotting the crow with one chevron on Bobby's sleeve. "You made E-four already?" R.J. walked up to Bobby and threw his arms around him. "Congrats, G. You done good!"

"Thanks, R.J." Bobby returned the hug and stepped back, inspecting his friend. "You look pretty good, too. Still know how to do the duck-walk?"

He laughed and looked at Billy Lopez. "This guy," Bobby started, pointing at R.J. who smiled sheepishly. "He don't like authority, see? So when the company petty officers were chosen back at good ol' Camp Nimitz, R.J. decides he don't like his squad leader, who was a mealy-mouthed little fucker. Anyway, R.J. tells the guy to go fuck himself when the guy tells us to shut up and go to sleep. Well, the little pencil-neck puts R.J. on report. Next morning," Bobby started snickering at the memory. "After morning inspection, the Company Commander has R.J. fall out. He says he heard R.J. don't like to follow orders. So he makes R.J. squat down and put his hands behind his head." Bobby was starting to laugh so hard tears were coming out of his eyes. "Then he tells R.J. to walk like a duck all around the ranks of the company. R.J. goes all around the company, squatted down on his haunches, walking like a duck. When he gets back to the front of the formation, the C.C. makes him do it again, only this time he has to quack like a duck." Bobby wiped his eyes and shook his head. "Man, that was some funny shit. He quacked and duck-walked around the entire company, and then he did it again! Didn't have to do it again. He wasn't ordered to do it again. He's just stubborn, y'know? Wanted to make a point."

Bobby held his stomach and laughed hard enough to bring back the tears. "Sometimes after that day, we'd be in our racks at night after drilling and marching all day, everybody worn out. You know what boot camp's like, Billy. Then out of the dark R.J. would let go with this loud 'quaaaack—quaaaack—quaaaack! Cracked everybody up!"

"Good story," Billy smiled charmingly. "But we need to talk to you about our supplies, Bobby."

Bobby's smile faded slowly from his face and he turned to look at Billy. "That's all there is," he stated firmly. "Everybody had to be cut back a little. We didn't get everything we ordered from Pearl."

"That's the same story we always get, man," Billy protested, his charming smile gone. "The guys on the Brister said they don't have any problem getting all their supplies."

"Well," Bobby retorted. "Maybe that's because they don't have a big-mouthed, pig-faced bully coming around here *fuckin'* with everybody."

"C'mon, man," Billy pleaded. "He ain't one of our favorite people, either."

"Sorry," Bobby said adamantly. "That's all I can give you. Try again in a couple of weeks."

"We're going on patrol next week," Billy said desperately. "That stuff ain't gonna last us, Bobby."

R.J. stepped between them. "Let me talk to him, Billy," he whispered. "Wait outside and I'll talk to him."

Billy reluctantly stepped outside. He needed a little air, anyway. When the door closed behind him, R.J. turned, his hands spread out palms up and smiled at Bobby Gamboa. "So how's your family, Bob? You probably spend a lot of time with 'em."

"They're good, man. I'm home almost every weekend. They're poor, you know, but happy." Bobby started moving paperwork around as he talked with R.J. "I help out with some money every month, so they're doin' okay. They still live the way Guamanians have lived since forever, ten of them in that small trailer, roof leaks, a lot of mouths to feed, but they're happy."

R.J. thought for a moment, then asked, "Do they like to eat barracuda?"

"They love it, why?"

* * * * *

Pea and Billy Lopez stood leaning on the bed of the pickup, which was loaded with the ship's supplies. They smoked cigarettes and argued about who was foxier, Connie Stevens or Suzanne Pleshette.

"You know nothin' about women, Pea," Billy chided him. "Connie's a dumb blonde with big knockers. That's why you like her."

"That's true, but she's sexy," Pea retorted. "Got that 'come over here and nail me' look on her face." He nodded slowly. "Much sexier."

"Suzanne is a classy brunette," Billy argued. "She looks cool and contained, but I know her type. She turns tiger in bed."

"Suzanne couldn't carry Connie's bra," Pea insisted. "She a cold fish. Just look at the way she..."

They were interrupted by R.J.'s return. He walked to the truck, deposited a small canvas bag in the bed and turned to Billy. "Bobby is gonna fill the rest of the order, and have it ready this afternoon." He smiled broadly at the working party. "He's gonna throw in some extra eggs, some fruit and a bunch of chicken." He looked around at the members of the working party, who were staring at him with their mouths open. "But this is the best part," R.J. said mysteriously, patting the canvas bag.

"What?" Pea asked.

"What?" Billy demanded.

R.J. made a big production of pulling the bag out of the truck and slowly opening it. He stuck his hand into the bag and, winking at the other men, delicately removed one of three silver film canisters which he held up in the air. On the front of the film canister, printed on a piece of adhesive tape was the title, *"Dr. No."*

"How in the hell...," Billy started.

"What?" Pea asked, confused, looking from R.J. to Billy. "What?"

"Bobby and I made a deal," R.J. explained, matter-of-factly.

"What kind of deal?" Billy asked.

"What?" Pea pleaded, staring at the canister, and pulling Billy's sleeve.

"We bring him twenty barracuda a week for his family, and we don't have any more supply problems...and we get movies first when they come in from stateside."

"No shit!" Pea exclaimed.

"What about Sablan?" Billy asked. "And Queen and Crawford?"

"Screw them!" Pea said.

"When we tell Queen and Crawford about the deal, they won't complain," R.J. said. "Besides, they only catch about ten a night. We can pull another twenty a week out of the harbor easy."

"So Sablan still gets his fish?" Billy asked, mostly to himself.

"Screw Sablan!" Pea said.

"One more thing," R.J. cautioned.

"What?" Billy asked.

"What?" Pea echoed.

"Bobby's going to Pearl next month for two weeks' training on a new supply inventory system, and I kinda promised him we'd look out for his people while he's gone."

"Look out how?" Billy asked suspiciously. Pea stood looking back and forth at R.J. and Billy, still a little confused.

"Just make sure they get the fish, and you know..."

"Is there something you're not telling us?" Billy asked suspiciously.

"What?" Pea demanded.

"Well," R.J. began. "I kinda promised him we'd help fix up their trailer."

"Here we go," Billy warned. "We gotta baby-sit Bobby's whole clan? There must be a hundred of them."

"So what?" R.J. asked. "It's worth it, isn't it? Hell, plenty of supplies and good movies. Besides, it's only once a week."

"Just once a week, right?" Pea asked. "We go up there once a week and help out?"

"That's right," R.J. nodded. "Look at it as community relations."

"Get me in a room with Connie Stevens," Pea said. "I'll show you some community re-lations!"

Billy climbed into the cab of the pickup and started up the engine. R.J. hopped into the passenger side, calling "Shotgun!" The other sailors climbed into the back of the truck and found handholds to grip on to.

"Hold on!" Billy yelled, and popped the clutch, sending the old pickup darting down the gravel road, spewing rocks and dirt in its path.

Pea sat with his back to the cab and braced himself against the wooden boxes as Billy gathered speed. Soon the wind was blowing across the roof of the cab and the working party bounced around in the truck, laughing and enjoying the cooling breeze.

Once back aboard ship, Billy Lopez held a brief meeting with Queen in First Division's compartment, then caught up with Crawford in the forward engine room while Pea was meeting with Snively. All agreed that R.J. had cut a sweet deal, and promised to cooperate with two conditions: R.J., Billy and Pea had to catch the barracuda for the Gamboas, and Queen, Crawford and Snively were exempt from repair duty on the Gamboas' trailer. Queen offered to come along and supervise, but Billy convinced him that would be unnecessary.

The Haverfield scuttlebutt network spread the word through the ship in record time. Several sailors from different departments volunteered their time to help out with the trailer repairs and unanimously acknowledged R.J. for cutting the deal with Bobby Gamboa.

"Only got one problem as I see it," Crawford pointed out. "Gotta keep Chief Twitchell away from the supply depot." He picked his teeth and observed, "Might not be that easy."

"Let me take care of that," Queen said.

"Y'all goin' to talk to him?" Crawford drawled.

"Nope," the big man said. "I'm gonna talk to Whipple and ask him to talk to Mr. MacDonald and ask him to talk to Mr. Almogordo so he'll talk to Twitchell."

Later that afternoon Chief Twitchell left Mr. Almogordo's stateroom with explicit instructions not to interfere with the supply chain, and to stay away from Bobby Gamboa, the supply depot and anyone who worked there. Twitchell was not happy being so instructed, but agreed. When he came out on deck, his face was red with humiliation and he cornered Crawford, who told him the whole story of what happened at the supply depot. The news enraged Twitchell. *Davis? That new shit-head was looking for trouble.* Chief Twitchell made a mental promise to get even with that wise-ass, no matter how long it took.

R.J worked with Tanner's crew for the rest of the day, learning about seamanship. Working on the focsul, Tanner taught him how to properly tie a square knot as opposed to a granny knot, and R.J. learned how to tie a bowline knot, a half-hitch and a clove-hitch. He picked up the knot-tying quickly, and soon learned he had a knack for knots. He learned to properly coil up line and store it in the bosun's locker. Tanner warned him about coiling up line.

"Coil the line under your bicep and around your hand, as neatly as you can. Remember, someone is going to need that line and it should uncoil smoothly. And one more thing," he grinned slyly. "Watch the free end of the line when you're coiling it, because if you let it fly around free, it will whip up and hit you right in the balls." He chuckled and left R.J. to his line coiling.

R.J. laughed. Tanner always had some funny thing to say, and R.J. was sure he was putting him on about the line, until he let the free end fly around and it hit him right in the balls, just like Tanner had warned. "Ow, shit!" R.J. exclaimed, bending over and trying to fight the sick feeling in his stomach. He looked up, embarrassed, and saw Tanner watching him from the 02 level.

"I warned you about that free end, Wog!" he yelled, laughing at R.J.'s discomfort.

That evening, after chow, R.J. showered and put more witch hazel on his worsening sunburn and sprinkled baby powder on the rash that was beginning to form on his crotch. He had been warned by several First Division crew members about the tropical "crotch-rot" and was determined to arrest it before it spread. It seemed the crotch-rot had different ideas, and R.J. gingerly spread the baby powder around his crotch area in an attempt to fight off the tropical fungus.

Even though it was Friday night, most of the crew stayed aboard to watch 'Dr. No.' Only the married men with dependents on the island and a few Mocombo Club-bound liberty hounds left the ship.

As R.J., Pea and Billy Lopez came up the ladder to the fantail, several sailors broke into applause. The trio bowed and waved, graciously indicating each other with hand gestures and soaking up the attention.

Cotton came up to them as the trio pulled themselves into sitting positions on the torpedo tubes. "Don't know how you guys did it," he said, smiling. "But life just got a little easier on the ol' Haverbucket."

"Well, we promised Bobby we would have this movie back by tomorrow," R.J. explained. "They're having a dinner party followed by the movie at the Officer's Club tomorrow night, and I guaranteed it would be back."

"That's cool," Cotton said. "Tomorrow's Saturday, and we're planning an assault on the Mocombo Club." He squinted at R.J. "You up for it?"

"Okay," R.J. agreed. "Think they'll sell me some tequila this time?"

Snively called for quiet and started up the projector. As the music began its dramatic melody and the titles began to play, the men on the fantail broke into a raucous cheer. James Bond was walking along in his dapper suit, viewed through the rifled barrel of a gun. He turned, drew his Walther PPK and fired, bringing more cheers from the audience. Later in the film, when Ursula Andress emerged from the surf in a white bikini, the men on the fantail went crazy, yelling, hooting, whistling and howling like dogs at the moon.

R.J. sat on the torpedo tubes with his shipmates and smiled happily at the scene around him. He was becoming more comfortable on board this ship with every passing minute, and felt satisfied that he had made friends and actually contributed to the health and welfare of the crew in the past three weeks. The newest sailor on the Haverfield, R.J. was beginning to feel he belonged to this crew, and instinctively felt they were beginning to accept him as one of them. Everyone except for Twitchell, who had taken every opportunity to treat R.J. like crap. He glared and growled at R.J. every time he encountered him, and R.J. had heeded Jefferson's advice to stay away from him, but he couldn't help but feel there was a confrontation coming. He couldn't just let the chief continue to browbeat him. It pissed him off just to think about it.

The movie ended, and the men left the fantail, laughing and joking, kidding each other about the movie. Several waved thanks to R.J., Pea and Billy as they left to go below to their compartments where they would lie awake in their bunks, late into the night, fantasizing about Ursula Andress in a white bikini.

R.J. stayed on the fantail after everyone else had left. He leaned back on the three-inch gun mount and lit a cigarette, blowing the smoke out through his nose. It was quiet and peaceful on the fantail. Mr. Thompson, the OOD on the quarterdeck, paced back and forth in front of the brow, lost in thought.

As the ship began to fall asleep, weary from the day's work, R.J. looked up at the clear night sky and tried to compute in his head just how far he was from Longmont, Denver and San Diego. He remembered a poem by Henry Reed called 'Judging Distances' in which a World War One Army trainee was asked to judge the distance between his platoon and the figures of a man and a woman, lying gently together under swaying elm trees. The trainee judges that the distance between himself and the young lovers is, *"...roughly a distance of about one year and a half."*

R.J. had been in the Navy for a little over a year and a half, and had about two and a half years left on his enlistment. He judged that the distance between him and Longmont, Colorado was roughly a distance of two and a half years. San Diego was a little closer. *San Diego.* The trouble he got into with the rest of the Straps seemed farther away than almost six months ago. He wondered how Big Lenny, John-John, Cool Richard and Frankie were doing in their new duty stations.

TWELVE

U.S. Naval Training Center
San Diego, California
Saturday, October 20, 1962

"We're going to war!"

R.J. awoke at 0600 as Radioman First Class Bill Crenshaw, head instructor of Radioman School Class 22 of 1962, stalked up and down the aisle of the barracks bellowing at the top of his lungs.

"We're by-God going to war, boys," he bellowed. "Hop out of those racks!" He was over six feet and close to two hundred twenty pounds, and none of it was fat. He moved with a certain quiet grace, up on the balls of his feet, always pacing, be it in front of a classroom or in the barracks. He never stopped pacing.

R.J. and the other students slowly began to stir. They rubbed their eyes, and jumped out of their bunks, gathering around the big table in the middle of the barracks room. They were sleepy and confused. Crenshaw wasn't making any sense. Was he drunk? What was going on?

'By-God' Bill Crenshaw hopped up on top of the table and surveyed his charges. They were babies, really. Few of them had much experience and none of them had been in a war. But this was a war, by-God, no doubt about it. That bearded spic Fidel Castro had been asking for this for a long time, and now he was by-God going to get it.

Bill Crenshaw knew about war. He had joined the Navy during the Korean Conflict and had patrolled the Sea of Japan in a tin can for almost a year. He had been shot at from shore batteries, harassed by PT boats, and had ferried Marines to and from the action on the Korean Peninsula.

"All liberty is cancelled," By-God Bill announced, pacing back and forth on top of the table. Groans erupted from the men of class twenty-two. "Knock off the belly-aching. This is by-God serious." He waved a decoded message slip at them. "President Kennedy has declared an emergency for all branches of the service. You boys ain't goin' on liberty for a while."

Questions were fired at the head instructor from all over the barracks.

"What war?"

"You drunk, Crenshaw?"

"I got a 48 hour liberty, man!"

"Calm down," Crenshaw bellowed. "Here's what we know. There is a problem in Cuba, don't know what it is." He stopped pacing and held up his hand at the questions. "But we're going to by-God do something about it!"

The truth was that neither By-God Bill nor anyone else on base knew exactly what was wrong. They only knew it to be serious. Crenshaw hoped it wasn't another aborted invasion like the Bay of Pigs fiasco last year. Surely Kennedy had learned his lesson on that one! This time he was mobilizing the armed forces, and that was enough for By-God Bill Crenshaw to determine that war was imminent. He glared around the room at the radio school students.

"Get cleaned up, square away this barracks and go to chow. When you get back I want you to pack your seabags and stand by at your bunks." He started to climb down off the table, paused, and then added dramatically, "And no phone calls. But you might as well write to your honeys back home, fellas. They probably won't see you for a long time." By-God Bill Crenshaw was clearly excited at the prospect of going to war.

The men of Radio School class 22 of 1962 stood staring at each other for several moments after Crenshaw had returned to his office. Slowly, one by one they began drifting off to the showers, making up their bunks and getting dressed for chow. They headed out in large groups, quietly walking the half-mile to the chow hall where breakfast was being put together. On the way, R.J. and Frankie ran into Big Lenny and some of the Straps from other classes, also making their way to the chow hall. The two groups fell in with each other, no one talking, and they entered the chow hall quietly.

R.J., Frankie and the other Straps moved through the chow line quickly and found a table near the rear of the big hall. Once seated, the excited conversations began.

"What do you think is going on, Lenny?" R.J. asked.

Big Lenny just shrugged and forked a large portion of scrambled eggs into his mouth. "Hell, I don't know," he said, chewing and talking at the same time. "Probably invading again. Kennedy screwed it up royal last time. Probably wants to make up for it."

Frankie considered this for a minute. "Then how come ALL the armed forces are on alert?" he asked. "Cuba's not that big. I mean, a couple of platoons of Marines can handle that Castro fucker." Nods and grunts of agreement came from the other men at the table.

John-John Baxter leaned forward to look down the table at Lenny. "Maybe the Russians are involved," he suggested.

Lenny nodded his head, thinking. "That would make sense. Maybe..." He frowned at his eggs. "That's maybe why this big alert." He put his fork down on his tray and looked around at the Straps, frowning. "Shit! Maybe we goin' to war with Russia!"

The Straps sat silently, not eating, deep in thought. If it was the Russians, this was going to be an ugly war. They, too, had a lot of those nuclear bombs and the means to deliver them.

"Oh, shit," Carl Foretti said, pointing toward the chowline. "Here comes that asshole Fellows."

"I don' like that sumbitch," Tyrone 'Splib' Walker announced. "He a fuckin' loan shark. Man hit me for seven dollars to borrow five!"

'Cool' Richard Martinez agreed with the 'Splib.' "Guy's a fuckin' leech," he spat. "Also a rat-fink. Tells the instructors everything. He's the one got everybody pissed off about our straps." 'Cool' gestured with his thumbs, hooking them into a pair of imaginary suspenders.

"I'm gonna catch that asshole on the beach some night and jack his ass up," Big Lenny stated, picking his teeth with a wooden toothpick. "Seven for five ain't right, no matter how broke a guy is."

"He's coming over here," R.J. said. "Let's split."

The Straps picked up their trays and started toward the scullery. Fellows came up to the table as they were leaving.

"What's happening, Strap-Guys?" he smirked. "Lost your appetites?" Fellows was medium height, medium weight and had a medium complexion. He wore black, horn-rimmed glasses which sat perched on his medium nose. There was nothing special or remarkable about him. He was a very ordinary man.

The Straps ignored him.

"Heard the Shore Patrol busted you Strap-Guys last night and sent you home to Momma!" Fellows said, smirking.

R.J. turned back to say something, but Big Lenny grabbed his arm. "Not now, partner," he cautioned. "Not here and not now. But soon."

"Hey, Splib!" Fellows called to the Straps as they left the chow hall. "You still owe me seven dollars!"

Tyrone called back, "Screw you, Fellows. Only my friends call me 'Splib.'"

Back at the barracks, the men of Radio School Class 22 busied themselves with packing their seabags and writing letters. 'By-God' Bill Crenshaw was in his office, door closed, pacing and listening intently to the radio for news of the Cuban situation. He hung a 'Do Not Disturb' sign on his door, and passed the word that he was unavailable.

R.J. finished packing his seabag, hung it on his bunk and took his writing paper and pen to the long table in the middle of the barracks. Many Radio School students were sitting at the table, writing letters home.

"So, R.J.," Big Lenny smiled as R.J. sat next to him on the bench. "How many letters you gotta write? I know you got a whole bunch of chicks back home."

R.J. clicked his ballpoint pen. "No, just one in Longmont and one in Denver," he replied. Then, thinking about what he said he added, "And one in San Diego."

"Oh," Frankie said. "You mean Tonya?" He cupped his hands under his chest. "This Tonya?" Everyone laughed, including R.J.

"You're gonna get writer's cramp," Arnie 'Stretch' Johnson warned.

"He's gonna get cramps somewhere else when he goes home on leave," Frankie said. "He likes to spread the wealth among several fortunate young ladies."

R.J. sat quietly and composed letters to Renee in Longmont and Janice in Denver. Janice had been his first real girlfriend when he was fourteen and she was thirteen. They had broken up and got back to together so often, he was never sure if their friendship was on or off, but he wrote to her anyway. The letters were similar, but not exact copies. R.J. prided himself in writing personalized letters to each girl. He felt it would be wrong to send the same letter to three different girls, like 'Cool' Richard always did, claiming it saved time.

Saturday passed with no news, and Sunday was the same. Crenshaw stayed in his office, coming out only to shower, go to chow and sleep. The students were becoming bored, the excitement of Saturday morning faded into routine, and the students played hearts or poker or showed each other card tricks to pass the time.

Meanwhile, in Washington, D.C. President Kennedy spent the entire day in conference with his advisors. They worked to decide the level and type of the American response to the Soviet threat. Two options were discussed: A naval blockade of the island, or an air strike to eliminate the missiles and their launchers. It was decided that a blockade would be the prudent course of action, but because the term 'blockade' suggested an act of war, the President decided to call it a 'quarantine.' It was further decided the President would meet with congressional leaders the next morning, Monday the twenty-second, and would address the nation on Monday evening. Orders were sent to the Navy to organize the quarantine and refuse any Soviet attempt to deliver more weapons to Cuba. It was known that Soviet cargo ships were en route to Cuba with more missiles and an escort of warships. The stage was set for confrontation.

* * * * *

Monday dawned and nothing seemed different. The students arose, showered and went to morning chow. Then they returned to the barracks, gathered their class materials and mustered in the courtyard between the barracks. 'By God' Bill Crenshaw stood on the steps in front of the barracks doors with his clipboard. When he was satisfied everyone was there, he began calling the roll.

"Abercrombie!"

"Here!"

"Andrews!"

"Here!"

"Baxter!"

"Here, by God!" Snickers from the students as Crenshaw looked over his glasses at John-John Baxter. "Very funny. Davis!"

"Here!"

When the roll-call was finished Crenshaw set down his clipboard and clasped his hands behind his back. He paced in front of the students, scowling at them over his glasses.

"They say no news is good news, so I guess the news is good this morning," he said loudly. "We carry on as usual. Anything new happens you will be informed." He stopped and picked up his clipboard. "Now, let's march to class and I want a by-God tight formation all the way. Youse are sailors, so behave in an orderly military fashion!" Crenshaw moved down the steps and took his place in front of the class. "Ten-hut! Column right march!"

Radio School Class 22 marched down Nimitz Avenue with other classes, number 21 in front of them and number 23 behind. R.J. felt there was a big difference in this morning's routine. He couldn't quite put his finger on the change, but there was definitely a difference. Then it dawned on him; no good-natured banter among the students as they marched. There were no jokes, no laughter and no friendly ribbing. Everyone was silent, and the only sound was the stomp-stomp cadence of marching feet making their way to the classroom.

R.J. filed into the classroom with the rest of the class and took his seat at his typewriter near the front of the room. The work stations were assigned alphabetically, so R.J. was always near the front row. He put on his earphones and rested his fingers on the typewriter keys, A S D F J K L. The typewriters had no letters or numbers on the keys. The students referred to a large chart on the wall at the front of the classroom for the locations of letters and numbers. The idea was to listen to the code, and type the correct key without looking at the typewriter keys. They were nearing the end of their fourth month of Radio School, and were getting quite accomplished typing out the code. R.J. was particularly good at typing without looking at the chart, having memorized the locations of the keys. And he loved taking code. He loved the rhythm and meter of the *dits* and *dahs* coming through his headphones, and he discovered he could copy the code and daydream at the same time. It was becoming automatic. His speed was approaching forty words per minute. When the majority of the class could copy at a certain speed, 'By-God' Bill Crenshaw would speed up the tape, and the students had to adjust quickly to the new speed. Slowly, over time, they would master the faster speed. Crenshaw would then increase it again. By the time graduation arrived, they were required to copy Morse code at fifty words per minute. R.J. knew he would be faster than that.

R.J. and his classmates rotated from copying code to electronics class where they learned to tune in and repair the big, cumbersome transceivers, a combination transmitter and receiver. During the World Series, Big Lenny had managed to tune in the games, and the students, along with their instructors, enjoyed the contests between the San Francisco Giants and the New York Yankees. The Yankees had won in seven games, second baseman Bobby Richardson making a great play on a line drive by Willie McCovey to end the series. Naturally, money changed hands.

Before the class broke for lunch, Bill Crenshaw made an announcement. President Kennedy was going to address the nation at 1900 Washington time, 1600 San Diego time. Classes were going to end at 1500 to give the students a chance to return to their barracks and listen to the speech. The students were abuzz with excitement all through lunch, speculating on what the President might say. Many thought it would be a declaration of war.

By 1600 hours the streets and courtyards of the Naval Training Center were deserted, and all of the radio school students were gathered around radios in their barracks. Crenshaw had wired his radio into the barracks loud speakers and the students gathered around the big table, or sat on their bunks, awaiting the President's address. He began at precisely 1600.

"Good evening, my fellow citizens: This government, as promised, has maintained the closest surveillance of the Soviet military buildup on the island of Cuba. Within the past week, unmistakable evidence has established the fact that a series of offensive missile sites is now in preparation on that imprisoned island. The purpose of these bases can be none other than to provide a nuclear strike capability against the Western Hemisphere."

For the first time R.J. could remember, the barracks was completely silent. The students listened intently as the President, in his strong Massachusetts accent, continued to make his case.

"The characteristics of these new missile sites indicate two distinct types of installations. Several of them include medium range ballistic missiles capable of carrying a nuclear warhead for a distance of more that one thousand nautical miles. Each of these missiles, in short, is capable of striking Washington, D.C., the Panama Canal, Cape Canaveral, Mexico City, or any other city in the southeastern part of the United States, in Central America, or in the Caribbean area."

The radio school students began to murmur and shift in their seats. The President went on to describe the false assurances by the Soviet Union that the missiles were for defense only, and made a convincing case for Soviet duplicity. He described how the Soviet Union, assisted by Fidel Castro, had begun a large military buildup in Cuba contrary to international law. He cited the Rio Pact of 1947, the joint resolution of the 87th Congress and the charter of the United Nations.

"Acting, therefore, in the defense of our own security and of the entire Western Hemisphere, and under the authority entrusted to me by the Constitution as endorsed by the resolution of the Congress, I have directed that the following initial steps be taken immediately."

He then outlined a seven-step program to defuse the crisis, including a naval quarantine of the island to turn back any Soviet ships approaching Cuba, directing the American military to prepare for any eventuality, and a policy of regarding any nuclear missile launched from Cuba as an attack by the Soviet Union on the United States, requiring a full retaliatory response upon the Soviet Union. He announced the reinforcement of the base at Guantanamo and called for an immediate meeting of the Organization of American States to examine the threat to the Western Hemisphere. He also asked the United Nations to convene an emergency meeting of the Security Council to take action against the Soviet threat. Finally, he called upon Chairman Krushchev to cease and desist from the military buildup and join in an historic effort to end the perilous arms race.

R.J. stared at the deck, trying to picture a war waged with nuclear weapons. It brought to mind the drills in elementary school designed to protect the children of America against a nuclear attack. Ducking under their desks and covering their eyes seemed oddly naïve, considering the prediction that half the United States would be destroyed in such an attack.

President Kennedy then called on the Cuban people to rise up and throw out the tyrant, Castro, and be welcomed back into the international community.

He then directed his words directly to the American people:

"My fellow citizens: let no one doubt that this is a difficult and dangerous effort on which we have set out. No one can see precisely what course it will take or what costs or casualties will be incurred. Many months of sacrifice and self-discipline lie ahead—months in which our patience and our will will be tested—months in which many threats and denunciations will keep us aware of our danger. But the greatest danger of all would be to do nothing.

The path we have chosen for the present is full of hazards, as all paths are. But it is the one most consistent with our character and courage as a nation and our commitments around the world. The cost of freedom is always high, and Americans have always paid it. And one path we shall never choose, and that is the path of surrender or submission.

Our goal is not the victory of might, but the vindication of right. Not peace at the expense of freedom, but both peace and freedom, here in this hemisphere, and we hope, around the world. God willing, that goal will be achieved.

Thank you and goodnight."

The silence was palpable in the barracks. The students sat at the table and on their bunks, deep in thought. Some leaned against the bulkheads smoking cigarettes. No one spoke for a long time. Then, someone from the back of the room asked softly, "What do we do now?"

All heads turned toward Bill Crenshaw. He stood up and looked around the room. "We wait," he said. "We by-God wait."

* * * * *

For the next week, R.J. and his radio school classmates fell into a numbing routine. Up early and off to chow. Back for roll-call and march to class. Copy Morse code for hours and then more hours studying electronics. Then back to the barracks to catch the latest news on the Cuban Missile Crisis. No liberty, although they were allowed to make phone calls. Not much was happening with the confrontation. The American Navy had successfully quarantined the island of Cuba and Soviet ships, laden with missiles and other war-making materials, had wisely declined to try and penetrate the quarantine. The situation had all the earmarks of a stalemate.

A week went by with no significant developments. That changed on Saturday, the twenty-seventh, while the students were complaining and grousing about the lack of liberty. Word came down that the Cubans manning a SAM missile site had shot down an American U-2 spy aircraft and killed the pilot. The consensus at the San Diego Naval Training Center was that now, finally, the United States would unleash a bombing strike to retaliate. But hours dragged on and there was no retaliation, leading to frustration among the students and instructors.

On Monday, October 29, Soviet Premier Khrushchev went on worldwide radio and announced that the Soviet Union would remove the missiles from Cuba if the United States promised not to invade the island. For all practical purposes, the crisis was over.

"Fuckers backed down!" Bill Crenshaw burst into the barracks shaking his fist in the air. "The Russkies by-God backed down." He was more than a little disappointed. By-God Bill Crenshaw wanted a war. He felt that it was just a matter of time before war happened between the U.S. and Soviet Union, and he wanted it to happen now, when America was much stronger than the Russians.

The students cheered the end of the crisis. Not because war had been averted, but because once again they could leave the base on liberty. No more boring routine. They were back to normal. In a few days, the Cuban missile crisis faded from their memories, and in a few weeks, it was as though it had never happened.

'By-God' Bill Crenshaw stood leaning against the doorjam of his office, smoking a cigarette and watching his radio school charges celebrate the end of the missile crisis and their forced confinement to the base. He shook his head sadly, knowing that these kids, and that's basically what they were, had no real appreciation of the fact that the world had recently teetered on the brink of self-destruction. The Cuban crisis and face-off of two of the world's nuclear powers, pushed to its logical conclusion, could have resulted in a horrible war of destruction like nothing ever seen on the planet.

"Stupid kids," Crenshaw muttered to himself. He crushed the butt of his cigarette in the butt-kit and turned back to his desk. "A bunch of stupid fucking kids, by God."

THIRTEEN

Apra Harbor, Guam
April 3, 1963

Captain D. Paul Oliver was pleased with the results so far. The ship was beginning to look like a Navy vessel and the crew was getting squared away, thanks mostly to MacDonald and the department chiefs. Fresh paint covered the decks and bulkheads, and engineering spare parts suddenly began to trickle in. Captain Oliver had heard rumors about a deal which was negotiated between supply and some of his crewmembers, but he didn't inquire as to what or whom. Things were going well, and he wasn't one to look a gift horse in the mouth. Besides, this was the coconut Navy and you had to scrounge for everything. By the time they returned to port on the twentieth, he would be ready to host the dinner party for the admiral and the other ships' captains. Lorelei would be there. He had thought of her almost constantly during the past few weeks. He thought about how she would react to his ship. He walked the decks, examining the new paint job, the shine of polished brass and the improvement of the crew's appearance, and tried to imagine what impression all of it would make on Lorelei. *Wait a minute,* he thought. *Why am I trying to impress her? It's the admiral I want to impress.* But despite his protests, he knew he wanted to impress Lorelei. He tried to tell himself he didn't know why, but...

He was anxious to get underway and put the crew through its paces. The next couple of weeks at sea would tell him much about his ship and crew, and what effect the new training program had had on both.

* * * * *

R.J. was excited about going to sea for the first time...finally! The Haverfield was scheduled to survey several islands in the U.S. Trust Territory and return to Guam on the morning of Saturday, April 20. R.J. knew the patrol would reveal much about him and his ability to function as a part of the Haverfield crew.

R.J. stood on the fantail before reveille and watched the sun creep over that mountain to the northeast. *I've got to find out the name of that mountain,* he thought. Reveille sounded, and R.J. decided to go below to the compartment and get a fresh pack of cigarettes from his locker. As he came down the aft ladder into the compartment, the deck crew was beginning to stir, and he was surprised to hear laughter and shouting coming from the First Division quarters so early in the morning.

He reached the bottom of the ladder and saw that several sailors had gathered around Jefferson's bunk and were chiding him in a friendly, but obscene way. Jefferson lay back on his bunk, eyes wide open, with a sheet covering him from the waist down. The sheet rose up into the air as if it was being held up by a tent pole, and when Jefferson removed the sheet (to the cheers of the deck crew) R.J. could see what the commotion was about. Jefferson had a huge erection, his large member much bigger than any R.J. had ever seen before. His penis stood proud and thick, bouncing slightly in the air.

"Get back!" Jefferson warned. "I'm taking 'im up to the shower and I don' want nobody gettin' hurt!" He swung his legs over his bunk and the sailors around him backed up in mock awe and respect. Jefferson hopped out of the bunk and hit the deck lightly on his feet, his big member bouncing up and down as he landed. He gently laid a towel over it, and with his head held high in an air of superiority, he marched slowly toward the forward ladder, led by his proud, towel-draped erection.

"Torpedo in the water!" Pea called out.

"Better holster that hog-leg, Jefferson!" Sonny laughed.

"Watch out for that thing," Queen cautioned seriously. "You can put somebody's eye out with that!"

Jefferson saw R.J. standing at the bottom of the ladder.

"Step back, R.J.," he warned. "I'm takin' Buster for a walk."

"Buster?" R.J. asked, staring at the bouncing towel.

"That's 'is name!" Pea yelled, laughing and nodding enthusiastically.

"That's jus 'is first name," Jefferson explained.

"What's his last name?" R.J. asked, shaking his head in wonder.

"Hymen," Jefferson said, proudly, and started climbing the ladder.

"Buster Hymen?" R.J. asked as Jefferson vanished into the after crew's head.

Sonny saw the look on R.J.'s face and started laughing. "You ain't never seen Buster before?" he asked. R.J. shook his head.

"That's right," Pancho said. "He's always up on the fantail in the morning. Whatta ya do up there, R.J.? Pray or something?"

"Something like that," R.J. replied.

"No wonder you ain't never seen big Buster," Sonny said. "Impressive, huh?"

"To say the least," R.J. agreed.

"Wasn't for ol' Buster," Queen observed, absently picking his massive teeth, "we'd have room for one more deck ape in here."

* * * * *

R.J. joined the Havernauts for morning chow and then went back to the compartment to stow away gear and get ready for the patrol.

"Set the special sea and anchor detail!" the 1-MC blared. "Make all preparations for getting underway!"

The ship was abuzz with activity. Men from the deck crew scurried about, lashing down anything that was loose and could shift around during steaming. Deck hatches were closed and dogged down, leaving only small, round openings in the larger hatches for sailors to squeeze through. Condition Able was set to insure water tight integrity. Line handlers from the Brister gathered on the pier, ready to help the Haverfield cast off.

On the bridge, Captain Oliver took the conn and prepared to pilot the ship away from the dock. Tanner was on the helm, as usual. Cotton was on the leehelm. Chief Lyons and Lieutenant Barkman huddled over the chart table, manually plotting courses and establishing time frames.

Captain Oliver came into the pilot house from the flying bridge and pointed to the chart table. "How we coming?" he asked.

"Good, Cap'n," Mr. Barkman replied. "We're plotted and ready to proceed." He moved aside so the captain could see the chart and the courses plotted there. The Haverfield was going to patrol elements of the Yap Islands during this survey.

"Okay." The captain studied the chart. "South to Gafert, then down to Faraulep Atoll, Woleal Atoll and Eauripik Atoll. Then west to Sorol Atoll, north to Fais and a straight shot northwest to home." He nodded to himself, satisfied with the course plotting. "Good job, let's stay on schedule."

"Aye, sir," Lieutenant Barkman said.

"The ship's ready to get underway, sir." Mr. MacDonald arrived on the bridge to report the ship's readiness.

"Very well. Single up all lines."

Mr. MacDonald leaned over the starboard wing bridge and called to the line handlers on the focsul. "Single up all lines!" The order was repeated on the focsul, amidships and on the fantail.

R.J. was stationed amidships with Pea. Together they singled up lines amidships and hauled the big manila line aboard, coiling it neatly on the deck.

"Cast off two and three!"

The dock line handlers removed lines two and three from their cleats and tossed them off the pier. Pea and R.J. pulled the lines in quickly, before they hit the water, and coiled them on the deck.

"Cast off number four!" The fantail line was pulled in and coiled up. The only connection left to the pier was the single number one line on the front of the bow. Sonny and Pancho stood by to bring that one aboard and Queen stood by to oversee the focsul operations.

Captain Oliver came out on the wing and looked up and down the pier. The ship was drifting slightly away from the dock. "Cast off one!" he called. The last line was cast off and pulled aboard.

"All back one third!"

"All back one third, aye sir!"

"Left standard rudder!"

"Left standard rudder aye, sir." Tanner eased the helm to the left and the Haverfield swung away from the pier, the ship's whistle blew and she swung in a smooth arc into the channel.

"We're underway," Pea said.

R.J. looked at the pier fading farther away, and realized the ship was moving. It was a strange sensation after a month in port. He felt a little unsure of his footing and leaned his hand on the bulkhead to steady himself. The ship came almost to a stop as the bow came around and pointed down the channel to the breakwater.

"All ahead one third!" the captain ordered.

"All ahead one third, sir." Cotton repeated the order.

"Come to course one eight zero."

"One eight zero, aye." Tanner made small adjustments with the helm and brought the ship gently on course. The Haverfield moved down the channel and past the Brister whose sailors lined the side, waving to the Haverfield crew.

"This ain't too bad," R.J. said, standing with his legs apart on the deck, trying to maintain his balance.

"Yeah?" Pea asked. "Wait till we hit the breakwater, then we'll see if you got sea legs."

The Haverfield continued down the channel, her crew dragging the mooring lines forward and down into the bosun's locker for storage while at sea. R.J. and Pea stored their lines and stood by, watching the activity. As the ship approached the mouth of the harbor, the captain ordered all ahead two thirds and the ship picked up speed. R.J. felt the increase in speed through the soles of his feet as he watched the mouth of the harbor drawing closer. The ship rocked gently in the channel, cutting easily through the calm water of Apra Harbor. Then she hit the breakwater. The change in the ship's attitude was dramatic when her bow pitched past the breakwater, making contact with the Pacific Ocean. She began to bob and roll in a steady rhythm, and R.J. stumbled on the deck and almost fell.

"C'mon, boy!" Pea yelled. "Follow me." He headed forward to the focsul. He moved smoothly along the pitching and rolling deck, walking a little bow-legged to steady himself. He made it look easy, leaning left or right, matching the rolling of the ship. R.J. struggled to keep up with him and balance himself against the rolling motion. It wasn't working. He felt like he was standing on a big, bobbing cork being tossed around in the sea. Looking down at the ocean only made matters worse. As he struggled toward the focsul, swaying and stumbling, he tried to keep close to the bulkhead and maintain his handhold. The men on the focsul saw his dilemma and pointed at him, laughing.

"Look at that stupid Wog!" Lester yelled. "Them's land legs. He gonna fall over the side!"

Sonny grinned widely as R.J. finally made his way to the focsul. "You walk like Frankenstein, man!" He began walking around stiff-legged, imitating R.J.

"Got to loosen up those knees," Queen advised him. "Get your balance from the knees down. Everything else will follow." He motioned R.J. over. "I want you to go down the port side to the fantail, then up the starboard side back here. Do that ten times and report back to me."

R.J. frowned and looked aft toward the fantail. It seemed like a long way off. He was bent over, holding on to the capstain. "Okay," he said and started aft, weaving and stumbling against the motion of the ship.

"And stay off the lifeline!" Queen called. The others stood on the deck, steady and balanced, riding the ship like experienced sailors. R.J. envied them. *Will I ever get that kind of balance?* He doubted it.

By the time he finished the tenth circuit along the deck, R.J. was beginning to feel more comfortable with the rolling of the ship. He didn't have to hold onto the bulkhead as often, and he quit looking down at the water to get his bearings. He concentrated on the deck ahead of him, and found he could anticipate the ship's roll and pitch.

"Secure the special sea and anchor detail!" came the announcement. "Duty section three assume the watch!"

R.J. wasn't scheduled for watch until 1600, so he made his way aft to First Division's compartment. Big Queen was in his usual spot between bunks, overseeing activity there.

"Let's get this compartment squared away and get up on deck. I want the landing rafts checked and secured and I don't wanna see no rust nowhere."

The Havernauts scrambled around the compartment, storing gear and cleaning up. Tanner pulled R.J. aside.

"You're in my duty section," he said. "Let's go topside and make sure everything is secure." He led R.J. up the ladder and through the small hatch to the fantail. "We check everything and then we check it again," Tanner explained. On the fantail, three large black rubber life rafts outfitted with gasoline powered outboard motors were lashed to the deck. Each life raft had six life jackets tied to the manila line which encircled the raft like a life-line. "This is how we land on the islands," Tanner explained.

"I thought we used the motor whaleboat," R.J. said.

"Too hard to get off the beach," Tanner explained. "See, landing on the beach is a breeze. We just ride the surf, you know, kinda like Cotton and his surfer buddies back in California."

"So landing is the easy part?" R.J. asked, curiously examining the life rafts.

"Coming back through the surf is the hard part," Tanner said patiently. "We got to push the rafts hard into the surf, jump in and start paddling. Soon as we get past the first wave, we fire up the outboard motor and drive through the surf. It can be pretty dangerous. Last year we had a guy who fell out of the raft and got dragged along the coral reef. He got cut up pretty bad and then got a bad infection from the coral."

"Will I get to go on a landing?"

"Probably. Check the Plan of the Day. It's posted outside the mess-decks. Gives us the schedules for the landings and lists the guys going in."

R.J. followed Tanner as he made his rounds on deck. Lester was on the focsul with his crew doing the same, and Sonny had his crew on the 02 and 03 levels. Everywhere he looked, R.J. saw sailors moving around, going up starboard and down port in a steady stream of activity. Gone was the relaxed atmosphere of in-port routine. Men were going about their jobs seriously, professionally. R.J. felt a thrill as he took in the scene. The crew bustling about, the ship cutting through the waves, the vast sky, the American flag fluttering from the main mast, all filled R.J. with a sense of adventure and pride. This was how he had imagined it would be when he first enlisted.

When noon chow was announced, R.J., and Tanner joined Pea and Billy Lopez in line. They collected up their trays and silverware and picked their way through the galley, accepting servings of beef stew and biscuits. Tanner stopped at the milk dispensing machine and handed R.J. a cup.

"You feelin' a little queasy?" he asked.

"Not yet," R.J. answered. He had forgotten about the dreaded seasickness.

"Milk is the secret," Tanner advised. "You feel a little queasy, drink some milk and eat some saltines. Works all the time."

"Does everyone get seasick his first time out?"

"No, not everyone," Tanner replied. "Unless *they* have something to do with it." He pointed toward a booth in the middle of the messdecks. Queen, Sonny and Lester were sitting there, looking at R.J. and making comments under their breath. "They're gonna try to make you sick, so stand by."

Oh great, R.J. thought. *Another initiation.*

R.J. and the other three sat in a booth across from Queen, Sonny and Lester. As soon as they sat down, Lester started in.

"So I run over this skunk, and it smelled pretty bad, but it tasted real good," he said, smacking his lips. "I licked it off my tires and washed it down with some cod liver oil."

R.J. felt his stomach complain, but he drank his milk and started on his beef stew, trying to ignore the trio across the aisle.

"I seen a guy puke all over the fantail one time," Queen rumbled. He pointed at R.J.'s tray. "Looked a lot like that stuff there."

R.J. ignored them and continued to eat his beef stew.

"Uh oh," Tanner said. "Don't look at him, R.J."

R.J. involuntarily looked over at the other booth. Sonny was smiling widely and beef stew was dribbling through his teeth and dropping onto his tray.

"Hey," Queen said. "If you ain't gonna eat that, I will." He started to scoop some up with his spoon, but Sonny stopped him.

"That's *my* lunch, Queen. Regurgitate some o' your own!'

They kept it up until R.J. had finished his lunch. His stomach did feel a little sour, but he was damned if he was going to let them get to him. He got up with his tray and made his way to the scullery.

Queen, Sonny and Lester looked at each other and shrugged. It didn't work. Tomorrow they'd pick on someone else.

R.J almost did get seasick when he stepped into the passageway outside the messdecks and caught a strong whiff of diesel fuel. He forced the feeling down and studied the schedule for island landings. He was listed on the fifth landing, at Sorol Atoll with Lester's raft. Along with them were Mr. Thompson, Anselmi, Pancho and Jefferson. The second raft was led by Mr. Anton, accompanied by Tanner, Billy Lopez, Kelly 'Doc' Gysler, the corpsman, Pea and Cotton. R.J. was disappointed they weren't going to hit Sorol Atoll until Saturday, the thirteenth. He was looking forward to the landing, having heard so much about them from the veteran sailors in First Division. A small announcement on the bottom of the POD listed three promotions in rank. Pea had been promoted to Seaman, E-3, as had Billy Lopez, and Tanner had been promoted to Boatswain's Mate Third Class, E-4. Crawford had made first class Machinist Mate. R.J. turned back to return to the messdecks, but Tanner was just coming out.

"Hey, man!" R.J. exclaimed, pointing at the promotion list.

Tanner ran his finger down the POD and smiled broadly. "Made it my first try," he said with a satisfied look. "Got my fuckin' crow!"

They returned to First Division's compartment together and the other deck crew sailors began filing in.

"Tanner made Third Class!" R.J. announced, and the compartment erupted in cheers. Nobody deserved the promotion more than Tanner. He was a real sailor who 'knew his shit' and had the respect of everyone in the deck force.

"Too bad we ain't in port," Lester said. "We'd throw his ass over the side to celebrate." He put his arm around Tanner's neck and pointed to his own Third Class Crow. "I'm still senior," he pointed out.

Queen picked at his big teeth thoughtfully and suggested, "Let's throw 'im over the side anyways. See if he can swim."

At 1300 the announcement came over the 1-MC, but this time the announcement was preceded by a shrill bosun's whistle. "Turn to! Commence ship's work!"

"Okay, girls, you heard the call," Queen said. "Hit the deck and make 'er look pretty!"

The deck force surged up the ladders and onto the decks, spreading out toward their work stations. R.J. found he was walking more steadily and could match the ship's motion better than he could that morning.

"Lookey here!" Sonny exclaimed, pointing at R.J. "Man's getting' his sea legs already!"

R.J. smiled and gave Sonny the OK sign with his forefinger and thumb. It felt good to be at sea. The salt spray fanned over the ship from the bow, and R.J. got his first face-full. The sun would dry the water soon, leaving a thin layer of salt on his face, turning R.J. into an 'old salt' his first day out. He felt as though he had been at sea for a week rather than a day, and his confidence rose as he learned to master his sea legs.

Duty section two relieved the watch at 1545 and R.J. stood his first underway watch with Tanner, who was assigned to teach him how things worked. They began on the leehelm, and Tanner explained how the ship's telegraph worked. Since the ship was steaming at a steady twenty knots, there wasn't much to do. No speed changes meant the leehelmsman merely stood there, sound powered phones on his head, watching the activity on the bridge. The sun poured through the hatch of the starboard wing bridge as the Haverfield continued south toward the first island group. Mr. Winters, the OOD, stood on the flying bridge, a pair of binoculars hanging from his neck. He occasionally lifted them to his eyes and scanned the horizon, but there was nothing to see but blue water.

After thirty minutes on the leehelm, the watch rotated and R.J. and Tanner moved to the helm position. Tanner took the helm and showed R.J. how to gently make adjustments so that the ship stayed on the designated course, which was 180 degrees. It looked quite easy when Tanner did it, but when R.J. took the helm the ship began to drift off course. All his attempts at bringing it back to course resulted in compass swings of five degrees or more to each side.

"Mind your helm!" Mr. Winters ordered, noticing the variations.

"Aye, sir," Tanner answered, and reached across to steady the helm back on course. After thirty minutes as helmsman, R.J. was convinced he would never master that position. Then they rotated again, and took the watch position on the port wing bridge

Tanner explained the responsibilities of the port wing look-out and showed R.J. how to sweep the horizon from the bow to the port beam. R.J. enjoyed looking at the ocean through the binoculars. The sun was dropping lower in the sky on the starboard side of the ship, and the sea was turning a slate-blue color. The wind was rising and white caps dotted the dark surface as choppy waves began to form. After thirty minutes on the wing, the watch rotated again, and Tanner and R.J. took up position as lookout on the 04 level, port side. From there, the highest lookout post, R.J. could see the bow of the ship pushing into the waves, throwing spray back over the foc-sul. The feeling was like being on a roller coaster, the ship plowing head-first into the sea, then rearing back and plowing in again. The wind was strongest up on the 04 level. Following Tanner's lead, R.J. put his steaming cap in his back pocket and held on to the forward railing, feet apart, riding the bucking ship as it bounced back and forth on the teeming sea.

Their thirty minutes completed on the 04 level, Tanner and R.J. went aft and took position as the aft look-out, on the 02 level looking down at the fantail.

A group of sailors was gathered around a large cardboard box on the fantail, many of them holding brooms. R.J. watched them as one by one they peeked into the box and laughed and nodded at each other.

"What's going on?" R.J. asked.

"They musta caught a sea bat," Tanner explained.

"What's a sea bat?"

"It's pretty rare, but not unheard of," Tanner said, a twinkle in his eyes. "We usually catch at least one each patrol. They fly low over the ship, and the guys knock them down with brooms and drop a box over them." R.J. wondered what nonsense the crew was up to with this tale. He didn't believe the story about a mysterious sea-bat.

"Watch this," Tanner said.

The cardboard box was intriguing Kelly, a young electrician's mate. Lester had one foot on the box and warned Kelly to stand back.

"Don't mess with it or it'll get away," he cautioned.

"What is it?" Kelly asked, inspecting the box.

"It's a sea-bat, boot. Ain't you never heard of a sea bat?"

Kelly shook his head. "Can I see it?" he asked.

"Maybe if you're careful," Lester said seriously. "I'll pick the box up just a little and you can look under it, but do it quickly."

"Will it bite?" Kelly asked.

"Naw, but it'll fly away if it gets the chance, so get down close to the deck and take a quick peek."

Kelly got down on all fours and Lester made a production of slowly lift-ing the box so Kelly could see under it. "Careful," Lester warned.

As Kelly peeked under the box, five sailors swung their brooms and hit him hard on the ass. Kelly jumped up, red faced, and looked around. Everyone on the fantail was pointing at him and laughing. He looked con-fused, then finally got the joke and smiled sheepishly, rubbing his buttocks with both hands. Another new guy had been had by the sea-bat trick.

R.J. laughed along with the rest of them, privately glad he wasn't the object of this particular practical joke. He vowed to be on guard in the future. He donned the sound powered phones of the aft look-out and sat up on a vent, watching the ship's wake leaving a trail on the ocean. The wake was waving a little, the helmsman having a little trouble keeping her on course. R.J. imagined what the wake had looked like when he was on the helm. *Probably like a winding road through the mountains.*

Tanner tapped him on the shoulder to let him know it was time to rotate. Tanner led R.J. forward to the starboard wing and climbed the ladder to the 04 level, stationing him as the starboard lookout. From there they rotated down to the starboard wing, and then into the pilot house as the messenger of the watch. Their four-hour watch was almost over, and R.J. couldn't believe how fast the time had passed. Relaxing in the rear of the pilot house, smoking cigarettes and chatting about the various watch stations, Tanner explained that one of the messenger's jobs was to round up the watch's relief which was due to come on duty at 2000. The messenger began rounding up the relief at 1930 to give them plenty of time to take positions at 1945.

"It's time," Tanner said softly, looking up at the chronometer on the aft bulkhead. It was important for everyone to keep quiet when in the pilot house. The members of the watch spoke to each other in undertones. The sun had set and the ship was dark except for red steaming lights positioned around the pilot house. "You go round up duty section three," he instructed R.J. "I'll wait here."

R.J. went below to First Division's compartment and let everyone know it was time to relieve the watch. Lester and a few others were playing hearts on a blanket spread on the deck. "Okay," he said. "Let's relieve those pussies in Section Two." He gathered up the cards and folded the blanket, tossing it on his bunk and slipping the deck of cards under it. R.J. returned to the bridge through the messdecks and up the forward ladder. When he got topside, he found he couldn't see. The sun had finished setting and it was very dark. R.J. bumped into Tanner as he came into the pilot house.

"Whoa, man," Tanner said quietly. "Stand by over there until your eyes adjust to the dark."

R.J. leaned back on the bulkhead and blinked. Slowly, his eyes became used to the darkness and he could see the interior of the bridge. The gyroscope compass was the brightest-lit object in the pilot house. It illuminated the helmsman's face with a soft green light, distorting his features. To R.J. it looked like he was holding a flashlight under his chin, as R.J. used to do to frighten his little brother at night.

"Let's see if we can grab some late chow," Tanner suggested. They went below to the messdecks where Hawkins was polishing his pots. "Anything to eat, Hawk?" Tanner asked pleasantly.

"I lef' a little out," Hawkins replied, pointing to a couple of steaming trays of food, set off to the side. "Don' make no mess!" he scolded.

They took trays, selected a couple of pieces of fried chicken and some mashed potatoes, and found a booth near the middle of the messdecks.

"Well, you stood your first underway watch." Tanner said, shoveling potatoes into his mouth. "Whatta you think?" He chewed slowly, watching R.J.'s face.

"I loved it," R.J. beamed. "Being at sea is a gas."

Tanner washed down his food with a cup of milk. "That's 'cuz it's new. It'll get real boring, you watch and see."

R.J. nodded, but he couldn't believe he would ever get bored standing watch at sea. There was just too much to experience. Duty section two had

the morning watch, beginning at 0400, and R.J. found he was looking forward to it. He loved the early morning, and he was anxious for 0400 to
arrive.

"One more rotation," Tanner was saying. "And then you on your own.
Think you can handle the watch on your own?"

"Yeah, except for the helm. Steering the ship is the hardest part," R.J.
said.

"You'll get used to it," Tanner encouraged him. "Soon you'll be as good
as me."

R.J. smiled and nodded his head, but he didn't believe he would ever
be the helmsman Tanner was.

The days went quickly on patrol, full of routine. The watches grew
longer, it seemed to R.J., just as Tanner had predicted, and R.J. was getting
a little better on the helm, though he still struggled with it. He watched his
first island landing from the fantail where he and other deck crew members
were responsible for lowering the rafts into the water and bringing them
back aboard when they returned.

At first sight, the island of Gaferut looked like a big clump of crabgrass
sitting on the surface of the ocean. As the ship grew closer, R.J. could make
out the sandy beach and the waves crashing on the reef. The ship anchored
about four miles out, maintaining a safe distance from the coral reef that
surrounded the island. The rafts were lowered into the water, and the
crews climbed down a bosun's ladder and arranged themselves in the rubber rafts. They pushed off from the ship, started the outboard motors, and
began moving toward the island. R.J. looked through binoculars as the
crews reached the surf and rode it in, sweeping down rapidly on the beach.
They jumped out of the rafts and pulled them up the beach to a safe distance from the surf. Then they disappeared into the forest of palm trees
toward the center of the island.

About two hours later, the aft lookout pointed toward the island and
announced, "They're coming back!"

Through the binoculars, R.J. watched the crews pull the rafts into the
surf, running hard. The rafts hit the waves and reared up, showing their
black undersides briefly, then crashed back down while the crews paddled
furiously to get them through the surf. The outboard motors started up
again and the rafts were on their way back to the ship. R.J. yearned to go
on a landing, and he wished his landing on Sorol Atoll were tomorrow,
instead of a week away.

The two rafts arrived back at the ship and the deck crew manipulated
the manual davit to hook onto them and bring them aboard. The crews had
brought back many interesting items, including coconuts, carvings from
wood made by the natives and some large, colored glass balls. R.J. helped
bring everything aboard and held one of the glass balls, a bright red one, up
to the light. It was a little smaller than a basketball, but heavier.

"What's this?" he asked Sonny, who took it from him and hefted it in
one hand.

"It's a fishing net float," Sonny explained. "Japs use them to float their nets. Sometimes they break loose and wash up on the beach. We find 'em all over the place."

"I thought the Japs weren't supposed to fish these waters," R.J. said.

"True, but they do," Sonny replied. "You know what sneaky little bastards they are." He tucked the ball under his arm and went down below, squeezing through the small opening in the aft hatch, and pulled the lid down behind him as he disappeared down the ladder.

The deck crew washed down the rafts, replenished the gasoline in the outboard motors, and secured the rafts with nylon line to the fantail. They were ready for the next island landing.

Finally, the day for R.J.'s turn on the landing rafts arrived. Sorol Atoll popped up on the horizon just after breakfast and R.J. had trouble containing his excitement. The atoll, like most Pacific islands, was surrounded by a coral reef, which created a natural boundary around the atoll. The water over the reef was too shallow for the Haverfield to get very close, so the ship lay off the island, well away from the reef, and the landing rafts putt-putted toward the island in some of the most remarkable aqua-colored water R.J. had ever dreamed of.

Only about six feet deep in some spots, the water was crystal clear and R.J. could see the coral bottom as the raft cruised over. Fish of all sizes, shapes and colors darted among the coral, and the color of the reef changed every few feet. R.J. spotted a huge sea tortoise moving effortlessly away from the raft, its big flippers guiding it through the aqua water like the big wings of a bird. Reef sharks darted along the bottom, scooting away as the raft drew close to them.

"Heads up!" Lester called, pointing ahead to the beach. White surf about two feet high washed up on the sand where the water was deeper close to the shore. Lester held the outboard engine's screws out of the water and the raft cruised toward the beach, riding the surf. They were ashore in no time. They pulled their rubber rafts up on the beach and secured them by tying them to palm trees.

R.J. jumped out of the raft and helped pull it up the beach. He looked around at the tropical island, amazed at the pristine white beach and thick, lush, deep green vegetation.

"C'mon, Wog!" Lester urged him. "Ain't no time for sight-seeing." He led R.J. up through the palm trees and down a narrow path to the tiny village near the center of the island. Under the canopy of palm trees, the sun was blocked from view and the smell of the island was harsh and pungent. No breeze cooled the landing party and the humidity was stifling. Soon, they came upon a clearing in which stood several thatch-roofed huts. The sing-song language of the natives filled the air and they came forward to greet the sailors.

Men were dressed only in loincloths, with a few of them wearing cut off dungarees they had traded for with previous landing parties. R.J. was shocked to see the women. They wore only loin cloths or short, wrap around skirts and were bare-chested. They grinned at the sailors with brown, rotting teeth and offered carvings and trinkets they had fashioned from wood and coral rock. It was impossible to tell their ages. Mostly they all looked alike, that same blank expression, even when they smiled. R.J. thought island life was probably a lot tougher than he'd imagined.

Mr. Thompson and Doc Gysler were involved in a conversation with the village elder, using a combination of sign language and pig-latin to convey their meaning. Doc set up a make-shift examination area and began treating minor cuts and bruises among the natives. Other sailors bargained for trinkets with cigarettes, soap and candy bars.

R.J., Tanner and Billy Lopez walked along the beach, looking for the tell-tale glass bulbs that washed ashore, signifying the presence of Japanese fisherman. They found three floating in the shallow coral pools near a small inlet. R.J. picked up a large blue glass ball and held it up for the others to see.

"Got one!" he announced, standing knee-deep in the water.

"You better get out of there!" Tanner called to him, pointing at R.J.'s feet.

R.J. looked down and yelped. Four small reef sharks were darting in and around his ankles, brushing against him in a threatening way. R.J. splashed ashore, holding his new blue orb like a football.

Billy Lopez laughed. "They will bite your ass," he said of the reef sharks. "But they don't eat much."

R.J. grinned sheepishly and strode up the beach toward the rafts. Mr. Thompson was calling the crew back. Doc Gysler had finished examining the natives and found no serious injuries. R.J. was disappointed that the survey was over so soon. He was enjoying himself.

"Now comes the hard part," Tanner said seriously, pointing toward the surf which had been whipped up by a stiff wind. The waves were bigger than when they landed, and they crashed white foam on the coral beach.

"Gotta get back through that," Tanner said, his jaw set.

"Let's go!" Mr. Thompson ordered. "Hit the surf!"

The two crews picked up their rafts and trotted toward the surf, building up speed as they ran down the beach. They crashed into the water and pushed the rafts into the waves, jumping into them at the last moment. Each man grabbed an oar and began paddling furiously through the surf. At first R.J. didn't think they were going to make it. Then the rafts reared up and slammed down on the waves. Lester and Tanner started their outboard motors and the propellers took hold, pushing the rafts through the waves and into deeper water. They had made it through the surf.

R.J. looked around at the sailors in the rafts, soaking wet, sweating and grinning at each other. He wiped salt water from his face and lay back on the side of the raft, taking in the sun, watching the white clouds drifting above him. He had never felt more content or more at peace. His first landing had gone off without trouble, and he felt a genuine affection for the men in the rafts. They had landed and come back through the surf together, the teamwork paying off. He was a little closer to full membership in the Havernauts and it felt good to him.

The landing parties reached the ship and climbed the bosun's ladder to the fantail. R.J. helped pull the rafts aboard and went below to change clothes and store his glass ball in his locker. He was very familiar with the ship now, and he found he could move up and down the ladders and through the hatches with little effort. The underway watches were becoming easier, more routine. He walked the rolling decks with more confidence, balancing himself with his feet apart, almost bow-legged the way the more experienced sailors walked the deck.

The landing on Fais, the last of the Yap islands they would survey on the patrol, went off smoothly and without incident. The Haverfield set course back to Guam in the late afternoon of the fifteenth, the arrival scheduled for Saturday, April 20. The patrol had been successful. No major health problems were reported among the native islanders, and there had been no confrontations with Japanese fisherman. The crew was in good spirits and looked forward to going home, even if home for them was Apra Harbor, Guam.

* * * * *

The day before they were to arrive back on Guam, Captain Oliver met with his officers in the wardroom to review the patrol, and assess the ship's performance. He was pleased with the progress the crew was making, and with the way the officers had implemented his rehabilitation strategy. His plans for the admiral's reception aboard the Haverfield were final and the dinner was set for Wednesday, the twenty-fourth. His officers were almost as enthusiastic as he was. They looked forward to having the admiral aboard, too. When the meeting was adjourned, he asked Mr. MacDonald to stay behind.

"I understand you're researching some of the Pacific battles in World War Two," he said matter-of-factly, lighting his pipe and sitting back in his chair.

"Yes, sir," MacDonald replied.

"Ever do any teaching, Mac?"

"No, sir."

"I think you'd be good at it," he said, puffing at his pipe. "And I'd like you to give it a try."

"Sir?" The lieutenant was a little confused.

"Part of instilling pride in this crew, Mac, is giving them a sense of what the Navy is all about." The captain puffed his pipe, found it had gone out, and struck a kitchen match to the bowl. "I want you to share some of the history with them, in an informal way. Just get a bunch of them together and tell them the stories. You know the history well, and I think they would get a lot out of it."

"Yes, sir." The idea was beginning to appeal to him. Mr. MacDonald thought about it for a moment and nodded. "The naval campaigns in the Pacific are fascinating history," he agreed. "I think they'd get a lot out of it, too."

"Good." The captain blew pleasant smelling pipe smoke into the air. "And I think you should conduct these history lessons at sea. You agree?"

He looked over his pipe at the lieutenant. It didn't sound like a question.

MacDonald nodded in assent. "Yes, sir. That would make them seem more real, I think."

"Put the first one together for our next patrol," the captain suggested. "We're going out on May twenty-fourth for two weeks. Pass the word and make sure you have a good turn out." He smiled pleasantly. "Any ideas what you want to talk about?"

MacDonald thought for a moment. "The battle of Midway, I think," he said, almost to himself. Mr. MacDonald loved to tell stories, and he was very good at it. He loved naval history and often wove it into his stories for color and charm. He often said that once he retired, he was going to write a book about the myth of the Japanese Imperial Fleet. His premise was that Japan was never a significant naval power. She had the ships, but not the admirals. The battles they won, they got lucky. He often pointed out the many errors in judgment committed by Japanese admirals in the Pacific war in battles at Pearl Harbor, Midway and his own personal favorite, Leyte Gulf.

* * * * *

Except for the duty section on watch, the crew was peacefully asleep at 0300 the morning of the twentieth. Lieutenant Westerman had the conn, with Pea on the helm and Billy Lopez on lee-helm. It was quiet on the bridge, and the men on watch were relaxed, sleepy and content. They'd be back on Guam in a few hours, and they looked forward to the easy routine of being in port. The ship seemed sleepy and anxious to return to port too, as if she somehow knew she had performed well and earned her trip home.

Captain Oliver stepped out of his stateroom and onto the bridge. Billy Lopez spotted him and called out, "Captain's on the bridge!"

The rest of the watch was startled, including Mr. Westerman. The captain on the bridge at 0300 could only mean one thing: A surprise drill.

"Morning, Cap'n," Mr. Westerman greeted him.

"Seems quiet, Bill," the captain said, looking into the radar scope.

"Yes sir," the OOD agreed. "Very quiet." He had an idea what was coming.

The captain looked around the bridge, then turned back to Mr. Westerman. "We have a hostile submarine contact bearing 030," he said matter-of-factly. "Sound general quarters, and make it 'no drill.'"

"Aye, sir." The OOD turned to Pancho, who was the bosun of the watch. "Sound general quarters, man ASW battle stations," he ordered.

"Aye, aye, sir!" Pancho replied and stepped to the 1-MC. He pushed the ON button and blew 'attention' with his bosun's pipe. "General quarters, general quarters! This is not a drill! All hands man your anti-submarine warfare stations!" He reached down and pulled the handle on the GQ alarm, sending the blaring BONG-BONG-BONG-BONG throughout the ship.

R.J. was startled awake and it took him a few seconds to get his bearings. What the hell was going on? The deck crew sailors were leaping from their bunks and pulling on trousers and boots, hurriedly rushing up the aft ladder. R.J. fell in with Tanner and rushed to his GQ station, which was on the fantail.

The Haverfield awoke quickly, her decks teeming with sailors rushing to battle stations. Finally, the annoying BONG-BONG-BONG of the GQ alarm stopped and all stations began reporting readiness to the bridge.

R.J. and Tanner took turns looking through the binoculars, trying to spot the submarine's periscope cutting through the ocean. There was nothing to port, nothing to starboard and nothing aft. Tanner relaxed and leaned on the three-inch gun mount.

"Another fuckin' drill," he announced.

Captain Oliver looked at his watch, timing the crew as they scurried to reach their battle stations. When all stations had reported in, he smiled and looked up at Mr. Westerman. "They made good time," he said, still smiling. "Tell the crew to secure from general quarters." He headed back to his stateroom. "And wake me at 0600," he said over his shoulder.

Mr. Westerman and the members of the watch grinned at each other in the dark pilot house. The crew had been rudely awakened at an un-Godly hour by the call to general quarters. They had responded quickly and efficiently, far more quickly and efficiently than ever before. Now they could head for the barn.

FOURTEEN

When the ship arrived at Apra Harbor and tied up starboard-side to the pier, three new crew members were waiting to come aboard. Chief Twitchell stood on the 02 level with Chief Risk, scowling down at the trio on the pier. Two of them were black, and looked like brothers, carrying the same strong build and mannerisms. They were tall and athletic looking, but one was a light, almost caramel color, the other was very black with strong African features. Still, it was obvious they were brothers. The third was a tall, skinny white guy with a large nose and a protruding Adam's apple. All three were staring at the Haverfield, their disappointment in the ship's age evident in their expressions.

"Goddammit!" Twitchell spat. "More niggers. That's all we need."

"Stay calm, Chief," Risk said impatiently. "Try to keep your feelings to yourself."

"Chrissakes, we already got enough niggers on this ship to remake *King Kong!*" The fat chief was fuming.

Chief Risk shook his head and walked away. Chief Twitchell stood at the lifeline and glared down at the newcomers. "Takin' over is what they're doing," he mumbled to himself. "Oughta call this ship 'The African Queen.'"

R.J. was washing down the fantail with fresh water, and heard Chief Twitchell's tirade on the new sailors. He felt the anger rising, and his face was reddening. He was developing a deep hatred for the chief, and it was becoming more and more difficult to hide it. He felt like yelling at the fat chief, calling him a bigot and a redneck, but he bit his lip and swallowed down the anger. The time would come, he knew, when he wouldn't be able to swallow it down anymore.

When the ship had been washed down with fresh water, and the fantail awning erected, R.J. and the Havernauts hurried down the aft ladder to their compartment. They wanted to greet the newcomers.

Queen was getting the new men situated; assigning bunks and helping them get their gear stored. The Havernauts gathered around, appraising the newcomers and introducing themselves. The two blacks were indeed brothers, Rafer (the light skinned one) and Andy Sample from Alabama. The third was Gino Karras from Brooklyn, New York and had the accent to prove it. All three had been assigned to the deck force.

"We gonna have a triple thunder party!" Sonny Metzner drawled.

"Three for one special," Tanner said, looking over the three new guys. "Don't think we ever had one of them."

The Sample brothers calmly stowed their gear in their lockers, paying little attention to the banter of the deck crew. Gino Karras took the bait.

"What's a thunda pawty?" he asked in Brooklyn-ese, his head bobbing as he talked.

Several of the Havernauts looked to R.J., smirking. They would leave it to him to enlighten the new guys.

"It's a little initiation we all go through," he explained. "No big deal."

"Boot camp was enough initiation for me," Gino grinned. "Like ta kill me with all that marchin' shit."

"Let's get this compartment squared away," Queen bellowed. "Turn in your laundry and trice up those racks. You wanna hit the beach or what?"

"Yeah," Billy Lopez said. "It's Saturday. Let's hit the Mocombo Club!"

"Wait a second," R.J. said. "We promised Bobby Gamboa we'd help fix up his folks' trailer." He held his hands out, palms up. "Remember Dr. No?"

"That's right," Pea agreed. "It's still early. Keep your dungarees on, men. We can come back and change into our whites after we done."

Queen grinned his big ugly grin and growled, "Anybody goin' to the Gamboas' jump in the truck. Billy, you take it easy on those roads up there. Don't want the ship's limo all beat to shit."

"I'll be as careful as ever," Billy replied.

"Yeah," Queen rumbled. "That's what I'm afraid of."

Rafer Sample looked at R.J. questioningly. "Who the Gamboas?"

R.J. explained the promise they had made to Bobby in exchange for some good movies and better supplies. Rafer and Andy spoke quietly for a moment and Rafer asked, "Mind if me and my brother help out?"

"Hell, no," R.J. replied. "We can use the help." He decided he liked Rafer Sample right away. He also liked Gino, but Andy was sort of a mystery. He spoke very little and seemed to be a bit shy.

R.J. was a little surprised by the number of men who volunteered to help with the Gamboas' trailer. He had so many willing to go, he had to turn some away, promising they could go on the next trip. The Gamboa

Working Party, as it came to be known, assembled ten men on the quarter-deck. Chief Tom Lyons had the deck, and when he learned what the working party was for, he offered a suggestion.

"Just before you get to the main gate," he told Billy, "there's a junk yard off to starboard. Go in there and see if you can find some materials. Maybe some corrugated tin, or some wood. There's bound to be something you can use."

"Thanks, Chief," Billy said, leading the crew down the brow.

Seven of them piled into the bed of the truck, and R.J. and Pea got in front with Billy. Tanner and Sonny sat with their backs against the cab, and Jefferson, Rafer, Andy, Gino Karras and Cotton arranged themselves around the bed. Just before Billy started the truck, Lester, who had the duty on the quarterdeck, came down the brow with a large canvas bag.

"You dumb shits gonna need these," he chided, and handed over the bag. It was full of tools: hammers, screwdrivers, marlin spikes, crowbars and a large assortment of nails and various screws.

"Good thinkin' Lester," Tanner said, and rummaged through the bag. He looked up at Lester with a pained expression. "No sandwiches?" he whined.

"Here's your sandwich," Lester retorted. He grabbed his crotch and backed up the brow to the quarterdeck.

"Hold on!" Billy yelled as he gunned the engine.

Sonny pointed at the new guys. "Y'all better get a hand hold. This boy's nuts." He hooked a thumb at Billy Lopez.

Billy popped the clutch and the old gray truck groaned down the pier, fishtailing and screeching rubber as it went, the passengers in the bed bouncing and flailing around.

On the quarterdeck, Lester shook his head and smiled at Chief Lyons. "Boy's gonna kill himself one of these days."

"Yep," the chief agreed, frowning. "And probably a bunch of others, too."

The junkyard yielded a trove of materials which were usable. The working party threw sheets of tin, several spare two-by-fours, some plywood and even a wooden window frame in surprisingly good condition into the bed of the truck. Billy approached the main gate and leaned out of the cab to talk to the Marine guard. After a brief conversation they were waved through and hit Highway One toward Agana.

Billy sped through the small town of Agana, passing various shops and Talagi's drive-in hamburger stand, then turned right on an unpaved road which led up to the mountains. The Gamboas lived outside a tiny village near Sinajana. R.J. spotted Bobby Gamboa standing in front of his family's dilapidated trailer, shirt off, feeding two goats. Bobby looked up at the sound of the pickup truck and broke into a big smile when he saw all the men in the bed.

"Hafa dai!" he called. He turned toward the trailer. "Hey pop, c'mon out here and look at this!"

Bobby's father was an older, heavier version of Bobby, but his teeth weren't as good. He showed them anyway in a huge grin and came forward to greet the Haverfield sailors. He was followed by his plump wife and his other eight children.

Billy Lopez slid to a stop, sending billows of dust flying everywhere. He jumped out of the truck and slammed the door, turned to greet the Gamboas, and instantly fell in love.

Bobby's younger sister, Teresa, stood on the wooden steps of the trailer, a short, tight flowery skirt wrapped around her body, coming just above the knees and showing off her ample curves. She held her baby sister, Maria, on her hip. Little Maria was about two years old and a miniature version of Teresa. She clung to her older sister and stared out at the sailors gathering around her home.

Teresa was seventeen years old. Her black hair was pulled back in a ponytail and she wore no makeup. When she smiled, she showed remarkably white teeth and her dark eyes danced with mischief and mirth. She was almost painfully beautiful and all her attention was directed at Billy Lopez.

Billy froze as if a falling safe had hit him on the head. His mouth was agape and his eyes were wide with wonder. Standing in the settling dust, he seemed unable to move his limbs, and when he tried to speak all that came out of his mouth was, "We...uh..the truck..uh.."

"I do believe the boy is smitten," Sonny drawled, looking back and forth between Billy and Teresa.

Tanner nodded in agreement, a big grin on his face. "I don't think I ever seen Billy at a loss for words." He gave Billy a gentle push in the back. "Go on and say hello, stupid."

Billy walked stiff-legged toward the trailer and took off his whitehat. "I...I'm..." he stammered.

Bobby interceded on Billy's behalf. "This is Billy Lopez, sis," he said. "Billy, this is my sister Teresa."

"Nice to meet you," Teresa said in a voice that sounded to Billy like the promise of heaven.

"I...uh..," Billy stammered. "Oh, hell...Hello, I mean..."

Teresa shook his hand and giggled. Billy stared, a silly look on his face. He tried to speak, but words failed him. His face was reddening and he was having a little trouble breathing.

R.J. turned to Tanner. "I don't think we better let him drive back."

"Shit," Tanner replied, grinning at Billy and Teresa. "That boy's gonna FLY home."

Bobby grabbed R.J. in a bear hug and lifted him off the ground. "You are a man of your word, buddy," he said, and put R.J. down.

"I thought you were going to Pearl," R.J. said when he regained his feet.

"Next week," Bobby explained, and walked R.J. toward the trailer with his arm thrown over R.J.'s shoulder.

Bobby introduced his family to the Havernauts and it was decided Billy would drive Mr. Gamboa to the store to pick up a couple of cases of beer. R.J. took up a collection from the crew and handed the money to Billy.

"Coors," R.J. instructed him. "Good Colorado beer."

Billy nodded, but was looking at Teresa. Mr. Gamboa grinned widely and motioned for Teresa to join them. "C'mon, little one. You go with us."

Teresa smiled happily and slid into the cab of the pickup between Billy and Mr. Gamboa. Billy started the truck, put it in reverse and slowly, very carefully backed down to the road. He shifted again, none of his trademark grinding of gears this time, and slowly headed down the hill.

"Last time I seen him drive that careful," Sonny drawled, "he had Twitchell with him."

"Bet he likes this better," R.J. laughed.

When Billy, Teresa and Mr. Gamboa returned with the beer, the Havernauts were already busy working on the trailer. The Sample brothers were on the roof repairing holes, Tanner and R.J. were putting up framing for a porch, and the rest of the crew busied themselves inside the trailer. The Gamboa children were running around, playing and laughing, and Mrs. Gamboa was cooking something delicious-smelling in a big pot on her wood burning stove.

Billy got out of the truck and ran around to the passenger side to help Teresa step down from the cab. As she slid across the seat she deliberately let Billy get a look at her thighs. She smiled sweetly at him and pulled her dress down. Billy gulped hard and tried to catch his breath. Mrs. Gamboa stood in the doorway of the trailer with her arms crossed, scowling at Teresa, who pretended not to notice.

"Beer!" Pea yelled and the crew took a break and gathered around Mr. Gamboa, who passed out cans of beer.

"I hope you got a church key," Cotton said, wiping his hands on his dungaree trousers.

Billy and Mr. Gamboa looked at each other and shrugged as if to say, "I thought you got the church key."

"Let me guess," Cotton said, glaring at Billy. "No church key, right?"

"Here you go!" Bobby came out of the trailer with a can opener. "One beer can opener," he said.

R.J. inspected the beer. "Hey, I said Coors. This is San Miguel."

"That's all they had," Billy said. "Didn't have no Coors."

"You boys will like this beer," Mr. Gamboa announced, holding up a can of San Miguel and inspecting it appreciatively. "It's good beer from the Philippines."

R.J. shrugged and began opening beers and passing them around.

The Havernauts sat around, some on the ground, some leaning against the truck, and sipped cold beer. A slight breeze rustled the palm trees and they listened to Mr. Gamboa reminiscing about World War Two when the Japanese occupied the island.

"We took to the hills," he said, pointing high in the mountains. "We stayed up there a long time and snuck into their camps late at night to steal food and ammunition. We couldn't fight them very well, but we sure made them miserable." He chuckled, remembering his youth. "We were young and dumb. Kinda like you boys." He grinned, showing his blackened teeth, and drank down his beer. R.J. opened another for him and Mr. Gamboa nodded thankfully. "We were too dumb to understand we could get killed or tortured, but we hated having those yellow bastards on our island." Mr. Gamboa looked off into the distance, and his eyes seemed to be slightly out of focus as he remembered. "They rounded up the men and boys, anyone young or strong enough to work, and marched us into the jungle to help them build their pillboxes and dug-in defensive positions. Some of us ran away and hid out. The girls they rounded up for different purposes." He sighed a big sigh and lit his corn-cob pipe. It smelled like he was smoking horse manure. "At least we didn't do what they did on Saipan." A dark, saddened look came over Mr. Gamboa's face. "That was a terrible thing," he whispered.

"What happened on Saipan, Mr. G.?" Pea asked.

Mr. Gamboa gazed off into the jungle. He shook his head quickly and puffed on his pipe. "One of these days I'll tell you about it," he said softly. "But not today."

After a few beers, the crew got back to work. They were thoroughly enjoying the day, pounding and sawing away at the trailer. After a few hours the old trailer was starting to improve in appearance. Tanner stood back and admired their handiwork.

"We're gonna need some paint," he observed.

"No, no!" Pea protested. "Please let's not paint it gray!"

Mr. Gamboa patted Pea on the back. "Maybe we paint it red. I always wanted a red house. Got any red paint?" he asked.

R.J. and Tanner looked at each other and said at the same time, "Red lead!"

And so it was decided to paint the Gamboas' trailer red. They would come again next Saturday and bring some red lead with them, after first getting permission from Queen.

Mrs. Gamboa came to the door of the trailer, Teresa behind her, and called to the crew, "Time to eat!"

Mr. Gamboa opened the spigot on his water tank so the Havernauts could wash up, and everyone crammed into the trailer for Mrs. Gamboa's fish stew. It didn't look like it tasted good, but R.J. took the small bowl and sipped the broth from it. It was delicious.

"You like?" Mrs. Gamboa asked, smiling maternally.

"This is great!" R.J. said. "What's in it?"

"Barracuda," Bobby replied. "The barracuda you caught for us."

R.J. sipped the stew with his eyes closed. He was afraid a barracuda eyeball might be floating in it. Mrs. Gamboa bustled about, filling bowls and breaking off pieces of home-made bread for the crew to dip into the soup. Teresa sat at a dilapidated formica table, little Maria on her lap, and stared at Billy, who stared back. They hadn't touched their lunch.

Before the Havernauts left it was decided they would return next Saturday with more scraps from the junk yard and some red lead paint. Bobby would be in Hawaii but he encouraged the crew to come anyway. Mrs. Gamboa, beaming happily, agreed enthusiastically. Sonny told Mrs.

Gamboa he would help her start a garden, which greatly pleased her. Tanner remembered some canvas that was stored in the bosun's locker and promised to finish the porch framing and cover it with the canvas. Their plans set for the next week, the tired but happy crew piled into the pickup truck and prepared to return to the ship. Teresa sat on the steps to the trailer, bouncing little Maria on her knee, and smiled sweetly at Billy. With new-found courage Billy approached her. He was trying to decide if he should try to kiss her goodbye, but the decision was made for him by a scowling Mrs. Gamboa who appeared in the doorway. Billy took both of Teresa's hands and squeezed them. She smiled and squeezed back. Billy backed toward the truck, his eyes on Teresa, and banged into the truck's fender. He giggled and climbed into the driver's seat, started the truck and slowly backed down the hill. Teresa stood in the doorway, Mrs. Gamboa behind her, and they waved at the crew, who waved back.

"Y'know," Tanner observed. "That's one thing we're missing around here."

"What?" R.J. asked.

"Romance, my friend. Old fashioned romance."

R.J. thought a moment, then began reciting a favorite poem.

> *"Romance who loves to nod and sing,*
> *with drowsy head and folded wing,*
> *among the green leaves as they shake*
> *far down within some shadowy lake.. "*

He grinned at Tanner who looked at him suspiciously.

"Edgar Allen Poe," R.J. explained. Tanner shrugged.

Sonny looked at the Sample brothers and Gino. "Y'all some hard workers," he said. "I'm not gonna enjoy thundering y'all like I did R.J. here."

R.J. winced and felt his chest. The bruise was long gone, but the memory lingered.

Andy and Rafer looked at each other. "What you mean, thunder?" Andy asked suspiciously in his deep voice.

"Man, you got one of them 'Mr. Bassman' voices," Gino said to Andy. "You do any singing?"

"I sang in our church's choir," Andy replied. "Our daddy's the minister."

Billy Lopez turned on Highway One and accelerated. The wind swept over the cab and cooled the occupants in the truck's bed.

"We had street groups in Brooklyn," Gino said. "Stood on the corners and sang to the chicks."

Andy grinned. "Y'mean like this?" He began snapping his fingers and singing the bass part of the Marcels' 'Blue Moon.'

> *"Bomp ba ba bomp ba bomp ba bomp bomp,*
> *Ba ba bomp ba ba bomp, ba dang a dang dang*
> *A ding a dong ding Blue Moon, Blue Moon, Blue Moon,*
> *Dip da dip da dip..."*

All the others joined in. *"Blue Blue Blue Blue moon, dip da dip da dip!"*

Gino started singing the lead. *"Blue moon, you saw me standing alone, without a dream in my heart, without a love of my own!"*

The others stopped singing and stared at the skinny kid from Brooklyn. They couldn't believe the beautiful voice that came out of his mouth. The clear soprano tones floating delicately in the air amazed them. They sat and stared. Gino looked around at their faces.

"Wha?" he said.

"Man, you are good!" Tanner said. "Let's take it again." And he began snapping his fingers while Andy restarted the bass. Billy Lopez had the truck up to fifty and they breezed through Agana, past onlookers in their shops who stopped and stared at the truckload of sailors speeding down the highway singing *'Blue Moon.'*

Back aboard ship, the deck crew showered and changed into whites for the trip to the Mocombo Club. It was past 1700 and Tanner was anxious to get going. He walked up and down the aisles of the compartment, snapping his fingers and urging the others to hurry and get dressed.

"C'mon, c'mon you deadheads. Let's roll. Won't be any tequila left by the time we get there." Tanner noticed the Sample brothers were not in whites.

"You guys comin' or what?" he asked.

"Naw, we gonna stay here," Rafer replied. "Gonna look around the ship, see what we can see."

"You're gonna miss out on your free shot of tequila," Tanner said disapprovingly.

"That's okay, man," Andy replied. "We don't never drink more than a beer or two. Our daddy wouldn't like it."

"Your daddy ain't here," Pea said.

Rafer tapped his chest with his hand. "He here. He always here."

The shuttle bus pulled up on the pier, brakes squeaking as it came to a stop. The Havernauts piled on board and the bus chugged up the hill toward the Mocombo Club.

* * * * *

It was almost midnight when the shuttle bus dropped the crew off at the foot of the Haverfield brow. Ensign P.J. Jones had the deck, Riley was the Petty Officer of the watch and Pancho was the messenger.

The returning sailors stumbled out of the shuttle, walking unsteadily up the brow. R.J. and Tanner carried a comatose Gino up the brow, his shoes dragging along behind him, his big feet unable to support him.

"Tequila?" Riley asked as they pulled Gino aboard and laid him down on the deck.

"Yep," R.J. smiled. "Dude can't hold his liquor."

Gino moaned and rolled over, becoming semi-conscious. "Blue Moon," he sang, slightly off-key. "You saw me standing..." He fell back asleep.

"Let's get him below," Tanner said. "Toss him in his rack before he expires."

Down in the compartment the crew put Gino in his rack. Everyone undressed, crawled into their bunks and fell asleep. R.J. looked around the darkened compartment that had become his home. The Sample brothers were sleeping soundly, looking quite peaceful. Cotton turned on the small light above his bunk and began reading a novel, as he always did before falling asleep. Lester was snoring loudly and Jefferson was tossing and turning. R.J. smiled to himself, realizing he was beginning to look upon these men as family. It was true they were becoming closer, unavoidable for men thrown together in small spaces. Good friendships were being forged within this crew, and it was obvious through their teasing banter that they were developing real affection for each other. R.J. decided to go up on deck and smoke a cigarette. He couldn't sleep anyway. The Mocombo Club had been loud and boisterous, and he was glad when they had taken Gino outside and he had succumbed to the tequila and the humidity. R.J. knew he was lucky it had not happened to him. His baby face had saved him from that particular humiliation.

Up on the fantail R.J. lit a cigarette with his Zippo and blew the smoke out through his nose. He leaned against a torpedo tube and smiled up at the dark sky, sprinkled with stars. Everything seemed right to him: the stars, the calm water of the harbor, the quiet, sleeping ship. He felt at peace with the world. He didn't see Chief Twitchell coming up behind him.

"Watcha doin' up here, shitbird?" The chief was drunk, his voice raspy and he slurred his words. "You ain't on watch, are you?"

R.J. turned around and looked at the chief. *Oh, great,* he thought.

"Just takin' the night air, Chief," he replied, irritated that his peaceful evening had been interrupted. He continued to lean against the torpedo tube, looked up at the stars and blew smoke out his nose.

"Stand up straight when I talk to you, boy!"

R.J. felt the anger and resentment rise and he was tired and still a little high from the beers at the Mocombo Club. He stayed where he was and tried to ignore the fat chief.

"I said stand up!" Twitchell roared.

Ensign Jones and Riley were becoming interested in the scene. They didn't hear all of what Twitchell had said, but as they came closer to R.J. and the chief, they did hear what R.J. was saying.

"I'll stand up for you when you get a gold bar on your collar." R.J. looked away from Twitchell and took a drag off his cigarette. He was sick of this fat drunk, and he felt defensive and insolent.

"You'll stand now!" the chief bellowed, coming around in front of R.J., getting in his face.

R.J. threw the cigarette in the harbor, stood looking down at Chief Twitchell, and exploded. All the resentment and anger at the chief that had been building since he came aboard finally came gushing forth. "Fuck you, you fat-ass bastard!" He spat at the chief's face.

Twitchell backed up, staring in disbelief at R.J., who sneered at the fat chief.

"What did you say?" Twitchell asked.

"I said fuck you, you horse's ass." R.J. poked his finger in the chief's chest and backed him up. "Fuck you and everybody related to you!" He continued poking Chief Twitchell in the chest. Ensign Jones stepped in, putting a stop to the confrontation.

"That'll do!" he ordered. "Get below, Davis."

R.J. looked at Mr. Jones and decided not to backtalk the ensign. Riley stood behind the OOD, frowning at the situation. Chief Twitchell fumed.

"Your ass is on report!" he yelled at R.J.

"Go below," Ensign Jones ordered.

R.J. looked over at Riley who nodded. R.J. sighed and started down the aft ladder to the compartment.

"I'm gonna run your ass into the brig you shitbird!" Twitchell yelled.

R.J. lifted his middle finger in the air and disappeared down the ladder.

"You both saw the whole thing," Twitchell said to Mr. Jones and Riley.

"Why don't you go to your quarters, Chief," Mr. Jones said. "Sleep on it and we'll talk about this tomorrow."

"I don't need to sleep on it," the chief said sarcastically.

Ensign Jones was a twenty three year old reserve officer who didn't have much experience in the Navy. He knew Twitchell, a senior chief machinists' mate, had been in for almost twenty five years, and he felt a little intimidated by him. Still, he was not going to let the chief know that.

"I think it's customary, Chief," Mr. Jones said, calmly and evenly, "for a petty officer to address an officer as 'Sir.'" He stared into the chief's eyes and thought he saw a glimmer of doubt. He continued, "I said to go to your quarters. That was not a suggestion."

"Yes sir," the fat chief said. He turned on his heel and stomped off.

Mr. Jones returned to the quarterdeck, Riley following close behind. "Riley, I want you to write this up in the log. Chief Twitchell is not going to let this go, and I want a record of it."

Riley opened the log. "You know, sir," he began, "Twitchell has been pretty hard to deal with, especially when it comes to this Davis kid."

"A seaman apprentice cannot talk to a chief petty officer in that manner," Mr. Jones said, "whatever the provocation may be." He sighed and shook his head. "Hell, I know Twitchell's a hard ass. But there are a lot of hard asses in this man's Navy, and kids like Davis need to understand they can't smart talk a chief petty officer."

"Yes, sir," Riley said. He began writing in the log. He tried to downplay the confrontation as much as possible. He knew Davis was going on report, and he liked the kid, even though he was obviously a hard head. He showed the log entry to Mr. Jones who initialed it, saying nothing. Riley disliked Chief Twitchell and had ever since the fat chief reported aboard a year ago. There were few in the crew who cared for Twitchell, except for Crawford and a couple of other rednecks. The chief was definitely not well thought of among the crew, but the officers seemed to think he was the second coming, or something. Riley shook his head. *That's the Navy for you,* he thought.

* * * * *

The next morning, Sunday, the word spread quickly around the ship about the confrontation between R.J. and Chief Twitchell. Several sailors from all the ship's divisions congratulated R.J., patting him on the back, grinning at him. There was little love lost for Twitchell among the crew, and they admired R.J. for doing something many of them wished they had done, or could do. The deck crew was unanimously behind R.J., with the most notable exception being Queen. The big man pulled R.J. out of line at breakfast and motioned for him to follow him out a hatch to the 01 level. Once outside he pointed a fat, hairy finger at R.J.'s chest.

"You're about as dumb a fuck as I ever seen," he grumbled. "You damn well better learn to keep your smart mouth shut. Where you think you're at, your momma's house?"

R.J. felt the resentment rise up. "That fat asshole has been on my case since I got here," he complained. "Last night he was drunk on his butt and got in my face. I got tired of taking it."

Queen took a deep breath. "You ain't a bad kid," he began. "You work hard and you get along with everybody, but if you think you can fight the Navy, you're wrong." The big boatswain's mate leaned against the bulkhead and spread out his big hands. "This shit is gonna land you in the brig, you know."

R.J. looked at Queen and frowned. "They wanna throw me in the brig for standing up for myself, then I guess I go to the brig."

Queen shook his big ugly head, turned around, and returned to the messdecks. R.J. was leaning on the railing, smoking a cigarette when Tanner found him.

"C'mon, man," Tanner said, beckoning R.J. toward the messdecks. "Twitchell's in there and he's got you written up."

R.J. followed Tanner to the messdecks where Twitchell and Riley were waiting. The fat chief handed R.J. the report chit and told him to sign it. R.J. looked at the chit. 'Insubordination to a superior officer,' it read. Riley had already signed it as a witness. R.J. looked up at Riley who shrugged slightly, a sympathetic look on his face. He signed the chit hurriedly and tossed it back at Chief Twitchell who caught it and walked away.

"Sorry," Riley said to R.J. The radioman walked out of the messdecks.

"What now?" R.J. asked.

Tanner sighed and shook his head. "Tomorrow you go to captain's mast and Twitchell will tell the captain what happened, then you tell the captain what happened, then Riley tells the captain what happened, then the captain decides what to do to you."

"What can he do to me?"

"For insubordination? Best case is restriction, worst case is the brig."

* * * * *

Captain's mast was set up on the 02 level, a wooden podium the centerpiece where the captain would hear the case and make his decision. R.J.'s was the first case to be presented.

The captain sat in his cabin, smoking his pipe and reviewing the engineering reports when the exec knocked on his door.

"Come in."

"Excuse me, Captain," the exec said, slipping in the door and closing it behind him. "I have the file and report chit on the Davis kid."

The captain nodded, pipe in mouth and took the paperwork from the exec. "Insubordination to Chief Twitchell?" he asked, quickly reading the report.

"Yes sir. The incident was witnessed by Mr. Jones and Riley."

The captain rubbed his chin. "This is the third report for insubordination Chief Twitchell has written since I've been aboard," the captain mused. "He's a little rough around the edges, don't you think, Chet?"

The executive officer handed a personnel file to Captain Oliver. "This is the kid who got into that mess in San Diego," he said. "I took away his clearance and tossed him in the deck force. You may recall."

Captain Oliver waved away the personnel file. "I've seen it, Chet. What do you think would be an appropriate punishment?"

"Brig, Captain. He's obviously a hard learner. Put him in the brig for thirty days and let him cool off. If that doesn't do it, I say we send him home."

"The last two men Twitchell wrote up got a month's restriction to the ship," Captain Oliver observed.

"This man is a trouble maker, sir." The exec was pushing for the brig. "He needs to learn a lesson."

Captain Oliver nodded and puffed on his pipe. The exec certainly had it in for this man. Captain Oliver thought about it and decided he would get C.C. Edgars transferred. The man was not a leader. It was obvious he didn't agree with what Captain Oliver was trying to do with the ship, and he allowed his personal feelings to color his judgment. After a few moments Captain Oliver looked up at the exec. "Get all parties ready," he said. "I'll be right there." He excused the exec and picked up the personnel file on Ruben James Davis, SA, and began leafing through it. Very high marks in Radio School, especially in Morse Code. Belonged to a group called the 'Straps,' who used to run around wearing suspenders. No disciplinary problems until...

The captain closed the file, threw it on his desk and put on his hat. He walked down to the 02 level where R.J., Ensign Jones, Twitchell, Riley and the exec were waiting. Snively stood off to the side, ready to record the proceedings.

"Attention on deck!" Riley called. All came to attention. The captain stepped up to the podium and nodded to the exec.

"Davis, R.J., seaman apprentice, has been put on report by Chief Twitchell for insubordination." he stated.

R.J. and Chief Twitchell stepped forward.

"Talk to me, chief," the captain ordered.

Twitchell's face was red, his eyes blurry and he sweated as he recounted the confrontation on the fantail. He embellished the story as much as he dared, glancing sideways at Riley as he did so. The captain nodded and waved Twitchell back.

"Davis. What do you have to say for yourself?" he asked.

"Nothing, sir." R.J. replied. *Screw it,* he thought. *I'm not going to give that fat bastard the satisfaction.*

"Do you dispute anything the chief just said?"

"No, sir."

"Do you have anything to say in your defense?"

"No, sir."

Chief Twitchell seemed to relax. Riley looked confused. The exec smiled to himself, a satisfied look on his face.

Captain Oliver looked from R.J. to Twitchell. This was unusual. Sailors at captain's mast always had something to say in their defense. They always presented mitigating circumstances, or sometimes just excuses. This kid seemed determined to go to the brig.

"You understand you can tell your side of the story," the captain said.

"I understand, sir," R.J. replied stubbornly.

The captain sighed. Perhaps this sailor was a hard learner. "Well, you leave me no choice," the captain said. "I'm going to send you to the Marine brig for thirty days."

R.J. said nothing. Twitchell smiled. Riley frowned. He wasn't going to get to testify. The exec smirked. Mr. Jones stood passively, staring straight ahead.

"You're dismissed," the captain said. He closed his folder and left the 02 level. The exec turned to Snively.

"Tell Chief Whipple to pack up this man's locker and present him to the OOD for transport to the brig."

"Yessir," Snively said. He cast a sideways glance at R.J. and went below. R.J. went down to the quarterdeck to await transportation to the brig. He was not disappointed, and he was not particularly upset. In fact, he felt nothing but numbness, in his mind and in his body. He had stood up to Chief Twitchell, and that in itself provided him with a small feeling of pride. More than anything, he was anxious to get the thirty days behind him. After all, this was inevitable, wasn't it?

Tanner came up on the quarterdeck wearing a duty belt and a shore patrol armband. "I'm your escort," he said flatly. "Whipple told me to accompany you."

"That's fine," R.J. said, as if he had any choice.

Billy Lopez appeared on the quarterdeck and frowned at R.J., then went down the brow to retrieve the ship's truck. Ensign Jones joined R.J. and Tanner, a file folder under his arm.

"I'm going to check you in at the brig," he explained.

"Yes, sir," R.J. answered, not looking at the ensign.

"If you had spoken up at Captain's mast, you probably would have been restricted to the ship," Mr. Jones said. "Why didn't you say something? Chief Twitchell was not completely in the right, you know."

R.J. shook his head. "Doesn't matter," he mumbled. He followed Mr. Jones and Tanner down the brow and got into the truck next to Billy. Mr. Jones rode shotgun and Tanner climbed into the bed.

Billy slammed the truck into first gear and started down the pier. Mr. Jones looked at R.J. and shook his head.

"What did you mean, it doesn't matter?" he asked.

"Twitchell's been determined to get me into the brig," R.J. answered quietly. "It was just a matter of time. Now maybe he'll get off my case."

"You can get him off your case by getting rid of your attitude," Mr. Jones said gently. "Avoid situations that can cause trouble for you. Don't be so damn stubborn. This is the Navy, not high school."

"Yes, sir," R.J. said.

The truck pulled up in front of the Marine brig and the occupants got out. R.J. looked around. The brig looked like the many barracks buildings on the Naval base. It had been converted to a brig by erecting a tall, chain link fence around the building and fitting the windows with wire mesh. A Marine lance corporal opened the fence's gate and examined the file Mr. Jones handed him. The guard looked at R.J. and sneered. R.J. stared straight ahead. The guard motioned for R.J. to come through the gate. "Stand over there at attention," he barked, pointing to a spot inside the fence.

"So long, R.J.," Tanner said. He and Billy waved to him.

"Take care of the Gamboas," R.J. called to them.

"We will," Tanner said. Billy gave him the 'thumbs up' and the two of them climbed back into the truck. Mr. Jones looked at R.J. for a few minutes and nodded slowly. R.J. smiled weakly and nodded back.

Another Marine guard, a sergeant armed with a billy-club, came out of the brig entrance and motioned for R.J. to follow him. This Marine was definitely what they called 'gung ho.' His uniform was tailored to his lean body and his posture was ram-rod stiff. He marched forward with purpose and confidence, his face an expressionless mask. R.J. fell in step next to him and when they approached the locked steel door, the Marine sergeant knocked on it with his billy-club. It made a hollow sound as if he had banged on an empty oil drum. The door opened and R.J. walked into the Marine brig. The big door slammed shut behind him with a loud, deep thunk, echoing down the passageway, and R.J. flinched involuntarily.

FIFTEEN

"Goddammit!" Bobby Gamboa threw his clipboard across the supply depot office. It slid across the floor, papers fluttering, and slammed against the bulkhead. Billy Lopez and Pea stood quietly, hands in pockets, staring at the floor.

"He got thirty days, that's all," Pea said, trying to calm Bobby. "He'll be out before you know it."

"He'll be out in twenty five, with five days off for good behavior," Billy explained. "In the meantime, everything goes on like before. We'll be at your trailer on Saturday, and we'll bring the red lead paint."

"That asshole Twitchell!" Bobby yelled. "Something's gotta be done about that fat fuck!"

"It's gonna be okay, Bobby." Billy tried to soothe him, but he was really only thinking of Teresa. If Bobby got really pissed, he might call off the trailer repairs, the first choice movies and extra supplies. Billy might not see Teresa again. The thought made him wince, and his stomach felt empty.

Bobby frowned and chewed his thumb nail. "I'll go see him in the brig when I get back from Pearl," he muttered, then he looked up at Pea and Billy. "You guys gonna bring my barracuda?"

"Hell yes!" Pea exclaimed. "R.J. is gonna be back soon, and everything will be back to normal." He hoped he sounded more confident than he felt.

"You guys understand, don't you?" Bobby asked. "R.J. is the best guy you got on that ship." Billy and Pea nodded. They hadn't thought about it that way, but Bobby was right. The Haverfield had seemed to gain new life since R.J. came aboard.

* * * * *

R.J. was led to a wire mesh enclosure with a locked gate and the guard motioned for him to stand to the side at attention facing the gray painted bulkhead. Another guard inside the wire jingled some keys and unlocked the gate. R.J. was directed to enter. He was led to an office door with a small sign which read, 'Commanding Officer, Marine Brig.' The sergeant pointed to a spot on the floor and R.J. stood on the spot at attention. The sergeant knocked on the door.

"Come in." The sergeant opened the door and waved R.J. into the office. A Marine lieutenant sat with his hands folded on top of a gray metal desk. The sergeant put R.J.'s file on the desk and stepped back.

"New prisoner, sir," he said smartly.

Lieutenant Charles Shepard was a slim, good-looking man in his late twenties. His short blonde hair was parted neatly on one side and he sat ram-rod straight in his chair as he looked R.J. over. His blue eyes were cold and unemotional. His lips were pressed tight and R.J. figured it had been awhile since they last saw a smile.

"You are here for thirty days," the lieutenant said, reading R.J.'s file. He did not look up. "You will learn the rules of my brig and follow them to the letter. Is that understood?" He looked up from the file and stared at R.J. with those cold eyes. They seemed to be staring into R.J., searching his soul.

"Yes, sir," R.J. replied.

The Marine sergeant stepped up behind R.J. and shouted into his ear. "The first and last words out of your mouth, maggot, are SIR! You got that?"

R.J. winced. "Sir, yes sir," he said.

The lieutenant nodded. "From now on you will refer to yourself as prisoner Davis, R.J. You have no other identity. You will not use the terms, 'I' or 'Me.' Do you understand, prisoner?"

"Sir, yes sir."

Lieutenant Shepard opened a drawer and placed the file inside. He closed the drawer and looked over at the Marine sergeant.

"Sergeant Leftowitz, get this man's hair cut and have him unpack his seabag. I want his shirts stenciled at once. Then give him to prisoner

Pinney to teach him the ropes."

"Aye, aye, sir."

R.J. started to turn back toward the door. Sergeant Leftowitz stepped in front of him and snarled at him. "Who told you to move, maggot?" he yelled in R.J.'s face. "You don't move, you don't wriggle you don't scratch unless you are told to. Got that?"

"Sir yes sir," R.J. said meekly. He stood at attention, staring at a point just above Lieutenant Shepard's head.

"About face!" Leftowitz barked. R.J. did a crisp about face.

"Forward, marrrch!" R.J. stepped out of the office and marched down the passageway, following a yellow line painted on the floor. They came to another wire-mesh enclosure and a guard, this one an Air Force airman, opened the gate with a key from a large ring.

The Air Force guard stood in front of R.J. and ordered him to take off his shirt. He was made to hold his whitehat in one hand, his shirt in the other and spread out his arms and legs. The guard quickly frisked him and nodded to Leftowitz, who gave R.J. a not too gentle push in the back, propelling him through the gate.

R.J. found himself in a large barracks with wire mesh on all the windows. At the end of the barracks in yet another wire mesh enclosure, he could see several bunk beds, and to his left he could look into a large head with showers along one wall. There was only one other prisoner that he could see, swabbing the deck with a large mop, and R.J. wondered how many men were serving time there.

Sergeant Leftowitz led R.J. into the sleeping area and assigned him a bottom bunk. Two small footlockers stood at the end of each set of bunk beds, and Leftowitz pointed to the footlocker which would be R.J.'s.

"Put everything in that footlocker except your dungaree shirts," he ordered. "And fold everything neatly, as if you're getting ready for a bag inspection. Then take your shirts over to that table." He pointed to a long, wooden table with picnic type benches along its sides. He indicated the other prisoner. "That's prisoner Beatty. He'll give you a haircut and help you stencil your shirts. Then you wait right here."

"Sir yes sir."

Leftowitz turned and strode smartly back to the gate, his posture perfect. He sat at a small table off to the side. He opened a paperback book and began reading, his lips moving as he read.

Prisoner Beatty stepped up and offered his hand. R.J. shook it and whispered, "What do we stencil on our shirts?"

Beatty grinned. He had a friendly face and a pleasant grin. His red hair was cut burr-style and he had freckles all over his face and arms. R.J. could even see freckles on his scalp. Beatty turned around and showed R.J. the back of his shirt. It was stenciled with a large, black 'P' covering almost the entire back of the shirt.

"Okay, sit here," Beatty said, indicating the bench alongside the table. Beatty put a towel over R.J.'s shoulders and produced an electric barber's shear. "Everybody gets the same haircut," he said, and quickly mowed off

R.J.'s hair, starting at the front of his head, shearing all the way to the back, making four or five passes. R.J.'s hair fell onto the towel and down to the floor. In minutes he had the same haircut as Beatty.

"Just like boot camp," R.J. said, running a hand over his head.

"'Cept here we do this every week," Beatty explained, wrapping the cord around the shear and setting it on the table. "There's a broom over there." He pointed to a broom leaning against the wall. "Sweep the hair up off the deck and toss it in the shit-can. Don't miss any," he warned.

"Sir yes sir," R.J. replied, smiling.

Beatty smiled back. "You're catching on." He spread the first of R.J.'s shirts on the table and set the stencil on the back. With a short, stubby brush dipped in stencil ink he filled in the big 'P' on the first one and went to work on the others.

"Aren't there any other prisoners in here?" R.J. asked, looking around.

"They're out in the bush," Beatty replied, as if that explained everything. "They'll be here in a few minutes. It's past 1600 now."

"How many guards are there?" R.J. asked, carefully sweeping up the hair.

"Four," Beatty replied. "They rotate every day. We got four or five Marines, a couple of sailors and two Air Force guys."

R.J. nodded surreptitiously at Leftowitz. "What's his story?"

"Him?" Beatty chuckled. "He's The Duke of Earl."

A commotion outside the brig entrance interrupted their conversation. The sound of marching feet echoed down the passageway and R.J. looked up to see several prisoners approaching the interior gate. The Air Force guard opened the gate and the prisoners, one by one, stepped forward, hat in one hand, shirt in the other, and spread-eagled for the body search.

The first prisoner through the search walked briskly into the barracks, putting his shirt back on and tucking it into his dungaree trousers.

"That's Pinney," Beatty said. "He's numero uno around here."

"Numero uno?" R.J. asked, looking at Pinney as he approached.

"Yeah, number one, 'cause he's been here the longest. 'Bout six months, I think."

Pinney approached the other two prisoners with a wide smile on his face. He had curly hair cropped short on his head, though not as short as R.J.'s and Beatty's. He was tall, strong and muscular and walked with a casual air. His skin was deeply tanned and he offered his hand to R.J. who shook it. Pinney's grip confirmed the impression of strength. His hand was rough and calloused.

"Greg Pinney," he smiled. "You gotta be Davis."

"Yep, I gotta be," R.J. replied, smiling. He liked Pinney at once.

"I'm gonna help you learn the routine," Pinney said. "Just remember a few things." He began ticking off points on his fingers. "One, stare straight ahead, don't look at directly at the guards. Two, first and last words out of your mouth are 'sir.' Three, always refer to yourself as 'prisoner.' Four, keep your mouth shut, don't complain or back talk the guards. Five, watch me closely and always do what I do. Got any questions?"

"Sir, no sir," R.J. replied, grinning.

Pinney returned the grin. "That's the spirit."

R.J. nodded toward Leftowitz. "He got in my face about a few of the rules already. I thought he was gonna go up side my head with that billy club."

Pinney shook his head. "No, he won't do that, unless you attack him. The guards can yell at you, call you names, hell, they can even make you stand on your head and fart 'Yankee Doodle Dandy.' But they can't touch you physically unless you get violent."

"I always heard the Marine guards at the brig were brutal," R.J. said.

"Not here," Pinney explained. "This is more like a reform school." He looked around behind him at the other prisoners filing into the barracks. "These guys are all in here for minor shit. You know, like being AWOL, stealing stuff, insubordination, or just being a fuck-up." Pinney looked R.J. over as if he was trying to determine if the new man fit the latter category. "Anyway, the bad-asses get sent to Pearl or San Diego, or worse, Portsmouth Naval Brig back in New Hampshire."

"What're you in here for?" R.J. asked.

"Him?" a voice behind Pinney broke in. "He a regular entray-panoor."

A small, skinny black prisoner came up to R.J. and hooked a thumb at Pinney. "In fact, he a celebrity on this here island." He looked R.J. over and decided he liked him.

Pinney grinned and put an arm around the black prisoner's thin shoulders. "Meet Bobby James Johnson. We just call him Bobby Jim or B.J." He laughed and squeezed Johnson's shoulders. "You know, like blow job."

"Don't pay him no never mind," Johnson said to R.J. "He been in here so long his brain done got stiff. Can't think right no more."

R.J. looked at Pinney, wondering what had sent him to the brig for so long. "So, an entrepreneur, huh? What'd you do?"

Beatty and Bobby Jim were grinning at Pinney, but the big man just shrugged. "I'll tell you about it later," he said. "We gotta wash up for chow, and then it's Duke of Earl time."

R.J. was about to ask a question, but Sergeant Leftowitz strode into the barracks and yelled, "Let's go, maggots. Get in that head and clean up. Time for chow!"

R.J. hurried into the head behind Pinney and washed his hands and splashed water on his face. Pinney motioned for him to follow and led R.J. back into the barracks. A red line was painted along the far wall in front of the wire-meshed windows, and prisoners were lining up on it. Pinney spoke quickly to R.J.

"I'm the first prisoner in this formation. You're new, so you're the last prisoner in this formation. When I sound off, everyone down the line sounds off. You are last. Here's what you say: 'Sir, prisoner Davis, what's your initials, R.J.? Sir, prisoner Davis, R.J. is the last prisoner in this prisoner formation, sir!' Got it?" Without waiting for an answer, he strode to the front of the line and took his place.

When Leftowitz was satisfied with the formation, he took a position in front of the prisoners, feet apart and hands behind his back. His Marine cap was cocked forward on his head, resting on his thick eyebrows. "Sound off!" he ordered.

"Sir, prisoner Pinney G.P. is the first prisoner in this prisoner formation, sir!"

Each prisoner sounded off one by one. Leftowitz moved down the formation, nodding solemnly. When he got to the end of the line, he stood directly in front of R.J. and stared at him. R.J. picked out a spot on the far wall just above the Sergeant's left ear and fixed his gaze on it. The man next to R.J. sounded off.

"Sir, prisoner Wilson, D.L., sir!"

R.J. took a breath and sounded off. "Sir, prisoner Davis, R.J. is the last prisoner in this prisoner formation, sir!"

Leftowitz smiled. It was more akin to a grimace than a smile. R.J. couldn't imagine the sergeant actually smiling with that face. Someone up the line muttered, "Way to go." Leftowitz shot a look up the line but everyone was staring straight ahead.

"All right maggots. Left, face!" The prisoners pivoted on their left feet and brought their right feet up in unison. A loud 'clump' sounded as their boondockers all hit the floor at once.

"Hands on shoulders, hut!"

The prisoners brought their right hands up and placed them on the right shoulders of the men in front of them. R.J. quickly put his hand on Wilson's right shoulder.

"March in place, hut!" Leftowitz barked.

Twenty pairs of boots began marching in place, all in perfect unison. The clump, clump, clump echoed like a drum beat in the barracks room. The Air Force guard had both wire gates open, anticipating the prisoners' march to chow.

Leftowitz took his place near the head of the formation. "Forward on the half-step! Duke of Earl! Marrrch!"

The prisoners began marching on the half step, boots clumping in perfect rhythm, hands on shoulders and chanting, "Duke, Duke, Duke, Duke of Earl, Duke Duke, Duke of Earl Duke Duke, Duke of Earl!"

Leftowitz strutted along proudly at the head of the line. His billy-club was tucked under his left arm like a baton, his body turned slightly sideways. He held his chin up in the air and smartly returned the guards' salutes as the formation half-stepped out the front door of the brig and down the sidewalk toward the chow hall. "Duke, Duke, Duke, Duke of Earl, Duke Duke..."

Several sailors and Marines stopped on their way to the chow hall, or hung out the barracks windows watching the line of prisoners marching to chow, chanting The Duke of Earl. It was a daily event, and sergeant Leftowitz enjoyed showing off for an audience. He also enjoyed the humiliation he knew the prisoners felt, being forced to perform like chimpanzees.

As they marched into the chow hall, R.J. watched the other prisoners for clues as to what to do. They stood at attention facing the food line and sidestepped to the left as food was put on their trays. They held the trays up to their chests and stared straight ahead. When Leftowitz led them to the tables in the rear of the hall, they stood at attention in front of their chairs.

"Seats!" Leftowitz barked and they sat down, placed their trays on the table and dropped their hands into their laps.

"Eat!" Leftowitz yelled.

Pinney sat across from R.J. and began eating. R.J. looked at him and opened his mouth to ask a question, but Pinney shook his head quickly and held a finger to his lips. R.J. concentrated on his food, which was surprisingly good.

Back in the barracks, after the body search, the prisoners began preparing for their nightly shower. They hung up their dungarees at the foot of their cots and tied towels around their waists. They lined up outside the head and stood at attention, waiting for the order to proceed. Leftowitz had been relieved for the evening and a second class Boatswains's mate named Culver took over. Culver was a stocky, muscular man in his mid-twenties. He had jet-black hair and a kindly look on his face. He didn't bark and yell like Leftowitz, but spoke in a quiet, confident manner, like someone used to having his orders followed.

Culver ordered the men into the shower and stood in the middle of the head, overseeing his charges as they showered quickly and toweled down. They were allowed only three minutes under the shower spray, and R.J. moved quickly to finish. After his first time at sea, he had mastered the quick 'G.I.' shower.

Showers finished, the prisoners had two hours to themselves before 'taps' at 2130. No one was allowed on the bunks until time to go to sleep, so the prisoners sat at the big table in the middle of the barracks or sat around on the floor, writing letters and talking quietly. Pinney sat in a semi-circle with R.J., Beatty and Bobby Jim Johnson, explaining brig procedures and personnel to R.J.

"Reveille is 'bout the worst time, as you'll find out," Pinney said. "They make a huge racket at 0500 and you have to jump out of bed, grab the sheet and blanket off your mattress, hold them up in your hands and run in place until everyone's up."

"Yeah," Beatty agreed. "It sucks, man."

"Whatchoo expect, man?" Johnson chided Beatty. "You in the brig, not the Waldorf Astoria." He had a way of making everything he said sound funny, and R.J. was getting a big kick out of the little guy. He reminded R.J. of a black Pea. *That was it*, R.J. decided. *He's a black Peacock. Same cocky attitude, same curious sense of humor, always cracking everyone up.*

"Anyways," Pinney continued. "Then we make our beds, very carefully, and line up for razor blades."

"Line up for razor blades?" R.J. asked.

"Yeah, you gotta shave every day, even Sundays, and you gotta ask permission for a razor blade." Pinney mused about it for a moment. "Guess they don't want anyone slashing his wrists," he concluded.

"So let me guess," R.J. said. "Sir, prisoner Davis, R.J. requests a razor blade, sir?"

"Close," Beatty said. "Requests the use of one razor blade, sir."

Pinney nodded. "They break out a blade, put it in your razor, and you march into the head and shave. When you're done, you line back up and return the blade."

"Then what?"

"Then we go to breakfast, climb into the truck and hit the bush." Pinney smiled. "That's what will break your back if you let it." Beatty and B.J. nodded sadly. Pinney went on. "We get to chop the jungle away from military roads and sometimes the runways at Anderson Air Force base."

"Yeah, I like that duty," Johnson nodded. "The Air Force chow is a lot better'n ours."

R.J. remembered the threats Whipple had made to him when he first came aboard. *"I'll have you chopping boonies in the Marine brig,"* was what he had said.

"What do we chop the bush with?" R.J. asked.

"Machetes," Beatty replied.

R.J. looked confused, then began smiling. "So, let me get this straight. They don't want us to have razor blades but they issue us machetes?"

The other three laughed. "I never thought about it like that," Pinney said. "But you're right."

Culver approached the group frowning. It was his subtle way of letting them know they were too loud with their laughter, and the four prisoners quieted down. Culver walked back to his post and R.J. looked over at Pinney.

"So, what did you do to get thrown in here?" he asked.

Johnson and Beatty looked at Pinney and smiled big smiles, their eyes twinkling. "G'head, tell 'im," Bobby Jim said, smirking.

"I worked at the base PX, see?" Pinney began. "It all started when a buddy of mine wanted to buy a watch, but didn't have enough money. So I slipped a Timex out one night, fixed up the inventory so they wouldn't know it was gone, and sold it to him for half price." Pinney pointed a finger to his temple. "Then I got to thinking. Maybe this was a way I could make some money. So I started screwing around with the inventory so certain items never showed up as delivered, and I sold stuff at half price."

"He's just being modest," Beatty said. "You're looking at the main black marketer on this island."

"It was going good," Pinney continued. "For six months I smuggled stuff out of the PX, not big things, you know, cameras, watches, cigarettes, stuff like that. I made about three thousand dollars."

"Three thousand?" R.J. said, a little too loudly. Culver looked over and frowned. R.J. lowered his voice. "Three thousand dollars?"

"Yep," Pinney grinned proudly. "Put it all in the bank and never spent a dime."

"That's why his white ass ain't in Leavenworth," B.J. explained.

"How did they catch you?' R.J. asked.

"It was just a matter of time," Pinney shook his head. "They pulled a surprise inventory inspection and compared the shipping forms from Pearl and San Diego against my inventory sheets. I was busted." Pinney chuckled. "My signature was on everything. They had me cold. Sent me here for nine months, busted me to E-2."

"But you didn't get sent to Leavenworth or Portsmouth?"

"Nope. Kept all that money in the bank. It just sat there. I gave it all back to them along with over two hundred in interest." Pinney grinned proudly. "Hell, they made money on the deal."

R.J. rolled backward on the deck, laughing so hard he couldn't breathe. Soon the other three were laughing uncontrollably, and Culver come over and scowled at them.

"What's so damn funny?" he demanded.

Johnson wiped tears from his eyes and pointed at Pinney. "Sir, Prisoner Pinney just 'splained what he did to get put in here, sir."

Culver smiled sardonically. He had heard the story, too. "Well, keep it down. You clowns sound like a bunch of drunken loons."

Taps was sounded and the prisoners filed into the wire-mesh cage that held their bunks. Culver locked the gate and ordered them to hit the sack. They were required to lie at attention until they fell asleep, but R.J. couldn't sleep. He smiled at Pinney's story and worried about the next morning, his first in the bush. The brig wasn't as bad as he had imagined, in fact it was kind of fun, so far. But R.J. knew he was locked up, and he felt claustrophobic. He tried to counter the feeling by thinking of his girlfriends, and his thoughts drifted to Tonya and San Diego. He remembered the last time he saw her, just before he got put on restriction for that incident with the loan shark, Fellows.

SIXTEEN

San Diego, California
November, 1962

It was Sunday night and the Straps mustered around the fountain at the little park on Broadway and Fifth Streets. They were gathering for their weekly pilgrimage to the Tropics, a dance club down at the end of Fifth Street. The Cascades were performing there, and they were opening their show with their hit single, *Rhythm of the Rain*, so the Straps wanted to be there. To get to the Tropics, they had to walk all the way down Fifth Street, through the downtown area known as 'Black Alley' because mostly blacks hung out there. Several bars lined both sides of the street, and black people milled around in front of them, drinking, dancing and sometimes fighting.

The blacks never bothered the Straps. They were used to seeing them. Besides, these white boys were cool. They dressed cool, they walked cool, and they sure as hell didn't dance like white guys. The Straps were friendly to the blacks on fifth street, exchanging greetings and joking with them as they strolled down the street, heels clicking on the concrete and jackets folded neatly across their forearms.

"White boys!" yelled a tall, angular black man named Oscar who was leaning against a brick wall sipping out of a half-pint of whiskey. "Slip me some skin!" He held his hand out, palm up, and Frankie reached out and drew his palm across Oscar's palm. Both pulled their hands back and snapped their fingers.

"Lookin' good!" Oscar called, taking a pull of the whiskey.

R.J. had his arm around Tonya's waist and was whispering in her ear. She giggled and pushed him away, and he pretended to stumble so he could grab her shoulder and hold on. His hand snaked down toward her bra, but she deftly moved it back to her shoulder.

"Don't do that in public," she warned him.

"Well, you won't let me do it in private."

Tonya smiled and winked at him. "Maybe someday," she whispered.

R.J.'s stomach jumped as he contemplated the chance to feel her breasts. They were such beautiful breasts. He found himself staring at them, imagining their pink nipples and softness under his hand.

"R.J.!" she snapped, pretending to be offended. "You're staring at my chest."

"Can't help it, baby," R.J. pleaded. "You know how crazy I am about you."

"I know how crazy you are, that's for sure." She giggled.

They arrived at the Tropics night club and the strains of the music inside drifted out to the parking lot. The club band was playing Chuck Berry's 'Roll Over Beethoven' and the Straps danced into the club in a Pony line, their heels clicking on the floor. Several other dancers joined the line and they danced around and around the dance floor until the song ended. R.J. grabbed Tonya by the hand and led her to a table in the corner, far away from the crowd.

"We need to talk," he said in her ear.

"I know what you want to talk about," she said, frowning at him.

"We got less than a month of school left," R.J. began. "In three weeks I'll be going on leave and then overseas. Probably to the Mediterranean. I put in for it. I'll probably be on a ship for two or three years." He held her hands and gazed into her eyes with what he hoped was a serious, sincere look. "We won't see each other for a long time, baby."

"I'll wait for you, R.J.," she promised.

"You say that now, but in a year or two you'll probably forget all about me."

Tonya smiled and her blue eyes lit up. "I won't forget you. But you'll forget me the first time you meet a French girl or an Italian girl over there."

R.J. saw an opening. "We won't forget each other if we have something to remember each other by." He looked into her eyes sincerely.

"I know what you're getting at, R.J.," she said disapprovingly. "And I'm afraid if you get what you want, you'll just move on to the next girl."

This was getting frustrating. He took a deep breath and tried again.

"Baby, I love you. I know you love me. It's just something people do when they love each other."

"So you've done it before? Back in Denver or Longmont?"

"No," he lied, putting on his sincere look. "You're gonna be my first."

"Unless I don't go along with it, right?"

"Baby," R.J. held his hands out, palms up. "Why do you have to make things so difficult?"

"I'm making things difficult?" she said sharply, anger in her eyes. "You're the one making things difficult." She poked him in the chest with her finger. "You're putting too much pressure on me, and I'm not ready." She got up from the table, tucked her purse under her arm and stomped toward the ladies room, ignoring his pleas to stay.

R.J. sighed and looked up at the ceiling. Frankie came over and sat down at the table. "Still no go, huh?" he asked, grinning at R.J.'s frustration.

R.J. just shook his head and stared at the ceiling.

"Maybe she's just a good girl," Frankie offered.

"Yeah, too good." R.J. put his hands on the table and pushed himself up. "Let's go get a smoke," he said.

Outside the evening was becoming cool, and a light mist was forming, blurring the lights on the building into soft, hazy colors. Frankie and R.J. stood smoking, shivering slightly in the damp air.

"The thing is," R.J. said after a while, "I really like her, you know? She's one of the sweetest girls I ever met."

"She just won't put out, huh?" Frankie asked.

"Yeah," R.J. said. He dropped his cigarette on the pavement and crushed it with his heel. "Guess I'm gonna strike out on this one."

"Lots of fish in the sea, buddy." Frankie offered. He flipped his cigarette across the parking lot and motioned R.J. back into the club. "In fact," he said, looking around as they entered the warm building, "lots of fish in here."

R.J. found Tonya sitting back at the table, pouting. "Where were you?" she asked.

"Outside for a smoke," he replied, sitting next to her and putting his arm around her shoulder. "You wanna dance, baby?"

"No. I want to go home." She pouted.

"But the Cascades haven't come on yet," R.J. argued. "Why you wanna go home?"

"I just want to go home," she insisted.

R.J. stared at Tonya, trying to decide how to handle her. She did have those great boobs, but she was very moody. "Okay, baby. I'll take you to the bus," he said resignedly.

They left the dance and walked up Fifth Street to Broadway, hardly speaking to each other. R.J. waited at the bus stop with her, and when her bus came down Broadway and stopped in front of them, she turned to R.J.

"Coming with me?" she asked quietly.

"No, I'll call you tomorrow," he said, looking down at the ground.

"My folks aren't home," she whispered. R.J. jumped on the bus.

* * * * *

A few hours later, R.J. got off the bus on Broadway in front of the YMCA just after 2330. Several Straps were at the bus stop, waiting for the next bus to the Naval Training Center. Cool Richard came up to R.J.

"Where you been, boy?" he asked.

"Up at Tonya's." R.J. grinned. "Her folks weren't home, so we made out on the couch for a couple of hours."

"Yeah?" Cool said, disinterested.

"That girl is a little strange," R.J. said almost to himself.

"Well, you should have been with us. We got in a fight with that asshole Fellows and a few of his cowboy friends down at the Tropics."

R.J. stared at Cool Richard. "What happened?"

Splib Walker joined the conversation. "Fellows started in with his bad mouthin', you know? Drunk on his ass. Big Lenny popped him in the mouth, and the shit was on!"

R.J. looked around. "Where's Frankie and Lenny?" he asked.

"Shore patrol got 'em," Splib said. "Got John-John and Stretch, too." He shook his head. "Frankie punched one of the cowboys. They got took back to the base in their civvies."

"That fuckin' Fellows filed a complaint," Cool said. "Said they attacked him for no reason."

"Sonofabitch!" R.J. spat. "We're gonna have to do something about this crap." He looked around the street. It was getting late, and the air was crisp and cold. He could see his breath when he talked. The NTC bus was coming down Broadway. "Where's Fellows?" he asked.

"Dunno," Splib answered. "The dude was drunk, but I don't think the SPs got 'im."

The bus pulled up to the curb and the Straps piled aboard and found seats. Very few passengers were on the bus, and the lights were off, so it took them a while to realize that Fellows was passed out in the back, stretched length-wise across the back seat, snoring softly.

"There's that loan-sharkin' sumbitch!" Splib pointed to the prostrate figure in the back of the bus. "I'm gonna kick 'is ass right here."

"Hold on," Cool Richard said, taking hold of Splib's arm. "I gotta idea."

The bus pulled up in front of the locker club across Rosecrans Boulevard from the NTC, and the Straps got off, half carrying a passed-out Fellows between them. They went into the locker club and sat Fellows down on the floor. He groaned and rolled over on his side. The Straps quickly changed into uniforms and dragged Fellows out of the locker club. Looking both ways up and down the street, and finding no traffic, they dragged Fellows across the street and propped him up against the wall which surrounded the NTC.

Cool Richard took charge. "R.J., climb over the wall and stand by. We're gonna push this asshole over and then jump over after him."

R.J. shrugged, climbed the wall and dropped down on the other side as quietly as possible. He found himself in the Base Commander's garden, right next to Captain Proctor's Chevrolet Impala. *Oh, shit,* he thought, looking up at the adobe, tile-roofed house, hoping no one heard him. Apparently, no one had. The house was dark, and there were no sounds of anyone stirring. R.J. was glad the captain didn't have a dog.

Fellows was beginning to come to as he was pushed to the top of the wall and dropped to the ground in front of R.J. He landed with a dull thud on top of some ice plant in the garden.

"Ugh, wha' the fuck...?" He groaned, looking up at R.J.

Cool Richard and Splib came over the wall, dropping to the ground and crouching down, looking around. Cool held a finger to his lips.

"Whatta you guys doin'?" Fellows moaned, looking at them with bleary, unfocused eyes.

"Getting even, asshole," Cool said, and punched Fellows in the eye. Fellows put both hands in front of his face and moaned again.

"Let's pants him and put him in the car," Cool said.

Splib and R.J. quickly removed Fellows' trousers, pulled off his shorts and threw him into the back seat of Captain Proctor's Chevy. Fellows rolled over and vomited on the floor of the car, hacking and coughing.

"I got his wallet," Splib announced, looking through the billfold. "He got like two hundred bucks in here."

"Take it and let's get going," Cool said. He was fiddling with the Impala's steering wheel. He jammed a ballpoint pen into the space between the steering wheel and the chrome lever which sounded the horn. The car's horn began to blare and the three Straps ran out of the captain's compound and made their way behind several other barracks until they reached their own. They scrambled up the stairs, got undressed quickly, and hopped into their bunks. The Impala's horn was still blaring in the night air.

SEVENTEEN

Marine Brig, U. S. Naval Base
Guam
April 23, 1963

R.J. was startled awake by the clatter of a big, metal garbage can thrown on the deck. The can made a clanging, ear-splitting din as it bounced and screeched and rolled in front of the wire mesh cage that contained the prisoners' bunks. R.J.'s eyes popped open and he lay motionless on his back, staring at the bottom of the bunk above him. His mind could not process the clanging metal noise made by the trash can, and he was stunned, unable to move.

"Rise and shine, maggots!" Sergeant Leftowitz yelled through a bull horn. "Get those legs pumping now!"

The other prisoners were on their feet, their sheets in one hand, blankets in the other, running in place. R.J. quickly jumped up and began running in place with his sheet and blanket in his hands. He was not quite awake, his head fuzzy and his thoughts scattered, but he was waking up fast. It was a rude way to be awakened.

"Stand at attention!" Leftowitz bellowed. The prisoners snapped to attention, backs straight, staring ahead, not moving at all.

"All right, get those bunks made, then file out and shave those ugly-lookin' faces!"

R.J. fell in behind Beatty as the prisoners lined up in front of the guards' office. Leftowitz stood in the door of the office. A cabinet on the wall had been unlocked and was standing open. One by one, the prisoners approached Leftowitz and repeated the same request.

R.J. waited for his turn, and when it came he stepped forward and called out, "Sir, prisoner Davis, R.J. requests the use of one razor blade, sir!"

Leftowitz sneered at him and carefully dropped a double-edged razor blade into the top of a safety razor, then screwed the top closed and handed it to R.J.

"You ain't gonna cut yourself, are you, boy?" Leftowitz sneered.

"Sir, no sir!" R.J. replied, and filed into the head to shave with the other prisoners. When they were finished, the prisoners lined back up in front of the office and Leftowitz collected the razor blades, put them back in the cabinet and closed the door, locking it with a padlock. It was time to dress and go to chow.

The prisoners lined up on the red line and stood at attention. "Duke of Earl time?" R.J. whispered to Wilson out of the side of his mouth.

"No," Wilson whispered. "That's only for evening chow."

The column of prisoners marched at the half-step into the chow hall and moved through the line with trays held up. They stood in front of their chairs and awaited the command to 'sit' and then 'eat.' R.J. was beginning to get used to and anticipate the routine. He felt a strange comfort in its predictability. He didn't have to really think about anything, just go along with the routine. But he knew that was one of his problems, going along.

Breakfast over, they lined up outside the barracks and stood at attention. After a few minutes a large panel truck pulled up and the back doors were unlocked and opened by Leftowitz.

"Climb in, maggots!" he yelled. "Time to attack the bush!"

R.J. filed into the truck and sat on one of the wooden benches that lined both sides and were bolted into the floor. Leftowitz slammed the double doors closed and R.J. heard the sound of a padlock being snapped shut. No one was getting out, that was for sure.

Leftowitz climbed into the cab along with the driver, an Air Force non-com who threw the truck into gear and hit the gas. The truck lurched forward, sending the prisoners tumbling in the back. The non-com and Leftowitz laughed. *This guy drives like Billy Lopez,* R.J. thought. He smiled to himself thinking about Charming Billy and Teresa and their crush on each other.

The truck wound around the Naval base over dirt roads and came to a stop. The back doors opened and the prisoners jumped out and lined up along the road. They were on the far side of the base, and the tropical vegetation was beginning to creep onto the road. R.J. took a deep breath of morning air. It was relatively cool and quiet at this time of morning. The sounds of seagulls singing in the harbor filtered up and over the hills, and R.J. looked up, expecting to see the birds circling above.

"You praying, prisoner?" The Air Force non-com, a short, fat Mexican named Calderon asked, smiling.

"Sir, no sir," R.J. answered.

"Then get your head out of the clouds, prisoner, and let's get to work." Calderon was a pleasant, easy-going guard who treated the prisoners with respect. It was soon obvious to R.J. that Calderon was the favorite guard among the prisoners.

"Prisoner Davis is just wondering what happened to his freedom, sir," Pinney volunteered, grinning at Calderon and swinging his machete at the bush.

"Well, he's looking for it in the right place," Calderon mused, "because it's evaporated into thin air." He looked up at the sky. "There it is," he pointed up. "Drifting away in the wind." The other prisoners laughed.

"Knock off the gab fest!" Leftowitz yelled, coming around the truck, carrying a seabag. "Grab a tool and get to work!" He threw the seabag onto the ground and it made a clinking sound. Pinney emptied the bag and several machetes fell out. Calderon pulled four rakes out of the truck and threw them down on the ground. They were quickly picked up by four prisoners who scrambled to be the first to reach them.

R.J. picked up a machete and hefted it with his hand, testing its weight. Pinney came up behind him and nudged him with his elbow. "Let's chop some boonies," he said, motioning R.J. to follow him off the road and into the bush, where Pinney began hacking at the vegetation with slow, practiced strokes. R.J. copied him and soon was chopping vegetation away from the road. The prisoners with the rakes were raking the chopped vegetation into large piles on the side of the road, to be picked up later.

Pinney spoke without missing a stroke with his machete. "Tomorrow try to grab a rake," he said. "Raking is a lot easier than chopping, but you gotta be quick."

"They sure grabbed them up fast," R.J. said.

"Pace yourself," Pinney advised. "You don't wanna get too worn out your first day. Tomorrow you're gonna be plenty sore."

R.J. fell into a measured pace with the rest of the boonie-choppers, swinging the machete easily and chopping away at the plant life. The machete was very sharp and it cut into the vegetation easily. Before he knew it, they had chopped away almost a half-mile of it. The sun beat down hard on him, and he was sweating through his dungaree shirt. He noticed other prisoners were taking off their shirts and tying them around their waists.

"Take off your shirt," Pinney suggested. "You don't have to ask permission. They let you do it anytime you want." He gestured toward the guards who lined the road and watched the prisoners work. They each had a billy-club, but none of them carried a shotgun as R.J. had imagined. It seemed strange, the prisoners outnumbered the guards and were armed with

121

machetes. It would be easy to overpower them and escape. But to where? How would they get off the island? R.J. amused himself thinking about it as he worked. It felt good to swing the machete against the many kinds of plants, chopping them away and moving up the road. He was making good progress, and was getting ahead of the other prisoners when Calderon blew his whistle and called a water break.

"Break time!" he hollered, and the sweating prisoners lined up behind the truck where Calderon handed out paper cups and drew water from a cooler sitting in the back of the truck.

"Hey, man," Bobby Jim said quietly as he came up behind R.J. "You in a race or somethin'?" He drank down his water and held his cup out for more. "Cool it, man. Take it easy, you makin' the rest of us look bad." He winked and walked over to the road and sat down with the other prisoners. R.J. joined them.

"I guess I just got carried away," R.J. explained, his face flushed. "I was day-dreaming."

"Well, day-dream a little slower," Bobby Jim said. The other prisoners laughed.

"Okay girls," Calderon called. "That's enough resting. Let's get at that bush!"

R.J. learned to pace himself better as the morning passed. The heat and humidity wore heavily on him and he felt light-headed. Sweat stung his eyes and blurred his vision. He stood up straight to stretch his back, stumbled and fell to the ground. His legs didn't seem to work properly and he sat on the road, staring at the jungle. He didn't seem able to hold a thought in his head. Calderon came over with a cup of water and two large pills.

"Take these," he said. "And don't drink that water too fast."

R.J. looked at the pills in his hand. "What's this?" he asked weakly.

"Salt tablets," Calderon answered. "Take them and swallow them down with some water. Wait a few minutes before you try to stand again." He left R.J. and resumed patrolling the perimeter.

R.J. began to feel a little better and returned to his boonie chopping, a lot slower than before. His head felt like it was stuffed with marshmallows and he swung the machete slowly and steadily, almost in a trance. He was already exhausted, and was thankful when lunch time came.

Leftowitz called the prisoners to the truck and handed out baloney sandwiches and cartons of milk. R.J. sat down and leaned up against the truck with Pinney, Beatty and Johnson. They ate their sandwiches and drank their milk in silence. R.J. felt beat, and lay back on the road, his hands folded across his chest, his eyes closed.

"See?" B.J. said, pointing to R.J. "He done kilt himself with all that hurryin'."

"First guy I ever seen die from choppin' boonies," Pinney said. "Maybe we should kick him, see if he's alive."

R.J. raised an index finger into the air.

"Sadly I know I am shorn of my strength,
and no muscle I move as I lie at full length,

but no matter. I feel I am better at length."

Pinney looked at Beatty who looked at Bobby Jim who looked back at Pinney. They frowned and shrugged at each other. R.J. continued.

"And I rest so composedly now in my bed,
that any beholder might fancy me dead.
Might start at beholding me, thinking me dead."

"That's scary shit, dude," Beatty observed. "What the hell is that?"

R.J. pulled himself up and rested on one elbow. "Edgar Allan Poe," he replied, wiping sweat from his red face. "Best American poet ever born."

"That so?" Pinney asked. "I always thought Hank Williams was the best American poet ever born."

"No way, man," Bobby Jim argued. "Best poet ever born is Smokey Robinson." He stood and began singing. "I don't like you, but I love you...""

"Knock off the bullshit, prisoner Johnson!" Leftowitz came around the truck. "Get your asses back to work. You can sing that stupid shit at Show and Tell. Now git goin'!"

R.J. pulled himself up and picked up his machete. He was already getting sore, and he felt the beginnings of blisters on his right palm. He decided to chop with his left hand for the rest of the day. Maybe that way he could avoid the blisters. "What's this Show and Tell?" he asked Bobby Jim.

"You'll see," Bobby Jim replied. "Friday night. That's when we have Show and Tell, and I hope you can sing." He laughed and headed into the bush, swinging his machete. The afternoon sped by quickly, and before R.J. knew it, he was back in the truck, bouncing along toward the Marine brig. He sighed. His first day in the bush really hadn't been that bad. He figured he could do his thirty days without too much trouble.

The next morning he wished he were dead. The trash can came scuttling down the passageway and banged into the wire enclosure, echoing loudly against the walls and ceilings. R.J. started to jump out of bed, but his legs gave way and he fell face-first on the deck. He scrambled up and grabbed his blanket and sheet. Every muscle in his body ached. He had a terrible headache, his arms and legs felt heavy and limp, and he had huge blisters on the palms of his hands. His legs wouldn't run in place for him, so he went through the motions, waist-up, hoping he wouldn't be noticed by Leftowitz. He wasn't. He didn't think it would be possible to be any more miserable than he was at that moment. He proceeded dream-like through the day's routine and fell asleep that evening against a bulkhead while talking with Pinney and Bobby Jim. The next day was a little better. At least he felt he might live.

The rest of R.J.'s first week went by quickly and without incident. Up early in the morning to the sounds of the trash can bouncing off the deck, shave, go to breakfast, then hit the bush. The heat almost got him again a few times, but R.J. learned how to slow down and breathe deeply, which seemed to help. Chopping away at the jungle was back breaking, mind numbing work, but R.J. was becoming quite proficient with the machete, and declined the rake when it was offered to him. He had blisters on both hands and a few had broken and were painful for awhile, but they soon began hardening into calluses. He was sunburned on his face, neck and back, and was already beginning to peel.

The prisoners usually lunched by the side of the road, then back to work all afternoon, then to the barracks to be frisked and clean up. Then *Duke of Earl* to chow, back to shower, and spend some quiet time writing letters, reading or sitting around talking quietly with the other prisoners. The routine was becoming familiar, and R.J. felt a strange comfort in being incarcerated. It gave him a great deal of time to think and plot his revenge against Chief Twitchell.

On Friday, during the lunch break, R.J. shared with his new friends the conflict between himself and Twitchell. He told them how the fat chief had singled him out from day one, finding fault in everything he did, and how he was planning to get back at him. Somehow, someday, some way, he was going to get even.

Pinney smiled and nodded slowly, as if he understood everything R.J. was feeling and thinking. "Let me tell you something, brig meat," he said patiently. "In all the time I've spent in the Navy, I've learned some basic truths which I am happy to pass on to you. If, of course, you're willing to listen." He looked at R.J. questioningly. Johnson and Beatty grinned at R.J. Beatty hooked a thumb at Pinney.

"Listen up, R.J.," he said. "You're about to get the word according to G.P. Pinney."

"Okay," R.J. agreed. "Lay it out for me." He sat back and folded his arms across his chest.

"The Navy is all about going along," Pinney explained. "In reality, you can get away with all kinds of shit in the Navy as long as..." Pinney paused and looked into R.J.'s eyes. "And this is important," he said. "As long as the Navy *thinks* you are going along with the program." He grinned and raised his eyebrows. "You understand?" he asked.

R.J. studied Pinney's expression. "Meaning?" he asked.

"Act as if you are doing everything the Navy way. Never back-talk a superior regardless of how stupid the man is. Get real good at your job, whatever it is, and be pleasant, agreeable and respectful to officers." Pinney pointed a finger at R.J. "They eat that shit up," he explained.

"The guy who got me thrown in here is a complete moron," R.J. said, shaking his head. "The man is a pig and a drunk, yet he gets away with it."

"That's 'cause he know how to play the game," Johnson said. "You gotta look at it like a game."

"Yeah," Beatty agreed. "Like you're acting a part. You do that, you can get away with all kinds of shit when they ain't looking."

"You're gonna be under a magnifying glass when you get back to your ship," Pinney explained. "They're gonna watch everything you do, so you won't be able to screw around. But soon as they see you've learned your lesson, the heat will be off."

R.J. thought for a moment. "So, play the game, huh?"

"Play the game," Pinney echoed. "Just play the game."

Back in the bush, swinging the machete, R.J. thought long and hard about what Pinney, Johnson and Beatty had said, and it made sense. Trying to get back at Twitchell would only cause him more grief, and R.J. wasn't eager to absorb any more grief. He definitely didn't want to come back to the brig, so he decided to give it a try, to play the game the Navy way. What did he have to lose?

That night after chow and shower time, Sergeant Leftowitz lined up the prisoners according to time served and ordered them to sing out. At the start of the formation, Gregory Pinney called out.

"Sir, prisoner Pinney, G.P. is the first prisoner in this prisoner formation, sir!"

All along the line the prisoners called out their names.

"Sir, prisoner Beatty, W.M., sir!"

"Sir, prisoner Johnson, B.J., sir!"

"Sir, prisoner Alesandro, P.D., sir!"

The roster sang out until the end of the formation where R.J. anchored the end of the line.

"Sir, prisoner Davis, R.J. is the last prisoner in this prisoner formation, sir!"

Sergeant Leftowitz strutted along the formation, his Marine uniform crisp and neatly pressed, the creases sharp and defined. His Marine hat was tilted jauntily on his head and he gazed upon his charges with an arrogant sneer. It was time for Show and Tell.

"Show and Tell, maggots!" he ordered. "Let's see what you got."

B.J. Johnson took two paces forward and saluted sergeant Leftowitz. "Sir, prisoner Johnson, B.J. wishes to sing for the Sergeant, sir!"

Leftowitz nodded solemnly. "Proceed, prisoner."

B.J. took a deep breath and began singing a Smokey Robinson song.

"I don't like you, but I love you.

"Seems like I'm always thinking of you.

Though you treat me badly, I love you madly,

You really got a hold on me."

"Belay that!" Leftowitz yelled. "That's the same song every Friday, prisoner Johnson."

"Sir, that is prisoner Johnson's favorite song, sir!" Bobby Jim looked hurt.

"Let's get somebody new up here. We already heard your song." Leftowitz looked up and down the formation and his gaze fixed on R.J.

"Prisoner Davis!" he barked. "Front and center!"

R.J. stepped two paces forward and stood at attention.

Leftowitz looked R.J. over as if he expected to see a stain on his trousers. "Let's hear you sing, prisoner," he ordered.

R.J. stood at attention, not moving.

"I said sing, asshole!" Leftowitz ordered.

The barracks grew quiet. The other prisoners looked at R.J. beseechingly, silently urging him to go on.

"Sir, prisoner Davis, R.J. cannot sing, sir!" R.J. pleaded.

Leftowitz sneered, his lip curled up like a dog getting ready to bite. He had this new prisoner by the balls, and it felt good to him. "Well, if you can't sing, then you will dance," he said, smiling sadistically. "C'mon, prisoner Davis. Let's see you dance."

"Sir, prisoner Davis, R.J. cannot dance, sir!"

The sadistic smile faded from Leftowitz's face. "Well, if you can't sing and you can't dance," he sneered, hands on hips, leaning forward, "What the fuck you gonna do for Show and Tell?" He stood in front of R.J., his scowling face inches from R.J.'s face.

R.J. took a deep breath. "Sir," he said softly, "Prisoner Davis, R.J. would like to recite a poem, sir!"

"A poem?" Leftowitz asked, his eyebrows raised in mock contempt. "You want to recite some faggot poem in my brig?" He smiled and sneered at the same time. "Any of you other faggots wanna hear a poem?" he asked, staring at the other prisoners. They stood quietly at attention, staring straight ahead.

"Okay," he sneered. "Prisoner Davis is gonna recite some faggoty poem." He stepped back smirking, and motioned for R.J. to take center stage. R.J. stepped forward, turned and looked at the line of prisoners standing at attention before him. He thought he had the perfect poem for these guys.

R.J. cleared his throat and began:

"He did not wear his scarlet coat,
for blood and wine are red.
And blood and wine were on his hands
When they found him with the dead,
The poor dead woman whom he loved,
And murdered in her bed."

The prisoners stopped staring ahead and looked at R.J. This was definitely unusual. Usually they sang or danced at Show and Tell. No one had ever recited a poem before. And this was a spooky poem! Leftowitz stood at parade rest and said nothing. His face was a mask of indecision, and he was a little stunned. He thought he should interrupt, put an end to this, but he was fascinated despite himself and did not want to stop it. He stood and stared like the prisoners, cocking his head at R.J.

"He walked amongst the trial men
In a suit of shabby gray,
A cricket cap was on his head,
And his step seemed light and gay;
Yet I never saw a man who looked
So wistfully upon the day."

The other prisoners stared open-mouthed at R.J.

"I never saw a man who looked
With such a wistful eye,
Upon that little tent of blue
We prisoners call the sky,
And at every drifting cloud that went
With sails of silver by.

I walked with other souls in pain,
Within a different ring,
And was wondering if the man had done
A great or little thing,
When a voice behind me whispered low,
'That fellow's got to swing.'

Dear Christ! The very prison walls
Suddenly seemed to reel,
And the sky above my head became
Like a casque of scorching steel;
And, though I was a soul in pain,
My pain I could not feel."

The brig barracks was silent as all the prisoners stared dumbfounded at R.J. Sergeant Leftowitz opened his mouth to say something, then closed it.

"I only knew what hunted thought
Quickened his step, and why
He looked upon the garish day
With such a wistful eye;
The man had killed the thing he loved
And so he had to die."

Leftowitz stepped in and ordered R.J. to stop. "That's enough of that queer shit!" he yelled. "You maggots get ready for taps!" He stared at R.J. with what might have been respect, frowning, obviously not comprehending what just occurred. R.J. recognized the look of the uneducated, unable to accept something beautiful, regardless of the circumstances. R.J. knew instinctively, though he was the prisoner and Leftowitz was in power, that he, R.J. Davis, had captured a moment on behalf of all the prisoners. It was a delicious moment, one which would not last. He knew Leftowitz would see to that. The Marine sergeant did not like being upstaged.

"You just earned the watch for tonight," Leftowitz told R.J. as the prisoners filed into the wire mesh compound and climbed into their bunks. "Here's what you do." Leftowitz led R.J. to the window and pointed through the wire mesh to the harbor, far below in the distance. "You stand at parade rest in front of this window and keep an eye on the harbor. If you see any communist bastards trying to attack the fleet, you sound off loud and clear." The sergeant scowled. "And you don't move, you don't wriggle, you don't scratch, understand?"

"Sir, yes sir!"

"And you stand there until you are relieved, prisoner!" Leftowitz turned and marched out of the compound. He locked the wire-mesh door behind him and turned off the lights.

When the sergeant had returned to his post outside the brig office, R.J. whispered to Pinney, who was settling into his bunk. "How long is this watch? Four hours?"

"All night, pal," Pinney replied. "They do that to punish a guy. You are gonna be tired tomorrow."

"Oh well," R.J. sighed. "Play the game, right?"

"That's right, man," Pinney said. "Can I ask you something?"

"Sure."

"That poem. It was cool. Was that Edgar Allan Poe again?"

"No," R.J. replied, staring at the harbor. "Actually, that was Oscar Wilde."

"Well," Pinney said, pulling his blanket up to his chin and closing his eyes, "It sure was cool."

R.J. stood and watched the ships in the harbor. It was a long way off, but he thought he could pick out the Haverfield tied to her berth. He felt a little homesick for the ship, even though he had only been aboard a couple of months. He imagined his buddies at the Mocombo Club, drinking tequila and dancing with Tiny's hogs. He smiled to himself. Then a flashing light caught his eye. A signalman on one ship was trying to raise another ship, probably to shoot the bull during a boring watch. R.J. tried to follow the dits and dahs being sent back and forth between the ships. They weren't sending particularly fast, and, over time, as he stood there watching, concentrating, he began to pick up whole words. The longer he watched, the better he could read the code. He was suddenly excited. He could read the flashing light! The two signalmen talked about their home towns, their girls and their cars, and after a time R.J. could read everything they sent. After they had stopped, R.J. went over the flashing light in his mind, writing letters in code to Tonya and the others until he felt he had a good handle on it. The code had been transformed from audio to visual in his mind, and R.J. grinned and secretly thanked Leftowitz for giving him the opportunity. He was still grinning and reading code in his mind when the big metal trash can hit the deck almost seven hours later. It was 0500! Time had passed so quickly that R.J. hadn't noticed how long he had stood there at the window.

EIGHTEEN

Captain Paul Oliver sat at his desk in his stateroom and reviewed, for the hundredth time, the plans for the dinner he was hosting for the admiral that night. It was Saturday, May 3, and every one of the port ships' commanding officers had RSVP'd the invitation. *Three captains and their wives, the Haverfield's exec and five department heads, and Lee Piper, the admiral and his wife...his wife!* Paul's heart jumped again at the thought of Lorelei. The wardroom would seat sixteen comfortably, with perhaps a little crowding. Hawkins and his ships' servicemen worked hard on the meal and the table setting. Somehow, Hawkins had managed to locate real silver settings for the table through his friends at the Naval base, and his menu of potato leek soup, waldorf salad, roast prime rib and baby carrots was sure to please the palates of his guests. Hawkins had also located several bottles of a good cabernet sure to make a fine accompaniment to the prime rib. A knock at the door interrupted his thoughts.

"Come in."

"Excuse me, Cap'n." Cotton, messenger of the watch, removed his whitehat when he stepped into the captain's cabin to give him the message from the quarterdeck.

"Thank you," Captain Oliver said, unfolding the message. "That'll be all."

"Aye, aye, sir," Cotton put his hat back on, saluted and backed out of the room. Captain Oliver read the message. It was from the admiral requesting he call back as soon as possible. He put the message down on his desk, put on his hat as he left his cabin, and headed toward the quarterdeck, where the telephone land line was located. *Christ, I hope he isn't canceling,* he thought.

On the quarterdeck the captain returned the OOD's salute and picked up the phone. He dialed the admiral's office number and waited, listening to the ringing of the phone. After four rings it was picked up. "Admiral Prescott's office," Captain Pollack's voice boomed clearly over the phone line.

"Good morning, sir," Paul began. "This is Paul Oliver from the Haverfield and I'm returning the admiral's call."

"Morning, Paul," Captain Pollack seemed preoccupied. His voice was friendly but tense. "Wait one, please."

Admiral Prescott came on the line, and wasted no time on preliminaries. "Paul, I know how much trouble you went to for the dinner tonight, but I'm afraid I won't be able to make it." Captain Pollack in the background was giving orders to someone. "I've been ordered back to Pearl for a conference, something going on in Southeast Asia." In the background Paul could hear several voices all talking at once. "We're getting ready to head out now to catch a plane."

"I'm sorry to hear you won't be able to make it, sir," Paul said, disappointed. "But duty calls, right sir?" He used one of the admiral's favorite expressions.

"Right," the admiral chuckled. "Indeed it does. I don't want to disappoint your guests, however, and I have a favor to ask you."

"Yes sir, what can I do?"

"I'm not taking Lorelei to Pearl with me, she'd just get bored, and I would appreciate it very much if you would escort her to your dinner party. I don't want her to miss it after all the hard work and trouble you went to."

Paul said nothing. He stood dumbly with the receiver at his ear, not quite certain he had heard correctly.

"Paul, are you there?"

"Yes, sir," Paul quickly recovered his wits. "I...it would be an honor to escort Mrs. Prescott tonight."

"Good. I'll tell her you'll pick her up a little early. She can serve as your hostess. Shall we say 1900?"

"Yes, sir. Dinner is at eight, so that will work out..."

"Good, good." The admiral seemed preoccupied too. "Have a great dinner and Paul...thank you."

"Thank you, sir. Have a safe trip." Captain Oliver put the phone on the receiver and returned to his cabin. His heart was thumping and he felt again like a high school kid. He sat at his desk and stared at Hawkins' dinner menu, not really seeing it. His thoughts were on Lorelei. She would be his date for the evening; that was exciting enough. He would pick her up and take her home. He felt anxious, anticipating the evening. It was 1000 and he was picking up Lorelei at 1900. *Nine hours until then.* It seemed more like nine days, and Paul quickly busied himself with ship's routine to fill the time.

In his cabin, Captain Oliver showered and shaved carefully, then splashed on a liberal amount of after shave. It burned a little and he winced, a small price to pay for smelling good. The admiral's car would pick him up at a quarter to seven and take him to the admiral's residence to collect Lorelei. He was glad of that. He wouldn't have to use the Haverfield's pickup truck driven by Billy Lopez. Even Captain Oliver was leery of Billy's driving.

On the fantail, Mr. MacDonald met with Chief Whipple and Queen to insure the ship would look its best for the dinner reception. They didn't yet know that the admiral wasn't coming, so they discussed the military etiquette of piping the admiral aboard, setting up the honor guard and polishing up the quarterdeck. The OOD for the evening, Ensign Thompson would be in dress whites, as would the petty officer of the watch, the messenger of the watch and the members of the honor guard. The brow was decorated with a new white banner with large blue lettering: USS Haverfield DER-393. The honor guard would man the quarterdeck on both sides of the brow so the admiral and his guests would walk between them as they were piped aboard. The members of the honor guard would then escort the officers and their ladies to the wardroom. At the end of the evening the honor guard would escort the guests back to the quarterdeck. Mr. MacDonald was pleased with the appearance of the ship.

"We are looking good, men," he told the other two, who smiled. "It's been two months since the captain instituted his rehab program and there has been a marked improvement not only in the appearance of the ship, but also in the appearance and attitude of the men." Mr. Mac knew the men were as proud as he was of this ship, and everyone was looking forward to the admiral's visit. "We are beginning to look like regular Navy around here," he said, smiling and looking around the fantail.

"The crew has responded well," Chief Whipple said, nodding. "With the ship looking as good as it does, it allows us to concentrate on training, making everyone better at their jobs."

"I gotta agree," rumbled Queen in his heavy voice. "Seems to be a new enthusiasm on board, especially in the deck force."

"Yep," Mr. Mac agreed, smiling. "The Havernauts are becoming a crew. They have a long way to go, but they are beginning to bond."

Captain Oliver looked at the chronometer on his wall for the umpteenth time. It seemed that the hands of the clock had slowed down to a painful crawl, and time seemed to go by agonizingly slow. But it was finally 1830 and he expected any minute to hear from the quarterdeck that his transportation had arrived. When the expected knock came at his door, he forced himself to be calm. "Come in," he said, looking over the menu one last time.

"Captain." Pancho Cortez had the duty as messenger and stepped into the captain's cabin. "The car is here for you, sir."

Captain Oliver made a show of looking at his watch as if he hadn't realized the time. "Very well," he said. "I'm on my way."

Pancho left and Captain Oliver picked up his hat and took a last look in the mirror. He hoped he looked like a proper Naval officer in his starched dress whites. He put on his hat and forced himself to walk slowly in the direction of the quarterdeck. He appraised the quarterdeck crew appreciatively and smiled as he returned their salutes.

"Haverfield departing," came the announcement over the 1-MC. Captain Oliver saluted the OOD and walked calmly down the brow to the waiting gray Navy sedan, its rear door held open by the driver.

The sun was setting slowly, spreading warm golden hues across the horizon and creating darkened chasms between the hills. The Navy sedan negotiated the twists and turns, climbing above the Naval base toward the admiral's residence, set atop a hill, back from the road. The driver slowed as he turned into the driveway. The car stopped in front of the admiral's residence, the front door opened and Lorelei stepped out onto the porch. Paul Oliver stared at her through the car window, waiting for the driver to come around and open his door. She was beautiful standing there in a lovely beige dress which hung on her body like it was tailored for her. It accentuated her figure without being bold. The dress was high-necked and the hem came below her knee, but even with the lack of skin showing, it was an incredibly sexy sight. She shielded her eyes against the slanting sun and waved to him with her other hand.

Paul walked up the three steps to the porch and Lorelei came forward to greet him, her hand held out in welcome. He took it.

"Captain Oliver," she said sweetly. "I want to thank you for serving as my escort this evening, and the admiral asked me to apologize for his absence. Something important in Pearl." Her sweet voice was musical in a soft, sultry way, and it reminded him of Brenda Lee.

"My pleasure, ma'am," he replied. "I hope you will enjoy the evening."

"I will on one condition," she smiled. "You must stop calling me ma'am. Please call me Lorelei, or Lorrie if you like."

Captain Oliver nodded dumbly. He couldn't possibly be familiar enough to call her Lorrie, it didn't sound respectful. Besides, he felt it would be silly to shorten a lovely name like Lorelei. "Okay, Lorelei," he said, smiling and holding her hand as she descended the stairs. He walked her to the car and waited for her to slide into the back seat, then slid in next to her, closing the door behind him. She held a folded shawl on her lap. "Alright, driver," he said, with as much authority as he could manage. The car began moving down the driveway, turned onto the road and gained speed as it headed down the hill. Paul stole little sideways glances at her. She was looking ahead, through the windshield, with a slight smile on her face. Her perfume filled the car with a subtle, sweet aroma that smelled like heaven to him. She looked at him and spoke softly.

"The admiral seems quite taken with you, Captain." She turned in her seat to look at him. "He says you are a comer. Just what is a comer, Captain?" It seemed to Paul that she was teasing him. She obviously knew what the term meant.

"I suppose it means this is my first command, and if I don't screw it up I might get another."

She laughed and the musical sound made his heart thump. "The admiral is a very good judge of character, Captain," she said, still smiling sweetly. "And he's very seldom wrong about people."

He turned in the seat to look directly into her violet eyes. "If I'm going to call you Lorelei," he said, "then perhaps you should call me Paul."

She smiled and her eyes lighted up brightly. "You've got a deal," she said. "Paul."

They rode in silence, the car winding its way down the hill toward highway one. Paul felt the warmth from her, sitting there across the back seat, though there was a good eighteen inches of space between them. He settled back and stared out the side window. It seemed to him to be a perfect evening, a perfect car-ride and would no doubt be a perfect dinner. After a few minutes, she spoke.

"I feel I must warn you, Cap...I mean Paul," she said in her sweet sounding voice. "I'm here tonight as a spy."

Paul turned and looked at her. Damn, she was beautiful. "A spy? How so?"

"The admiral wants a full report on your command," she cooed. "He wants me to look over your ship and crew, from a woman's point of view, and report back to him on your progress." She had a sly little smile on her face, looking quite amused.

"I see," Paul replied, also smiling. "Then I guess I'd better be on my best behavior and make a good impression."

"You've already made a good impression," she said. "The admiral was apprehensive about his assignment here. He had heard many reports about the slovenliness of the ships stationed here in what he called 'the coconut Navy." Paul smiled at the familiar term. She went on. "You made a favorable impression on him at our reception, and he thinks you can be an example of regular Navy to the other commands." She looked at the ring on his finger. "You're an academy man. The admiral favors academy men."

"We've worked hard to bring our ship up to standards," he said, seriously. "I think you'll be able to give him a positive report."

Lorelei smiled and looked out the window. "It's really beautiful here, isn't it?" she asked absently.

"Yes, it is. Not like Pearl, but still very beautiful."

"I like it here," she said. "It's more private, more intimate than Pearl."

He nodded, replaying her words in his mind. *Was he getting some sort of subtle signal, or was he reading too much in her comments?* He shook the thoughts from his mind and concentrated on the scenery. They rode the rest of the way in silence, she staring straight ahead with a slight smile on her lips, and he looking out the side window, eyes closed, breathing in her hypnotic perfume.

Anselmi and Becker stood on the starboard wing bridge, enjoying the cooling of the evening when the Navy sedan pulled up close to the brow. Captain Oliver didn't wait for the driver to come around and open the door. He stepped out of the car and put on his hat, holding his hand out for Lorelei, who took it and emerged from the car.

"Wow," Anselmi whispered. "That's a fine-looking woman."

"The admiral's wife," scolded Becker. "You're leering at the admiral's wife."

Anselmi whistled softly. "Way to go, Skipper!" he exclaimed, watching the captain escort her up the brow, with a hand on her elbow to steady her.

"Haverfield arriving!" came the announcement.

As the captain escorted Lorelei to the wardroom he noticed her looking around the ship appreciatively. He was proud of the job the crew had done. The Haverfield was spit and polish, regular Navy, its paint gleaming, its brass shining in the dimming light.

They were the first to arrive, and Paul escorted Lorelei to the head of the table in the wardroom and held out a chair for her. She sank down on the navy blue cushion and placed her handbag under the chair. "This is lovely," she said, indicating the flowers in the table centerpiece and the silver settings. "Quite lovely."

Paul put his hat on the chair to her right, signaling the seat was taken just in case one of the other diners tried to sit there.

"Brister arriving," the 1-MC announced Captain Piper's arrival. Paul excused himself and moved toward the door so he could greet Lee Piper. When Captain Piper came in he looked surprised to see Lorelei there without the admiral. Paul explained the situation and led Captain Piper to the chair on Lorelei's left. She smiled at Captain Piper and offered her hand.

"Nice to see you again, Captain," she said.

Lee Piper shook her hand and shot a quick glance at Paul. "A pleasure, ma'am," he said, sitting down next to her.

Paul was pleased. He had arranged the seating of Lorelei between the two bachelors so it would look as if she had two escorts for the evening. He was relieved that Lee Piper immediately engaged her in conversation. Now Paul could greet his guests without feeling he had to entertain the admiral's wife.

The dinner was a huge success. The small wardroom afforded the attendees the opportunity to get to know each other, and conversations were bright and friendly. Lee Piper certainly did his part. He talked with Lorelei all evening, laughing at her little jokes and lighting her cigarettes. He was attentive and courteous, the perfect gentleman. Paul sat back and watched, pleased, as Hawkins and his crew removed the dinner dishes and brought coffee and dessert, a large white cake with an anchor decorated in blue frosting. Lorelei raised her coffee cup and proposed a toast.

"To our host," she said, nodding toward Paul. "Thank you for a lovely dinner and a wonderful evening." She smiled and sipped her coffee as the other guests echoed the sentiment. Paul reddened just a bit before standing and raising his coffee cup.

"Thank you, Mrs. Prescott," he said. "I'm sorry the admiral couldn't make it, but he could not have sent us a more gracious representative." He sipped his coffee and went on. "And thank you all for making this a successful evening. Now," he looked around the wardroom. "Who's going to host the next dinner party?"

The guests laughed and looked around at each other. "I will," Lee Piper volunteered. "How about tomorrow night?" There was more laughter around the table.

The dinner guests began looking at their watches and fidgeting around, signaling that the evening was just about over. Lee Piper, ever on the ball, stood and announced, "It's getting late, and I still have some paperwork to do. A guy shouldn't have to work on the weekends," he grinned, straightening his tie and his collar. "It's un-American."

Slowly the guests began saying their goodbyes and filing out the hatchway, to be escorted to the quarterdeck by deck-force sailors in sparkling dress whites. Paul stood at the wardroom door and said goodnight to his guests one by one. He shook every hand offered, bussed every cheek offered and thanked everyone for coming. He was the perfect host. Lorelei sat in her chair, turned slightly, one ankle crossed over the other, and watched him with amusement in her eyes.

Paul pulled the door shut behind the last guest and leaned back against it, letting out an exaggerated whoosh of air. He smiled at her and began walking toward the table. "Did we pass inspection, madam spy?" he asked, smiling down at her.

"Quite," she smiled back. "Seriously, Paul, you've done a brilliant job with this ship."

"The crew did most of the work," he replied, sitting next to her. He cherished any chance to talk about his ship and his men. "They've worked hard and trained hard. They're becoming a pretty good crew."

Lorelei listened, smiling as Paul talked about his ship. He described to her the poor condition he had found aboard the ship when he assumed command. The sloppiness of the crew, the lax attitude of the officers and petty officers, the tarnish and rust throughout the decks and the terrible level of training had appalled him. He had not expected to take command of a sea-going garbage scow.

She listened patiently, occasionally encouraging him to continue by asking questions at strategic moments. She was having a good time, sitting relaxed in the Haverfield's wardroom, sipping coffee and enjoying the company of a man she found incredibly attractive. She loved the way his brown eyes sparkled when he talked about his ship. She felt comfortable with him as he told her about his plans to rehabilitate the ship and retrain the crew. He was proud of the progress so far, and he detailed the many areas of improvement, including the training program he had instituted. *After all, he reasoned, as long as she was going to give a full report...*

"I want this vessel to be ready to take her place in the fleet. We aren't always going to be assigned crap duty like island surveys." He stopped abruptly and looked at her, hoping he hadn't insulted the admiral.

She waved him away. "Don't worry, Captain," she cooed. "The admiral doesn't much like crap duty either."

He looked at his watch and stood, straightening the crease on his trousers. "I'm sorry, I didn't realize the time..." He fumbled with his tie and his collar. He didn't want the time he spent alone with her to become shipboard scuttlebutt. That kind of gossip could spread very quickly and maybe reach the admiral's ears.

"Yes," Lorelei reluctantly agreed, perhaps thinking the same thoughts. "I've got Cinderella liberty, you know." She picked up her wrap and allowed him to drape it over her shoulders. He stared down at the back of her neck as he arranged the shawl neatly on her shoulders, and caught a whiff of that lovely scent. What was that? Chanel?

She turned and looked up at him, and for a moment they just stood there, staring into each others' eyes. He reached over and picked up the sound powered phone from its cradle on the bulkhead and raised the quarterdeck. He continued looking at her as he told the OOD, "Find the admiral's duty driver and have him get the car ready." He put the phone back in its cradle. She was watching him closely, her violet eyes searching his face as if she were trying to read him.

Paul escorted Lorelei down the aft ladder to the fantail and across to the quarterdeck. The duty driver had the car ready at the bottom of the brow, engine running and back door held open, awaiting his passengers.

Paul returned the salutes of the quarterdeck watch and took Lorelei's elbow, guiding her down the brow to the waiting car. He slid in next to her in the back seat and told the driver to return them to the admiral's residence. They rode in silence through the darkened hills. It was still warm, but a cooling breeze was picking up strength through the canyons, and Lorelei pulled the shawl around her tighter, shuddering slightly in anticipation of the cool evening.

The car pulled into the circular driveway in front of the admiral's residence and slowly came to a stop. The driver hurried around the car and opened the door for Captain Oliver. Paul stepped out and held out his hand for Lorelei. She took it and held it tightly as she pulled herself out of the car, and the breeze caught her hair and blew it straight back. Paul felt that thump again and closed the car door a little too hard, causing it to slam shut and startle the driver, who jumped. They all laughed nervously and Paul led Lorelei up the front steps to the door. The driver turned his back to the scene and leaned against the driver's side door. He lit a cigarette and stared across the road at the thick vegetation.

At the top of the steps, in front of the door, they stood staring into each others' eyes, neither knowing what to say; or afraid to say what was really on their minds. Finally, Paul touched the tip of his visor with a casual salute and said, "Well, goodnight, Lorelei. It was a very successful evening, thanks in no small part to your presence."

"It was delightful," she replied, smiling sweetly. "I thoroughly enjoyed it, and I intend to give the admiral a very favorable report." She had a little twinkle in her eye, as if she was half-putting him on. Then she stepped close to him, reached up and kissed his right cheek. She whispered, "Good night," and vanished through the front door into the house, leaving her haunting scent swirling in his nostrils.

Paul stood on the porch, staring at the closed front door and touching his fingers to the spot on his cheek where she had kissed him. He took out his handkerchief and wiped at his cheek. A touch of lipstick showed on his handkerchief, and he folded it carefully and put it into his right trouser pocket. He turned and started back down the steps. The driver heard him coming and threw his cigarette away, pulled his hat square on his head and ran around the car to hold the door open. Paul got into the car and took off his hat. The driver closed the door and ran back around the sedan, jumping in behind the wheel. "Back to the Haverfield, sir?" he asked into the rear view mirror.

Captain Oliver nodded, looking through the side window up at the front door of the admiral's residence. As the car began to pull away, a curtain in the big front window moved aside and he saw Lorelei standing there in the dark, looking out the window. One hand held the curtain open, the other played absently with her hair as she watched the car make its way down the driveway.

Lorelei on the Rhine, he thought, watching her standing in the window. He could almost hear her siren song in his head...or was that the wind?

Lorelei stood in the window and watched the gray sedan disappear, its taillights blinking and fading through the trees. She held her hand to her throat and felt a little breathless. It had been a wonderful evening. She felt young and attractive, and thoroughly enjoyed the attention she received from Paul and Lee Piper, though she felt the difference between them was that Lee Piper was being friendly and attentive because he thought he should. Paul Oliver did not fawn over her, but she knew the attraction was there, behind those big brown eyes of his. She smiled to herself. It had been a long time since she had felt these longings, and she was not ashamed of them. Not that anything could ever come of it, she knew. Still, it was a delicious feeling.

NINETEEN

With only two weeks to go on his sentence, R.J. and the other prisoners were informed they would be clearing vegetation from the runways at Anderson Air Force base on the far side of the island. It was the first time R.J. had seen the base, and it amazed him that it was so big and sprawling. The morning was spent chopping boonies from the main runway, and then they headed to the chow hall for lunch. The prisoners liked working around the Air Force base because they knew they would eat lunch in the big, new chow hall. Most of the time they were far out in the bush and it wouldn't be practical to haul them back and forth to the Navy chow hall, so they brought their lunches with them, usually consisting of baloney sandwiches and milk.

Bobby Jim was right. The food was excellent. The chow hall was very large, the formica tables polished and shined, and the trays and silverware were like brand new. R.J. thought he could get used to eating at the Air Force base.

They left the chow hall feeling well fed and content. Bring on those boonies! Calderon grinned at them as they filed past him to the waiting truck.

"Have a good lunch, boys?" he asked playfully.

"Sir yes sir!" B.J. sang out. "And that's no baloney, sir!" Calderon and the prisoners all laughed. Leftowitz stood by the truck and glared.

The brig prisoners were transported to an airfield on the far side of the base, away from the main buildings and airstrip. It was an isolated and lonely spot, and R.J. wondered at the shape of the airstrip. It was longer and much narrower than the main landing strip. It was very clean of debris and seemed to have been swept by street sweepers. The prisoners were ordered to clean the vegetation from an access road about two miles from the pristine landing strip. Calderon saw R.J. admiring the strip and came up beside him.

"Are we sightseeing today, prisoner Davis?" he asked.

"Sir, no sir," R.J. replied.

"Know what you're looking at?" Calderon asked, staring at the narrow landing strip.

"Sir, no sir," R.J. answered. He liked Calderon. The airman was a pretty decent guy, not a hard ass like Leftowitz.

"That there is a take off and landing strip for the U-2 reconnaissance aircraft."

R.J. turned and looked at Calderon. "Sir, do you mean like the one the Russians shot down? Sir?" Some of the other prisoners began gathering around R.J. and Calderon.

"That's the one," Calderon nodded. "We might get a look at one today," he said. "If we're lucky." He glanced over his shoulder at Leftowitz who was looking their way and frowning. "Get back to work," Calderon ordered. "I'll let you guys know if I spot one."

R.J. picked up his machete and began chopping away at the vegetation that was starting to infringe on the access road. The sun felt good on his back and he shed his shirt. He was working up a good sweat. The blisters on his hands didn't bother him as much as they used to, having pretty much turned into hard calluses. The prisoners had been back to work for almost an hour when Calderon called out.

"Here she comes!" He pointed to the end of the runway where a small tractor was towing an aircraft onto the strip. The aircraft was long and sleek-looking. It was painted black and its long, thin wingtips draped down, riding the pavement on small wheels. The fuselage was very slim. It looked like a long black bullet and it glided down the strip gracefully, almost majestically, and stopped. The tractor disengaged and turned back, leaving the U-2 parked alone on the strip.

Leftowitz allowed the prisoners to take a break and watch the U-2. He was as intrigued as the rest of them. They lined the access road and stared across the field at the black reconnaissance plane. The guards stood a few feet behind them. They were as curious as the prisoners. The air around the plane shimmered as the U-2's engines fired and revved. It began rolling forward down the runway, slowly at first and then faster and faster as it picked up speed. Suddenly the plane was airborne, and roared into the air, the sound of its afterburners taking a moment to reach the working party. The men stared as the U-2's nose came up dramatically and the plane seemed to fly straight up into the sky like a rocket being launched from Cape Canaveral. In just a few moments, the U-2 disappeared into the clouds. The sound of its engines reached the prisoners well after the U-2 had vanished, enveloping the men in a deep rumbling roar.

No one said anything for a few minutes. They all stood and stared at the spot where the U-2 had disappeared, mouths open, heads shaking.

"Holy shit!" Bobby Jim exclaimed. "Did y'all see that?" He looked around at the others. "Did y'all *SEE* that?"

Pinney slapped Bobby Jim on the back. "That was some amazing Buck Rogers shit," he said excitedly.

"That was the Air Force's best aircraft," Calderon said, smiling at the sky. "At least in my opinion."

Beatty stood with his hands on his hips, looking up at the spot where the U-2 had disappeared. "I seen those Navy Phantom jets takin' off from the deck of the Kitty Hawk," he said. "I thought those were some awesome planes, but that," he pointed to the sky. "That was somethin' else!"

Leftowitz broke the spell. "That's enough eyeballin', maggots," he yelled. "The boonies are growing back. Start swinging those blades."

For the rest of the afternoon, the prisoners chopped vegetation and talked quietly about the U-2. They kept an eye out for the recon plane's return, but it didn't come back. It was on an extended reconnaissance mission over Southeast Asia, in a part of the world most of the prisoners had never heard of...yet.

On Sunday Bobby Gamboa visited R.J. and brought him a carton of cigarettes. "Here's the smokes I owe you," he said. "I didn't want you to think I forgot about you. I just got back from Pearl."

"Thanks, Bob. How's it goin' with the trailer?" R.J. was pleased to see his friend, and was grateful that Bobby came to visit.

"Good," Bobby replied. "Real good. It's now red, and we have a porch and a roof that don't leak. Thanks to them Sample boys. Those guys sure work their asses off."

"Good upbringing," R.J. said absently. "How're Billy and Teresa getting along?" R.J. was anxious for some news. He was looking forward to finishing his sentence and getting back to his ship and his friends. He missed them more than he thought he would. His biggest fear was that the ship would get underway before he got out and he'd end up spending three weeks in the transit barracks. That would be almost as bad as the brig.

"Great," Bobby replied, grinning. "They're in love, but my mom, she's gonna be sure they don't do anything about it." He chuckled at the thought of his mother watching over his sister. "But Billy, he's a gentleman, you know? They hold hands and kiss good-bye, but that's all. My mom won't let her go out with him alone. And Billy treats my mom really nice. She likes him, but she don't trust him."

"Can't blame her," R.J. said wearily, rubbing his eyes. "He's a sailor. She has a right to be suspicious."

"Anyway, I got some good movies for the crew. Sorry you can't be there, R.J. We're having a good time out at the trailer. Lots of guys from your ship come out to help. My dad loves it 'cause he gets to drink beer with them and tell all his World War Two stories. The guys eat it up."

"Two more weeks," R.J. said quietly. "I'll be back in two weeks."

Bobby looked at his friend, frowning with concern. "You okay, buddy?" he asked. "You ain't your usual cheerful self."

"It's not much fun in here, Bob," R.J. answered, looking around for the guards. "They aren't brutal or physical with us, but they work our asses off. The first day I almost passed out from the heat, and I don't think I'll ever get rid of the calluses." He sighed heavily. "The worst thing is I'm locked up in jail. It's not someplace I wanna come back to anytime soon."

"You hang in there, R.J.," Bobby said. "We're gonna party when you get out."

After Bobby's visit, R.J. became more homesick and anxious to return to the Haverfield. He began counting down the days, which only made the time go by more slowly. He concentrated on the daily routine and staying out of trouble, working hard to be the perfect prisoner. *Play the game*, he thought, *play the game*. At night, during quiet time, he spent as much time as possible standing by the window, reading flashing lights in the harbor below. Pinney, Bobby Jim and Beatty liked to stand there with him as he read aloud what the signalmen were sending to each other. The guards left them alone as long as they were quiet and posed no discipline problems.

With a little less than a week to serve, R.J. was dressing in his dungarees, having returned his razor blade to the guard's locker, when Leftowitz strode up to him. "Come with me, prisoner Davis," he ordered.

Uh oh, R.J. thought. *What did I do now?* "Sir, yes sir," he answered, and fell in just behind Leftowitz who led him into Lieutenant Shepard's office. R.J. stood stiffly in front of the brig commander's desk, waiting for the lieutenant to look up from the file folder in front of him.

Finally, Lieutenant Shepard closed the folder and looked at R.J. "I've been getting some good reports about you, Davis," he said. "Sergeant Leftowitz and the other guards tell me you've become a model prisoner. They say you're one of the hardest workers we've got and that you're a natural leader with the rest of the men."

R.J. swallowed hard. "Sir, thank you, sir," he said meekly.

"I think you've learned your lesson, don't you?"

"Sir, yes sir," R.J. said quietly.

"Good, because tomorrow we're releasing you back to your ship."

R.J.'s mouth dropped open. He had almost a week left to serve.

"You're getting five days' reduction in your sentence for good behavior," the lieutenant continued, as if he had read R.J.'s mind. "It doesn't happen as often as I'd like, but when it does, it's usually because the prisoner has demonstrated a desire to reform. Anyway, congratulations. You'll be released tomorrow morning right after breakfast." He looked amused at the surprised expression on R.J.'s face. "That's all, Davis." Lieutenant Shepard opened another file and began studying it.

"Sir, yes sir," R.J. stammered. "Thank you, sir."

"About face!" Leftowitz barked. R.J. swiveled around. "Forward, maaarch!" R.J. marched out of the office with a big grin on his face. Leftowitz pretended not to notice. R.J. hurried into the barracks to inform his friends that he was going home. They cheered and slapped him on the back, congratulating him, joking that he must have kissed Leftowitz's ass or something to get an early release. They were clearly happy for him.

That day in the bush, R.J. worked harder than he had ever worked before, trying to prove he deserved the early release. He chopped away at the vegetation furiously and chided the others to keep up with him. He didn't care about the heat, or sunburn or passing out. He was getting out of there and the thought cheered him, energized him.

"Lookit that fool," Bobby Jim laughed. "Now he tryin' to get promoted to head prisoner or something."

"Hell, he probably wants Shepard's job," Pinney suggested. "We're all gonna be working for him from now on."

"You gotta admit, though," Beatty observed. "He is definitely one boonie-choppin' sumbitch!"

"I just wanna make sure I get most of this stuff off the road," R.J. countered. "I know I can't depend on you dead-heads after I'm gone." His last day was the most pleasant he had spent in the brig, and he wanted to savor it, enjoy it as much as possible, laboring in the hot sun, bonded to the other prisoners by circumstance.

That evening, after the prisoners had cleaned up and lined up on the red line for chow, Leftowitz strode to the middle of the barracks and stood in front of the column, staring up and down the line. "Sound off!" he barked.

"Sir, Pinney, G.P. is the first prisoner in this prisoner formation, sir!"

All down the line the men sounded off, one by one until finally it became R.J.'s turn. "Sir, Davis, R.J. is the last prisoner in this prisoner formation, SIR!" he called.

Leftowitz nodded. "Left face!" he barked. The column did a smart left face, clomping their boondockers down in unison. Leftowitz stepped back two paces. "Prisoner Davis, front and center!" he ordered.

R.J. looked confused by the break in routine, but he did a sharp right-face and took two paces forward.

Leftowitz smiled at R.J. It was a genuine smile, not the sneer R.J. was used to. It startled him a little. Leftowitz really wasn't that bad looking when he smiled like that. Or maybe it just seemed that way because R.J. was getting out and everything looked good to him today.

"Since you're leaving us tomorrow, prisoner Davis," Leftowitz said, "tonight you are the Duke of Earl. Take your place at the head of the column!"

"Sir, yes sir!" R.J. marched quickly to the head of the column and stood at attention, grinning widely.

"Take us to chow, prisoner Davis," Leftowitz ordered.

"Sir, yes sir! Hands on shoulders, hut!" R.J. called out. The prisoners brought their hands up in unison and placed them on the shoulders of the men in front of them. They were all grinning.

"March in place, hut!" R.J. ordered, clearly enjoying himself. The column began marching in place, their boondockers clomping as one.

"Forward at the half-step. Duke of Earl, march!" RJ. barked in his best Leftowitz impression, and led the prisoners out the door and into the passageway where Calderon and Culver stood at attention saluting. R.J. and Leftowitz returned their salutes smartly as the column passed.

"Duke Duke Duke, Duke of Earl, Duke Duke..."

* * * * *

R.J. found it almost impossible to sleep. Knowing he was leaving the brig in the morning kept him wide-eyed and awake even though he wanted more than anything to fall asleep and wake up the next morning, his last morning in the brig. He tossed and turned through the night, and an hour before reveille he finally dozed off, only to be awakened by the clattering trash can. For the last time he jumped out of his bunk and ran in place with his blanket and sheet in his hands. For the last time he requested his razor blade and shaved with the others. For the last time he made up his bunk, top sheet pulled so tight he could bounce a quarter off it, and for the last time he lined up on the painted red line and sounded off with the rest of the prisoners.

After breakfast Leftowitz led the prisoners to the waiting panel truck to transport them to the morning's designated boonie-chopping area. R.J. stayed in the barracks and packed his seabag. Calderon came up behind him.

"You ain't a prisoner anymore, Davis," he announced. "So you're gonna need this." He tossed R.J. a new dungaree shirt, one without the big black 'P' stenciled on the back. R.J. put on the shirt and tucked it into his trousers.

"Thank you," he said gratefully.

"You're welcome," Calderon said. He was smiling. "Now get your ass outta my brig."

"Sir, yes sir!" R.J. replied, grinning wide. He hefted the seabag onto his shoulder and walked out the front door. Culver smiled at him as he passed, and R.J. smiled back.

On the front steps of the barracks, R.J. stopped and dropped his seabag down onto the concrete. He looked around and took a deep breath of fresh, free air, savoring the moment. The big gray panel truck with the prisoners in the back drove past him with Leftowitz riding shotgun. As the truck went by R.J.'s and Leftowitz's eyes met. The sergeant nodded slightly and R.J. nodded back, still grinning. The truck turned down the road and headed for the main gate. In the back window R.J. saw Pinney, Bobby Jim and Beatty looking at him through the glass, all three of them with their middle fingers pointed in the air. R.J. laughed, waved and headed down the front steps toward the street. He would have to catch the shuttle bus back to the Haverfield.

He waited in front of the shuttle kiosk for the bus. It felt good to be out of the brig, knowing he would not have to get up in the morning and swing that machete. He was tanned and fit, having lost a few pounds and firmed up a great deal. He put his head back and soaked up the warm sun with his eyes closed. Down the street he heard a familiar and happy sound. Truck gears ground loudly, and an engine revved plaintively, coming up the hill. He smiled, eyes still closed. *That's gotta be Charming Billy,* he thought, and opened his eyes.

The Haverfield's pickup truck screeched to a stop in front of the kiosk, swirling dust all around. Tanner was leaning out of the passenger window with a big grin on his face. Billy Lopez, smiling charmingly, leaned his head back to look past Tanner. "Anybody going to the Haverfield?" he called.

Tears welled up in R.J.'s eyes at the sight of his friends. He grinned and tossed his seabag into the bed of the truck and slid into the cab, shaking hands with Tanner and Billy.

"You miss me?" he asked.

"Why?" Tanner asked, a look of mock surprise on his face. "You go somewhere?"

"Thanks for picking me up, fellas," R.J. said. "I appreciate it."

"Well shit, boy," Charming Billy replied. "You didn't think we was gonna let you take the bus home, did you?"

"You look good, Wog," Tanner said. "You're all tan and fit lookin'. The brig musta done you some good."

"It did," R.J. said quietly. "It definitely did."

"Gotta surprise for you," Tanner said.

"What?" R.J. asked.

"Complete Control Edgars got rotated back to the states," he said. "We got us a new exec. Academy man, named Edward J. Martin, and he seems to be a really good guy."

"That's good news," R.J. said. "Now please tell me Twitchell's gone, too."

"No such luck," Billy replied. "He's the same old asshole."

Billy swung the truck into its parking place next to the Quonset hut on the pier and the three of them headed for the brow of the Haverfield. R.J. smiled at the ship. She was a welcome sight after almost a month in the brig. He looked up at the quarterdeck and saw that Twitchell was the OOD. R.J. groaned to himself, hefted the seabag onto his shoulder and walked up the brow. He saluted the flag on the fantail, then saluted the OOD, who threw him a hurried, sloppy salute in return.

"You learn anything in the brig, shithead?" Twitchell asked, his pig face sweating, leaving a dark stain on his shirt collar.

"Yes chief," R.J. answered. "I learned to keep my mouth shut." *And so should you*, he thought.

Twitchell nodded, scowled and turned away. He opened the ship's log and notated the return of SA Davis, R.J. He did not look up. R.J. picked up his seabag and went down the aft ladder to First Division's compartment. Big Queen was standing between two bunks, shoveling ice cream into his mouth with a small plastic spoon.

"Davis," he said matter of factly. "'Bout time you showed up for work. Stow your shit and get up on deck. We're getting underway in the morning and I want you to help lash down the landing rafts."

"Okay, Boats," R.J. replied and headed for his locker, smiling at the big boatswain's mate. Sitting on his bunk was a large piece of cardboard on which someone had scrawled, 'WELCOME HOME SHITHEAD!' R.J. grinned as he stowed his gear into his locker. He was home.

* * * * *

After evening chow, R.J. sat in the messdecks with Tanner, Billy Lopez and Pea, playing hearts and catching up. R.J. told them all about his time in the brig, how he learned to read flashing light, standing by the window and watching the signalmen in the harbor. The others got a big kick out of the stories about Greg Pinney, Bobby Jim Johnson, Sergeant Leftowitz and the Duke of Earl. Tanner told R.J. about the triple thunder party held for the Sample brothers and Gino.

"It was like an assembly line," he explained. "We lined 'em up on the deck of the bosun's locker and gang-thundered them." He chuckled as he recounted the event, and Pea and Billy laughed along with him.

"When they was done," Pea said, laughing, "they went up on the focsul to kiss the Union Jack and we threw Gino in the drink. Then both the Samples climbed over the lifeline and did these beautiful swan dives into the harbor. It was neat." He shook his head at the memory. "We all applauded when they came to the surface."

"Good thunder party," Billy agreed, smiling and sipping his coffee. "And Gino put together a singing group."

"A singing group?" R.J. asked.

"Yeah," Tanner answered. "And we're pretty good. Come up on the focsul tonight and listen to us practice."

"Okay, I will," R.J. agreed. "I feel like fishing, anyway. I'll be there."

Chief Whipple came into the messdecks and poured himself a cup of coffee. He sipped at the cup, his eyes taking in the four sailors in the back booth. He walked slowly toward them, stopped and looked down at them until their chatter subsided.

"How was the brig, Davis?" he asked.

"Not too good, Chief."

"You got five days off for good behavior, huh?" The chief sipped his coffee. The others at the table sensed something was coming and began fidgeting.

"Yes, Chief."

Whipple nodded, his face expressionless. "Tomorrow, right after we hit the breakwater I want you to report to Hawkins for scullery duty." He said it quietly, staring at R.J. "See, I think if a guy is sent to the brig for thirty days, he oughta do thirty days."

"Scullery duty?" R.J. asked, surprised.

"That's right. You spend five days working here in the galley with Hawkins, cleaning trays and silverware, taking out the garbage, peeling potatoes and swabbing the galley deck. Any other shit job he's got. Then I'll consider your sentence to be finished. Questions?" The chief sipped his coffee, studying R.J. over the rim of the cup. His eyes were cold and humorless. He neither expected nor wanted any questions.

"No, Chief," R.J. replied meekly.

Chief Whipple nodded. "We're gonna be gone for three weeks, so after your five days in here you'll be eligible for landings, and I'll make sure you get on an island or two. Fair enough?" He didn't wait for an answer. He turned on his heel and walked out of the messdecks.

R.J. looked around at his buddies. "What was that all about?"

"He's just making a point," Tanner answered, staring at the messdecks hatch where Whipple had left. "He don't want you getting cocky. That's just his way of telling you he ain't gonna take no shit."

"Yeah," Billy agreed. "He wants to be sure you learned your lesson. Kinda like showing you who's boss."

"Well, I just got outta the brig. I guess I can do five days in the scullery," R.J. said.

While most of the crew stayed on the fantail to watch *Operation Mad Ball* with Jack Lemmon, R.J. took his fishing pole up to the focsul to catch some barracuda for the Gamboas. Bobby would stop by later to pick them up. R.J. heard the music just as he stepped through the port hatch and started toward the bow. It was soft harmony, sung a cappella, and it sounded good. He reached the focsul and looked around. Seven or eight sailors sat around the deck or leaned against the gun mount, smoking cigarettes. Charming Billy was the focsul watch. Gino was standing in the middle of a four man group. Andy Sample was the base, Tanner did the baritone, Cotton was the alto and Gino was singing the lead to '(I'll Remember) In the Still of the Night.' Their voices blended beautifully, and R.J. thought they sounded at least as good as the Five Satins. He leaned against the gun mount and listened as the group finished the song. He stood up and applauded enthusiastically with the rest of the audience. Gino and the group bowed and grinned.

"Wow, you guys been practicing!" R.J. exclaimed.

"Told you we sounded good," Tanner said proudly.

"Got any more songs?" R.J. asked.

"We got a bunch of 'em," Gino said. "How 'bout this?'

"*I sit in my room, looking out at the rain,*
My tears are like crystals, they cover my window pane,"

The rest of the group joined in and began singing the backup to what

R.J. recognized as *'Teardrops'* by Lee Andrews and the Hearts. Gino's voice filled the evening air with a resonant beauty. He sang with his eyes closed, swaying slowly back and forth with the gentle rhythm.

> *"I'm thinking of our lost romance,*
> *and how it should have been,*
> *Oh, if we only could start over again."*

R.J. baited his hook with a piece of cheese and dropped the line into the harbor. He leaned the pole against the lifeline and sat back on the capstain, listening to Gino's group. It felt good to be back aboard ship, fishing for barracuda, laughing and joking with his friends. The weather was beginning to warm up, the tropical summer not too far off. As he sat there, smoking, listening to the music and awaiting the first barracuda strike, his mind drifted off to Longmont, Colorado and the last springtime he had spent there; the last time he had heard *'Teardrops.'*

He sighed aloud as he thought of those warm, dark nights in Sunset Park with his buddies and their girlfriends. Together they had pondered the mysteries of the universe, had learned to smoke cigarettes and French kiss. It was on one of those warm, dark nights in Sunset Park that Dino Phillips first brought up the idea of joining the Navy. R.J. had at once become enthusiastic over the idea, though Renee did not share that enthusiasm. After a lot of tears and more than a few arguments, R.J. had joined the Navy. Dino had chickened out to stay home and get married. R.J. wondered how things were going for Dino.

"R.J.!" Snapping back to the present, R.J. saw Bobby Gamboa coming up the port side toward the bow, pointing. "Get your line, man!" he shouted.

R.J. looked over and saw his fishing pole being pulled over the lifeline. "Oh, shit!" he yelled, and grabbed the handle of the pole just before it vanished over the side. He had hooked a good-sized barracuda with the cheese bait. He would cut it up into pieces and use it for bait to catch other barracuda. It was a curious fact that barracuda liked to eat other barracuda more than anything else. That's why they made the best bait. In fact, as R.J. had discovered, once a barracuda was hooked and thrashing about, he had to reel in quickly or it would be devoured by other barracuda.

"Good save," Bobby said, laughing. "How many you got so far?"

"This is numero uno," R.J. replied, holding the fish so Billy could bonk it on the head with his nightstick. "I'll cut 'im up for bait. Why don't you grab a pole?"

Bobby picked up a pole and baited his hook with a piece of barracuda flesh. He winked at R.J. and turned to Billy. "Teresa says she's gonna miss you a lot, Billy," he teased. "You guys are gonna be gone for about three weeks. I hope she doesn't find someone else." He saw the painful look on Billy's face and backed off. "Just jerking you around, Billy," he said. "Teresa is so much in love with you she doesn't even see anyone else."

Billy beamed happily and Bobby winked again at R.J.

After Bobby had left with his fish and a long letter from Billy to Teresa, and Gino and his group had gone below, R.J. went up to the signal bridge to try his hand at the light. He raised the Raptor across the harbor and began shooting the breeze with Washington, an SM-3. R.J. loved the fact he could read the light, but he had a hard time sending the code. The damn handle kept making that clacking noise. He was afraid his coded characters were impossible to read, but Washington seemed to have no trouble with them. *Practice,* R.J. thought. *Practice makes perfect.*

TWENTY

The next morning, May 18, the Haverfield got underway for the Marshall Islands. Once the ship hit the breakwater and began bouncing, pitching and rolling east, R.J. reported to Hawkins in the galley. Hawkins was polishing his pots and pans lovingly, making them shine like mirrors. He looked suspiciously at R.J.

"How come the Chief done sent you to me?" he asked, fogging a pan with his breath and wiping it clean.

"Said I owe five days," R.J. replied.

Hawkins nodded. "Okay, here what you gonna do." He led R.J. to a small locker. Inside was a large bin of potatoes and a sink. Next to the sink was a large tub-like contraption, obviously electric because it was plugged into the wall socket. Everything was painted gray, as usual.

"What's that?" R.J. asked.

"That there the potato peeler," Hawkins explained. He walked over and turned the contraption on. The tub began turning, groaning and grinding as it warmed up. Hawkins turned on a faucet and water began running into the tub. "You don' never turn this thing on without you got water goin' in it. Unnerstan?"

R.J. nodded and looked into the tub. The inside chamber was turning around and around slowly. The chamber was coated with what looked like the same sandy, non-skid material used on deck to keep sailors from slipping and sliding. Hawkins dropped a potato into the tub. As the chamber turned, it rubbed the potato until the peel was almost gone. Hawkins turned off the tub.

"This thing will do most of the peelin' for you," he explained. "Soon as most of the skin is rubbed off, all you gots to do is dig out the eyes and scrape off the rest of the peel. Cool, huh?" He grinned at R.J. proudly, showing white teeth. Hawkins was proud of his galley and equipment. "And don' never overload it neither," he warned. "Bout six or seven potatoes, that all."

"I got it. But you know Whipple told me I had to work in the scullery. You sure this is gonna be okay with him?"

Hawkins flared and looked at R.J. angrily. "Don' nobody run this here galley but ol' Hawkins," he snapped, pointing a finger at his thick chest. "I gots all the scullery rats I needs for now. You do this here job and we get along fine." He frowned at R.J., then broke into a toothy grin. "This the easiest job in the galley," he proclaimed.

"Thanks, Hawk. I'll do my best." R.J. studied the potato peeling machine.

* * * * *

The Haverfield steamed east across the Marianas Trench and into the magnificent deep blue of the Pacific Ocean. There was very little wind, and the early summer sun scorched the ocean, turning it into a smooth, glassy surface. The ship made eighteen knots, sailing effortlessly across the calm and quiet sea, creating a welcome breeze for the duty section on deck.

R.J. stood lookout on the 04 level with Pancho Cortez, thankful for the wind blowing in his face. It was hot and getting hotter as the sun climbed in the cloudless sky and the noonday watch rotated around the ship. He watched as silvery flying fish sailed out of the water ahead of the ship, airborne for a few seconds and then diving back into the ocean. He and Pancho made a contest out of it, judging how far the fish could fly until they disappeared into the water. The Haverfield's bow cut swiftly and cleanly through the smooth water, sending foam-capped waves surging on both sides, chasing the frantic flying fish.

R.J. was happy and at peace. The galley duty was pretty easy, and he got to make salads for lunch and dinner. He was only responsible for cleaning his small locker and keeping the bin full of potatoes. He had discovered a time-saving method for peeling them. Instead of taking them out of the tub when they still had a little skin on them and digging out the eyes, R.J. found that if he left them in the tub, and allowed the non-skid surface to rub at them longer, the potatoes came out clean, with no skin and no eyes. Of course they came out of the tub a lot smaller, which meant that he had to use more potatoes, but it saved time, and Hawkins seemed happy with his work. The head cook did wonder aloud, on occasion, why the crew was eating so many potatoes.

The Marine brig seemed like a distant memory, though it had only been a few days since he returned to the ship. He fell back into the shipboard routine easily, and he enjoyed the underway watches. His sea legs were well established, and he was becoming adept at walking the decks and balancing himself with the pitch and roll of the ship. He could even navigate the decks with a cup of coffee in his hand. He was beginning to feel like a sailor.

His attitude had changed. He could feel it. He made fewer wisecracks and kept his anger and insolence under control. He was melding with the ship and the crew, becoming a part of the machinery, eager to do his job. He had a better understanding of how each man aboard, each piece of the puzzle, fit together in the overall scheme of things. He was more confident in his ability to carry his share of the load, and he was becoming a very good deck seaman. It felt great.

"There!" Pancho yelled from the starboard side. "Didja see that one? Had to go at least twenty five feet!" He was pointing to the bow where the flying fish frolicked. R.J. smiled and nodded. He took off his steaming cap and put in his back pocket. The Pacific Ocean was the deepest color blue he had ever seen. For as far as he could see in every direction the Pacific stretched on and on. He was in the center of the earth, on the most beautiful ocean in the world. Holding on to the forward railing and leaning backward, he let the hot sun beat down on his face. He was developing a pretty good tan, thankfully, because he suffered less from sunburn. With his eyes closed, he could feel the rhythms of the ship pass through the railing and into his arms, his torso and his legs. He was in total synch with the movements of the small DER and could anticipate her bobbing and weaving. *Yes,* he thought, *this is why I joined the Navy.*

TWENTY ONE

Mr. MacDonald and Snively huddled around the mimeograph machine in the yeoman's office. Morning chow had just ended, and Mr. MacDonald was eager to finish the preparations for his lecture that evening, June first. The lieutenant had drawn a map of the battle of Midway and intended to pass out copies to the men who attended. He was excited about the material, having become more and more enthusiastic about the idea since Captain Oliver first suggested it.

"Pass the word, Snively," the lieutenant said, studying his map. "I want a good turnout tonight. Tell them 1930 on the fantail, before the evening watch and before sunset." MacDonald made some notes on his copy of the map. He was deep in thought and didn't notice when Snively took several copies and left the office to distribute them.

Frank MacDonald had done a great deal of research into the battle of Midway, and knew his material well. There was a wealth of information available at the Naval base at Pearl Harbor, and he had pored over those resources for hours on end. The battle had taken place twenty one years before and had turned the tide in the Pacific war. Mr. MacDonald wanted to express to the men the importance of that battle and that war, but had nagging doubts about his ability to explain it properly. The captain had told him to 'let them feel your passion' for the material, and that was what the lieutenant hoped to do.

* * * * *

Captain Oliver paced the flying bridge, sipping his morning coffee and scanning the horizon with his binoculars. The OOD, Mr. Barkman, watched the captain pace, deep in thought, and figured the captain was going over the details of the cruise in his mind. Mr. Barkman knew the captain was a stickler for detail, and missed nothing, always aware of what was happening everywhere aboard his ship when they were at sea.

Captain Oliver was deep in thought, but the lady he was thinking about wasn't the USS Haverfield, and he wasn't on the bridge at that moment. He was back on Guam with Lorelei Von Dulm Prescott. He imagined them cruising through the hills with the top down on Lorelei's car, the sun on their faces and their happy laughter drifting upward to be swept away with the wind. They would find a little picnic spot high up in the hills, where they could put down a blanket, sit back, and enjoy the scenery. His heart thumped again, fantasizing about her. *This is no good*, he thought. *I can't get her out of my mind, but I still can't picture her face.*

Lorelei was the most compelling woman he had ever met. *She smoked cigarettes, laughed lustily and flirted with him shamelessly. She had the face of an angel and the body of...*

"Captain?" Mr. Barkman poked his head through the porthole from the bridge. He held a clipboard in his hand and offered it through the porthole. "Engineering reports, sir."

The image of Lorelei evaporated and Paul Oliver came back to the present. "Very well," he said, taking the clipboard and leafing through the report. Mr. Almogordo wanted to take number one engine off line for maintenance. That was okay. The Haverfield could steam efficiently on three engines. The bad news was with the evaporators. Chiefs Risk and Twitchell were working on them, but the prognosis wasn't good. They would get them running for awhile, then they would go down again. Risk believed the entire system needed an overhaul, but that would mean time in the yard, and the Haverfield's patrol schedule was pretty busy for the next few months. Chief Twitchell stubbornly believed he could single-handedly fix the problem, and spent many hours working on the evaporators, with little success. The fresh water supply was low and dwindling, which meant no fresh water showers. The captain initialed each page of the report and handed it back through the porthole to Mr. Barkman.

"Ask Mr. Almogordo to come to the bridge," the captain said, and returned to scanning the horizon.

Pedro Almogordo came up to the bridge wiping his hands on an oily rag. His face was gleaming with sweat and his khakis were soaked through in many places. He smiled and nodded to Mr. Barkman, then joined the captain on the flying bridge.

"You wanted to see me, captain?"

"Pedro, your men are doing an incredible job down there in engineering, and I've read the reports, but I like to get information first hand. Any hope for the evaps?"

"Well sir, as we speak Chief Twitchell has the evaps up and running, though I don't know how long they'll be on line." Mr. Almogordo shook his head in wonder. "That Twitchell is a hell of an engineer, sir. He's working his butt off down there. I don't know how he did it, but we're producing fresh water."

The captain nodded. "Let's continue the rationing for a few days and give the evaps a chance to catch up. We'll be back in port in a week. I'll see what I can do to get us a little yard time."

"Aye, sir." The engineering officer left the bridge smiling, and as he slid down the ladder to the 02 level Captain Oliver could hear him singing, "I'm a ramblin' wreck from Georgia Tech and a hell of an engineer!"

* * * * *

Sailors began gathering on the fantail just before 1930. Except for the on-duty watch, almost all the deck force was there to hear Mr. MacDonald's lecture, and men from other divisions had joined them. They weren't sure what to expect. Many were there out of curiosity, some out of boredom, and some, like the deck force, were there because they respected and liked the First Division commander.

It was a warm evening, the sun just beginning to touch the horizon where it would sink into the water slowly, spectacularly. In about half an hour the sun would disappear and the sky would darken. The wind would pick up and bring a welcome breeze across the faces of the men gathered on the fantail. Many smoked cigarettes and chatted quietly, waiting for the lieutenant to appear.

It was Mr. MacDonald who had assigned the deck crew the nickname, 'Havernauts.' He identified them with the story of Jason and the Argonauts and the search for the golden fleece. As he was fond of saying, "Out here in coconut country, away from the prying eyes of the fleet, we tend to be a relaxed and slap-happy group. We don't get the scrutiny a regular fleet ship gets, but we also don't get the fresh supplies or spare parts. We are on our own most of the time, yet we, too are on a quest. Not for the golden fleece, but for something more important: Our identity. We must each seek that identity inside ourselves. And we must seek it as a team, each man bonded in loyalty to the other, each man willing to sacrifice for his shipmates." That night he would tell them a true story of teamwork, of loyalty, and of sacrifice.

Mr. MacDonald came up the aft ladder to the fantail with his mimeographed pages under his arm and smiled, a little embarrassed by the scattering of applause. He pulled himself up on one of the torpedo tubes and looked around at his audience. *Pretty good turnout,* he thought.

"Good evening, men," he said cheerfully. He was answered by a chorus of 'good evenings.' MacDonald smiled and went on. "How many of you had fathers or other relatives in World War Two?" Most of the men raised their hands. "Good. And how many of you had relatives in the Navy in World War Two?" Many of the hands stayed raised. "Well, I'm sure you heard a lot of stories about the Navy, right?" Heads nodded up and down. "Then how many of you can tell me what incident brought the United States into the war?"

Tanner raised his hand and MacDonald nodded to him. "The Japanese attack on Pearl Harbor?" he ventured.

"Correct. The American Pacific fleet was stationed at Pearl Harbor. The strength of the American Navy in 1941, and of most all naval powers for that matter, was the battleship. As many of you know, we lost several battleships in that attack. They were in port and almost defenseless. The most famous of these was the USS Arizona. Over two thousand sailors died on that ship, including the man our ship was named for, James Wallace Haverfield." He looked around at the men gathered in front of him. He had their attention. Most had forgotten about Ensign Haverfield. MacDonald was determined they would not forget again.

"The Japanese planned to destroy the American Pacific fleet at Pearl Harbor. If successful, they would have become the masters of the Pacific from Hawaii to Japan. But naval power was changing at that time in history. The battleship was slowly being replaced by the aircraft carrier as the main power of the Navy. The Japanese knew and appreciated this. That's why they built so many aircraft carriers and that's why Admiral Yamamoto, the architect of the Pearl Harbor strike force was desperate to find and destroy the American carriers. But thanks to an admiral by the name of Halsey, our carriers were at sea that Sunday morning, and escaped the attack. And that is the reason, my friends, the American Navy was able to survive to harass the Japs across the Pacific. An American carrier actually bombed the Jap homeland for the first time. Anyone remember the Doolittle raid on Tokyo? That was launched from the USS Hornet, one of our carriers. Then in May, the Americans stopped the Japs from invading Port Moresby in the battle of Coral Sea." Mr. MacDonald gathered up the mimeographed sheets and held them in the air. "But the battle which turned the tide in the Pacific and set the Japs back on their heels took place almost exactly twenty-one years ago, in June, nineteen forty two, and its focal point was the island of Midway." He began passing out his mimeographed maps. "The Japs wanted Midway because of its strategic location, and because the island had one of the biggest landing strips in the area, a place where the Japs could station aircraft and use as a jumping off point for attacks on Hawaii and eventually the American west coast. Midway also provided an eastern defensive line which would make further attacks on their home island impossible." The men began to look at their maps.

"Those were the early days of the Pacific war, and America was still reeling from the Pearl Harbor attack. The Japanese were the power in the Pacific, having spent many years building up their naval forces. In June 1942 America was scrambling to catch up and hoping to stall the Japs long enough to allow our great industrial machine to gain momentum. We were outnumbered, outgunned and outmanned. We were, you might say, a prohibitive underdog.

"But the American command at Pearl Harbor had a significant advantage. They had broken the Japanese naval code and knew the next big attack was going to be against Midway." Mr. Mac looked around at the men, all of whom were studying their maps or listening intently. "The Japs' plan was to feint an attack on the Aleutian Islands to draw the American carriers away from Midway, allowing them to take the strategic island with little or no resistance. The Marines defending Midway were greatly outnumbered, but they dug in and waited, doggedly determined to fight off the Japanese attack when it came.

"They planned to attack and destroy the American carrier forces as they turned back from the feint on the Aleutians to help defend Midway. It might have worked, too, if the Jap naval code hadn't been compromised." Mr. Mac looked at his notes and stuck an unlit cigar in his mouth. The men remained silent, waiting for the story to continue. A soft, steady breeze wafted over the fantail, bringing with it the refreshing smell of salt air.

"The American Navy had taken up positions northeast of Midway Island where they would wait, watch and listen for the approach of the Jap fleet. Task Force sixteen, as it was known, was commanded not by Bull Halsey, but by Rear Admiral Ray Spruance. Halsey was in the hospital in

Pearl Harbor fighting a case of the shingles." He chuckled and looked around at the men. "That musta pissed him off something awful," MacDonald said, grinning at the thought of Bull Halsey in a hospital bed instead of pacing the deck of the USS Enterprise.

"And the Americans had another surprise for the Japs. The USS Yorktown, the carrier severely damaged in the Coral Sea and thought by the Japs to be sunk, was quickly repaired in Pearl. Task Force seventeen was formed around her under Rear Admiral Jack Fletcher and sent to support Task Force sixteen." He slowly lit his cigar and blew the smoke into the breeze. "The Japs didn't expect the American carriers to be anywhere near them, and they certainly didn't expect the Yorktown to be involved. They thought they had approached Midway completely undetected, but scout planes from Midway, searching for the Japanese fleet, had spotted the main battle group and radioed the course and distance to Admiral Nimitz in Pearl, and he forwarded it to the *two* American task forces." First Division's lieutenant took a deep breath and continued.

"That's when things started to get a little dicey," he said, referring to his notes. "Here's what happened: Along with support ships of all types, there were four Jap carriers, named Akagi, Kaga, Soryu and Hiryu. This is important for you to know, so write it down and I'll explain later." He repeated the names again, slowly. The men wrote on their maps. "These four carriers were going to pull double duty that day, first arming their planes with bombs and bombing Midway in preparation for the invasion; then rearming the planes with torpedoes to repel the expected counter-attack from the American carrier task force returning from the feint on the Aleutians. But remember," Mr. Mac held his cigar up like a pointer. "The Japs didn't know there were two American task forces, and they didn't expect to see the Yorktown, they thought they had sunk her. But the biggest surprise was that those American carrier task forces were not rushing back from the north. They were just over the horizon." MacDonald stuck the now dead cigar between his teeth and grinned, staring over the men's heads to the darkening horizon behind them. The men turned and looked back. The last of the sun's light was ebbing slowly into the horizon, brushing the low clouds with colors from all over the spectrum. It wasn't hard to imagine that battle fought between two powerful navies; the battle that would turn the tide in a world war.

"It was fought in these waters, this ocean, roughly half-way from here to Pearl Harbor," Mac continued quietly. The men stared at the horizon. The fantail was completely silent and the only sounds that could be heard belonged to the Pacific Ocean.

R.J. believed if he strained very hard to listen, the Pacific would whisper up those sounds from many fathoms deep and he would be able to hear the clamor and roar of that battle. In his imagination he heard the sounds clearly, and he stared down into the deep blue ocean, trying to see through the dark waters to what lay below. *What did Uncle Lloyd used to say? A lot of good men are sleeping at the bottom of the Pacific.*

"The Japs attacked Midway hard and heavy," Mr. MacDonald went on.

"Their bombers dropped holy hell on the island and their fighters, Zeros, or Zekes as they were called, pretty much destroyed the Marine fighter planes defending the island. Amazingly, they didn't do much real damage to the island installations."

Mr. Mac's cigar had gone out and he paused to re-light it, puffing hard until the tip glowed orange. Silhouetted against the graying sky, his hair blowing in the wind, it was easy to imagine him on the deck of one of the American aircraft carriers, steaming headlong toward the overpowering Japanese fleet. "The three American carriers launched their torpedo bombers at the Jap carriers. Remember these squadrons, men. They were VT-3, VT-6 and VT-8. These were the true heroes of the Battle of Midway, even though none of them made hits on the Japs. In fact they were almost completely wiped out by the Zeros guarding the Jap fleet. But they continued their torpedo runs at those carriers, diving through exploding flack from the Jap ships and a rain of fire from the Zeroes. Can you imagine the bravery of those pilots? They undoubtedly saw the systematic destruction of the planes ahead of them, and still they attacked right into the teeth of the Jap anti-aircraft fire. In VT-8 only one pilot survived. A few others were shot down and captured by the Japs, who interrogated them, then executed them, throwing their decapitated bodies into the ocean. But those brave torpedo pilots accomplished one thing: They pulled the Jap air cover away and the skies were open for the American dive bombers to attack the Jap carriers with impunity, catching their bombers on deck, switching their payloads from bombs to torpedoes. They attacked swiftly, one after another making his bombing run, dropping his bombs and pulling up and away. In six minutes three Jap carriers were burning. Six minutes!"

The men's eyes were bright and attentive, some smiling and nodding, others sitting mesmerized. MacDonald continued.

"The Kaga and Akagi were destroyed by planes from the Enterprise and the bomber pilots from the Yorktown got the Soryu. A lot of Jap pilots had to ditch in the ocean because they couldn't land on the burning carriers."

"Tough shit!" someone said. Nervous laughter and nods of agreement rippled through the audience as Mr. Mac continued his story.

"The remaining carrier, the Hiryu, managed to launch her planes against the Yorktown and severely damaged her. She was attacked again and eventually had to be abandoned. The Enterprise's dive bombers caught up with Hiryu later that day and destroyed her. For all practical purposes, the battle was over. The Japanese admiral commanding the fleet, Nagumo was his name, transferred his flag from the burning Akagi, tucked his tail between his legs and retreated west."

The lieutenant sat back on a torpedo tube and let the story sink in. "We had no right winning that battle," he said, slowly shaking his head. "We got lucky when we broke the Jap code and those incredibly brave torpedo bomber pilots sacrificed their lives so the dive bombers could attack without getting torn up by the Zekes. We got all the luck that day. Every American in that battle was a hero, especially the men from VT-3, VT-6 and VT-8. God bless them. The Japs had lost the momentum they gained on

December seven. They were no longer the supreme naval power in the Pacific. The odds had been evened, and the Japs never recovered." MacDonald blinked away tears and took a deep breath, exhaling slowly. "And those four Jap carriers, the Akagi, the Kaga, the Hiryu and the Soryu?" He made eye contact with every man on the fantail, slowly looking from man to man, making certain they were listening. "Those were the four Japanese aircraft carriers that attacked Pearl Harbor." He let his words hang in the air. Smiles broke out among the men.

"You know what they say, fellas. Revenge is sweet!"

The men sat quietly, some nodding and staring at the deck, some gazing out at the horizon as Mr. MacDonald bid them goodnight and returned to officer country. No one wanted to leave the fantail. They stood and mingled at the lifeline, staring into the Pacific, each alone with his thoughts.

R.J. strained again to listen to the ghosts of the torpedo bombers from VT-3, VT-6 and VT-8. He could almost hear them yelling and shouting as they attacked the Jap carriers and were blown out of the sky, crashing into the sea. *So many brave men*, he thought. He stared at the Pacific, rolling gently in the warm tropical night, and imagined those pilots roaring down at the Jap carriers and being systematically destroyed. "God bless you," he whispered. He turned and walked down the ladder to the First Division compartment.

TWENTY TWO

The tropical summer heated up. The days grew longer and the work seemed harder because of the heavy heat and humidity. Even early in the morning, on the fantail to watch the sunrise, R.J. could feel the oppression of the humid air. Battling bouts of depression, the men moved more slowly, more deliberately as they maintained the appearance of the ship. Painted spots seemed to take forever to dry, and perspiration soaked through the crew's shirts in a matter of minutes.

The ship was in port through the end of June and the first week of July, so the crew couldn't depend on ocean breezes to cool them as they did when they were underway. Tempers grew short and the animosity between R.J. and Lester finally came to a head. It was late afternoon and a rare June rainstorm pelted the ship for about an hour. The deck crew went below to get out of the rain, and the compartment was stifling with heat and too many bodies in too small a space. Lester was leaning against his bunk when R.J. entered the compartment and tried to squeeze past him, bumping him slightly.

"Fuckin' Wog!" Lester spat. "Watch where the fuck you're goin'!"

"Screw you, Gomer!" R.J. answered, curling his lip and pointing his finger into Lester's chest.

R.J. saw the punch coming and ducked. Lester's fist sailed over R.J.'s head and R.J. countered with an overhand right. It wasn't a particularly hard punch, but it caught the surprised Lester square on the jaw and his knees buckled as he grabbed R.J. in a bear hug. They held on to each other and wrestled standing up until Tanner and Sonny stepped between them and broke it up.

"Knock it off!" Tanner warned. "We don't throw punches at each other. You both know that!"

Big Queen came into the compartment and noticed the commotion. "What's this all about, ladies?" he demanded, scowling at the knot of sailors gathered around the two combatants.

"Nothin', Boats," R.J. said, staring at Lester.

"That right Lester?" Queen asked, cocking his head and squinting.

"Nothin'," Lester said, and turned to his bunk. Queen nodded, looking at R.J. and Lester. "Good," he said, and climbed the aft ladder to the fantail.

"You guys done now?" Sonny asked, looking to R.J. then to Lester. Both nodded. "'Cause y'all oughtta be ashamed of yourselves." He looked at Lester. "You been givin' this guy a lot of shit since he came aboard," he observed. "And you," he looked at R.J. who stared at Lester with an insolent look. "You been runnin' your mouth every chance you get. I think it's 'bout time y'all buried the hatchet."

"Yeah," Tanner agreed. "We're a team, y'know? This shit can't go on in this deck crew. I say you find a way to work it out so's you can get along."

R.J. and Lester stared at each other self-consciously. Neither wanted to fight, but neither wanted to be the first to apologize. Finally, R.J. put out his hand to Lester. "Sorry," he mumbled. "Just lost my temper." *Play the game.*

Lester nodded, relieved. "Yeah, sorry," he said, taking R.J.'s hand and shaking it. Then he grinned and rubbed his jaw. "You can't hit for shit," he said.

R.J. rubbed his hand, wincing. "You got a hard head, man." The conflict was over.

"I'll get you back in a couple of weeks, Wog," Lester said. "When we cross the equator."

The conversation picked up in the compartment as the Shellbacks among the deck crew began talking about the equator crossing scheduled for the middle of July.

"Equator!" Tanner shouted. "Man, I'm gonna enjoy this!" He looked around at Pea, R.J. and the Sample brothers. "But you ain't!" He pointed at them.

"What happens when we cross the equator?" Andy asked.

"You'll see, Wog," Tanner answered. The other Shellbacks laughed.

"Alright deck apes!" Queen yelled down the hatch from the fantail. "The rain has stopped. Get yer lily-white asses on deck and turn to!" The deck crew filed up the ladder and began swabbing the water off the fantail.

"So what's this equator crossing about?" Andy asked no one in particular.

"If you ain't been across," Jefferson explained, "you a pollywog and you got to go through an initiation." He stopped swabbing and wrung out his swab in a bucket.

"How many fuckin' initiations you got on this ship?" Gino asked incredulously. "Man, I shoulda stood in Brooklyn!"

TWENTY THREE

On Monday, July 8, the Haverfield set sail for another round of island surveys. This patrol was to take them southeast through the Truk islands and south to the equator, where they would cross, conduct the traditional initiation ceremonies, and return to Guam with a one hundred percent 'Shellback' crew.

From the time they hit the breakwater and steamed into the open sea, the Shellbacks began harassing and tormenting the pollywogs. Shellbacks were allowed to grow out their beards, pollywogs had to shave every day. Shellbacks were allowed to don pirate clothing; bandanas on their heads, patches on their eyes, gold rings attached to their ears and large brass buckles adorning their dungaree trousers. When a Shellback confronted a pollywog asking, "What are you, slimeball?" the pollywog was required to answer, "A scurvy pollywog, sir!"

No harassment was allowed in sensitive compartments such as the CIC (Combat Information Center), bridge, radio shack, engineering spaces, sonar or pilot house, and no harassment of pollywog officers was allowed until 1600 on the day before the crossing. Any pollywog standing a watch was immune until he came off watch. The ship's arrival at the equator was planned for 0500 on the morning of the nineteenth.

Part of the initiation was the manufacturing of the Shellback 'shillelagh' which consisted of manila line woven together into a wide, flat paddle-like weapon used to 'spank' the pollywogs as they crawled through a gauntlet of Shellbacks during the initiation finale. One favorite method of 'seasoning' the shillelagh was to soak it in saltwater for several days, then let it dry out in the sun. The result was a very hard, stiff paddle which could raise welts on a pollywog's hindquarters, which was, of course, the point. The Shellbacks paraded around the ship with their shillelaghs attached loosely onto their belts, swinging threateningly as they walked.

During island landings it was business as usual, with no Shellback/pollywog interaction allowed. The landings went smoothly on the first three islands, but early on the morning of the seventeenth, steaming south toward the island of Nukuoro Atoll just two days before the equator crossing, radar picked up a surface contact which appeared to be steaming away from the island. It was 0400 and the morning watch had just come on duty. Mr. MacDonald was the OOD, R.J. was at the starboard wing lookout position, and Sonny Metzner was on the helm.

"Sir, I have a contact bearing dead ahead," Cotton called. His face, peering at the radar scope, had an eerie green glow to it.

Lieutenant MacDonald came in from the flying bridge and studied the radar scope. R.J. lifted his binoculars and scanned the horizon ahead, trying to spot the contact. MacDonald came out on the starboard wing and looked up at the 04 level lookouts.

"You men see anything?" he called.

Pancho and Andy Sample on the 04 level had their binoculars trained straight ahead, scanning for the contact. "Nothing yet, sir,"

156

Pancho called down.

"I've got a port running light just off the starboard bow, sir," R.J. announced, his binoculars trained on the contact.

"Contact, sir!" Pancho yelled. "Starboard bow!"

"I got 'im too, sir!" Andy announced.

Mr. MacDonald stood on the wing next to R.J. and focused his binoculars on the contact. "Looks like he's moving away to port," he mumbled. "Away from the island." He turned back to the pilot house. "Give me a bearing on the contact," he ordered.

Cotton peered into the scope. "Bearing one four five degrees, sir!"

"Very well. Helmsman, come to course one four five," MacDonald ordered. "Let's intercept him. Probably a Jap fisherman." He kept his binoculars trained on the contact.

The atmosphere on the bridge became electric. Everyone was instantly alert and focused. "Messenger!" MacDonald called. "Wake the captain and tell him we have a surface contact that appears to be a fishing boat. Advise him we are steaming to intercept."

"Aye, aye sir!" Jefferson replied and stepped through the passageway toward the captain's cabin.

Cotton looked up from the scope. "He's speeding up, sir," he said.

"All ahead full!" MacDonald ordered. "Bearing to the contact!"

"One three zero, sir!"

"Come to course one *two* zero!" MacDonald ordered. "We'll cut the bastard off."

"One two zero, aye sir!" Sonny smoothly eased the ship onto the new course.

The captain arrived in the pilot house looking immaculate in his starched khakis, as usual. Captain Oliver always looked like a Navy recruiting poster, even when he had been awakened in the wee hours of the morning.

"What's the situation, Mac?" he asked calmly, peering at the radar scope.

"We have a surface contact just off the starboard bow, sir," MacDonald reported. "He's moving off to port, away from the island, and we're moving to cut him off."

"Very well," Captain Oliver replied, and calmly drew himself a cup of coffee from the pilot house pot.

"Do you wish to take the conn, sir?" MacDonald asked.

"Not necessary, Mac," the captain replied, sipping the hot coffee and making a face. "Continue the pursuit."

Mr. MacDonald and the crew on the bridge grinned at each other. This was going to be their show.

Nukuoro Atoll seemed to rise out of the sea and move to starboard as the ship came closer to the island in pursuit of the slow-moving fishing boat. The Haverfield was closing the gap quickly.

"He's slowing down, sir!" Cotton called.

"Very well," MacDonald answered, his binoculars trained on the boat.

Captain Oliver stood on the flying bridge. He watched the fishing boat through his binoculars held in his right hand and sipped the coffee with his left.

"It appears he stopped, sir," Cotton called.

"Very well." MacDonald smiled. *Well, at least he's not stupid,* he thought.

The captain poked his head into the pilot house through the porthole from the flying bridge. "Mr. MacDonald," he said calmly. "A moment of your time, please."

MacDonald joined the captain on the flying bridge and they spoke quietly, their heads close together. When MacDonald returned to the pilot house he was grinning broadly.

"Jefferson," he called. "It's 0500, and we're going to wake up the crew a little early this morning."

"Sound General Quarters, sir?" Jefferson asked.

"No, just sound reveille," MacDonald replied. He nodded toward the Japanese fishing boat. "This bird isn't armed."

"Aye, aye sir," Jefferson replied. He stepped to the 1-MC and took his bosun's pipe out of his pocket. He pressed the 'on' button and blew 'attention.' "Reveille, reveille, all hands heave out and trice up!"

MacDonald, still grinning, motioned for Jefferson to come into the pilot house where everyone could hear his next order. "Pass the word," MacDonald said. "Tell the crew we've intercepted a Japanese fishing boat and I want all hands to man the starboard side. Especially the Shellbacks. Tell 'em to don their pirate gear." He looked around the bridge, grinning. "We're going to give these people something to think about." The men on the bridge were grinning, suddenly aware of what was about to happen.

Normally, a crew hates to be awakened before reveille because it usually means the ship is conducting another tedious drill. This morning, as the word was passed from compartment to compartment, the men jumped out of their racks and cheerfully took positions on the starboard side, most of them wearing pirate garb.

The Haverfield slowed and took position about fifty yards from the fishing boat's port side. Dawn was casting a pale light on the morning, and the fishing boat was clearly visible, its net booms neatly secured. Rust spotted the bulkheads of the boat, and it was obvious the crew didn't spend a lot of time on maintenance. They weren't fishing, yet. Mr. MacDonald picked up the radio telephone and dialed the transceiver to the international frequency. He spoke loudly and clearly into the mouthpiece. "Japanese fishing boat, this is the U.S.S. Haverfield! You are encroaching in United States Territorial waters. You are not allowed to fish these waters. You must leave the area immediately or stand by to be boarded! Over."

R.J. watched the crew of the small fishing boat come out on deck. He smiled at the shocked looks on their faces. When they spotted the Haverfield 'pirates' they were clearly terrified. The Shellbacks were unshaven and dressed in various pirate gear. They relished their roles, snarling and sneering, waving their fists in the air and swinging their shillelaghs in wide circles at the Japanese crew, who simultaneously bowed to the Haverfield over and over again.

The bridge became very quiet as everyone waited for the Japanese to reply. After what seemed like minutes, but was actually only a few seconds, a crackling static came over the speaker, then a faint voice replied in broken English, "Haberfill, this Kioshi Maru. We no fish. We leave now."

"What are we gonna do with them, sir?" R.J. asked Mr. MacDonald.

"Nothing we can do," the OOD answered, "unless we catch 'em red-handed. But we sure scared the crap out of 'em!"

The captain stood on the flying bridge, watching through his binoculars as the Kioshi Maru moved away, with as much haste as it could muster, toward international waters. He chuckled softly to himself. Those fishermen were going to have quite a story to tell when they got home.

* * * * *

Chief Twitchell was fuming. They had only been out to sea a little over a week and he had completely exhausted his supply of scotch. That shithead at the supply depot he bribed so he'd sell him more whiskey had shorted him, telling him there was no more in inventory. It had taken a long time to cultivate the relationship with that senior supply chief. He suspected that gook Bobby Gamboa was behind it. He couldn't buy enough from the Mocombo Club to last him. That would look suspicious. Besides, he'd have to pay retail. Now he was fresh out, and he was not pleased.

To make matters worse, the ship was headed for the equator. Chief Twitchell had been across the equator several times, but had never earned a Shellback card. Twitchell didn't believe in that stupid tradition, and had made it clear to Lieutenant Almogordo and everyone else in engineering. He didn't believe in it. Period. He wasn't about to participate in that humiliating initiation, crawling around on the deck in his skivvies with common sailors, most of them niggers. He'd be damned if he was going to cavort with niggers!

On previous ships and previous cruises, the chief had stayed in the engineering spaces, taking care of the machinery while the monkeys and apes conducted their ridiculous ceremony up on deck. Maybe it was time to get out of the Navy before the dirt people took over completely. Was a time when white people meant something to the Navy. Now that fucking Kennedy and his liberal asshole family were perpetuating the criminal desegregation that was started by that cocksucker, Harry Truman. They all ought to be shot, goddammit! He rifled through his locker one more time, tossing clothes on the deck in a desperate search for more scotch. Shit! Nothing there.

The crew knew about Twitchell's refusal to participate in the crossing ceremony, and it did not endear him to them. Behind his back, they mocked and made fun of him, calling him the seventh fleet's oldest pollywog. When he came up on deck in the morning, hungover and unsteady, his hands shaking, he earned his Haverfield nickname. Rafer Sample looked at him, amused, and said, "Here come Chief Twitchy." Of course, he said it low enough that Twitchell couldn't hear it, but the nickname stuck.

Mr. Almogordo tried to persuade Twitchell to participate in the equator crossing initiation. He cornered the chief just after the confrontation with the Japanese fishing boat and tried to reason with him.

"The captain wants a one hundred percent Shellback crew when we return to Guam," he said. "He's not going to like it if you screw it up for him."

"Is there anything in Navy regulations that says I have to participate?" the fat chief asked stubbornly.

"No, chief, and you know that," the engineering officer said. "But the whole crew is looking forward to it, and you are a part of this crew, are you not?"

"I do my job, sir," Twitchell replied, frowning. "I think the tradition is juvenile and unless I'm ordered to take part, I'll stay in engineering while it's going on."

"I'm not ordering you, chief..."

"Thank you, sir." Twitchell excused himself and went below. He was still a little unsteady, and he wanted to grab a quick cat-nap before the next island landing. He crawled into his bunk with his clothes on and fell to sleep at once, snoring loudly and sweating profusely.

At 1600 on the eighteenth, ship's work was knocked off and the Shellbacks held a meeting in the bosun's locker. It was close quarters with fifty-odd Shellbacks crammed in, but their spirits were high and they had some planning to do. The pollywogs would have their chance to rally and try to take over the ship, which meant reaching the signal bridge and hauling down the Jolly Roger the Shellbacks had hoisted on the starboard yardarm. The traditional pollywog revolt would take place after evening chow, between 1800 and 2400, by which time the Shellbacks would be back in total control, and would continue to be in control until after the crossing at 0600 the next morning. But for a few hours, the pollywogs were allowed to fight back. They started by congregating on the focsul, locking down the deck hatch and jumping up and down on the deck, creating a distracting din in the locker below.

The pollywogs had to adhere to certain rules. No punches were allowed to be thrown. No violence of any kind would be tolerated except good-natured wrestling. Pain was not allowed to be inflicted, but they could throw water balloons and hose down the Shellbacks with salt-water hoses. If they 'captured' a Shellback they could tie him up, shave his head or mustache, rub him down with axle grease mixed with coffee grounds, and similar antics. The Shellbacks were allowed to do the same types of things to the pollywogs. If the Jolly Roger was captured, a pollywog victory would be claimed and the Shellbacks humiliated. The goal of the Shellbacks was to prevent the capture of the Jolly Roger until midnight when the pollywogs' revolt was officially over, and the traditional Shellback hazing began.

The Haverfield pollywogs were well organized and outnumbered the Shellbacks by about two to one. They were at a disadvantage because the Shellbacks held the high ground and possessed all but one of the available fire hoses. Still, the pollywogs put up a valiant fight to capture the Jolly Roger. They started by isolating the Shellbacks in the bosun locker. Rafer and Andy, along with Gino and Pea, tied down the aft hatch to the locker and resisted the Shellbacks' attempts to force it open. As a result, the Shellbacks had only one way to escape the bosun locker. They had to climb the ladder and crawl out the small deck hatch on the focsul. They could only come out one at a time, and were met by R.J., armed with a fire hose equipped with a suicide nozzle, a small-bored nozzle that sent out a power-ful, narrow stream of water. As they popped out of the hatch, R.J. took their feet out from under them with the hose and they were pelted with water balloons and various other non-lethal objects. Meanwhile, the signal bridge was under siege, with several pollywogs trying to charge up the lad-der to the 03 level, only to be repelled time after time by Anselmi, Sonny Metzner, Tanner and Pancho Cortez who were armed with water balloons and two fire hoses. The signal bridge defenders threw back several polly-wog attempts to storm up the ladder, and by dark the Jolly Roger's position was secure.

The pollywogs were forced to fight a retreating action, being steadily pushed back to the fantail by the force of the fire hoses, where most of them broke and dropped through the aft hatch to First Division's compartment. There they were 'captured' by Queen, Lester, Cotton and Jefferson who had assembled a large contingent of Shellbacks. The pollywogs were forced to lie at attention in the deck crew's bunks, awaiting the bewitching hour and being constantly harangued by Shellbacks in pirate garb. Except for R.J. Since he was largely considered one of the main leaders of the pollywog revolt, he was tied spread-eagled to a landing raft on the fantail and soaked down with saltwater every half hour until midnight. The Sample brothers, Gino and Pea were captured in the bosun's locker and lashed to the deck with half-inch nylon line. The pollywog revolt had been crushed.

At midnight, R.J. was untied (after being soaked down one more time) and brought to the messdecks where several Shellbacks had gathered for pollywog rickshaw races, consisting of teams of two pollywogs, one in front and one in back. The man in front would balance on his hands, in push-up position, his feet held up by the man in back, who 'wheelbarreled' the front man, propelling him down the deck as fast as he could. The race course led down the messdecks, across the passageway to the engineering compart-ment, through the compartment and down the passageway back to the messdecks, ending at the starting point. It was a time trial, and Queen kept the times with a stopwatch. All along the race course, Shellbacks lined the passageways, yelling encouragement to the pollywogs and throwing blan-kets and pillows in their path to slow them down. Two laps were required to finish each time trial, and the pollywogs would change position after the first lap, the man in front moving to the back, the man in back assuming the 'wheelbarrel' position. It was great fun...for the Shellbacks.

Rafer was stationed on the port side of the ship and Andy was stationed on the starboard side. Both had whistles around their necks and grappling hooks at the end of about six fathoms of line. They were required to throw the grappling hook into the ocean and try to catch the equator. They would reel in the grappling hook, blow the whistle and announce, "Sir, this scurvy pollywog has not caught the equator!" Then they would repeat the procedure.

Ensigns P.J. Jones and Rodney Thompson were the only officers who were not Shellbacks. They stood in their skivvies on the 04 level, each with a long, three inch brass pipe which they used as telescopes. They held the heavy pipes up to their eyes and searched the horizon for the equator. When a Shellback would order them to report, they would call out, "Sir, this scurvy pollywog has not spotted the equator!"

On the fantail, Lester, Sonny Metzner and Queen had assembled several pollywogs and were conducting close order drills. The pollywogs stood shoulder to shoulder and followed commands to 'left face,' 'about face,' 'forward march,' 'to the rear march,' and all the time they had to maintain shoulder to shoulder contact. Any pollywog who broke contact was dispatched to the messdecks to participate in the rickshaw races. The marching orders were barked quickly, one after another, and almost guaranteed the pollywogs would stumble and fall.

Finally, at 0200 the word was passed from the bridge to knock off pollywog punishment and allow the pollywogs a little sleep time. The actual equator initiation would begin at 0600 and the pollywogs would need their rest.

It seemed to R.J. that he had just closed his eyes when reveille was sounded. Half asleep and in a dreamlike state, he imagined that pirates had taken over the ship and were throwing the crew overboard. In fact, Shellbacks dressed as pirates came storming into the compartment, yelling and slapping their shillelaghs on the sides of the bunks and on the metal lockers, creating a numbing din in the small compartment.

R.J. shook himself awake and rolled out of his bunk, dropping gingerly to the deck. He was having a hard time waking up, and as he looked around the compartment, it was obvious the other pollywogs were in the same shape.

"Shower shoes and skivvy shorts only, you scurvy pigs!" Tanner yelled, swinging his shillelagh like a lariat. "Up on the focsul for your shower! Go!"

The pollywogs scrambled up the ladder in their skivvies and made their way to the focsul. It was a cool morning, the sun not quite breaking through the cloud cover, which hugged the horizon. The ship was steaming at twenty knots, plunging its bow into the sea and sending a heavy blanket of salt spray showering over the pollywogs, who huddled together on the focsul trying to stay warm.

R.J. looked up at the signal bridge and saw the Jolly Roger flying proudly from the yardarm. The Shellbacks had gathered on the 02 level, safe from the spray, and they yelled and chanted obscenities, swinging those damn shillelaghs in the air. He couldn't believe how cold it was near the equator. It got worse when fire hoses from the 02 level erupted and shot more salt water over the focsul, soaking the already cold and shivering pollywogs.

It was time for pollywog chow. The miserable group of pollywogs was marched into the messdecks and issued metal trays with no silverware. As they passed through the chow line, Hawkins, dressed as a pirate and grinning broadly, two of his teeth blacked out with shoe polish, heaped onto their trays a mixture which appeared to be garbage. There were eggshells, potato peelings, coffee grounds, corned beef hash and various pieces of vegetables all mixed together, floating in a gray-green sauce. The pollywogs were ordered to sit on the deck and eat with their hands.

"I don' want no slimey pollywog sittin' in my booths," Hawkins declared. "Y'all ain't even good enough for the deck!"

"Eat it all, Wogs!" Lester yelled, walking up and down the deck between the pollywogs. "When you done, you better tell me how delicious it is!"

"Anybody pukes you gotta eat that too!" Big Queen bellowed. He had a red bandana tied around his head and a patch covering one eye. He looked uglier than usual. "We don't waste no food on the equator!"

Tanner moved among the pollywogs with a squirt-type oil gun in his hand. "This hot sauce is my own private concoction," he said, squirting a nasty, foul smelling yellow liquid on the pollywogs' trays. "It'll make everything taste better."

He grinned at R.J. and squirted the liquid on his food. R.J. winced at the smell.

"Eat up, Wog!" Tanner ordered.

R.J. closed his eyes and picked up some of the chow with his fingers, sticking it into his mouth. He gagged at the taste. Tanner's special sauce tasted worse than it smelled. It seemed to be a mixture of diesel fuel, Tabasco and orange juice. R.J. swallowed quickly and gagged again.

Tanner squatted down next to R.J. "Ain't that delicious?" he demanded.

"Yes, sir, honorable Shellback sir," R.J. replied. "That's delicious, sir." Tanner seemed pleased and moved among the rest of the pollywogs, liberally dispensing his special sauce and asking the question the wogs had grown accustomed to hearing.

"What are you, slimewads?"

"We are scurvy pollywogs, sir!" came the reply.

Chow time came mercifully to an end, and the pollywogs were marched aft to First Division's compartment. As they filed into the compartment, Shellbacks smeared numbers on their backs with black shoe polish. R.J. received the number twelve. They were then ordered to sit on the deck with their heads between their knees and await the calling out of their numbers.

Up on the fantail the Shellbacks were making a lot of noise, jumping up and down, pounding the deck with their shillelaghs and screaming down the hatch at the pollywogs, who were huddled shivering with cold and nervous with anticipation. R.J. just wanted it to be over. Jefferson walked among them, swinging his shillelagh and threatening them with various forms of physical suffering.

Up on the fantail, Sonny Metzner stuck his head down through the hatch and yelled, "Number one, get your scurvy ass up here!"

The first pollywog climbed the ladder and squeezed through the hatch, aided by Jefferson's shillelagh popping him on the ass from the bottom of the ladder, sending him shooting through the hatch. The noise on the fantail increased and Sonny once again stuck his head through the hatch.

"Number two, get your slimy ass up here!"

One by one the pollywogs went up the ladder, helped by a stinging shot from Jefferson's shillelagh. He cackled loudly with each crack of his shillelagh. The noise on the fantail was deafening. Shouts, screamed obscenities and raucous laughter came drifting down into the compartment, increasing the discomfort of the pollywogs huddled below.

R.J. was almost relieved when Sonny stuck his head through the hatch and called, "Number twelve, get your scurvy ass up here!"

R.J. climbed the ladder as quickly as he could, trying to avoid the smack on the ass, but Jefferson was quick and accurate, no doubt from a great deal of practice, and the shillelagh caught R.J. on the buttocks and propelled him through the hatch. *Damn, that stung!*

Up on deck R.J.'s head was forced down, preventing him from seeing what was going on. "Keep your scurvy head down on the non-skid, pollywog!" Tanner yelled into R.J.'s ear. "Do what I tell you and you'll get through this quickly. You understand?"

"Yes sir!" R.J. howled.

Tanner looped a line around R.J.'s neck and led him to the imperial 'judge' who was actually Chief Lyons wearing a wig made from a mop head. He sat behind a small barrel on top of which was placed a two-foot by two-foot piece of plywood, serving as the judge's 'bench.' R.J.'s head was pulled up and his chin placed in a glob of axle grease at the end of the bench.

Chief Lyons looked down at him sternly. "You slimy pollywog," he began, reading from the indictment. "You are charged with fomenting treason and mutiny against our honorable Shellbacks. How doest thou plead?"

Before R.J. could say anything, Chief Lyons brought a large rubber mallet down on his side of the bench, rattling the plywood board, snapping R.J.'s head back. "Guilty as charged," the imperial judge roared. "Take him through the torture chamber!"

Tanner jerked the leash and led R.J. to the first stop. Cotton was the Royal Barber and would give R.J. a haircut, consisting of an inverted Mohawk. Cotton ran a pair of shears down the middle of R.J.'s head and held a mirror to his face. "Lookin' good, huh?" R.J. winced at the sight and was jerked to the next stop.

Big Queen was the Royal Baby. He sat on a folding chair, his knees apart, dressed only in an oversized diaper. His huge belly hung over the diaper and was smeared with axel grease, coffee grounds and a selection of the morning's breakfast.

"This is the Royal Baby," Tanner advised. "Ain't he cute?"

R.J. looked up. Queen still had that red bandana wrapped around his big head. He wore a pair of swimming goggles and had a large brass ring in his nose. He smiled down at R.J. His teeth had been blackened out with shoe polish.

"Yes, he's very cute," R.J. replied, giggling nervously.

"Well, if you think he's so fucking cute, kiss his cute little tummy."

R.J. leaned up to kiss the Baby's tummy and Queen grabbed him by the back of his head and pulled his face in, rubbing it into the goo on his belly. R.J. couldn't breathe and when Queen finally let him go, he gasped for air. Tanner jerked the leash and led him to the next stop. R.J. scrambled along the deck, trying to keep up, and skinned his knees on the non-skid.

Machinists Mate first class Crawford was sitting on another folding chair, a mop on his head. He was dressed in a sheet draped over his shoulders and tied at the waist. His face was made up with mascara and lipstick and two large breasts in the form of battle helmets protruded from his 'gown.'

"This is our Royal Queen," Tanner said, jerking the leash so R.J. had to look up. "Ain't she beeootiful?"

R.J. looked at Crawford and winced. "Yeah, she's beautiful," he replied weakly.

"Nice boobs, right?" Tanner asked.

"Yeah," R.J. replied, a sour look on his face. "Real nice."

"Well then," Tanner said. "Grab a lip-lock on her left boob."

R.J. looked at the Royal Queen's left boob. There was a hole in the sheet covering it and a strange liquid was oozing out of the 'nipple.' Previous pollywogs had already had their mouths on it and R.J. hesitated. Tanner jerked the leash.

"You are insulting our Royal Highness," he bellowed. "You wanna start all over again?"

R.J. put his mouth on the 'boob' and Crawford squeezed the squirt gun he had hidden inside the battle helmet, shooting a sour, terrible tasting liquid into R.J.'s mouth. R.J. sputtered and started to spit it out when Tanner jerked the leash again.

"You spit out the Queen's milk and you start all over again," he warned.

R.J. grimaced and swallowed the nasty liquid. It was hard to keep from upchucking. Tanner jerked him to the next stop.

Chief Whipple, as King Neptune, sat on a chair like the others, a mop on his head, a sheet draped over his shoulder like a Roman tunic. He was wearing a large pair of glasses and held a trident in his right hand. Around his neck he wore a gold medallion. He looked down at R.J. with a royal air and asked softly, "Is this pollywog good enough to be a Royal Shellback?"

"We believe him to be so, your Royal Highness," Tanner replied solemnly.

"Very well," Neptune replied. He looked down at R.J. "Are you eligible to become a Royal Shellback?" he asked.

"Yes, your Royal Highness!" R.J. croaked.

"Very well. Kiss the Royal Toe and crawl the gauntlet!" Neptune commanded.

R.J. looked down at Neptune's toe. It was covered with more grease and coffee grounds, but R.J. leaned down and kissed it. Just as he kissed the toe, Tanner hit him hard on the buttocks with his shillelagh.

"Now comes the fun part," Tanner said, smiling deviously. "But not for you." He jerked the leash and led R.J. to the gauntlet. Several Shellbacks lined the deck on both sides ahead of him, swinging their shillelaghs and yelling and snarling. As R.J. was led slowly through the gauntlet the Shellbacks beat him on the buttocks and hurled insults at him. R.J. tried to speed up, to get through the gauntlet more quickly, but Tanner held him back. Finally they came to the end.

"Now for your Royal Bath," Tanner announced. He led R.J. to a long, canvas tube which was filled with saltwater, grease, stale milk and two weeks' worth of garbage which Hawkins had set aside for the occasion.

"Swim through that and you're a Shellback," Tanner said, pointing to the garbage-filled tube. He leaned down and whispered in R.J.'s ear. "And when they pull you out and ask you what you are, you better say you're a Shellback or you start all over." Tanner winked.

R.J. didn't hesitate. He held his breath and threw himself into the garbage pit, scrambling frantically until he reached the end. Lester was there waiting for him and pulled R.J. up by what was left of his hair.

"What are you?" he screamed into R.J.'s ear.

R.J. sputtered and coughed, gagging at the taste and smell of the garbage. His eyes stung and he could barely see. "I'm a fucking Shellback!" he managed to yell.

Lester smiled benevolently. "Then what are you doing in there?" he asked calmly. "Get out and take a shower, fellow Shellback." He helped R.J. out of the garbage chute and shook his hand, slapping him on the back. Lester grinned broadly at R.J. Something passed between them, and instinctively R.J. knew that his problems with Lester were over.

"I ain't a fuckin' Wog anymore!" R.J. sputtered. Grease and garbage stuck to his face.

"You shore ain't, shipmate," Lester grinned. He wiped R.J.'s face with a towel and handed it to him. "You shore as hell ain't."

R.J. smiled weakly and climbed the ladder to the 02 level where saltwater hoses had been set up. He stood under the hose and washed the garbage, grease and oil from his hair and body. He ached all over and his rear end stung like crazy when the saltwater hit the welts on it, but he didn't care. He was happy. He had finally become a Shellback, and nobody could call him a Boot or a Wog. He had passed an ancient maritime test, and he had emerged a sailor.

After the saltwater shower, R.J. went below to the after crew's head and joined other newly initiated Shellbacks who were taking quick, fresh water showers. He toweled off, dressed in clean dungarees and returned to the 02 level so he could watch the rest of the initiation. His hair felt strange, with the wide swath taken out of the middle, and he knew he was going to have to get a buzz cut. He could still taste that rancid stuff they shot into his mouth, but he didn't care. He was a Shellback, by God.

R.J. stood on the 02 level watching as the last of the scurvy pollywogs were converted into honorable Shellbacks. It was comical, the way they crawled around on leashes, being led to each station and then through the dreaded gauntlet and into the garbage chute. He didn't laugh, though, as funny as the scene was. About twenty minutes had passed since he was crawling along the fantail, and the pain continued to be vivid in his memory, the stinging still felt on his rear end. He wasn't about to laugh at those poor pollywogs. Still, he couldn't help but feel slightly superior to them.

Captain Oliver was not happy returning to port with less than a one-hundred-percent Shellback crew, but there was little he could do about it. There was nothing that said a sailor *had* to participate in the ceremony, but Chief Twitchell was the first man he had ever heard of who declined to take part. Captain Oliver decided not to mention it to anyone. Still, it irritated him because the men were beginning to become a solidified crew. They were getting better and faster responding to the many drills he ran at them, and he could see a bonding, a developing pride between shipmates. As good as Chief Twitchell was at his job, Paul Oliver sensed a belligerence in the man, and vowed to keep informed about the chief's behavior. He knew it only took one bad apple to screw up the barrel, but he didn't want to transfer Twitchell and lose his engineering expertise. After all, the chiefs ran the Navy, and good chiefs were critical to having a good crew.

The captain was glad for a few weeks back in port to rest and work on improving the evaps and the power plant. He was anxious to see Lorelei and he knew she was anxious to see him. He reminded himself to tread lightly with the admiral's wife.

* * * * *

R.J. grinned broadly at the small card he received for crossing the equator:

Domain Of Neptunus Rex

Know ye, that **R.J. Davis, SA** On the 19ᵗʰ day of July, 1963 aboard the
U.S.S. Haverfield (DER-393) Latitude 00-00, Longitude **154-53°E**
appeared into Our Royal Domain, and having been inspected and found worthy
by My Royal Staff, was initiated into the:

Solemn Mysteries of the Ancient Order of the Deep
I command my subjects to honor and respect the bearer of this certificate as
One of Our Trusty Shellbacks.

Lt. William Westerman	**Lt. Francis MacDonald**
Davy Jones	Neptunus Rex
His Royal Scribe	Ruler of the Raging Main

It proclaimed him as a trusty Shellback, something he was very proud of. Since he had first come aboard the Haverfield in March he had been regaled with stories about the equator crossing and the importance of the initiation which would make him a Shellback, transforming him magically into a real sailor. Now it was in his hand, and he did feel transformed. He and the other new Shellbacks were treated differently by the rest of the deck force crew. Even Lester treated him like a shipmate. Now, coming into Apra Harbor after the crossing, R.J. happily took part in tying the ship to the pier and erecting the awning over the fantail. He enthusiastically joined in the washing down of the ship with fresh water, the storing of the survey rafts and other underway gear, and converting the ship to in-port status. He was anxious to join the others at the Mocombo Club, confident that now that he was a trusty Shellback, they would certainly serve him tequila. He was mistaken.

TWENTY FOUR

In late August, Captain Oliver was informed by COMCRUDESPAC that a British destroyer, H.M.S. Triumph, was coming to Guam to conduct underway exercises with the Haverfield. British sailors would come aboard to observe the Haverfield as she ran ASW drills. They would also serve as judges, grading the effectiveness of the Haverfield's crew. Sailors from the Haverfield would board the Triumph and do the same for her crew. These joint exercises would be conducted under the banner of SEATO (South East Asia Treaty Organization) and were designed to further cement the relationship between the two allies.

Captain Oliver was instructed to treat the British as guests, and to see to it that his crew behaved diplomatically, graciously and with maximum courtesy toward the Triumph's crew. The captain assumed that the British were given the same instructions.

At quarters the morning of the twenty-eighth, Captain Oliver was to address the crew and make the announcement. The men stood at quarters and anxiously awaited the captain's word. They already knew what was going on because Snively had typed up the captain's remarks, and had passed the word to the crew. They were excited and looking forward to the exercises, which promised to break up the boredom and monotony of the Haverfield's day-to-day routine.

A bosun's whistle sounding 'attention' broke the early morning quiet, and the captain's deep, resonant voice came on the 1MC.

"Good morning, men," he began. "Today at 1200, this ship will get underway and rendezvous just east of Rota Island with the British destroyer Triumph. We will exchange some personnel by motor whaleboat and conduct nighttime ASW drills together. The submarine USS Silverfish will lay off Rota and begin mock attacks on both ships beginning at nightfall. Our men aboard the Triumph will serve as observers, and grade the Triumph's performance. Their personnel aboard our ship will serve the same purpose.

"It is critical that we not only perform in a highly efficient manner, but that we treat the British with respect and dignity. You men are diplomats, representatives of your country and your Navy, and I expect you to conduct yourselves accordingly. Any questions should be addressed to your division commanders. I want all officers to assemble in the wardroom in five minutes. Carry on."

The crew of First Division broke ranks and began to make preparations for getting underway. Before he left them to go to the wardroom, Lieutenant MacDonald was pleased to note the men had a little extra energy, a little lift to their steps as they went about their pre-underway tasks. *This is our chance to really show what we can do as a team*, he thought. He smiled broadly and bounded up the ladder to the wardroom, looking forward to the day.

The other officers were already gathered in the wardroom, awaiting the captain. MacDonald poured a cup of coffee and took a seat. When the captain stepped through the hatch, MacDonald called, "Attention on deck!" and the officers all rose to their feet. "As you were," the captain said. The officers sat.

"Gentlemen, we have an opportunity before us," he said, looking around the room. "This is our chance to show that we're good for more than just island surveys and fishing enforcement detail." The officers nodded agreement. The captain looked around the wardroom table, meeting each of his officer's eyes. He paused and consulted his notes. "The Silverfish will begin its mock attacks just after dark, and I want to make damn sure we detect her before the Brits do. Understand?" The officers all nodded.

"All right," the captain said, rubbing his hands together in anticipation. "Give me the readiness report."

One by one the officers reported the readiness of their divisions. The only officer not present was the supply officer, Lieutenant Wallace Winters, who had taken Billy Lopez and the ship's truck to the base supply depot for some last minute additions to his inventory. Also missing was the exec, who was busy writing the plan of the day to be posted prior to getting underway.

"You have plenty of concussion grenades, Bill?" the captain asked the weapons officer.

"Yes sir," Lieutenant Westerman replied. "Any idea how many runs the Silverfish will make at us, sir?"

"No, not yet, but I do know we will operate from dark until 2400," the captain replied. "Then we'll make our way slowly back to port, arriving at approximately 0800." He again checked his notes. "After we wash down the ship and perform the necessary maintenance, we will host the captain of the Triumph and his executive officer for dinner here in the wardroom. I'm counting on you officers to tell the men they will host the Triumph's crew at the Mocombo Club tomorrow evening." He pursed his lips thoughtfully and added, "And please impress upon the men that the British are our guests. They are to be accorded every courtesy. I do not want any reports of conflict between our crew and the Brits. Understood?" The officers all nodded.

Captain Oliver looked directly at Lieutenant MacDonald. "Mac, that goes double for those buccaneers in First Division." The other officers laughed as Lieutenant MacDonald nodded.

"Okay, men." Captain Oliver was satisfied. "You're dismissed. Let's make preparations for getting underway." The officers filed out of the wardroom and headed to their respective divisions.

As MacDonald was leaving, Captain Oliver took his arm and pulled him back into the wardroom. "I mean it, Mac," he warned. "Those Havernauts of yours seem to get into a lot of scrapes ashore, and I want them to fully understand the gravity of this situation."

"They'll behave like gentlemen, Captain," MacDonald assured him. "I'll impress on them the importance of displaying good conduct."

At 1145 the 1MC barked, "Single up all lines!"

The First Division crew sprang into action, singling up the lines and coiling them neatly on the deck. MacDonald nodded, pleased at the well-drilled efficiency his men were displaying. As the announcement came to cast off lines four, then two and three, and finally line one from the bow, the Haverfield blew her whistle and announced she was underway. The captain had the conn and issued orders to back the ship gently out into the harbor and away from the dock.

"All back one third," he instructed.

"Back one third, aye, sir," came the lee-helmsman's reply.

"Ten degrees left rudder."

"Ten degrees left, aye, sir."

The Haverfield slowly slipped away from the pier and pivoted into the harbor, her bow slowly coming around to point toward the mouth of the harbor and the breakwater just beyond.

"Rudder amidships," the captain ordered.

"Rudder amidships, aye, sir."

"All stop."

"All stop, sir."

The ship slowed its reverse course and almost came to a stop. The captain smiled slyly at the exec and winked. He wanted to give the men a little charge of adrenaline, and he knew how to do it. He would hit the breakwater going as fast as he could, and catapult the Haverfield into the open sea.

"All ahead full!"

The bridge crew looked at each other and grinned. "All ahead full, sir!" the lee helmsman called.

The four Fairbanks Morse geared diesel engines began turning revolutions and the twin screws under the fantail churned up the water in the harbor as the radar picket ship began to pick up speed. The Haverfield steamed faster and faster toward the mouth of the harbor, gently rolling side to side, the wind increasing as the ship sped toward the breakwater.

R.J. and Pancho were on watch on the 04 level and noticed the unusual speed the ship was making as they plowed through the harbor.

"Hold on, Pancho!" R.J. called above the wind. "This is gonna be fun!"

Pancho smiled back and nodded, pumping his fist into the air. "Yeah, baby," he called into the wind. "Go! Go!"

The ship's rolling increased as it approached the breakwater, then suddenly pitched up and down as it made contact with deep water and drove its bow into the choppy blue waves. The effect was like being shot out of a cannon, and cheers of appreciation went up throughout the ship as saltwater spray flew off the bow and sprinkled the decks all the way aft to the fantail. The skipper was really driving the old Haverbucket, and the crew was excited and pumped up. They would show those limeys how to track a submarine!

Settling down easily to eight knots, the Haverfield covered the thirty miles to the rendezvous point off Rota in about three and a half hours. Arriving on station, and finding no sign of the Triumph, the Haverfield began patrolling off Rota, ten miles north and then back ten miles south waiting for contact with the British ship.

"Beat those limeys out here, didn't we?" R.J. yelled from his starboard lookout position.

"Yeah," Pancho called back. "They been steaming from Midway. Shoulda been here by now!"

At 1545, as the Haverfield was completing its northern leg and turning south, Sonny and Cotton came up to relieve the watch. Just then R.J. spotted a speck on the horizon to the east of their position. "Contact off the port bow!" he called to the bridge below.

The exec had the conn and stepped out onto the port wing bridge with his binoculars trained on the contact. "What you got, radar?" he asked Lieutenant (J.G.) Anton who was manning the radar scope.

"Contact bearing 090, sir," Anton called. "No other contacts in the area, sir."

"Very well," the exec said. "Come to course 090 and close on the contact," he ordered.

Tanner had the helm. "090, aye, sir," he replied and turned the helm left, easing the ship gently until his compass read 090.

"All ahead two-thirds," the exec ordered. "Quartermaster of the watch, alert the captain we've made contact with the Triumph!"

Anselmi was standing quartermaster of the watch, and closed the steaming log, tucking it into the drawer under the QM table. He made his way to the captain's stateroom and knocked gently on the captain's door.

"Enter!" the captain called. He was writing in his journal at his small, teakwood desk when Anselmi stuck his head into the stateroom.

"We got contact with the Limeys, sir," he reported.

"Very well," the captain said. "Anselmi!" The signalman had started to leave, but turned as he heard the captain call his name.

"Yes sir?"

"These British sailors are our allies. They are not Limeys. They are British, or English if you wish. Do not refer to them as Limeys."

"Yes sir," Anselmi smiled sheepishly.

"And Anselmi," the captain said.

"Yes sir?"

"Pass the word to the rest of the crew about that Limey stuff."

"Aye, sir."

Even though R.J., Pancho and the other men in their duty section had been relieved, they stayed at their posts, anxious to get a look at the British ship. By 1700 the two ships were laying to, about a half-mile from each other. The Triumph began signaling with her flashing light.

"What they saying, R.J.?" Pancho asked.

R.J. was busy reading the code. "They are ready to proceed with the personnel transfer," he explained. "They are asking permission to use their motor whaleboat for the transfer."

A few minutes later, Anselmi flashed back Captain Oliver's reply.

"What we sayin'?" Pancho asked.

"The captain concurs and says he'll have the men ready at 1630. He wants us all to have chow first."

Pancho shook his head at R.J. "Man, you really good at that flashing light shit, ain't you?"

"I can read it pretty good now," R.J. said, nodding.

"You need to be a signalman, R.J. You're wasting your talents on the deck force," Cotton observed.

"Tell it to Mr. Mac," R.J. smiled. "I'll put in the chit anytime he says he'll approve it."

At precisely 1630 the British motor whaleboat cast off from the Triumph and began slowly making its way to the Haverfield. Lieutenant Barkman led the Haverfield contingent along with Ensign Thompson and three enlisted men, Crawford from engineering, Chief Lyons and Riley. As the whaleboat tied up alongside the Haverfield, a bosun's ladder was lowered to the British contingent and they climbed aboard carefully, which was no easy task because the sea was a little choppy, and the whaleboat bounced around quite a bit. The Haverfield men then moved down the ladder and took positions in the boat. The coxswain signaled he was ready, and the lines were cast off. The whaleboat turned and the coxswain accelerated back toward the Triumph.

The British personnel were escorted to the bridge, met there by the captain and the exec. It was decided that two of them would remain on the bridge, and the other three would take up positions on the fantail to observe the depth charge attack on the sub.

As dusk became dark, R.J. joined the men on the fantail. He had never seen ASW drills with a real submarine and he wanted to watch the operation and talk a bit with the British sailors.

Several other Haverfield sailors were already gathered on the fantail when R.J. arrived. The three British sailors were sitting in a group apart from the others, smoking pipes and laughing among themselves. R.J. approached them and offered his hand.

"Welcome aboard, allies," he said, a friendly, ally-kind-of-a-smile on his face.

The biggest of the group, a large red-faced sailor with blond hair looked R.J. over and shook his hand. "I'd much rather be aboard me own vessel," he said in a cockney accent. "Tell you the truth, lad, this old tub don't look seaworthy to me and me mates." He puffed his pipe and blew smoke in R.J.'s face.

R.J. smiled diplomatically. "Well, if she goes down, you'll have a little problem. You see, we don't have enough life jackets for you and your mates."

Tanner, Lester and Sonny stepped up behind R.J. and scowled at the

British sailors. The big blond seemed to appraise the situation, then broke out laughing. "That's a good one, Yank," he said, turning to his shipmates. "Some Yanks have a sense of humor," he laughed.

The tension broken, R.J. joined the rest of the Haverfield sailors on the starboard side near the depth charge racks. The British remained on the port side of the fantail, talking among themselves.

Lester looked over at the British and said to Tanner, "How come those shitheads don't have to be diplomatic? Don't they know we're allies?"

"Don't matter," Tanner replied. "Just be cool and smile, Lester. Don't start no shit."

"I ain't gonna start nothing,'" Lester grumbled, squinting at the Brits. "But I ain't gonna take no shit, neither."

Bixby, Second Class Gunner's Mate, stood near the depth charge racks with a set of sound-powered phones on his head. The mouthpiece was mounted on a flat, metal breastplate and bobbed on his chest.

"We got contact!" he yelled, and moved to a large wooden box which held the concussion grenades. He chose one and stepped up close to the stern. "Depth charge ready!" he shouted into the sound-powered phones. The Haverfield had detected the sub first.

"What's he doin'?" R.J. asked.

"Watch," Tanner replied, "this is really cool. Bixby throws the concussion grenade to simulate a depth charge. It don't hurt the sub, but they can register the blast on their antennae, and if we score a hit, they turn on their lights. It's really cool."

Bixby held up a hand palm out to indicate he was getting an order over the sound-powered phones. "Aye, sir," he called. "Fire depth charge!" He pulled the pin on the concussion grenade and threw it high and aft of the fantail. The grenade hit the water and began to sink. Suddenly, a deep, muffled explosion rumbled below the surface and a spout of water shot up into the night air. Then silence.

All the sailors on the fantail stared into the water aft of the ship. After a wait of about fifteen seconds, the sub turned on her lights below the surface and an eerie blue-green glow spread in a wide circle under the fantail, bubbles dancing up through the deep. Then it was gone.

"Hit!" Bixby yelled into the phones, and cheers went up on the fantail. Even the British sailors were cheering. "Good on ya, lad," one of them shouted at Bixby.

The submarine made a total of ten passes at the Haverfield, and Bixby scored seven hits with his concussion grenades. The British were quietly observing and making notes on their clipboards.

"Aye, aye, sir!" Bixby yelled into his phones. He took off the sound-powered set and tossed it into the wooden box. "We're secure back here," he said, obviously pleased with himself. "Now it's the Brits' turn."

"Seven out of ten is gonna be hard to beat," Tanner said.

"You've not seen the British Navy, yet," Big Blond Guy said. "We'll give that sub a proper thrashing!"

"For how much?" R.J. challenged.

"What have you got, Yank?"

R.J. consulted with his shipmates. Together they pitched in a total of twenty-seven dollars. R.J. held out the money. "Here you go, mate," he said. "Match it. Winner takes all."

"How much is that in sterling?" Big Blond Guy asked his mates.

"About eighteen pounds, more or less," one of them answered.

"You're on, Yank," Big Blond Guy said.

"Let's see your money," Lester piped in.

Big Blond Guy and his friends went into their pockets and produced eighteen pounds in British currency. "There," he exclaimed. "Done and done!"

Lester peered at the British currency suspiciously. "That shit looks like Monopoly money to me, dude."

"No problem," Tanner interjected. He gathered up the British money and put it with the American dollars and handed the lot over to Bixby. "You hold the bet, Bix. When we win we can exchange that funny-money on base." Bixby nodded, counted out the money and put in into the pocket of his dungarees.

"I trust your man is reliable," Big Blond Guy said, eyeing Bixby.

"You mean Bixby?" Sonny asked in his Oklahoma drawl. "Hell, he so honest he steps out of the shower to take a leak."

The British thought that was funnier than hell and laughed heartily. "Then we have a bet, lads," Big Blond Guy said.

A flashing light, green for starboard, began blinking on the Triumph.

"What they sayin?" Sonny asked R.J.

"They're ready to make their run," R.J. answered.

Big Blond Guy and his shipmates began cheering on their fellow Brits aboard the Triumph as the British destroyer sped up and came about, plowing through the sea, searching for the sub. They made contact after about fifteen minutes and commenced their depth charge attack. The sub dived and circled, making a total of ten runs at the Triumph. R.J. had to admit that the British ship looked good cutting through the sea. She was much newer than the Haverfield, and obviously much faster.

The Triumph crew scored hits on their first three tries and Big Blond Guy began to chide the American crew. "That, lads, is how it's done!" he shouted.

"Quite!" another said. "We'll score ten out of ten tonight lads!"

"Wanna double the bet?" Tanner challenged. The Brits looked at each other and shook their heads. All their money was already riding on the outcome.

After seven runs, the Triumph had four hits. Three more runs to go and they could only tie. The Brits grew quiet on the fantail as the Triumph missed her next two shots, and scored a hit on her last try. Final score: Haverfield seven, Triumph five.

The Havernauts cheered and yelped, jumping around on the fantail.

"Remember, boys," Tanner warned. "We're ambassadors, so be diplomatic."

The British were obviously disappointed, and the Americans all came over to shake their hands and congratulate them on a good contest before going below to get some sleep. The Havernauts hit their racks a happy lot.

Up on the bridge, the captain turned the conn over to Lieutenant MacDonald, the OOD for the midwatch.

"Good exercise, Mac," the captain said, pleased with his ship's performance. "Stay on patrol until oh four hundred and then head for the barn."

"Aye, sir," MacDonald replied. He turned to the helmsman. "Come right to course zero, zero, zero," he ordered.

"Zero, zero, zero, aye, sir." The helmsman turned to starboard and settled on the course. The Haverfield turned slowly right, rolling gently in the sea. Down in First Division's compartment, the rolling of the ship, familiar and comfortable to the Havernauts, eased them into a deep sleep. Quiet consumed the ship and she steamed easily through the night, leaving a wide, white swath in her wake.

The bosun's whistle shrilled into the 1MC and a voice boomed "Reveille, Reveille! All hands heave out and trice up. The smoking lamp is lit in all authorized spaces...Reveille!"

R.J. was already awake, trying to shake the feeling of a dream he couldn't remember. It had something to do with whales singing deep in the ocean, and it left his head fuzzy and thick. He swung his legs over his rack and rubbed his eyes. The ship rolled gently to port and then to starboard. Timing the roll just right, R.J. jumped from his rack and landed on the balls of his feet on the deck, adjusting instantly to the motion of the ship. *At least my sea legs are awake*, he thought as he tried to shake the numbness out of his head.

He had the watch beginning at 0800 and the Haverfield was due to dock at 0900, so he hurried to the head to wash his face before heading to breakfast. When he reached the messdecks, the British sailors were already there, seated together in one of the forward booths.

"Morning, fellas," R.J. offered. No answer. The Brits stared into their coffee mugs and ignored him. R.J. shrugged and began moving down the chow line, piling scrambled eggs, potatoes and toast on his metal tray. He picked up a fork and knife and put them in his shirt pocket as he made his way to the big coffee urn.

Hawkins was polishing up the coffee urn and looking around for something else to tidy up when R.J. drew coffee into his mug.

"R.J.," Hawkins whispered, motioning for R.J. to join him in the scullery around the corner. He took hold of R.J.'s arm and whispered, "I heerd those Limeys talkin' a little while ago." He looked around to make sure no one was listening. "They dint see me behind them."

"What?" R.J. asked, curiously.

"They gonna bomb us on that underway evaluation," Hawkins whispered. "They pissed off 'cause they lost that bet." He nodded and winked conspiratorially and peeked around the corner before returning to his cleaning and polishing chores. He turned back to R.J.

"And they makin' a big mess on my table." He frowned.

"Thanks, Hawk," R.J. said.

R.J. found Tanner, Sonny and Lester sitting at a rear table and joined them. He told them of his conversation with Hawkins. Lester was ready to go to blows with the Brits, but Tanner and Sonny calmed him.

"Not now, Les," Tanner cautioned. "Let's just wait awhile. They wanna be bad sports, don't mean we have to." He thought a moment, then added, "Besides, we don't want Mr. MacDonald or the Skipper to find out about the bet. They frown on that sort of stuff."

"Psst," Sonny warned as the Brits came toward the rear exit. They passed by without a word, not looking at the American sailors.

"Yeah, they up to somethin'," Sonny agreed. "I'd like to deck that big blond fucker." He held up a fist and shook it.

The shrill call of the bosun's whistle interrupted their conversation. "Now hear this, now hear this! Set the special sea and anchor detail. All hands make preparations for arrival!"

The Haverfield rolled and pitched toward the harbor, a mile ahead of the Triumph. She passed the breakwater, and the rolling and pitching lessened as she entered the smooth, aqua-green water of Apra Harbor. She approached her designated berth at the dock, and a party of line handlers stood and began to receive her. Haverfield sailors dropped fenders over the side and secured them to stanchions to prevent any damage as the ship and the pier came together.

On the focsul, Lester hurled the leader line high up into the air and over the end of the pier. The heavy weight on the end bounced on the dock and the line handlers scrambled to grab it and pull it in. Lester smiled at his accurate throw.

"Nice toss, Lester!" Cotton called to him from his post on the starboard wing-bridge. Lester turned, looked up at Cotton and bowed deeply, arms spread out to his sides. The detail on the focsul and the watch on the bridge laughed happily. They were in port, it was Thursday, and tonight they would celebrate their successful ASW drills at the Mocombo Club.

"Shift colors," ordered the 1MC. The American ensign flying on the main mast came down, and the in-port ensign went up on the fantail while the union jack went up on the bow. The Haverfield was docked.

Lester leaned over the sideline and called to the line handlers, "Honey, I'm home!" The line handlers laughed and blew him kisses.

First Division turned to, hooking up the fresh water hoses to the pier and washing the salt off the ship, forward to aft. The tarp went up to cover the fantail, and the quarterdeck desk was set up on the fantail just aft of the starboard hatch. The control point of the ship was shifted from the bridge to the fantail, and the bridge was secured. Sound-powered phones were returned to engineering and the duty section took their stations. It was just past 1000.

Down in First Division's compartment, big, ugly Queen was at his usual post, between bunks, lounging against his rack, eating ice cream. He smiled his big, ugly smile as the crew came into the compartment to clean things up and change out of their salt-encrusted clothes.

"Clean laundry is on your racks," Queen grumbled. "Get it stored and get cleaned up. Time to turn to. We got rust to fight!"

Pea came into the compartment and stared at Queen. "Where'd you get ice cream?" he asked, amazed. "Hawk tol' me there wasn't any."

"There ain't any for you, Pea," Queen answered, licking his spoon loudly. "Old Hawk and I got an arrangement." He began to lick the bowl, peering at Pea over the rim, eyes filled with amusement. Pea shrugged disgustedly and began folding his laundry.

R.J. went up to the head and quickly wiped himself down with a damp towel. No time to get a shower. That would have to wait until the evening. He was looking forward to the party at the Mocombo Club, but he had a nagging feeling something was going to happen. The rest of the crew felt it too, and wanted to make sure they were there in force in case trouble broke out with the British. They had abandoned their pledge to play gracious hosts when Hawkins' information was revealed. Everyone aboard had heard the story.

Up on deck the five British sailors were leaving the ship and heading back to the Triumph. Sonny and Tanner were standing on the 02 level, watching the departure. As the Brits began climbing into Charming Billy's truck, Sonny called out to them.

"God save the Queen!"

"Fook the Queen," Big Blond Guy yelled back. "And fook you too, Yank!"

Sonny turned to Tanner. "Did you hear that fucker?"

"Yeah," Tanner replied, smiling wryly. "I heard that fooker." He motioned to the pickup truck. "Billy'll give 'em a ride," he grinned.

Charming Billy didn't warn the Brits, he just raced the engine and popped the clutch, sending the truck bolting forward and sending the Brits tumbling around in its bed. As Billy raced down the pier, grinding gears and smiling charmingly, the Brits bounced around and scrambled frantically to hold on to something.

Tanner and Sonny grinned at each other. "Let's see what tonight brings," Tanner said, nodding. Sonny agreed.

* * * * *

The shuttle bus was filled with Haverfield sailors, and it chugged along the steep rising road toward the enlisted men's venue, the Mocombo Club. The club was situated on top of a hill only seven miles from the harbor below. As the bus groaned and whined its way toward the club, the sailors aboard sang bawdy songs, known to all branches of the service. Lester began the sing along.

"I know a girl lives over the hill!'
Chorus:"Honey, honey!"
"I know a girl lives over the hill!"
Chorus:"Babe, babe!"
"I know a girl lives over the hill, she won't do it but her sister will!"
Chorus:"Honey, Oh baby of mine!"

All: *"Gimme your left, your right, your left,*
Gimme your left, your right, your left!"

With each new ditty the chorus became louder and more raucous, the sailors laughing loudly at each verse, though they had heard them all many times before. It was a festive, happy group, flushed with victory and the knowledge of a job well done, and looking forward to whatever the evening held in store.

As the bus approached the club, Pea offered the finale.

"See the girl all dressed in pink!"
"Honey, honey!"
"See the girl all dressed in pink!"
"Babe, babe!"
"See the girl all dressed in pink, she's the one made my finger stink!"
"Honey, oh baby of mine!"

The bus pulled up to the Mocombo Club and the sailors spilled out, laughing and singing, "Gimme your left, your right, your left..."

The Mocombo Club was an old World War II quonset hut surrounded by palm trees, sitting up on the crest of the hill. The doors were closed against the tropical heat, and colored lights splashed across her front entrance, reflecting into the gravel parking lot and painting the front of the building in soft hues of blue, red and green. There were three old clunker cars sitting in the lot, along with a brightly colored bus with the legend, "Tiny's Band of Renown," and "Girls—Girls—Girls" painted neatly in large yellow and green letters. Music from a rock & roll juke box filtered through the closed doors, and Gino began singing along with the song,

"I need your lovin' every day..." His high falsetto voice rang clear in the night air, and R.J. shook his head in wonder.

"That boy can sing!" he said to Pea as they scrambled off the shuttle bus. Sonny came up behind them. "Naw," he drawled. "That boy can *sang!*"

The Havernauts busted through the doorway and discovered that the Triumph's crew had already arrived. Several of the Brits were busy building a big pyramid of emptied beer cans on top of one of the tables. It was clear from the height of the pyramid that the Brits had been there awhile. They were pretty juiced, singing and talking loudly, little of what they said completely understood by the Americans.

The Brits quieted down when the Haverfield crew came in and occupied several tables toward the bandstand. Tiny, a large, hulking Guamanian in a bright, flowing Hawaiian shirt stood in front of the band with a baton, ready to direct the band's first set as soon as the juke box stopped playing *'I Need Your Lovin'* by Don Gardner and Dee Dee Ford.

A half dozen young Guamanian girls in tight Japanese-style dresses of various colors sat near the bandstand, smoking cigarettes, drinking beers and looking very bored. They were there to entertain the sailors with dances and conversation (nothing more, as Tiny often insisted on pointing out).

The Brits did not acknowledge the Americans' presence and the Americans ignored the British. There was a certain tension in the air as the

Havernauts ordered beers from the bar and returned to their respective tables.

Tanner took a quick head-count of the British and Americans and determined that his shipmates outnumbered the Brits by almost two-to-one. He turned to Sonny and Lester and proposed that they build a pyramid of their own.

"We got twice the guys, and we can build a bigger pyramid than those mutts," he said. "Let's pass the word. We're gonna out-build those Brits!"

"Yeah," Lester agreed. "Just like we out-sailed them last night!"

The Havernauts began drinking beer and adding cans to their pyramid. The Brits noticed and accepted the challenge, stepping up their drinking and pyramid building. Tiny stood in front of the band, scowling. No one was dancing with the girls or sitting with them, buying them drinks. How could these girls earn any tips this way? Tiny increased the tempo of his direction, and his band, pitiful on a good night, played faster and louder. The girls sat, smoked and frowned at the sailors. A feeling of anticipation hung in the air.

The Americans' pyramid soon overtook the British pyramid and as the night wore on, both crews got drunker and more surly. Insults were tossed back and forth across the room, growing louder and nastier in their content. It was getting close to 2330 and the shuttle buses were pulling up in front of the club, ready to take the crews back to their respective ships.

Sonny Metzner, full of beer and feeling cocky, stepped up on one of the plastic, molded chairs and raised a beer toward the British table. "A toast to our British allies!" he yelled above the din. The Mocombo Club grew quiet as the Brits stood drunkenly, staggered slightly and raised their beers.

Sonny smiled his biggest smile, raised his can high into the air and declared, "Fook the Queen!"

The Americans laughed and raised their cans high into the air. "Fook the Queen," they toasted in unison.

Suddenly, a full beer can flew through the air and crashed into the Haverfield's pyramid, sending empty beer cans scattering all over the floor. Pea threw a full beer at the British pyramid with the same result, and both crews surged toward each other, swinging fists and chairs, throwing beer cans and cursing.

Sonny caught one of the Brits with a sharp left and the Brit grabbed him, sending them both to the floor, swinging, scratching and biting.

Lester went after Big Blond Guy and decked him with a beautiful right hand. R.J. tagged another Brit, then got blindsided by a punch to his left eye. He reeled around and caught another punch to the mouth before he threw three punches of his own, one catching the Brit on the nose, the other two sailing harmlessly into the air.

Tanner had a British sailor on the floor, pummeling him with lefts and rights. Two Brits jumped on top of Tanner. Lester and R.J. jumped on top of the Brits, kicking and punching until Tanner wriggled out and leapt to his feet.

"Thanks, fellas," Tanner yelled, and ducked a beer can aimed at his head.

Rafer and Andy stood back to back in the middle of the dance floor, landing crisp, clean punches on any Brit unlucky enough to get near them. Six British sailors lay at their feet.

Damn, R.J. thought, *those Sample boys can fight!* As he was admiring Rafer and Andy, he got hit in the back of the head with a chair and went down. He tried to scramble out of the way of several kicking feet and was getting pummeled pretty good when he felt strong hands grabbing him. He looked up to see Andy who grinned and pulled R.J. to his feet. "Thanks," he mumbled, and jumped on the back of the nearest Brit, riding him to the floor.

The melee continued until it was obvious the Brits were out-manned. They re-grouped and pushed their way out the door, jumped on the first shuttle bus and slammed the doors. The bus lurched and coughed and shot down the hill, spraying gravel back at the pursuing Americans, who threw rocks and beer cans at the retreating bus.

"Run you fookers!" Tanner yelled. The bus fishtailed hurriedly down the road, black exhaust spewing from its tailpipe.

Tiny rushed his band and his girls onto their bus and they also sped down the hill in another shower of beer cans and rocks. Tiny had locked the doors of the Mocombo Club and the Haverfield sailors kicked at them, attempting to return for one more beer.

The driver of the remaining shuttle bus honked the horn, signaling his desire to bring the evening to an end, but the Havernauts milled around the parking lot, congratulating each other with hugs and handshakes and laughing drunkenly.

Lester came over to R.J. and put his arm around his shoulders. He inspected R.J.'s swollen lip and quickly-blackening eye and asked, "You okay, shipmate?"

"I feel like I been in a fight!" R.J. answered, touching his swelling eye and wincing.

"Shit, I lost my whitehat!" Lester exclaimed, rubbing the top of his head. "I'm gonna get written up, for sure!"

R.J. took off his own whitehat and placed it ceremoniously on Lester's head. "Wear mine, ol' buddy," he slurred, grinning through his bleeding lip.

"Yeah, but then you gonna get written up without a cover," Lester warned.

"I got a cover," R.J. replied, and held up a British Navy hat. A dark blue ribbon around the front of the hat proclaimed, 'HMS TRIUMPH.' The hat was scuffed and dirty, having been stepped on and kicked around the dance floor.

R.J. put the hat on the back of his head and grinned through bloody lips at Lester who broke out laughing. The rest of the crew noticed the hat and joined in the laughter. Together, arm in arm, Lester and R.J. led the men onto the shuttle bus.

Billy Lopez announced he would drive, and pulled the Guamanian driver out from behind the wheel and passed him toward the rear of the bus where he was grabbed and passed on until he reached the back seat, cursing and yelling at the sailors in a mixture of broken English and Chamorro.

Rafer grinned at him and pushed him down into the back seat. "Tonight you gonna ride in the back of the bus," he announced.

Billy gunned the engine, popped the clutch and the bus stalled. The Havernauts hooted and yelled at him until he got the bus running and ground the gear shift into first. "I got it!" he yelled over his shoulder. "I got it!"

The bus pulled away from the Mocombo Club slowly as Billy began to master its controls. He gained momentum, moving down the hill toward the harbor and the Havernauts broke into song. They stood in the aisle, holding on to the railing that ran across the roof and sang loudly and off-key, a variation on a barracks song R.J. had heard as a kid.

Mr. MacDonald hung up the telephone on the quarter deck and said thanks to Mr. Anton, who was the OOD and had summoned MacDonald up to the quarter deck to answer the phone call. It was Fat Tiny calling to report the evening's events and complain about the 'rowdy Haverfield thugs,' as he put it.

The shuttle bus, full of drunken, singing sailors came down the pier slowly, weaving dramatically as Billy sang and swung the steering wheel left and right. The Guamanian driver was still cursing and yelling from his seat in the back. The Havernauts were rocking back and forth, making the bus roll to one side then the other like the Haverfield on choppy seas. The windows were open and the men on the quarterdeck could distinctly hear the words of the Havernauts' theme song as the bus weaved toward the ship.

"Oh, we're the Havernauts, we're riders in the night!
We're dirty sons of bitches, we'd rather fuck than fight!
Oh, idey-didey Christ a mighty who the hell are we?
Zim zam! Hot damn! We're the men of the three-nine-three!"
"Now, Mister Mac's our leader, he's full of wisdom and wit,
He likes to work our asses off, but we don't give a shit!
Oh, idey-didey Christ a mighty who the hell are we?
Zim zam! Hot damn! We're the men of the three-nine- three!"

The bus lurched to a stop at an angle in front of the brow and the Havernauts tumbled out onto the pier, singing the last verse of their bawdy song.

"We castrated Chief Twitchy with a piece of rusty glass,
We found an old bamboo pole, and rammed it up his ass!
Oh, idey-didey Christ a mighty who the hell are we?
Zim zam! Hot damn! We're the men of the three-nine-three!"

While the happy, singing sailors were being deposited on the pier, Mr. MacDonald was waiting on the quarterdeck, a deep frown on his face. The Guamanian driver reclaimed his seat at the controls, still yelling and cursing, and pulled the lever to close the front door. The bus roared away and the Havernauts headed up the brow.

Coming aboard, one by one, the Havernauts simmered down when they saw their division commander and the look on his face. Humbly, quietly they assembled on the fantail, straightening their hats and their neckerchiefs and trying to look innocent. It wasn't working.

Mr. MacDonald paced in front of the men, his arms folded across his chest, scowling and glaring at the disheveled lot. Finally, he broke the silence.

"You men were instructed to behave like gentlemen. I just got a report on the riot that took place at the Mocombo Club, and I'm inclined to send each and every one of you to mast." He stopped and narrowed his eyes, glaring at the crew, who shuffled and fidgeted. "Now what the hell happened?" MacDonald demanded.

After a short pause, Tanner began to explain. "We didn't start it, sir," he said, a little too loudly.

"That's right, sir," Sonny agreed. "We didn't start it."

The rest of the men joined in, protesting their innocence.

"You didn't start it?" MacDonald asked, incredulous. "Why did you let it happen? You were supposed to be ambassadors, for Chrissakes!"

"We didn't start it, Mr. MacDonald," Andy Sample offered. "But we damn shore finished it!"

"That's right, sir," the men chimed in.

"Yeah, we finished it!"

"Damn shore did!"

"Quiet down!" MacDonald barked. "Who wants to explain to me what happened with the British sailors?"

The men looked down at their feet and shuffled and fidgeted a little more. R.J. stepped forward reluctantly, the British hat cocked on the back of his head, his eye almost swollen shut.

"Well, sir. It was like this..." He began to sing:
"They ran through the briars
and they ran through the brambles
and they ran through the bushes where a rabbit couldn't go!"

The rest of the men joined in, almost shouting.
"They ran so fast that the hounds couldn't catch 'em,
down the Mississippi to the Gulf of Mexico!"

MacDonald lowered his head, partly because he was incredulous about the entire situation, and partly because he didn't want the men to see the smile that was creeping onto his face. He glanced back up at them with what he hoped was a disgusted and disapproving look.

"Get your drunken asses below," he ordered in a quiet, controlled voice. "I hope you realize we're all going to catch heat because of this." He glared at them. "And go to sick bay so Doc can clean up those cuts and bruises."

The Havernauts came to attention, saluted Mr. MacDonald and filed down through the aft hatch loudly singing, "They ran through the briars and they ran through the brambles..."

MacDonald turned to the quarterdeck where Mr. Anton and Cotton stood grinning widely. Their smiles faded when they saw the look on MacDonald's face, and they busied themselves with the ship's log. Mr.

MacDonald broke into a broad grin and shook his head. Tomorrow he was sure to get his head handed to him, but tonight, by God, these guys were a crew!

Early next morning, before reveille, MacDonald held a meeting with Chief Whipple and Queen in the deserted messdecks. He explained the events of the previous evening and told them to prepare for the captain's wrath. He knew the captain would hold him and the two senior bosun's mates responsible for the behavior of the men of First Division, and he wanted his petty officers to prepare a disciplinary action he could present to the captain. He hoped he could mitigate the situation by demonstrating that he was handling the problem at the division level. While he held no great hope that this would ameliorate things in the captain's mind, Mr. MacDonald knew he couldn't just sit back and wait for the captain to decide on discipline.

The three men sat in a booth and sipped black coffee, while Hawkins prepared for the morning meal and polished his galley.

"I want you two to investigate last night's fight at the Mocombo Club," Mr. Mac instructed the two bosuns. "Bring these men in and question them one at a time, talk to the people at the Club and find out what happened, why it happened, and who instigated the fight."

Chief Whipple and Queen sat quietly, nodding and taking notes. They knew better than to talk. Each had been in the Navy long enough to know when to keep their mouths shut.

"There have to be consequences to this," MacDonald continued. "I don't think the old man knows about this yet, but when he finds out, he's going to take it out on the exec and me, and I'm going to take it out on you and the men. That's the chain of command, fellas. I want the captain and the exec to know we have the situation under control, and we will see to it that the guilty parties are held responsible." Lieutenant MacDonald sipped his coffee and winced. "Damn, Hawkins has the cleanest galley in the Navy, but his coffee has to be the worst I've ever tasted."

Whipple nodded agreement, though he truly liked Hawkins' coffee. Queen sat stoically, not speaking a word.

"If a captain's mast is in order," the lieutenant continued, "then we must put on report those who instigated this fight and see to it they are brought before the skipper for punishment." He stopped and sighed. Things had been starting to go so well. He was molding his division into a well-oiled, well-trained team of sailors. Now this.

"Others involved in the fight will receive restriction, extra duty and anything else we decide after your investigation. Let me know what you find. And men," he looked at them with a tired, resigned expression. "Do it today."

MacDonald left the messdecks and Whipple and Queen stayed to formulate their strategy. Queen finally spoke.

"You know this is bullshit, Chief," he growled. "Sailors have a God-given right to get drunk and fight. That's just bein' sailors."

"Under normal circumstances I would agree with you, Queenie," the chief replied. "But all hands on board this ship were instructed to treat the British sailors with respect and courtesy, and I don't think beating the shit out of them falls within the parameters of those instructions."

"I haven't heard anything about what happened last night, except what that fat gook Tiny told Mr. Mac, and to tell you the truth, I always thought Tiny was a pimp." Queen finished his coffee and made a face. "Mr. Mac is right about this coffee," he said. He turned toward the galley and yelled at Hawkins. "Hey Hawk, you strain this crap through a gopher's ass?"

"Y'all don' like it, don' drink it," Hawkins replied, neatly stacking metal trays and putting out silverware.

"Well, all I know is the captain had a very successful dinner with the Brits last night, and he's instructed us to give them a glowing report for their part in the ASW operation." Chief Whipple lowered his voice and spoke in a conspiratorial tone. "We already heard rumors that their report on us won't be good, and something like this fight on top of a bad report is really going to piss him off."

"I'll find out what happened, Chief," Queen assured him. "But I want to get our side of the story, too."

"That's fine, as long as I have someone's ass to present to Mr. MacDonald."

Reveille sounded at 0600 and Queen was already in First Division's compartment. He turned on the lights and stalked between the bunks, yelling and growling in his deep raspy voice at the slowly awakening, hungover crew.

"Get out of those racks, fender-heads! Drop your cocks and grab your socks! Heave out and trice the fuck up!" He pulled blankets and sheets off the men and threw them in their faces. "Anybody in this fuckin' compartment wanna fight *me* this morning? C'mon, who's the bad-asses in here? You wanna fight? I'll kick your lily-white asses all over this island. Now get the fuck outta those racks!"

R.J. swung his feet over the edge of the bunk and put his aching head in his hands. The crew was beginning to stir, groaning and moaning, sore and hung over from the previous night, but Queen wasn't letting up. R.J. took a deep breath, gingerly touched his swollen lip and blackened eye, and hopped down to the deck, swaying a bit as he landed. He felt nauseous. *I feel like shit warmed over. This has to be what seasickness feels like.* This particular sickness came from ashore, though and R.J. managed to smile as he thought, *this is GROUND-sickness.* Instinctively, he knew that sailors across the world would understand completely and relate closely to that term.

"Let's go! Get your feet on the deck! Drag your sorry asses to the head and get ready for a new day! You shitbirds have a lot to account for, now get the fuck up!"

Queen looked around at the men disgustedly. They all averted his stare. No one dared look him in the eye. They sheepishly began to file out and up the ladder to the after crew's head.

"And I want this shit hole compartment cleaned from stem to stern! When I come back from chow this space better be ready for inspection."

Queen made an ugly face, even more ugly than usual, and stalked out of the compartment.

"We in some deep shit," Jefferson moaned, legs hanging over his rack. His aching head was cradled in his hands, and his huge reveille erection was stiff and sniffing the air of a fresh and new morning. Buster was the only one in the compartment welcoming the new day.

The word got around the ship in a hurry. By breakfast the whole crew had heard and passed on the news. The general consensus was that the men of First Division were in some deep shit.

R.J. was always amazed how quickly scuttlebutt was disseminated aboard the Haverfield. *Hell, I can't send code that fast.* As the men of the deck force came into the messdecks, hung over and hurting, most of the tables were occupied by other sailors, already enjoying breakfast. They smiled at the deck crew sadly and shook their heads in sympathy. It was going to be a tough day for the Havernauts.

Mr. MacDonald did not have breakfast with the other officers. He didn't want to face the captain just yet, not this early, and not until he, Chief Whipple, and BM-1 Queen had the opportunity to formulate a plan.

At 0900 a black Navy sedan pulled up in front of the ship and the Triumph's commanding officer and executive officer climbed out and strode purposefully up the brow, briefcases in hand. They sported creased, starched white shorts and sparkling-white calf-length stockings. As they saluted the flag on the fantail and then the OOD, the 1MC announced, "Triumph arriving!"

Here comes the bad news, MacDonald thought, pacing the fantail, coffee cup in hand. He looked mournfully at the harbor, wishing he could jump in and swim back to the states. Drowning in the ocean would be preferable over what was in store for him this morning.

At 0945 the British officers left the ship as the 1MC announced, "Triumph departing."

At 0950 the word came over the 1MC. "Now hear this, now hear this. The captain requests all officers assemble in the wardroom at ten hundred."

MacDonald made his way slowly to the wardroom as if he could delay this morning's meeting. As he climbed the ladder to the 02 level, he felt anxious but determined to face the captain with his head held high.

The other officers were already gathered around the wardroom table, awaiting the captain's arrival. When MacDonald walked in, no one looked at him, and he could tell by their posture that they had already heard about the fight. If they had heard about it, the captain surely had.

The door to the wardroom banged open and the exec strode in, followed by the captain. "Attention on deck!' the exec ordered. The officers sprang to their feet as Captain Oliver entered the room. He was smiling! In fact, he was absolutely beaming!

"At ease," the captain said, and sat at the head of the table.

MacDonald stared in disbelief at the smiling countenance of the Haverfield's skipper. Laughing and joking with the other officers, he seemed downright happy.

"Gentlemen," Captain Oliver began, laying the British operations report on the table, "I want to congratulate you on an outstanding operational evaluation."

Lieutenant MacDonald stared at the captain, not certain he had heard correctly. He tried to look at the other officers out of the corner of his eye, but they were all staring at the captain in confusion.

"Commander Carlisle and his team have given us a three-eight on our operational efficiency, and he told me that he wanted to give a four-oh, and would have had we not missed those three depth charge attacks." Captain Oliver looked around the room, smiling broadly. "The officers and crew of this ship have every right to be proud today," he said. "You have proven to me that this ship is capable of more than island-hopping. I believe we can steam with any ship in the fleet!"

The officers looked around, smiling uncertainly.

"To show my appreciation," Captain Oliver went on, enjoying the officers' confusion, "I'm requesting the admiral reward the Haverfield with an R&R cruise...to Yokosuka, Japan."

This brought a cheer from the officers, and they nudged, winked at each other and smiled broadly. Japan! They were going to Japan!

Mr. Jones spoke up, and instantly wished he hadn't. "What...what about the fight last night, sir?"

The wardroom became quickly quiet. Some of the officers winced, others lowered their heads, and Mr. Jones' face became red with embarrassment. *Why didn't he just keep his mouth shut?*

"Oh, that," the captain chuckled. "Well, how did Commander Carlisle put it? He said he heard it was a 'right proper donnybrook' enjoyed by one and all."

The smiles came back and Ensign Jones breathed a huge sigh of relief.

"Pass the word to the men," Captain Oliver ordered. "Today is Friday. Knock off ship's work at noon and give them the rest of the day off. They deserve it." The captain stood and beamed at them. "You are dismissed, gentlemen."

As the officers filed out of the wardroom, the captain called MacDonald back. "Mac, wait a moment, will you?"

Lieutenant MacDonald turned and stood before the captain, who was still smiling.

"Did we win the fight, Mac?" the captain asked, cocking his head and grinning at the lieutenant.

"Well, sir," MacDonald replied. "The way the men told it, the British, 'they ran through the briars and they ran through the brambles and they ran through the bushes where a rabbit couldn't go.'"

Then the captain did something MacDonald had never seen him do in the eight months he had served with him. Captain Oliver threw back his head and laughed. He laughed loudly, uproariously, obviously delighted.

MacDonald left the wardroom and closed the door, shaking his head in utter amazement. As he headed down the passageway to First Division's compartment to announce the good news, he could hear the captain still roaring with laughter in the wardroom.

When the deck crew returned to the compartment, Queen and Whipple were already there waiting for them, along with Mr. MacDonald. They didn't look happy. The men filed in and stood sheepishly by their bunks, ready for inspection. The compartment had been cleaned and polished before morning chow, and the men had shaved, showered and put on their cleanest dungarees. The compartment was as quiet as a church. The Havernauts awaited their fate, resigning themselves to it. They were feeling more than a little contrite, and their heads ached with hangovers. Whipple and Queen glared at them disapprovingly, and Mr. MacDonald stepped forward.

"I've tried my best to mold you men into a proud and efficient crew," he started, his eyes sweeping over the men, most of whom were staring at the deck. "Today I'm proud to say we have achieved that."

Heads came up slowly and the men looked around at each other confused, questioning each other with their eyes, wondering what the hell...

"Sometimes you're good, and sometimes you're lucky," the lieutenant said, smiling for the first time. "The past couple of days, you've been both."

He went on to relate the outcome of the operational report, and the reaction of Commander Carlisle to the Mocombo Club fight, along with the captain's reaction. He saved the best for last. They were going to Yokosuka for a week of R&R as soon as the captain could obtain the orders. Then he dismissed the men and went up the aft ladder to the fantail. He had to think this over. *Were they really that good, or was this favorable report politically influenced,* one ally stroking the other?

The Haverrnauts stood motionless, staring at Queen, Whipple and each other. No one spoke a word. They were stunned and a little amazed at what had just happened. In their diminished capacity, they were having trouble fully comprehending the morning's events, and they remained stunned and silent for several seconds.

R.J. broke the silence. "Well, it's about time we got some fookin' appreciation around here!"

Up on the fantail, Mr. MacDonald was jolted from his thoughts by the loud, raucous laughter and cheering coming from the compartment below.

While the celebration in First Division's compartment continued, MacDonald, staring wistfully at the harbor, spotted something out of the corner of his vision. He stared, realized what he was looking at, and ran to the aft hatch to yell at the crew below, "All hands on deck! Get on deck now!"

The deck crew scrambled up the ladder and fell into ranks on the fantail. Mr. MacDonald looked them over, glanced back at the ship coming down the channel headed for the breakwater, and ordered, "Attention to port!"

The H.M.S. Triumph was departing Guam, slowly slipping down the channel, call sign flags and British ensign fluttering in the soft, warm breeze. Her crew was assembled on her port side to salute the Haverfield. The sailors on the Haverfield prepared to do the same from their port side.

As the Triumph approached and began to pass the Haverfield, the crew snapped to attention. Mr. MacDonald barked "Hand salute!" and the Haverfield crew saluted the Brits, who in turn saluted the Americans.

"Two!" barked Mr. Mac and R.J. dropped his salute and stepped close to the sideline, waving the British Navy hat high in the air so the Brits could see it.

The Brits on the fantail of the Triumph laughed and pointed to the yardarm above their decks. Flying and fluttering from one of their signal lanyards was a genuine American Navy whitehat.

The Brits yelled and hooted while the Havernauts stood at attention and stared blankly at the lonely whitehat being kidnapped by the British Navy.

"Goddamn Limeys!" Lester yelled, pointing at the Triumph. "That's my fookin' whitehat!"

Mr. MacDonald smiled and waved at the Triumph. Both crews had managed to come away with something positive. Both crews could retell a face-saving story, and each crew had earned a grudging respect from the other. Both ships could brag among themselves about their operational evaluations, and build on those evaluations for the further training and molding of their respective crews.

Haverfield Captain D. Paul Oliver stood on the port wingbridge, watching and saluting the passing of the Triumph. Today was a great day for the Haverfield, a great day for Anglo-American relations, and a great day for Lieutenant Commander D. Paul Oliver. He was a happy man. All was right with his world. Over the past six months he had worked hard to remold the crew and this ship in his own image, and he had proven that even a post-war reject, a ship stationed out in the far-reaches of the world and not in day-to-day contact with the fleet, could perform as well as any line cruiser or destroyer. He was anxious to visit Japan and size up the rest of the seventh fleet. He wanted his men to know they stacked up with those vessels. And of course there was Lorelei. He smiled to himself. Yes, Captain Oliver was enjoying life.

Chief Twitchell, however, was not enjoying life at all.

TWENTY FIVE

On Wednesday morning, August 28 (the 27th in the States) Chief Twitchell was in a rage. He had spent an uncomfortable night passed out in the chief's quarters after a bender the previous evening, and he was hung over, frustrated and angry. His source of anger this particular morning was the planned civil rights march on Washington D.C. scheduled for the next day, Wednesday the 28th in the States. He had been listening to the Armed Forces radio network the previous afternoon. When he learned about the plans for a hundred and fifty thousand people to march on Washington in support of civil rights he headed for the Mocombo Club where he sat on a bar stool the entire evening, guzzling scotch and railing against the civil rights movement, President Kennedy and all black people in general.

"Goddam niggers!" he was heard to complain. "They're tryin' to take over the whole country!" Unfortunately, Chief Twitchell had several supporters at the bar, and their encouragement only made him more vehement. The fact that his supporters hung around because he was buying drinks was lost on him.

As he came up on deck that morning, the sun hit him like a bolt of lightning. He squinted against the glare and, coffee cup in hand, sat unsteadily on a vent on the 02 level to breath in some badly needed fresh air. He held the cup in both shaking hands to keep from spilling the coffee all over the deck. Looking down on the fantail, he spotted Rafer, Andy and Timothy Jefferson standing with several other black sailors. They were laughing and joking with each other in a friendly way that for some reason pissed off the chief.

Twitchell got up and leaned over the rail. "Hey, all you porch monkeys need to get back to work!" he shouted. "Or you don't get no watermelon!"

The men on the fantail looked up at the chief, and Jefferson made a comment under his breath that made the others laugh. This enraged Twitchell even more.

"I said break it up!" he screamed. He was holding onto the railing and his knuckles were whitening under his tight grip. He twitched uncontrollably, partly from anger and partly from his horrendous hangover. His fat face was red and wet with perspiration and his eyes were bloodshot and blurry.

The men on the fantail started slowly to disperse, casting dirty looks at Twitchell as they made their way through the port side hatch and into the engineering compartment. They had to pass under the spot where the chief was standing and as they passed below him, he colored the morning air with insults.

"You black bastards!' he yelled. "Whadda you doin', organizing a zebra hunt? You got work to do, you lazy spooks. Why are all you niggers so fuckin' lazy?"

Most of the blacks ignored him, but Rafer Sample looked up at the chief with anger of his own. "Only nigger on this ship is you!" he spat, pointing up at Twitchell.

"What was that, Sambo?" The chief came down the ladder quickly, much faster than his fat body could handle, and just before he reached the bottom, he stumbled and fell to the deck, scrambling to get his feet under him. He was puffing hard, his face beet-red. Rafer had disappeared into the compartment and Twitchell started to follow him, but was stopped by Mr. Almogordo.

"My office, Chief," he ordered. "We need to talk."

Twitchell's anger quickly subsided in the face of the engineering officer and he mumbled, "Yes, sir," and meekly followed the lieutenant into his stateroom. Mr. Almogordo closed the door.

"Sit down, Chief." he said, gesturing toward a chair. Twitchell sat.

"I don't want to hear another public outburst like that again," the engineering officer said, staring directly into Twitchell's blood-shot eyes.

"They act like they own the place," the chief complained. "They hang out in groups, by themselves, like street gangs. I don't trust any of them.

They're all thieves."

Mr. Almogordo was a patient and understanding leader, but Chief Twitchell was pushing his patience to the limit. The lieutenant took a deep breath. "You know as well as I that on board a Navy ship everyone lives closely together," he said, calmly. "We have to get along together if we're going to work together. When it comes down to doing the job, do you really care what color the man next to you is?"

Chief Twitchell was an ignorant man, but he wasn't so stupid that he didn't understand he was pushing the lieutenant too far. He backed off.

"I just want the ship to run smoothly." he said, contritely. "I don't like people separating themselves from the rest of the crew."

Mr. Almogordo smiled patiently and relaxed a little. "Times are changing, Chief. What was true in the old Navy is no longer true today." The engineering officer lit a cigarette and offered one to the chief, who declined.

"It wasn't too long ago, blacks weren't aboard Navy ships unless they were ship's servicemen, you know, cooks and bakers and such."

The chief sat quietly and nodded, remembering fondly those good old days.

"I'm a Mexican from Texas, Chief," Mr. Almogordo continued. "Wasn't that long ago you wouldn't see a Mexican officer in the Navy, either." He grinned and took a drag on his cigarette. "But more than anything, I'm an American. I'm proud of that."

"Me too, sir."

"Then what say we concentrate on our jobs and not who's doing them, okay?" The lieutenant was not comfortable with this type of conversation, and he wanted to wrap it up quickly. The chief was prejudiced, sure, but he was an excellent engineer, and Mr. Almogordo depended on him.

"Aye, aye sir," the chief agreed.

"You're a good engineer, Chief, and you know it. If you want to make Master Chief, you've got to learn to be more diplomatic." The lieutenant stood, indicating the conversation was over. Chief Twitchell stood also and started toward the door.

"I'll watch my temper, sir," he said.

"Good." Mr. Almogordo opened the door for the chubby chief and let him out. When the chief had gone and the door was closed, the lieutenant sat back down and drummed his fingers on his desk, deep in thought. *This isn't going to be the end of it,* he thought. *Maybe I'd better talk to the exec about this. Just to cover my ass.* He reached for the sound-powered phone and made an appointment to see the exec that afternoon.

* * * * *

"Stay outta his way for a while, Rafer," R.J. cautioned. He was sitting in the messdecks with Rafer, Andy and Tanner discussing the most recent outburst by Chief Twitchell. Lunch was over but the four lingered past the allotted time for the noon meal. Chief Twitchell was becoming more and more a subject of conversation among the men of First Division.

"Good advice." Tanner nodded.

"That cracker's lookin' to get 'is ass whooped," Rafer said vehemently.

"Maybe I go up side his head," Andy offered, raising his open hand and making a slapping gesture. "Whack! Hit 'im a lick!"

Tanner laughed. "Shit, Andy, big as you are, you'd probably kill him."

"Not a bad idea," Rafer said thoughtfully, chewing on his thumbnail.

"Maybe one dark night at sea we stick him in a weighted bag and drop his sorry ass over the side," R.J. suggested, only half-kidding.

"Hmm." Rafer pondered that for a moment.

Jefferson came walking through the messdecks and stopped at the booth where the others were sitting. "We gotta do something 'bout ol' Twitchy."

R.J. nodded agreement. "We were just exploring some possibilities," he said. He brought Jefferson up to date on the conversation.

"Hey," Jefferson brightened with an idea. "When we get to Yokosuka, we hire a dude to bump 'im off. You can get a muh-fuh killed for five bucks American in Jay-pan."

Everyone laughed but Rafer. His anger was too deep, too personal to joke much. His anger for the fat chief was smoldering and growing.

The others continued coming up with ideas for bumping off Twitchell. Tanner suggested they drop a chipping hammer on his head from the 04 level. R.J. recommended slipping rat poison in his whiskey. Andy wanted to go up side his head. Their good humor cheered Rafer a little, and his anger subsided. They were laughing about the various ways they dreamt up to commit homicide when Chief Whipple came into the messdecks.

"Having a little party, are we?" the chief said, eyebrows raised in mock surprise. "If it don't inconvenience you ladies too much, perhaps we could get busy with the ship's work."

"Right, Whip," Tanner agreed and got up from the table.

The chief rubbed his hands together. "We got less than two weeks before we set sail for Yokosuka and I want this ship to shine like a new penny. I want the decks lookin' like Hawkins' galley." He attempted a sardonic smile, but it didn't quite establish itself on his face. It was almost as if the smile was afraid to venture onto that face. "This old broad might not be the youngest ship in the fleet, but when we hit Yokosuka, she's damn sure gonna be the prettiest. Now let's turn to!"

* * * * *

Lieutenant Edward X. Coleman, new executive officer on the Haverfield was a quiet, self-assured officer who went about his business in a calm and organized manner. He too was an Annapolis graduate, and he and Captain Oliver had forged an immediate bond. The captain had been a class ahead of Mr. Coleman at the academy, and although they had not known each other in school, they shared many of the same memories and experiences.

Mr. Almogordo sat opposite the exec in the wardroom, sipping coffee while discussing engineering problems and their possible solutions. The repairs on the engines were coming along nicely, and Chief Twitchell had solved the difficulties with the evaps. Mr. Almogordo was quick to give his chiefs credit for the progress, and he cited Chief Risk and Chief Twitchell as two of his best. There was, of course, a small problem with Twitchell.

"What problem, Pete?" The exec asked, looking up from the engineering report.

Pedro Almogordo quickly summed up the confrontation between Twitchell and the blacks earlier in the day, and recounted the conversation he had had with the chief machinists mate.

The exec listened patiently and made a few notes. He was frowning, his brow furrowed. "Is this a problem, or just a passing thing?" he asked the engineering officer.

"I'd like to think it's just a passing thing, sir." Mr. Almogordo said. "I've spoken with the chief, and he's a little rough around the edges, but it's my considered opinion he'll calm down."

"I reviewed the personnel files on everyone on this ship when I came aboard a couple of months ago." Lieutenant Coleman said. "Senior Chief Twitchell has an exemplary record, Pete. He wears the gold hash-marks. He's never been in trouble in over eighteen years."

"That's true, sir."

"Your evaluation reports on him have always been very good. Glowing, in fact."

"He's a damn good engineer, sir. Saved our butts more than once in that engine room." Pedro Almogordo rubbed his chin thoughtfully. "He works like a dog, but..."

"But what?"

"I don't want to see a bad mark on his record, and this is just my opinion..."

"What, Pete?" The exec was becoming impatient.

"Just between you and me, I think Chief Twitchell might have a drinking problem."

The exec snorted through his nose. "Hell, Pete, half the engineers in the seventh fleet drink too much. The question is can he continue to function at a high level? The other question is can you control him?"

"I think we have an understanding, he and I."

"Good." The exec initialed the engineering report and stood. Mr. Almogordo stood also. "Keep an eye on the situation, Pete. And keep me informed of any further situations. I'll take the engineering report to the captain."

Mr. Almogordo nodded. "Yes sir."

"And, Pete. You've done a helluva job down there."

"Thank you, sir." The engineering officer was pleased. "It's nice to be able to get the parts we need."

When Mr. Almogordo had left, the exec sat at the wardroom table, drumming his fingers on the engineering report and thinking. He decided not to inform the captain of the confrontation on the fantail. He would monitor the situation closely and rely on his engineering officer to manage it. No use burdening the captain unless it happened again.

Down in the chief's quarters, Twitchell was venting his anger and Chief Risk was sitting on his bunk, going over some paperwork and listening patiently. They were alone in the compartment.

"These fuckin' darkies are forgetting their goddam place!" Twitchell yelled. "That asshole Kennedy is lettin' 'em get away with murder. Marching on Washington! What the fuck is that stupid mick lettin' 'em get away with that for?" He paced back and forth in the narrow aisle, fuming. "That's what we get, electing a fuckin' Catholic!"

"Chief," Risk said soothingly.

"I'm telling you, Phil, it's either them or us in this man's Navy. Ain't room for both races. Send 'em back to Alabama to pick cotton, those black sonsabitches!"

"Control your temper, Jasper," Chief Risk said quietly. "It's gonna get you in trouble one of these days."

"Bullshit!" Twitchell spat. "No one's gonna take the side of a bunch of niggers over a white man."

TWENTY SIX

Early in the morning of Monday, September 9th, the Haverfield set sail to Japan for two weeks' R&R in Yokosuka. The crew was ecstatic. Many of the crew had never been to Japan, and the older members like Tanner, Sonny and Lester regaled them with stories of Japanese women, the bars in the Alley and the many attractions of that land. Anticipation was high, and spirits were even higher. The ship was looking good, freshly painted, all the brass shined up, and decorative knots painted white adorned many places on the ship. They had only to drop off some supplies at a Naval radio installation on an island called Chi Chi Jima, and then it was straight to Japan!

Before they sailed, R.J. had begun to practice semaphore in front of a mirror every chance he got. Mr. MacDonald already knew R.J. was practicing on the flashing light almost every evening, shooting the breeze with signalmen on every ship in the harbor. The lieutenant had questioned Anselmi about it. The second class signalman had told the lieutenant the truth; R.J. sent the purest code he had ever seen, and the kid could read it faster than anyone he had ever known.

"He's a natural on that light, sir," Anselmi had said. "He'd be a good signalman if only..." He became thoughtful, trying to formulate a way to get R.J. up on the signal bridge. He sure could use the extra help up there.

"If only what?"

"If he could learn semaphore and the flags in the flag bag, get to handling flag hoists and stuff like that, I think he'd be one of the best." Anselmi thought for a moment and added, "Watch him some night, Mr. Mac, you'll be amazed."

MacDonald did get the opportunity to watch R.J., though it was quite by accident. One night, he was on the bridge of the USS Pelican, a minesweeper which had made a stop in Guam on its way to Japan. He was there as a dinner guest of the Pelican's captain, an old friend, and had joined his friend on the bridge for an after-dinner cigar. The Pelican's chief signalman was on the signal light, shooting the breeze with another ship. While MacDonald watched the other ship and tried to follow the code, he realized the other ship was the Haverfield.

"Boy this sumbitch sends code like he's spreading butter!" the chief exclaimed, sending *dit-dah, dit-dit-dit,* or *AS* which meant, 'Please Wait." He turned to the captain. "Skipper, you can read code. Watch this guy."

Bill Bartkowski, the Pelican's commander, also a lieutenant, nodded and the chief blinked the light rapidly to raise the Haverfield back. Once he had reestablished contact he sent rapid code for a few minutes, asking the other signalman where he was from, when had he joined the Navy, and how had he learn Morse code so well.

The response came back immediately in quick, even flashes, red dits and dahs arranged beautifully into the English language, each series of dits and dahs immaculately constructed and sent very fast, very smoothly, and with perfect grammar. And this guy even used punctuation! No one used punctuation except in official messages. Hell, most guys didn't even know the codes for any punctuation signs with the exception of the period, which everyone used to mark the end of a sentence and went *dit-dah-dit-dah-dit-dah.* This guy used parentheses, exclamation points and semi-colons, for chrissakes! This guy was smooth!

Bartkowski, 'Bart' to his friends, shook his head quickly as if trying to clear it and asked the chief, "What was that about radio school, Chief? He's too damn quick for me."

"Sumbitch is an E-2!" the chief shouted, flashing "Please Wait' again and turning back to the captain. "Says he's an E-2 and he went to radio school, even graduated, and learned the code there. He also said he's on the deck force." The chief laughed and slapped the back of his signal light. "Shit! Pardon, sir, but SHIT! This guy is almost too fast for me and I'm an E-7! Who the hell is this guy?"

"Davis," Lieutenant MacDonald said quietly, exhaling blue cigar smoke and watching it spiral up into the evening breeze. He stared thoughtfully across the harbor at the Haverfield. "His name is R.J. Davis and he's one of mine." MacDonald looked at the end of his cigar and blew gently, the tip glowed and threw a soft, orange hue across his face. "In fact, he's becoming one of my best."

"How come he's not in the radio shack, sir?" the chief asked.

"Why don't you ask him, Chief?" MacDonald said, smiling and pointing toward the Haverfield with his cigar.

The chief turned back to his light and flashed the question. R.J. responded quickly: "It's a long story."

"I got that," Bart said proudly. "Long story, huh?" He looked at MacDonald.

MacDonald shrugged. "Some trouble back in Dago," he said. "Our old exec was a hard-ass sometimes, and he took the kid's clearance away. Stuck him in First Division."

"Trouble in San Diego, huh?" Bart asked his friend. "And you don't want to talk about it, right Mac?"

Lieutenant MacDonald nodded absently, watching in fascination as R.J. sent code in beautiful characters that MacDonald could almost read. He could damn sure appreciate it! The chief was right. This guy was smooth. *Gonna have to watch his progress a little more carefully,* he thought, *I knew there was something about this kid...*

The next morning MacDonald went to Anselmi and procured a set of playing cards with all the flags in the flag bag illustrated on them, and a set of semaphore signal flags, red and orange in color. He found R.J. on the fantail and he instructed R.J. to learn more than Morse code if he expected to be a signalman. The lieutenant had smiled wryly, handed the items to R.J., and walked away, leaving him standing stunned and dumbfounded, yet deeply touched by the gesture. R.J. decided then and there he was going to memorize the flags, learn to assemble and fly a flag hoist, and solve the problem of semaphore. It was the damned semaphore R.J. was having trouble with. Sending it was no problem; he knew where the flags were placed for each of the letters of the alphabet, but reading it was a different matter because everything was reversed. A *'K'* sent to the receiver looked like a *'V'* to the sender. A *'P'* looked like a *'J,'* a *'B'* looked like an *'F'* and so on. R.J. couldn't get his mind around it...yet. He was determined to learn to read semaphore. He was prepared to stand in front of the mirror and practice for hours until his arms grew tired and he could barely lift them.

Now, out at sea, steaming toward his first visit to Japan, R.J. stood the rotation of watches happily, looking forward to his first visit to another country. *Tijuana doesn't count.* He was anxious to get to Japan and was pleased they were not stopping at any of those insignificant, shitty little islands they always had to visit while on patrol. Tanner called it "Poacher Patrol" because they were mainly keeping the Japanese fishing fleet from plying their trade inside the U.S. Trust Territory. Not this time. Just one short stop to drop off supplies, and they were headed to Japan!

After his first few times at sea and after several rounds of underway watches, R.J. decided that the mid-day watch and the morning watch were the prime watches to stand. The mid-day watch began at 12:00 hours and ended at 16:00 hours while the morning watch began at 04:00 hours and ended at 08:00 hours. Each watch had its distinct advantage. The mid-day watch occurred during the ship's busiest time, and R.J. found that the watch went by very quickly indeed, especially during those times he rotated to messenger of the watch, and was responsible for delivering all the messages between the bridge and the various departments. This kept him busy in a hectic rush fore and aft, starboard to port, for at least one hour out of his four-hour watch. The other three hours he rotated with the rest of the watch and enjoyed his turn at the helm and lee-helm. He was getting pretty good at steering the ship, and he held very close to course, even in rough seas. He wasn't as good as Tanner, though. No one was. Tanner could handle the helm with just the fingertips of one hand, and gently guide the ship, always straight on course, through any weather. There was no waving line of a wake behind the Haverfield when Tanner was at the helm.

His wake was straight and even, right on course.

The morning watch, however, was a completely different animal. The morning watch occurred during the ship's quietest time and R.J. had ample opportunity to reflect on the day's events at sea. The early pre-dawn quiet on the slate-blue ocean enraptured R.J., and he rarely missed an opportunity to experience it. The ever-brightening sky, the white, soft, pillow-like clouds and the intricate lace patterns of white caps decorating rolling waves as they crashed into each other, the dramatic sunrises on the blue Pacific always left R.J. a little breathless. He stood in the vortex of all that power; the power of nature and an American Naval vessel, and thought how one related to the other. It was a symbiotic relationship, R.J. figured. The ship couldn't function as a ship without the sea. Conversely, the sea couldn't exist without the ship, for it brought men to the sea to witness its terrible power. And the sea, showing its appreciation, often behaved outrageously in order to impress its power upon the sailors.

R.J. stood and watched, soaking up the salt air carried by the warm wind blowing directly across the bow. He smiled at the first red and orange hint of sunrise and thought of how people loved to worship in churches and cathedrals. *Why would they spend the time and money to build these monuments to their faith, when all they really had to do was step outside just before dawn and watch all the wonderment the world has to offer unfold before their eyes...in nature's cathedral?*

It's not possible to fully appreciate day-time steaming if you are the messenger assigned to mid-day watch, because there is too much going on. Every message that flowed between the bridge commanded by the Officer of the Deck and all other departments aboard the ship had to be delivered quickly by the messenger. Many messages were sent and received via the sound-powered phones or the ship's electronic intercom, but the messenger carried the written messages received and sent by the radio shack and the signal bridge. The messenger was responsible for rounding up (and in the case of the morning watch, waking up) the next duty section to take over the watch.

R.J. loved being at sea. He loved the action and the motion of the ship as the Haverfield steamed through its busy day. Everyone was working, doing the jobs they were trained for, their success evident in the ever-forward thrust of the ship, drawing closer and closer to its next objective. Everything came together, neat and in order, as was expected. The crew was happy and morale was high. They did their jobs with a high degree of professionalism, good-naturedly and with enthusiasm. The normal carping and complaining was at a minimum, and the normal daily slur of insults took on a friendly, affable nature.

R.J. liked delivering messages aft more than forward while at sea. Going down the deck aft on a steaming ship creates the illusion of faster movement. R.J. felt like he was moving faster, as the ship steamed forward, and it was a good feeling. He was feeling progress. Going forward was more like a chore because it felt less like progress and more like treading water, trying to keep up with the forward thrust of the ship. Sometimes it felt like he was on a treadmill, going nowhere, unable to exceed the ship's forward speed.

Three days out from Yokosuka, on a warm day, wind blowing and salt spraying over the bow, the bosun's whistle cut the air with high-pitched urgency.

"Man overboard! Man overboard starboard side!"

Someone on the bridge had tossed Oscar, an orange-colored, stuffed and very crudely made mannequin over the side, hoping to catch the aft look-out daydreaming, failing to notice poor Oscar floating past him. The aft look-out this day was Pea, and he didn't miss much of anything. Shouting into his sound-powered phones, Pea alerted the bridge of the 'man' over-board's being spotted and advised them that 'Oscar' was on the starboard side. This was important, because the ship would immediately turn to whichever side was identified, swinging the stern of the ship away from the sailor in the water, and preventing him from being sucked down into the screws and becoming hamburger. At the same time, the 'Oscar' flag for the letter 'O' was raised on the outer, starboard signal lanyard, advising anyone in the area that the ship had a man overboard.

"Right standard rudder!" barked Mr. Barkman, OOD. "All ahead one-third."

"Right standard rudder, aye, sir!" the helmsman repeated, spinning the helm to the right.

"All ahead one-third, aye, sir!" the lee-helmsman repeated, grasping the handles of the ship's telegraph and signaling all ahead one-third to the engine room. The answer of ahead one-third was answered by the engine room immediately, and the indicator arrows on the lee-helm moved to match the arrows on the handles at ahead one-third. The ship slowed.

"Engine room answers all ahead one-third, sir!"

"Very well," nodded Mr. Barkman. "Get ready to lower the motor whaleboat and let's go get that poor bastard."

The stern of the ship swung around to port, away from Oscar, who bobbed and floated, waiting patiently for his rescue. As the ship complet-ed a one hundred and eighty-degree turn, the men on the bridge could see Oscar riding the ocean swells ahead of them now by about four hundred yards.

"All stop," Mr. Barkman ordered. "Rudder amidships." The helmsman and lee-helmsman responded and the Haverfield came slowly to a stop, rolling gently with the swells of the Pacific and waiting patiently for the motor whaleboat to reach and retrieve Oscar.

R.J. had not yet been scheduled motor whaleboat duty during a man overboard drill, but he really wanted to go. He wanted to climb down into the whaleboat and take out across the ocean to rescue Oscar, that poor, stuffed, orange-colored bastard who always needed rescuing. That duty was held in high regard by the crew, who fought, argued and jockeyed for position in the motor whaleboat. Only the best hands were assigned to it; Tanner, Sonny, Lester and Cotton were fixtures, along with Anselmi, signal-man of the boat, and Chief Lyons, who commanded the boat.

Anselmi didn't much like motor whaleboat duty. He preferred to stay on the signal bridge and watch the man overboard recovery, but since Becker, Signalman First Class spent almost every steaming day in his rack battling severe sea-sickness, Anselmi was assigned the motor whaleboat as a permanent duty. On the rare occasions he was required to communicate with the ship, Becker would be dragged from his bed and assisted to the bridge where he would read the incoming message, send the instructed answer, and crawl pitifully back into his rack to continue his suffering.

R.J. wasn't on duty, so he hung around the bridge area to watch the man overboard drill play out. The motor whaleboat bounced around on the waves as several hands reached over the gunwales and pulled Oscar up into the boat. Tanner and Sonny held Oscar high in the air, as custom dictated, signaling the recovery to the men on board ship who cheered and waved. With Oscar safe in the boat, Lester, the boat coxswain, gunned the motor and spun the boat around in a wide circle, gathering speed and beginning his return to the Haverfield. The boat's engine coughed and sputtered and then gave up, winding down to a stop, refusing Lester's frantic attempts at restarting.

"Shit!" Lester yelled. "Shit!"

On the bridge of the Haverfield, Mr. Barkman frowned and studied the frantic efforts of the whaleboat crew through his binoculars. "What the hell...?" he muttered. "They are laying-to out there. What's the problem?"

"Sonofabitch!" Lester screamed at the whaleboat's engine. "Come on, come on..." He ground the starter over and over, but his efforts only resulted in wearing down the battery, and it ground down painfully to a slow rumble of a death.

"Battery's dead," Chief Lyons observed, to no one in particular. "Salami, get on your light and tell the ship we need a tow."

"Great," Anselmi grumbled. "We ain't gonna hear the end of this." He opened the small carrying case and removed the miniature, hand-held signal light. Checking to see that the battery was charged, smiling when he verified it was, Anselmi pointed the light at the ship and blinked the trigger several times to get the attention of the ship. He waited patiently for a response. Becker would have to be pulled from his rack and brought up to the bridge. Anselmi smiled as he imagined the First Class Signalman being escorted to the bridge, trying to keep from puking all over the deck.

"We're getting a signal from the motor whaleboat, sir," the port lookout called, pointing toward the blinking light.

"Get Becker up here to take this message," Mr. Barkman ordered. "Tell him to shake a leg. It's going to be dark in about an hour, and I don't want to try to recover that boat in the dark."

Mr. MacDonald came into the pilot-house and looked around. They weren't securing from the man overboard drill as fast as they should be, and the captain was going to show up pretty soon. Mr. Barkman could do without that, so Mr. MacDonald stood by to help in any way he could.

"Where the hell is Becker?" Barkman demanded.

The messenger of the watch was just returning from the operations compartment where Becker was moaning and writhing in his rack.

"He can't make it, sir," the messenger explained.

"What is that supposed to mean?" Mr. Barkman asked, frowning down at the messenger.

"He's really sick, sir," the messenger replied. "He's got a big ten gallon milk can secured to his rack with some baling wire, and he been pukin' in it. It's almost half full!" The messenger laughed and looked around the bridge, trying to find someone to share his humor. His smile faded when Mr. Barkman scowled at him and walked out to the port wing bridge. He raised his binoculars and focused on the motor whaleboat, which was beginning to drift farther away from the ship.

"We're taking on water, Chief!" Sonny yelled and pointed to the whaleboat's deck. Water was seeping in from the engine compartment. Chief Lyons pulled the top off the motor housing and looked into the small compartment.

"Hell, that's what happened to the engine," he explained. "Flooded her out. We got problems, men." He looked around the whaleboat. "No oars to paddle with, nothing to bail with. Anselmi, raise the ship and tell them we got a water problem, maybe get a landing raft out here to tow us."

"Signal from the whaleboat, sir," the port lookout cried. Mr. Barkman was already looking at the dim flashing light coming from the whaleboat.

"Mac," Barkman summoned Mr. MacDonald over to the wingbridge. "Can you read that?" he asked, pointing toward the flashing light.

MacDonald squinted and blinked his eyes rapidly, trying to focus. "Nope, too fast for me." He turned to the OOD with a smile on his face. "But I know someone who can."

"Who?" the OOD asked.

MacDonald kept looking at Mr. Barkman and called back over his shoulder, "R.J., get up here!"

R.J. came around to the wing from his vantage point on the signal bridge and grinned at Mr. MacDonald. "I can read it, sir."

MacDonald nodded and R.J. stepped up to the port signal light, turned it on and pointed it toward the motor whaleboat. *Dah-dit-dah*, he sent the letter 'K' which meant, 'go ahead."

The small light blinked rapidly from the motor whaleboat while dusk began to creep across the ocean. Whitecaps started to form and the sea began to get choppy.

R.J. read the code easily, and when Anselmi had finished, R.J. flashed *dit-dah*, *dit-dit-dit*, or 'wait' and turned to Mr. Barkman.

"They're taking water in the engine housing, sir," R.J. interpreted the code. "The engine's dead and they are going to need a tow. Chief Lyons said they don't have any bailing equipment and no oars, so they are depending on that tow."

Mr. Barkman stood staring at R.J. for just a moment. He had no idea this kid could read Morse code. "Can you send something for me?" he asked R.J.

"Yes, sir," R.J. replied, pointing the signal light at the motor whaleboat.

"Tell them we are dispatching a landing raft to tow them in, and I'll move the ship a little closer," Mr. Barkman dictated and R.J. sent the message.

On the motor whaleboat, Anselmi knew immediately who was operating the flashing light aboard the Haverfield as soon as R.J. sent the 'K' for 'go ahead.' The beautiful brevity of the *dits* and *dahs* continued to amaze Anselmi. It was like sitting in an easy chair reading a well-written novel, the way this kid sent code. Anselmi smiled at the others in the boat and receipted for R.J.'s message with *dit-dah-dit*, or 'R' for 'received.'

"They're sending a landing raft to tow us in," he said to Chief Lyons.

"Great," the chief replied. "And they'll all be hanging over the side with their cameras, no doubt." The chief shook his head and frowned. The crew of the motor whaleboat was not going to live this down anytime soon. A landing raft towing the captain's gig back to the ship. Chief Lyons shook his head again disgustedly and continued frowning.

The ship lowered the landing raft into the water, and a crew of four manned the raft and pushed away from the ship. The coxswain pull-started the outboard motor and accelerated toward the whaleboat. Anselmi signaled again with his portable light and R.J. sent 'go ahead.' They sent code back and forth for a few minutes and the crew in the whaleboat looked at Anselmi questioningly.

"It's R.J. on the light," Anselmi explained. "Becker was too seasick to get out of his rack and R.J. was hanging out on the bridge. Mr. MacDonald told him to get on the light. That was R.J. sending that code."

Sonny, Tanner, Cotton and Lester looked at each other, grinning proudly. "That's the way things get done in this here Navy," Sonny drawled. "The deck force has to come out and rescue us, and a 'deck ape' handles the communications." He threw his head back and laughed, quickly joined by the others.

"It's like Mr. MacDonald says," Cotton agreed. "The Havernauts are the best damn deck gang in the Seventh Fleet!"

Chief Lyons watched with amusement as the whaleboat crew congratulated themselves, each other, and R.J. Davis for the great work they did today. "Okay, okay," he sighed, laughing along with them. "Let's get this over with and face the music aboard ship."

The landing raft reached the whaleboat and threw a towline across her bow. Tanner locked the rudder amidships, pulled the tiller out of its slot above the boat's rudder, and laid it carefully on the deck. Sonny grabbed the towline and secured it to the boat's bow, and the landing raft took the strain and slowly began to pull the boat toward the ship.

A half-hour later, just as the last of the day's light was slipping slowly below the horizon, the motor whaleboat was secured in its davits, and the landing raft was pulled back onto the fantail and washed down before being stowed away. There had been only a few kidding remarks when the motor whaleboat crew returned to the ship by the grace of a landing raft's tow. There existed aboard ship a common feeling of accomplishment. The man overboard drill had gone wrong when the whaleboat's engine got swamped, but the ship's crew had reacted to the crisis with cool professionalism. Like a well-practiced team, they responded at once, solved the problem quickly and avoided any injury. The high spirits of the deck force infected the entire crew. They were in control of their ship and they were on their way to Japan! Morale was very high, and Captain Oliver could not have been happier. The ship was due for the annual UED, Underway Evaluation Drills which judge and measure the underway efficiency of the ship and crew as they are run through one drill after another. Captain Oliver believed they were ready, especially after the joint operations with the Triumph, and looked forward to the UED. He too wanted to see the big, white 'E' painted on the ship's stack, proof of a 'squared-away' crew.

A team consisting of Tanner, Queen, Chief Whipple and Lester were walking around the motor whaleboat, looking up at her keel, trying to find the water leak. By midnight the leak would be found and repaired, the engine taken apart, cleaned and re-assembled. Tomorrow the motor whaleboat would be seaworthy again.

The Haverfield returned to her base course and continued her slow, steady steaming toward Yokosuka. R.J. stood on the wing bridge and watched as the day became night in the South Pacific. He felt good, really good. He had operated the flashing light in an official capacity for the first time. He showed Mr. Barkman, the operations officer, what he could do with a signal light, and he noticed Mr. Barkman talking quietly with Mr. MacDonald, both of them glancing his way when the motor whaleboat was brought aboard and secured.

He wasn't surprised when Mr. MacDonald slid in next to him on the wing bridge. "That was a good job on that light, Davis," MacDonald said. "You're damn fast on that thing."

"Thank you, sir," R.J. replied. "I like sending and reading code."

"Mr. Barkman asked if you had any interest in the signal bridge," MacDonald said, watching R.J. closely from out of the corner of his eye.

R.J. stood staring at the dark ocean and listening to the sounds of sea spray as it sprinkled and scattered across the deck. He loved being a Havernaut, and he loved being in the deck force. But he knew he belonged to the mysterious code, with communications, up here on the bridge where everything that happened could be seen and experienced. Mr. MacDonald had been good to him since he first arrived on the Haverfield, and now he was a little afraid he would disappoint the First Division commander.

"I'm a Havernaut, sir," R.J. said quietly. "I got a lot of good friends in First Division. I don't want to let my shipmates down."

"You'll always be a Havernaut, Davis," MacDonald replied. "Anyone who works as hard as you do, and has the talent you have, should go wherever that talent can take him." MacDonald put a hand on R.J.'s shoulder and squeezed affectionately. "You gotta see life as a series of steps, kid. Some of the steps you take are forward and some of them are backward. Some of them are lateral, like treading water. That's what you're doing now. You're stepping laterally." MacDonald cocked his head at R.J. and looked into his eyes. "Any of this make sense to you?"

"Yessir," R.J. replied, staring out at the sea.

"Good, because this step you're about to take to the signal bridge is what kind of step, lad?"

R.J. grinned at the lieutenant. "It's a forward step, sir."

"One of many forward steps to come, I think," MacDonald said. "You put in your chit tomorrow and I'll approve it and give it to Lieutenant Barkman." He smiled as he began to walk away. "You're lucky, really," he chuckled, turning back. "At least Complete Control Edgars isn't aboard any longer."

R.J. laughed while Mr. MacDonald went aft, and thought to himself, *Now, if we could just get rid of Chief Twitchy...*

The next morning R.J. submitted a request chit for transfer to the signal bridge. While he was filling out the chit, he decided to make a small addition. He also checked the box indicating a promotion in rank and wrote in, "...from SA (Seaman Apprentice, E-2) to SN (Seaman, E-3)." As long as Mr. MacDonald was in a good mood, R.J. figured he might as well test the limits of his benevolence.

That afternoon Mr. MacDonald stopped R.J. in the passageway and handed him the approved chit. "You are a signalman as of 0800 tomorrow, Davis. Report to Mr. Barkman in the OPS office right after chow." He smiled as he walked down the passageway, and called over his shoulder, "Nice touch with that promotion thing. I told Barkman it was my idea." He stopped and turned around. "Wanted you to know it didn't slip past me, *Seaman* Davis." Mr. MacDonald looked at R.J. for a few moments, then turned back around and went down the passageway.

After chow, R.J. sat at the rear booth of the messdecks, playing pinochle with Tanner, Sonny and Pea. He was taking some good-natured ribbing for 'running out on the deck force' as Sonny put it, but R.J. didn't mind. *One step forward.*

"We gettin' to Chi Chi Jima in a couple days," Sonny drawled. "Mr. MacDonald is going to talk about the battle for Iwo Jima tomorrow night on the fantail." He closed his cards and put them face down on the formica table. "I sure liked that last one, the one about Midway. That was cool."

Tanner put his cards down and lit a cigarette, blowing smoke rings up into the fluorescent light fixture. "My ol' man was in the Navy during the war," he announced. "He was with the fleet that run the Japs out of Leyte Gulf. He told us hundreds of stories about it. I hope Mr. MacDonald knows about that battle."

"He talks about the World War Two battles sometimes on the mid watch," R.J. said quietly. "Says he might write a book about it when he retires."

"All I know," Tanner said, picking up and sorting his cards, "is he shore do know his shit."

The game broke up and R.J. headed to First Division's compartment, looking forward to spending his last night there before moving to the more spacious and less crowded Operations Division compartment. When he got there, everyone seemed to be asleep, though it was only 2100. The only light on was the red steaming light which barely illuminated the compartment. R.J. reached his rack and felt something was wrong, out of place. He felt around with his hands and discovered his mattress was missing.

"Okay, wise-asses," he called out in the dark, "gimme back my mattress."

The sounds of bare feet hitting the deck all over the compartment made R.J. squint and peer through the darkness, trying to see where the sounds were coming from. Slowly, through the red-tinted dark several shapes began to appear. Men dressed only in skivvies were slowly surrounding him, and they were each carrying something big and white...

"Yo rack is up on the Signal Bridge," a deep voice bellowed out. "Where it belong!" It sounded like Andy Sample.

"Yeah," shouted another, (Lester?) "Where YOU belong!"

Something large and lumpy slammed into the deck at R.J.'s feet. He looked down at the thing and recognized it. *My seabag?*

"All yo shit's in yo seabag, Mr. Signalman," the first voice bellowed. "You gone from First Division now, and we all only got one thing to say to you."

Slowly and quietly the crowd closed in on R.J. He saw what they had in their hands, and he grabbed his seabag and tried to duck out, but was pushed backward and pummeled with pillows as the Havernauts pounded him to the deck. He was laughing so hard he couldn't get his feet under him. The crew continued pounding as R.J. scrambled on all fours to escape. Softly at first, then louder until they were chanting, almost shouting:

"Duke, Duke, Duke,
Duke of Earl, Duke, Duke,
Duke of Earl, Duke Duke
Duke of Earl."

Gino began to sing the lead while R.J. continued to try to flee:

"As I, I walk through this world,"
Pound, pound, pound.
"Nothing can stop me, the Duke of Earl!"
Pound, scramble, pound, pound.

R.J. dragged his seabag and squeezed between someone's legs to reach the hatch leading forward to escape and freedom. While he ran up the ladder, dragging his seabag, coughing and laughing, the Havernauts sang on below:

"And when they know you're my girl,
nothing can harm you—Oh nooooooo!"

R.J. reached the Operations compartment and found an empty rack, its mattress folded in two toward the head. He looked around. No sheets, no pillow cases. He resigned himself to sleeping on the bare mattress and opened up his seabag to get his gear when he discovered that his seabag had been packed neatly and carefully, everything clean and folded with regulation creases. On top was a new steaming hat. On the front of the hat was affixed a brass pin in the shape of crossed signal flags, the insignia for the signalman rate. R.J. smiled, running his fingers over the crossed flags. A little going away present from the deck force.

He stretched out on the bare mattress and put his hands behind his head, staring up at the overhead. He always liked to be in the top bunk, because he could stare at the overhead, trying to follow the paths of the various pipes until he fell asleep. And with no one sleeping above him, there was no chance someone would leap out of the top rack without looking and land on him. R.J. was always careful to look before he leaped. He stared at the overhead maze of pipes and swayed and rolled with the motion of the ship until he fell gently to sleep.

TWENTY SEVEN

Mr. Barkman was his usual cheerful self as he smiled at R.J. over the small desk in his stateroom, which he shared with Lieutenant (j.g.) Anton. He signed the order accepting R.J. into Operations Division and closed the personnel file. "I read about that stuff in San Diego, sailor, and I have to tell you, I think you've grown up a lot in the past six months." Mr. Barkman smiled pleasantly. "Anyway, bygones being bygones I expect you to make a contribution, Davis." He looked up from his desk and smiled again. "You receiving me, sailor?"

"Yessir," R.J. answered, smartly.

"Good. Well, I know you know your way around the Signal Bridge, so why don't you go up, report to Anselmi, and he'll keep you busy for today."

"Thank you, sir."

"It'll take me a couple of days to put together a training program for you. Try to look busy until then." Mr. Barkman smiled, stood up and held out his hand. "Welcome to Operations," he said.

R.J. took his hand. "Thank you, sir, it's good to be here." He turned and left, feeling like his boots were pillows and he was walking on clouds. He hurried to the signal bridge, hoping another ship would come by so he could signal her. Maybe take an important message, warning the ship of trouble ahead. He'd take it, write it out and present it to the captain. *Maybe save the ship his first day on the job!*

When he got to the signal bridge, Anselmi greeted him with a huge smile. "Hey, striker!" he called. "Boy am I glad to see you."

R.J. smiled. "Glad to be here."

Anselmi put his arm around R.J. and started leading him around the signal bridge. "See these belaying pins here, the ones we wrap the signal lanyards around to hold the flag hoist? They are made out of brass, and they tend to get a little corroded by all the sea air and all the neglect." He stopped and grinned. "Now since I ain't had time to do it, and since Becker is busy puking in his rack, you, my boy, the low man on the totem pole, must shine these pins until they sparkle in the moonlight." Anselmi stepped back, arms crossed and smiling.

R.J. looked around. There had to be thirty toggle pins to shine, many of which weren't even being used. "All these?" he asked, motioning with his arm. "This will take me all day."

"Take all the time you need," Anselmi smiled broadly. "Make sure you hit every brass surface you can find. If you do a good job, I'll put you on the light when we pull into Tokyo Bay.

R.J. knew that meant he would be taking all flashing light messages when they pulled into port. Yokosuka was a major Naval base. *Had to be hundreds of ships coming and going. Got to be a lot of signal traffic.* R.J. grabbed the bottle of Brasso and an old torn up tee-shirt. "Okay, Salami," he said. "They're gonna sparkle in the moonlight."

"Atta boy," Anselmi called as he slid down the ladder to the 02 level.

R.J. used the entire can of Brasso to polish the pins and all other brass surfaces on the signal bridge. The brass gleamed beautifully and gave the signal bridge a certain air of efficiency. When Anselmi returned and saw the job R.J. did, he gave him the rest of the day off. R.J. hung around the bridge anyway, watching the operation of the ship until evening chow was called, and then he drifted into the messdecks. He wanted to eat and get squared away in the new compartment before 2000, when Mr. MacDonald was going to give his lecture. R.J. wasn't about to miss that.

Fifteen minutes before 2000, the men began showing up on the fantail to stake out a place to sit. By the time Mr. MacDonald arrived, the deck, torpedo tubes and depth charge racks were filled with sailors, patiently waiting for the First Division commander.

The ship cut quietly and softly through the warm sea; the only sound of her journey was the gentle hiss of the waves sliding along her sides, port and starboard, like soft sighs in the moonlight.

Mr. MacDonald leaned against the forward bulkhead and glanced through a sheaf of notes in his hand. He looked up and scanned his audience, all bright, eager faces. He took out a cigar, slowly and purposefully unwrapped it, and stuck it in his mouth unlighted. He paced the deck slowly, and in the shadows of a warm, bright moon, Mr. MacDonald told them the story of Iwo Jima.

"The island we are visiting, Chi Chi Jima," he began, "is the little sister of a bigger, meaner, *nastier* island called Iwo Jima. You'll know what I mean when you see it. It was in the battle for Iwo Jima that American Marines, caught in a bitter struggle against a determined enemy who was well dug-in, lost more men than in any other battle of the war." Mr. MacDonald had a rapt audience. "Tomorrow morning, at zero-five-hundred hours, this vessel will pass within five miles of Iwo Jima and we will get a chance to see, up close, that disgusting blood-sucking island." He paused to make certain they were listening. They were. "Iwo Jima is not considered a naval battle per se, although Navy forces were certainly involved. The reason we are discussing this battle tonight is because we are passing close to that battle site tomorrow morning."

The men were sitting attentively, some on the deck, some on the 3-inch gun mount, some on the vents and some on the torpedo tubes. It looked as if both the off-duty sections were present. A bright canopy of stars and one of the most beautiful moons in history went unnoticed among the men gathered there, as Mr. MacDonald, cigar held between his thumb and forefinger and used as a pointer, began to spin the terrible tale.

"Iwo Jima was a strategic island," he began, "because the Japanese had built three airstrips on the island so they could launch their kamikaze attacks on U.S. Navy ships. We wanted the island as a base for the big B-29 bombers to conduct raids on the Japanese homeland. Taking this island meant the Japs had to fall back to Okinawa for their kamikaze operations, and we would have an air base halfway between Okinawa and Guam." He paused and looked around at the rapt faces of his audience. "You all know where Guam is, don't you?" he joked. Everyone laughed nervously. MacDonald lighted his cigar and blew the blue smoke up into the air where the wind took it and scattered it into the night.

"Hell, the carriers' planes bombed the damn island for over two months, and the battleships and cruisers bombarded the island for three days prior to the Marines' landing. Yes, Sonny?" he recognized the raised hand of Sonny Metzner. Lieutenant MacDonald enjoyed answering the crew's questions and encouraged the men to ask them.

"When exactly did this battle happen, sir?" Sonny asked.

MacDonald opened his notebook and flipped a few pages. "The Marines landed on February nineteen, nineteen forty five," he explained. "But the island wasn't secure until the end of March." He let that sink in for a few moments, then continued. "During that month and a half, those Marines caught living hell on that lousy island, and the Navy ships surrounding the island caught hell from the kamikazes." He closed his notebook and began reciting the story from memory.

"There were over seventy thousand American Marines and twenty-seven thousand Jap defenders involved in the battle. The Japs dug tunnels and built pillboxes all over the place. The little yellow bastards had themselves really well dug in. See, in previous invasion landings on Saipan and Tarawa, the Japs conducted massive banzai charges against the Marines and were mowed down by the thousands. This greatly shortened those battles, but the Japs weren't going to do it that way at Iwo Jima. They became more defensive. They didn't launch banzai attacks and, as a result, the battle for Iwo Jima took a long time and resulted in thousands of American casualties." He stared off into space for a few moments, alone with his thoughts.

"At one end of the island is a volcanic mountain called Mt. Suribachi," he went on. "This mountain had spewed volcanic ash all over the island and the Marines had to plod their way through it, carrying about a hundred pounds of equipment. The ash was slippery and soft and knee-deep. Kinda like advancing through quicksand. But they advanced, those brave Marines. They advanced all day and all night for three days against a horrendous hail of gunfire coming down on them from the high ground the Japs controlled. The Marines had to fire uphill as they attacked, and the angle was very bad. Plus, the Japs rained mortars down on them and the beach was littered with anti-tank mines, which made bringing the armor ashore difficult. The Marines had to take Suribachi quickly or the Japs would slaughter them from their high-ground firing positions." MacDonald began pacing back and forth in front of his audience, stabbing the air with his cigar.

"By the end of the first day, our Marines had only advanced a short dis-tance, capturing only half of their objectives, but they had over thirty thou-sand men ashore and were poised to advance on Mt. Suribachi. It took them three days to reach the peak, all the time taking heavy fire from the Jap positions. The kamikaze attacks continued all that time, and the Bismark Sea, an American carrier, was sunk. The Saratoga, another carri-er, was severely damaged. But the Marines came on," his voice faltered and his eyes teared up, "and they kept coming straight into the face of the Japs' resistance. With flame throwers and satchel charges the Marines slowly began to wipe out the tunnels and pillboxes the Japs were holed up in. They even set fire to the brush in the ravines to drive the little fuckers out of their holes. The Marines fought and died for small amounts of ground, sometimes measured in feet, but they kept coming on." He paused a moment and drew on his cigar again.

"Finally, on the twenty-third of February the Marines planted the flag on Mt. Suribachi. You guys have all seen that famous picture, right?" Everyone nodded silently.

"But the battle was far from finished," he cautioned. "The Fourth and Fifth Marine divisions launched an attack on the morning of the twenty-fourth and the Third Marine division led the attack on the center of the Jap position. With tanks coming ashore and pressed into the battle, the Marines made better progress and captured the first and second airfields. The Japs had positions high in the hills above the third airfield, and the Marines were determined to take those positions. The battle raged day and night, with heavy casualties on both sides. The Japs attacked over and over again, only to be beaten back by Marine tanks and artillery, but they fought on and on. On March 25 the Marines captured Kitano Point and the battle for Iwo Jima was all but over." Mr. MacDonald glanced again at his notes. "But that night the Japs snuck in behind the American lines and tried to disrupt their organization. By morning all but a few of the Japs were dead on the ground, sometimes only a few feet away from Marine positions." MacDonald sat back on a torpedo tube and looked into the faces of the men staring raptly at him. "Can you imagine what it was like, fighting for their lives in that dark night?"

R.J. closed his eyes and tried to put himself in their place. Whispers of the battle seemed to seep into his mind, across the two decades since Iwo Jima. He swore he could hear the sounds of the fighting, the shouts and screams, the explosions, the desperate struggle to stay alive.

"Boys, this battle was the bloodiest of the war for the U.S. Marines, but they finally took all three airfields and secured the island. Of the twenty-seven thousand Japanese involved in the battle, over twenty thousand were killed."

Several of the men responded. "Yeah, good!' Sonny shouted.

"Fuckin' ay," Pea spat.

"Too bad they didn't kill all those bastards," someone else said.

Mr. MacDonald waited for them to quiet down. "Just remember," he warned, "the Marines lost about seven thousand killed and another twenty thousand wounded. It was a dear price to pay for only eight square miles of rock. Remember that next time you see a Marine on liberty. Buy him a drink or give him a sharp salute. Show him the respect his daddy earned on Iwo Jima."

When Mr. MacDonald finished, the men sat stunned and quiet. Slowly, they began looking around at each other, trying to communicate the special feeling they were experiencing, and seeing it in others' eyes, smiled acknowledgment and lowered their heads.

"That's a true story of World War II, boys." Mr. MacDonald stubbed out his cigar in the butt kit and started forward, toward officer country. He sighed as he ducked his head and disappeared through the starboard hatch. "Good night, fellas," he whispered.

Hesitantly, one by one, the sailors got up, glanced around one more time, and drifted down to their compartments where they would lie awake in their racks, deep into thought, thinking of Iwo and the blood that was spent there.

The next morning at 0500 the sideline was crammed with sailors who wanted to get a glimpse of that "terrible island." They expected something sinister-looking and they were not disappointed.

Iwo Jima squatted on the horizon like a worn out sea cow. As the ship drew closer, the island quickly became more defined, seeming to etch itself harshly upon the new day. Mount Suribachi rose like an infected boil at one end of the island, and the men standing behind the lifeline, looking at it, swore they could smell its stench. They stood affixed, staring at Iwo Jima and thinking of the lives lost there. Tanner stepped up close to the lifeline and came to attention. Slowly, deliberately he raised his right hand and saluted sharply. All the Haverfield sailors followed, stepping forward without a sound, coming to attention and saluting. They held their salute quietly, tears rolling down their cheeks until Iwo slipped past their stern. Then they returned to their compartments without a word. R.J. stood on the fantail, awaiting reveille, and watched as the island of Iwo Jima faded and evaporated in the ship's wake, disappearing from the sea, almost as if it were never there. R.J. had the strange feeling that he had traveled back in time to see that horrible place, to experience that desperate battle, and was now returning to the present. He shuddered and went up to the signal bridge to polish some brass.

* * * * *

Later that morning Chief Twitchell roused himself from a drunken and fitful slumber and headed toward the chief's quarters to freshen up. He had spent the night passed out on a pile of spare life preservers in the forward storage compartment and he hadn't slept well despite downing a fifth of scotch. Chief Twitchell was in a bad mood, and was anxious to demonstrate to someone, anyone, just how bad his mood was. Unfortunately for Rafer Sample that morning, he just happened to be in Twitchell's path.

Rafer came around the corner from the ship's store, carefully tearing the wrapper off a chocolate bar with almonds, and didn't see Chief Twitchell until it was too late. Twitchell, head down and hurrying to his compartment, actually head-butted Rafer as they collided in the passageway. The chief bounced off Rafer and stumbled, falling to the deck. His chief's hat flew off his head, got caught in the wind, and sailed aft over the side and into the sea. Chief Twitchell went into a horrible rage, swearing, threatening and calling Rafer names. The confrontation lasted only a few moments, and ended abruptly when Chief Twitchell exploded in Rafer's face.

"You fuckin' niggers think you own the Navy now!" he screeched. "Wasn't too long ago you weren't welcome on board ship. Now you're all acting like you got the same rights as white people." Twitchell was red in the face and sweating profusely. A few sailors witnessed the confrontation and began to walk away, not wanting to be the next target for the furious chief. He pointed his finger in Rafer's face. "You're all shit as far as I'm concerned," he shouted.

Rafer shrank away from Twitchell. Not because he was afraid of him, but because the chief's breath was making Rafer sick. He stepped aside to allow the chief to pass, saying, "Don't call me that name." Rafer was outwardly calm, but his mind was seething, and his vision was filled with red. "In fact," he continued, "I want an apology."

Chief Twitchell turned and yelled at Rafer. "Don't back-talk me, Buckwheat! I'll put your ass on the pad so fast it'll make your head swim!"

"You wrong this time, Chief," Rafer said calmly. "You oughta apologize." He stared down directly into Twitchell's bleary, wet eyes.

"Your black ass is on report!" Twitchell shouted. "Assaulting a superior officer, disrespect to a superior officer, and anything else I can think of!"

Twitchell barked at Snively, who was one of the sailors watching the incident, "Go get me a fucking report form!"

Snively returned from the yeoman's office with the report form and gave it to Twitchell. The chief snatched it out of Snively's hands and waved it at Rafer. Then he turned his back and waddled off.

Rafer shrugged, looked around at the other sailors who were standing and staring, and stepped out the port-side hatch, calmly unwrapping his chocolate bar. He wasn't going to allow anyone to see his anger. He had a reputation for being cool under pressure, and that was exactly how he was going to act. If Chief Twitchy put him on report, he would just explain to the captain what had happened, and get some of the others who were present to testify. He knew he was in the right, and he knew Chief Twitchy was a racist asshole. But he didn't realize the fear that Twitchell inspired in the crew. When Twitchell returned with the report form filled out, he had two machinists mates with him as witnesses. Neither of them had been on deck during the confrontation, but both had signed the report chit and sworn that Rafer attacked the chief.

Rafer read the report chit and looked at the smiling, smirking face of Chief Twitchell. He looked over at the two witnesses who avoided making eye contact with him, and shook his head slowly and sadly. "This ain't how it happened," he said flatly.

"Sign the fucking chit!" Twitchell shrieked. "You ain't admitting anything, just sign."

"I ain't signin' anything that says I done somethin' I didn't," Rafer stated firmly. He folded the chit in half and stuck into Chief Twitchell's pocket. Then he glared at the two witnesses, turned around and walked away, toward the fantail.

Behind him the chief was apoplectic. "Get back here, you black sonofabitch!" he shouted. But Rafer didn't turn around. He clenched his teeth as hard as he could and tried to fight back the tears of rage welling up in his eyes. All his life he had swallowed the racial insults from teachers, storekeepers and restaurant owners who didn't want 'colored' in their establishments. He had broken the faces of a lot of red-necked white boys who bought into the theory that blacks were inferior. He and Andy had proven, with their fists, the fallacy of that argument, but this was a different thing altogether. This racist asshole was a chief petty officer aboard a Navy ship, and he held a lot of power Rafer could not fight with his fists. As angry as he was, Rafer realized that he had to be cool, try to think this out, find a way to get back at Twitchell without a direct confrontation. The Captain's mast would be his chance. He would get his witnesses together and make 'Twitchy' squirm at the Captain's mast. Rafer found Andy on the fantail and pulled him aside, explaining what had happened with Twitchell. Andy's big eyes got wider as Rafer told him the story and asked him to round up the guys who were there and saw what happened.

Andy nodded, jaw clenched and set, his hands forming tight fists at his side. "I'll get R.J.," he said. "He know how to go about this." Andy grinned at Rafer. "R.J. been to Captain's mast," he said. "And he don't play that racist shit."

"OK," Rafer nodded. "Talk to R.J."

By the time Andy made his way to the signal bridge, R.J. had already heard what had happened. In fact, the word had already spread throughout the ship by that fastest of all forms of communication; the scuttlebutt network.

Andy and R.J. talked for over half an hour. It was R.J.'s considered opinion that the captain wouldn't hold mast until after the ship had returned to Guam, so Rafer needn't worry about having his Japanese liberty suspended. But R.J. cautioned Andy that once back on Guam, it would be easier to send Rafer to the brig without considering lesser punishment such as restriction or extra duty. R.J. didn't believe the assault charge would hold, especially considering there were witnesses, but he warned Andy that if that charge did stick, Rafer was sure to go to the brig.

"If that happens," R.J. explained to Andy, "I'll give Rafer a lot of hints about the brig that'll make his time a little easier." He grinned and spread his hands out in front of him. "After all, I did my thirty days in there."

"Les hope that don't happen," Andy said seriously. "I don't want my brother in the brig for somethin' he dint do."

* * * * *

"Come in!" Captain Oliver called when someone knocked on his stateroom door. It was just after evening chow and the captain was writing in his journal and reviewing the steaming logs. He was pleased that the ship had made an average of twenty knots after leaving Guam, even with the delay of the man overboard drill, and would pull into Yokosuka tomorrow morning at 0900.

The stop over at Chi Chi Jima to drop off supplies only lasted a few hours as working parties labored quickly to load the supplies onto a motor driven barge for transfer to the island. Those men not on the working parties had broken out the fishing poles and caught several bonita off the focsul. Hawkins had cleaned them and the crew enjoyed an old fashioned fish fry that evening.

Captain Oliver smiled when he realized that the next day was Friday the thirteenth. He always considered Friday the thirteenth to be a lucky day for him.

The exec put his head in the door and asked, "Got a minute, Cap'n?"

Captain Oliver waved him in and gestured toward his bunk. "Sit down, Ed. What's up?"

"We've got a situation," the exec said.

"What kind of situation?" the captain asked, suspiciously.

"It's Chief Twitchell, Captain," the exec explained.

Oh, no, the captain thought. *Now what?*

"He put one of the deck force crew on report," the exec continued, handing the report chit to the captain. "Claimed that he was assaulted."

"Physically assaulted?" the captain asked, his brow furrowing and his mouth turning down into a scowl as he read the report chit.

"Yessir," the exec answered.

The captain groaned. "Who's the accused?"

"Rafer Sample, but it's a little thin, this accusation," the exec went on. "It seems it was more a case of Sample bumping into Twitchell, according to a few witnesses, and then back-talking him and refusing to sign the report chit."

Captain Oliver sighed. He was growing weary of Twitchell and all his confrontations with other sailors. The man was a hell of an engineer, but the trouble he caused diminished his efficiency in the captain's eyes. "Well," he said to the exec, "I'm not holding mast while we're in Japan. Tell the chief and young Sample that we will take this up after we return to Guam. I'm not going to let anything negative creep into this trip." The captain nodded and handed the chit back to the exec. "Give it to me after we're home, Ed."

Mr. MacDonald was furious when he heard about the confrontation between Rafer and Chief Twitchell. MacDonald didn't care for Twitchell and was glad he wasn't in First Division, but he recognized the chief's clout with the engineering department, and he knew the captain often deferred to Twitchell, especially when it came to the ship's power plants. The fact that Twitchell decided to turn in his report chit directly to the exec, without

MacDonald's getting the opportunity to talk to Twitchell and possibly dissuade him, really pissed off the lieutenant.

MacDonald headed for the exec's stateroom with the intention of stifling this report chit. *It was all bullshit, anyway.* If Rafer Sample had actually hit Twitchell, the chief would still be in sick bay. Rafer was a big, strong guy, and Twitchell was a fat drunk. The First Division lieutenant didn't believe Rafer had hit the chief, and he wanted to intercede before the exec took it to the skipper. He met the exec coming down the bridge ladder.

"I was hoping to talk with you," Mr. Mac said. "In private, if possible."

"Is this about Sample and Twitchell?" the exec asked.

"Yessir."

"Well, it's gonna have to wait until we get back to Guam, Mac. Captain doesn't want anything to detract from this trip."

"Twitchell should have come to me, sir," Mr. Mac said angrily. "Sample's my man and I don't like being kept out of the system."

"I know, I know, Mac," the exec said soothingly. "Let's put it on hold. We'll be back on Guam on the twenty-third. I'm going to talk to Twitchell and Pedro Almogordo about this, and I want everyone to just cool down until we get back."

MacDonald sighed and nodded. "Yes, sir," he replied, and turned around to leave.

"Mac," the exec called him back. He wanted to smooth things over and keep things under a lid until their return. MacDonald was one of the best officers aboard ship, and the exec had a great deal of respect for the First Division commander.

"Yes sir?" The lieutenant turned.

"That kid, Davis," the exec said. "You did the right thing moving him to the signal bridge." He smiled warmly at MacDonald and put his hand on his shoulder. "I saw him on the signal light. He's good."

MacDonald smiled widely and nodded. "That he is, sir. That he is."

"Keep up the good work, Mac," the exec said, patting MacDonald on the shoulder. "The captain and I are damn proud of that deck force."

MacDonald beamed. "Thank you, sir," he said, saluting sharply.

The exec returned the salute and watched MacDonald slide down the ladder to the 02 level. *Good man,* he thought. *Damned good man.*

TWENTY EIGHT

Next morning R.J. was up early, before reveille, and stood on the port wing sipping coffee and looking at the islands of Japan as they loomed out of the horizon. The main island, Honshu, looked a lot bigger than it did on the nav charts. The charts didn't show it was an island full of flourishing green trees on lush green hills. The ship slowed to two-thirds as they grew closer to Japan and encountered a little shipping traffic, mostly big, rusty cargo ships flying various national flags and carefully keeping to their shipping lanes. Anselmi stood on the 02 level, holding the lanyard to the steaming flag, waiting orders to dip, but only if the other ships dipped first. American Naval ships do not dip the American flag first, only in answer to another country's ship dipping hers. And the American flag was never, ever dipped to a Soviet ship or any other communist nation's ships, regardless of whether or not they dipped first.

Becker came staggering up to the bridge carrying a ten-gallon milk can, the top cut out and a loop of nylon line holding the can around his neck. He was seasick as usual, and R.J. was astonished to see that the man was actually green! His face was a pale green color, and he looked as if he were on his death bed. R.J. had heard that seasickness will turn a man green, but he always thought that was just an expression. Now, looking at Becker, he realized it was true.

"Davis," Becker gasped, "I heard you were striking to be a signalman. Welcome to the signal bridge."

R.J. thought it was curious that Becker was welcoming HIM to the signal bridge. He had spent much more time on the signal bridge than Becker did over the past couple of months, but he just smiled and said, "Thanks, Flags."

Becker smiled weakly, then got a sick look on his face and turned around to barf into the milk can. R.J. turned away, listening to the sounds Becker made, and decided he wasn't in the mood for breakfast.

Becker wiped his mouth on his dungaree shirt sleeve and turned back toward R.J. "Sorry," he gasped. "Fucking seasickness. Sorry."

"No problem," R.J. said, smiling sympathetically.

"Anyway, I won't be here when we pull in to port, so you and Anselmi gotta handle things. I'll be up when this fuckin' ship stops bobbing around."

"We'll take care of it, Flags," R.J. assured him. "We can handle it."

"Okay," Becker said, holding on to his milk can. He staggered back down the ladder to the 02 level. He was headed straight for his bunk. R.J. hoped he would make it without decorating the deck.

Anselmi arrived on the bridge just after reveille, sipping a cup of coffee and munching on a piece of toast. He motioned for R.J. to join him back by the flag bag.

"Becker won't be around for docking," he said.

"Yeah, I know. He was just up here."

"He share his milk can with you?" Anselmi chuckled.

"He offered, but I said I already ate breakfast." R.J. replied. "He was green. I mean, the man was actually green!"

"Yeah, they get that way." Anselmi sipped his coffee and studied R.J. over the rim of the cup. "You want the light coming in to port?"

"Damn straight I do," R.J. replied, grinning broadly.

"Okay, here's the drill." Anselmi finished his toast and brushed his hands together, getting rid of the crumbs. "The tower in Yokosuka is the only thing you worry about. If another ship tries to flash us on our way in, I'll take it. You just concentrate on that tower."

"Okay," R.J. acknowledged. "What's the tower gonna ask us?"

"They'll give you the berthing instructions and welcome us to Yokosuka," Anselmi explained. "Then, as we head to our berth they will send several action messages for the captain. These messages indicate the air and water temperatures, wind speed and direction, weather reports, standing port orders and any special instructions for the captain from the Port OOD."

"Sounds simple enough," R.J. observed.

"Not simple!" Anselmi scolded him. "These guys on that signal tower are the best in the fleet. There's a three-year waiting list for assignment there, and everyone who gets assigned there is a career man. They have to ship over for six years to get that two-year assignment, but for a signalman, that's the top, understand?"

"I think so."

"And they aren't bashful about showing off, so they'll hit you with one message after another, very fast code, and they'll do everything they can to snow you." Anselmi stared at R.J., making sure he understood.

"I'm ready, Salami," R.J. assured him.

"You better be," Anselmi said, "because every signal bridge in the port is going to be watching you, and if they think you fucked up, we'll never hear the end of it in the Alley."

"The Alley?" R.J. asked.

"That's where all the Navy bars are located downtown," Anselmi said. "They call it the Alley."

"Let 'em watch," R.J. said, head raised in a cocky fashion. "They wanna rock and roll, we'll rock and roll."

"Atta boy!" Anselmi said. "You do good and I'll take you to the 'Texas' tonight." He winked and nudged R.J. with his elbow.

"The Texas bar?" R.J. asked.

"Yeah, you heard of it?"

"Tanner and Lester rave about the place. Said they had the best Jap pussy in Yokosuka," R.J. said, laughing.

"That be true," Anselmi agreed. "That be true." He grinned and headed back to the flag bags, where he unbuttoned their canvas covers and reached in, fluffing the flags with his hands. He checked the lanyards on both sides of the ship and turned his attention to the signal lights, checking that they came on quickly, and inspecting the bulbs for signs of burn out. He noticed the brass on the signal bridge was freshly polished and gleamed in the early morning mist. He glanced toward R.J. and smiled to himself. *Nothing like shiny brass to make a signal bridge look four-oh.*

Just as the ship was approaching the mouth of Tokyo Bay, Captain Oliver came onto the bridge and checked the charts. He then went to the radar scope and checked that. "I'll take the conn," he said to Ensign Thompson.

"Aye, aye, sir," Mr. Thompson replied. "The special sea and anchor detail is set, sir."

"Very well."

"The captain has the conn!"

"Stick close, Rod," the captain instructed Mr. Thompson. "I want you to learn how to handle a ship coming into a large port."

"Aye, sir." Mr. Thompson stood on the flying bridge, out of the way where he could observe without interfering.

"All ahead one third," the captain ordered. He wanted to slow down a bit while they maneuvered through the channel.

"One third, aye, sir."

"Come to course three five zero," the captain called.

"Three five zero, aye, sir." Tanner was at the helm, as always during the special sea and anchor detail.

The ship began to pick its way around jutting islands and vegetation covered hills, slowly steaming into the bay toward Yokosuka, which was at the mouth of Tokyo Bay. R.J. thought Japan was beautiful, with all the green hills and blue-green water. The shipping traffic was heavy in Tokyo Bay, mostly merchant ships headed here and there, with a few American Navy ships mixed in. The Haverfield was too far away for the flag dipping tradition, so Anselmi stayed on the bridge and watched the activity with R.J.

As they turned the corner and began to make their way into the port, the sight was unforgettable to R.J. Dozens of Navy ships were tied up, all flying the Stars and Stripes. R.J. had never seen so many Navy ships in one place, not even San Diego. This was the fleet; the powerful, undefeated American Navy in all its glory. Destroyers, aircraft carriers, cruisers and supply ships lined the piers or were tied up next to each other. They passed the tender, Prairie, tied stern to pier with destroyers lined up along both her sides. And everywhere R.J. looked, that proud, beautiful flag was flying from every fantail in sight. Those 'broad stripes and bright stars' fluttered and flowed in the wind, proclaiming the power and invincibility of the American Navy. R.J. never felt so proud to be a part of something. He felt like he was coming home. He stood and stared, in a trance, at those beautiful flags flying from every ship in the harbor.

"Hey, R.J. wake up!"

R.J. snapped out of his trance and saw Anselmi on the starboard wing pointing toward the hills above the harbor. A light was flashing furiously from the signal tower, high up in the hills, surrounded by trees of unusual shape and texture. *Oh well. Back to reality.*

R.J. snapped the light on, spun it around and pointed it at the tower, and sent *dah-dit-dah*, or 'K' for 'go ahead.' Cotton appeared at R.J.'s elbow, message pad and pencil poised. R.J. smiled at Cotton, who smiled back.

"Okay," R.J. said, "here we go."

The tower began flashing a message. The sender was very fast, but sent in short spurts of code, obviously trying to impress. R.J. began reading and Cotton began writing.

"To Commander USS Haverfield from port commander, Yokosuka," he read. Cotton wrote it down quickly, not looking up. "Welcome to Japan. Best wishes for a pleasant visit."

The signalman on the tower didn't use any punctuation, so R.J. decided he either didn't know it, or was lazy. "Please proceed starboard side of USS Prairie and tie up to outboard ship." R.J. smiled as he read it aloud. Couldn't very well tie up to the inboard ship, could they? He deliberately held the light open so the signal tower could continue to send without stopping for the usual flash of acknowledgement after each word. Then the tower sent 'K' for go ahead. R.J. looked at the message form in Cotton's hand and, satisfied he had written it down correctly, flashed *dit-dah-dit*, or 'R' for received. Cotton took the message to the captain who studied the layout of the harbor, found the Prairie and realized he was about to sail past it.

"All stop!" he ordered.

"All stop, aye, sir."

"Right standard rudder! Come to course zero one zero!"

"Right standard rudder, coming to course zero one zero, sir."

The tower flashed again, the first of several low-priority messages sent to all arriving ships, and R.J. took each message with the light wide open, and receipted for them immediately after the tower had sent them.

The Haverfield pivoted and swung into its turn, the stern sweeping to port until she came broadside to the fleet in plain view of every ship docked there. Just as she began to move backward, the captain smiled. "All ahead one-third," he said calmly. The Haverfield came out of the turn beautifully, just like a car backing out of a driveway, turning, stopping, shifting gears and moving forward. She pointed her bow to the tender and began easing slowly toward the outboard destroyer, the William Collins. The line handling party stood at the Collins' lifeline, awaiting the Haverfield's arrival.

"Signal bridge!" the captain called. R.J. rushed into the pilot house.

"Yes sir?"

"Thank the tower for the greeting and advise them we will comply with berthing instructions. Ask them if our mail has been forwarded."

"Yes, sir," R.J. said and ran back to his light. *My turn.*

Sailors on almost every ship watched the Haverfield complete the clever maneuver and slide smoothly toward the tender. They smiled and waved at the Haverfield, acknowledging the expert ship handling. The sailors on the Collins were grinning and shaking their heads in wonder. *That was one hell of a slick move!*

R.J. flashed the tower and when he got the 'go ahead' he grinned and began to transmit his message. He didn't send too fast, but matched the speed of the tower. It soon became obvious that, while he wasn't sending faster than the tower, he sure as hell was sending smoother. He was acutely aware he was being watched by the other ships in port, so he included various punctuation marks which the tower had a little trouble recognizing, and when the message was sent and receipted for, he sent *dah dah-dit-dah dit-dit-dit*, which stood for 'TKS' or 'thanks.'

* * * * *

High up in the hills in the signal tower, senior chief signalman Joe Williams stood behind SM1 Carruthers and shook his head. "That guy is smooth," he said, tapping Carruthers on the shoulder. "He's as fast as you, but his code is perfect. Easy to read."

"Must be a chief or first class," Carruthers remarked.

"Ask him his name," the chief said.

Carruthers flashed the Haverfield and when R.J. answered, asked the question. 'Davis, R.J.' came the reply.

"Tell him we would like to buy him a drink at the Black Rose tonight," the chief instructed. Carruthers sent and R.J. replied, 'You got a deal!'

Carruthers receipted for the message, but turned to the chief and said, "I didn't quite get that last little bit."

The chief looked at Carruthers and grinned. "That last little bit, my friend," he said, "was an exclamation point. You ever see or send an exclamation point?"

"Nope, never seen one before."

"Well, I haven't seen many. I can't believe I actually remembered the code. Exclamation point. Who the hell sends exclamation points?" he asked no one in particular.

* * * * *

"All stop!" the captain ordered. "Rudder amidships!"

"All stop, aye, sir!"

"Rudder amidships, sir!"

The Haverfield drifted toward the William Collins, slipped into position about three feet away, and stopped. The Haverfield line handlers grinned at each other, reached over and handed the mooring lines to the William Collins line handlers, who shook their heads in wonder.

"Mind if we park here?" Lester asked the Collins sailors.

Most ships would have stopped farther away, thrown the lead lines over, and once moored, would have used the capstain to bring the ship in. The Haverfield was in perfect position as soon as the drifting stopped, and it took only minutes to drop the fenders over the side and tie her up.

"We're tied up, Captain," Mr. Thompson said.

"Very well." The captain was smiling. "Switch to shore power and wash down the ship fore and aft. Once the ship is squared away, announce liberty."

"Aye, aye, sir," Mr. Thompson said, grinning broadly as the captain left the bridge. *The Skipper was one smooth son of a bitch*, he thought.

Tanner let go of the helm, stepped back, flipped open his Zippo and lit a cigarette. "That was cool," he said, snapping the lighter shut and blowing a perfect smoke ring up at the overhead. "VERY cool."

As soon as Anselmi lowered the steaming ensign and raised another on the fantail, flashing lights came from four, then five, then six different ships. R.J. rushed to the light and found he had left it on. It was hot as hell and he burned his hand slightly as he swung the light around and sent 'K' to the nearest flashing ship, the carrier Oriskany, carrying the Admiral's flag.

'To Commander, USS Haverfield. From COMCRUDESPAC. That was one hell of a maneuver and some great shiphandling. Please join me and my staff for dinner aboard the flagship, 1700 hrs.' 'K'

R.J. receipted for the message and turned his light toward the next flashing ship, another destroyer escort. 'K'

'Quite a show you guys put on coming into port. Nice move to the berth. Who is sending that code?' 'K'

R.J. receipted and replied. 'Davis, R.J.'

He then turned to the next ship and the next and the next until he had taken congratulatory messages from six or seven of them. He watched as several ships flashed others and chatted about the dramatic entrance to Yokosuka by the DER from Guam. One of the main topics was the perfect code being sent by the Haverfield's signal bridge. R.J.'s chest puffed just a bit as he eavesdropped on the conversations.

"Don't get a swelled head kid, but you done a good job."

R.J. turned and dropped his jaw at the sight before him. Becker was standing on the wing. He had showered and shaved and was outfitted in clean, pressed dress blues, with a beautiful spit shine on his shoes. He looked good, incredibly good compared to when R.J. had last seen him.

"Thanks, Flags," R.J. said. "You look good."

"I'm gonna be first down that gangway when they call liberty," Becker said. "I'm gonna get on solid ground, then I'm gonna go down to the Texas Bar, get drunk and snatch me some of that Jap poontang before the fleet gets liberty!"

"Save some for the rest of us," R.J. called to him as Becker disappeared down the bridge ladder.

Anselmi came up on the signal bridge with a big grin on his face. "I been watching all the signal activity. I guess we made a hell of an entrance, huh?"

R.J. smiled and looked around at the sea of Navy gray in the harbor. "You know something, Salami?" he said, patting the bulkhead. "This old gal is the most squared away ship here." He pointed to the fleet. "Not one of them looks as good as us."

He was right. Even the Oriskany was in need of a paint job. The William Collins, the ship the Haverfield was tied up next to, looked like it had been through a battle. Sailors were scurrying around, sanding rust spots and working on all types of equipment. Her brass fixtures were green from salt spray, and her crew was sloppy in dress and manner.

"Kinda reminds you of us a few months ago, don't it?" Anselmi asked.

"Captain done us proud," R.J. said quietly, almost to himself.

"Light!" Anselmi pointed toward the signal tower. They were flashing the Haverfield's abbreviated call sign: *dah-dit-dit   dit-dit-dit-dah-dah*, or 'D-3', short for DER-393.

R.J. turned on the signal light and sent the 'K'. *dah-dit-dah.*

The signal tower asked if R.J. was on the light. When he responded with *dah-dit-dah-dit* or 'C' for correct, the tower asked him to be at the Black Rose Bar at 1900 and ask for Chief Williams.

R.J. receipted for the message and turned to Anselmi. "Guess I gotta date," he grinned.

"Those guys are gonna want you to ship over and join the tower crew," Anselmi said. "That's how they find their new talent."

"Well," R.J. replied. "They're gonna be disappointed, 'cause I'm here for four and no more."

Anselmi winked at R.J. and left the bridge. "Have fun," he called as he slid down the ladder. "I gotta beat Becker to the Texas, or he'll have all those chicks spoiled, throwing yen around."

"You better hurry," R.J. warned. "He's got a head start on you." R.J. pointed to the stern of the tender Prairie where Becker was scurrying down the brow and heading for the main gate.

"Sonofabitch!" Anselmi complained. "How did he..." He waved at R.J. absently and rushed below to change into his dress blues.

R.J. didn't have 'open gangway liberty' like all E-5's and above, so he stayed on the signal bridge, fidgeting with his signal light, cleaning the lens and oiling all the working parts. He polished the light lovingly, checking for rust spots and working the oil into the handle and louvers. There wasn't much to do, since he had polished all the brass before they came into the bay, and Anselmi had tightened up all the signal lanyards and neatly folded the canvas covers to the flagbags, storing them in the cabinet behind the signal bridge.

R.J. stood on the bridge, taking in the sights of the morning, eavesdropping on signal traffic and sipping black coffee. The harbor was cool, the dark gray water calm and a bit oily, and it smelled of dead fish. *Much different from the aqua green water of Apra Harbor.* All around him the sounds of the fleet permeated the air. Chipping and sanding, shouting and cursing, machinery blaring, cranes groaning up and down the docks, all made R.J. feel that the Haverfield had taken her place with the fleet. She didn't feel like a 'Coconut-Navy' ship now. She felt more like an orphaned daughter reunited with her estranged parents. It was a good feeling.

* * * * *

The ship's officers gathered in the wardroom for lunch, buzzing about the arrival in Japan and the slick maneuver the captain executed coming into port. They fell silent and rose to their feet when Captain Oliver stepped into the wardroom. Then they started applauding.

"As you were," the captain said, a happy smile on his face. The officers sat down, grinning and waited patiently for the captain to speak. Hawkins and one of his Filipino ship's servicemen came in with lunch and distributed the plates of food and glasses of iced tea around the table. The captain waited until they left. The door closed and the captain picked up his glass and held it up for a toast. "Gentlemen," he began. "Here's to a successful voyage. I'm proud of you and the crew for your performance during this trip. And I'm proud of the condition and appearance of our ship."

The officers raised their glasses and said in unison, "To a successful voyage."

Mr. MacDonald cleared his throat. "If I may, Captain?" he said. The captain nodded. Mr. Mac raised his glass and toasted, "To one of the slickest ship-handling maneuvers I've ever seen." The other officers raised their glasses to a chorus of, "Here, here!"

"Thanks, Mac," the captain responded. "I'm having dinner with the admiral tonight on the flag ship and I intend to ask for our UED time table to be advanced so we can participate in the evaluations on our way back to Guam." He looked around the table at his officers. "I think we're ready."

The officers all voiced agreement with the captain. They were all anxious to prove that their training for the past six months was paying dividends. A good UED would prove that beyond doubt. And each officer, in his own mind, felt a degree of pride with the improved appearance of the ship and the crew. They knew they could hold their heads up at the Officer's Club, confident in their abilities and the abilities of their ship. Maybe they were an older, smaller ship from Micronesia, part of the 'Coconut Fleet,' but they were Navy and anxious to prove it.

The rest of the lunch went pleasantly, with every officer in high spirits and a good mood. No one could remember a more successful, better executed steaming trip. Bring on the UED, they were indeed ready.

TWENTY NINE

R.J. tied the square knot in his neckerchief and adjusted it so it sat precisely on the 'V' of his jumper, which was regulation and was where the thundering had taken place. It was impossible not to remember where to place the knot after being thundered there, but R.J. knew as soon as he left the ship he would readjust the knot higher, closer to his neck like a real Navy 'Salt.' It was going on 1700 and he had promised Tanner, Lester, and a few others that he would stop at the Texas bar for drinks before joining the tower signalmen at the Black Rose. He was anxious to get off base and into the Alley. He had heard a great deal about the bar section of Yokosuka and he wanted to experience it first hand, in all its infamous glory. As he stood on the quarterdeck of the Prairie with his liberty card in hand, waiting for his turn to leave the ship, Cotton and Gino came up next to him.

"Goin' to the Texas?" Cotton asked.

"That's affirmative," R.J. answered, nodding his head and snapping his fingers.

Gino picked up the beat and began singing, "Goin' to the chapel and we're gonna get ma-a-arried." He grinned his big Greek grin at the others. "Man I been lookin' forward to coming here," he said, sweeping his hand over the harbor.

"Well, pace yourself, good buddy," Cotton said. "We got two weeks, so don't blow your whole wad on one night." He patted Gino on the back. "Know what I mean about blowing your wad?"

"Yeah," Gino said, lapsing into jive talk and grabbing his crotch. "You be talkin' 'bout my munny."

"Speaking of money," R.J. cut in. "How come they paid us in this Monopoly money?" He held out several bills of military scrip. The bills were smaller than the dollar and printed in elaborate red designs.

"Can't use greenbacks over here," Cotton explained. "And don't ask me why 'cause I don't know." He thought about it for a second. "AND, I don't give a shit."

The trio left the ship and hurried down the brow. They walked quick-ly down the pier, across the base and out the main gate, where they piled into one of the Japanese taxis lined up just outside the gate. "Texas Bar," Cotton instructed, climbing in the front with the driver. "And hayaku, if you please."

The taxi driver smiled big and nodded. He slammed the transmission into first gear and exploded down the street, screeching tires and careening through the congested traffic, throwing his passengers across the backseat.

"Shit!" Gino howled. "What's 'hayaku' mean, drive like a muddafuc-ka?"

Gino and R.J. held on to the back of the driver's seat as the taxi bounced along the narrow, pot-holed street. "This dude drives worse than Billy Lopez!" Gino exclaimed.

R.J. tried to get a look at the passing scenery, but the taxi was going too fast to focus on anything, so he sat back and enjoyed the myriad of sights and sounds whizzing past the speeding car. Before they knew it, they squealed to a stop in front of the EM Club, the passengers bouncing back and forth in the rear seat.

"This ain't the Texas Bar," Gino observed, looking out the window at the big stone building.

"No go Alley!" the taxi driver yelled.

"Okay, okay," Cotton assured him. "No go Alley."

The trio crawled out of the cab, a little shaken but no worse for wear and Cotton handed the driver a hundred yen. The driver smiled big and gunned the engine, popped the clutch and shot down the street, careening and weaving his way through the maddening traffic.

"How much you give him, Cotton?" R.J. asked.

"Hunnerd yen."

"How much is that?" Gino inquired.

"Three hunnerd-sixty yen to a dollar," Cotton replied. "'Bout thirty-five cents."

"Man, the Cyclone roller coaster at Lakeside Park in Denver costs more than that," R.J. said, straightening his whitehat. "And the ride ain't nearly as scary."

"How come he wouldn't go to the Alley?" Gino asked.

"Can't," Cotton replied. "Streets are too narrow for cars, so they ain't allowed. Only wheels in the Alley are bicycles."

"What about rickshaws?" Gino asked.

"Naw, man. You thinkin' of China." Cotton laughed.

"Chinese, Japanese, what's the difference?" Gino retorted.

Cotton led them into the Enlisted Men's Club, where they climbed a long staircase to the main floor.

"Where we goin?" R.J. asked. "This ain't the Texas bar."

"Gotta get some whiskey and beer," Cotton said, motioning them to follow.

"I thought we were gonna drink at the Texas," Gino whined. "I don't wanna drink with just a bunch of fuckin' sailors my first night in town!" He looked at Cotton and R.J. "No offense."

"We buy a bottle of Jack Daniel's and a case of beer here where the prices are really low," Cotton explained. "Then we take it to the Texas and Mama-san keeps it behind the bar and gives us a beer or a shot when we order it." He smiled at the neophytes with him. "She only charges a hunnerd yen to check it in, and she keeps track of it for us."

"How do they make any money?" R.J. wondered.

"From the chicks, my man," Cotton explained. "From the chicks."

They all pitched in for a fifth of Jack Daniel's and case of beer, San Miguel because they didn't have any Colorado beer, and headed out of the EM Club and down the avenue toward the Alley. The avenue was crowded with foot traffic, mostly sailors wandering down the street, either toward the Alley or the EM Club.

Cotton led them around the corner into a narrow street teeming with hundreds of people. There were sailors everywhere, bicyclists maneuvering their way through the crowd with trays of fried rice for delivery, Japanese pimps who tried to tempt the trio into bars and whorehouses, and shopkeepers who tried to lure them into the various shops. These included gift shops, where the sailors could buy everything from fancy knives to Oriental lingerie to send home to wives and girlfriends. There were novelty shops that custom-made coffee mugs with whatever message a sailor wanted baked on, food stands offering sashimi, octopus and other delicacies, and the ever-present tattoo parlors with pictures of the tattoo artist's work proudly displayed in the windows. Everywhere was the bustling sound of hawkers. In the doorway of every bar they passed, scantily clad Japanese bar girls begged and chided the sailors to "come in, havva good time!"

R.J. took it all in, the sounds and smells of commerce, Yokosuka-style, and he loved it. This was much better than Tijuana, with its dirty streets, dirtier whores and filthy bars. This was the Orient he had imagined, and he was thoroughly enjoying it. Everywhere he looked, neon signs blinked and blared a rainbow of bright colors in the cool evening air. Bars with names like the Blue Fox, the Night Hawk, the Tennessee Bar and Grill, Sasebo Sally's and of course, the Black Rose, glittered along Broadway Avenue, the actual name of the main street in the Alley.

R.J.'s head was on a swivel, trying in vain to take it all in at once. When they approached the New Texas, Cotton motioned for them to follow. They stooped down under the door jam as they entered the small, dingy alcove leading to the bar. Almost at once, mama-san appeared and bowed to them, smiling inscrutably in her red and blue flowered kimono. She had spotted the whiskey and beer they were carrying and figured they were serious customers who would stay awhile and fraternize with her girls. She led them to the bar where they plunked down a hundred yen and she took the alcohol into the back room, returning with two small cardboard cards, one numbered from one to twenty four (for the beer) and the other numbered from one to forty (for the whiskey.) Mama-san could easily squeeze forty shots out of a fifth of whiskey.

"You sit," she directed. "You havva good time!" She bowed and went back behind the bar to bring them a shot and beer.

The trio spotted the other Havernauts at a table across the small dance floor and headed that way. Sonny, Tanner and Pancho were sitting with three brightly dressed bar girls and Pea and Lester were dancing with two others, grinding obscenely to the strains of Barbara Lynn's 'You'll Lose a Good Thing' which blared from the juke-box at the end of the room.

Tanner saw them approaching and called out, "Hey boy-san, you come here, havva good time!"

R.J. and Gino followed Cotton as he navigated his way across the smoky dance floor, weaving in and around the sailors and bar girls until they reached the table where their shipmates sat. Pancho's white hat was on his girl's head, and he was nuzzling her ear. Sonny and Tanner had their hats on the backs of their heads and their sleeves rolled up, both against uniform regs, and they were flushed with alcohol. Smiling bright-eyed at the newcomers, Sonny scooted three chairs out for them with his foot and yelled above the music, "Y'all take a load off!"

As the trio sat down, three more bar girls in brightly colored, form-fitting dresses appeared and sat down with them. R.J. looked at the dark haired girl next to him. She looked like she was in high school, but then so did he.

"You buy me drink?" she cooed, snaking her arm around R.J.'s neck.

"Sure, why not?" he shrugged. "Bring this girl a shot and a beer!" he called to mama-san who came scooting over to the table to admonish him.

"She no drinkee whiskey," she scolded. "She havva champagne cocktail." She frowned and pointed at R.J. disapprovingly. "You buy!"

R.J. looked at Tanner and Sonny. They grinned and nodded. Pancho was whispering something obscene in the girl's ear.

"Okay, I buy," R.J. agreed.

"Me too," Gino said. "I buy too!" He put his arm around his girl and pulled her close.

"Yeah, yeah," Cotton agreed. "Bring all three of 'em drinks."

Mama-san scurried off and returned with three wine glasses filled with a pink bubbly liquid. She put the drinks in front of the girls and handed them each a colorful plastic chip that looked like a large guitar pick. The chips had holes drilled in one end. The girls took their chips and threaded them onto key-rings which already held several other chips.

Sonny saw R.J. and Gino looking questioningly at the chips. "That's how they get paid," he explained. "You buy a drink, they get a chip. At the end of the night, they turn their chips in and get money from mama-san."

The girls were nodding and smiling. R.J. looked at his girl and asked, "So, what's your name, Toots?"

She smiled, giggled and pointed to herself. "No Toots!" she squealed, "my name Susie." She pointed to the other two girls. "Her name Tammy, and she Patty."

Cotton gulped down his whiskey, made a sour face and chased it down with several gulps of beer. "Pleased ta meetcha," he said, wiping his mouth on his sleeve. "C'mon baby, let's dance." He took Patty's arm and they moved out onto the floor where they began doing the twist to a Chubby Checker song.

"You want dance?" Susie asked R.J.

"No dancee!" R.J. answered, smiling mischievously. "Me want drinkee!"

Susie looked at him curiously, trying to decide if he was making fun of her.

R.J. saw her expression and smiled his most charming smile. "So, you are surprised I speak your ranguage," he said in his best Oriental accent. "You see, I was educated in your country. At UCRA."

Susie squinted at R.J. and finally decided he was making fun of her. "You crazy, boy-san!" she yelled and stood up. "I go now!"

"Sure, sure, Toots," R.J. replied, waving her away. "You go now."

"No Toots! My name Susie!" She turned on her heel and left in a huff, throwing a disapproving look at her friends.

"Now why did you go and do that?" Tanner asked pleasantly. "You're throwing away perfectly good pussy." Pancho's head came up when he heard 'pussy' and he looked around blearily.

R.J. leaned close to Tanner so the other girls couldn't hear him. "Don't like Japs," he said in a low voice.

"And why not?" Tanner asked.

"Because they tried to kill my father."

"Mine, too," Tanner replied. "Look at it as revenge."

R.J. frowned and sipped his beer. "You take revenge for me," he said. "I gotta date with a chief signalman."

"Just 'cause you don' like these gals," Sonny drawled, "ain't no reason to turn queer."

R.J. laughed and finished his beer. "Speaking of signalmen, where's Becker and Anselmi?"

Sonny pointed to the ceiling.

"What's up there?" Gino asked.

"Rooms," Tanner replied.

"They went up there with a coupla chicks?" R.J. asked.

"Yep," Sonny said. "Went up there with a coupla chicks...each."

"Two?" R.J. exclaimed. "What's a guy gonna do with two chicks?"

"Same as what you do with one," Tanner explained. "Only faster."

Gino shook his head. "Shit, and I thought boatswain's mates were strange." He grinned at Tanner and Sonny. "No offense."

"Oh, shit," Sonny said, looking up at the stairs which led to the second floor bedrooms. "Here he comes again."

They all looked up at the stairs. Riley was staggering down the steps, his neckerchief missing and the sleeves to his jumper rolled up, showing brightly colored twin dragon patches sewn into the inside of the cuffs. He was naked from the waist down except for his navy blue socks, and he had his arm around a bar girl. He gave her a quarter and, weaving slightly, pointed her toward the juke box. She scampered down the stairs and deposited the quarter in the box, punching two buttons and scrambling back up the stairs.

"Great," Tanner said disgustedly. "Now we gotta listen to that damn song again."

The juke box deposited the 45 RPM record on the turntable and the beautiful voice of Tony Bennett filled the air. Riley stood on the stairs and sang along drunkenly.

"I lef my heart...in Shan Franchishco!"

Most of the other sailors in the bar groaned along with Tanner and Sonny. R.J. smiled at the scene. When Riley spotted him sitting with Tanner, Sonny and Pancho he lurched down the stairs, missed the last step and stumbled toward their table.

"R.J.!" he yelled. "You shoulda seen this little chink's ass! She had the cutest little ass!" Riley stood swaying in the middle of the dance floor. He squinted around at the crowd, and interpreted their laughter as encouragement. "Really cute!" he assured everyone seriously. He staggered slightly and regained his balance. "Ha ha ha! Cute little chink ass!"

R.J. and the Havernauts laughed along with everyone else in the bar. Riley grabbed the bar girl by the ass and announced, "These japs got dumpy asses, not like my sweet little chink!"

Mama-san came bustling up and shooed Riley and the girl back up the stairs. Riley climbed the stairs slowly, supported by the bar girl who was scolding him. Everyone in the bar laughed as Riley's bare bottom disappeared up the stairs.

"High up on a hill, she callsh to me!"

Tanner shook his head, grinning at the stairs. "That's about the hundredth time we heard that song tonight," he said.

It was getting close to 1900 so R.J. excused himself and made his way to the front door. Susie was seated with another sailor as R.J. passed and she stuck her tongue out at him. R.J. smiled pleasantly and flipped her the finger, then slipped out the front door. He stood outside for a moment, screwed his whitehat down on his head and looked around for the Black Rose.

The Alley was much more crowded as the fleet sailors poured into the street. They moved about in groups of three and four, the patches at the tops of their right arms denoting their ships' names. U.S.S. Oriskany, U.S.S. Prairie, U.S.S. Turner Joy and many other ships were represented. Night had fallen and with the dark the neon lights blinked and flashed even brighter than before. R.J. looked around at the sea of neon and realized he was lost. He asked a passing group of sailors how to get to the Black Rose and they pointed down the Alley to his right. He thanked them and headed that way.

The Black Rose Cabaret was located near the end of the Alley just across from a garishly lit sign that read "Broadway Avenue" in big pink neon letters. In the middle of the sign was a representation of the Statue of

Liberty formed of white neon, her red neon torch held high in the air. Below the sign in more white neon was the word, "Yokosuka."

Bring me your tired, your poor, your huddled masses yearning to breathe free... R.J. thought. *And we'll sell them champagne cocktails.*

R.J. slipped through the curtain covering the entrance of the Black Rose, removed his whitehat and stepped inside. The decor looked pretty much like the New Texas, but the Black Rose was bigger, darker, smokier and more crowded. He didn't know how he was going to locate Chief Williams among the dozens of sailors, but he took a deep breath and plunged into the crowd, asking everyone if they knew Chief Williams from the signal tower. Finally, one sailor jerked his thumb toward a large table in the back. R.J. made his way over to the table and stood there looking around. There were at least a dozen sailors sitting around the table, laughing, smoking and drinking. R.J. didn't see anyone ranked lower than a first class petty officer, and many of them were chief petty officers.

"Excuse me," R.J. said.

The conversations at the table stopped as the men gathered there turned to look at R.J. "Whadda ya want, boot?" a first class quartermaster demanded.

"I'm looking for Chief Williams," R.J. answered.

A big, red-faced chief signalman with a stogie stuck in the side of his mouth stood up. "I'm Williams. Whadda ya want?"

The others eyed R.J. suspiciously. He was an interloper, interfering with their party. "You invited me for a drink, chief," R.J. said.

The chief looked R.J. over skeptically. "I invited you?" he asked.

"I'm R.J. Davis. From the Haverfield."

The chief frowned at R.J. He looked at the three white stripes on R.J.'s jumper sleeve and the realization slowly began to creep onto his face. He started to smile and then he began laughing. "You gotta be shittin' me!" he roared.

"He's a fuckin' E-3!" yelled Pete Carruthers, SM-1, shaking his head in disbelief. "In fact, he's a fuckin' kid!"

"You sent that code?" Chief Williams asked, flabbergasted.

"I sure did, Chief," R.J. replied, proudly.

"Well, I'll be a sonofabitch!" the chief exclaimed. "Sit your ass down here, boy." He pulled out a chair and R.J. sat. "You old enough to drink, kid?"

"I am in *this* country," R.J. replied and the table burst into laughter.

R.J. sat and drank beer while the others at the table were downing boilermakers. At Chief Williams' urging, R.J. told them about learning Morse Code in radio school, and he alluded to the fact that he got into a little trouble in San Diego, got put on restriction, and had his Top Secret clearance stripped away by C.C. Edgars. Then he was relegated to the deck force.

"What kinda trouble?" the chief asked.

"It's a long story," R.J. replied.

"We got all night, boy!" Carruthers hollered above the din.

"Not this kid," Chief Williams said. "He's got pumpkin written all over him."

"That's right," another chief said. "Cinderella at the ball."

R.J. nodded. He did indeed have to return to the ship before midnight. In fact, he figured he should get back to the New Texas and round up his friends. He excused himself from the table and prepared to leave.

"Why don't you visit the tower tomorrow?" Chief Williams suggested. "Take a look at how white boys live."

"I'd like that," R.J. replied. "Got any blue bunting we can have? Some of our flags need to be repaired, and blue is in short supply."

"You come up to the tower tomorrow morning," Carruthers said. "I'll give you all the blue bunting you need." He stood and shook R.J.'s hand. "You send some sweet code, kid."

"Thanks, Flags." R.J. shook his hand, smiling. "See you in the morning."

R.J. stepped outside the Black Rose and checked his watch. 23:30. The Havernauts had a half hour to return to the ship. He headed toward the New Texas just in case his friends weren't paying attention to the time. He didn't know it, but the Havernauts at the New Texas had their hands full at that moment.

He made his way down the Alley slowly, dodging the hundreds of sailors who clogged the street, and side-stepping the food deliverymen on their bicycles. He heard a ruckus behind him and looked back. The teeming mass of blue-uniformed humanity parted like the Red Sea as a dozen sailors were double-timing it down the Alley toward the Texas Bar. They ran in formation and chanted, "LST 1055! LST 1055! LST 1055!"

"What's goin' on?" R.J. yelled as they passed.

"Fight at the New Texas!" one of the LST sailors yelled back.

"LST 1055, LST 1055!"

R.J. picked up his pace and reached the New Texas in the wake of the chanting formation. They were pushing on the double glass doors, trying to force their way into the bar. R.J. looked past them and noticed four sailors on the other side of the doors, pushing them closed against the rush of LST 1055. He looked closer and realized the harried defenders were Tanner, Sonny, Lester and Pea. Cotton, Pancho and Gino stood behind them, urging them to hold against the tide.

"LST 1055! LST 1055!" The sailors chanted, surging against the door. It was obvious to R.J. that the Havernauts couldn't hold out much longer. They were sorely outmanned. He decided to try to do something about it.

He yelled as loud as he could at the LST sailors, "Hey, you guys off an LST?"

"Yeah, why?" one of them answered, pushing against the door.

R.J. pointed back up the Alley.

"Some LST crew is in a big fight at the Black Rose!" he yelled. "They look like they need help!"

The LST 1055's sailors quit pushing on the New Texas' doors and regrouped in formation. Their leader pointed toward the Black Rose and yelled, "Forward, men!" The formation began double-timing it to the Black Rose.

"LST 1055! LST 1055!"

R.J. approached the doors of the New Texas and motioned for his buddies to let him in. Pea put his mouth to the crack between the doors and asked, "They gone?"

R.J. put his mouth close to the crack and assured Pea the LST sailors had left. Sheepishly, the Havernauts opened the doors and piled out of the bar.

"Maybe we oughtta go help the guys at the Black Rose," Sonny said. "Don't hardly look like a fair fight."

"What fight?" R.J. asked, grinning. "Ain't no fight at the Black Rose."

The Havernauts looked at each other and started laughing. "We better get a fast cab," Tanner warned. "They're gonna be back."

The Havernauts hurried down the street and flagged down the nearest cab, a tiny, dented Toyota. The chanting returned as the LST sailors realized they had been duped and headed back toward the New Texas.

"LST 1055! LST 1055!"

The Havernauts piled into the cab. Gino tapped the cabbie on his shoulder and instructed, "Drive like a muddafucka!"

The cabbie looked at Gino, confused.

"Hayaku!" Cotton yelled. The cabbie nodded, grinned and popped the clutch. The cab lurched forward toward the entrance to the Alley, sending pedestrians scurrying to get out of its way and bouncing its passengers around the interior.

As they approached the main gate to the Naval base, Tanner started giggling and soon the cab was rocking with uncontrolled laughter.

"R.J., we owe you!" Tanner said, putting his arm around R.J.'s neck and planting a wet kiss on his cheek. "You saved our lives."

R.J. wiped the kiss off and made a disgusted face. "Ain't no reason to turn queer," he admonished.

The little Toyota taxi cab squealed to a stop at the main gate and the Havernauts crawled out, stumbling and falling over each other. They took up a collection, paid the smiling driver and watched as he sped away, fishtailing down the avenue in search of his next fare, or victims.

"You know," R.J. said when they had passed through the gate onto the Naval base, "we left Anselmi and Becker back at the New Texas."

"Don' worry 'bout them ol' boys," Sonny drawled. "They drunker'n a coupla shit-house rats. Besides, they probably stayed upstairs with the chicks." He laughed again at the thought of the LST sailors being duped. "Them shallow-water sailors sure are dumb."

"Time for Prairie burgers, men," Tanner announced, and they climbed the two-tiered brow which led to the tender's quarterdeck.

"What's a Prairie burger?" Gino asked suspiciously. "Some new initiation you guys haven't hit us with yet?"

"No, you gonna like this," Cotton explained. "Long as we on the tender before midnight, we ain't UA and we can get a burger before we go home." He smacked his lips in anticipation of the tasty burger. "They give us a chit shows we was aboard the tender before 2400 so we legal."

"The cooks on the Prairie make burgers for all the pumpkins who got Cinderella liberty," Tanner said. "Good stuff, too. They got a little group of guys who play rock and roll, and sometimes they entertain the troops."

"Well, by all means," R.J. agreed. "Let's go get us some Prairie burgers!"

* * * * *

It was 00:30 when R.J. and the others made their way across three destroyers and onto the Haverfield quarterdeck. Their good humor was immediately extinguished when they came aboard and realized Chief Twitchell was the OOD. The fat-bodied machinist glared at them venomously, his round face red and his eyes glowing yellow. He looked like a wolf in the night, a very fat wolf.

"You shit-birds are UA!" he spat, moving to the desk and opening up the log. "Gimme your whitehats, I'm gonna write your dumb asses up!" The easiest way to identify a sailor was by taking his whitehat which had his name and service number stenciled inside.

Tanner smiled and spoke softly to Twitchell. "We were on the tender, Chief," he explained patiently, not wanting to further aggravate him. "We got some Prairie burgers and Pepsis." Tanner handed his chit over and the others dug into their jumper pockets and produced their chits.

Chief Twitchell examined the chits slowly, as if trying to spot a forgery, then grudgingly allowed them to go below. He seemed genuinely disappointed he didn't get to write them up for being unauthorized absentees.

As they passed by the chief on their way below, R.J. flipped him the finger. The chief turned toward them quickly as if he expected something like that, and R.J. just as quickly pulled his hand to the back of his head and pretended he was scratching. He smiled at the chief. The chief glowered.

"Score one for the 'Nauts," Tanner said, winking at R.J. as they went down the aft hatch.

THIRTY

R.J. was on the signal bridge early the next morning, sipping coffee, smoking a cigarette and admiring the fleet. He was looking forward to morning colors when the Stars and Stripes would appear on every fantail in the harbor, all at the same time. The dark water in the harbor was calm, with a soft mist floating above it. Seagulls and pelicans darted and dove around the ships and the pier, trying to scrounge up breakfast, and the harbor smelled like fish.

Anselmi came up on the signal bridge, shuffling slowly and stiff-legged, holding a coffee cup in both hands as if he were afraid he'd drop it. His whitehat was askew on his head, his eyes bloodshot and bleary, and he swayed unsteadily.

"Mornin', Salami," R.J. greeted him cheerfully.

Anselmi winced and held a finger to his lips. "Shhhh, not so loud," he whined. The second class signalman sat gingerly on the rung of the flagbag and set his coffee down next to him, his hands shaking. Some of the hot, brown liquid sloshed on his hand and he winced in pain. "Ow," he said weakly.

"You guys musta had a good time up there with those little jap girls," R.J. said, grinning. "You missed the fight we almost had."

"Wha?" Anselmi whined.

"We almost got into it with a bunch of LST sailors at the New Texas last night," R.J. explained.

"Man, I feel like I been ate and shit out by a grizzly bear," Anselmi moaned.

"Yeah, and you look it, too," R.J. observed, again cheerfully.

Anselmi looked up with bleary eyes at R.J., a pained expression on his face. "Do you have to be so fucking happy this morning?" he whined.

R.J. chuckled. "It's a great day to be alive and in the Navy."

"Good morning, men!"

R.J. and Anselmi looked around and saw Becker coming up the ladder from the 02 level. He was clean-shaven and in a freshly pressed uniform. His whitehat was squared perfectly on his head and his shoes sparkled with a beautiful spit-shine. His eyes were bright and shiny, and he smiled broadly as he joined them.

R.J. stared at Becker not believing what he was seeing. Anselmi looked up at the first class signalman with a pained expression on his furrowed face. "Jesus!" he moaned.

"Close, but no cigar!" Becker said cheerfully. "C'mon, Salami, greet the beautiful new day!"

"Ooh, my head!" Anselmi groaned.

Becker rubbed his hands together. "Let's go get some chow." He grinned.

"No, no, no," Anselmi moaned. "Please don't talk about food."

R.J. laughed. "I'm gonna wait for colors, Flags," he said to Becker.

"Later, men." Becker slid down the ladder to the 02 level, a bounce in his step.

"Man, I don't believe it," R.J. said, shaking his head in wonder. "How does he do it?"

"I dunno," Anselmi groaned. "Dude had as much to drink as me." He put his head in his hands and whimpered softly. "Shit. That guy can't get out of his rack when we're underway, but he never gets a hangover."

"Must be God's way of compensating him," R.J. laughed.

"I wish God would compensate me," Anselmi whined.

A bugle blew on the Oriskany, the flagship, and the call to colors echoed across the water as each ship prepared to salute the colors.

"I gotta go down to the fantail, raise the ensign," Anselmi moaned, trying to stand. It didn't work and he plopped back down on the rung.

"I'll get it," R.J. volunteered. He took the tri-folded flag and hurried to the fantail just in time for colors. As he raised the flag on the fantail he stood back and saluted. Out of the corner of his eye he saw the same ceremony taking place on the dozens of ships all around him. On carriers and cruisers, destroyers and escorts, oilers and transports, the red, white and blue of the American flag unfurled all across the harbor in a beautiful display of color and pride. R.J. felt a lump in his throat at the sight, and tears formed in the corners of his eyes. The American Navy was awakening and showing off her colors. The gentle morning breeze accommodated the awakening by reaching out and touching each ship's flag, bolstering them with wind, proudly waving them to the world as if to say, "This is the greatest Naval fleet the Earth has ever known!"

R.J. ended his salute and turned, wiping the tears from his eyes. He looked up and saw Mr. MacDonald on the 02 level. The First Division commander was at attention facing the fleet, and he held a handkerchief to his eyes, dabbing at tears. When he saw R.J. he nodded slowly in acknowledgment of the shared moment. Then he turned and walked forward, toward the officers' wardroom.

* * * * *

Back up on the signal bridge R.J. checked with a cheerful Becker and got permission to visit the signal tower, ostensibly to pick up some blue bunting, but mostly because he wanted to see how the tower operated with so many ships in port.

"Don't let 'em Shanghai you, kid," Becker warned. "They'll try to romance you into shipping over."

"Not me, flags," R.J. replied. "Like I told Salami, I'm in for four and no more!" The truth was that R.J. loved being at sea, he really enjoyed the Navy, but he had plans, and a Navy career wasn't part of them.

R.J. left the ship, crossed over three destroyers and the Prairie and walked down the pier toward the base shuttle bus. Activity was increasing in Yokosuka harbor as the fleet began the day's work. Cranes moved up and down the pier on tracks and constantly beeped warnings as the huge arms swung around, carrying various loads high above the ground. Acetylene welding torches flared on metal, hammers chipped away at rust and everywhere the sound of sailors yelling at each other pierced the morning air.

The base shuttle picked up R.J. at a small kiosk at the front of the pier, and he sat in the back with a half dozen other sailors on similar missions. The bus moved slowly around the base, making its rounds, dropping off and picking up passengers at various stops. When they reached the base of the mountain where the signal tower was located, R.J. hopped off the shuttle and looked up at the many steps leading up the hill. A line from Poe's "The Bells" popped into his head. *And the people, ah, the people, they that dwell up in the steeple all alone.* There had to be a hundred steps to climb to reach the tower. *No elevator? Sure glad I don't have Anselmi's hangover.*

By the time he reached the top of the stairs, R.J. was puffing and perspiring. He stopped for a minute to catch his breath and then walked into the tower. He found himself in a large, glassed-in room with a catwalk outside that ran in a semi-circle across the front of the mountain. On the catwalk stood six regular signal lights and two of the new, bigger carbon-arc lights. R.J. had only heard about the carbon-arcs, but had never seen one.

They looked powerful next to the smaller lights.

At the rear of the tower's big room was a small, enclosed office where Chief Williams sat talking into a telephone. When he saw R.J. he waved him over, still talking on the phone. R.J. stepped into the office.

"Well, look who's here!" first class signalman Carruthers announced. "The boy genius!" He shook R.J.'s hand and indicated a chair. R.J. sat.

"Chief'll be done in a minute," Carruthers whispered. "Then we'll give you the tour." R.J. nodded.

The chief was arguing with someone on the phone. "I don't give a shit, Brad," he barked into the mouthpiece. "Those filters have to stay on at night, and they gotta keep 'em in good shape. A filter with scratched glass is like having no filter at all. Shit, they almost blinded us with that damn thing!"

Chief Williams finished his conversation and hung up the phone. He stuck a stub of a stogie in his mouth and looked over at R.J. "You don't look like you suffered much from the party last night," he observed.

"I just had a coupla beers, Chief. Didn't want to push my luck."

The chief smiled and nodded, looking at R.J. intently, sizing him up. Then he turned to Carruthers. "Will you please send two new red filters over to the Maddox?" he asked politely. "They say they haven't got any good ones. That's why their light is so damn bright." He shook his head in disgust, chomping on his stogie.

"No problem, Chief," Carruthers replied. "They'll have them this afternoon."

"Well, Slick, how do you like the tower?" the chief asked R.J.

"Very impressive," R.J. answered, looking around at the operation. "You must handle a lot of traffic up here."

"A shit load," Carruthers replied. "Some days it's a big shit load."

"This is the place to be if you want to be a serious signalman," the chief added. "With your skill on the light, you could be E-6 in no time. Maybe three years." He chewed his stogie and studied R.J.

"I really like being at sea, Chief," R.J. said, staring down at his hands.

The chief nodded. "Yeah, I know," he said. "That's a good looking ship you got there."

R.J. looked up and grinned. "We got a good skipper, and he's really got us squared away."

The chief winked at Carruthers. "Well, we're gonna see just how squared away you are," he said to R.J. He opened a file folder on his desk and handed R.J. a message slip. "Give this to your Ops officer when you get back," he said.

R.J. looked at the message. It was from COMCRUDESPAC instructing the tower to conduct communications drills with all destroyers, cruisers and escorts in port. The drills were to start the next day.

"Ever been through a communications drill?" Carruthers asked R.J.

"No, not yet."

"Well, it ain't like shootin' the breeze on the light," the chief warned. "The competition for the green 'C' is tough and we got some good signal bridges and radio shacks out there." He indicated the ships in the harbor.

"They'll all try to snow you, make you look bad," Carruthers said. "Throw all kinds of shit at you, like coded groups and stuff like that." He cocked his head and looked R.J. in the eye. "You guys up to it?"

"Hell yes!" R.J. exclaimed, excited at the possibility.

"Okay, kid," Chief Williams said. "We'll see. And think about coming up here and joining us." He shook R.J.'s hand and got back on the phone.

Carruthers walked R.J. to the front door and handed him a big ream of blue bunting. "Take it easy, man," he said. "Good luck on the comm Exercises."

R.J. thanked him and trotted down the steps to the shuttle kiosk. He was anxious to get back to the ship and turn the message over to Mr. Barkman. On the way back he looked over the other ships in the harbor, trying to predict which would be the most competition.

* * * * *

The communications drills began at 0900 the next day, and lasted until noon. A total of sixteen ships were involved in the exercises, which amounted to a round-robin format, each ship communicating with the others, radio shack versus radio shack and signal bridge versus signal bridge. The harbor was ablaze with flashing lights and fluttering flags. The signal crews competed in three areas: Flag Hoist, Semaphore and Flashing Light. Each ship studied the flag hoist code manual for the most difficult and obscure signals they could find. The testing ship would raise a flag hoist to the top of the yardarm and time the ship they were testing for speed in recognition of the message. The ship being tested would run up the identical flags half-way up the yardarm and then pore over the manual to decode the message. Once they had decoded it, they would raise the flag hoist to the top of the yardarm. Then by semaphore or flashing light they would verify the message. The Haverfield's signal crew correctly identified all the flag hoists, but were a little slow on a few of them.

Semaphore was tested for speed and correct positioning of the semaphore flags. Anselmi was the resident semaphore expert, and Becker stood behind him, helping him read the signals from the testing ship. Becker could read semaphore like no one in the fleet, and he constantly amazed R.J. with his ability. He didn't have to help Anselmi much, though. Anselmi usually read along with Becker, and throughout the exercises they weren't snowed once at semaphore.

The flashing light testing was last, and R.J. proudly took over the light. The signals came quick and with great speed from the cruiser Long Beach, sent by a chief signalman who could send very fast. Normally, a word or code group would be sent and the receiver would open the light for one dah to acknowledge he read it correctly. R.J. could read code at any speed being sent, so he just held the light open and allowed the chief to send as fast as he could. R.J. didn't miss a single word or code group, and when the flashing light exercise was over, Becker and Anselmi slapped him on the back in congratulations.

When R.J.'s turn came to test the Long Beach on the signal light, he scanned the message of coded groups and nodded to Becker, who semaphored their readiness. The signal bridge of the Long Beach flashed a quick message: ' Let's see what you got.'

R.J. grinned and handed the message to Anselmi, who held it up in front of R.J.'s face so he could read the paper and send the message. He started at a brisk, but not extremely fast pace and the Long Beach signal chief opened his light to let him know he was reading it fine. Slowly, R.J. picked up the speed, trying to make the Long Beach chief close his light, not able to read, but the light stayed open.

Halfway through the message R.J. hit his stride and he began to send faster and faster until Becker and Anselmi looked at each other and shook their heads, amazed at the speed of the light. R.J. felt separated from his body, looking down on the scene on the signal bridge from somewhere above. His hand flicked the signal light handle smoothly and steadily, making almost no sound. Becker estimated he was sending code at about fifty words per minute, unheard of for a fleet signalman.

Finally, with only six more coded groups left in the message, the light closed on the Long Beach. R.J. patiently resent the coded group the Long Beach missed, then sent the remaining groups a little slower, allowing the Long Beach to catch up. The Haverfield had 'aced' the flashing light drills.

Up in the signal tower, Chief Williams and Carruthers stood on the outside catwalk, watching the comm exercises in the harbor below. When the Haverfield signal bridge secured from the flashing light drills, the chief and first class signalmen looked at each other and grinned.

"Kid can cook, huh?" Carruthers said.

Chief Williams nodded his head and chomped down on his stogie. "Cleanest code groups I ever seen."

At noon chow, the radiomen and signalmen sat together comparing notes. The radio shack had performed as well as the signal bridge, and spirits were high. Everyone in communications believed they had done very well on the exercises, but just how well they had done was to be determined by the Yokosuka signal tower, and the staff at COMCRUDESPAC after all the data was analyzed. One thing was certain: The Haverfield's performance clearly had met fleet standards. They would get the results in about thirty days.

* * * * *

Lunch in the wardroom was a pleasant affair. Lieutenant Barkman made his report to the captain about the communications exercise and how well he felt they had done. The captain was in a good mood, having convinced the powers that be the Haverfield was ready for their UED, and having received the okay to proceed with the evaluation. The U.S.S. Phillips was designated to conduct the evaluation of the Haverfield, and Captain Oliver was very pleased to note that his academy classmate, Lieutenant Commander Thomas Jolicoeur, was commanding the Phillips. He knew Tom wouldn't cut him any extra slack during the drills, but Captain Oliver felt comfortable having his old friend as proctor of the UED.

"The UED will be held on our way back to Guam next week," Captain Oliver told his officers. "I want the officers and crew to enjoy their liberty here in Yokosuka, but remind everyone that we cannot let our guard down." The captain shook his finger at them. "We've worked hard to get this vessel squared away, and I don't want any backsliding. Understood?"

It was understood.

THIRTY ONE

R.J. and Gino left the ship at 1600 and made their way across the three destroyers and the tender. They had promised Tanner and Pea they would meet at the New Texas Bar later in the evening, but R.J. wanted to see some of the sights first. Before they left the ship, they asked Rafer and Andy Sample to meet them at the New Texas. The Sample brothers said they would be there.

Wandering around the market in Yokosuka, checking out all the stalls of available goods was an eye-opening experience for R.J. and Gino. Everything imaginable was being sold in the market, from exotic vegetables to live squid and octopus. Tuna was cut up and made into sashimi, which R.J. refused to sample, though Gino gathered the courage to do so. He made a sour face and swallowed the raw fish whole, shaking his head and asking the proprietor for something to wash it down. Gino took the offered cup of what looked to him like water, so he drank it down quickly. It was warm sake, and Gino choked on it, coughing and wheezing, trying to catch his breath.

"What the hell you doin' to me, old man?" he shouted at the little Japanese man who just smiled back and nodded, offering Gino another cup. "Hell no!" Gino waved his hands at the old man. "You tryin' to kill me?" The old man smiled and nodded, bowing low and offering Gino the cup.

R.J. laughed at the scene and led his friend away. Gino was coughing and spitting, trying to get the taste out of his mouth. Just before they reached the New Texas, the sake began to warm his belly and he looked at R.J. "You know, that stuff ain't half bad." He grinned. His eyes were bright and he was becoming flushed. As they were about to enter the bar, the Sample brothers came up behind them.

"Whoa, Lordy!" Andy exclaimed, looking around the neon Alley. "Lookit all them pretty lights!" Passing sailors were staring at them, and R.J. stared back.

"What's their problem?" he asked.

"Dunno, let's get some beer," Gino slurred.

The four walked into the New Texas and conversations stopped. The bar had grown quiet except for the juke box which wailed a Patsy Cline ballad. There were sailors from many ships sitting in the booths and piloting girls around the dance floor, but everyone stopped and stared at the newcomers. R.J. spotted Tanner and Pea sitting with a couple of girls in a booth off to the side and headed that way. Slowly, the activity in the bar began to resume. Conversations started back up but were muted. R.J., Gino and the Sample brothers squeezed into the booth and the girls got up and left.

"Was it something I said?" R.J. asked, looking around the bar.

"Naw," Tanner replied, slightly drunk. "They ain't used to seeing black guys in here." He raised his beer to the Sample brothers in a salute. "Welcome, shipmates," he toasted, and downed the beer.

"So, this a segregated place?" Rafer asked, looking around, amused.

"Fuck 'em!" Pea spat. He was a little drunk and when Pea got drunk he became belligerent. "They don't like our shipmates, fuck 'em!"

"Yeah, fuck 'em!" R.J agreed. "Hey, mama-san!" he called. "Four more beers!"

Mama-san came shuffling quickly over to the table. "So sorry, you leave. No want trouble here!" she pleaded. "You all go now!" She looked toward the back of the bar where a group of sailors were standing and staring at the Haverfield crew.

"Well, well," Tanner observed. "Looks like somebody don't want us in here." He grinned at the others. "Might just have to kick some ass."

"I gots to stay and fight," Andy said. "I got me a bum leg, and I can't run."

"Well, I gots to stay too, then," Rafer added. "My momma tol' me to take good care of my little brother, so I can't run neither."

"Fuck 'em!" Pea said. "Let 'em start some shit, boy. I'm just in the fuckin' mood."

A stocky chief petty officer pushed mama-san out of the way and growled, "Your kind ain't welcome here, spooks. Take off!" It was a drunken Chief Twitchell, rocking unsteadily and sneering, his lip curled.

"You go now!" Mama-san pleaded.

"I ain't goin' nowhere," R.J. stated stubbornly. "Bring us some beers."

Rafer got up slowly from the booth and stared down menacingly at Chief Twitchell. "I'm gettin' a little tired of yo shit, Chief," he warned. Andy stood up behind Rafer. R.J. jumped up, followed by Pea, Tanner and Gino.

"You go now. I call shore patrol!" Mama-san shuffled back behind the counter and began yelling in Japanese into a phone. Several sailors came up behind Chief Twitchell to back his play. None of them was from the Haverfield.

The chief was drunk. His face was blood red, his eyes were unfocused and he was sweating profusely. His lip curled in a sneer and he stuck a finger in Rafer's face. "Go back up in the 'Hole' where you darkies belong!" he slurred.

Rafer slapped the chief's hand out of his face so quickly that everyone just froze. The chief was thrown off balance and he stumbled backward, caught by two sailors behind him. "You lousy nigger!" he yelled. "I'm gonna kick your black ass!" He lunged toward Rafer, who stepped aside and Twitchell crashed onto the table, upsetting it, sending him sprawling on the deck. The sailors behind the chief took a step forward and the Haverfield crew stepped up to meet them. They stood face to face for a few seconds until a shrill whistle sounded, startling them, and four members of the Yokosuka shore patrol came rushing into the bar, nightsticks at the ready. The combatant sailors all stepped back.

The shore patrol began pushing the two sides back away from each other. Then they stood back, nightsticks up, and a tall, mean looking boatswain's mate first class stepped in front of them, allowing them to relax. BM-1 Carl Simpson was in charge of the shore patrol in Yokosuka. He was a muscular black man over six feet tall with a reputation for no nonsense. He glared at the combatants, narrowing his eyes when he saw Rafer and Andy.

"What you boys doin' in here?" he demanded.

"They're with us, Boats," R.J. said.

"Shut the fuck up!" Simpson ordered, still looking at Rafer and Andy. "I ain't talkin' to you, boy." He pointed at the Sample brothers. "I'm talkin' to these here boys."

"They ain't supposed to be in here!" yelled Chief Twitchell.

Simpson slowly moved his gaze to the fat chief. "You wanna go in the wagon, Chief? Take you back and turn you over to your OOD?" he asked menacingly. Chief Twitchell turned around and went back to his table. Simpson looked back at Rafer and Andy. "I don't like trouble in my Alley," he said calmly. "Maybe you boys oughta just leave."

Rafer stared at Simpson who stared back. Rafer slowly nodded. "Why don' we just leave, then?" he said, just as calmly.

Simpson nodded. He turned and stared down the sailors who were backing Chief Twitchell. They backed off and retreated to their table.

"You go now!" Mama-san pleaded, pointing at Rafer and Andy.

"See you guys," Rafer said. He picked up his whitehat and headed toward the door, Andy following behind.

"You know what, mama-san?" R.J. said, standing and popping open his whitehat. "My friends ain't welcome here, fuck you. I go now."

"I go now, too!" Pea said. He looked around the bar in disgust. "Fuck all you Jap bastards!"

Tanner and Gino joined them and they all left the New Texas. Out on the street R.J. looked at Tanner and asked, "What the hell was that all about?"

Tanner shrugged. "Black guys usually hang out in a section of Yokosuka called 'The Hole," he explained.

"Forget it, R.J.," Rafer said calmly. "We used to that shit. We from Alabama. Lots of that shit happen there."

"Bullshit!" R.J. spat.

"Fuck 'em!" Pea yelled and staggered into the street just as a bicycle deliveryman was weaving his way through the foot traffic carrying a large, round tray stacked high with food containers. Pea spotted him and stared, trying to focus, weaving a little in the middle of the street. As the deliveryman maneuvered his bicycle around closer, Pea took aim and swung wildly, a sweeping roundhouse punch that caught the bicyclist in the middle of his chest, knocking him off his bike. Pea staggered sideways, falling into the street. "Fuck 'em!" Pea yelled again, trying to stand. Fried rice, sashimi and various foods were scattered all over the street and the deliveryman started screaming in Japanese. Tanner grabbed Pea and yelled at the others, "C'mon, let's get the hell out of here!" They all started running toward the entrance to the Alley, dragging Pea and laughing so hard they could hardly run. They heard the shore patrol whistle behind them as they piled into the nearest cab.

"Everybody got his whitehat?" Tanner took inventory. Thankfully, no whitehats were lost. "Hayaku!" he yelled at the driver, who nodded and popped the clutch, sending the passengers careening around in the back seat.

"What do hayaku mean?" Andy asked, trying to find something to hold on to.

"It means drive like a mudda fucka," Gino explained.

Rafer held on to the back of the driver's seat and laughed. "It shore do!" he exclaimed.

"Tanner," R.J. said seriously. "I'm gonna quit hitting the beach with you. I been out with you twice and we barely escaped each time."

"Third time's a charm," Tanner said, laughing and sitting back in the seat. "Let's get some Prairie burgers."

Sitting at a large table in the Prairie's messdecks, the Havernauts munched on the burgers and sipped Pepsis. Sailors from all the ships tied up to the tender were scattered around the large messdecks with more coming in as Cinderella liberty expired.

R.J. swallowed a bite of Prairie burger and looked over at Tanner. "I don't understand this black-white shit in the Alley," he said. "The Navy ain't s'posed to be segregated."

"Don' let it bug you, man," Rafer said. "If it don' bug us, it oughta not bug you."

"Fuck 'em!" Pea said, his mouth full of burger. His chin was covered with mustard and ketchup. He held the burger in one hand, waving it around like a club.

Andy put his arm around Pea's shoulder. "You a funny little dude," he said in his deep voice. "You pretty mean for yo size."

Pea grinned and some of the half-chewed burger fell out of his mouth and landed on his lap. "Fuckin' ay," he mumbled, brushing off his lap.

Tanner finished his burger and wiped his hands with a paper napkin. "I agree with R.J.," he said. "Guys who work and live with us oughta be able to drink with us."

"Cept these guys don't drink," Gino observed, indicating Rafer and Andy. "I never seen either of them drink more than one beer."

"Don' smoke neither," Rafer added.

"Well, they should be able to go anywhere we go," R.J. said stubbornly. "Look around." He pointed to the sailors gathered at the various tables. "There's lots of black guys in here." He thought for a moment. "Lots of black guys all over the Navy," he added.

"Shit's changing back home," Tanner observed. "Civil rights is gettin' to

be a big thing. Lots of people marching together, trying to put that segregation stuff behind us."

"Won' happen overnight," Rafer said. "You gotta live in the South to
unnerstand it."

"It a way o' life in the South," Andy agreed. "It be what it be."

"Too many assholes like Twitchy in the Navy," R.J. said.

Rafer nodded solemnly. "He one o' the worst I ever seen."

"Fuck 'em!" Pea exclaimed, and the others nodded their heads in agreement.

* * * * *

R.J. decided to stay aboard ship the next few nights, studying for the
Third Class exam. The test wasn't held until the first of the year, but R.J.
was determined to get his 'Crow.' Anselmi was delighted that R.J. was staying aboard, and offered him five dollars to stand by for him, meaning take
his duty.

"I ain't gonna charge you, Salami," R.J. told him. "I still owe you for
helping me get up here."

"Cool," Anselmi said. He headed down to the compartment to change
into his dress blues. "Don't forget to polish the brass!" he called over his
shoulder.

R.J. smiled at Anselmi as the second class signalmen skipped down the
ladder. Actually, R.J. didn't mind polishing brass. It gave him time to think,
and it appealed to his sense of order and organization. He tore off a piece
of old tee-shirt and shook the can of Brasso 'well before using', as the
instructions indicated. He was busy polishing belaying pins and didn't see
the captain come out on the wing. Captain Oliver was standing over R.J.
before he noticed him. R.J. jumped to his feet and saluted, standing at
attention.

"At ease," the captain said, returning the salute. "How's it going, Davis?
Keeping you busy, are they?"

"Yessir," R.J. answered, relaxing a bit.

"I need you to do me a favor," the captain said. "I'm having trouble getting this damn collar to fold down. Help me with it, will you?" He turned
around and R.J. quickly wiped his hands and reached up, pulling the back
of the captain's collar over his tie.

"There you go, sir," R.J. said, satisfied with the result.

The captain turned around, adjusting his tie. "Mr. Barkman said you
men did a great job on the comm exercises," he said, looking R.J. in the eye.

"We aced the flashing light drill, sir," R.J. replied, pleased by the captain's comments. "I think we did good on the flag-hoist and semaphore,
too."

The captain nodded, still looking R.J. in the eye. "I also heard you're a
holy terror on the light." He smiled at R.J. with a look of amusement in his
eyes.

"Thank you, sir."

The captain nodded and adjusted his coat. "How do I look?" he asked.

"Four-oh, sir," R.J. replied.

"Fine. I'm off to a dinner at the Officer's Club. You keep up the good work, sailor."

"Aye, aye, sir." R.J. straightened to attention and saluted the captain.

The captain returned the salute and went down the aft ladder to the 02 level. He was pleased with this kid Davis' progress. He didn't seem like the same surly young man he had had to send to the brig last spring. He appeared to be growing up. Well, the Navy had a way of either making you mature or sending you home. Most of the time it was that simple with the Navy; you either make 'em or break 'em. This kid was turning out okay. In some respects, he was a microcosm of what was happening to the U.S.S. Haverfield. This kid was growing and maturing, becoming better at his job every day, just like the ship and the crew were maturing, getting better every day. Commander D. Paul Oliver sensed a new professional attitude, a new pride in the crew, and sensing that pleased him.

What Captain Oliver did not sense, perhaps because of his distracting infatuation and obsession with Lorelei Prescott, was the growing friction aboard his ship that existed between the black sailors and the white sailors; a friction that would, inevitably, result in the dramatic and unprecedented incident which would come to define his command and, moreover, his career.

* * * * *

On the morning of Monday September 30, the Haverfield got underway for her return to Guam and the UED exercises to be conducted with the USS Phillips. Their visit to Yokosuka had been just what the crew needed, and after blowing off steam for two weeks, they were well rested and eager to get on with the UED.

Normally it would take four days steaming from Japan to Guam, but because they were participating in the UED, they were scheduled to arrive in Apra Harbor on Sunday, October 6th.

The Haverfield sailed out of Tokyo Bay and hit the breakwater just after ten A.M. They were scheduled to rendezvous with the Phillips on Tuesday morning to start the drills. After the special sea and anchor detail was secured and the watch was set throughout the ship, the off-duty sailors began to turn to in their work places, performing the hundreds of tasks it took to keep the ship steaming toward its objective. The gunners' mates cleaned and polished the two three-inch guns, the engineers struggled with the evaporators and the four powerful diesel engines, the deck force swarmed topside, chipping and sanding, applying red lead and fresh paint. On the flying bridge, Captain Oliver sat in his chair with his binoculars hanging around his neck and reviewed for the fourth time the readiness reports from the department heads. Everything seemed to be going pretty well. *Hell*, he thought, *even the evaps were working at full capacity*. Captain Oliver was anxious to begin the UED and get back to Guam. He had not seen Lorelei in almost a month, and the sweet memory of their last encounter was stamped indelibly on his mind. He missed her and he wanted badly to see her. He imagined laying his head in her lap and feeling her playing with his hair. He shook the thoughts from his mind impatiently and concentrated on the readiness reports.

On the fantail, the Sample brothers, Tanner, Pea and Charming Billy worked on the lifelines. Rafer and Andy tightened up the turnbuckles until the lifelines showed no slack, and Tanner and Billy busily replaced the canvas wrap that covered the wire lines. Pea moved behind them wearing rubber gloves and carrying a can of white paint. As Tanner and Billy sewed the canvas tight around the wire, Pea dipped a cloth into the white paint and wrapped his hand around the new canvas on the line, holding the soaked paint cloth tightly and running his hand up and down the lifeline until the entire canvas wrapping was painted white. As Pea did so, he carried on a running monologue about Japan and Japanese women.

"I'll tell you this much," he said, dipping the cloth into the paint. "That Riley's right. The jap broads got dumpy asses."

"Watch what you're doin', Pea," Tanner warned, pointing to the deck where Pea had dripped some white paint. "You're making a big mess!"

Pea leaned over and wiped up his spill. "That chick Tammie at the New Texas wanted two thousand yen to go upstairs with her. Two thousand yen!" He shook his head in disgust.

"You wanna play you gotta pay, little man," Andy chuckled in his deep voice. "A little scrawny dude like you always gotta pay." Andy smiled to show Pea he was teasing him. "Big, pretty black man like me don't never have to pay."

"You ain't pretty," Pea protested. "You just tall, that's all." He soaked the cloth in the paint thoughtfully. "Everybody got to pay for pussy, that's just the way it is."

"Not me," Andy said, pointing a thumb at his chest. "I gets me all the pussy I needs." He grinned and straightened his whitehat on his head, then turned to show Pea his profile. "Cause I'm pretty," he said flatly.

Pea stared at Andy, cocking his head and grinning. "So you never have to pay, ever?" he asked mockingly.

"Nope," Andy replied. "I always gots lots of cooze back home 'cause I won't take no for an answer from them ho's." He raised his hand as if to strike Pea. "Don' wanna gimme that pussy, whack!" he brought his hand down in a slapping motion. "Whup that ho, she give it up."

"Uh oh," Pea warned, looking over Andy's shoulder. Andy and the others turned to see Chief Twitchell strolling out on deck. He looked aft and watched the island of Japan fade into the horizon, then looked over at the group of sailors.

"I hope that fat fuck doesn't come over here," Pea hissed under his breath. He concentrated on painting the lifeline. The conversation stopped in anticipation of more venom from Chief Twitchy. But the chief just sneered in their direction, turned and disappeared through the port side hatch.

"Boy, I hate that fat asshole," Pea spat. "He put Rafer on the pad."

Rafer nodded. He had almost forgotten he was facing a Captain's mast when they returned to Guam. "That dude's asking for trouble." Rafer stared angrily at the hatch where the chief had left. "Maybe I just throw his ass over the side and let the barracuda get him."

"Naw," Andy said, grinning and winking at Pea. "The barracuda just spit his ass out."

"The man is an embarrassment to the Navy," R.J. stated. "He's always drunk and staggering around, like he can't keep his balance." He looked at Rafer, trying to determine if Rafer really would throw the chief overboard. "Hell, that asshole is probably gonna fall over the side one of these days."

"I tell you this much," Rafer said, turning to face the others. "I ain't gonna take any more of his shit. I been thinkin' about this a lot." His jaw was set, his mouth was tight, and his eyes were angry. "That cracker is gonna go too far one of these days, and I'm gonna knock him on his ass." No one on the fantail doubted Rafer could do it. They worked in silence, their good mood gone, each alone with his thoughts.

Pea broke the silence. "Fuck 'im!" he stated firmly, looking around at the others, who broke up in laughter. Chief Twitchell could hear the laughter as he went down the ladder to engineering, and he knew they were laughing at him. *Those niggers and their nigger-loving friends,* he thought. *They are going to answer to me.*

* * * * *

The Phillips was on station waiting when the Haverfield appeared over the horizon and began closing the distance between the two ships. A flashing light began blinking rapidly from the Phillips, and R.J. rushed to the light, grabbing the handle just before Anselmi could reach it.

"Go ahead, Slick," Anselmi smiled and nodded toward the Phillips.

R.J. grinned sheepishly and spun the light around, pointing it at the Phillips. He sent the go ahead and the Phillips' light blinked quickly. R.J. receipted for the message and stuck his head into the flying bridge.

"Phillips says they're ready to proceed with the drills, Captain," he reported.

"Very well," the captain said calmly. "Let's proceed by all means."

For two days the Phillips and the Haverfield steamed together, like two boxers circling and stalking each other. The Phillips signaled ship maneuvers and course settings. They drilled the Haverfield in all types of exercises including man-overboard drills, anti-submarine warfare drills, and mock attacks by superior surface forces. The Phillips threw one drill after another at the Haverfield crew and timed them on how quickly they responded to each situation. Phillips proctors were on board the Haverfield to grade the various departments on their responses to the manufactured crises. Toward the end of the two days, it was obvious the Haverfield was performing very well.

The captain stood on the bridge, just inside the port hatch. He held the radio microphone to his mouth and pressed the 'send' button. He was responding to a call from his friend, Tom Jolicoeur, on board the Phillips. "Go ahead, Phillips."

The radio crackled with static, then the message came through clearly. "Well done, Paul," Captain Jolicoeur said. "That's as close to four-oh as you can get. Over."

"Roger," Captain Oliver replied, smiling proudly. "Thanks for the help, Tom. Drinks are on me at the O-club when we get back to port."

"Roger. I'll take you up on it next time. We're being called back to Pearl for some high-level conference. Seems something's up in the South China Sea. Over."

Captain Oliver frowned. His friend and classmate was heading to where the action was and briefly Paul felt resentment toward his old friend. "Roger. Well, next time you're in our neighborhood. Over."

"Roger. God speed, Paul. You've got a squared away ship there. Congratulations. Over."

"Roger, thanks. Over and out." Paul put the receiver back in its cradle and sighed. *Well, at least the UED went well.* He knew he would get a good report from Tom Jolicoeur, but all he really wanted at that moment was orders to join the fleet, wherever they were headed. He turned back to the bridge and saw that the members of the bridge crew were looking at him anxiously. He looked back at them, grinned and turned his attention to the OOD, Mr. MacDonald, who was pretending not to overhear the radio conversation.

"Mac, set a course for home," the captain said pleasantly. "Looks like we got a good UED report."

"Aye, aye, sir," Mr. MacDonald answered crisply. He too was smiling as he bent over the chart table and began plotting the course that would take them back to Guam. Mr. MacDonald was aware that the captain was a regular Navy man, a graduate of the Naval Academy and one hell of a ship handler. He knew the captain yearned to steam with the regular fleet, and was a little disappointed over his current duty station, commanding an island-hopping, over the hill ship that had seen better days. But Mr. Mac also knew that Paul Oliver was a professional. He had proven that in more ways than one. At that moment Frank MacDonald wished with all his heart that Captain Oliver would get the fleet command he wanted. He had a lot of affection and respect for Paul Oliver, and he felt a fierce loyalty to the Haverfield's skipper.

R.J. stood on the signal bridge as the Haverfield crossed the breakwater into Apra Harbor. It was a very warm morning, and the sun beat down on the harbor, seeming to wilt everything in sight. After the cool climes of Japan, the heat seemed oppressive and heavy, steam rising up from the vegetation and evaporating into the air. The ship seemed to relax as it made its way to the designated berth on the pier where a team of line-handlers stood by. She was home after a successful R&R trip, and she was a proud ship. Her UED had gone well, and the communications exercises in Yokosuka had gone very well. R.J. smiled at the thought that he had less than a year to serve on this ship, and his mind went back to the night he first arrived in March. A lot had happened in those six plus months. R.J. felt as if years had gone by. He was different, he knew. His attitude was better, and he had developed real friendships among the crew. Friendships, he was convinced, that would last years after his Naval service ended.

The ship approached the pier and Pea stood on the focsul with the leader line, ready to toss in to the waiting line handlers. R.J. leaned over the side of the signal bridge and watched as the leader line sailed high into the air and landed with a thump on the dock. *Nice throw, Pea,* he thought, smiling down at the diminutive sailor. A mail truck was on the pier with a few weeks' mail in several canvas bags. Cars with wives and dependents lined the pier, their occupants out in front of the vehicles, waving happily as the ship tied up and shifted colors. They had been gone over three weeks and everyone was anxious to get home and fall back into the familiar routine.

R.J. frowned as he thought of Rafer's captain's mast. Surely the captain would understand the nature of Chief Twitchell's report and maybe put Rafer on restriction for a couple of weeks. R.J. watched the officers and petty officers who had families on the island disembark first from the ship. They hurried down the brow and into the waiting arms of their loved ones. R.J. felt a twinge of regret that he didn't have someone on Guam welcoming him back home. He silently resented the men who had someone waiting for them, and wished to himself that he would meet a girl with whom he could share his life, at least until he was rotated back to the States. Oh, well, there was something he could depend on. The routine aboard ship was familiar, and his friends were people he could trust to watch his back. He was becoming a cracker-jack signalman, and the Haverfield felt more and more like home. Life was settling into a comfortable daily routine that fit like a soft pair of slippers on tired feet. He was content in the knowledge that his months on board the Haverfield would continue in the same easy way, predictable and comforting.

There was no way he could have known that near-future events would threaten that comfort; that love would soon enter his life and make him miserable, and that the dynamics aboard ship were changing in ways he couldn't see or understand. It would begin with incidents that would disrupt the harmony aboard the Haverfield and severely divide the crew. It all started when a terrible typhoon named Mabel attacked Guam with a vicious vengeance, hurtling down from the heavens like the angry wrath of God.

PART THREE:

STORM

THIRTY TWO

Apra Harbor, Guam
October 9, 1963

Captain Oliver tossed the personnel file on his desk and flopped down heavily in his chair. The exec, Lieutenant Martin, sat across from the captain on his bunk. They sat there silently, neither saying a word, each thinking about how badly Rafer Sample's captain's mast had gone. It had seemed like a pretty simple case, really. Twitchell had accused Rafer of insubordination, making threats to a superior officer and had hinted that Rafer had attacked him not once, but twice; the first time on the ship, and later at the New Texas bar in Yokosuka. He had produced affidavits from the non-Haverfield sailors who were with him at the New Texas, and MM-1 Crawford had testified about the incident aboard ship.

Rafer had declined the offer from R.J., Tanner, Pea and Gino to attend the mast and testify on his behalf, saying that he didn't think the captain would believe the fat chief. "This is on me," he had said. "I can handle this myself. The truth is on my side."

When Twitchell described the two incidents Rafer interrupted him constantly, calling him a liar, despite the captain's warnings to keep quiet and wait his turn. When Twitchell introduced the witness affidavits, Rafer had blown up and accused the fat chief of racism. When told to shut up by the exec, Rafer had exploded that the exec and the captain were racists, too. When it came Rafer's turn to tell his side of the story, he had clammed up, stubbornly and sullenly refusing to defend himself, despite the urgings of the captain and the exec. When it was over, the captain had no choice but to sentence Rafer to thirty days in the brig, although Chief Twitchell had argued for a much stiffer sentence.

Captain Oliver knew there was more to the story than had been presented at mast. He urged Rafer to defend himself, but the black sailor had set his jaw stubbornly, seething with anger, and remained silent.

"We need to keep a close watch on Chief Twitchell," the captain said finally. "I don't want any more problems between the crew members on my ship." He struck a kitchen match against the side of his desk and lit his pipe.

"I concur, captain," the exec replied. "But you really had no choice but to send Sample to the brig. He was uncommunicative and sullen, defiant even. He could have made a case for himself, and I, for one, don't believe all that Twitchell said about the situation."

Captain Oliver sat and smoked in silence for a few minutes, pondering the problem. Finally he leaned forward and spoke in a low, even voice. "Ed, this ship is coming around. The crew is performing better than I had hoped for at this stage in their training, and I'm convinced we are going to receive an excellent UED report. I can't have these petty problems cropping up."

"Absolutely not, sir," the exec said. "But with your permission, Captain, I don't think this problem is petty at all." Lieutenant Martin took a deep breath and tried to choose his words carefully. "The civil rights movement is gaining momentum back home. There are powerful feelings on both sides of the issue. The country is becoming divided over it, and I think it's inevitable that this issue will ripple into the Navy, and into all branches of the service, for that matter." He spread his hands out in front of him. "We must be aware of what is happening back home and be prepared to deal with the feelings of the crew."

Captain Oliver nodded silently, puffing his pipe to keep it from going out. "Let's try to address this at the department level," he said, setting his pipe in the ashtray and standing, indicating the meeting was over. "Talk to Pedro and to Mac. Advise them I want a tight lid on this issue. There will be no racial conflict aboard the Haverfield."

"Aye, aye, sir." The exec nodded and left, closing the door gently behind him. He stood for a moment in the passageway outside the captain's cabin, trying to think of a way to prevent the situation from gaining momentum beyond his or the captain's control. He sighed and headed to engineering.

R.J. stood on the 03 level with Tanner, Pea and Gino, watching as Rafer got into the cab of the pickup and sat between Charming Billy and Mr. MacDonald. Lester, sporting a shore patrol armband, hopped into the bed of the truck. Andy stood at the driver's door, his head in the window, speaking to Rafer as Billy leaned back to allow them to converse. Andy stepped back and patted the side of the truck. Billy put the truck in gear, spotted Chief Twitchell standing on the fantail watching, and gunned the engine, a defiant look on his face. He popped the clutch and laid rubber noisily down the pier. Mr. MacDonald looked over at him and frowned, but Billy ignored him. Rafer sat stiffly, staring straight ahead, his jaw muscles flexing.

R.J. and the others watched the truck disappear toward the Marine brig and Andy came up on the 03 level to join them. No one said a word until the truck's taillights could no longer be seen.

"That fuckin' Twitchell is a big asshole!" Pea yelled at the top of his lungs, aware that the fat chief was on the fantail just below them.

Twitchell looked up at the 03 level, sneering at the five sailors. R.J. and the others glared directly at him, scowling. The chief dropped his gaze and went below down the aft ladder.

* * * * *

Andy Sample kept mostly to himself for the next few days. He didn't talk much, and resisted attempts by R.J. and the rest of the men to cheer him up. By Saturday he was beginning to come around a little, but declined to join the Gamboa working party.

Billy Lopez pulled the truck up near the brow and the Gamboa working party, consisting of R.J., Gino, Tanner, Lester, Cotton, Pancho and Pea climbed into the bed. Gino was concerned that their a capella group hadn't practiced in three days because Andy declined to participate.

"Got to practice, man," he complained. "We gonna lose our edge."

"Andy will be okay," Tanner soothed him. "Think about how pissed off we are about Rafer and then imagine it from Andy's point of view. It's his brother, man."

They sat in silence until Billy brought the truck onto Highway One and gained speed. Pea stood behind the cab, holding on to the sides and letting the wind blow into his face. As they roared through Agana he yelled at the people on the sides of the road. "Fuck Chief Twitchy! Fuck that fat-assed bastard!" The people stopped what they were doing and stared at the speeding truck.

"Get back down here, you dumb shit," Lester warned him. "You're gonna fall out on your ass!"

"Fuck Twitchell!" Pea hollered into the wind.

R.J. stood up next to Pea. "Fuck Chief Twitchy!" he yelled, grinning down at Pea. One by one the other sailors in the truck stood and yelled into the wind, their heads back. "Fuck Twitchy! Fuck Twitchy! Fuck Twitchy!"

By the time they reached the Gamboas' trailer they were all laughing and jumping up and down in the bed of the truck. Mrs. Gamboa came out of the trailer with a frown on her face. She glared at the sailors with a disapproving look and the men quieted down. They might take on Chief Twitchell, but no one wanted to mess with Mrs. Gamboa.

Teresa came running down the steps and threw her arms around Billy. They embraced and walked to the trailer arm in arm, whispering to each other. Mrs. Gamboa followed them with her eyes.

Since their first visit, the condition of the trailer had improved greatly. The red lead paint had been applied in two coats, the porch was finished and awaited a paint job, and the roof was free of leaks. A small garden had been started on the side of the trailer and sprouts were beginning to break through the soil. The working party decided it was time to remodel the inside.

Mr. Gamboa came out of the trailer with a big grin on his face. He sat on the steps and motioned for the men to gather around. "I got a big surprise for you," he said mysteriously. The men crowded around him.

Mr. Gamboa pointed toward the road at a cloud of dust coming up the hill. An old 1949 Oldsmobile screeched to a stop next to the truck and a large Guamanian man got out. He looked a lot like Mr. Gamboa.

"Oscar," Mr. Gamboa called. "Come over here and meet my friends." He stood and embraced the other man. "Boys," he explained. "This is my brother, Oscar."

The men shook Oscar's hand and greeted him. Oscar grinned, showing his bad teeth and winked at Mr. Gamboa. "What you think?" he asked him.

Mr. Gamboa walked around the Oldsmobile, inspecting it and nodding appreciatively. "That's a nice car," he remarked.

The old car was painted a dark primer gray and had a few dents. Its front bumper was missing and the rear door handles had been removed. The windshield was a little pock-marked and the hub caps were gone. But the interior was in pretty good shape and Oscar assured everyone that the engine ran perfectly.

"You guys been a big help to us," Mr. Gamboa said, smiling at the working party. "Oscar's had this old heap for a long time, and he wants to sell it. You boys can have it for a hunnerd fifty bucks."

"Fuckin' ay!" Pea exclaimed and jumped into the driver's seat. He moved the steering wheel and bounced up and down on the seat. "Wheels! We got wheels!"

R.J. and Gino decided to go in with Pea on the car. The others looked skeptically at the old heap and shook their heads. "It's all yours, boys," Tanner said, "I think I'll stick with Billy and the truck."

R.J. quickly set up a payment plan with Oscar while Pea sat bouncing behind the wheel, honking the horn and pretending to drive, a big grin on his face.

After the transaction was concluded, work began on the interior of the trailer. Mrs. Gamboa had cooked up a terrific lunch and Mr. Gamboa sat on the porch, drinking San Miguel and regaling the men with stories about Guam during World War Two. Soon it was time to leave.

"I'm driving!" Pea announced and slid in behind the wheel. Gino and R.J. got into the front seat with him and they followed Billy down the hill and onto Highway One. When they reached the gate to the base, the guard explained to Pea that without a Navy sticker, he could not park the 'Bomb' as Pea named the car, on the base. He would have to park it in the lot next to the gate where other non-registered cars were kept. Pea wasn't happy, but locked up the Bomb and climbed into the truck with the others.

"Let's get cleaned up and come back to take her for a cruise," Pea said, grinning widely. R.J. and Gino quickly agreed.

* * * * *

With the admiral spending more and more time in Pearl Harbor, Paul Oliver and Lorelei Prescott had many opportunities to get together. It was difficult to maintain secrecy, Guam being a small island with many curious eyes and ears, but they managed to meet in out of the way places. One of their favorites was the parking lot at the USO beach, which was usually deserted in the evenings. Paul would borrow Lee Piper's Ford Fairlane and park it in a remote area of the parking lot. When Lorelei arrived in her Buick convertible, Paul would climb in and they would head into the hills for some privacy. Alone among the palm trees and under the star-studded sky they would hold each other, kiss passionately, and talk of their affection and the hopelessness of it. Both had little doubt that, given the opportunity and a safe place to get together, their relationship would naturally proceed to the next level. They talked about it often; about the strong feelings they had for each other, balanced by their sense of honor and loyalty to Admiral Prescott.

Before midnight they would return to the USO parking lot and Paul would kiss her goodnight and climb back into Lee Piper's Ford. Returning to the base he would tell himself that they could not continue seeing each other, but it was a poignant, delicious feeling, and he spent more and more of his time planning to see her again, fantasizing about holding her naked in his arms, trying to decide if they had a future together. A little voice in the back of his head repeatedly warned him that wanting her was a more intense feeling than having her would be. He chose to ignore the voice.

$$* * * * *$$

R.J., Gino and Pea caught the shuttle bus to the main gate and hurried over to where the Bomb was parked. Pea caressed the fender lovingly and jumped behind the wheel. The Oldsmobile started up at once and they grinned at each other. Its outward appearance was not pretty, by any stretch of the imagination, but the engine was in great running condition. Pea grinned at the others as he raced the engine. Soon they were speeding down Highway One to Talagi's drive-in diner, the only one of its kind in Agana. There they parked and sat in the car while the Guamanian car hop brought them hamburgers and Pepsis. They had no radio, but Gino kept them entertained by softly singing the tunes he and the group had practiced. Life was good, and in the next few minutes, was about to get better.

Another car rolled slowly into the parking lot, and R.J. nudged Gino in the ribs. Gino looked over at the new arrival and nudged Pea in the ribs. They stared appreciatively at the other car. It was a 1959 Chevrolet Impala convertible with large cat-eye taillights. It was black with a white top and red interior, sitting on white sidewall tires, and it glowed in the lights of the drive-in.

"Nice fuckin' sled!" Pea exclaimed, letting out a slow whistle.

"It's what's inside that's nice," R.J. said, hooking a thumb toward the Chevy.

In the front seat sat three young women in their early twenties, and obviously American. The driver was heavy-set with a large round face and an ample bosom. In the middle sat a slim, pretty brunette, and next to her, riding shotgun, was a great looking blonde, brushing hair from her eyes and looking around with a bored expression.

"Wow," R.J. said softly.

"Three of 'em," Gino observed.

"Hubba, hubba!" Pea grinned, looking over at the driver. "I like 'em hefty!"

The girls looked over at the three sailors in the beat up Oldsmobile and whispered to each other, giggling.

Pea started up the Bomb and backed out of the parking lot. "Where the hell you goin'?" Gino asked.

"Just getting a little closer," Pea replied, putting the Olds in first gear and easing it up next to the Chevy. R.J. leaned out of the window and called to the girls.

"Wanna race?" he asked, trying to duplicate Billy's charming smile. The girls giggled and whispered to each other, pretending to ignore him.

"Wanna trade cars?" R.J. asked, smiling charmingly.

The brunette leaned across the driver. "Think you boys can keep up?" she challenged. The heavy-set driver backed the Chevy out of the parking lot and pointed it toward Highway One.

Pea wasted no time getting the Bomb running, and he began backing out of the parking space, the car-hop's tray still attached to his window.

"Pea, the tray!" Gino yelled. Pea pulled the tray off the window and threw it into the gravel parking lot. As they sped away in pursuit of the Chevy the car-hop picked up the tray and stood in the lot cursing them.

The Chevy picked up speed and hurtled down Highway One, the old Oldsmobile in pursuit. "Don't lose them, Pea!" R.J. called. "They're getting away!"

The Bomb was no match for the Chevy, and soon the girls were far ahead, the big cat-eye taillights disappearing around a corner. Pea struggled to catch up, weaving around the sparse traffic on the highway. They finally spotted the Chevy ahead.

"They slowed down," Gino observed.

"They want us to catch them," R.J. observed.

"The driver's mine!" Pea announced, scooting closer to the wheel and pressing down hard on the gas.

"Take it easy, Pea," R.J. warned. "You're goin' too fast!'

The Impala's big cat-like taillights glowed as the convertible slowed and began easing off to the side of the road.

"Look!" Gino exclaimed, pointing ahead to the black Chevy. "They're pulling into the USO beach!"

Pea slowed the car and shifted down to second gear. The big Olds shuddered and the engine roared, slowing the car down. Pea pulled into the USO beach parking lot and followed the Chevy as it made its way to the rear of the lot. R.J. noticed a Ford Fairlane parked there and thought it looked familiar, but concentrated on the Impala which had pulled to a stop under a clump of palm trees. The driver killed the lights, but left the engine running and the radio on. As Pea pulled the Bomb up next to the Chevy, the Impala's radio was playing Doris Troy's 'Just One Look.' Gino picked up the song.

"Just one look, and I fell so hard, hard hard in love, with you..."

For a few minutes no one said anything. The evening was cooling down and the surf was coming up, making crashing sounds on the beach below. The music and the sound of the surf seemed to be in synch and the six of them sat in their cars, staring out at the ocean.

"Well?" Gino asked no one in particular.

"R.J.," Pea pleaded. "Go talk some shit to 'em."

R.J. smiled and got out of the car. He walked around the rear of the Bomb and leaned casually against the passenger side door of the Impala. The blonde looked up and R.J. found himself looking into eyes so blue they reminded him of the deep Pacific. When she smiled the night seemed to light up and R.J. was smitten.

"Hi," she said sweetly.

R.J. swallowed hard and heard himself answer, "Hi. I'm R.J."

"I'm Annie," the voice sang. "Who's your buddies?"

R.J. stared down at her and motioned to his friends to join him without taking his eyes off of Annie.

Pea jumped out of the Olds and hurried around to the driver's side of the Impala. "Hey, there," he grinned at the driver. She grinned back and got out of the car. She was indeed hefty and Pea appraised her appreciatively, looking her up and down.

"My name's Peacock, but everyone just calls me Pea, you know, for short."

"Well, you certainly are short," the driver agreed, looking down at Pea, smiling. "I'm Carol." She was a head taller and outweighed him by about seventy-five pounds. Pea stood staring at her as if she were the most beautiful woman he had ever seen. Actually, he was staring at her chest, which was at eye level for him.

Gino slid out of the Bomb and joined R.J. on the passenger side of the Impala. R.J. opened the passenger door and held out his hand to Annie. "Wanna take a walk on the beach?" he asked.

"Let's talk here," she suggested. She took R.J.'s hand and slid out of the car. Gino quickly slipped into the passenger seat next to the slim brunette and introduced himself.

"Gino Karras," he said, offering his hand. The brunette shook it and smiled.

"Betty," she said.

"Pleased ta meetcha," Gino grinned. He turned to R.J. and winked.

R.J. leaned against the Olds and looked Annie over. She leaned against the Chevy facing him. She wore a light blue blouse over blue jeans. She was short, about five foot two and had long blonde hair which she wore pulled back and tied in a ribbon. Her blue eyes smiled at him with a mischievous twinkle and her mouth was slightly crooked as she grinned at him. She wore almost no make-up, but she didn't need any. R.J. figured she was about his age, twenty or so.

"You guys on the same ship?" Annie asked.

"Yeah," Pea answered, grinning at Carol's boobs. "We all in the same boat, you might say." Gino was talking softly to Betty, their heads close together, Betty giggling quietly.

"So," R.J. said. "You three aren't in the Navy, are you?"

"No," Annie answered. "We're dependents."

"Your fathers are in the Navy?" R.J. asked.

The three girls giggled at each other. "No," Annie said, suddenly serious. "Our husbands. They're all on the Raptor." R.J. knew the Raptor, a minesweeper stationed in Guam. He had shot the breeze with their head signalman many times. He also knew the Raptor was not in port. It was on a three week cruise to the Philippines.

R.J. stared at her stupidly as if he hadn't heard her. Gino's head snapped up and he jumped out of the Chevy.

"Shit," he said to R.J. "They're fucking married, man!" Betty and Annie giggled again. Carol was staring down affectionately at Pea, who stared back affectionately at her breasts.

"So what?" R.J. finally said. "We're just talking here, right?" He looked to Annie, who nodded and smiled demurely. Betty sat in the Impala with her arm on the back of the passenger seat, looking up at Gino.

Gino shrugged. "What the hell," he said and slid back into the Chevy.

"Cmon," Pea said to Carol. He took her hand and they walked up the beach and sat beneath a palm tree, talking quietly. Carol's laughter rippled down to the parking lot. They were obviously getting along well.

Gino sat talking with Betty, holding her hand and describing his neighborhood in Brooklyn and explaining why he had joined the Navy. Betty listened quietly.

R.J. and Annie stood looking at each other, not saying a word. She looked great in the warm evening, leaning back on the Impala, looking up at him with her head slightly cocked to one side, that crooked little smile on her face.

"How old are you?" she asked.

"Twenty last September," R.J. answered. "How about you?"

"It's not polite to ask a lady her age," Annie admonished him. Then she smiled sweetly and asked, "How old do you think I am?"

"Probably about nineteen or twenty," R.J. ventured.

She giggled again. "Actually, I'm twenty three," she said.

"How long you been married?"

The smile faded. "Too long," she said quietly, looking down at her feet.

R.J. watched her until she looked up at him. She had a sad expression in her eyes and she glanced around nervously.

"Wanna take that walk on the beach?" R.J. offered.

Annie looked at the surf, then back toward the highway. "It's too public here."

"Would you like to go somewhere more private?" he asked hopefully.

"Where?" she asked, looking into his eyes.

"I dunno, maybe up in the hills." He returned her gaze. "Where we can be alone?"

"I think we better go," Annie said, looking around for her friends.

"C'mon," R.J. objected. "Stick around for a while. Your friends don't seem to be in a hurry."

Annie looked around again. Betty and Gino had their heads together, talking softly and seriously. Pea and Carol were making out under the palm tree. R.J. pointed to them and laughed.

"Your friend doesn't waste any time, does he?" Annie said, smiling sweetly.

"He's a bearcat's ass," R.J. said, grinning at Pea and Carol, wrapped in each others' arms under the palm trees.

Suddenly, headlights swept over the beach and a Shore Patrol pickup truck came bouncing into the parking lot.

"Oh, shit!" Annie exclaimed, and turned her head away from the lights.

"Don't worry," R.J. said. He walked up the parking lot to meet the Shore Patrol truck. As he approached the truck he broke into a big grin. Sitting in the passenger seat with an SP armband was Radioman Third Class Fred Riley.

"Got the duty, Sparks?" R.J. asked, walking up to the truck and leaning against it, blocking Riley's view of the beach.

"Yeah," Riley answered disgustedly. "Wait till you make third class, R.J. Then you'll be wearing this armband and patrolling the boonies." He craned his neck to see around R.J. "What you guys doing down there?"

"We met a coupla girls and we're just talking, that's all," R.J. answered with a proud grin.

"Are they chinks?" Riley asked hopefully.

"Naw, round eyes."

"Chink chicks got the nicest asses." Riley turned toward the driver to explain. Riley looked back at R.J. "Take it easy, man."

"See ya," R.J. answered and stood as the driver put the truck in gear and began to move slowly up toward the highway. As they drove away, R.J. could hear Riley talking to the driver. "Did I ever tell you about my one true love in San Francisco? No? Man she was fucking beautiful..."

R.J. chuckled to himself and strolled back to the Impala. Carol was back behind the wheel and Annie had slid back in next to Betty. Gino and Pea stood around the car with disappointed looks on their faces.

"Where you goin'?" R.J. asked Annie as he joined them.

Gino shook his head. "They got spooked by the SPs," he said disgustedly. "They wanna go home."

R.J. leaned against the passenger side of the convertible and looked down at Annie who was staring straight ahead. "Where you goin'?" he repeated.

Annie looked up at him with that sad look in her eyes and his heart melted. "We're going home," she said. "It's too public here."

"Why don't we go somewhere else?" he offered.

"It's getting late," Annie answered, looking down at the watch on her wrist.

"Can we see you again?" R.J. asked desperately.

"I don't know..."

"We'll have a picnic in the hills," R.J. pleaded. "It'll be very private."

"I don't know..."

Betty leaned over and whispered something in Annie's ear. Annie nodded and looked up at R.J. "Maybe Monday night," she said. "Give me the phone number to your ship and we'll call you Monday and let you know." Gino wrote down the ship's phone number and gave it to Annie.

R.J. backed away from the Impala and folded his arms across his chest. "I know a brush off when I see one," he said stubbornly.

Carol leaned over from the driver's side. "We'll call you," she promised. She put the Chevy in gear and backed out, then pointed it toward the highway and drove off, leaving the three sailors standing in the parking lot, watching the cat-eyes fade into the night.

"Whooee!" Pea yelled. "That is one hot chick!"

R.J. and Gino stared at Pea for a moment, then began laughing.

"Pea, you one smooth lil' dude!" Gino said.

"You got some moves, boy," R.J. agreed.

"Wait till Monday night," Pea promised. "I'll teach you guys some things."

"Ain't gonna be no Monday night," R.J. said. "We just got the bum's rush."

"Think positive, m'man," Gino said, slapping R.J. on the back. "They gonna call. I know they gonna call." R.J. smiled, but he doubted it.

They climbed into the Bomb and headed up Highway One toward the Naval base. Gino tapped his hand on his knee and sang softly, "Just one look, that's all it took, just one look..."

R.J. and Pea joined in and sang along with Gino while they sped toward the base. They were enjoying themselves and didn't notice the maroon Buick convertible pass them on its way to the USO beach.

THIRTY THREE

Lorelei killed the headlights when she pulled into the parking lot and cruised slowly to where Lee Piper's car was parked. Paul climbed out of the passenger side and put on his cap while he walked to the driver's side to say goodnight. He leaned in to kiss her and she turned her head. The kiss ended up on her cheek.

"You okay?" he asked.

"I don't know," she said, staring through the windshield at the surf. "I feel pretty rotten sometimes." She turned to look up at him and he thought that in the dim light of the USO beach she was the most beautiful woman he had ever seen. The sad look on her face only added to her beauty as far as he was concerned.

"I don't want to leave when you're feeling like this," he said softly, staring into her violet eyes.

"It's just that..." her voice trailed off and her eyes welled up with tears. She stared out at the surf softly rolling up onto the beach.

"You're feeling guilty," he said flatly. "I understand, but..."

"But what?" she turned to look up at him.

"You...we haven't done anything wrong."

"Nothing wrong?" she challenged, dabbing at her eyes with a hanky. "I'm deceiving my husband."

Paul stood there silently, looking at the ocean and wishing he were out on it, steaming to...where? Anywhere but here. He sighed and looked down at her pretty face.

"If you don't want to see me again..." he started.

She became angry. "Don't want to see you again? What's the matter with you? You don't understand women at all, do you?" She put the Buick in gear and roared out of the parking lot, leaving Captain Oliver standing alone wondering what the hell he'd said to set her off.

He opened the door to the Fairlane and sat in the driver's seat, gripping the steering wheel and shaking his head. *Well,* he thought, *maybe I don't understand women, but who in the hell does?* He stuck his unlit pipe in his mouth and started up the Ford, maneuvered through the parking lot and pulled up onto the highway where he gunned it and sped toward the base.

THIRTY FOUR

Andy rejoined the focsul singing group on Sunday evening. Nothing was said when he just came up on the focsul and began singing the base part of Ray Charles' 'What'd I say?" The others in the group smiled and began snapping their fingers, getting into the rhythm of the song. R.J. stood near the lifeline, fishing pole in hand, lowering the cheese-baited hook into the harbor. It was just after dark and the barracuda would be biting soon. Pea sat on the capstain head and smoked a cigarette, grinning slyly, thinking of Carol. Of Carol's chest. *That magnificent chest!*

Jefferson had the focsul watch and leaned against the gun mount, snapping his fingers to the music and moving back and forth slowly to the beat. Pancho Cortez lay on the deck, staring at the star-filled night. Billy Lopez had taken the ship's truck to visit Teresa and wouldn't be back until Mrs. Gamboa kicked him out, usually around midnight.

R.J. enjoyed the evenings on the focsul almost as much as he enjoyed the mornings on the fantail. The difference was that on the fantail he was alone with his thoughts as he welcomed the creeping dawn. On the focsul in the evenings, with his friends and shipmates, listening to the group sing and the friendly banter of the men, he felt bonded with them. Though he was now a signalman striker, he was still welcomed and accepted by the deck force. He was an honorary deck ape in their eyes, and would always be a part of First Division.

The group took a break and lit up cigarettes, talking excitedly about the songs they had learned and the new ones Gino wanted them to try. Voices came up the port side and Crawford and Queen arrived on the focsul, carrying fishing poles and a bucket. When Crawford appeared the conversation stopped. He had lied for Twitchell at Rafer's captain's mast and the men of First Division would not forgive him for that.

Queen looked around at the now silent men and frowned. "Let's hear some music, fellas," he said pleasantly.

"We're just knocking off, Boats," Tanner said and began walking down the starboard side toward the hatch. One by one the others followed, glaring at Crawford as they left the focsul. R.J. pulled in his bait, picked up his bucket, gave Crawford a dirty look and followed the others through the starboard hatch.

Crawford shrugged. "Hey, more fish for us, huh?" he asked Queen, who stood staring at the hatch through which the deck apes had disappeared.

"Yeah," he said absently. "I guess so."

Crawford dropped his line into the water and almost immediately got a hit. He pulled in a fair-sized barracuda and held it tightly while he removed the hook. "Hey Jefferson," he called. "Bonk this here bad boy on the head for me!"

"Bonk 'im yourself," Jefferson said bitterly. "I got the watch up here." He turned and walked up the focsul to the point of the bow, staring out at the harbor, his back to Crawford.

Crawford started to follow him, but Queen stopped him. "Forget it,

Crawford," he advised. "We'll do it ourselves." He removed a marlin spike from the scabbard on his belt and snapped it down on the wriggling fish, which stopped wriggling.

"Guess those guys are gonna hold a grudge, huh?" Crawford drawled.

"They're pissed off about Rafer Sample," Queen explained.

"Yeah, well fuck them," Crawford spat. "Who gives a shit what they think?"

Queen thought for a moment. "I do, for one," he replied. "Here." He handed the marlin spike to Crawford. "Make sure you clean it before you give it back." Queen stared at Crawford for a moment, then turned and walked down the focsul and through the starboard hatch. Crawford stood on the focsul holding the dead barracuda in one hand and the steel marlin spike in the other. He shrugged, dropped the fish into the bucket and lowered another cheese-baited hook into the water, whistling softly to himself. Jefferson stood at the bow, looking out at the water of the harbor. The focsul was quiet.

* * * * *

R.J. busied himself on the signal bridge Monday morning, hoping against hope that the girls would call to set up a rendezvous for that evening. Every hour on the hour Pea would holler up at him from the 02 level, "Hey, R.J., you hear anything yet?"

"Not yet, Pea," R.J. would yell down. "I'll come and get you as soon as they call."

"You think they gonna call?" Pea would ask hopefully.

"Yeah, they'll call. Be patient." But R.J. was not nearly as confident as he sounded. *Besides,* he thought, *they were married. It would probably be best for all of us if they didn't call. Married women are trouble.*

The brass was all polished, the flagbag aired out and R.J. was mending the lanyard on the Bravo flag when Cotton came up on the signal bridge, wearing the duty belt of the messenger of the watch.

"R.J.!" he called. "Phone call on the quarterdeck."

R.J. smiled to himself and nodded. He knew they would call. He followed Cotton to the quarterdeck.

"Some broad on the phone," Cotton explained as they made their way aft to the fantail. "Who is she?"

"Some chick I met," R.J. answered and picked up the phone. Pea and Gino had been alerted to the call and stood a few feet away, anxiously looking at R.J. as he answered the phone.

"R.J. Davis speaking," he said into the mouthpiece.

"Do you know who this is?" a soft voice asked.

R.J. grinned. "Mom!" he exclaimed. "You're calling me from Denver?"

Pea and Gino let their faces drop in disappointment. R.J. winked at them.

A giggle on the phone, then, "You're a funny guy. Want me to hang up?"

"No, I'm just kidding. Of course I know who you are." R.J. gave the thumbs up to Pea and Gino. "You're that gorgeous woman I met the other night at Talagi's."

"My friends want to know if you and your buddies want to get togeth-er?" Her voice had a soft, musical quality that sent a chill across the back of his neck.

"Is this a trick question?" R.J. asked dramatically.

She giggled. She said something to someone in the background, proba-bly Betty and Carol because he heard more giggling. "Meet us at Talagi's at eight o'clock. Carol knows a place where we can get together, you know, in private."

"We'll be there," he assured her. "And Annie," he said softly.

"Yes?"

"I been thinking about you."

"I've been thinking about you, too." The phone became silent and R.J. thought for a moment that she had hung up. "See you tonight," she said softly and R.J. heard the click as she set the receiver in its cradle.

R.J. turned to Gino and Pea, who stood there watching him, anxious looks on their faces. "Well?" Gino asked.

"Yeah, what the fuck, R.J.," Pea demanded impatiently. "We gonna get together or what?"

R.J. smiled at them. "Yahoo!" he said, giving them the thumbs up with both hands.

"Yahoo!" Pea yelped and began dancing around the fantail. "Yahoo!"

Gino grinned crookedly and returned to his task of applying red lead to a freshly sanded spot on the deck.

* * * * *

Lieutenant MacDonald sat in his stateroom studying the paperwork from Rafer Sample's captain's mast. He read over the affidavits provided by Chief Twitchell and the testimony of Crawford. *Something stinks. Rafer had had no witnesses, why was that? He presented no ex*planation, nor did he defend himself. The captain had no choice but to send him to the brig.

Mr. Mac did not like Chief Twitchell. The fat chief was an embarrass-ment as far as he was concerned, but MacDonald knew why the captain put up with him. He was the only man aboard who could repair the evaps, and he spent many hours in the engine room on the problem. But the man was obviously an obnoxious drunk who hated everyone, especially blacks. The First Division commander knew that times were changing. *If we don't change with them, this man's Navy is going to be in big trouble,* he thought sadly. He closed the file and threw it on his desk. He would talk with Pedro Almogordo the first chance he got. He knew something had to be done to nip this situation in the bud or it would only get worse.

* * * * *

Later that afternoon Lee Piper leaned against the bulkhead in Captain Oliver's stateroom smoking a cigar and talking about the Brister's recent patrol. The Haverfield's sister ship had returned to port that morning and Captain Piper was there to pick up the keys to his car.

"Thanks for taking care of my baby, Paul," he said, puffing on the stogie. "I appreciate your keeping an eye on it for me."

"No problem, Lee," Paul replied, distracted.

"What's going on, Paul?" Piper asked, his brow knitted in a frown.

"What do you mean?"

"I got eyes," Piper said. "I can see."

Paul Oliver felt a small twinge of panic. "I don't know what you're talking about."

"Look, old buddy, I'm your friend. Probably the best friend you got on this island and I got a feeling you're hiding something from me." He pointed his cigar at Captain Oliver. "Tell me I'm wrong."

"Just a lot on my mind, Lee."

Captain Piper decided to take a chance and just say what was on his mind. "This have anything to do with Lorelei Prescott?" he asked quietly.

Paul Oliver felt his face redden, and he knew Piper had put it together. *If he had figured it out...*

"Don't sweat it, man," Piper said cheerfully. "I'm not about to say anything to anyone, and I doubt seriously that anyone else has figured it out." He sat down on Captain Oliver's bunk and rested his forearms on his knees. "Want to talk about it?"

Paul took his time lighting his pipe and puffing to get it going. His mind was racing. Could he confide in his friend? Did he dare? He set his pipe down on the desk and turned to face Lee Piper. "How did you know?" he asked softly.

"I've seen the way you two look at each other when you think no one is watching. But I'll tell you how it all came together in my mind." He relit his cigar while Captain Oliver waited expectantly. "Every time you return my car I can smell her in it." He grinned at Paul. "That Chanel she wears is a very distinctive aroma."

Paul sat and stared at his desk. He didn't know what to say. He felt as if he had been caught stealing, and he was embarrassed.

"You want to talk about it?" Lee asked again.

"Yes," Paul replied, slowly nodding his head, "but not here."

"Okay," Lee said and pulled himself up. "How about we hit the beach tonight? I've got a little surprise for you." He smiled conspiratorially and put on his hat. "I'll pick you up at 1900."

Paul sat in his chair and smoked his pipe thoughtfully. *I know I can trust Lee Piper, but if Lee could figure it out, isn't it reasonable to believe others could? Perhaps I ought to end this friendship with Lorelei before it goes too far; before others figure it out.* But he knew he wouldn't do it. He couldn't. He was in love with the admiral's wife and he knew she was in love with him. He tried to look into the future, to get a glimpse of what lay in store for them, but all he saw was dark skies and stormy seas. A knock at his door brought him out of his reverie and he welcomed the interruption.

"Enter!"

RM-1 Paul Murray opened the door. He was beaming, his big smile filling his face. He handed the captain a clipboard with a message on it. "Just came in, Cap'n," he grinned.

Captain Oliver scanned the message quickly, looked up at Murray and then read the message again, slowly. A smile began to creep across his face as he read the text:

From: Comcrudespac
To: Commanding Officer, USS Haverfield DER-393
Date: 15 October 1963
Subj: Underway Evaluation Drills, results of

Be advised this date USS Haverfield performed exceptionally well in UED exercises last month. You are authorized to display "E" for efficiency on ship's stack.
Haverfield is also authorized to display "C" for communications excellence, having posted third highest score in Seventh Fleet area of operations.
Congratulations on a four-oh job.

Rear Admiral Thomas Boddicker, USN
COMCRUDESPAC

Paul Oliver sat and stared at the message, his mind reeling with a thousand different thoughts. They had made it! All the hard work, all the training had paid off. He had forgotten about Murray.

"Thank you." He grinned up at the radioman, who was beaming at him. Paul initialed the message, took his copy and returned the clipboard. Murray saluted and did an about face, marching sharply toward the radio shack.

Captain Oliver looked at the message again and took a deep breath. He reached for the sound-powered phone and rang up the quarterdeck.

"Quarterdeck, Chief Risk speaking, sir."

"Chief, send the messenger to Mr. Almogordo and Mr. MacDonald and have them report to my cabin at once."

"Aye, sir." The chief put down the phone and pondered. Was something wrong? Were the engineering department head and the First Division department head in some kind of trouble?

Pancho Cortez was the messenger of the watch and was just returning from an errand. "Pancho," the chief said. "Go tell Mr. Almogordo and Mr. MacDonald the captain wants to see them at once."

"Okay, chief." Pancho headed to engineering first. He wondered what was up. Did this have something to do with Chief Twitchy? He hurried down the passageway toward Mr. Almogordo's office.

THIRTY FOUR

Though they weren't meeting the girls until eight, Pea was ready to go at five-thirty. He had spent a long time in the head, showering, washing his hair five times, shaving, lathering on several layers of deodorant, and soaking himself in aftershave. He stood in the hatchway of the head urging Gino and R.J. to hurry up and get ready.

"C'mon guys, let's shake a leg. We don't wanna miss 'em, do we?"

"Shut up, Pea!" Gino yelled from inside the shower. "We got over two hours before we meet them." He peeked around the shower curtain, his hair full of shampoo. "Play it cool, little dude," he grinned.

Pea shifted his attention to R.J. "You gettin' ready, R.J.?" he pleaded.

"For Chrissakes, Pea," R.J. answered from inside the shower stall. "You act like you never had a date."

Pea couldn't stand still. He paced back and forth in the head until Gino and R.J. emerged from their showers. "Pee-yoo!" Gino exclaimed, waving his hands in front of him. "What the hell is that smell? What you got on, boy?"

Pea grinned and grabbed his crotch. "I got a hard on, but I didn't know you could smell it!"

Gino shook the water from his hair like a dog climbing out of a lake. The water splattered on Pea and he jumped back. "Hey, man, these are clean whites!"

"Then get the hell out of here and let us get ready," Gino warned.

Pea left the head pouting and went up to the fantail. Sailors in dress whites were lining up on the quarterdeck with their liberty cards, waiting to leave the ship and climb on the shuttle bus to the Mocombo Club. Some were walking down the pier toward the main gate to hitch-hike into town. Mr. Jones was the OOD and he smelled Pea before he saw him.

"Whoa, Peacock," he said, holding his nose. "You smell like a French whore!"

"Thank you, sir!" Pea beamed proudly.

"You going ashore?" Mr. Jones asked, looking Pea up and down. He couldn't remember ever seeing the diminutive sailor looking so squared away.

"Yes sir, soon as my buds are ready."

"Well, stand down wind from me, will ya?" Mr. Jones pleaded, a sour smile on his face. "You're bringing tears to my eyes."

Pea paced the fantail, waiting for his friends. It seemed like hours before Gino and R.J. finally came up the aft ladder and joined Pea on the quarterdeck.

"Permission to leave the ship, sir," R.J. saluted Mr. Jones and the flag on the stern, then walked slowly down the brow. The tide was coming in and the ship rose in the water, making the brow slant down at an angle. Gino and Pea joined him on the pier.

"Let's go to the Mocombo Club and have a few beers before it's time to meet the ladies," Gino suggested, rubbing his hands together in anticipation.

"No, no," Pea protested. "We're gonna miss 'em!"

"Pea," R.J. reasoned, looking at his watch. "We got almost two hours before we're supposed to hook up, so why don't you cool it?"

"What if they're early?" Pea whined. "What if they get there, we ain't there and they split?"

Gino and R.J. looked at each other and shook their heads. "Okay," Gino gave in. "We'll go hang out at fuckin' Talagi's and sip Pepsis for two hours."

The sharply dressed, good-smelling trio made their way slowly down the pier toward the main gate where the Bomb was parked. Mr. Jones stood on the quarterdeck watching them, a sardonic smile creasing his face. He turned to Tanner who was the petty officer of the watch. "Those guys are not going to sneak up on anybody tonight," he laughed, holding his nose.

"No, sir, they sure ain't," Tanner grinned back.

* * * * *

R.J., Pea and Gino sat at a patio table in front of Talagi's, drinking Pepsis and feeding the juke box which had speakers all around the outside of the drive-in hamburger stand. There were a few tables inside, but they wanted to be in clear view of the girls when they arrived.

Buddy Holly's 'That'll Be the Day' echoed through the patio and Gino nudged R.J. with his elbow and pointed toward Highway One. The black Chevy Impala convertible, its top down, rolled slowly into the gravel parking lot and stopped next to the Bomb. It was just before eight o'clock and dark had settled over the island, showing off a clear night sky resplendent with stars.

"Hey, guys," Pea whispered. "They're here."

"Yeah, Pea, no shit," Gino replied impatiently. "Now play it cool, don't be too aggressive or you'll scare 'em off."

Pea got up and strode over to the Impala's driver's side and placed his hands on the door, leaning forward. "How ya doin', baby?" he asked Carol.

"Just fine, Shorty," she giggled up at him. "You sure smell good."

Pea turned and grinned at the others with satisfaction. Gino and R.J. rolled their eyes in disgust and sat sipping their Pepsis, pretending to pay no particular attention to Pea or the girls. This situation required cool, they had agreed, but Pea was making a fool of himself. He sure had a lot to learn about women.

Annie leaned back and looked over from her shotgun seat. She caught R.J.'s eye and smiled sweetly. R.J. smiled back, sipping his Pepsi from a straw. Betty was watching Gino closely, and Gino pretended he was intrigued with the bottom of his Pepsi bottle.

"You guys gonna follow us?" Carol asked playfully.

Pea leered down at her. "Do a bear shit in the woods?" he asked as charmingly as he could manage. The girls giggled and Carol put the Impala in gear and began backing out of the lot. Gino and R.J. joined Pea in the Bomb and the two cars eased out onto Highway One.

Pea followed along closely behind the Chevy. "Wonder where they takin' us?" he mused.

"This looks like a fuckin' setup," Gino warned. "They might have some guys waitin' to roll us."

"For what?" R.J. asked. "Between the three of us we got maybe five bucks."

"Well, maybe they just gonna jump us," Gino offered.

"Growin' up in Brooklyn has made you paranoid, Gino," R.J. laughed.

"Brooklyn makes everybody paranoid," Gino replied thoughtfully.

The Impala turned off Highway One onto a narrow road leading up into the hills with the Bomb following close behind. Pea was grinning broadly and tapping his fingers on the steering wheel, singing loudly, *"That'll be the day, when you say good bye-aye, that'll be the day, when you make me cry-aye, you say you gonna leave but you know it's a lie-aye..."*

"They're slowing down," R.J. observed, pointing at the black Impala as it slowed and turned onto a rutted, dirt road. The Bomb followed and within a few minutes they came bouncing into a small clearing, surrounded by palm trees and thick vegetation, and came to a stop behind the Impala. It was an isolated, lonely looking place, and R.J. got out of the car, looked around and saw no one else in sight. The vegetation was very thick, and no light came into the clearing except for the overhead blanket of stars. R.J. motioned to Gino and the kid from Brooklyn got out of the car and looked around suspiciously, as if he were expecting to be jumped.

Pea sauntered up to the Impala as the girls got out. Carol had a large blanket in her arms, which she spread out at the soft edge of the clearing. She left the Impala running, radio playing. The girls sat on the blanket and Betty produced a six pack of San Miguel beer.

"No Coors?" R.J. asked, sitting down and accepting a bottle of beer offered to him by Annie. She looked great in the light of the stars, and she smelled a lot better than Pea. R.J. drank a long pull of beer and stretched out on the blanket, resting on his elbow, staring at Annie. Gino stood next to the Chevy talking with Betty. Everything seemed perfect, the night, the stars, the girls, the music. Then the mosquitoes swarmed in on them with a vengeance.

"Ow, shit!" Pea yelled and jumped up, slapping at the air around his head.

"Damn!" Gino yelped. "These bugs're eating me up!"

R.J. slapped at the mosquitoes, jumping to his feet. "Retreat!" he yelled, laughing. "We're outnumbered!"

All six of them, waving frantically at the bugs, decided to jump into the Bomb for protection. Pea and Carol were in the front seat and Gino and R.J. got into the back with Betty and Annie. It was crowded but they didn't seem to mind much. R.J. liked the feel of Annie's leg pressed up against him. They sat in silence for awhile, trying to figure out what to do next.

"We can't all stay in this car all night," Betty said. "We need to go someplace else."

"Where?" Gino asked, snaking his arm around her.

"Yeah, where?" Annie asked.

Betty looked at Annie and raised her eyebrows.

"Oh, no, you're asking for trouble if you're thinking what I think you're thinking."

"Wha?" Pea asked. "What you thinking?"

"Well," Betty began slowly. "We can go to my place."

"Where do you live?" Gino asked.

"Naval housing."

"Oh no. Shit that's all we need," Gino complained. "Get busted in Naval housing without a good reason and we all go to the fuckin' brig!" He looked at R.J. "No way, right, pard?"

"The Raptor's on a cruise, right?" R.J. asked Annie, who nodded slowly.

"You can't be serious, man," Gino said quietly, but the idea was beginning to appeal to him. "How we gonna get into Naval housing? The SPs'll bust us for sure."

"My car," Carol said, smiling wickedly at Pea, "has a really huge trunk."

"Sounds good to me," Pea said, smiling wickedly back at her.

"So lemme get this straight," Gino said seriously. "You're gonna sneak us past the shore patrol in the trunk of the car?" He looked around at the others. "Can we do that?" he asked, but his mind was already made up.

"Why the hell not?" R.J. asked, staring into Annie's big blue eyes.

They sat quietly for a while, thinking about what they were about to do.

"Well, let's go then!" Pea decided. "Let's do it!"

"This is what we're gonna do," Betty said, and explained her plan to the others who nodded agreement. The girls got out of the Bomb and piled into the Impala, swatting at mosquitoes. Pea backed the Bomb onto the narrow road, allowing the Chevy to take the lead. Soon they were speeding up Highway One toward the base. Pea fell back and followed at a distance of a mile or so. They didn't want to go through the main gate directly behind the girls. That might cause suspicion with the Marine SPs manning the gate. They were very protective of Navy dependents.

When the Bomb passed through the gate to the base, the Impala was nowhere in sight. Pea parked the Olds in the lot and locked it up. The trio made their way up the road toward Apra Harbor. They went around a bend in the road, out of sight of the gate and spotted the Impala pulled to the side, lights off, the trunk open and Carol standing next to the car.. They looked around to make certain no one was watching, then climbed into the trunk of the Chevy. Carol closed the lid and slid back behind the wheel. She was right, the Impala had a large trunk and the three sailors were uncomfortable but not crowded.

"This is stupid," Gino whispered when the Chevy pulled out and gained speed. "We're gonna get busted."

"Shhhh!" Pea scolded. "It's too late to back out now."

"One of these days we're gonna look back on this and laugh," R.J. said, shifting his weight, trying to find a comfortable position.

"That Carol is a hot chick," Pea whispered. "She digs me, too."

R.J. and Gino laughed nervously. "Y'know, Pea," R.J. said. "You really are a funny little dude."

"Fuckin' ay," Pea whispered and they all laughed.

"You guys be quiet back there," Betty's muffled voice came from the front seat. "We're pulling in to Naval housing now."

The Impala came to a stop in a designated parking area and the men waited nervously. The trunk came open and R.J. looked up, almost expecting to see the shore patrol looking down at them, but it was only Carol. They climbed out of the trunk and looked around. R.J. thought that Naval housing looked a lot like the projects in North Denver. Two-story, apartment-like dwellings, connected four to a building sprawled as far as he could see, all the same color. *How did anybody find the right house?* he wondered.

"Look there," Betty instructed, pointing to the rear of the nearest building. Concrete slabs lay behind each unit, serving as back porches, and each had a porch light next to the back door. "It's the second one from the left," she said. "We'll go in the front door and let you in through the back." She leaned over and kissed Gino on the mouth. "Hurry," she whispered, and followed Carol and Annie around to the front of the building. It was still early, just past nine o'clock, but the area was deserted.

R.J. led the way as they hurried from the parking lot, across the rear greenbelt to the second door from the left. So far so good. They lined up outside the back door and waited. What the hell was taking so long? Suddenly, the back porch light came on, bathing the three furtive sailors in bright light. The back door opened.

"Turn off that fuckin' light!" Gino whispered hoarsely. The light went out and the three sailors ducked into Betty's house. They found themselves in a small kitchen and Gino went immediately to the window and looked up and down the parking lot. Apparently no one had spotted them.

"We'll leave the lights off," Betty said, leading them through the kitchen to the living room. R.J. and Gino sat on the overstuffed couch and lit cigarettes. Annie sat down next to R.J. and took the cigarette out of his mouth, putting it into her own. R.J. smiled and lit another.

Betty put on the radio in the kitchen and music began filtering through the house. She came in and snuggled next to Gino on the couch. He put his arm around her and she laid her head on his shoulder.

"Where's Pea?" R.J. asked, looking around. "And where's Carol?"

Betty giggled and pointed to the stairs. "Up there," she said. "Your buddy moves right along, doesn't he?" Squeaky bedspring noises and giggles came through the floor clearly.

"Yeah," Annie added, looking up at the ceiling. "He's a regular Pepe LePew."

Gino and R.J. looked at the ceiling and then at each other. They burst out laughing.

"What's so funny?" Annie asked.

"We told Pea to take it slow so's he wouldn't scare her off," Gino explained.

"That why you're taking it slow?" Betty asked. Gino looked at her and she pulled his head down and planted her mouth on his in a deep, passionate kiss.

"I'm gonna get a Pepsi," Annie said, and got up from the couch and walked into the kitchen. R.J. followed. The radio was playing Johnny Mathis singing *'Chances Are'*, and Annie handed a bottle of Pepsi to R.J.

R.J. sipped the Pepsi and looked at Annie. She was leaning against the kitchen sink, her head cocked to one side, studying him with those beautiful blue eyes. She looked young and lovely, her blonde hair framed in the dim light coming through the window.

"Let's dance," he said and took the Pepsi from her hand and put both bottles on the counter. She came to him and snaked her left arm around his neck. He held her close and they began swaying with the music. He maneuvered her backwards until he backed her up against the counter just as the song was ending. She looked up and he kissed her tentatively, exploring her mouth. She responded and they stood locked in the embrace until she broke it off and backed away.

"Whew," she said, waving her hand in front of her face. "I need to sit down."

THIRTY FIVE

Lee Piper guided the Ford Fairlane one-handed through the winding roads above Agana. Paul Oliver sat in the passenger seat, silently puffing on his pipe and watching the vegetation pass by in what seemed like slow motion. Lee had said he had a surprise for him, but Paul had no idea what he was talking about, which was fine. He was content to sit and puff and daydream about Lorelei.

The Ford pulled off the road into a private driveway that sloped down toward a small cottage set against a sloping hill. The car came to a stop, Lee Piper killed the ignition and got out, waving for Paul to follow him. Captain Oliver got out of the car and surveyed the cottage.

"What do you think?" Lee asked.

"Nice," Paul answered. "Who does it belong to?"

"Me," Captain Piper answered. "At least for now. I'm renting it from my ex-operations officer. You remember Bill Maguire? He was transferred back to San Diego last month, and had six months to go on the lease, so I took it over. Figured it would make a good bachelor pad." He chuckled and led Paul toward the front door. "Guess what Bill named this place?"

Paul shrugged, looking around at the cozy little cottage.

"The 'Id,'" Lee said, laughing. He unlocked the front door and held it open for Captain Oliver. "Welcome to the Id!"

Inside, the cottage opened up into a living room with a large, sectional couch set in the far corner. A teakwood coffee table sat in front of the sectional and two end tables sat on either side, with small lamps sitting on them. Lee turned on both lamps and Paul looked around appreciatively.

"Wow," he said. "Nice pad."

Lee went into the kitchenette and pulled two bottles of San Miguel from the small refrigerator. He opened them and handed one to Paul. "Little kitchen, but functional," Lee began the tour. "One bedroom in the back, one bath but it's pretty good-sized." Lee opened the bathroom door and Paul looked in. It was a pretty good-sized bathroom, but the most distinctive feature was the large, free-standing bathtub. It wasn't lost on Paul that the bathtub was big enough to accommodate two people.

"I know what you're thinking," Lee laughed and opened the door to the bedroom.

A large, double bed dominated the small room. A wardrobe sat against one wall and a large window occupied the opposite wall. Lee pulled back the curtains and Paul looked out. For as far as he could see, rolling hills and jungle vegetation spread out before him. *This is very private*, he thought.

"Let's talk," Captain Piper said, leading Paul back into the living room where they sat on the sectional and sipped at their beers. Paul sat staring at his pipe, which had gone out, and Lee tossed his Zippo lighter over to him. "Tell me about Lorelei," he said softly. Paul Oliver slowly lit his pipe and leaned back on the couch, nodding to his friend. It would be good to talk it out.

* * * * *

Annie sat down at the chrome and formica kitchen table and motioned R.J. to a chair. She took two cigarettes from his pack and lit them both, passing one over to him. "Tell me what you're thinking," she said.

"I'm thinking that the shore patrol is going to come busting in here and arrest all of us," R.J. replied. "They patrol Naval housing pretty regular, don't they?"

"Don't worry," she said soothingly. "We'll get you back to your ship safely."

"So, you've done this before?"

"Certainly not," she said, pouting. "I'm as nervous as you are."

"Well," he said, pointing to the ceiling. "Sounds like Gino and Pea have made themselves at home."

Annie looked up and cocked her head to one side, listening to the unmistakable sounds of men and women thoroughly enjoying each other's company. Bed springs were squeaking in both upstairs bedrooms, and muffled sounds of female giggling and male laughter drifted down through the ceiling. She blushed slightly and looked back at R.J.

"I'm not going to bed with you tonight," she said firmly.

"Did I ask you?" R.J. challenged.

"Well, no," she admitted.

"Then why don't you wait until I ask you before you turn me down?"

"Fair enough," she said, glad that particular issue had been dealt with. "Would you like to go in the living room? It'll be more comfortable."

They moved to the overstuffed couch where R.J. sat down. Annie climbed onto his lap, putting her arms around his neck. They kissed, tentatively at first, then with more feeling until they were grinding their mouths against each other. She pulled back and started to stand, but he pulled her back down on his lap and kissed her again, snaking his hand under the back of her blouse and deftly unsnapping her bra with two fingers.

"Wait a minute," she gasped. "You're pretty light fingered, aren't you?"

He pulled her bra and blouse up in the front and buried his face in her breasts. She sighed and fell back on the couch. "Remember what I said," she whispered.

"I know, I know," he said, his voice muffled in soft, smooth flesh.

"This is as far as we go," she whispered.

"I know, I know."

They lay next to each other, kissing deeply, he fondling her breasts, she running her fingers through his hair and moaning. She sat up suddenly.

"Wait," she said. "I hear something."

She hurried over to the window and peeked out, refastening her bra and pulling down her blouse. "The shore patrol just went by," she said, turning back to him.

"As long as they keep just going by," he grinned and patted the couch next to him.

She sat down next to him. "What time is it?" she asked.

R.J. looked at his watch. "Ten-thirty," he said. "Still early." He reached for her and she pulled away.

"I thought you dug me," he said, disappointed.

"I do like you," she replied. "That's the problem, I like you a lot. Let's just take it slow."

"Slow it is," he agreed, and pulled her down next to him. She didn't resist. He kissed her and smiled at the squeaky sounds seeping down through the ceiling.

* * * * *

"And that's how it's been," Paul Oliver was telling the story to his friend. "We get together maybe twice a month, drive up in the hills, park and talk." He smiled and finished his beer. "Sometimes we make out, but we've never gone all the way."

"Is it love?" Lee asked seriously. "I mean, where is this going?"

"Hell, Lee," Paul said, a frustrated tone in his voice. "I don't know. Sometimes I think we should just break it off, then I start thinking of her and I know I'll never be the one to end it."

"How does she feel?"

"Same as me, I guess," Paul answered. "She's always happy, you know? Never says a discouraging word, never talks about her husband...much." He relit his pipe while Lee went into the kitchenette and produced two more beers. "She's always smiling, always gracious, always incredibly beautiful." Paul Oliver shook his head slowly. "Maybe she's just in it for the excitement, I don't know." He thought for a moment. "Maybe she's just bored."

"The two of you have to work it out together," Lee advised. "Tell you what," he threw a key onto the table. "I made you a key. You can use this place anytime I'm at sea."

Paul picked up the key slowly, examined it and turned it over in his hand. *The key to paradise, or maybe to hell,* he thought. Aloud to Lee he said, "I feel like I'm slipping down into a situation over which I have no control." He shrugged and put the key in his pocket. "Guess I just have to ride it out."

"Just be careful, friend," was all the advice Lee Piper gave him.

＊＊*

It was late when Gino came bouncing down the stairs in his skivvy shorts and walked by R.J. and Annie as if they weren't there. He went into the kitchen, asking, "You got anything to drink in here besides Pepsis?" Betty came down after him in her panties and bra. She didn't seem to notice R.J. and Annie either as she followed Gino into the kitchen. "I got some wine, I think," she said and put her arms around him from behind. After a few minutes, they emerged from the kitchen and stood staring down at Annie and R.J. on the couch.

"You guys wanna use the room?" Betty asked, pointing up at the stairs.

"Not tonight," Annie answered and snuggled up next to R.J.

Gino looked down at his friend, disappointed that he wasn't going upstairs. R.J. and Annie snuggled close and held on to each other lovingly. "You two ain't fallin' in love, are you?" Gino asked, frowning.

"What if we are?" Annie asked.

Gino shook his head sadly. "Shit," he said and grabbed Betty's hand, leading her to the stairs.

"Hurry up," R.J. called to him. "It's after midnight and we gotta get back sometime tonight."

"Tell Pea!" Gino laughed as he chased a squealing Betty up the stairs. "That little dude is layin' some serious pipe!"

＊＊*

Lee Piper dropped Paul Oliver off at the Haverfield's brow. Captain Oliver got out of the car and stuck his head in the passenger window. "Thanks, Lee," he said sincerely. "Thanks for the key, and for the talk."

"Anytime, buddy," Piper said and drove off down the pier. Captain Oliver walked up the brow, acknowledged the salutes of the quarterdeck crew and made his way to his cabin. The cottage's key felt heavy in his pocket. He could feel it growing warm against his leg.

＊＊*

"The shore patrol just went by," Annie said, peering out the front window. "That means we got a half hour before they come around again." She looked at the three sailors, fully dressed and lined up behind her. "Let's go quickly."

Betty went out the back door first and opened the trunk of the Impala. She gave a signal and R.J., Gino and Pea followed quickly, looking around, hoping they weren't being watched. They piled into the trunk and Betty closed the lid.

The three girls got into the front seat. Carol started up the car and backed out of the parking place. Before they knew it, they were out of Naval housing and on the road to the harbor. Carol pulled over under some palm trees and opened the trunk. The sailors climbed out and into the back seat. As they headed toward the harbor, Gino began to sing a Sam Cooke song:

"Cupid, draw back your bow, and let your arrow go..." He pretended he had a bow and arrow and he shot the imaginary arrow at Annie, who giggled at him. *"Straight to my lover's heart, for me!"* R.J. scowled at him.

Carol stopped the Chevy about fifty yards from the Haverfield and the boys got out. Pea jumped over the closed door and came around to the driver's side. "See you, baby," he leered at Carol. She looked up and hooked a finger at him.

"C'mere, shorty," she said and pulled his head down, planting a wet kiss on his mouth. "You take care of yourself, y'hear?"

Gino said goodbye to Betty and R.J. said goodbye to Annie and the three sailors walked backwards toward the ship, waving to the Impala as it sped away down the pier.

Back aboard, they undressed quietly in the dark and fell exhausted into their bunks. In Operations Division's compartment R.J. lay awake in his rack, staring at the overhead. *I'm the only one didn't get any,* he thought before he fell asleep.

THIRTY SIX

Senior Chief Jaspar Twitchell was angry. He didn't like being called into Lieutenant Almogordo's office, especially on a topic they had already discussed. The engineering officer laid down the law: There would be no racial conflict on the Haverfield. Chief Twitchell was instructed to maintain a low profile in his dealings with black sailors, to keep his opinions to himself, and cause no trouble. The chief had agreed to Mr. Almogordo's orders but he had no intention of following them. He would lay low for a while, gather support from like-minded crew members, and force a confrontation when the time was right. One thing was certain: Jaspar Twitchell would not kow-tow to niggers, regardless of what that spic Almogordo said.

* * * * *

At morning quarters a smiling Lieutenant Barkman read the results of the UED and instructed SM-1 Becker to have the green 'C' for communications excellence painted on the bulkhead just below the signal bridge.

"I want it in plain sight for all to see," the grinning lieutenant instructed. "First Division is painting the white 'E' on the stack this morning." He looked around at his men from operations division. "Hell of a job, men," he said. "Hell of a job." He dismissed them from quarters and walked away, a happy bounce in his step.

The First Division men cheered when Mr. MacDonald gave them the news. "Now that we know how good we are," he cautioned, "we must maintain this level of performance. You men have set a standard which you must live up to. Nothing else will be acceptable." He was clearly proud of them, and he walked up and down the ranks, shaking hands and offering individual congratulations to each man. When he dismissed them from quarters, the men milled around, slapping each other on the back and arguing about who got to paint the "E' on the stack. It was decided that Pea would do the job, and the little sailor puffed with pride, not really understanding they let him do it to shut him up.

R.J. visited Riley in the radio shack and obtained the ships movement schedules which would tell him when the Raptor was due to return to port. He then went aft to the fantail where Gino and Pea were working and advised them that the minesweeper was due to return to Guam the coming Friday, October eighteenth.

"We got a few days," Pea observed, looking at the report. "We can get together tonight."

"We don't know how to contact them," Gino replied. "They got our number but we don't have theirs."

"Why not?" Pea asked. "You guys didn't get a number?" He stared at the other two, his mouth agape. "I can't believe you didn't get a number."

"Did you get a number?" Gino asked.

"No, I was too busy," Pea retorted, making thrusting movements with his hips.

"They'll call," R.J. said, more confident than he felt.

"I got the focsul watch on Wednesday night," Gino said.

"I got the messenger watch that night," Pea said.

R.J., who didn't have to stand watches, reassured them. "We got tonight and tomorrow night," he said. "They'll call today, I'm sure of it."

"What if they don't?" Pea whined.

"Then we'll hit Talagi's and wait for them to show up."

The call came just before noon chow. It was Annie and she told R.J. what he already knew. The Raptor was due back on Friday, so they only had Tuesday and Wednesday to get together. None of the girls wanted to go out on Thursday night, the day before their husbands were to return. They made arrangements to meet at Talagi's that evening. The rest of the week would be problematic.

"Tomorrow is no good," R.J. told her. "Pea and Gino have the duty, so they'll be stuck aboard ship." He paused, then suggested, "But you and I can get together tomorrow night."

He waited for her to reply, but the phone was quiet. "Annie?" he asked.

"I like it better when we're all together," she said quietly.

"Whatever," he said, disappointed.

"I just feel better when my friends are there," she explained.

"Whatever," he said. "See you tonight." He hung up before she could answer, angry that she didn't want to be alone with him. He passed the word to Gino and Pea and returned to the signal bridge to busy himself with housekeeping duties. He shined all the brass, aired out the flag-bags, swept and swabbed the deck and oiled the two flashing lights, one starboard and one port. He was concentrating on the tasks, forcing Annie out of his mind and did not see SM-1 Becker come up the ladder from the 02 level.

"Man, will you look at this striker work!" Becker exclaimed good naturedly. "You're makin' the rest of us look bad, R.J."

R.J. grinned and wiped the sweat from his brow. "Hey, Flags," he said, "what's happening?"

"Take a break, I want to talk to you," Becker said, more serious. They sat next to each other on the port flagbag. Becker pulled a chit from his shirt pocket and studied it for a moment. "One of the reasons we got the green 'C' is because of your performance in Yokosuka," he said. "I talked to Mr. Barkman and he agrees with me." He handed the chit to R.J. "It's all filled out, but you're gonna have to do the work," he said.

R.J. looked at the chit. It was a request for Davis, R.J. to take the third class signalman's exam coming up in January. It had already been approved by Becker and Mr. Barkman. All it needed was R.J.'s signature.

"I just made E-3 a couple of months ago," he murmured.

"This ship needs two petty officers on the signal bridge," Becker explained. "And we need one signalman striker, which I hope you can find in the deck force."

"We already got you and Anselmi," R.J. said, a little confused.

"Not no more we don't," Becker said, grinning. "I got my orders. I'm outta here!"

"Where to?" R.J. asked, staring dumbfounded at the older man.

"Pensacola," Becker grinned. "Shore duty!"

"When?" R.J. asked.

"Tomorrow," Becker replied, smiling broadly. "I gotta go get my family ready to move. I go tomorrow and they follow next week."

Becker handed him a ball-point pen and R.J. quickly signed the chit.

"This afternoon," Becker said, "I'll give you the materials you're gonna need to study for the exam." He started back down the ladder. "Don't let us down, Slick," he called.

R.J. grinned happily, watching Becker descend the ladder and stride across the 02 level toward the fantail. The first class signalman was getting shore duty. Well, that was good, R.J. figured. The guy just wasn't made for sea duty.

* * * * *

Paul Oliver smiled to himself as he read the ships movement schedule. Lee Piper's ship, the Brister, was scheduled for an R&R trip to Japan. They would leave on the following Monday, October 21 for a three week cruise. He was happy for his friend, and excited about the prospect of finally being completely alone with Lorelei. Admiral Prescott was due back from Pearl in a few days, and Paul tried to think of a way to get together with Lorelei with the admiral at home. It would not be easy. She refused to meet him unless Admiral Prescott was away, but that was before he had the key to the 'Id' where they could relax without always being watchful of prying eyes. He was tired of the sneaking around, meeting in the USO beach parking lot, taking rides up in the hills, then sneaking back to the parking lot, stealing kisses and going their separate ways, always frustrated, unfulfilled, wanting more. Now they could have more, if only the admiral wasn't coming home so soon. He decided to call her and tell her about the 'Id.' He wondered how she would react.

He called the quarterdeck and instructed Chief Lyons, the OOD, to have the ship's truck brought up. He was going to the officers' club for lunch. He would call Lorelei from there. He put on his cap, took a look around his cabin to make sure everything was ship-shape, and went down to the quarterdeck. Billy Lopez had the truck waiting at the bottom of the brow when Paul reached the quarterdeck. He saluted the OOD, the flag on the stern and went down the brow, getting into the cab of the truck.

"Haverfield departing."

Charming Billy smiled at the captain and put the truck into gear, slowly gathering speed down the pier toward the winding road which would lead them up the hill to the officers' club. He drove carefully, only grinding the gears a few times.

* * * * *

R.J. sat in the chart house leafing through the study guide Becker had left for him. He was familiar with a lot of the material, but he realized there was a whole hell of a lot about being a signalman that he did not know. While he was poring over flag dimensions and flag hoist protocol Anselmi walked in with a can of cola in his hand and leaned against the door jam, grinning.

"Guess you heard about Becker," he said.

"Yeah, he told me earlier. Good thing he's getting shore duty."

Anselmi chuckled. "It ain't gonna be the same around here without old puke-boy." He sipped his cola and narrowed his eyes at R.J. "You gonna pass that third class exam?" he asked.

R.J. tossed the study guide on the chart table. "A lot of it I'll ace, but some of this stuff is gonna be tough, like recognizing flag hoists quickly."

"I'll help you with that," Anselmi assured him. "We'll use your flash cards and practice every day." The second class signalman started to leave, then turned back. "Unless you're too busy chasing pussy."

"Huh?" R.J. asked, surprised. "How did you know?"

"Couldn't sleep last night and I saw you guys getting out of that sharp-looking Chevy down the pier." He smiled again. "Some guys get lucky, my boy, and you are on a roll."

R.J. sat staring at the table after Anselmi left. He thought of Gino, Pea and the girls and realized they were going to have to be more careful. That Impala was too easy to spot, and Apra Harbor was a small place. It was like Longmont, a small town where everybody knew everybody else. It wouldn't take a genius to identify the Impala convertible with the USS Raptor. He'd have to talk to the boys about this.

THIRTY SEVEN

The officers' club was about half full when Paul Oliver stepped through the door and took off his hat. He looked around for a table and spotted

Lorelei sitting in the back, lunching with a few officers' wives. He took a deep breath and approached the women.

"Good day Mrs. Prescott," he said pleasantly as he reached the table. The women all looked up. "Ladies," he said, nodding to her lunch companions.

"Hello Captain Oliver," Lorelei said, smiling up at him. "You know everyone here, don't you?"

"Yes ma'am," he smiled at the other wives.

"Would you like to join us, Captain?" one of the others said.

"No, thank you," he replied graciously. "I'm meeting Lee Piper for lunch." He looked around as if he were trying to spot Captain Piper. He had no such lunch date, but he didn't want them to know that. "Anyone seen him?" he asked.

The women began looking around the room, shaking their heads. Lorelei was looking at Paul, smiling. Did she know he was lying?

"I don't see him," Paul said. "I'll wait for him at the bar."

"Drinking on duty?" Lorelei teased.

"Just coffee, ma'am," Paul answered. "I wouldn't want the admiral to think I was drinking in the afternoon...ma'am." The women giggled at him.

"Well, he's still in Pearl," teased one of them. "We won't rat you out." They all giggled again, except Lorelei who just kept looking at him.

"Yes," she said sweetly. "And unfortunately he's not returning until next week. Some sort of delay."

"That's the Navy for you," one of the women said. "There are always delays." The others nodded in agreement.

Paul excused himself and went to the bar where he ordered coffee and made a display of looking at his watch, as if he were expecting Lee Piper. To the women at the table the exchange was innocent, but Paul understood what Lorelei was saying to him. The admiral was not returning in a day or two, and she would meet Paul at the usual place at the usual time that night. He smiled to himself and ordered a club sandwich. The key to the 'Id' felt heavy and warm in his pocket. He felt that quivering feeling in his loins and tried to shake it off, concentrating on his coffee. He would ask Lee for use of the 'Id' tonight.

* * * * *

R.J., Gino and Pea cruised in the Bomb down Highway One toward Talagi's. "Damn, Pea," Gino complained. "Roll down the window and let some air in here." He held his nose. "Your aftershave would gag a maggot."

"Chicks dig it," Pea retorted with a grin. "Carol says I smell real good."

"Something's wrong with that girl's nose," Gino said.

"Nothin' wrong with her tits, though," Pea said, beaming.

R.J. sat quietly, looking out the window at the foliage speeding past them.

"What you so quiet about, R.J.?" Pea asked, looking straight ahead as he piloted the Bomb down the highway.

"Nothing," R.J. said. He thought for a moment and added, "I'm gonna take the third class exam in January."

"No shit!" Gino exclaimed. "Way to go, buddy."

"Third class, huh?" Pea asked, grinning. "You striking for captain or something?"

"You better hope not," R.J. replied. "If I make captain I'm gonna burn your liberty card."

They were laughing happily when they pulled into Talagi's parking lot. The Impala convertible was sitting off to the side. The top was down and the girls were sipping Pepsis and looking bored. R.J. met Annie's eyes as the Bomb pulled in next to them and she smiled sweetly, brushing her blonde hair from her eyes. R.J. felt a little short of breath, and was about to wave to her when she frowned and shook her head slightly. R.J. looked around and realized what she was trying to tell him. Three sailors from the Brister sat at an outside table, drinking Pepsis and playing the juke box. R.J. knew two of them by sight, but didn't know their names. They were leering at the girls in the Impala, who were ignoring them.

One of the Brister sailors, a tall skinny sonarman, walked up to the Bomb and started talking to Pea. "Hey, Pea, nice boat, where'd you get it?"

"Hi Jim. We bought it off a guy in the hills," Pea said proudly. "Hunnerd and fifty bucks."

"At least you got wheels," the sailor said. "How 'bout giving us a ride back to the base. It's dead around here and we're going to the Mocombo Club." He looked over at the girls in the Chevy. "We're getting nowhere with them," he said sadly.

Pea looked over at the girls who ignored him. "Now, that's a nice boat," he said.

"Yeah, nice car, but cold girls, y'know?"

"Maybe they just don't like sailors," R.J. offered.

"Yeah," Jim agreed. "Lots of chicks don't like sailors." He turned to Pea. "How 'bout that ride back to the base?"

Pea looked over at Gino and R.J. who shrugged. "Might as well," Pea said. "Nothin' going on here."

The Brister sailors jumped in the back seat and Pea slowly backed out of the parking lot. R.J. looked over at Annie quickly and winked. Annie winked back.

They passed through the main gate and Pea headed toward the parking lot. "I got no sticker so I have to leave the car in there," he said.

"Hey!" Jim shouted. "Here comes the shuttle, let's go!"

"You guys go ahead," Pea said. "I got to lock up the car. We'll see you later."

"So long. Thanks for the lift." Jim waved and climbed aboard the shuttle with his shipmates. Pea, R.J. and Gino stood in the parking lot and watched as the shuttle disappeared toward the Mocombo Club.

"Now what?" Pea asked. "Should we go back?"

"Naw," R.J. answered with more confidence than he felt. "The girls will be here soon." He motioned for the others to follow him. "Let's get out of sight of the gate."

They began walking slowly up the road toward the harbor, looking back, hoping the girls got the hint and were following. Headlights bathed them in yellow and the Impala pulled up next to them.

"You boys need a ride?" Annie asked from the passenger seat.

R.J. grinned. "We were hoping you'd follow us," he said, smiling down at her. Her blonde hair was swirling in the breeze and she brushed it back with her hand. It was a beautiful gesture, very female and R.J. couldn't help staring at her.

"What's wrong?" she asked, puzzled by the look on his face.

"I think I'm in love," he grinned. He wasn't really kidding. He was beginning to think he was falling for her hard, and it wasn't an unpleasant sensation.

"Yeah, yeah," Betty teased. "We're all falling in love. Get in the trunk and let's go."

Pea went around to the driver's side and kissed Carol on the lips. "Don't fall in love with me, baby," he warned, "'cause I'll just break your heart." She giggled and Pea climbed into the trunk with the others.

* * * * *

Captain Oliver sat in the USO beach parking lot waiting for Lorelei to show up. Lee Piper had agreed to let him use the 'Id' that evening, saying nothing more than, "Be careful, my friend. You know you're playing with fire."

"Roger that," Paul had replied. Now he sat impatiently, constantly looking at his watch and at the rear view mirror. Finally, the Buick rolled slowly into the parking lot and came to a stop next to the Fairlane. Paul got out, locked the Ford and slid into the passenger seat. He planted a tentative kiss on Lorelei's cheek and put his arm around her. He inhaled her scent and sighed.

"You okay?" she asked, amused at the look on his face. She was dressed in Bermuda shorts and a sleeveless, cotton blouse. Her hair was pulled back in a ponytail and she looked like a teenager. He marveled at her beauty, and when she looked at him with those soft, violet eyes his heart melted.

"Lee Piper knows about us." He blurted it out before he could stop himself and immediately regretted it. She stared at him with her mouth open.

"What?" she demanded.

"It's all right, he's a friend. He won't say anything."

She gripped the steering wheel and stared straight ahead. "I...what did you tell him?" She seemed angry.

"Nothing. He put it together. Said he could smell your perfume whenever I returned his car."

"That's all?" She was definitely angry. She turned in the seat and leaned back against the door, crossing her arms as if she were trying to put as much space between them as possible.

"It's all right, Lorelei," he said, a little desperately. "Lee's got a cottage up in the hills and he gave me a key. Let's go up there and talk."

She stared at him as if he had suggested they set fire to her car. "Oh, no...no...I don't like this, Paul." She was shaking her head slowly and biting her lower lip. Cruising in the hills and making out in the car was one thing, but the thought of taking their relationship to the next level clearly frightened her, especially because now someone else knew about them.

"It's just a place to be alone and talk comfortably," he pleaded. "I'll be a gentleman, I promise." He looked into her eyes. Being a gentleman was becoming increasingly difficult, and he knew that, if they were alone, he would be hard pressed to keep it up.

She sat staring blankly at him, seemingly looking through him. Finally she spoke. "I'm going home. I have to think."

"Lorelei..."

"No! I'm going home. Please get out of the car." She shifted in her seat and started up the Buick.

"Lorelei, please don't go. Let's talk this thing out."

"I'll call you in a few days," she said, putting the Buick in gear. He shook his head sadly and climbed out of the car. Without looking at him she sped out of the parking lot and turned on to Highway One, leaving Paul standing in the middle of the lot trying to figure out what the hell just happened. He took the key to the 'Id' out of his pocket and looked at it. *This strangely shaped little piece of metal seemed to be the key to paradise only a few short hours ago. Now it was just a piece of metal.* He put it back in his pocket and got behind the wheel of the Fairlane. Gripping the steering wheel tightly with both hands he took a deep breath. "Shit," he swore softly, and started the car.

* * * * *

"Coast is clear," Betty said to the trunk of the Impala. She opened it and the three sailors climbed out and looked around. "You know what to do," she said and headed for the front of the apartment building. The boys made a bee-line to the back door and waited.

"I hope she doesn't turn on that stupid light," Gino said, glancing around nervously. She didn't and the back door opened. The trio rushed in and closed the door behind them, standing quietly in the kitchen, listening for sounds of the shore patrol.

"We're cool," R.J. said, and walked into the living room. Annie was seated on the couch, leaning forward with her knees together and her hands folded on her lap. She looked like an angel. R.J. plopped down next to her and put his arm around her shoulders. Gino and Pea followed Carol and Betty up the stairs and into the two bedrooms. Soon, giggling and muffled sounds of intimate physical contact seeped through the ceiling and R.J. looked up and grinned.

"Didn't waste any time, did they?" he whispered, snuggling up close to her and nibbling on her ear.

"Ooh, don't do that," she whispered back.

"Why not?" He continued nibbling.

"Because that makes me...you know..."

"Hot?"

"Yes, hot, now cut it out." She pushed him away playfully.

He leaned back on the sofa and lit a cigarette. She took it from his mouth and he lit another. "Now what's wrong?" he asked impatiently.

"I like you, R.J.," she said softly. "I like you a lot, but I'm scared."

"Me too," he said, blowing smoke at the ceiling. "Think I wanna get caught up here with a married chick?" He grinned at her. "I don't look good in stripes."

She looked at the glowing ember of her cigarette and began to cry, her tears rolling gently down her cheeks. He put out his cigarette, took hers and put it out, then held her in his arms, letting her sob softly into his chest. "It's okay, baby," he soothed her. "We can take it slow if you want. Just don't cry. I can't stand it when a girl cries."

"I'm so miserable," she said, sitting up and dabbing at her tears. "I'm sorry, I like my husband, but we got married young and I just don't think I want to be married and have kids, you know?"

"Why don't you tell me about it?" R.J. leaned back and patted her thigh.

"You probably think I'm a real weak sister."

"I think you probably just need someone to talk to."

"You're very sweet," she said, laying her head on his shoulder. "We got married right out of high school in McPherson, Kansas. Gary was my boyfriend all the way through high school and it was kind of expected of us." She looked up at him. "You sure you want to hear this?"

"Sure," R.J. assured her. *Not much else is gonna happen tonight*, he thought, looking up at the ceiling and listening to the sounds coming from the upstairs bedrooms.

* * * * *

Captain Oliver parked the Fairlane next to the Haverfield's pickup truck and walked slowly up the brow. It was almost 2200 hours and he was tired. Lorelei had sapped his energy the way long nights on the bridge will do, and he wanted more than anything to fall into his bunk and sleep for about three days. He knew he probably wouldn't see her for a while, perhaps a long while, and in his present state of mind he was glad of it. He knew he had fallen in love with her. He felt he had misjudged her because he had thought she felt the same way about him, but when push came to shove she had bolted.

"Good evening, Captain," Big Queen was the OOD and saluted when Captain Oliver came aboard. "Early evening, sir?"

"Early evening, Boats," he replied, returning the salute. "All quiet tonight?"

"Yes sir," the big boatswain's mate said, smiling his big ugly smile. "'Course the boys ain't back from the Mocombo Club yet."

The captain nodded wearily and headed for his cabin. Big Queen stood on the quarterdeck frowning as he watched the captain go up the ladder to the 02 level. Something wasn't right with the skipper tonight. Maybe he was just a little tired. Queen shrugged and opened the ship's log, entering the time the captain returned. Two more hours on watch and the big boatswain's mate could hit the sack, too. He yawned, stretched and scratched his crotch.

* * * * *

"So as soon as Gary made E-5 I joined him in the Phillippines. Then he got assigned to the Raptor and we came here. We've been here for six months." Annie snuggled close to R.J. and looked up into his eyes. "You're a good listener," she cooed.

"What's his rate?" R.J. asked. "What does Gary do on the Raptor?"

"He's a radioman," she replied.

"No shit," R.J. said. "I went through radio school."

She sat up and looked at him, surprised. "How did you get to be a signalman?" she asked, pointing to the crossed flags above the three stripes on his jumper.

"It's a long story," he said automatically. "I'll tell you about it sometime." He drifted off in thought and she laid her head back on his shoulder.

"R.J.?"

"Yeah?"

"You don't think I'm a tease, do you?"

"No, sometimes it's right and sometimes it isn't." He pointed up at the ceiling. "Two out of three ain't bad."

She looked up at the ceiling sadly. "It'll happen when I'm ready."

"Yeah," he said. He got up from the couch and went into the kitchen. He opened the fridge and took out a bottle of beer. Annie sat on the couch and stared at the rug on the living room floor. R.J. stood in the kitchen staring at the linoleum on the kitchen floor, wishing his buddies would come down so they could go back to the ship. He didn't want to stay there anymore, but he couldn't quite tell why. He felt the evening was over, and he was anxious to get back aboard ship so he wouldn't have to talk to her anymore. She made him weary and he hung his head until his chin was on his chest. *What the hell was taking those guys so long?*

Annie came into the kitchen so quietly he didn't know she was there until she whispered, "R.J., are you mad?"

"Naw," he lied. "Just a little tired."

"Tired of me?" She looked hurt.

"No, just tired."

They stood there looking at each other until the sound of feet pounding down the stairs interrupted them. Gino and Betty came bursting into the kitchen in their underwear.

"Any more beer?" Gino asked. He took one look at R.J. and Annie and stopped. "You kids ain't fighting, are you?" he asked, his head cocked to one side.

"Naw, we ain't fighting," R.J. answered, looking into Annie's eyes.

"Love!" Gino spat. "It's overrated, you know."

R.J. laughed. "Yeah, it sure as hell is."

Annie started crying and ran out of the kitchen.

"I think that's my cue," R.J. said, gulping down the rest of his beer. "Let's head back to the ship."

Gino stood there looking at him for a few moments. Then he nodded. "Okay, bud. Lemme go get the little fucker."

He left the kitchen and Betty stood by the small table, arms folded in front, frowning at R.J. She shook her head slowly and turned and followed Gino up the stairs.

Annie decided to stay in the apartment while Betty and Carol took the boys back to the harbor. Inside the trunk no one said anything. When they got back near the ship and stopped, Betty jumped out of the passenger side and opened the trunk.

"Okay, fellas," she sang, "you are home safe and sound."

"See ya, babe," Gino planted a kiss on her mouth. "I'm gonna miss you."

"Me too," she answered, throwing her arms around his neck. "But they'll be back at sea in a few weeks and we'll get together."

"Keep thinkin' about me, will ya Toots?" Pea said to Carol, squaring his hat on his head and trying to wipe the lipstick off his mouth. "Don't be gettin' all weepy, okay?"

She smiled down at him, kissed his cheek and slid in behind the wheel. "Don't you be gettin' all weepy, okay Shorty?"

Pea saluted smartly and walked backwards down the pier, grinning widely.

The shuttle bus pulled up in front of the Haverfield as Gino, R.J. and Pea were arriving. They fell in behind the drunken sailors and walked up the brow. Queen was standing at the quarterdeck returning the salutes of the men coming off liberty and he assumed R.J., Pea and Gino were returning on the shuttle bus.

"You boys didn't do any damage to the Mocombo Club tonight, did you?" he asked as they stepped onto the quarterdeck.

"You know we're lovers, not fighters, Boats," Pea replied, grinning widely.

"Yeah, you're lovers all right," Queen said and began laughing his wounded buffalo laugh. "That'll be the day when you get laid, Pea."

Pea turned to say something but R.J. and Gino grabbed his arms and led him down the ladder to First Division's compartment.

"See you manana," R.J. said wearily, after Gino and Pea climbed into their racks. He went up the forward ladder to Operations Division's com partment. He kicked off his shoes and climbed up into his rack with his whites still on, too tired to undress. He closed his eyes tightly and pushed all thoughts of Annie out of his head, willing himself to sleep.

THIRTY EIGHT

"R.J.! Wake up!"

Slowly awakening, R.J. squinted at Tanner who was shaking his arm, trying to rouse him. Tanner wore the duty belt of petty officer of the watch

"What the hell..." R.J. mumbled, trying to focus his eyes on Tanner. "What's wrong?" he asked sleepily, pulling himself up on one elbow and looking around the dark compartment where men were sleeping and snoring.

"You got a phone call, boy," Tanner said quietly.

"Huh?" R.J. tried to shake the numbing slumber from his head. "What are you talking about? What time is it?"

"It's oh-one hundred and you got some chick on the phone. C'mon, get up." Tanner waited until R.J. swung his legs over the side of his bunk, then returned to the quarterdeck. R.J. jumped down to the deck and adjusted his wrinkled jumper. He put on his whitehat and made his way to the quarterdeck.

Crawford, the OOD on the mid watch, nodded to R.J. and motioned to the phone on the quarterdeck desk. R.J. picked up the receiver. "Hello?" he asked, still partly asleep.

"Hi R.J., this is Betty."

"Hi, what's happening?" He shook his head to clear it. Why was Betty calling him?

"Annie wants to see you. Can she pick you up?"

R.J. paused while it began to sink in. "Where is she?" he asked.

"She's here."

"Then why isn't she calling me?"

"She thought you might be a little pissed off and she didn't want...you know."

"Put her on," R.J. said impatiently.

He could hear murmuring voices in the background as the phone changed hands. "Hi, R.J.," said that sweet voice. "Do you want to see me?"

R.J. frowned at the phone, a little confused. "Yeah, sure," he said slowly. "When?"

"How about right now?" the soft voice asked. "Betty is gonna stay over with Carol and we can have the apartment to ourselves."

R.J. stood silent, the phone receiver at his ear. He hadn't expected this and didn't know quite how to respond.

"R.J.? Are you still there?"

* * * * *

Paul Oliver paced his small cabin, trying to occupy his mind with repair status reports. It wasn't working. He lit his pipe and picked up the novel he was reading, *To Kill a Mockingbird*, by Harper Lee. That didn't work either. Nothing worked. Nothing he tried could push Lorelei from his mind. He walked out onto the starboard wing bridge and looked up at the night sky. It was peaceful on the bridge late at night when the ship was in port. The liberty hounds had since returned from the Mocombo Club and were (hopefully) tucked away in their racks, dreaming sailor dreams. The harbor was calm and the pier was deserted. The focsul watch stood near the bow, leaning on the lifeline and staring into the water. A white-clad figure walked down the brow from the quarterdeck and up the pier toward a waiting car parked in the darkness. It looked like a Chevrolet convertible, its white top up. The sailor got into the passenger seat and the car swung around and headed down the pier. *Who was that?* Captain Oliver pondered. It looked like the signalman, R.J. Davis. *Wonder where he's going?* The captain shrugged and relit his pipe.

* * * * *

R.J. ducked down in the front seat as Annie maneuvered the Impala through the streets of Naval housing. She parked behind Betty's apartment and got out. Without saying a word she made her way to the front door while R.J. went up to the back door and waited. He heard the lock click and the door open. He slipped inside.

Annie led him to the living room and stood a few feet away, watching his face, trying to gauge his mood. Finally she said, "I've changed my mind about going to bed with you."

"Yeah? Maybe I changed my mind, too." He felt irritable, being awakened in the middle of the night, sneaking into Naval housing so she could make an announcement.

"So, now you don't want to go to bed with me?"

"I think you're playing with my head," he said with what he hoped was sarcasm.

Annie smiled ruefully and slowly unbuttoned her blouse, letting it slip to the floor. She stepped out of her skirt and stood there in her bra and panties. "I could take you back to the ship if you want," she said, smiling sweetly.

R.J. went to her and scooped her up in his arms. As he carried her up the stairs toward the bedroom Andy Sample's favorite saying echoed in his mind. *Whoa, Lordy!*

* * * * *

Captain Oliver looked at his watch. 0200, time to try to get some sleep. He yawned, stretched and left the wing bridge, returning to his cabin. He undressed and lay across his bunk, trying again to get interested in *To Kill a Mockingbird*. Fifteen minutes later he fell asleep, the novel open on his chest. He dozed off with the image of Lorelei in his mind, her head thrown back, laughing; her dark hair billowing in the wind as they drove through the winding roads in the hills above Agana.

* * * * *

R.J. and Annie lay naked on their backs, smoking cigarettes and staring at the ceiling, basking in the afterglow of lovemaking.

"Now I know what he meant," R.J. said softly, a thoughtful look on his face.

"What who meant?"

"I always thought he was talking about death and dying, but now I understand."

She rolled over and put her head on his shoulder. "Who are you talking about, R.J.?"

"Edgar Allan Poe." He replied in almost a whisper. "He wrote a poem for this moment. He even named it after you."

"You're talking in riddles. What poem?"

"For Annie. He wrote it in eighteen forty nine. He wrote it for you." He put out his cigarette in the ashtray on the nightstand and rolled over to look into her eyes. "Would you like to hear it?"

"Sure, what's it about?"

"It's about this feeling. Right now, you know, after we've made love."

"Is it spooky? I always thought he was a spooky guy."

R.J. smiled, lay back and closed his eyes. He began to recite:

"Thank Heaven! The crisis—
The danger is past,
And the lingering illness
Is over at last—
And the fever called 'Living'
Is conquered at last.
Sadly, I know
I am shorn of my strength,
And no muscle I move
As I lie at full length—
But no matter! I feel
I am better at length.
And I rest so composedly,
Now, in my bed,
That any beholder
Might fancy me dead—
Might start at beholding me,
Thinking me dead."

She lay quietly on his shoulder, listening to the cadence of the poetry, feeling herself giving in to the words and the meter and the rhyme as R.J. softly quoted the stanzas.

"And ah! Of all tortures
That torture the worst
Has abated—the terrible
Torture of thirst
For the napthaline river
Of passion accurst:—
I have drank of a water
That quenches all thirst:—"

"God," she whispered, "that's exactly how I feel." She snuggled as close to him as she could get, sighing softly.

"Of a water that flows,
With a lullaby sound,
From a fountain a very few
Feet under ground—
From a cavern not very far

Down under ground.
And ah! Let it never
Be foolishly said,
That my room it is gloomy
And narrow my bed;
For man never slept
In a different bed—
And to sleep, you must slumber
In just such a bed."

She nuzzled his neck. "You recite that so nice," she whispered.

"Just getting to the good part," he whispered back.

"And so it lies happily,
Bathed in many
A dream of the truth
And the beauty of Annie—
Drowned in a bath
Of the tresses of Annie.
She tenderly kissed me,
She fondly caressed,
And then I fell gently
To sleep on her breast—
Deeply to sleep
From the heaven of her breast."

He pulled her closer and whispered in her ear.

"And I lie so composedly,
Now in my bed
(Knowing her love)
That you fancy me dead—
And I rest so contentedly,
Now in my bed,
(With her love at my breast)
That you fancy me dead.
That you shudder to look at me,
Thinking me dead:—
But my heart it is brighter
Than all of the many
Stars in the sky
For it sparkles with Annie—
It glows with the light
Of the love of my Annie—
With the thought of the light
Of the eyes of my Annie."

Annie rolled over on her back and wiped tears from her eyes with the back of her hand. "No one has ever recited poetry to me before," she sniffled.

"That's too bad," he said. "That poem was written for you." He turned his head on the pillow so he could look into her blue eyes. "For Annie," he whispered.

"It's really beautiful, R.J. Thank you."

"What time is it?" he sat up and squinted at the clock on the nightstand. "Holy crap, it's three o'clock!"

"Just a couple more minutes," she pleaded, and pulled him back down, resting her head on his chest. "You know any more poems?"

"Sure, I know a lot of 'em," he answered.

"Will you do another one for me?"

"Next time," he answered, "if there is a next time."

She sat up and looked at him curiously. "What makes you think there won't be a next time?"

"The Raptor is due back Friday, right?" he asked.

"Yeah, so?"

"So, maybe you'll start feeling guilty and want to stick it out with your husband."

"R.J.!" she snapped. "Why do you say things to piss me off?"

"I guess it's just my nature," he grinned. "I better get back."

She sat up and swung her legs over the side of the bed, looking around for her underwear. "I've never cheated on him before, you know," she pouted.

"I know. It's just that I'm crazy about you, baby."

"Now you sound like Pea!" She threw a pillow at him and he ducked, laughing. She was laughing, too. She put on her panties and adjusted her bra. "I better take you back before the sun comes up," she said absently.

He thought about making a wisecrack about the cold light of day, but decided against it.

* * * * *

She pulled to a stop down the pier from the sleeping Haverfield and R.J. got out and came around to the driver's side. "Call me when you can," he said, kissing her softly on the lips. He broke off the kiss before she wanted him to, and she grabbed his neckerchief, pulling his head down for one more.

"I promise I will," she said sweetly. She shifted into drive and drove slowly down the pier, the cat-like taillights blinking in the cool morning air. R.J. walked to the ship and up the brow to the quarterdeck. Crawford and Tanner were still on the mid watch, just as they had been when R.J. first reported to the Haverfield. *Was that really seven months ago?* The ship had certainly changed in seven months. She looked nothing like she did when R.J. first laid eyes on her. He looked up at the big white "E" painted on the stack and the smaller green "C" on the side of the signal bridge and smiled. Her decks and bulkheads were cleanly painted, the hull number was bright white with black shadowing and the water line was painted a solid, even black. She was a squared away fleet vessel and R.J. felt a glowing pride warming his chest.

"Y'all fall asleep in the jungle? Crawford drawled.

R.J. smiled wearily and nodded to Tanner who grinned and nodded back.

"'Night, fellas." R.J. waved and went through the port hatch toward his compartment. Reveille was in a couple of short hours, but as tired as he was, he was not sleepy. As he lay in his rack, staring at the overhead, he wished he had asked Annie for a picture.

THIRTY NINE

R.J. stood on the signal bridge on Friday the eighteenth scanning the breakwater at the entrance to the harbor with binoculars, hoping to catch sight of the Raptor as it returned to port. It was just before noon. Becker had transferred stateside and Anselmi had spent the last few days helping R.J. prepare for the third class exam. Anselmi had proven to be a strict taskmaster, grilling R.J. on coded signals, flag hoists and semaphore. R.J. was getting to the point where he could read semaphore pretty well. Not as well as Anselmi, but a lot faster than when he first came on board.

The second class signalman came up on the signal bridge and watched R.J. scanning for the Raptor. "Don't you got any brass to polish, Slick?" he asked good naturedly.

"All done, Flags," R.J. answered without lowering the binoculars.

"How 'bout those flag bags, they neat and organized?"

"Lookin' good," R.J. said.

"Code book updates in?"

R.J. lowered the binoculars and turned toward Anselmi smiling. "We're all squared away up here, Flags," he said.

Anselmi looked around the signal bridge. It surely was squared away. He liked the way this kid took his job seriously. He like R.J. and he especially liked the way the kid saved him work. "Then I guess we might as well grab some chow."

"Go ahead," R.J. answered, raising the binoculars back up to his eyes.

"What you lookin' for?" Anselmi asked.

"The Raptor's due back about now and I promised Pea I'd let him know when they get in." He looked back at Anselmi and explained, "He's got a buddy on the Raptor and he wants me to raise him on the light, set up a date at the Mocombo Club." He turned back to his scanning, hoping Anselmi couldn't detect the lie.

"Hey, Slick, you're not kidding me," Anselmi said.

R.J. froze. "Whadda you mean?" he asked quietly.

"You just wanna impress their signal bridge with your Morse code. Hell, boy, everybody in this port already knows you the best. Why you wanna rub their noses in it?" Anselmi laughed and scooted down the ladder to the 02 level. R.J. let out a sigh of relief as soon as Anselmi left. *Damn,* he thought, *I'm getting paranoid. In fact, I'm getting Brooklyn paranoid.*

The Raptor hit the breakwater ten minutes later and moved smoothly into the harbor. The small 'Agile' class minesweeper with its snub-nosed bow and single forty mm gun slowed as it made its way to its assigned berth, a half mile aft of where the Haverfield was tied up. Its call sign waved and floated in the wind from both port and starboard lanyards and the ship looked as if it needed a paint job. Rust spots streaked down the sides from the scuppers on its forecastle and R.J. could see the crusted sea salt shimmering on its decks and bulkheads as it sparkled in the noon sun. She'd been at sea a long time.

R.J. moved to the starboard side and trained the binoculars down on the pier where line handlers and the Raptor's dependents gathered to greet her. The black Impala convertible was sitting off to the side of the crowd with Carol at the wheel and Betty and Annie next to her. They seemed bored as they waited. Annie looked down the pier at the Haverfield and R.J. caught a glimpse of her blonde hair and blue eyes under a scarf tied beneath her chin. She seemed to be looking directly at him and he lowered the binoculars and put them back into their case. He hung the binocular case inside the bridge and went below to chow.

When he walked into the mess decks he spotted Gino, Pea and Billy Lopez sitting in a booth to the rear. They waved him over and he went through the line quickly, picking up small amounts of Hawkins' lunch fare which consisted of corned beef hash and O'Brien potatoes. He ignored the boiled carrots. Hawkins stood in the back of the galley, instructing one of his charges on the proper way to scrub pots and pans.

"Ask us why we're grinnin' like a bunch of jackasses," Pea said as R.J. slid into the booth next to Charming Billy.

"Okay," R.J. said, spooning hash into his mouth and talking around it. "Why you grinnin' like a bunch of assholes?"

"Jackasses," Pea corrected. "Billy's got an announcement." He nodded to Billy who was grinning like a jackass.

"Saturday I'm gonna ask Mr. Gamboa if I can propose to Teresa," the charming one said. "I got a feeling he'll say yes." Billy smiled proudly and charmingly.

"Pretty cool, dude," Gino said. "But what about Mrs. Gamboa?"

Billy stopped smiling. "I figure Mr. G will handle her," he said seriously.

"You think Teresa will say yes?" R.J. asked.

"Well, we kinda talked about it," Billy said, suddenly doubtful. It had never occurred to him that Teresa would turn him down. He frowned, then brightened. "Oh, hell," he sputtered. "Of course she'll say yes. We're in love."

Gino picked up his coffee cup and raised it in the air. "To love," he toasted. "And all the good things it does for a man." He threw a look at R.J. "And to all the bad things, too," he said, quietly and more solemnly.

R.J. gave him a dirty look and drank a toast to Billy and Teresa. He was looking forward to going up to the Gamboas' on Saturday, and he was genuinely happy for Billy. "What about our dear mother, the United States Navy?" he asked. "You gotta get a chit signed to get married."

"I talked to Mr. Mac and he said he would approve it and pass it along," Billy said. "He don't think I'll have any trouble." He got up from the table and carried his tray to the scullery. "You guys are coming Saturday, right?" he called over his shoulder.

"Wouldn't miss it, shipmate," R.J. called back. Billy smiled and stepped through the hatch and into the passageway.

Pea waited until Billy had disappeared and turned to R.J. "They here?" he asked.

"Yep, just before I came down."

"Well, looks like we're gonna be lonely for a while," Gino said sadly. Pea and R.J. nodded, saying nothing.

* * * * *

Lee Piper closed the door to Paul Oliver's cabin and pulled his cap down on his head. He was saddened by the conversation they had and wished he could be more help to his friend. It looked like Paul's friendship with Lorelei was over, but was that such a bad thing? They had been heading for disaster, and in Captain Piper's judgment, it was just a matter of time. *Speaking of time, that was exactly what his friend needed to rid himself of these destructive feelings...time; time to heal and forget.* Lee Piper decided that in time Paul would come to realize that all this was for the best. Still, he felt helpless, wanting to do something or say something that would make the sadness more palatable.

Captain Oliver sat at his desk, smoking his pipe and thinking about the talk he had had with Lee Piper. Lee was a good friend, someone he could trust, and he was soothed and encouraged by his friend's understanding. It was good to have someone he respected and could talk to about this situation. He sighed and picked up the sheath of radio messages which needed his attention and initials. He would lose himself for a while in the dreary daily minutiae of shipboard routine.

* * * * *

Lorelei Prescott sat alone on the veranda of the admiral's residence, sipping iced tea and smoking cigarettes. She stared off into the jungle vegetation, her mind cluttered with so many painful thoughts. A brief Guamanian rain had darted quickly through the area, leaving a wet mist on everything it touched, and a clean, fresh smell in the heavy, humid air. The sun returned and threw a beautiful rainbow across the valley below, and she imagined the pot of gold that might be found at the rainbow's end. She recited the colored bands of the arc the rainbow cast. "Red, orange, yellow, green, blue, (no indigo) and violet." *Almost every color of the spectrum was represented.* She thought it was the most beautiful rainbow she had ever seen, and tears welled up in her eyes. She suddenly felt the urge to pick up the phone and call Paul, but she shook the feeling off and threw her cigarette off the porch, disgusted at her weakness. "Damn it!" she said bitterly. "God damn it!" She sat back, sighing, tucked her legs under and lit another cigarette.

* * * * *

Charming Billy pulled the truck up to the foot of the brow and honked the horn impatiently. It was Saturday morning and the Gamboa working party gathered on the fantail. They carried no tools because most of the work on the trailer had already been done, and today was a special day. There would be no work today. Andy leaned over the lifeline and called to Billy.

"You in a hurry, boy?" Billy honked the horn again.

Andy turned back to the others. "He in a hurry all right," he grinned. "S'pose we oughta go get in the truck."

Pea, R.J., Gino, Pancho, Cotton and Tanner followed Andy down the brow and climbed into the truck. They sped out the main gate after being waved through by the Marine posted there and made good time to the Gamboas' trailer. Teresa was waiting out front for them and broke into a huge smile as Billy pulled up and came to a stop, dust and dirt swirling around the truck. The sailors piled out and went to meet Mr. Gamboa, who came out of the trailer to greet them, a happy smile on his face.

"Hafa dai!" he called. "C'mon up, let's drink some beer!"

Mrs. Gamboa stood in the doorway, frowning at her husband. She broke into a smile when she spotted Billy and waved to them all. Billy bounded up the steps to the trailer and gave Mrs. Gamboa a big hug and kiss. She playfully slapped him on the arm, giggling, and went back inside to tend to whatever she was cooking.

Billy whispered to Mr. Gamboa and the older man took on a serious look, nodding and motioning toward the rear of the trailer. He and Billy went around back as the Havernauts lounged on the porch and steps. Bobby opened beers and passed them around. He hooked a thumb in the direction Billy and his father had gone and said conspiratorially, "Well, here we go."

"You already know about this?" R.J. asked, taking a long drink of beer.

"Of course," Bobby said. "Billy came to me first. I told him I was all for it and that he should ask my dad."

"So now it's up to Teresa," Tanner said.

"And my mom," Bobby cautioned, holding his index finger in the air.

"Oh, yeah," Andy said, nodding. "Mrs. G gonna have to say okay."

Bobby and Mr. G came back around the trailer. Both were smiling happily. Mr. G went into the trailer and shooed the remaining Gamboa children outside. Billy sat down nervously and accepted a beer from Bobby who winked at him.

"It's gonna be okay, Billy," Bobby assured him. Billy looked frightened and downed his beer in one drink. Teresa sat next to him quietly, holding his hand and staring into his eyes. Everyone sat silently, waiting for the final decision. Would Mrs. G give her blessing or would she kick them all out?

"Aieeee!" The scream came from inside the trailer and everyone on the porch jumped to their feet. Mrs. Gamboa came running through the front door, slamming the screen against the trailer and waddling as fast as she could, reaching out her arms to Billy Lopez. She grabbed the shocked Billy in a great bear-hug and lifted him off his feet, bouncing him up and down like a rag doll. Then she smothered his face with kisses, tears running down her cheeks. She then grabbed Teresa and did the same to her. Mr.

Gamboa stood in the doorway of the trailer, showing his bad teeth in a wide grin.

"I am so happy!" Mrs. Gamboa cried and grabbed Andy Sample in a big hug, then R.J. and Gino. She reached for Pea but he was too quick for her. He ducked under her arms and she chased him around the porch, caught him and lifted him off his feet, squeezing him until his eyes began bugging out of his head.

"Does this mean she approves?" Pea gasped as Mrs. Gamboa covered his face with kisses.

"I think she approves." Bobby laughed and hugged Teresa and Billy. Soon everyone was hugging everyone else and wiping tears. Mr. Gamboa brought out more beer and a half-gallon jug of what looked like cloudy white wine. Mrs. Gamboa bustled about in the kitchen, preparing food for the party and speaking in rapid Chamorro.

Billy leaned against the trailer, a dopey look on his face, grinning like a jackass. He raised his hand into the air and yelled over the celebration, "Hey, hey, hold it!" Everyone quieted down and turned to him. He led Teresa to a chair and she sat down, smiling up at him. Billy knelt down on one knee and pulled a small box out of his pocket. "Teresa, I adore you and I want to live my life with you." He opened the box and displayed a small diamond engagement ring. "Will you marry me?" he asked softly, staring up into her eyes.

With tears streaming down her face she accepted the ring. "Yes, yes, yes, I'll marry you, Billy," she said. She threw her arms around him and kissed him.

"Whoa Lordy!" Andy exclaimed and the celebration continued with everyone hugging everyone else. Mr. Gamboa passed the jug around and began opening beers. The Gamboa children gathered around Teresa, admiring her ring. The youngest, little Maria, climbed up on Teresa's lap and threw her arms around her neck.

R.J. wiped a tear from his eye and looked around self-consciously. Gino was wiping away a tear too, and when their eyes met they burst out laughing. "Y'know, bud," Gino said, grinning. "Maybe this love stuff ain't so overrated after all."

R.J.'s smile faded and he sipped his beer. He thought of Annie and her blonde hair and pretty blue eyes. Then he thought of the Raptor and shook his head to clear it, forcing thoughts of her from his mind.

FORTY

Captain Bill Pollock rushed up the stairs to Admiral Prescott's office on the second floor of the Naval Command Center. It was a warm, late afternoon in Pearl Harbor, and he hurriedly buttoned up his collar as he reached the admiral's door. He knocked softly and entered. The admiral was standing by the window, a piece of paper in his hand, looking out on the fleet moored below.

"You sent for me, Admiral?" Captain Pollock asked.

Quentin Prescott turned and Captain Pollock saw the curious look on the admiral's face. He looked pleased, but serious and a little concerned.

"Come in, Bill," he said. "Have a seat. In fact, have a drink." He motioned to the small bar set up against the wall.

Bill Pollock frowned slightly. It wasn't yet 1600 and tradition dictated that you didn't drink until after 1700. "Sir?" he asked, confused.

"And pour one for me," the admiral said, and strode across the room, holding out the paper which appeared to be an official message.

Captain Pollock took the message and began scanning it with one hand while he picked up a bottle of scotch with the other. He stopped and set the bottle back on the bar, staring at the message slip. "Sir?" he asked. "Does this mean we're..."

"That's right, Bill. I've been promoted. As of the first of the year you'll be working for the new COMCRUDESPAC." The admiral smiled. "Now, how about that drink?"

"Yes sir," Captain Pollock splashed scotch into two glasses and handed one to the admiral. "Congratulations, sir," he said, raising his glass in a toast. "What about Admiral Boddicker?" Boddicker was the current COMCRUDESPAC.

"Going to Washington," Admiral Prescott explained. "He's joining the Joint Chiefs on the staff of Admiral Benson."

"That's great, sir," Captain Pollock was genuinely pleased for his boss. "Congratulations."

"It means another star for me, Bill," the admiral said, smiling. "It also means I rate a rear admiral as my chief of staff." He handed Captain Pollock a small box. "Open it, Bill."

Captain Pollock opened the box and couldn't conceal the surprise on his face. The box contained the two-star collar pin of a rear admiral.

"Those were my stars, Bill," Admiral Prescott explained, still smiling. "I'd be pleased if you'd wear them...admiral."

Bill Pollock stood staring at Admiral Prescott. It took a few moments to sink in, then he broke into a large grin. "Yes sir, I would be honored."

"It isn't official until it's blessed by Congress," the admiral said. "But that's a formality." He took a drink of scotch. "By the way, we'll be moving to Subic Bay the first week of January. Better get your affairs in order on Guam. We're being replaced there."

Bill Pollock knew it wouldn't take him long to get his affairs in order. He was a bachelor and could be ready to go in a couple of days. "Have you told Mrs. Prescott yet?"

"No, but we'll be returning to Guam this Friday. I think she'll welcome the change. She doesn't say anything, but I don't think she likes Guam very much. She's seemed out of sorts lately. I think the excitement of the Philippines will perk her up."

"To Subic Bay and the new COMCRUDESPPAC," Bill Pollock raised his glass in a toast.

"To Subic Bay," Admiral Prescott said, and they touched glasses.

* * * * *

The party broke up after 10:00 P.M. and the happy, slightly drunken Havernauts piled into the pickup for the trip back to the ship. It was decided Andy would drive because he'd had very little to drink and Billy was happily inebriated. He insisted on riding shotgun so he could keep an eye on Andy's driving.

As Billy and Teresa embraced and kissed good night, Mr. Gamboa reminded the sailors of his intent to throw a proper engagement party for Billy and his daughter in two weeks, on Saturday, November 2nd.

Andy backed the truck slowly down the driveway and headed toward Highway One. Mr. and Mrs. Gamboa stood on the porch, arm in arm, their brood gathered around them, all waving to the pickup.

The truck pulled up next to the Quonset hut across the pier from the Haverfield and the sailors piled out. Andy was glad the trip was over. All the way home Billy had instructed him on how to drive, and constantly criticized the way he maneuvered the truck. It was a good thing Billy was the guest of honor or Andy would have gone up side his head.

The next week dragged by slowly. With the Raptor in port R.J. and his friends had little to occupy them except the Mocombo Club, which they visited every night they didn't have duty. Billy spent almost every evening with the Gamboas, knowing he had duty the following weekend and wouldn't be able to spend it with Teresa. He and the others were looking forward to the engagement party on the second, and talked about it constantly. All the Gamboas' friends and relatives would be there, along with almost all of the Haverfield's deck force. Even big Queen was invited, and he readily accepted.

R.J. spent hours on the signal light upon returning from the Mocombo Club each evening. Unable to sleep and thinking constantly of Annie, he found refuge in shooting the breeze with the signalmen on watch on other ships. Concentrating on the code helped him push thoughts of Annie from his mind, and he rarely went to bed before 0100, yet was always up early, standing on the fantail, watching the sunrise. Those were the most difficult moments for him, when his thoughts were dominated by Annie. He became depressed and lonely early in the morning, but did not stop greeting the sunrise. When he had first come aboard, the morning dawn always energized him, filled him with hope. Lately the ritual had become a depressing chore, but still he arose early and made his way slowly to the fantail each morning, as if being drawn there like some love-sick lemming.

* * * * *

Captain Oliver's week dragged by, too. It had been more than ten days since he had last spoken to Lorelei, and he was certain he had screwed up that relationship for good.

She called on Tuesday, the twenty-ninth.

Captain Oliver hurried down to the quarterdeck to take the call, his mind racing with a jumble of thoughts and emotions. He picked up the receiver and tried to sound calm and matter-of-fact.

"This is Captain Oliver," he said officiously.

"Paul, I have to see you." Her voice was strained, urgent.

"Something wrong?" he asked.

"Yes, well, no...I just have to see you."

"I've been hoping you'd call. I've missed you."

She sobbed softly. "Oh, hell. I promised myself I wouldn't cry."

"What is it, Lorelei?" he asked, suddenly concerned.

"Can we meet tomorrow afternoon?" she asked. "About two o'clock. I can get away for a couple of hours."

"Sure," he said. "Where?"

"Tell me where Lee's cottage is and I'll meet you there."

He gave her directions and hung up, excited at the prospect of being with her again, this time alone in Lee's cottage. His step was quick and full of bounce as he returned to his cabin.

Unfortunately, Billy and Teresa's engagement party and Captain Oliver's date with Lorelei would be postponed by the interference of a fierce, wrathful and spiteful female. Typhoon Mabel was heading with a vengeance toward Guam, gathering force and speed, winds whipping to over one hundred miles per hour, and she would demand the full attention of the Haverfield crew.

It began with a red sky on the morning of Wednesday, the thirtieth. R.J. stood on the fantail admiring the bright, bold crimson color of the dawn. He had never seen such a brilliantly colored sunrise, but he had never before experienced a storm like the one coming at him.

* * * * *

"Captain?" the exec stepped into Captain Oliver's cabin, a concerned look on his face.

"Yes, Ed?"

"Sir, the barometer is dropping like a stone. I talked to the weather people on the base and they tell me we're about to get hit by a typhoon."

Captain Oliver stood up. "Let's get ready to get underway," he said. "I expect we'll get the order to put to sea soon, and I want to be prepared."

"Aye, sir." The exec nodded grimly and left the cabin.

Paul Oliver's mind was racing and he felt fully alert. He had ridden out a typhoon a few years before and had an idea what to expect. A ship couldn't remain tied up in port. It would be slammed against the pier and destroyed. The only way to deal with a typhoon was to ride her out. He put on his cap and left the cabin, heading to the chart room.

* * * * *

"I want everything lashed down or stowed away," Chief Whipple paced the fantail in front of First Division, whose members stood at quarters, looking at each other nervously. "I want extra lifelines run fore and aft on every deck, and Queen," he looked over at the big boatswain's mate.

"Yes, chief?"

"Send a working party to the forward storage locker and break out all the foul weather gear you can find. We're gonna need it." The ship's bosun was worried, his brow furrowed and his mouth set grimly. "This ain't gonna be no party, men," he snapped. "This bitch is gonna beat up on us plenty, and we're just gonna have to ride her out."

* * * * *

"Make sure those lanyards are tight," Anselmi was touring the signal bridge with R.J. "Tie 'em off as tight as you can, then tighten 'em some more." He looked up at the sky, which was beginning to turn darker, clouds moving in quickly. "Lash down both signal lights and snap those covers on the flag bags."

"This is gonna be bad?" R.J. asked.

"Man, a typhoon is as bad as it gets," Anselmi answered. "You got no idea. My advice is to stay off the decks. Stay below or inside the bridge, and get ready to be tossed around."

"How long does it last?"

"Depends. Last time we were out there for four days. When we got back, the whole fuckin' island was messed up. No electricity at all. Wasn't for our generators..." he stopped, looked at R.J. and nodded seriously. "It's gonna be bad, Slick."

* * * * *

Chief Twitchell was awakened by the increased motion of the ship as the harbor became a little choppy. Mabel had sent out her forward scouts to stir up and agitate the usually calm water, presaging what was to come. She jabbed at the harbor with short, snappy, wind-blown punches like a fighter circling her opponent, moving in for the kill.

Twitchell rolled over on his back and attempted to rise, stretching out his neck like a giant sea turtle that had found itself overturned, its legs pawing out on all sides, trying in desperation to right itself. He had passed out in his uniform again, and his clothes were soaked in sweat. His fat face was wet and blotchy-red, his eyes dark-rimmed and unfocused. He threw his stubby legs over the side of his bunk and grimaced as the hangover pain shot through his head like a lightning bolt. He groaned and lowered himself slowly to the deck. He stood unsteadily, trying to get his legs under him and stumbled toward the head. He knew instinctively from many years at sea that a storm was coming, but how strong he did not know. He peeled off his wet uniform and dropped it on the deck, crawling into the small shower stall in his skivvies and socks. He hung his head under the spray and turned down the hot water slowly until he was gasping in cold water. He knew he had to get down to engineering and make preparations for getting underway. Chief Twitchell had ridden out tropical storms before and knew what they were like.

* * * * *

The deck crew hurried to prepare the ship for the storm. Mr. MacDonald stood on the 02 level, drinking coffee and watching the activity on the fantail. The crew was performing well. They had disassembled the fantail awning quickly and stowed it away. They were running additional lifelines along the sides of the ship and had lashed down the depth charges on the fantail and secured the anchor chain on the focsul with block and tackle reinforcements.

Chief Whipple came up beside Mr. MacDonald and watched the hurried activity.

"Smells like a bad one to me, sir," he said, looking into the sky toward the southeast. "She's coming on strong."

"You're right, chief," Mr. Mac agreed. "You were here when Karen hit last year, so you would know."

"I hope she ain't like Karen," the chief said, slowly shaking his head. He looked up at the graying sky and frowned. "That was one mean bitch of a typhoon."

* * * * *

Guam lies in an area of the Pacific Ocean where most tropical cyclones, or typhoons, form up. During the rainy season which runs from July to December, several tropical depressions build up around and near the island. Coming mostly from a southeasterly direction, many of the storms bypass the island and play themselves out on the open sea. Their high winds and driving rains, however, often impact the island as they pass. Some storms hit the island directly, and, depending on the force of their winds, can cause a great deal of damage. Typhoon Karen in November of 1962 was such a storm. Her little sister, typhoon Mabel, would prove to be another.

Almost as if she felt she had something to prove in a sibling rivalry, Mabel threw herself toward the island, whipping up the sea around her in what is known as sea-surge, a condition akin to a tsunami. The sea-surge can overwhelm sea walls and capsize smaller craft such as fishing boats, hurling them up and over the land to crash down hundreds of yards inland. Most vessels will put to sea during the storm, but some simply cannot survive the punishment of a typhoon at sea, and must seek refuge in the inner harbor. There, helpless, they are almost always destroyed.

* * * * *

"Single up all lines and let's get moving." Captain Oliver was on the bridge, looking at the radar scope and reviewing the weather reports handed to him by the exec. "Damn," he muttered, "she's coming on fast!"

"All lines singled up, sir." Mr. Mac had the conn.

"Very well, cast off two and three," Captain Oliver ordered.

"Two and three cast off, sir!"

The captain smiled. The deck crew was reacting very quickly. A sense of urgency spurred them on as the storm clouds grew darker and closer. "Cast off four!"

"Four cast off, sir."

"Very well." Captain Oliver stood on the starboard wing bridge, watching the mooring lines being pulled in and coiled on the deck. "Cast off one, all back one-third!"

"One cast off, sir," MacDonald reported.

"All back one third." Sonny Metzner was on the lee-helm. Tanner was at his usual post on the helm.

"Come left ten degrees."

"Ten degrees, aye sir," Tanner repeated the order and eased the rudder to the left. The Haverfield slowly began to back away from the pier, making a wide arc in the channel until the bow came around toward the breakwater. Aft of the Haverfield, the Brister and Raptor began pulling away from their berths.

One by one the three ships' horns blew, indicating they were underway. R.J. popped the ensign on the main mast and unfurled the call sign flags on the port lanyard as Anselmi brought in the flag from the fantail. The wind was picking up and the flags began whipping about furiously.

The Brister and Raptor, with orders to form up on the Haverfield, Captain Oliver in command, followed the Haverfield out of the harbor and past the breakwater. The sea was getting very choppy, white caps appearing everywhere like angry white splotches erupting from beneath the ocean.

"Signal bridge!" Captain Oliver shouted.

"Aye, sir?" Anselmi poked his head into the bridge from the port hatch.

"Signal course two seven zero!"

"Two seven zero, aye sir." Anselmi turned back to the signal bridge but R.J. had heard the order and was hooking up the flag hoist. Anselmi raised the hoist signaling the course and watched as the Brister and Raptor duplicated the flag hoist on their lanyards.

"Signal answered, sir," Anselmi called to the bridge.

"Execute!" the captain ordered.

Anselmi snapped the flag hoist down and R.J. pulled in the flags, stowing them neatly in their assigned slots in the flag bag. On the Raptor and the Brister the signals were pulled down and all three ships turned west to two seven zero degrees.

Mabel's winds grew stronger and she pelted the small convoy with a hard rain. The sea was whipped up and a salt water mist swirled and sprayed across the Haverfield's bow as she dipped and drove into the angry ocean. She bobbed and lurched forward, trying desperately to flee the onslaught. The sun was fading as clouds stormed in overhead, turning the sky into a bubbling cauldron of gray.

The convoy moved forward at a speed of fifteen knots. Captain Oliver paced the flying bridge and called Mr. MacDonald over.

"Bring the lookouts in, Mac," he said. "It's going to get pretty bad and I don't want them out in the middle of it."

"Aye, sir," Mr. Mac said, and ordered the lookouts inside the bridge. Cotton and Billy came down gratefully from the 04 level, their foul-weather gear already soaked. Jefferson and Andy stepped in from the wing bridges. The pilot house was becoming crowded. Everyone was silent. Tanner concentrated on holding the ship on course. Sonny stood at the lee-helm, his hands resting on the handles, staring straight ahead. The lookouts did their best to stay out of the way. Captain Oliver and the exec huddled over the chart table, plotting courses of the storm and the convoy.

"If this is the lull before the storm," Mr. Martin said quietly, "we are gonna catch hell."

"You're right, Ed," the captain replied, frowning. "Maintain this course and speed for a couple more hours, then we'll reevaluate the situation. We might not be able to outrun her, but maybe we can get away from the worst of it." He turned to Lester, the boatswain's mate of the watch. "Pass the word. I want all hands below decks or inside."

FORTY ONE

There wasn't much the crew could do, except wait. The day grew darker until night fell, and the small convoy plowed west in a futile attempt at fleeing Mabel's wrath. After a few hours, the crew became used to the tossing and turning of the ship, and began to settle into a routine. They played cards in the mess decks and lay in their bunks reading or trying to catch some sleep.

R.J. sat in the mess decks playing hearts with Tanner, Lester and Cotton. He was becoming accustomed to the ship's motion, and rolled with it, swaying side to side.

"This ain't too bad," he commented. "I thought riding out a typhoon would be a lot worse than this."

The other three started laughing.

"What's funny?" R.J. asked.

"Man, you ain't seen nothin' yet," Lester said. "This is just the beginning. This bitch is gonna make you wish you joined the Marine Corps." Cotton and Tanner grinned and nodded.

"It gets worse?" R.J. said, looking first to Tanner, then to Cotton.

"It gets worse," Tanner said softly. "Much worse."

* * * * *

"The storm is changing course, Captain." Mr. Barkman had the conn and was plotting the course of the storm from the radio messages delivered to the bridge by Riley. It was almost 2300 and the captain was still on the bridge, declining suggestions he get some sleep.

"Changing course? What direction?"

"Due west, sir," Mr. Barkman said. "She's following us."

The captain came over to the chart table and looked at the pencil line plotting the storm's course. "Let's head north, Jim. Let's try to stay out of her way as much as possible."

"Aye, sir." Mr. Barkman plotted the new course. "Suggest course three six zero, sir."

"Make it so," the captain said. "Signal the Brister and Raptor."

"Aye, sir."

The three ships abandoned the westerly course and turned north.

* * * * *

R.J. had been asleep almost four hours when he was thrown out of his bunk by a severe roll of the ship to port. He hit the deck on his knees and tried to stand. The ship lurched to starboard and he grabbed frantically at a bunk to keep from ending up in bed with Riley, whose bunk was just below his. He slipped and fell again, this time landing on his back. "Shit!" he swore.

All around him books, boots, anything not lashed down went flying. He struggled to his feet and fell back against Riley's bunk as the ship rolled violently to starboard, was hit by a huge wave and bounced back to port.

R.J. stood between the tiers of bunks and held on to opposite bunks with each hand. "Shit!" he said. "This sumbitch is gonna capsize!"

Sailors were jumping or falling out of their racks, many cursing, and some getting sick and vomiting on the deck. The lights blinked on and off in the compartment as sailors hurriedly got dressed, pulling on their boondockers and looking around confused. The ship pitched violently, and R.J. fell again, landing hard on his knees.

R.J. looked down at growing blue bruises on both knee caps. He scrambled to his feet, reached for his dungaree trousers and nearly fell again, hanging on to his top rack like an orangutan holding on to a tree branch. It was 0300 and Mabel was closing in.

Due to take over as quartermaster of the watch at 0400, R.J. was unable to sleep and unwilling to remain below. He made his way slowly to the bridge through the mess decks. Pots and pans were flying around, food trays were clattering in the water sloshing on the deck and the entire galley crew was on duty, trying desperately to hold things together. Hawkins moved from one area to the other, frantically barking orders, seemingly unaffected by the bouncing and rolling of the ship. Morning chow was going to be an interesting experience.

He reached the bridge and lurched inside as a huge wave crashed into the starboard side, sending the ship reeling to port. Another wave hit the port side and violently pushed the ship to starboard. The inclinometer showed rolls of forty-five degrees to port and then to starboard. Sailors were holding onto anything available to keep from being tossed around the bridge. The captain was still there, watching the chart table.

"Keep her in the wind, Bill," he said to Mr. Westerman, who had the conn.

"Aye, sir." Mr. Westerman frowned and spoke quietly to Lester who had the helm. "Steady on course, helm."

"Steady on, sir," Lester replied. He had a silly grin on his face and R.J. realized Lester was enjoying himself.

R.J. stood next to Gino at the starboard lookout position, peering through the windows of the flying bridge. The storm raged all around them. The wind was so ferocious rain was pelting the ship horizontally, making it almost impossible to see. R.J. felt the ship shudder and slide into a huge trough. He looked up and saw the angry gray ocean high above the ship. Another wave crashed onto the focsul and the ship shuddered again, the bow being forced down and the stern being forced up. The screws came out of the water, spinning free, making a futile whirring sound. The stern crashed back down and the screws bit into the ocean, propelling the ship forward into another swell. R.J. had never imagined the Pacific Ocean could be so angry, so powerfully ugly. He looked around the bridge and saw the fear on the faces of everyone there. They were helpless against the raging storm, and they knew it.

"I came up through the mess decks," R.J. said to no one in particular. "The galley is a mess, and Hawkins is having a fuckin' stroke!"

The bridge crew looked at each other and chuckled softly. Even Mr. Westerman and the captain allowed themselves a grin. They all could picture a frantic Hawkins going apoplectic as the typhoon made a total mess of his galley. Yeah, they seem to agree silently, Hawkins would definitely have a fuckin' stroke.

* * * * *

All through the night and into the next day the Haverfield led the small convoy north by northwest, making course corrections to stay into the wind, trying desperately to escape Mabel's power. By the late morning of the third day the rain had subsided and the lookouts were posted on the wing bridges. The captain didn't want any lookouts higher than the 03 level, so the 04 level lookouts doubled up with the lookouts on the wings.

R.J. stepped onto the port wing and looked around. The Pacific Ocean swelled and crashed in all directions. The sky was dark, even at noon, and the wind blew hard in the face of the convoy. The scene looked like it came out of a black and white movie; no color, only varying shades of gray. It amazed him that he could look up and watch the ocean swelling high above the ship. As the so-called peaceful Pacific Ocean raged over the small, insignificant convoy, R.J. marveled at the display of stark power. The Pacific was putting on quite a show.

That night the wind quieted down enough for the crew to get some sleep without being tossed out of their bunks. It was calm enough for R.J. to climb up on the 04 level, hang on to the railing and brace himself against the still-strong wind. The cloud cover began to break up, drifting west, leaving open spaces showing dark night skies and the distant silvery beams of a full moon.

"Boy," R.J. said to himself. "Last night was a helluva Halloween!"

* * * * *

Early Saturday morning, the fourth day of Mabel, R.J. stood on the 02 level above the fantail, watching the scattering of clouds astern of the ship. The Haverfield and Typhoon Mabel were parting company for good, and no one on the Haverfield would miss her. The convoy turned east and the radar showed relatively calm weather ahead. A hint of dawn began to break over the horizon like a welcome-home greeting to the returning sailors who had been beaten so badly by the storm. The crews of every ship in the convoy took a deep breath and murmured private thanks.

Damage reports began filtering in to the bridge. It was obvious the Haverfield had taken a beating. Deck plates were buckled all over the ship. A retaining wire had snapped off and the stack listed to port, looking like it would tip over, the proud white "E" peeling and almost unrecognizable. On the signal bridge they had lost three lanyards, two on the port side and one on the starboard side. They would have to be replaced when they returned to Guam and R.J. did not look forward to crawling out on the yardarm to re-string them.

Below decks the damage was worse. Two of the four engines were offline and the evaporators were inoperable. Chief Twitchell estimated it would take a week to repair them, if they could get the parts. The electrical plant was barely being held together, and Mr. Almogordo advised the captain that little could be accomplished without an extended down time in port.

In the mess decks, Hawkins and his galley crew worked feverishly to clean up the broken cups and scattered silverware, trays, pots and pans. The potato peeler had broken off its base and lay damaged on the deck. Water was being swabbed up all over the deck and the scullery equipment was barely working. Still, Hawkins managed to prepare breakfast for the crew, and as they filed into chow, the sailors marveled at how he had managed to get his galley squared away in such a short time. When he came out of the scullery and started up the aisle to the galley, sailors eating breakfast in the mess decks applauded him, whistling and cheering. Hawkins grinned broadly and managed a low bow before he stepped into the galley and began barking orders at his charges.

Reports from the Brister and Raptor were no better. The storm had caused a great deal of damage to them, too. All three skippers were anxious to return to Apra Harbor.

Captain Oliver read with relief the weather report. Mabel had continued west after passing over Guam, her high winds had subsided, and she was blowing herself out in the Philippine Sea. He decided to set course for home, anxious to return. The crew and the ship needed some down time to effect repairs and lick their wounds. It occurred to him that he had not thought about Lorelei at all during the storm. *One thing about a typhoon*, he thought, *she'll take your mind off any human female.*

R.J. stood on the starboard side of the signal bridge as the Haverfield limped past the breakwater and into the outer harbor on the afternoon of Saturday, November 2nd. They had been at sea for four days. He thought about how he had hated Guam when he first arrived, had resented being stationed there. His contempt for the island had deepened during his time in the brig, but now, coming up on the familiar outer harbor, the island seemed like a haven after the experience with the typhoon. And then there was Annie. *Be it ever so humble*, he thought.

The rest of the crew felt the same way about returning to Guam. The island truly seemed like home to them, a safe refuge after the beating they took from Mabel. They were going back to the safety of Apra Harbor, where they could lie in the sun on the USO beach and dance and drink at the Mocombo Club. They looked forward to the familiar surroundings; the busy harbor, the lush green hills, the happy, smiling Guamanian people.

They were shocked and dismayed at what they found waiting for them.

FORTY TWO

Steaming slowly past Orote Point and into the outer harbor, the Haverfield led the Brister and Raptor toward their berthing places. R.J. watched from the signal bridge as the convoy made its way into the inner harbor. Something was wrong. The familiar landscape had been altered. Trees were uprooted and broken. Small fishing boats were lying on their sides far up on the beach. Power lines were down and telephone poles had been snapped in two. They approached the pier with line handlers and a group of dependents waiting for them. The outbuildings, mostly Quonset huts, were scattered in pieces all over the dock. The Haverfield's pickup truck, Billy Lopez' pride and joy, was overturned, battered and pounded, resting on its top. All the windows had been shattered, the rear axle broken and three of the four tires were missing.

The small crowd waiting on the pier was subdued. No one waved, no welcome home signs were displayed; frightened children hung on to their unsmiling mothers. After the ship was moored, R.J. left the signal bridge and joined Pea, Gino and Billy on the 02 level.

"Shit!" Billy exclaimed. "Look at my truck!"

Standing in front of the crowd was Bobby Gamboa, his arms crossed, a worried look on his face. His mouth was set in a tight line and his brow was dark and furled.

"What's Bobby doing here?" R.J. wondered.

Billy caught sight of Bobby and smiled. He started to wave to him, but the look on Bobby's face stopped him and his smile froze. "Oh, my God," he exclaimed, "something's wrong...oh, my God!"

Billy rushed down to the fantail and ran down the brow just as it was being attached to the ship. "Hey, Lopez," Mr. Winters, the OOD yelled at him, but Billy didn't hear him. Bobby came forward to meet him and they talked in quiet, hushed tones. Billy's head dropped, his knees wobbled and he held on to Bobby to keep from dropping to the ground. Bobby wrapped his arms around his friend and looked up at R.J., Pea and Gino. He shook his head slowly and patted Billy on the back.

"It must be Teresa," Gino said. "Let's go!"

The three of them rushed down the brow and joined Bobby and Billy on the pier. Billy was sobbing and Bobby was trying to console him.

"What happened?" R.J. asked as they reached the two sailors. "Did something happen to Teresa?"

Bobby nodded, tears streaming down his cheeks. "She's hurt," he sobbed. "She's got a broken leg and some internal injuries."

Billy raised his head and looked helplessly at his friend. "I've got to see her, where is she, Bob?"

"She's in Agana hospital," he replied. "But that's not the worst of it."

His eyes filled with tears again and his face took on an anguished look. "Little Maria," he said softly. "She's dead."

"Oh, God no!" R.J. said, shocked. "Why? What happened?"

"I gotta go to Teresa," Billy moaned. "I gotta go now!" He wandered around in a circle, unsure of how to proceed. The truck was destroyed. How would he get to the hospital?

"I took the shuttle down here," Bobby explained. "I don't have a car."

"We do!" Pea yelled. He ran up the brow and had a hurried conversation with Mr. Winters, who slowly nodded. Pea ran back down the brow with his car keys in his hand. "We got emergency liberty," he said, and ran down the pier toward the main gate and the lot where the Bomb was parked. The others joined him and all five sprinted down the pier. It was two miles to the main gate and they ran like madmen, past the Raptor and the Brister, whose sailors stood on deck and stared.

They reached the parking lot and were relieved to see the Bomb had miraculously not been damaged. They piled into the car and Pea started it up, swinging out of the lot and through the main gate, ignoring the Marine guard. As they sped down Highway One, shocked at the destruction all around them, Bobby told them the story.

During the worst of the storm Bobby, his father, mother and Teresa frantically tried to shore up one side of the trailer that looked like it was going to collapse. Little Maria, terribly frightened, had run outside to be with her big sister and had been blown down the hill by the ferocious winds. Teresa had run after her and had her in her arms when a large palm tree uprooted and crashed down on them. Bobby and his father had managed to get the two back into the trailer, but Teresa and little Maria were both unconscious. It wasn't until the next morning, when the storm began to subside, that they were able to get to the hospital. The doctor told them little Maria must have died during the night.

They worked over Teresa frantically, taking x-rays and setting her leg, trying to determine the extent of her injuries. She suffered some internal bruising, but was expected to recover. She had regained consciousness only that morning, but was drifting in and out, often delirious. They couldn't bring themselves to tell her about Maria.

Pea screeched into the parking lot and left the car in front of the hospital. They all jumped out and ran up the steps and in the front door, past several shocked nurses.

"This way!" Bobby led them up a flight of stairs and down a hallway. They slowed as they spotted Mr. and Mrs. Gamboa sitting on a bench at the end of the hall. When the Gamboas saw the Haverfield sailors they rushed toward them and threw their arms around them. Mrs. Gamboa was weeping and she held on tightly to Billy.

"Where is she?" Billy asked, looking around the ward.

"In here," Mr. Gamboa said softly. He opened the door and Billy rushed in. Teresa was in the last bed of a four-bed room. Her right leg was in a cast and had been elevated. Her head was wrapped in white bandages and her face was bruised, her lips swollen. Billy gasped and knelt down next to her, took her hand and kissed it.

"Oh," she moaned softly and turned her head toward him. "Billy?" She tried to raise her head but didn't have the strength and she lay back, tears running down the sides of her face. The others gathered around her bed. Mrs. Gamboa sobbed quietly and held on to Bobby. R.J., Gino and Pea all put their arms around her and Mr. Gamboa stood behind Billy, patting him on the back.

"You're gonna be okay, baby," Billy assured her. "I'm here now and you're going to be okay."

Mr. Gamboa motioned for the others to follow him outside so Billy and Teresa could be alone. Out in the hallway he sighed and sat down heavily on the bench. Mrs. Gamboa sat next to him.

"We're so glad you're here," he said, looking up at the worried sailors. He shook his head slowly. "We lost little Maria," he said sadly. "We're so glad you're here." Mrs. Gamboa began weeping again, holding her husband's hand tightly.

A nurse came hurrying down the hall, her white shoes squeaking as she walked. "No more than two visitors," she scolded. "You must leave now. Come back tomorrow." Mrs. Gamboa stayed and the nurse herded the rest of them down the hall toward the stairs.

Outside, they gathered beside the Bomb, shuffled their feet and stared at the ground. R.J. passed around a pack of smokes and everyone lit up. The storm had passed and all that remained were a few broken clouds drifting west, seemingly looking back over their shoulders, nodding with satisfaction at the havoc Mabel had inflicted on the island.

"That was a bad typhoon," Mr. Gamboa understated quietly, shaking his head. For the first time he began to cry, big tears dropping from his eyes. The sailors gathered around him, and held him, trying to console him.

"My baby," he moaned, holding his head in his hands, "my poor little baby."

FORTY THREE

On Sunday Captain Oliver sat at his desk, reading the updated damage reports. The initial estimates had been understandably pessimistic, but the damage was not as bad as first thought. Still, it would take some time to bring the Haverfield back to a state of readiness. A soft knock at his cabin door interrupted his thoughts.

"Enter," he called.

The exec stepped in and closed the door behind him.

"Morning, Ed," the captain greeted.

"Morning, Cap'n. I have a message you might be interested in." The exec handed the message slip to Captain Oliver, who scanned it quickly, looked up at the exec and re-read the message more slowly.

"Hmm, wonder what this will mean," the captain mused. South Vietnamese's president, Ngo Dinh Diem, had been assassinated the previous day in Saigon.

"It can't be good," Lieutenant Martin replied. "It's probably going to create more instability. I have no doubt it will embolden the communists in the north."

"So, you believe it's going to result in more American involvement?" the captain asked.

"I think we should prepare for the worst," the exec replied. "That area must be stabilized if we don't want the communists to overrun all of Southeast Asia."

Paul Oliver nodded slowly, deep in thought. Could this be the start of another protracted war like Korea? Would it end the same way, with half the country embracing communism and the other half democracy? Is that the pattern that would dominate the geopolitical scene for the next who-knows-how-many years?

"You're right, Ed," Captain Oliver looked up. "This can't be good news."

* * * * *

All the Havernauts, except those on duty, attended the funeral mass for little Maria at Our Lady of Guadalupe chapel in Agana on Monday. Mr. MacDonald attended, representing the Haverfield's officers, and sailors from other divisions, Fred Riley, Walt Bixby, John Anselmi and "Doc" Gysler came to pay their respects. It was a painful day.

Teresa had to be wheeled into the chapel in a hospital wheelchair, pushed down the aisle by Billy Lopez. Her leg was extended out and she was in obvious pain, her eyes closed tight, tears running freely down her cheeks. She dabbed at her eyes with a small lace hankie. Billy's face was set and he stared straight ahead, trying his best to be strong.

Mrs. Gamboa knelt in the front pew, her head down, praying, a dark scarf tied around her head. Mr. Gamboa sat next to her, a dull, shocked look on his face. Members of the Gamboa clan from all over the island filled the front pews. R.J. and the Haverfield sailors sat in the rear, silent and a little uncomfortable.

Outside the church, after the mass, the sailors gathered around in small groups, talking quietly. They turned when Teresa and Mrs. Gamboa came out to get into the black Buick provided by the funeral home. Mr. Gamboa came over to the sailors and shook each hand, thanking them for coming to honor his little girl. His eyes were red and unfocused, his speech slurred slightly. He had been given a mild sedative. When he got to R.J., Andy, Pea and Gino standing off to one side, he hugged each of them.

"I'm afraid most of your hard work has been destroyed," he said sadly. "The trailer got pounded pretty good."

"We'll rebuild it, Mr. G.," R.J. said reassuringly. "We'll be there Saturday...if you are up to it."

Mr. Gamboa smiled sadly and hugged R.J. again. "Yes, please come this Saturday," he said. "It'll be good to have everyone together again." He thanked them once more and joined his family in the car. Billy helped Teresa into the back seat and waved to the Havernauts before getting in beside her.

"Damn," Gino swore softly. "That was rough."

"Shore was," Andy replied, shaking his head.

"Let's go," Pea said, and walked over to the Bomb. Andy and Gino climbed into the back, and R.J. rode shotgun. They were silent until they passed through the main gate to the base and parked the Bomb in the auxiliary lot. Andy spoke quietly.

"I seen Rafer yesterday," he said.

"He should be getting out today," R.J. calculated. "With five days off for good behavior."

Andy shook his head. "He ain't gettin' out till Saturday. Gonna do the whole thirty days."

"How come?" Pea asked.

"He ain't been getting' along with some of the guards," Andy explained. "Rafer is, you know, kinda stubborn sometimes."

"Rafer got fucked over!" Pea spat. "That asshole Twitchell..."

"Drop it, Pea," Gino said, frowning. "Ain't gonna do nobody any good to go through all that again."

"Yeah, you're right," Pea conceded. "Today we gotta think about the Gamboas."

"Rafer made a friend in the brig," Andy said. "Fella's name is Washington, and he's a real militant guy. Rafer said he learned a lot from him."

They walked in silence back to the ship. Andy's last comment was lost on them, and they didn't give it much thought. Later, looking back on the conversation, R.J. realized they had missed something significant. Rafer's return would change things dramatically on the Haverfield.

FORTY FOUR

Paul Oliver was stunned. He sat in the passenger seat of Lorelei Prescott's Buick convertible and stared at her. She sat next to him, absent-mindedly playing with the steering wheel. She stared down at her lap and ran her hands around the wheel nervously. She looked lovely with her hair pulled back, wearing just a little lipstick. She had on a short-sleeved, powder blue shirt with the collar turned up in back and she wore a pair of white tennis shorts which showed off her nicely tanned legs.

"Subic Bay?" Paul repeated, staring out the front windshield at the USO beach.

"Quentin is leaving on the fifteenth. I'm leaving right after the first of the year." She bit her lip and stared at her lap. She turned in the seat to look into his eyes. "Paul, I..."

He stared at the beach, watching the white surf break and crash on the sand. "I don't know what to say," he whispered. He turned to look at her and she moved closer, putting her head on his shoulder. He put his arm around her shoulders and held her tightly.

"I want to be with you," she whispered. A little sob escaped her lips and she snuggled closer into his neck. "I want to be with you," she whispered again.

He sat up and took hold of her arms, staring into her beautiful violet eyes. "You mean a little fling?" he asked. "A little affair before you go?" He was angry and she didn't understand why. He didn't quite understand, either.

"I...I don't know what I mean...I just want to be with you." She pulled away from him and sat back behind the wheel. "Sorry," she said sarcastically.

"No, I'm sorry," Paul said, moving closer to her. "I don't care how long it lasts. I want you too, even if it's just tonight."

"Not tonight," she said. "After Quentin leaves."

"Okay," he agreed, sitting up straight in his seat.

"You're angry," she said.

"No, really I'm not," he protested.

"He leaves on Friday the fifteenth, and I have to host a dinner for the governor on Saturday." She started playing with the steering wheel again. "Can we get together on Sunday?"

* * * * *

Rafer had changed. Thirty days in the brig can change a man, if only a little, but Rafer had changed a great deal. When he returned to the ship on Saturday after being released from the brig, Rafer was welcomed back by Andy and R.J., who waited for him at the brow. Rafer and Andy embraced, and R.J. put out his hand, smiling. Rafer looked at him strangely, a dark anger in his eyes. He took R.J.'s hand but did not shake it, leaving his own hand limp. Then he brushed by R.J. and went below with Andy. R.J. watched them go down the aft ladder and wondered what was wrong. Rafer had always been friendly and gregarious, with a funny sense of humor. R.J. shrugged and began rounding up the Gamboa working party.

Late that night after a long day working on the trailer, R.J. was restless, so he went up to the signal bridge and raised the Brister on the flashing light. A signalman named Simpson was on duty on the Brister and they shot the breeze for awhile. They talked about the typhoon and the damage it had caused to the ships and the island.

Simpson complimented R.J. on his Morse code and asked him how he learned to send so fast. Automatically, R.J. answered, *it's a long story.* Later, still unable to sleep, he got a cup of coffee from the mess decks and returned to the signal bridge. He leaned against the flag bag and looked out on the calm, quiet harbor. It was November, he realized, a year since the captain's mast at the Naval Training Center in San Diego that had changed the direction of his life.

FORTY FIVE

Naval Training Center
San Diego, California
November, 1962

The base Master at Arms, accompanied by two investigators from the Navy Criminal Investigation Unit, came into the barracks just after evening chow while most radio school students were preparing for liberty. They handed a list of names to RM1 Crenshaw and went into his office.

A little later, 'By God' Bill Crenshaw stormed out of his office and marched through the barracks, pointing to the students who were members of the Straps, motioning them to follow him. R.J., Frankie, Cool Richard, Splib and a few others followed him into the office.

"They're all yours," Crenshaw said to the master at arms. He stared at the students, a disgusted look on his face, and left the office, slamming the door behind him.

"What's this all about?" Frankie asked.

"Shut up, sailor," the master at arms snapped. "Stand at attention against that bulkhead and I don't wanna hear a peep outta you."

The criminal investigators ignored the students. One was on the phone and the other was reviewing paperwork on a clipboard.

"Okay," the one on the phone said, hanging up the receiver. "We're ready to go." He stood and looked the students over. Kids. All of them kids. "We are taking you people to the administrative building," he said, "for questioning."

"Questioning about what?" R.J. asked.

"Ten'hut!" barked the master at arms. "Left face! Forward march!"

They marched out of the office, down the stairs to the first floor and out into the courtyard. Most of the other students were hanging out of the second floor windows, hooting and hollering, watching the procession make its way across the grinder toward the admin building. Once inside, they were ushered into a large room with benches along the walls. Already gathered there, sitting on the benches, were Big Lenny, Stretch Johnson, and the rest of the Straps.

R.J. felt a cold fear run up his spine. *Uh oh,* he thought, and looked around at the others. It was clear they were thinking the same thing.

One by one, the detainees were led into one of three interview rooms where they would be questioned by an investigator. Fellows had been too drunk to be able to identify any one person. He knew for sure, he swore to God they were all Straps, so the investigators had to question every one of them individually. The questions were always the same, and the answers were also always the same.

"Where were you on the night of the attack on Fellows?"

"At the dance at the Tropics, sir."

"Were you involved in the assault on Fellows?"

"No, sir."

"Do you know who was?"

"No, sir."

The Navy investigators threatened, bullied, intimidated and tried to play one Strap against another. The Straps held firm. No one knew anything, no one saw anything, and no one did anything. The Straps wouldn't budge and Fellows couldn't identify even one of them. They either all had to be charged, or they all had to be let go. Consequently, the largest Captain's Mast in the history of the U.S. Naval Training Center would be conducted two days before Thanksgiving, 1962.

Captain Proctor, commanding officer of the NTC, was a large, dour man with a face that resembled a very unhappy bloodhound. His eyes were brown, large and sad; his ears hung long and heavy jowls sagged down both sides of his face. He was in an ill temper. He resented being known as the officer who conducted the largest captain's mast in history, and he was angry at the group of young sailors who were responsible for it. He intended to teach them a lesson. They would rue the day they messed with Captain Proctor's car.

The twenty defendants were marched into the captain's office and stood at attention in four ranks of five. Captain Proctor looked at them, scowling. Just a bunch of damn kids! The charges were read, which included assaulting Fellows and taking his money, malicious mischief to Captain Proctor's car and garden, and conduct unbecoming sailors in the United States Navy.

As much as he wanted to send them to the brig, Captain Proctor was limited in what he could do to them because Fellows couldn't identify the actual perpetrators. That was the reason the case ended up in a captain's mast and not a court martial.

Captain Proctor knew the radio school class these men belonged to was graduating in a month. He restricted them to the base for the remainder of that time and ordered them to do two hours' extra duty every night except Sunday until they graduated. He also fined them one hundred dollars apiece. The so-called Straps actually looked relieved at the sentence. They were certain they would get brig-time, but they were unaware of Captain Proctor's limitations in sentencing them.

Captain Proctor dismissed the men and sat behind his desk, staring at the paperwork piled there. He smiled to himself, knowing there was one more punishment he could impose. He called his aide into the office and began going through the twenty personnel records of the Straps.

The last four weeks of class passed agonizingly slow. The Straps couldn't go to town, couldn't attend the dances, and couldn't hang out at Papa Joe's. They talked on the phone with their girlfriends, but that was all. They mustered after breakfast, lunch, evening chow and again at 2300. They did all sorts of odd jobs, picking up trash from the grinder, standing watch at remote places on base, painting the outside of the barracks, and anything else the master at arms could think of to fulfill their daily two-hour obligations.

During his leisure time, which was rare, R.J. took to going to the library and checking out books. He read mostly novels, checking out three or four every couple of days, reading them, returning them and checking out others. It helped to pass the time, and R.J. was fond of reading. He could lose himself in a story and stay up half the night finishing a novel.

One evening after chow, R.J. stood amid the shelves and stacks of books looking for something interesting when his eyes focused on a sign off in the corner. It read, "POETRY" and he wandered over, more curious than anything else. He picked up two volumes of world poetry and one of American poetry. As he was preparing to check out the books and leave, another title caught his eye. Lying on its side on a middle shelf was a small, worn, red-covered book entitled, "THE COMPLETE WORKS OF EDGAR ALLAN POE." R.J. picked it up and studied the first few pages. He decided to check out the book with the others.

R.J. spent hours with his poetry books. He read and re-read many poems until he had committed them to memory. He loved the poems of Coleridge and Wordsworth, but did not like Keats or Shelley. He thought Lord Byron was boring, but he loved Emily Dickenson and Edgar Allan Poe. Especially Poe, whose poetry spoke to him in a personal way that made R.J. think and wonder and imagine and dream. He took the books back to the library, and when the clerk had returned them to the shelves, R.J. slipped the Poe volume under his jumper and walked out with it stuck down the front of his trousers.

Late at night R.J. would read and read again the poems of Edgar Allan Poe. The only poem he didn't read was The Raven, because he thought it was too much of a project, and from what he had heard about the poem, it was all about death and sorrow and R.J. didn't want to feel any more depressed than he already did. One day he would take on that poem. In the meantime, he sat on his bunk, a dictionary next to him, and read the poetry of Poe, constantly referring to the dictionary to help him with the language. He was enthralled at how Poe's poems, written more than a hundred years earlier, could so clearly articulate his own feelings. He recited the poems to himself over and over again, finding new meanings, new nuances that crystallized and clarified his emotions. He was hooked.

The time dragged. Graduation and reassignment was coming, just not fast enough for R.J. and the others on restriction. All R.J. could think of was getting out of radio school, putting all the trouble behind him, and getting into the fleet. He wanted to go to sea. He spoke to Tonya every night, and she came out to the base to see him a couple of times, but all they could do was sit in the car and talk. Their conversations the last couple of times had been strained. She was bored, he knew, and he couldn't blame her.

Two weeks before graduation the orders came in for all members of Class 22 of 1962. R.J. was excited because he had put in for the Med and was anxious to find out what ship he had been assigned to. He ran up the steps to the barracks and down the passageway to the offices. The new duty stations would be posted outside the office door. By the time R.J. got there, many radio school students were clogging the passageway, pushing, elbowing their way closer to the duty station announcement. Big Lenny and John-John were coming down the passageway, having already seen their assignments. They were not happy.

"What's happening?" R.J. asked as he tried to get a look at the postings.

"Fucking Midway Island," Lenny said bitterly. "That's what's happening for me. Shore duty on Midway!" He hung his head and shook it sadly.

"I got stationed on Kwajalein Atoll," John-John said. "Stretch is on a minesweeper in the Philippines and Cool Richard is going to the Aleutians."

"Jesus," R.J. whispered. "All the shit assignments." He pushed his way to the front of the crowd and found his name near the top of the list.

Davis, R.J.——USS Haverfield DER-393——Apra Harbor, Guam

He let out a low whistle and looked up Findlay, F. R. Frankie was going to Wake Island. One by one he checked the assignments of the other Straps. Each of them got stationed somewhere remote, with little or no night life and nothing to do but mark time. Iceland, Greenland, Adak, Alaska, Wake Island, Midway Island, a sea-going tug in the North Atlantic, an oiler home-ported in Bremerton, and so on. Captain Proctor had assigned them all to bottom-of-the-barrel duty stations for terms ranging from one year to three years. Any thoughts they had of joining the real fleet were dashed by the type-written orders on a clipboard. R.J. ran his finger down the list until he found Fellows, D.R. He was assigned to the radio shack of the USS ENTERPRISE, CVA (N) 65. The newest aircraft carrier in the fleet, and nuclear powered to boot! *That sonofabitch!* R.J. thought.

Captain Proctor had done one other thing. Securing the orders of each of the Straps, he dictated letters to their individual commanding officers, describing what happened and why these men deserved some severe supervision. He referred to them as a street gang and indicated that had there been evidence, they would all be in the brig.

Over their last few weeks, the Straps came to realize what had happened to them. They were together at every muster of restricted personnel, four times per day, and had a lot of time to think and talk about it. After the initial anger and frustration had passed, they began thinking of the events that led up to the 'Fellows Incident,' and what they might have done to prevent it. The restriction and the fine were bad enough, but they had taken a lot of flak from fellow students who relished the opportunity to get a 'dig' in at the Straps. Then, as a final blow, they were being assigned to the crappiest duty stations in the world.

Little by little, humility seeped in. The night before they were to go their separate ways, home on leave for thirty days then to the next duty stations, their last night on restriction, the Straps hung around after the final muster to talk together for the last time. At first they stood around, shuffling their feet, smoking cigarettes and staring at the ground.

"I'll tell ya what I'm gonna do," Frankie announced. He looked around at the other Straps and grinned that big, friendly, freckled-faced, can't-help-but-love-him grin. "I'm gonna be the best fuckin' radioman that poor, unfortunate island of Wake has ever fucking seen!"

"Ladies and Gentlemen!" Big Lenny bowed and gestured toward Frankie with both hands, index fingers pointing the way. "I give you...Mickey *fuckin'* Rooney!" The other Straps laughed, except for R.J. He held up his right palm, signaling for silence.

"I have a question," he said, and let his words evaporate into the night. The Straps grew silent, looking around at each other with questioning eyes. R.J. was one of their leaders; this was their last night together, and R.J. had a question.

Big Lenny looked around at the Straps, whose eyes were all on R.J. "By all means, sir," Big Lenny bowed toward R.J. his arms spread to the sides, palms up. "Your question, sir." Lenny grinned sardonically at R.J. who pretended not to notice him. Big Lenny's sarcastic leer transformed into a real smile. "Seriously, m'man. Go ahead."

"Why did we get together in the first place?" R.J. asked, looking around at the group. "Why the Straps? Was it because we shared the same fashion sense?" He stopped and smiled humbly. "Okay, that was a big part of it...the sharp clothes...the straps." He hooked his thumbs inside an imaginary set of suspenders. "We were the best. We got the highest scores, the instructors loved us. We were cool!" He held his index finger in the air. "We *are* the best." He stopped and looked into the faces of his friends. "I'm with Frankie," he said, throwing his arm around Frank's shoulder. "I still wanna be the best."

"I'm already the best," Frankie said, patting himself on the chest. "I'm going to bring this talent to Wake Island. Shit," he said, strutting around, bobbing his head. "They won't know what hit 'em! It's probably a good thing there *ain't* no chicks on that island.""

"That attitude?" Big Lenny cautioned Frankie. "That'll get your butt kicked, little man."

"Not once they meet me," Frankie retorted, smiling as big as he could manage. "I'm what you call..." he smiled sweetly into Lenny's eyes and batted his eyelids. "Irresistible!"

Lenny laughed. "No, you ain't irresistible to me." He pushed Frankie back, laughing. "You just some nut from Denver." He looked at R.J. "Like him," he said, pointing at R.J.

"My point is," R.J. continued stubbornly, "we always talked about being the best." He waited and let it seep in. "We were always trying to beat each other at this stuff," he waved a hand around the school grounds. "That's what made it fun."

"Yeah, besides," Frankie joined in, "You get away with more shit if you the best!" He grinned broadly, freckles scurrying around his nose and eyes. "Tomorrow, guys, we are goin' home for thirty, then on to our new duty stations. We're goin' to the fleet. Let's leave all this bad horseshit behind us."

Big Lenny stood there staring at his shoes, thinking. The others waited quietly until Lenny raised his head and grinned. "We had a helluva run, didn't we?"

Everyone agreed that they did, indeed have a great run. The trouble with Fellows aside, the Straps had stayed away from any real trouble, choosing instead to dance and romance the girls. Fellows had deserved what he got, there was no doubt about that, but all in all, the Straps were happy to leave this place and move on. It pleased them they were all near the top of the list, academically.

The next morning the students busied themselves packing seabags and yammering about going on leave. The morale was very high. 'By-God' Bill Crenshaw walked into the barracks with a clip board in his hand and looked around.

"Another pain in the ass class finally gets outta my hair," he bellowed. "Outside for your final roll-call, girls, or you won't By-God catch that bus!"

The students hustled outside quickly and stood attention in their dress blues. One by one Crenshaw called off their names and one by one the students answered, "Here," and left the formation, heading to the main gate and the Rosecrans bus that would take them downtown to the airport, the bus station or the train station.

As the Straps' names were called, each answered up and left the formation. Before heading toward the main gate, each Strap walked up to 'By-God' Bill Crenshaw and draped a set of suspenders over his wooden podium.

Crenshaw just stood there at parade rest, watching each set of suspenders being laid across his podium. Splib Walker was the last to be called and added his suspenders to the pile.

"Ain't no Straps no more," he said sadly, shaking his head slowly while he looked into Crenshaw's eyes. "These'll make good additions to your wardrobe, Crenshaw."

Crenshaw smiled very slowly and began gathering the suspenders together. "Maybe I'll go to the swap meet and sell these to some other ignorant young fucks who got their heads up their asses."

"Get a good price," Splib said, smiling. He turned and began to double-time it toward his friends and the main gate.

FORTY SIX

Apra Harbor
Guam
November, 1963

Twitchell had been pretty quiet during the month Rafer was in the brig. He had not yet chosen his next 'target,' but he was in no hurry. He was savoring Rafer's incarceration too much to think about anything else...exccpt scotch whiskey *and those fucking evaporators!*

Rafer's return changed that. Twitchell once again had his lightning rod, someone who could inflame his resentment, stir up his hatred and compel him to react harshly. Rafer did not disappoint.

Once back aboard, Rafer began to organize the other black sailors. He would hold meetings, 'enlightenments' as he referred to them, and preach black pride and civil rights to them. He had learned a lot from Jeremy Washington in the brig. Jeremy was a righteous brother, a true revolutionary. He knew more about black history than Rafer had ever imagined. Jeremy was an informed expert on another subject, a subject he pounded into Rafer's head for thirty days: black slavery in America. It was a topic Rafer would spend a great deal of time talking about.

It was late afternoon in the middle of the week, and a rain squall had swept in over the mountains and drenched the ship in a short, but heavy rain. Having swabbed up the water on the fantail, Rafer, Andy, Timothy Jefferson and three other black sailors stood in a circle, leaning on the handles of their swabs, laughing and joking with one another. It was only ten minutes before ship's work would be halted and liberty-eligible sailors could leave the ship.

Chief Twitchell came up on deck in clean whites, his shoes shined and the black visor of his hat, along with the gold hash-marks on his sleeve, glimmering in the late afternoon sun. He was determined to be the first off the ship tonight. He had been aboard, working almost round the clock, for seven days. Mr. Almogordo insisted he take some time off, and Chief Twitchell was not going to argue with him.

Seeing the black sailors standing around during working hours, talking like a bunch of goddamned monkeys, infuriated him. He strode over to the quarterdeck and asked the OOD, Chief Lyons, "You pass the word to knock off work, chief?" Twitchell motioned to the black sailors.

Chief Lyons didn't like Twitchell and didn't bother to hide it. "You going ashore, Jasper?" he asked, impatiently.

"Soon's I do your job for you, officer of the deck." He turned and strode over to where Rafer and his group stood. "You nee-groes got nothin' to do?" he demanded. "It ain't time to knock off, yet, so get yer black asses back to work!"

"You the Chief Boatswain's Mate?" Rafer stepped forward and challenged Twitchell.

"Don't wise off to me, *boy*," Twitchell spat.

"Boy?" Rafer exclaimed, eyebrows up, eyes glaring. "Do I look like a boy to you?" He stepped closer and looked down into the sweaty face of Chief Twitchell. "*Boy* swings with Tarzan, man. Don't you know that?"

The other sailors surrounded Twitchell, glaring down at him. "I'm puttin' your asses...all your black asses on report!" Twitchell pushed his way out of the circle of angry black sailors and returned to the quarterdeck. Rafer followed him.

"Go ahead and put us on report, Twitchy," he mocked. "I got the same right under the Uniform Code of Military Justice to put *yo* ass on report, and I got more witnesses than you do!" He smiled back at the others, who were gathered just behind him, covering his back.

Chief Lyons broke it up. "You men get your gear stowed and knock off," he ordered sternly. "Get below and get cleaned up." The black sailors slowly began wandering down the aft ladder to the compartment.

Chief Twitchell saluted Chief Lyons. "Request permission to leave the ship," he said smartly.

Lyons returned the salute. "Granted," he said curtly. Chief Twitchell saluted the flag on the fantail and hurried down the brow to a waiting cab.

"That guy's a real pain in the ass, chief," GM2 Bixby, petty officer of the watch, had come up behind Lyons as the chief quartermaster stood watching the departure of the pugnacious, sweating Twitchell.

"Hmm," the chief seemed to be agreeing. He stood arrow-straight; his hands clasped behind his back, and watched the cab pull away from the pier. Then he turned and walked over to the desk. He picked up the ship's log, thought for a moment, and began writing up the incident between Twitchell and the black sailors. Something about what Twitchell said compelled Chief Lyons to make a record of the events. *"I'll do your job for you,"* he had said.

Twitchell turned in the back seat of the cab and looked back at the Haverfield. *Goddamn niggers,* he thought, *if they can get organized, we can get organized.* He vowed to talk to those on board who shared his contempt for blacks. He would bring them all together for the protection of the white sailors.

Chief Twitchell wasn't alone in his feelings. Many on board the Haverfield shared the chief's contempt for blacks, and it didn't help that the blacks were becoming more aggressive and assertive in their dealings with their shipmates. Rafer spearheaded the movement, vocally and vociferously touting black power and equal rights. Any innocent comment or innuendo was jumped on and held up as an example of racism. Many other sailors, such as R.J., Pea, and Gino among them, rejected being drawn into the fray, and refused to take sides. Andy, though completely supportive of his brother, maintained his relationships with many white shipmates, and always showed up on the focsul for singing practice. The group was getting good. Things settled down into a dulling routine, and the little animosities were put aside. The atmosphere aboard ship became more relaxed, even hopeful.

Then came that terrible Saturday morning.

* * * * *

Lee Piper wasn't a brilliant mathematician, but he could add two and two. The captain of the Brister sat back in his chair, feet propped up on his desk, thinking. Admiral Prescott was leaving for Subic Bay on Friday and Paul Oliver had asked to use the 'Id' on Sunday night. Captain Piper knew there was a political dinner being held on Saturday night, hosted by Lorelei Von Dulm Prescott. Sunday was the first night she'd be available. "Yep," he mumbled to himself. "Still adds up to four."

* * * * *

Anybody black was absent from Saturday's Gamboa working party. Andy had decided to stay aboard with Rafer, and Jefferson and a few of the others had self-consciously declined to come along. Jefferson was fond of Bobby and his parents, and he was disappointed that he couldn't go, but brotherhood was brotherhood. Rafer was asking the brothers to commit to brotherhood, beginning this weekend.

The trailer was in pretty good shape, and most of the repairs needed were of a cosmetic nature, but Mrs. Gamboa was anxious to get the work done so she could host the delayed engagement party for Teresa and Billy. She had willed that the party and official announcement would be held on the following Saturday, the twenty-third, and therefore it must be done.

Mrs. Gamboa stood on the front porch, wiping her hands with a dish towel and watching the sailors interact with her children. Everyone was happy and having a good time. Mrs. G liked that. She was a very happy woman. Even though God decided he needed little Maria with him, Mrs. G had a lot to be happy about. Her oldest daughter was to be married to a man Mrs. G liked very much. Soon she would have grandchildren to spoil and fuss over. She had taken a real liking to these American boys. They felt like family to her, and they treated her like family. She smiled with happy satisfaction. The party would be a wonderful success. She sighed happily and wished that the weekend would hurry up and get there.

But when Saturday finally arrived, Mrs. Gamboa wished the day had never happened.

* * * * *

Lorelei wouldn't join him until fifteen hundred, but Paul wanted to make sure everything was perfect at the cabin, so he got there before noon on Sunday and began tidying up and airing out the place. He brought some fish and some vegetables he was determined to cook later that evening, and he stowed them away in the small refrigerator. He found a bottle of white wine with an obscure label and put it in the fridge to cool.

He checked the bathroom and put out fresh towels. He fluffed up the bed and aired out the bedroom. He paced back and forth between the bathroom in the rear of the cottage and the screened-in front porch. He craned his neck to look as far as he could see down the driveway, before it ended by curving out of sight, disappearing into the green vegetation. He had over two hours before Lorelei was supposed to arrive.

* * * * *

R.J. sat on the starboard flag bag, reading and rereading the course materials for the Signalman Third Class exam. It was a lazy Sunday afternoon, with most of the crew ashore, and the majority of those on board asleep in their racks. R.J. heard steps coming up the ladder from the 02 level and turned to greet Pancho Cortez, the messenger of the watch.

"You got a phone call, hombre," Pancho said, holding his thumb and little finger spread to the side of his face like a telephone receiver. He grinned devilishly and moved his eyebrows up and down. "A chickee, hombre," he said, winking.

R.J. stood and put the book down. Must be Annie. Who else could it be? "Okay," he said to Pancho. "Let's go."

"I told her I would go looking for you, and she said she'll call back at fifteen hundred exactly," Pancho said over his shoulder as he led the way down the ladder. R.J. looked at his watch. Fourteen fifty-five. Five minutes to three. He slowed a little, taking time to light a cigarette and look around the harbor. Everything looked and smelled fresh. They'd had plenty of rain this season, and everything was green, lush and clean smelling.

"C'mon, hombre," Pancho hurried him along. "You don' wanna miss this little Chiquita."

* * * * *

Lorelei was fifteen minutes late when her car wound its way up the driveway and screeched to a stop in front of the 'Id.' Paul, pacing and puffing on his pipe, heard her arrive and stepped quickly into the kitchen to retrieve the wine. He didn't want her to think he was anxiously waiting for her, which, of course, he was. He screwed the corkscrew into the cork and began twisting it, waiting to hear her come in behind him. He heard the screen door shut and soft footsteps coming toward him, tentative, uncertain in an unfamiliar place. He smiled and pulled the cork out of the bottle, making a loud popping sound. Lorelei followed the sound into the kitchen.

I found you," she said, a little breathlessly. "I heard you fire a warning shot." He turned to face her, a glass of wine in each hand. She looked great. She wore a short, wrap-around white skirt with a white, short-sleeved tee shirt covered by a peach colored sweater which she wore draped over her shoulders with the arms tied around her neck. She accepted the wine and looked around the kitchen. "Nice place," she said, admiringly. "I mean, nice little bachelor's pad." She walked around, running her fingertips across the refrigerator, the stove, looking through cabinets filled with glasses, cups and plates. "All the comforts, huh, Captain?"

"All the comforts," he agreed, raising his glass to her before taking a sip. *Damn, she was beautiful!*

She drank down half her wine in one gulp and untied the sweater, pulled it off her shoulders and threw it on the counter. "Where's the bedroom?" she asked. She kicked off her shoes and moved toward him slowly, letting her hips roll just a little. She held the wine glass between her thumb and forefinger, rocking the glass, slowly, gently sloshing the wine around inside it. Her pinkie stuck out and swayed gently in the air like a conductor's baton, and Paul watched it move slowly from side to side, mesmerized by its movement, the way the cobra is mesmerized by the flute.

* * * * *

Mr. Benedetto was OOD and nodded to R.J. when he and Pancho reached the quarterdeck. Before anyone could say anything, the phone rang. Mr. Benedetto looked at the phone, looked at R.J., and nodded. "It's for you, I think," he smiled and walked to the harbor side of the fantail, followed by Pancho. They could keep an eye on the quarterdeck, but they couldn't hear R.J.'s conversation.

"R.J. Davis," he said into the receiver.

"I miss you," the sweet voice said.

"I miss you too."

"We haven't seen each other in a month." She sounded like she was pouting and R.J. could visualize the sorrowful look she took on when she was pouting.

R.J. grinned. "Yeah, since before the typhoon."

"Guess what," she said, almost whispering.

"What?" R.J. asked.

"The Raptor's going to join some minesweeping exercises near Saipan and they'll be gone ten days."

"That's great!" R.J. said loudly, looking around at Mr. Bennedeto and Pancho. They pretended to ignore him. "When they leavin'?"

"This Saturday, the twenty-third. We can get together Saturday night if you want."

"I want," he assured her. "I want. Anytime."

"Anytime?" her tone was teasing.

"Sure, baby. Anytime."

"How about tonight? Gary's got the duty and has to stay aboard. He couldn't get a stand-by. I could meet you somewhere."

R.J.'s mind started racing, trying to think of a place they could meet. Talagi's was too public, and there would be a crowd on Sunday night at the USO beach. Then he hit on it. "Remember that place up in the hills where we first tried to get together?"

"You mean with all the damned mosquitoes?"

"We'll stay in the car, the mosquitoes won't bug us."

He waited while she remained quiet, thinking it over. "Okay," she finally said, "tell me how to get there."

"You gotta car?"

"Yeah, I got Gary's car."

He gave her directions from Talagi's because that was the only way he knew to get to the spot. She promised to meet him there at five o'clock. He thought the timing was perfect, because it would get dark early. He rushed below to shower, shave and dress in clean whites.

Showered, clean-shaven and dressed, R.J. hurried by Pea's bunk and retrieved the key to the Bomb. Pea was half asleep and muttered something about gasoline. R.J. left the ship and walked briskly down the pier toward the main gate. He got the Bomb started and left the base, cruising easily down Highway One toward Talagi's.

The sun was sinking into the western horizon as R.J. easily piloted the Olds around the curving road. He stopped to put a dollar's worth of gas in the Bomb, which gave him a little more than a quarter tank. He was high in the hills, looking for the turnoff and hoping Annie wouldn't be too late. She wouldn't be because she was already there. He turned into the clearing, switching on his headlights because the jungle made it so dark, and spotted a white Ford parked in the back of the clearing, front end pointed out, with Annie behind the wheel.

As he parked the Olds and cut the engine, Annie got out of her car and slid into the passenger seat beside R.J. She kissed him lightly on the lips and he reached out, grabbing a handful of her hair behind her head. He pulled her close, molding his mouth to hers.

"Wow!" she said, kissing him back. "I really missed you."

"Me too, baby," he whispered. "Let's jump in the back." He nodded his head toward the back seat.

"Are you kidding?" she asked, trying to sound offended. "I haven't done it in the back seat of a car since I was in high school."

"No, no," he protested. "We're just gonna stretch out and talk. More room back there," he said.

"Talk?" she said, skeptically. She was enjoying this little game.

"C'mon, baby," he coaxed, pulling the seat back to allow her to crawl into the back. She did and he followed.

"Just talk, right?" she said, a devilish look in her eye.

"Yeah, sure," he answered. "Just talk." He took off his shoes and began pulling his jumper over his head.

"What're you doing?" she asked, frowning at him.

"I talk better without my clothes," he explained, unbuckling his belt.

Annie giggled. "I'll bet you do," she said and started unbuttoning her blouse.

* * * * *

Paul took Lorelei by the hand and led her into the bedroom. The wind was picking up a bit and it rattled the shutters on the window. Paul went over, closed the shutters and latched them, but left the window open. He turned back to the room and gasped. Lorelei had stepped out of her skirt and tee shirt and stood in the doorway with her clothes in her hand. The light behind her outlined her figure with a soft, warm glow. He stood immobilized, staring at the beautiful, glowing vision before him.

"I've had a lot of time to think, Paul," she began as she walked to the bed and sat down. She sipped her wine and set it down on the nightstand. "When I knew I would see you often, it was easy to resist the feelings I had...have for you." Paul sat down on the other side of the bed and she turned to face him. "Now that there's a good chance we'll never meet again..." he put his fingers to her lips. "No, don't stop me," she brushed his hand away gently. "I would hate myself forever if I didn't do something about the way I feel about you," she said.

"You talk too much," he said, and pulled her down on the bed close to him. "And you think too much, too." He kissed her slowly and deeply, much more passionately than he had ever kissed her before. She gasped for breath when he broke the kiss and looked deeply into his eyes.

"I love you," she said. "I knew it as soon as I laid eyes on you. I can't pretend anymore, I..." Paul smothered her words in another deep, breath-stealing kiss.

"Talking," he murmured. "You're still talking."

She wrapped her arms around his neck, ground her mouth against his and moaned softly.

"That's better," he whispered as he reached behind her and unsnapped her bra. "Much better."

* * * * *

Annie pulled her panties up her legs and buttoned her blouse. "My hair must look like a rat's nest," she said, fidgeting with hair and bobby pins.

"You look great," R.J. grinned. He was leaning back in the seat, his legs thrown over the back of the passenger seat. He was naked except for his black Navy socks.

"You better get dressed, R.J.," she warned him. "I gotta be home by ten o'clock 'cause Gary is gonna call."

R.J. fumbled around in his pile of clothes. "Where's my watch?" he asked, then found it on the floor. It was just past seven. "You got time," he said. "C'mere." He reached for her and she let out a yelp and pulled away, giggling.

"Wait till Saturday," she teased. "We'll spend the night together."

"Okay, okay," he relented, pulling on his pants and shaking out his jumper. "But Saturday seems a long way away."

"Bye, R.J.," she kissed him quickly and jumped out of the Olds. She leaned in the back window. "See you Saturday. Bye." She hurried over to the Ford and started it up.

"Bye," R.J. said softly as she drove past him, waving. He dropped his head back on the seat and closed his eyes. *This thing with Annie is getting serious. I'm crazy about her and I know she's* in love with me. She's married. What kind of future do we have? Would she get a divorce and... He snapped awake. "What are you thinking?" he asked himself. He finished dressing quickly and hurried back to the base, driving faster than he should, squealing around corners and roaring down Highway One well ahead of the speed limit. He tried to concentrate on his driving, force Annie from his mind, but it wasn't working.

* * * * *

Lorelei lay curled up next to Paul, her head on his shoulder, her arm draped across his chest. She dozed slightly, listening to his breathing and the steady, strong beating of his heart.

"You awake?" he asked in the darkness.

"Mhmmm," she murmured, cuddling closer and nuzzling his neck with her nose. "I'm awake but I'm not getting up."

"You hungry?"

"I guess I did build up an appetite," she murmured.

He sat up on the edge of the bed and lit his pipe. "I've got some fish and some veggies," he said flatly. "I'm gonna grill all of it and make some rice."

"Sounds wonderful," she said. She sat up and looked around for her tee shirt. She couldn't find it so she put Paul's shirt on and buttoned it halfway. "How does this look on me?" she asked, cocking her head to the side, modeling the shirt.

"Looks a damn sight better on you than it does on me," he said, puffing at his pipe. He got up and fumbled in the closet, bringing out a light robe.

"Are you okay, Paul?" she asked. She felt a distance between them, a coolness that wasn't there before.

"Sure, I'm okay," he said, tying the robe around him. He looked down at her. "Truth is, Lorelei, I'm not okay."

"I knew something was wrong." She reached up and touched his shoulder. "I know what you're feeling," she said soothingly.

"I thought I'd be satisfied," he said, caressing her hair as she looked up at him. "If I could be with you just one time like this." He smiled sadly. "Now I know I'll never be satisfied unless you belong to me, and I also know you aren't about to leave the admiral so I guess this is it and I just have to get used to it."

"Please don't ruin it, Paul," Lorelei said, staring sadly at his frowning face. "Each minute I'm with you is wonderful. This is wonderful. I can't think of it any other way." She took his arm and held it close, kissing his forearm.

"I love you," he said and she smiled and kissed his forearm again. He looked down at her. *Screw it,* he thought. *If this is all we're going to have, then we might as well make the most of it.* "How about that fish?" he asked, and kissed the top of her head.

Over dinner Paul talked about his ship and the tensions developing between the black and white sailors. "I want to think that this is a minor thing which can be worked out before it gets blown out of proportion," he told her between bites of fish, vegetables and rice. "We haven't had any violence or even loud arguments, but the tension is there. It's damn sure there."

"The admiral was talking about the same thing, Paul," she said it as if she were merely reporting to him. "The tension isn't just on your ship. It's happening all over the fleet." She sipped her wine and looked at him. "Want to hear what he has to say about the subject?" she asked. "The admiral, I mean?"

He nodded. "Sure I do," he answered. "Any ideas I can get."

"He gave instructions to his entire command to encourage open discussion, and to give the black servicemen the benefit of the doubt. He has no problem with black pride as long as it doesn't interfere with Navy pride."

"I never got those instructions," Paul said.

"That's because they're being issued tomorrow," she said.

Paul stared at her, an idea creeping into his mind.

"Paul?" she asked, worried. "What's wrong?"

"Navy pride," he said, nodding slowly.

"What about Navy pride?" she asked.

"I think I'll hold a full dress inspection, challenge the men to look their best and to work together. If I only give them a couple days to prepare the ship..."

"They'll have to work together quickly to be ready," she offered.

"Yes," he muttered, puffing at his pipe thoughtfully. "That'll do."

She stepped close to him and opened her shirt. She pulled his head into her bosom and ran her fingers through his hair. "That was a lovely dinner," she whispered. "How about some dessert?" She took his hand and led him into the bedroom. She let the shirt drop to the floor and lay back on the bed. "You can think about your ship later," she said, reaching up for him.

"What ship?" he said, grinning. He tossed his robe on the floor and lay down next to her.

* * * * *

On Wednesday, November 20, 1963 Captain Oliver held a meeting with his department heads and announced a full dress inspection for Saturday, the twenty-third.

"It's obvious to us all that there are tensions developing on board," he said, standing at the head of the green, felt-covered wardroom table, his hands behind his back, his pipe clenched in his teeth. "I think a lot of this is inevitable. We see the strides the civil rights movement is making back in the States." The captain set his pipe in an ashtray and sat down wearily in his seat. "Change is not necessarily a bad thing. Personally, I think the blacks in our country have plenty to be upset about, and those feelings are naturally shared by our black shipmates." Captain Oliver sat forward in his chair, his elbows resting on the table, his hands folded in front. "Let's make this clear: Everyone aboard this ship has a right to an opinion and the right to voice it...within reason. I don't want anything to interfere with the operation of this vessel, under any circumstances. Beyond that, I want everyone to give everyone else a wide berth." He looked around the table at his officers. "Announce the full dress inspection," Captain Oliver said, standing and relighting his pipe. "We'll appeal to their pride. Tell them we want to see who the squared-away divisions are." He grinned through the blue smoke. "Pride versus Pride equals Peace."

Captain Oliver believed if he could keep everyone's attention on the operation of the ship, the pride the men had in doing their jobs right would supercede any hostilities. The full dress inspection on Saturday would remind them of their duties to the Navy, and reinstill their pride in being part of the service. Full dress inspections were always good for morale, even though sailors would bitch and gripe about them. It was a good feeling to fall in on the pier in starched dress whites, shoes shined so bright the sun glared off them, then pass inspection and scramble below to change clothes and go on liberty. The best thing about an inspection is when it's over.

* * * * *

For the next two days leading up to the inspection, the crew busied itself with getting the ship in full-dress inspection mode. Most of the damage caused by Mabel was repaired quickly enough, the majority of the repairs cosmetic. The power plant, unfortunately, was another matter. The reports given Captain Oliver by the engineers did not paint a pretty picture. Pedro Almogordo wanted to take all four engines off line and work on them at once. The repairs would take a couple of weeks. Captain Oliver resisted the suggestion, not liking the idea of having all four engines off line at one time. What would happen if they had to get underway in a hurry? "Do what you can for now," he told the engineering officer.

FORTY SEVEN

Saturday morning R.J. checked the knot on his neckerchief, making certain it covered the 'V' on his jumper and was tied in a perfect square knot. He ran a nylon stocking over his spit-shined shoes and adjusted his white-hat squarely on his head. In every compartment on the ship sailors were dressing for inspection amid a happy, if nervous, hum of activity. He hurried to the fantail where the quarterdeck was set up. Many sailors were already on the pier, gathering in sloppy ranks, waiting for department heads to order them to attention. It was strangely quiet on the fantail. The OOD, Mr. Thompson, had a serious, set look to his face and several sailors were coming back aboard the ship, similar serious looks on their faces, their heads hanging down.

"What's going on?" R.J. asked RM-3 Fred Riley.

"The President got shot," Riley said. "Inspection's cancelled."

"What?" R.J. looked around, confused. He saw Chief Whipple coming quickly up the brow. He looked angry, his head was down and a frown creased his mouth.

"Chief?" R.J. said hesitantly. Whipple stopped and looked up at him.

"Some guy shot President Kennedy," the chief said slowly. "In Dallas. They took him to the hospital."

"Is he alive?" R.J. asked.

"Dunno," the chief said and started up the ladder to the 02 level. "I'll tell you one thing, though," he said, stopping at the top of the ladder and looking down at R.J. "We better get ready because the shit's gonna hit the fan. Those fuckin' Russians aren't gonna get away with this."

"The Russians shot him?" R.J. asked, but the chief had disappeared up the ladder, on his way to his quarters.

R.J. decided to go to the radio shack and get any news first hand. As he passed through the mess decks, he spotted Hawkins sitting in the rear of the galley. He had on his dress whites and his hat was on the back of his head. He sat slumped on a small stool, his head down, a half-smoked cigar in his hand. He heard R.J.'s footsteps, and when he looked up, R.J. could see that he was crying, big tears rolling down his black cheeks.

R.J. hurried up to the radio shack and slid in behind several others crowding into the small space. Murray had tuned in a transceiver and was listening intently as news reports began to filter in.

"...as his motorcade weaved its way through the streets of Dallas. The President and Governor Connolly, along with the first Lady were rushed to Parkland Memorial Hospital where he is being operated on by a team of doctors..."

"He's alive?" someone asked.

"Did she get shot, too?" someone else asked.

Murray held up his hand for quiet and strained to hear the broadcast.

"...Police say several people have been detained as officers spread out throughout the city in a frantic effort to bring to justice the perpetrators of this terrible..."

"We're just getting spotty reports," Murray said quietly. "Nobody knows nothing right now."

"Who shot him, the Russians?" someone asked.

"Don't know," Murray replied, shrugging his shoulders.

"...with a tear in his eye and a long, tired look on his face, Walter Cronkite has just announced to the country that President John Fitzgerald Kennedy is dead."

The crowd in the radio shack grew quiet, stunned by the radio's announcement.

'...took the oath of office on Air Force One en route back to Washington D.C. with the former first lady, Jacqueline Kennedy, and the new first lady, Lady Bird Johnson, looking on."

"Lyndon Johnson is the new president," Murray said, staring at the transceiver.

* * * * *

Captain Oliver stood at the head of the wardroom table and stared silently at the ship's officers gathered there. Everyone was in sharp, dress whites. "Gentlemen," the captain began, "today is a dark day in American history. Our President has been assassinated, and no one is sure who did it." He hung his head and shook it sadly from side to side.

"Should we get underway, sir?" Mr. MacDonald asked.

"We have no orders to that effect, Mac," the captain replied. "In fact, we have no orders at all. So we'll just stay put until we are told to do otherwise."

"What about the engine repairs?" Mr. Almogordo asked.

"We can't take them all off line now, Pete," the captain said. "Who knows when we're going to get the order to get underway. I have to believe we are going to get orders to put to sea, probably take a patrol position. You are going to have to do what you can to keep the power plant operational. At least until we know what we are expected to do."

Pedro Almogordo sighed audibly. He had been looking forward happily to being able to repair all four of the Fairbanks Morse geared diesel engines at once. God knew they needed it. And Mr. Almogordo was tired of juggling the four engines. Two on line, one off, or one on line and three off. They had seldom had all four engines working at once in the year he had been aboard.

Riley knocked on the wardroom door and opened it. The captain motioned him in. Riley made his way to the head of the table and handed the captain a message slip. Captain Oliver took it, receipted for it and dismissed the radioman.

The captain read the message and began passing it around to his officers. "We are to take no action until further instructed," he said.

"What does that mean, skipper?" Mr. MacDonald asked. "We just sit back on our butts and do nothing?"

"That's about it, Mac," the captain replied. "Nothing is going to happen today, so announce liberty for the sections not on duty." He tucked his cap under his arm and dismissed the officers. Captain Oliver then went to his stateroom and kicked off his shoes. He lay back on his bunk and tried to think of ways to prepare his ship for whatever lay ahead. He was certain they would be ordered to sea soon. He was sure the Navy and all other branches of service would soon go on high alert. For now, however, there was nothing to be done, and Paul Oliver was puzzled. If Washington even thought there might be Soviet involvement in the president's assassination, surely they would issue the appropriate alert and bring all forces to readiness. That meant all patrol craft at sea. But the standing orders were to stand by, take no action. *Curious.*

$$* * * * *$$

Chief Twitchell was dressing to go ashore and he was delighted. He despised Kennedy, his family, and all Catholics, so he was not unhappy that John Kennedy got killed. He didn't care who did it or why, though he secretly wished it to be an American who shot him. Kennedy was like a God to black people, Twitchell knew, with all his bullshit civil rights activism. *Wouldn't it be funny if a nigger shot him?* Twitchell grinned at the thought and straightened his tie, smiling smugly at his reflection in the mirror. He wanted to get to the Mocombo Club.

$$* * * * *$$

All of the black sailors who didn't have families on the island stayed aboard that weekend, and for the full thirty days' traditional mourning period for a dead president. As the other Havernauts got ready for liberty, Rafer and the black sailors hung together on the fantail, keeping to themselves, discouraging interruptions and talking in low tones with their heads together.

R.J. came into First Division's compartment, looking around for Pea and Gino. As the only non-deck ape Havernaut aboard, he was the only non-deck ape allowed in the deck force's compartment, except on official business. Everyone else knew to avoid First Division, allowing sleeping dogs to lie.

R.J. looked around curiously. The compartment was quiet, which in itself was highly unusual, but it struck him at once that there were no black sailors in the compartment. He spotted Gino slouching down in front of a mirror, combing his hair. He knew Pea was near. He could smell that disgusting after-shave.

"Where's all the brothers?" R.J. asked, sniffing around for Pea.

Gino pointed up at the overhead. "Up there," he said, turning back to the mirror. "They're havin' a pow-wow up on the fantail."

"They up there talkin' that racist shit," Pea said, coming in from the head and depositing his shaving kit on his bunk. "They all pissed 'cause Kennedy got shot. Rafer said it's gotta be some white racist who did it." He splashed on more after-shave. R.J. and Gino wrinkled up their noses and moved away.

"Things're getting' worse, m'man," Gino said, nodding his head slowly. "It's gettin' to be like we two different crews. One white and one black."

R.J. looked up thoughtfully at the overhead which was the fantail's deck. "I'm sorry he got shot, too," he said quietly. "He seemed like good people to me."

"Rafer says Kennedy got shot so's Johnson could be president," Pea said, straightening his hat and checking his neckerchief knot. "He says Johnson is a known bigot and hates all blacks." Pea turned around and looked at the other two. "He also said that all people from Texas were racists." Pea shrugged. "Let's go get some beer. Maybe later we'll get lucky and run into the girls."

"I don't think so, little buddy," Gino said. "Nobody's gettin' underway today. We might not see the girls for a long, long time."

Pea looked at Gino thoughtfully, as if trying to decide if he was right or not. "I guess that's true..." He shrugged. "Well, let's go get some beer, then."

They went up to the fantail, and as Gino and Pea made their way down the brow, R.J. walked over to where the blacks were gathered, heads down, talking in hushed tones.

"Hey, Rafer!" R.J. called. "We're goin' to the Mocombo Club. You guys wanna go with us?"

They turned to look at R.J., most of them scowling. Rafer pushed his way out of the crowd. He frowned and shook his head at R.J. "We stayin' aboard," Rafer said seriously. "You and the other chucks can go and party if you want, but we stayin' here in honor of President Kennedy."

"We ain't goin' to party, Rafer," R.J. replied, smiling pleasantly. "We want to pay our respects different, that's all."

Rafer stepped closer to R.J. and looked him in the eye. "You got an honest heart, R.J.," he said softly. "But you white, and you don't have any idea how black people feel today."

"I think I do," R.J. protested.

Rafer stared at him. He had anger in his eyes, but R.J. knew the anger wasn't directed at him. Rafer slowly shook his head and walked away, joining the waiting group of black sailors.

R.J. shrugged and turned to the quarterdeck. He saluted the OOD and the flag and joined Pea and Gino on the pier.

"What's a chuck?" R.J. asked.

"That's what the bloods call white dudes," Gino explained. "Charlie, Chuck, Charles, you know, white boys."

The shuttle bus arrived and they climbed aboard. The bus was about half filled with quiet, solemn looking sailors. As R.J. made his way to the rear seat, he made eye contact with many of the sailors on the bus. They all looked shocked. R.J. decided to remain silent, let the mood fill the bus and leave him alone with his thoughts.

* * * * *

Paul Oliver sat on his bunk, elbows on his knees, rubbing his hands together and staring at the deck. There was nothing he could do, and he felt helpless and inadequate. Reports were filtering in that the Dallas police had apprehended the assassin and were interrogating him. *One man?* Captain Oliver thought. *How did one man get close enough to the President to kill him?* It didn't make sense. Something else had to be going on, he reasoned. If there were only one man, one assassin, maybe the Soviets trained him. They were the acknowledged experts in political intrigue. If they didn't do it, who?

He shook his head as if to clear it and stood, putting on his hat. There was no reason for him to stay aboard. He decided to go to the officers' club. Maybe he would run into some friends and he could talk this out. What he really wanted was to run into Lorelei and talk it out with her. She understood him better than anyone else. The truth was, he only wanted to be with her.

He couldn't get Sunday evening out of his mind. He had been surprised at the way Lorelei had thrown herself into their lovemaking. She was a generous and thoughtful lover, gently aggressive and passive at the same time. It seemed that once she made up her mind not to fight the feelings she had for him, she welcomed his love eagerly, unhesitatingly, with no reservations and no inhibitions. His entire being ached for her.

As Captain Oliver approached the quarterdeck, the OOD, Chief Risk, was setting the telephone receiver down on the deck. He turned and seemed startled to see the captain standing there.

"Oh, excuse me sir," Chief Risk said. He motioned to the phone. "There's a call for you, sir. It's Captain Piper from the Brister."

Captain Oliver nodded and picked up the phone. "Lee?"

"Can you believe this shit?" Captain Piper's voice sounded angry, tense.

"I was just going up to the club," Paul said. "I gave my crew liberty since nothing is going to happen anytime soon."

"So did I," Lee replied. "I'll pick you up in ten minutes and we'll go to the club together."

"I'll be waiting." Captain Oliver glumly set the receiver down and turned to Chief Risk. "I'm leaving the ship," he said, saluting smartly.

"Aye, aye, sir," Chief Risk returned the salute and opened the log, making a notation indicating the time the captain left the ship.

"Haverfield departing!"

* * * * *

Lorelei paced the front porch and chain-smoked cigarettes. The admiral was in Subic Bay, establishing his command there. She hadn't spoken to him since he'd left over a week ago, and she was certain he had his hands full with the news of the president's death.

The president was dead! What was happening to the country? Did this mean a war was coming? Were the Soviets involved in the assassination? Would they have the guts to pull off something like this?

She paced and smoked. She wanted desperately to see Paul, but she felt a strong sense of responsibility to the admiral in this crisis. She knew she had to stay home and wait to hear from him. He might need her help, or he might just need to talk. Either way, she was going to be there for him.

She sat down on the porch swing and leaned back, closing her eyes. The image of Paul Oliver came rushing into her mind, and she yearned to see him, to be with him if only for a short time. She glowed inwardly at the memories of their lovemaking. *How could something that felt so right, so perfect, be wrong?* They had merged their bodies and their souls that night, and she wanted more than anything to go away with him, leave everything behind and just go. But Quentin came first. That was her duty, her responsibility, and she would see it through, even if in her heart she knew she was married to the wrong man.

* * * * *

The Mocombo Club was unusually quiet and solemn. It was not yet noon but the club was almost full. Sailors from all home-ported ships, plus many from the Naval base sat glumly at their tables, speaking softly and sipping beers.

R.J. sat at a table with Gino, Pea, Tanner and Pancho Cortez. They sipped beers and watched the scene around them. None of them had seen the Mocombo Club so crowded on a Saturday afternoon.

Chief Twitchell sat at the bar with Crawford and a couple of other engineering department sailors. A half-full bottle of scotch sat on the bar in front of him, and he was already drunk and becoming obnoxious, having arrived early at the Club.

"Here's to the Russkie sumbitch that got that fuckin' Kennedy!" he roared, holding his glass in the air.

Most everyone in the bar glared at the chief with disapproval, but a few stools away, Carter Green, a black first class boatswain's mate from the Brister, looked up from his drink and saw the reflection of Chief Twitchell in the mirror behind the bar. That fool again!

"Ignore him, Carter," another black sailor from the Brister said. "He's an asshole, just ignore him."

"The President of the United States gets shot and that asshole wants to celebrate?" Green clenched his teeth and stared at his drink. "Not while I'm here," he said bitterly.

"Getting rid of that Catholic fuck is the best thing that's happened to this country in years," Twitchell crowed, gulping down one shot of scotch and pouring another. "If it was up to him, the niggers and Catholics would be running our country!"

"That's it!" Green pushed past his friend, who was trying to restrain him, and strode over to where Twitchell and his buddies were sitting.

"Why don't you shut the fuck up?" he demanded of the fat chief.

Twitchell turned in his seat and faced the angry boatswain's mate. Green was a head taller and much slimmer than Twitchell, and he glared at the chief with unconcealed malice in his eyes.

"What's the matter, Sambo?" the chief spat. "Your nigger-lovin' hero get his head blown off?" Crawford and the other engineers laughed and gathered around Twitchell.

"You got a big mouth, Twitchell," Green said, moving closer. "Maybe

I'll close it for you." He stared into Twitchell's bleary eyes, his nose only an inch from Twitchell's face.

Green's friend came up behind him. "Take it easy, Carter," he soothed. "Let it go. Everyone's tense today."

Green relaxed a bit and seemed to gather himself. He was angry, but he knew the smart thing to do was walk away before things got out of control. He turned to leave, but Twitchell was not going to let it go.

"At least you coons can't say you never had a nigger president," the fat chief smirked.

Carter Green turned quickly and threw an overhand right. The punch caught Twitchell square on his left eye and he fell back against the bar. The stool shot out from under him, clattering on the floor. He steadied himself on the bar and picked up the bottle of scotch. He swung it at Green's head and caught him against his right ear. The bottle shattered, sending shards of glass everywhere, and Green backed up. He put a hand to his ear and examined it. It was bloody.

"You son-of-a-bitch!" Green lunged at Twitchell but was restrained by his shipmates. Crawford and a few others restrained Twitchell. Every sailor in the club was on his feet, bristling for a fight.

The bartender came running around the end of the bar, waving a baseball bat. "I called the shore patrol. They'll be here in a few minutes, so if youse don't wanna go in the wagon, youse'll get outta here!"

Crawford led Chief Twitchell out the door. Green and his friends returned to their stools and sat quietly. Green downed his drink and looked at the bartender. "Sorry," he said quietly. "We'll leave if you want."

"Not your fault," the bartender said. "That Twitchell is a real asshole. It was only a matter of time before somebody took a swing at him."

The club became quiet again as everyone went back to concentrating on their drinking. R.J. stood and stretched, looking around the club.

"It was great seeing Twitchy get punched in the mouth, wasn't it?" he said.

"Yeah, but man, he sure went up side that guy's head with that bottle!" Tanner said, shaking his head. "I'm just glad it didn't turn into a rumble between us and the Brister." He sipped his beer and lit a cigarette. "I wouldn't wanna fight the Brister over an asshole like that."

"Me neither," Pea said. "Fuck 'im!" He stood and finished his beer, looking around the quiet, crowded club. "Everybody's all up tight about the president." He looked toward the bar. "I'm gonna get another beer."

* * * * *

Several officers lined the bar at the Officer's Club as Lee Piper and Paul Oliver pushed through the swinging doors and deposited their hats on the front table. Standing near the door, looking around at the eerily quiet room, Paul was struck by the silence. The club where so many good natured, boisterous parties had taken place seemed more like a mausoleum than a social club.

Captain Piper commandeered a table near the side windows while

Captain Oliver went to the bar and ordered two vodka tonics which he carried back to the table. He sat down heavily in his chair and raised his glass to his friend.

"God bless John Kennedy," he said solemnly.

"Aye," Lee Piper nodded, "God bless JFK."

They drank in silence for a while and Lee got up and refreshed their drinks. Paul sat with his back to the front door, staring out the window at the neatly manicured garden and the jungle vegetation beyond the grounds. Even the plants and flowers seemed deflated today, hanging limp in the wet air. Rain had come and gone in squalls all morning, leaving a slick, wet film over everything.

Lee came back to the table and set down the drinks. Paul looked up, his thoughts interrupted, and accepted the fresh drink.

"Thanks," he said, sipping the cocktail. "That's good." He sighed, leaning back in his chair.

"Paul," Lee Piper said quietly, staring over Paul's shoulder toward the front door. Paul turned to look. Lorelei Prescott and four other officers' wives came in the front door and seated themselves at a table near the bar. A white-jacketed waiter hurried over and took their drink orders.

Lorelei had scanned the room when she first came in, hoping that Paul was there. She spotted him sitting with Lee Piper but did not acknowledge him as she continued to look around. Admiral Prescott's replacement had not yet arrived on Guam, so until he did, Lorelei Von Dulm Prescott represented the current command authority in all social functions. She did not disappoint. She was gracious and attentive as officers lined up to pay their respects and express their sorrow over the death of the president.

The crowd around the women's table thinned and Lee looked over at his friend. "Guess we should pay our respects, huh?" he asked. Paul nodded absently.

They approached her table as she was talking to a young lieutenant j.g. from the Raptor. "The admiral is greatly saddened too," she said in her angelic voice. "That's why we're here." She indicated the other women. "The admiral thinks it's important that we show solidarity during these sad times." She looked over the lieutenant's shoulder and made eye contact with Paul. For the briefest of moments, her violet eyes flashed warmly, and she quickly returned her attention to the lieutenant.

Lee stepped up and took Lorelei's hand. "Thank you for coming here, Mrs. Prescott," he said. "It means a great deal to see you ladies here today." He smiled at the other women at the table. "It means a lot to all of us."

"You are gracious to say so, Captain Piper," she said sincerely.

Lee moved back and watched as Paul took Lorelei's hand. "Thank you for coming, Mrs. Prescott. I trust the admiral is well," he said, feeling himself sink into the soft violet of her eyes.

"He's well, but he's angry about the assassination," she said. "I spoke to him for an hour this morning, and he expressed his regrets that he isn't here with us."

"It's a sad day for Americans," Paul stated flatly.

"It is indeed, Captain Oliver," she replied just as flatly.

"Well," Paul said softly, "it's a pleasure to see you." He shook her hand gently and turned to join Lee Piper.

"Feel better?" Lee asked as they made their way back to their table.

"No," Paul shook his head. "If anything, I feel worse."

"It'll pass, my friend. It'll pass."

Paul arranged his chair so his back was to the window and he could glimpse Lorelei out of the corner of his eye. *This isn't going to pass anytime soon*, he thought.

After what was considered an appropriate amount of time, the ladies stood and began making their way to the door. Lorelei Prescott was moving from table to table, shaking hands and smiling, speaking sympathetically to each officer, saying her goodbyes.

She reached Paul and Lee's table and shook hands with them. "Good day, gentlemen," she said in her sweet voice. "I'm going to go home and take a long, hot bath." She turned and joined the other women at the door. They waved goodbye at the door and vanished.

Paul sat down and opened his hand, inspecting the note that Lorelei had surreptitiously passed him when she shook his hand. *Call me!* He slipped the note into his pocket and picked up his drink.

Lee saw him read the note, but didn't say anything, preferring to concentrate on his vodka tonic. He hadn't seen her pass him the note, and he was sure no one else in the club had seen it. But no one else in the club had seen the light in Paul Oliver's eyes when he read the note. It could only mean one thing. She wanted to see him.

"I think I'll head back to the ship," Lee said, finishing his drink. "Maybe get engrossed in a novel." He looked around the club. "This place is depressing, anyway." He looked at Paul. "Coming?" he asked, but he already knew the answer.

"I'll stick around for a while," Paul replied, staring into his drink. "I'll catch a cab back, you go ahead."

"See you later, buddy," Lee patted him on the shoulder. "Be careful."

Paul smiled. "I will," he said, knowing it was far too late for that.

FORTY EIGHT

Pea deftly piloted the Bomb along Highway One toward Agana. The windows were all down and the ocean breeze cooled the three sailors as they stared out the window. Tanner and Pancho had decided to stay at the club and get falling-down drunk when Pea suggested they go for a ride.

R.J. gazed mindlessly out the window. The streets and roads were almost deserted. All shops along the highway were closed and the Bomb only passed a few other cars on the road.

"What a bummer!" Gino exclaimed. "I never seen the Mocombo Club so quiet. Shit, everybody lookin' like they were ready to bust out crying."

"Let's go up to the trailer," R.J. suggested absently. "I wanna see how the Gamboas are doing."

Pea turned right just before they reached Talagi's and shifted down into second for the climb up to the trailer. The big Oldsmobile's engine complained as it climbed, and Pea shifted to third as they crested a hill. They cruised easily up the driveway of the Gamboas' home and pulled to a stop next to the Haverfield's new pickup truck. It was not actually new, but it was a few years newer than the old one. Billy Lopez complained constantly about the new truck. He had broken in the old one over a period of several months, and the old truck had seemed like an extension of Billy's personality. The new truck was okay, but it was an *automatic*, for Chrissakes, and Billy couldn't get the same rubber out of first gear. Still, the new truck was not nearly as dented and worn as the old one, and Teresa liked it so Billy got used to it.

Mr. Gamboa sat on the front porch, sipping out of a bottle of San Miguel and staring out at the jungle, absently puffing away at his pipe, which had gone out. He brightened a little when he saw the Bomb coming up the driveway and stood, smiling sadly as R.J., Gino and Pea got out of the car and came up the stairs to the porch. Mr. G. hugged each one of them and pointed to the other chairs on the porch.

"Take a load off your feet," he said. "Hey Bobby!" he called into the trailer. "We got guests! Bring some beers!"

A subdued Bobby Gamboa came out of the trailer with four beers and handed one to his father and one to each of his friends.

"Good to see you boys," he said, tipping his bottle to them in salute. "Not a good day for America, huh?" He gulped down half his beer and wiped his mouth with the back of his hand. The others nodded, sipped their beer and sat down heavily on the porch, ignoring the chairs.

"Seems like lots of shit's happening back home," R.J. said, shaking his head slowly, frustration in his voice. "People marching all over the place, blacks and whites at each other's throats. Now the president gets killed."

Mr. Gamboa stared at the jungle, alone in his thoughts. He seemed older somehow, more gray in his hair. He moved a little slower and more deliberately. It seemed little Maria's death had taken something out of him. He stood, drank down his beer and accepted another from Bobby. He sat back down on the porch and leaned against the trailer, sipping his beer.

"The thing about America," he said, looking intently at the sailors on the porch, "is that its great strength is in its people." He took a deep breath and let it out slowly. "The American people are strong and resilient," he said quietly. "They can overcome anything because they pull together."

"But Kennedy was a hero to blacks," R.J. said. "All that suspicion and resentment is gonna boil over. Just look at what's happening on our ship."

"You gotta believe, R.J., that America will bounce back even stronger than before," Mr. G said, putting his hand on R.J.'s shoulder and squeezing it. "Growing pains is what the country is experiencing. As soon as blacks become mainstream, like every other ethnic group that came to America, they will become part of the fabric that is this great nation. Then their contributions will grow and also become part of American life."

R.J., Gino and Pea stared at Mr. Gamboa. They had never heard him talk like this. They were a little surprised at the depth of his wisdom.

"That's the reason the Japanese lost the war, you know," Mr. G said, staring off into the jungle. "No diversity in their culture. No room to grow individually. Everyone subscribing to the same ancient traditions; individualism discouraged and abandoned for the sake of the empire." He stood and walked to the edge of the porch, still staring into the jungle. "It's like what they did on Saipan," he said, his voice not much more than a whisper.

"The Japanese had a large civilian population on Saipan," he began slowly, as if he were trying to find the words to tell the story. The Havernauts leaned forward, listening intently. "And, of course, they had about thirty thousand soldiers on the island. The Americans invaded in June, 1944. They had underestimated the strength of the Jap army and they got caught up in a vicious battle. Lots of men died, but they slowly overwhelmed the Japs and pushed them toward the north end of the island. The Japs refused to surrender. They hid out in caves with the civilian population during the air and Naval bombing, and convinced the civilians that American soldiers were vicious beasts who would rape them, slaughter them and eat their children." He relit his pipe and continued. "The civilians didn't know any better, they only knew what they were told, so they tried to escape the invading Americans. They ran and scrambled in a panic up the steep slopes of the island's northern point. They climbed up the cliffs near Mount Marpi on the far north end of the island and threw themselves into the rocky surf below. Some were dragged to the cliffs and thrown off by Japanese soldiers. Many others, convinced that the American soldiers would do all sorts of terrible things to them, threw themselves off the cliffs. Entire families perished that day." He stopped and took a drink of beer. His eyes were tearing up and he breathed deeply in an attempt to get a hold of himself.

"Want to know how the families died?" he asked quietly. Heads bobbed up and down silently. "They would line up the children, youngest first, on the edge of the cliffs. The older children would push the younger ones off the cliff and step up to be pushed off themselves. The father then threw the mother off and jumped after her." Mr. Gamboa shook his head sadly. "Thousands killed themselves by jumping off Suicide Cliff and Banzai Cliff. The Americans were offshore in boats, pleading with the people through bullhorns not to jump. They jumped anyway. The sea was littered with bodies for days. They have monuments up there now."

"How...how could they do that?" R.J. asked, stunned by the story.

"Because they didn't know much about the outside world," he explained. "They only knew what they were told." He turned to face his young audience. "The day I heard about it, I made myself a promise," he said. "I promised I would learn as much as I could about this world and the people who live in it. Knowledge is the key to life, fellas. If those poor people knew anything about America they wouldn't have killed themselves. That's why I read so much. I never wanted to be ignorant."

R.J. leaned back and studied Mr. Gamboa. He dressed, spoke and lived simply, but he was obviously not a simple man. R.J. doubted that anyone who knew him would consider him ignorant.

"I had cousins who died that day," Mr. G continued. "Hell, everyone on Guam had cousins who died that day."

The porch became silent as Mr. Gamboa finished his story. The sailors stared down at the wooden deck, trying to imagine what made so many people jump off the cliffs to their deaths.

"That could never happen in America," Mr. G continued. "Americans are stubbornly independent and self-reliant. They are problem solvers, solution seekers and blessed with the knowledge that they can do anything they put their minds to."

Billy and Teresa were standing in the doorway, arm in arm, listening and nodding agreement. Mrs. Gamboa sat at the kitchen table. She, too, was listening between sobs of sorrow for John F. Kennedy.

"Every time America has been challenged with a problem, her people have solved it...together. Now everyone is nervous about the civil rights movement. Hell, I've heard people say the blacks are going to rise up and kill whites in their sleep." He grunted and drank down his beer. "That's just plain bullshit." He accepted another beer from his son. "Blacks just want their share of the American dream, and they will get it eventually. When they do, and mark my words, fellas, they will, you'll see black culture become as much a part of American life as hamburgers and hot dogs. They will add to the greatness of America, not diminish it."

R.J. sat back and pondered Mr. G's words. He was right. That was it of course, the solution to the racial divide: Working together, becoming one people. After all, his own Irish forefathers came to America as poor, uneducated indentured servants. And while that situation could not compare with the brutality and hopelessness of slavery, the Irish had to struggle a hundred years for acceptance. There was still a lot of anti-Irish sentiment in New England. Those feelings died hard. He could remember his great grandfather telling him stories of signs posted on the lawns of well-to-do people's homes: Irish and Dogs Stay off the Grass! As other ethnic races came to America, they started on the bottom of the economic ladder, taking jobs no one else wanted, working their way up to the point where they could claim their piece of the dream, passing on their work ethic and love of country to their children. That's what made America so strong, R.J. decided. *We are truly a melting pot of peoples from all over the world. Don't the blacks have the same right to the same opportunity?* Of course they do. To R.J., black people were just like Irish people. They faced the same societal problems and challenges. There was one glaring difference; the Irish came to America because they wanted a better life. Most blacks came because they were forced to.

"Y'know, Mr. G," R.J. said, "you should write a book."

"Naw," Mr. Gamboa replied, "I don't have the patience, but," he looked intently at R.J. "You could write one."

R.J. grinned at the thought. "I always wanted to write a novel," he admitted. "But what would I write about?"

"Write about us, and your ship and your friends," he said. "You boys are living an adventure and you don't even know it. You're a living part of American history. Write it down, R.J. I know you can do it."

R.J. sat and sipped his beer and felt better. He decided he would talk to Rafer and the other blacks on board ship. He would make them see that it wasn't a matter of black versus white. They were all Americans, after all. R.J. smiled. Things had become clearer, more in focus for him, sitting and listening to a wise and experienced Mr. G. Surely, his black shipmates could see a future where there was no distinction made of skin color, where everyone pulled together for the greater good of the country. He knew, of course, it would be a difficult, uphill battle.

He just didn't know how difficult it would prove to be.

* * * * *

Paul waited for an hour before he placed the call. He slid into the end phone booth in the Officers' Club and pulled the door closed behind him, splashing himself with light from the automatic bulb in the top of the booth. He dialed the number slowly, ready to hang up if one of the domestic servants answered.

"Hello?" Lorelei answered in her sweet, musical voice.

"I was afraid the maid would answer and I'd have to hang up," he admitted.

"I gave the entire staff the weekend off," she said sweetly. "When can you get here?"

"Up there?" he asked incredulously. Surely she didn't mean to suggest he sneak into the admiral's residence.

"Yes, Paul, up here. Why not?" She sounded as if she were pouting.

"Well," he looked around the club. It was very crowded, yet uncommonly subdued for a Saturday afternoon. Did he dare enter the admiral's house with the intent of screwing the admiral's wife? That seemed to him to be a disaster waiting to happen, yet he was drawn to her lovely voice and he wanted her with every fiber of his being. He knew he couldn't resist for long. The fresh memories of her naked in bed next to him clouded his judgment and distorted his reason.

"Don't you want to see me, Paul?"

Why did women do that? he wondered. *They always try to put you back on your heels, force you into a corner where the*re is only one possible right answer. "Of course I want to see you, but don't you think my coming up there is a little dangerous?"

She was quiet and he waited, listening to the soft sound of her breathing. "It'll be dark soon," she said finally. "I'll meet you at the cottage at seven o'clock."

"Seven o'clock," he agreed and hung up. He stepped out of the phone booth and looked around. Now, how was he going to get to the Id?

He called Lee Piper to make sure he wasn't using the cottage. "Be careful," was all Lee said, and Paul went back into the bar. He had an hour to kill.

* * * * *

R.J. drove back to the base. Pea and Gino sat silently in the front seat. No one said a word until they had secured the Bomb in the parking lot and started walking down the pier toward the ship. Gino broke the silence.

"I never knew that story...you know, about Saipan."

"Sad story," R.J. said.

"Fuckin' weird," Pea agreed.

They walked on in silence, their heads down, filled with images of Japanese bodies floating in the water around Marpi Point. They reached the brow of the Haverfield and climbed slowly on board. Lieutenant (j.g.) Anton was OOD, Snively was the petty officer of the watch and Cotton was the messenger. They were playing three-handed hearts on the desk and almost didn't notice the three sailors returning.

"Shit!" Cotton jumped when he saw the trio come aboard. "You guys scared the crap out of me, sneaking up on us like that!" He adjusted his duty belt and squared his hat on his head. "Man, it's spooky tonight. I never seen it so quiet."

"Sad day," R.J. said. He saluted Mr. Anton and headed for the signal bridge. Pea and Gino followed. The quarterdeck watch returned to their card game.

Up on the signal bridge the three friends sat on the rung of the flag bag and lit cigarettes. Pea lifted his jumper and produced three bottles of San Miguel beer. "Mr. G gimme these to drink on the way back, but I saved 'em," he declared proudly. "Only problem is, we got no church key."

"No problem," Gino said. He took a bottle of beer and set it on the edge of the flag bag, its lip just under the bottle's cap. Gino held the bottle in one hand and slapped down on the lid with the other. The cap popped off and the bottle foamed over. Gino caught it in his mouth before it spilled on the deck.

"Cool," Pea said and tried to open his. He hit it several times but the cap wouldn't budge.

Gino took it, gave Pea a dirty look and popped the cap off. He handed Pea his beer and popped the cap off of R.J.'s. "It's a matter of leverage," he explained.

"How'd you learn to do that?" Pea asked, looking at his beer bottle.

"Learned it in Brooklyn," Gino explained. He sat back down on the rung and stared at his beer.

"Mr. G makes a lot of sense," R.J. said quietly.

"Sure does," Pea agreed.

"We gotta quit separating ourselves from each other," R.J. said.

"We ain't separating ourselves," Gino replied. "Rafer and his troops are separating themselves from the rest of us."

"Then we gotta find a way to get together," R.J. said flatly. "One crew, remember? A hundred and fifty guys working as one, just like Mr. Mac always says."

"Tell that to Twitchy," Pea said bitterly. "He's the biggest problem we got on this ship. If he wasn't here, things wouldn't be this bad."

"We could bump him off," Gino offered, only half-kidding.

Pea and R.J. looked at each other seriously. "Wouldn't be a bad idea," R.J. said, smiling.

"We get out to sea," Gino offered, "and wait till that fat fuck comes out on deck drunk, you know, stumbling around like he does. We drop his ass over the side and let the sharks have him."

"It would be an accident," Pea said, becoming enthusiastic about the idea. "Everybody knows he gets drunk and stumbles around. Nobody would even question it."

QMC Tom Lyons had been working in the chart house when he heard voices on the signal bridge. He began heading that way. They were laughing about something, but Chief Lyons couldn't make out what they were saying.

The trio didn't see Chief Lyons until he was standing next to them. They stood up sheepishly, trying to conceal the beer bottles.

"You men drinking on board ship?" he demanded.

Pea looked at Gino who looked at R.J. "We're drinking a beer to President Kennedy," R.J. said.

Chief Lyons took the bottle out of R.J.'s hand and looked at the label. "San Miguel, huh?" he asked and took a long swallow. "Not bad." He handed the bottle back to R.J. "Drink them down, men," he ordered. "And throw the bottles in the drink. I'm going to forget I saw this because of the tragedy of the day, but don't ever let me catch you drinking aboard ship again." He walked down the aft ladder and across the 02 level.

R.J. watched him go and turned to the others. "You think he heard us bitching about Twitchy?" he asked.

"Naw," Gino finished his beer and threw the bottle into the harbor. "He woulda said somethin'."

"Chief Lyons is cool," Pea decided and the others nodded agreement.

Pea and R.J. finished their beers and threw the bottles into the water. They stood leaning on the railing, watching the beer bottles bob around and slowly fill with water until they sank. R.J. wondered how many beer bottles were resting on the bottom of Apra Harbor.

"I'm tired, man," R.J. said. "I'm gonna hit the rack." He waved to Pea and Gino and made his way below to operation division's compartment.

* * * * *

Lorelei sat on the couch on the cottage's enclosed porch, a bed sheet wrapped around her naked body. Paul came out of the kitchen, also dressed toga-style in a bed sheet, holding two glasses of red wine. He handed one to Lorelei and sat down next to her. "Hungry?" he asked.

She shook her head and stared off into the jungle. Their lovemaking had become frantic as they rolled and tossed around in bed. There was a sense of urgency to it, as if they somehow thought they could erase the day from their minds through their lovemaking. Now, in the soft evening air, they sat quietly, side by side in their bed sheets, each wondering what the other was thinking. Lorelei was the first to speak.

"Why did they kill Kennedy, Paul?" She looked up at him and her violet eyes were moist and bright.

"I don't know."

"Do you think it was the Russians?"

"I don't know."

"Well, tell me something you do know," she teased, cuddling closer to him.

"I know I love you. I know you're leaving. What else do I have to know?" He sounded a little bitter and she searched his face intently, trying to gauge his mood.

"For as long as it lasts, remember, Paul?"

"Yeah," he sighed. "I remember. It's been a bad day, you know?"

"Hold me, Paul," she whispered. "Hold me and never let me go. Let's just stay up here and never go back."

He smiled sadly and put his arm around her. He did love her, and he knew it couldn't last. She was married to an admiral. She would never give that up. He realized that. He also belonged to another. His ship, Lady Haverfield, sat in the harbor and beckoned to him the way the whale had beckoned to Ahab. As long as it lasts, he thought, and pulled her close to him.

FORTY NINE

Rafer was angry. It didn't seem to him that the crew mourned President Kennedy as much as Rafer and his friends did. John Kennedy was a righteous white man who understood the black struggle in America, and had dedicated himself to righting the wrongs heaped on American blacks for over two centuries.

He often told the other blacks on board, "Lincoln freed the slaves, but unfortunately, a lot of crackers didn't get the word. We still bein' treated like second class citizens and some whites don't even hold us in that low regard. Northern whites, southern whites, western whites, eastern whites are all alike. They are white! Don't trust anybody who is white! They are the enemy, the foe, or ofay if you wanna say it in pig-latin."

His rhetoric became more strident, more forceful, when talking about the struggle. His anger flared at the slightest perceived insult. He was pugnacious and confrontational, forcing most whites aboard ship to avoid him. R.J. did not. He took every opportunity to talk with Rafer and the other blacks. Smiling and friendly, R.J. countered every one of Rafer's arguments with the same point: Togetherness was how the struggle would be overcome. Separating the races was akin to going back to slavery. Blacks would ostracize themselves from the rest of society and nothing would get better.

"Like it or not, Rafer," he reasoned one day when he found himself alone on the focsul with the angry Rafer, "the power is with the white people. You can't just take over."

"Why can't we?" Rafer challenged.

"Because whites greatly outnumber blacks and control the entire country. You don't have a chance of overpowering the whole country."

"Then we take as many out as we can!"

"That won't get equality for black children in the future," R.J. countered. "It'll piss people off and turn them against you."

"Then what we supposed to do? Get back on our knees and kiss whitey's ass?"

"Work together with the white power structure to get blacks where they belong," R.J. said pleasantly.

"You got a honest heart, R.J.," Rafer said slowly. "You one of the few guys on this ship that tries to understand, but you can't never understand."

"Why can't I?"

"Because you got no idea of what it means to be black."

R.J. looked into Rafer's eyes. "I don't, huh? Lemme tell you something, Rafer. I grew up in the Lipan Street Projects in North Denver. I was one of the few white guys in the projects, and I had to prove myself every day just walking to school. I got my ass kicked plenty, and I kicked some ass. After awhile, I can't say I was accepted, more like tolerated."

The look on Rafer's face became softer. "It still ain't the same," he said softly. "You ain't black."

"Maybe not, but in the Lipan Street Projects I was the minority...I was the nigger." A sad look came over R.J.'s face. "The blacks and Mexicans didn't want to hang around with me because I was white, and the whites didn't want to hang around with me because I was a projects kid. Hell, nobody liked me. They didn't like me for the same reason: I was white."

Rafer chewed his lip and thought it over. "Ain't a whole lot of guys like you, though," he said. "Most white people just don't give a shit."

"Then you gotta change their minds," R.J. reasoned. "It's gonna take a long time, Rafer. It ain't gonna happen overnight."

"You sound jus' like my daddy," Rafer flared. "We don't have a lotta time. We want our rights now. We don't wanna wait another two hundred years before we can stand next to whitey!"

"You can stand next to me anytime you want," R.J. said soothingly.

"Stand next to the nigger from North Denver?" Rafer asked, his eyebrows arched, a slow smile spreading across his face.

"Yeah, somethin' like that."

"Later, R.J.," Rafer said as he spotted several blacks assembling in the chow line for lunch. He walked slowly and deliberately down the focsul and joined his friends. Some of them looked over at R.J. questioningly, but Rafer ignored them.

Inside the mess decks the blacks commandeered several booths and scowled at any white sailor who tried to sit in one of them. The whites sat with whites while the blacks sat with other blacks.

Thanksgiving came but there was little to be thankful for, as far as R.J. was concerned. Little Maria had died, the typhoon had wreaked havoc on the ship, he had fallen in love with a married woman, the crew was splitting itself in two, and the collective schizophrenia was widening the gulf between black and white sailors.

Hawkins cooked up a traditional Thanksgiving feast. Roast turkey, dressing, mashed potatoes, yams, cranberries and pumpkin pies were spread out all over the galley. As each sailor came through the line, Hawkins would greet him with a wide smile and, "Happy Thanksgiving!"

The blacks sat on the port side of the mess decks, the whites to starboard. They talked among their individual groups, but said very little to each other.

Pea, Billy, R.J. and Gino sat together in one of the rear booths and appraised the scene. "This is bullshit!" Gino said, gesturing toward the two groups. "It's Thanksgiving, for crap's sake!"

Timothy Jefferson and two other blacks finished eating and carried their trays to the scullery. As they passed the four whites in the rear booth, Pea smiled up to them. They ignored him.

"Thanksgiving!" Pea spat. "Big fuckin' deal!"

After Thanksgiving and into the Christmas season, tensions between the two groups continued to smolder. During the coming New Year, those tensions would simmer, come to a boil, and eventually, inevitably, bubble over.

FIFTY

A week after Thanksgiving P.T. Tanner received his orders. He was leaving the Haverfield and going to the Helena, a heavy cruiser based in Bremerton, Washington.

The entire deck force, including blacks, gathered on the fantail to say goodbye to one of the most popular men aboard the Haverfield. Tanner was a born leader, respected by everyone aboard ship for his skill as a boatswain's mate and for his cheerful personality. He walked through the knot of Deck Apes toward the brow and accepted congratulations and handshakes as he went. Pea marched behind him, proudly carrying Tanner's seabag on his shoulder. On the pier, at the foot of the brow, Charming Billy held open the door to the New Pickup, as it was now known. Tanner shook hands with R.J. and winked at him. "Don't forget to watch the free end of the line," he grinned. R.J. nodded and grinned back.

Pea threw the seabag into the bed and stepped back. He came to attention and saluted smartly. The men of First Division all saluted from the fantail, and Tanner, eyes tearing up, returned the salute and climbed into the New Pickup. He looked over at Charming Billy, still grinning. "Hit it, Billy," he said.

Billy smiled charmingly and put the automatic transmission into neutral. He gunned the engine loudly and dropped the gear shift into drive. The New Pickup shot forward, laying rubber down the pier. The sailors on the fantail cheered as the New Pickup fishtailcd down the pier toward the main gate. When the truck disappeared, the sailors separated again into black and white groups and wandered back to work.

R.J., Gino and Pea stood at the lifeline, watching the truck drive toward the main gate.

"There goes a helluva sailor," R.J. said.

"Best sailor I ever seen," Pea agreed.

"We gotta find a new baritone," Gino mused.

That night R.J. got a phone call. He knew who was calling. Annie wanted to tell him that the Raptor was leaving the next morning, Friday, December 6, for the ten-day exercises it had missed because of the typhoon.

"God, I missed you," she breathed into the phone. "I haven't seen you for such a long time."

"My grandmother used to say that absence makes the heart grow fonder," R.J. teased.

"It's not only my heart," she giggled. "The rest of me has grown fonder, too."

"Where's Gary?" he asked, wondering why she was taking the chance of calling him.

"He's working," she replied. "He'll be home soon. I just couldn't wait to call."

"I'm glad you did. Can we get together this weekend?" he asked hopefully.

"How about tomorrow night?" she asked. "USO Beach, seven o'clock?"

"We'll be there." He hung up and went below to tell Gino and Pea.

The next morning R.J. stood on the signal bridge and watched the Raptor get underway from their berth a mile aft of the Haverfield. The minesweeper pivoted from the pier and backed into the channel. Once pointed toward the outer harbor, she picked up speed, churning a wake in the calm harbor.

"Have a safe trip," R.J. muttered to himself as he watched the Raptor through a pair of binoculars. "God speed."

* * * * *

Pea and Carol followed Gino and Betty upstairs as soon as they had sneaked in the back door. Annie and R.J. sat on the couch. The apartment was dark and quiet, except for the kitchen radio playing soft and low.

R.J. put his arm around her, and Annie moved next to him, looking up into his eyes. The noises of physical contact came wafting through the ceiling and Annie looked up and giggled.

"Didn't waste any time, did they?" R.J. said, glancing up at the ceiling.

"So why are we wasting time?" she asked and pulled her blouse up over her head. She wasn't wearing a bra and her breasts bounced and swaycd, the dark nipples erect.

"Hellooo there!" R.J. exclaimed, burying his face between her breasts. Annie pulled his head into her bosom with both hands and leaned back, lifting up her hips so he could help her wriggle out of her jeans. In a few moments they were both naked and writhing around on the couch.

Later, the three couples, clad only in their underwear, sat on the living room floor, smoking cigarettes and drinking beers. It was getting late, just after midnight, and they all were getting tired. R.J. shook himself to stay awake. The last thing they needed was to fall asleep and not wake up until

341

the next morning. They had to remain awake so they could slither out in the darkness when no one was around. They had timed the shore patrol and knew they had about forty-five minutes between rounds, which was plenty of time to sneak out of Naval housing. They had to remain awake.

"Hey," R.J. said. "Know what today is?"

"What's today?" Pea asked, his head lay in Carol's lap and she played with his hair.

"Pearl Harbor day," R.J. answered. "Twenty-two years ago Mr. Haverfield died on the Arizona."

"Mr. Haverfield?" Betty asked. "You mean like the name of your ship?"

"Right," Gino replied. "James Wallace Haverfield was one of the men who died when the Japs attacked Pearl Harbor."

"Wow," Carol said.

"Yeah," R.J. agreed. "Wow."

"Can you imagine what that was like?" Annie said softly. "People dropping bombs on you and your ship blowing up?"

R.J. looked at Gino and Pea. "I can imagine it," he said. He got up and began pulling on his trousers. "We gotta go before we fall asleep," he warned.

Gino and Pea began dressing, and the girls sat on the couch, smoking cigarettes and watching the sailors struggle into their jumpers.

The harbor was eerily quiet when the Impala convertible deposited the sailors a safe distance away from the ship. After kissing the girls goodbye and promising to get together again the next night, Gino, Pea and R.J. walked the hundred or so yards to the ship. R.J. stopped at the brow and saluted the ship. "That's for Mr. Haverfield," he stated firmly. Gino and Pea followed suit, stopping at the brow and saluting the ship, then went up the brow to the quarterdeck and saluted the OOD, Ensign Thompson.

"Goodnight, men," Ensign Thompson said, returning the salute.

"Goodnight, sir," they answered in unison.

R.J. lay awake in his bunk, thinking of Annie. *Damn*, he thought, *I keep forgetting to ask her for a picture*. He opened his book on Poe and turned to 'The Raven.' After reading and re-reading the first few verses, he fell asleep with the book open on his chest and dreamt of a big black bird perched on a white statue. It opened its beak to squawk, but made no sound.

* * * * *

The weather cooled a bit in December. It was still hot and humid, but not nearly as hot as summer gets, and the crew seemed to relax a little, though there existed an unmistakable undercurrent of distrust and tension among the men.

Chief Twitchell was kept busy working in engineering, and had little time to create mischief. Mr. Almogordo was tired of working piecemeal on the engines one at a time. He wanted to pull all four engines off-line, tear them down and re-build them all at once. It would take three weeks of intensive, round-the-clock work to finish the engine overhaul. Mr. Almogordo and the rest of the engineers took their case to the captain.

Captain Oliver, Mr. Almogordo, and Chiefs Risk and Twitchell met in the wardroom to review and analyze the ship's overhaul. The captain didn't like having all engines off line at one time, but the engineers convinced him it would be the fastest, safest and most efficient way of doing the job. They were moored safely, and despite the frequent rainstorms, the weather wasn't too bad for the season.

"When we're done with her, Captain," Pedro Almogordo said, "She'll run like brand new." The rest of the engineers voiced agreement.

"I'm glad to hear that, Pete," the captain said, frowning at the engineering reports in his hand. "And I hope your schedule holds, considering the season."

"We'll get her done quickly, Captain," Pete replied. "We won't get caught here."

What was not said aloud, but understood by everyone around the table, was that they were still in the middle of the typhoon season. Getting caught in port, tied to a buoy in the harbor instead of putting to sea and riding out the typhoon was more than dangerous; it was downright humiliating. At sea, a ship can change course and speed, keep her bow to the wind and have a fighting chance against the storm. Any ship unable to get underway is towed to a mooring buoy in the middle of the harbor, defenseless, serving as a punching bag for the storm.

The captain and the engineers kept their fingers crossed and worked quickly, feverishly, through day and night. No one wanted to be trapped in port during a typhoon.

Unfortunately, that's exactly what happened. The typhoon hit just before Christmas, and it was only by God's good graces that Typhoon Wilhelmina wasn't nearly as harsh as that vicious shrew, Mabel.

* * * * *

While the engines were off line and the engineering department worked feverishly on the overhaul, Captain Oliver met with the exec in the captain's cabin. One of Hawkins' cooks brought up a tray of hot coffee and toast with marmalade and set it down on the desk.

"Thank you," Captain Oliver said pleasantly as the Filipino cook smiled and left the cabin. "Have some coffee, Ed." The captain began pouring steaming coffee into two Navy mugs.

"Thanks, sir." The exec took the cup and blew on it to cool the hot liquid. He sipped it and made a face. "Ol' Hawkins is one of the best cooks in the fleet, and God knows he loves his galley, but the man can't make a decent cup of coffee."

"Now you sound like MacDonald," the captain grinned. "I wanted to talk to you about something, Ed," the captain said, sipping his coffee and tamping tobacco into the bowl of his pipe.

"Yessir?"

"The crew has been working very hard on this overhaul, especially the engineering department." He lit his pipe with a kitchen match and blew the smoke toward the overhead.

"Yessir, that's true," the exec agreed.

"The tensions have eased between the black sailors and white sailors, wouldn't you agree?"

"Yessir," the exec acknowledged. "Everybody's been too busy to get into trouble."

"That's my point exactly, Ed." The captain stood and began pacing the small compartment, waving his pipe as he talked. "A busy crew is a happy crew. They can't concentrate on their differences if they are busy working together for the benefit of the ship."

"Agreed, Captain."

"Then let's make certain they keep busy." Captain Oliver sat down and sipped his coffee. It didn't taste all that bad to him. "We're going out on patrol for three weeks beginning January tenth. Pedro assures me the engines will be back on line and running perfectly by then." He unrolled a chart on his desk and put his coffee cup and ashtray on the edges to keep the chart from rolling back up. "We're going to survey the Palau Islands as far south as Helen's Reef," he explained, pointing his finger at the chart. The exec bent over the chart and nodded as the captain continued. "We'll be gone three weeks, and during that time we are going to run every drill I can think of. We'll do ASW drills, surface action drills, man overboard drills, fire drills and anything else in the book." The captain smiled at the exec. "We'll work the crew hard and as a result, they'll be a well-trained machine, working together, taking pride in their performance and in their ship." He sat back down and studied his executive officer, who was staring at the chart. "Well, Ed, what do you think?"

The exec nodded thoughtfully and raised the coffee cup to his lips. Thinking better of it, he scowled and set the cup down on the tray. "It's a sound plan, Captain," he said, running his finger down the chart. "This is a good crew. They work together well, and I have one suggestion."

The captain nodded. "Go ahead, Ed," he said pleasantly.

"Let's conduct all those drills, but let's make them time drills. We'll challenge the crew to beat their time on each drill. That'll give them even more incentive to work together."

The captain smiled. "Perfect. Let's start plotting our course changes and scheduling the drills." His pipe went out and he re-lit it with a kitchen match. "And let's keep the drill schedule between us and department heads only. I want everyone to be on his toes. We'll run the drills at odd hours, so they don't know what to expect. I don't want this patrol to be routine or business as usual. Questions?"

The exec shook his head.

"Fill in the department heads once you've worked out the schedule, Ed," the captain said. "Let me know when everyone's up to speed."

"Aye, sir." The exec put on his cap and left the captain's cabin. He was excited about the patrol and looked forward to setting up a schedule for the drills. The captain had it right: A busy crew is a happy crew.

Captain Oliver sat smoking his pipe and looking at the chart. As usual, Lorelei invaded his thinking and he sat back in his chair, remembering their last night together. Christmas was coming, and with it, the typical loneliness all servicemen experience when spending the holiday season away from home. Paul Oliver decided to make the holiday as pleasant as possible for the crew. They would obtain a Christmas tree and deck the halls of the mess decks with holiday decorations. He would have Hawkins bake pies and cookies and maybe he could get the crew to sing carols. They couldn't be home, but he could damn sure bring a little bit of home to them. He smiled. Maybe it would snow.

* * * * *

Andy Sample joined the singing group for practice on the focsul, and he brought with him a surprise. Timothy Jefferson came with him, and asked to audition for the vacant baritone spot. Gino was delighted and began teaching Jefferson the songs the group had perfected. Jefferson turned out to be a very good baritone, and he picked up the songs quickly.

R.J. leaned on the lifeline, his fishing line in the water, and smiled as the group sang one song after another. It was not lost on anyone that the focsul group was now half white and half black. Several sailors lounged around the focsul, as was the custom when the group got together. With Jefferson's addition to the group, more black sailors showed up for the evening concerts, and by the end of the week, blacks and whites were laughing together, smoking together, joking together and even singing along. Even Rafer showed up, snapping his fingers to the beat and clowning around. Gino's group had spanned the gulf between the whites and blacks, and though it was never said aloud, the evenings on the focsul did more to cement black and white unity than any program the officers could develop.

One evening, the group had just finished an up-beat and snappy rendition of *At The Hop*, when Riley came down from the radio shack and asked the group to sing *I Left My Heart In San Francisco*. His request was greeted by a chorus of catcalls and boos. Rafer and R.J. threatened to throw him over the side to the delight and encouragement of the crowd. Everyone was laughing and enjoying themselves. The mood was light and friendly, and the tensions between the two groups eased considerably. The unwritten rule was that the evening was for music. No animosities were allowed to surface, and the politics of the times were not mentioned. The atmosphere on the ship was improving, and would have continued to improve if it weren't for the interference of Chief Twitchell.

FIFTY ONE

On Saturday evening, December 21st, Chief Whipple and BM1 Queen stood on the starboard side of the 02 level, watching Haverfield sailors climb aboard the shuttle bus headed to the temporary barracks on base. Dark clouds gathered over the mountains and the air was eerily still, as though all life had been sucked out of it. The barometer was dropping rapidly, and everyone knew what that meant: Another typhoon was hurtling toward Guam from the southeast.

A sea-going tug made its way slowly across the harbor toward the Haverfield. With her engines off line, the ship was practically helpless and had to be towed to the middle of the harbor and moored to a buoy. The captain had ordered all but a skeleton crew ashore, billeting them at the temp barracks until the storm passed. All engineering personnel would stay aboard, and Chief Whipple had asked for volunteers among the deck force to remain and help secure the ship to the buoy. Everyone in First Division volunteered, including all the black sailors. Volunteers from other departments remained to secure their areas and stand by to render assistance. R.J. insisted on staying, so Anselmi happily joined the men going to the base.

"Damn," big Queen muttered. "All we needed was another week and we woulda been able to put to sea."

Chief Whipple nodded absently and sipped his coffee. "You ever been moored out during a bad storm?" he asked the big boatswain's mate.

"Nope, this'll be my first."

"Well, my friend," the chief warned, "it ain't gonna be fun."

*****

Captain Oliver hung up the phone on the quarterdeck and nodded to Mr. MacDonald, the OOD. "I'm afraid you're going to have to stand a double watch, Mac," he said. "Soon as we cast off, shift to the bridge."

"Aye, sir." MacDonald saluted the captain and turned to his quarterdeck watch, which consisted of Lester as P.O and Pancho as messenger. "Let's get the desk and phone secured," he instructed. "When shore power is disengaged, we're only gonna have battery power, and no one knows how long it will last." He looked up at the sky. "Let's hope this isn't another bad one."

Deck force sailors worked quickly to batten down all hatches and tie down anything that could become a missile during the storm. R.J. secured the signal bridge and hurried down to the fantail to help out the deck force.

"Whatchoo doin' down here, skivvy waver?" Sonny Metzner chided R.J. good naturedly. "How come you ain't goin' up to the barracks with the rest of the pussies?"

"I figured you knuckle heads would need some supervision," R.J. kidded back, helping Jefferson single up number four line.

"He just comin' back to his roots," Pea called across the deck. "He ain't really a flag-fag, he got the deck force in his blood."

"Sometimes I think he got some slave blood in his veins," Andy laughed as he tightened up turnbuckles on the lifelines. "He like to work hard in the hot sun. Maybe he come from a long line of cotton pickers."

"Yeah," Rafer chimed in. "Them freckles on his face are the same color as my pretty golden ass."

"And they seem to be getting' bigger," Jefferson observed. "He gonna be one of us in a coupla years."

Rafer finished dogging down the deck hatch and stood, wiping his hands on his dungarees. "He one of us already," he said seriously. "The deck crew all grinned and nodded in agreement. R.J. was one of them, no matter his color. The growing feeling in the deck force was that your color didn't matter. They were the best deck crew in the fleet, and they worked together, side by side. There existed only one color in First Division, and it was called Havernaut.

* * * * *

Captain Oliver closed the door of his cabin and sat down heavily at his desk, scanning the weather reports. This storm was smaller than Mabel, thank God, and probably wouldn't last more than a couple of days. The batteries could hold out for a few days, as long as they used electricity sparingly. He leaned back in his chair and thought of Lorelei.

Their last encounter at the 'Id' had been strained, their lovemaking desperate and tense, yet strangely wonderful. As they lay side by side in the dark, bodies glistening with perspiration, Lorelei began to cry.

"Please don't cry," he said.

"I can't help it," she sobbed. "I'm leaving for Subic Bay in a few weeks and we'll probably never see each other again."

"That's not necessarily true," he said soothingly, but he knew he was kidding himself. He already felt her distancing herself from him, becoming quieter, more private, as if she were trying to wrap herself in a protective shell. She was already in Subic Bay in her mind, and he could feel her pulling away. *As long as it lasts*, he thought. *It won't last much longer.*

They lay together silently, each immersed in private thoughts, he concentrating on his ship and she planning her life in Subic Bay. When they had first become lovers, they would talk for hours after making love. Now they lay next to each other in the same bed, but might as well have been in different parts of the world. Soon they would be. They both realized it was coming to an end.

* * * * *

Dark settled over the harbor as the Haverfield tied up to the buoy. R.J. stood on the port wing bridge and watched the Brister and the Raptor reach the breakwater and begin bobbing about in the choppy sea. The Raptor had been in port the previous week, so R.J. had not seen Annie. Now her husband was going back out to sea, but he still couldn't see her.

The captain came out on the wing and joined him. R.J. snapped to attention and saluted. "Evening, Captain," he said.

"Davis," the captain nodded. "Staying with the ship, I see."

"Yessir," R.J. replied.

"Good man," the captain lit his pipe and puffed it until the bowl glowed red. "The good news is this typhoon is a small one."

"That last one was a bitch, sir," R.J. grinned.

"It was, indeed," the captain agreed, puffing away at his pipe. "You've got a signal," he said, pointing to the breakwater. R.J. turned and saw the flashing light coming from the Brister. He pulled the canvas cover off his signal light and answered with *dah-dit-dah*, or 'K' for 'go ahead.'

As the Brister signaled the message, R.J. held the light open and read it aloud to the captain.

"From C.O. Brister, to C.O. Haverfield. Good luck. Sorry you can't be with us. Hope you can get to the Id after the storm." R.J. receipted for the message and looked up at the captain. "What does he mean, sir?"

The captain smiled sadly. "Send him this," he said. "Thanks, but it looks like we might have our hands full. God speed."

R.J. sent the message and the Brister receipted for it by sending *dit-dah-dit*, or 'R' for receipt. The Brister and Raptor faded into the horizon as the rain began to fall and the wind picked up. The Haverfield rocked slowly in the harbor.

"Carry on," the captain said, and returned to his cabin. R.J. put the cover back on the signal light and went below to the mess decks. Christmas decorations hung on the walls and colored lights were strung around the area, but had been turned off to save electricity. R.J. nodded to Hawkins, who was busy stowing away his pots and pans. There would only be sandwiches and cold cuts to eat, but Hawkins would keep the coffee urn full and hot. R.J. drew a cup of coffee and smiled at the small Christmas tree sitting in the corner. Someone had hung a sign on the tree. SANTA IS A FINK!

R.J. chuckled and returned to the signal bridge. He put on foul weather gear and checked the covers on the flag bags and signal lights. He wanted to watch Typhoon Wilhelmina arrive.

* * * * *

Wilhelmina made landfall late that night, and by Sunday morning the rain and wind were whipping around the helpless DER as she rolled and bobbed at her mooring. For two days the typhoon lashed Guam with torrential rains and winds. It became obvious to the skeleton crew aboard ship that this typhoon was much milder than Mabel had been.

Chief Whipple organized a pinochle tournament to help pass the time, and the teams gathered in the mess decks to play cards and drink coffee. Spirits were high, and the crew laughed and joked about the typhoon. There was no racial segregation. The blacks mingled freely with the whites and the skeleton crew developed a sense of camaraderie during the storm. Gino and his group met often in First Division's compartment and rehearsed Christmas carols, much to the delight of the deck crew.

On Christmas Eve it was apparent that Wilhelmina had done her worst and was moving on. The harbor remained choppy, and the ship continued to bob and roll, but more mildly, signaling the end of the storm.

At 2000 Gino and The Deck Apes, as their group had been named, mustered on the bridge. Big Queen unrolled some masking tape, taped down the button on the 1-MC intercom system and blew 'attention' on his bosun's pipe. He put his mouth close to the microphone and announced, "Now hear this! The deck force of the USS Haverfield wishes everyone aboard a very Merry Christmas. The following is our Christmas present to you."

The group began with *'Deck the Halls'*, sung in an upbeat and happy manner. They sang *'Jingle Bells'*, *'We Three Kings'*, *'We Wish You a Merry*

Christmas', 'Joy to the World' and 'God Rest Ye Merry Gentlemen'. When they sang 'I'll be Home for Christmas' most of the crew dabbed at tears. When they finished with 'Silent Night' there wasn't a dry eye on board, including the captain, who stood on the wing bridge watching the group perform and smiling proudly.

As the group filed down the ladder, headed to the mess decks, Chief Whipple and big Queen stood at the bottom of the ladder, shaking the hands of the group and patting them on the back.

The captain stepped out on the wing bridge just before midnight and looked up at the sky. The storm was moving on, leaving scattered clouds milling about in its wake. The captain sighed. He wanted Christmas to be special for the crew, and it would have been if not for the typhoon. Still, when he considered the relative mildness of the storm and the beautiful songs from the Deck Apes, all in all it wasn't bad. It could have been a hell of a lot worse.

The next day was Christmas and the storm had passed. The sea-going tug came out to return the Haverfield to her berth at the pier. When they arrived, the shuttle bus was waiting on the dock, and sailors who had weathered the storm in the temporary barracks were lined up on the pier, waving and whistling as the ship tied up.

Mr. Winters was the first to come up the brow. He saluted Ensign Benedetto and grinned widely.

"We have a little Christmas gift for you," Mr. Winters beamed, and pointed toward the shuttle bus. Sailors had returned to the bus and were filing out, carrying trays of food, plates, cups, and silverware. They had brought Christmas dinner for the skeleton crew who stayed with the ship.

Hawkins set everything up on the fantail so everyone could eat Christmas dinner together, and the crew gathered around with their plates, sitting on whatever they could find; vents, torpedo tubes, hatches and a few scattered chairs.

The crew was in a festive mood. They laughed and joked, shared stories of Christmas back home and passed plates of food around. The captain stood on the 02 level and watched the party. He had been a little disappointed that he couldn't give the crew the Christmas he had wanted to, but everything had turned out wonderfully, mainly because the men who stayed ashore looked out for the skeleton crew who stayed aboard. The captain was proud of his men, and hurried down the ladder to join them.

"Attention on deck!" Someone yelled as the captain reached the fantail. The crew rose to their feet as one, smiling a greeting to their skipper.

"As you were, men," the captain said. "Any turkey left?"

Several plates were offered to him, and he took one, nodding thanks. He accepted a cup of coffee and held it up in the air. "Merry Christmas," he said. He was answered by a chorus of "Merry Christmas," and he sat on the deck and began eating with the crew.

Hardly noticed was the absence of Chief Twitchell. The fat engineer was in his bunk, sweating off a drunk, squirming and rolling about like a land-locked walrus. No one on the fantail missed him.

* * * * *

R.J. got up before reveille as was his habit, and stood near the stern, drinking coffee and watching the last remnants of Wilhelmina break up over the mountains. The once dark, angry clouds were lightening, giving way to white, puffy cumulus that drifted over the peaks and caught the morning sun on their underbellies, reflecting pastel shades of pink and orange and yellow. *If there is a heaven,* R.J. thought, *this is what it looks like.*

During these solitary moments alone on the fantail, R.J. often considered how much his life had changed. It had been nine months since he had arrived on Guam, and he felt like a different person. He had grown, he knew, and had learned a great deal about the world. Nine months of gestation had produced a more mature young man; his defiant attitude had mellowed, he had made good friends and suddenly he didn't want to leave. For the first time since he had joined the Navy, he felt he truly belonged to something good. The Straps had been a loosely organized group whose only purpose was to dance and have fun. The Havernauts were a serious, dedicated group of men who relied on one another, depended on one another, and each knew how he fit into the scheme of things. The training had bonded them, black, white and brown, to the point where they functioned perfectly as a unit. Pride, R.J. decided, pride and training were the difference.

R.J. felt someone's presence, and when he looked over, he saw it was Rafer. The big man nodded to him and looked up at the fleeting clouds.

"You got the watch?" R.J. asked.

"Naw, just wanna see what's so interesting early in the morning," Rafer replied. He grinned. "So I figured I'd come up here and stand next to the nigger from North Denver."

R.J. chuckled and sipped his coffee. "Nice Christmas, huh?" he muttered.

"Yeah, that was fine," Rafer replied. He leaned on the lifeline and looked around the harbor. "I got a letter from my Daddy," he began. "Christmas was always a big deal at our church and our house. Reading his letter about Christmas and peace and love...he made me think a little." Rafer smiled at a private memory. "I think you right, R.J. I mean, about how to change things, you know, the right way." He turned and looked into R.J.'s eyes. "We gotta look ahead, far ahead if we want to take our place in American society. It's gonna take a long time, and we gotta stick with it." He nodded emphatically, and in that moment R.J. thought he saw a significant change in Rafer. He seemed to quiet down, relax a bit. His face was more thoughtful, more withdrawn. He was retreating into himself, into his faith.

"Your Daddy sounds like a very smart man, Rafer."

"He is," Rafer nodded. "He shorely is." He pointed up to the clouds. "They sure are pretty." He patted his face with both hands. "Not as pretty as me, though."

R.J. grinned at him. "You're so pretty, Rafer, I'm surprised you ain't been the playmate of the month."

"One these days they gonna have a Playboy Magazine for women, and when they do, I'll be the first centerfold." He shook his head and grinned. "Damn, I'm pretty."

The 1-MC began barking. "Reveille, reveille, all hands heave out and trice up. The smoking lamp is lit in all authorized spaces, now, reveille!"

"Know what I'm gonna do?" R.J. turned and faced Rafer, who shook his head. "I'm gonna write about this."

"What?"

"I'm gonna write a book about this whole thing, this ship, these people, all the things we been through. I'm gonna write a novel."

Rafer smiled and nodded. "You probably the only one who could do it," he said softly. "You got an honest heart and I know you'll tell it right." He clasped R.J. on the shoulder affectionately. "You write it, R.J.," he said sincerely.

They stood there looking at each other for a moment, and a special feeling passed between them.

"I'm gonna get me some chow," Rafer decided, and headed through the port hatch. "Later, R.J."

"Later," R.J. replied. He looked up again at the clouds and sighed.

FIFTY TWO

Chief Twitchell leaned over the sink in the chief's head and splashed cold water on his sweating face. He stared into the mirror. His undershirt was stained with perspiration and his puffy face looked back at him through bloodshot eyes. The remnants of the previous night's scotch oozed from his pores and he smelled stale and putrid, even to himself. He turned on the shower and climbed in, underwear and all. As he stood under the cold spray, he went over the plan he had formulated while the ship was tied up, riding out the typhoon. *The niggers were getting out of control, and white boys like that punk Davis were hanging around with them, laughing and joking like a bunch of jive-ass junior flips.* There had to be a reckoning. He counted on his fingers the number of men aboard who would be on his side. *Twenty. Mostly good southern boys who could be depended on.* He then counted the niggers and came up with seventeen, not counting what he considered good niggers, men like Hawkins who kept their mouths shut and didn't forget their place.

The New Year was coming. 1964 would be different. *This civil rights crap had to be fought, or white people would be forced to mingle with the dirt people. Before you knew it, blacks would be marrying whites and then what would happen to the Caucasian race? Nigger blood couldn't be allowed to mix with pure white blood, or all of society would crumble. Didn't people understand that?*

The chief finished his shower and wrung out his underwear. As he toweled off in the small head he grinned to himself. Nineteen sixty-four would be different, all right, if Jasper Twitchell had anything to say about it.

* * * * *

351

"Let's take a romantic ride in the hills like we used to, Paul." Lorelei's musical voice sounded good over the phone, and Captain Oliver was anxious to see her. It was Thursday night and the Brister was due back in port the next morning.

"Pick me up at the USO beach about seven," he said, hoping his voice didn't give away how anxious he was. "We'll drive up to that little spot where we can watch the moon rise up over the ocean. It's going to be full in a couple of days."

"That sounds wonderful," she cooed. "Then maybe we can go back to the cabin. Would you like to do that?"

"That is a rhetorical question, right?" he asked.

* * * * *

R.J., Gino and Pea sat at an outside table in front of Talagi's and sipped Pepsis, looking around, hoping to spot the black 1959 Impala. They hadn't heard from the girls, and the Raptor was due back in the morning.

"I tol' you to get a fuckin' phone number," Pea scolded R.J.

"She wouldn't gimme her number," R.J. protested. "How come you didn't get a number?"

"I figured you'd get a number," Pea replied petulantly. "Shit, you the big romantic operator." He turned his attention to Gino. "How come you didn't get no number, you skinny fuck?" he chided.

"Here's your number, short stuff," Gino replied, his middle finger sticking up in the air.

"Well," Pea demanded. "We gonna sit here all night jerkin' each other off?" He looked at his watch. "It's already twenty-two hundred."

"Screw it," Gino stood and flipped his cigarette in a long arc across the parking lot. It crashed in a burst of sparks and sat smoldering on the gravel. "Let's split. Ain't nothin' happening tonight."

"You got that right," R.J. agreed. "The Raptor'll be back tomorrow and we're going on patrol in a couple of weeks. We ain't likely to see the girls until the end of next month."

They piled into the Bomb and headed down Highway One toward the base, arguing over who was supposed to get whose phone number.

* * * * *

The Mocombo Club was crowded with sailors on New Year's Eve when R.J., Gino, Pea and Cotton made their way through the front doors and found seats at a table with Sonny Metzner and Lester.

"Big crowd tonight," Sonny drawled. "Hope nobody starts any shit."

"Let 'em," Pea snarled. "I'm just in the fuckin' mood."

"What's wrong with him?" Lester asked, grinning at Pea. "He on the rag?"

"He ain't had his shots yet," R.J. warned. "So don't try to pet him." Pea snarled again.

Gino and Cotton shouldered their way through the crowd at the bar and returned with six cans of beer. "Gotta fight your way to the bar," Cotton said, sipping his beer and wiping off his mouth on his jumper sleeve. "I ain't never seen it so damn crowded." He looked around. "The brothers better hurry or they won't have anywhere to sit."

Almost every table was filled with drinking sailors. Tiny and his girls sat off to one side, listening patiently to the music coming from the juke box. They were due to go on at eight o'clock, and the musicians were setting up on the band stand. Colorful crepe paper streamers had been stapled all over the walls and hung from the ceiling, tied together with multi-colored balloons. A large, hand-lettered banner on the wall behind the bandstand announced, "Happy New Year! 1964!" The juke box played Elvis' *Are You Lonesome Tonight?*

Rafer and Andy, followed by Jefferson and three other black sailors, stepped in the front door and stood looking around for a table. R.J. spotted them from across the dance floor and waved them over. Gino pulled over one of the few remaining tables and Pea commandeered six extra chairs.

"If we sit here, do we gotta listen to that Elvis Presley shit?" Jefferson asked, grinning at the others.

"What you got against the King?" Pea asked.

"You mean other than he a white boy?" Andy asked, his eyebrows arched comically.

"You gotta admit, though," Gino offered. "At least he *tryin'* to be black."

"Where you dudes been?" R.J. asked. "You supposed to be here at nineteen hundred. We barely held on to that table."

"We on colored people's time, m'man," Andy explained. He pulled out a chair and sat down. Everyone at the table laughed loudly. Across the room, Chief Twitchell sat with several of his redneck friends and looked disgustedly at the black and white sailors sitting and laughing together.

"See," he sneered. "That's what I'm talkin' 'bout. They mixin' the races already."

"Was a time in Mississippi a nigger'd get hisself hung for sittin' with white boys," Crawford drawled.

"Same thing in Texas," another redneck agreed. "We still don't play that shit in the Lone Star State."

"Problem is," Crawford went on, "niggers today don't know they goddamn place."

Chief Twitchell nodded and downed a shot of scotch, his fifth in the last half-hour. "Some white boys don't know they place, neither," he observed, sneering across the room at the Havernauts. "They just white niggers to me."

"Ain't nothin' worse than white trash," Crawford drawled. "And that asshole, Metzner. What the hell's he doin' over there? He from Oklahoma. Oughta know better."

"Oklahoma ain't really a southern state," Twitchell explained. "That's where all the white trash comes from anyway."

"Fuckin' nigger lovers," Tex said absently. The others nodded and drank.

* * * * *

"I wonder if they miss us at the Officers' Club," Lorelei said as she snuggled naked in Paul's arms. He smiled and pulled her closer. Almost all the Naval officers and their wives or dates were attending the New Year's Eve party at the Officers' Club. He would probably not be missed, but Lorelei certainly would. Lee Piper had given him use of the car and the cottage. Lee and his officers from the Brister were having a private New Year's party aboard ship.

"Hungry?" he asked.

"Not anymore," she giggled, nuzzling his neck.

"I mean for food," he scolded. "I got a couple of great steaks from our cook."

"Oh, that," she giggled again. "Sure. You want to fire up the hibachi?"

"What time is it?" he asked.

She rolled over and picked up his watch from the nightstand. The covers fell away and he looked appreciatively at her bare bottom. "Nice ass," he said.

"Thanks, you lecherous man." She pulled the covers back up and peered at the watch. "It's almost ten."

"You mean twenty-two hundred, don't you?" he mocked her. "How long you been in the Navy?"

"Now you sound like Quentin," she scolded, and immediately wished she hadn't said it.

Paul got up and pulled on a pair of pajama bottoms. "I'll light the grill," he said softly.

Lorelei sat in bed, holding the covers up to her neck and shaking her head slowly. The romantic mood had been broken by her comment about her husband, but she was determined to rekindle it. After dinner and some of the champagne she had brought along, they would return to the bedroom for another round of lovemaking and she would make up for her faux pas.

* * * * *

The noise was getting so loud it was almost impossible to hear the band above the roar, but no one seemed to mind. There remained only an hour before midnight, and the majority of the sailors at the Mocombo Club were already feeling little if any pain.

A few sailors maneuvered around the dance floor with Tiny's Hogs, but most were content to sit and drink, tell bawdy jokes and share stories of girls back home. The band tried to play over the din, which did little to improve their performance, and the sailors only became louder anyway. As the evening wore on, the musicians became more mechanical and less entertaining. In fact, they became practically irrelevant.

"These guys can't play music for shit!" Gino proclaimed, looking up disgustedly at the bandstand.

"Maybe you guys should get up there and show 'em how it's done," R.J. suggested.

"That's a good fuckin' idea," Pea agreed. "I'd rather listen to the Deck

Apes, anyway."

Gino stood and walked up to the bandstand, motioning Tiny to come over. The big Guamanian scowled but leaned over the bandstand, straining to hear what Gino was saying to him. He shook his head firmly and returned to directing the band.

"What he say?" Pea asked as Gino returned to the table.

"Said no," Gino replied. "Don't want no guest artists."

"Fuckin' gook," Pea slurred. "Fuck 'im anyway."

* * * * *

"The steak was excellent, Paul." Lorelei sat on the couch on the enclosed porch and tucked her legs under her. She wore only the tops of Paul's pajamas and shuddered slightly in the night air. A soft rain fell gently, summoning a cooling breeze that wafted through the screened-in porch.

"Thanks," he said absently, pouring two more glasses of champagne and handing one to her. "I'm glad you liked it."

"I'm sorry about that remark, Paul," she said, searching his face. "I didn't mean..."

"Forget it." He cut her off. "We both know you're leaving in a couple of weeks. I'll be at sea when you go." He seemed distant, as if she were already gone and he'd become used to it.

They sat silently and sipped their champagne. Paul checked his watch periodically, awaiting the arrival of nineteen hundred and sixty four. She shivered again and Paul went into the cabin, returning with a blanket. He draped it over her shoulders.

"Thank you," she said quietly.

"You're welcome," he replied stiffly. He walked to the front steps and stared out the screen door at the green hills. She sipped her wine and tried to think of something to say.

* * * * *

"You didn't ax him right," Rafer explained above the din in the club. He and Andy had returned from the head and learned that Gino's request to perform had been turned down by Tiny. "Lemme go talk to him." Rafer and Andy approached Tiny and waved him over to the edge of the bandstand. Tiny leaned over and listened, then shook his head emphatically. Rafer reached up and grabbed Tiny by the front of his brightly colored Hawaiian shirt and pulled him down so he could speak directly and privately into his ear. Tiny's eyes grew wide. Rafer pointed to the band, then poked Tiny in the chest with his finger and said something more in Tiny's ear. Andy glared menacingly at the fat bandleader. Tiny backed up, frightened, and motioned for the band to quit playing. Rafer and Andy returned to the table and sat down.

"It's all yours," Rafer said to Gino, who grinned and motioned for Cotton, Jefferson and Andy to follow him. They bounded up the steps to the stage and Gino grabbed the microphone stand. The crowd of drunken sailors, realizing the music had stopped, began hooting and yelling. Gino held up his hands and called for quiet. The crowd became rowdier, shouting insults at the four men on the bandstand who had interrupted the music. Pea jumped up on the bandstand and grabbed the microphone from Gino.

"SHUT THE FUCK UP!" he yelled into the mike. The crowd settled down, more curious than anything else, and Pea turned the mike over to Gino.

"I bet everyone here wishes he were home with his chick," Gino said. The crowd quieted. "I'm Gino and these guys are the Deck Apes." He motioned to the others. "We wanna give you a little something to remember her by." Gino looked back at the Deck Apes and smiled. He turned, took the mike in both hands and began:

"You're a thousand miles away,
   but I still have your love to remember you by..."

The group fell into the harmony and Gino's beautiful voice filled the crowded, smoke-filled club. Conversations stopped, drinking stopped, and every face turned toward the stage, mesmerized by the poignant, four-part harmony.

The Deck Apes finished 'A Thousand Miles Away' with the promise that daddy was coming home soon, and as their voices faded into the night, the crowd sat quietly for a long, silent moment, remembering, reminiscing, each alone in his own memory. Then R.J. and the Havernauts jumped to their feet and began applauding. Soon, every man in the club was on his feet, clapping, yelling, and whistling.

Gino turned and grinned at Andy, Jefferson and Cotton, who grinned back proudly. "Let's turn this joint out!" Gino yelled over the noise, and returned to the microphone. "This is for all you fools out there," and the group swung into the song made famous by Frankie Lymon:

"Doo wah, doo wah,
   do-oo wah doo wah,
   why do fools fall in love,..."

The Deck Apes sang most of the songs in their repertoire, much to the delight of the crowd, most of whom sang along with the lyrics. The Deck Apes swung into an upbeat version of 'Remember Then', and segued right into 'Blue Moon,' featuring Andy's deep bass. The crowd got on their feet and cheered and waved, singing along with each tune. Midnight came and Gino wished everyone a happy new year. Tiny had his bus packed and was ready to lock up, so Gino announced the last song. The room once again grew respectfully quiet as Gino stepped up to the mike and led the group into 'Daddy's Home.'

"You're my love
   you're my angel,
   you're the girl of my dreams.
   I want to thank you (rat-a-tat)
   for waiting patiently.
   Daddy's home,
   Daddy's home to stay..."

The club became very quiet as the strains of *'Daddy's Home'* faded into the night. It was just past midnight when Gino and the Deck Apes snapped back into the doo-wop beat of *'Remember Then'*. Gino led them off the stage and out the front door through a gauntlet of sailors who slapped their backs and shook their hands. The last shuttle was filling up, preparing to leave. The Havernauts, followed by a handful of well-wishers, approached the shuttle and found the doors shut. Inside the bus, standing next to the driver, a drunken Chief Twitchell closed the doors and instructed the driver to take off.

"We still got plenty room," the driver complained.

"Drive, you fuckin' moron!" the chief yelled. "Those nigger-lovers can walk back for all I care." The shuttle took off, leaving the remaining sailors standing in the near-deserted parking lot.

The driver stuck his head out the window and called, "I be back!"

"Shit!" Cotton yelled. "That asshole, Twitchell!"

"Relax, buddy," R.J. soothed. "He's says he's coming back."

"Yeah, in about an hour!"

"Well," Gino said resignedly, "I guess we wait."

R.J. looked up at the full moon, drifting high in the night sky. "Hey, Gino," he said. "Look, there's a moon out tonight."

Gino grinned. "One of my favorite songs," he said. "C'mon fellas, let's do it." The Deck Apes gathered around and began singing *'There's a Moon Out Tonight'*. It was 1964 and the beautiful melody and four part harmony lingered in the damp night air, gently tugging at the hearts of the sailors, conjuring up melancholy thoughts of home.

R.J. leaned against the Mocombo Club wall and gazed up at the full moon, smiling to himself. *'There's A Moon Out Tonight'* was his and Janice's song, and it never failed to bring back sweet memories of her. They were among the few good memories he had of Denver.

The remaining sailors leaned back on the side of the Club or sat on the curb while Gino and the group sang requests. When the shuttle returned over an hour later, all climbed happily aboard, snapping their fingers and singing along, trying to match the harmony of the Deck Apes.

* * * * *

"Happy New Year," Lorelei whispered, her arm around Paul's neck. "It's getting a little chilly out here. Shall we go in?"

Paul hesitated. "Maybe I should get back," he said uncertainly, staring out the screen door. His pipe was in his mouth, a wisp of smoke curling up from the bowl.

She looked at him curiously. "What's wrong?" she asked, coming up behind him and snaking her arms around his waist. "I'm sorry for the remark I made."

He shook his head sadly. "It's not that, Lorelei," he started. "It's just..."

"Just what?" She was becoming irritable. She walked across the porch and sat down heavily on the couch. She put a cigarette in her mouth. "Do you have a light?" she pouted.

He struck a kitchen match and held it to her cigarette. The flare of light bathed her face and she looked beautiful.

"I'm just thinking," he said slowly. "You're leaving on the fifteenth. I'm going out on patrol the thirteenth. Maybe we should just call tonight our last night."

"Is that what you want, Paul?" Her voice was quiet, strained.

"What I want..." he turned to look at her. He stood in the shadows next to the screen door so she couldn't see his face. "What I want is for you to stay. I want you to leave Quentin and marry me!" He blurted it out before he had time to think about it, and he regretted it instantly.

"Paul..." she stood and backed away, toward the interior of the cottage. She was obviously shocked by what he had said. *I love him, yes, but leave Quentin? That would never happen. I have responsibilities.* I can't just leave my husband. Imagine the scandal!

Paul read the look on her face. "Sorry," he muttered. "C'mon, I'll take you back to your car."

They drove down the hill toward the USO beach in silence. The stunned look on her face when he blurted out he wanted to marry her was all he really needed to know. That expression said it all. She wasn't about to leave her cushy life for him. *Maybe for another admiral,* he thought bitterly. When he pulled up next to her Buick, she got out of the Ford Fairlane and poked her head through the window. "Goodnight, Paul," she said.

"Goodbye, Lorelei," he replied.

"We'll see each other before I leave, won't we?" she asked.

"Sure," he answered. "Sure, we will." He put the car in gear and drove off, not looking back. She stood in the parking lot and watched him leave. She raised her hand as if to wave good-bye, but dropped it slowly to her side. He was gone. She sighed sadly and unlocked the driver's door to the Buick.

FIFTY THREE

Admiral Quentin Prescott sat back in his easy chair and sipped from a snifter of cognac. An opened envelope sat on the floor where he had dropped it. He held a single, handwritten page in his hand. He read the anonymous note again and shook his head sadly. His wife was having an affair, the note said. She had been seen driving through the hills in the officer's car, and there was a rumor that she had been sharing a cottage in the hills with him. The note writer had taken it upon himself (herself?) to investigate and had verified the whole thing.

Admiral Prescott downed his cognac in one gulp and stood to refill his glass. He had to think about this. The evidence was, apparently, overwhelming. What was he going to do about it? He wasn't sure just now, but he knew he had to do something in due course. He poured more cognac into the snifter and sat back down heavily, sighing. He shook his head again, trying to make sense out of it. Why had she done it? Why had his wife taken up with Lee Piper, the captain of the Brister?

* * * * *

A happy peace settled on the Haverfield, helped along by the change in Rafer's attitude. R.J. liked to think he had something to do with it, but he understood that Rafer did what he liked, and didn't allow anyone to be much of an influence on him, even Andy. In that relationship it was easy to see that Rafer was the leader, the one who made things happen. Andy, much more easy-going, was satisfied to follow Rafer's lead.

The deck force had finished painting the entire ship, from mast to water-line, and the old girl was looking good. R.J. re-painted the signal bridge, which made Anselmi very happy, mostly because he didn't have to participate. The ship was ready for a patrol cruise, and truth be told, so were the crew. In the meantime, they worked together to keep the ship polished and swapped tales of island hopping and bare-breasted native girls.

* * * * *

Pedro Almogordo beamed brightly as he led the captain on a tour of the engine room. All four of the Fairbanks Morse geared-diesel engines had been overhauled, polished, fine tuned and polished again. All four were running at peak efficiency and the engineering officer proudly boasted that the ship could hit 25 knots, if necessary. This brought a big smile to the captain's face. He seriously doubted Pedro's exaggerated claim, but not his enthusiasm. The ship's speed was rated at 21 knots, but Captain Oliver had yet to see her actually reach that speed. Their cruising speed was usually around 15 knots. Still, it might be fun to see what she could do.

* * * * *

With the Raptor in port, R.J. spent most nights either in the chart house, studying for the third class exam, or in his bunk, reading Poe. He was delighted when Billy Lopez announced he was going to strike for signalman and Mr. MacDonald had signed the chit. Training Billy in Morse code and semaphore filled the down time so he didn't have to think about Annie. He was genuinely glad the Haverfield was setting sail for the Palau Islands on Monday morning. They would be at sea for three weeks.

He was also looking forward to returning to Guam. Billy and Teresa were getting married on St. Valentine's Day, and R.J. was proud that Billy had asked him to stand up for him as best man. All the Havernauts were named honorary ushers and would line both sides of the aisle, saluting newlyweds Billy and Teresa as they walked between them, leaving the church.

Mostly, he wanted to see Annie again. It had been several weeks since they had been together, and R.J. thought about her constantly. Damn, why hadn't he asked for a picture?

* * * * *

Lorelei Prescott stood in front of her full-length mirror and admired her new cocktail dress. Since she was leaving for Subic Bay on the fifteenth, Guam's naval officers and their wives planned a going away dinner at the

Officer's Club on Saturday night. Lorelei was looking forward to it. She would be saying goodbye to people she had known since she arrived last year, many of whom had become friends, but mostly she wanted to see Paul Oliver before she left. In all likelihood, they would not see each other again. She stepped closer to the mirror and inspected her face. *Not bad for a thirty year old broad,* she thought. Paul's face appeared in her mind's eye and she winced.

"Well, what am I supposed to do?" she asked her reflected image. "Leave Quentin and go tearing around the South Pacific with Paul Oliver?" She shook her head emphatically. No, that was not going to happen. She enjoyed her pampered life, and she wasn't about to throw it all away. Of course she loved Paul, how could she not? But having an affair was different from divorce and scandal, and Lorelei Von Dulm Prescott had been raised to always behave properly, even when being indiscreet. *Just once more,* she thought, turning around to view her new dress from a different angle. *I just want to see him once more.*

* * * * *

Paul knew he wouldn't attend the going away party. He had sent his regrets to the organizing committee, begging off because he had to get his ship ready for patrol. He knew the ship was ready, and required no further tinkering on his part. He just didn't want to face Lorelei. He had poured his heart out to her, let down his carefully constructed guard, and revealed his deepest feelings. She responded by pulling away from him and looking at him like he was crazy. *Well, maybe I am crazy,* he thought, *but I'll be damned if I'm going to give her another chance to step on me.*

As long as it lasts, they had said to each other. But that was when everything was new and exciting. It was easy to be cavalier about it when they were locked together in a naked embrace. All those wonderful feelings made it impossible to imagine that things would somehow change and those delicious feelings of love and lust would metamorphose into pain and regret.

Paul Oliver stood on the wing bridge on Saturday night, watching the blinking lights of the harbor, sipping a cup of coffee he had laced generously with brandy. Up at the Officer's Club everyone would be toasting the admiral's wife, wishing her a pleasant journey and promising to keep in touch. The least he could do was join that toast. He held his cup up in the air and toasted Lorelei Von Dulm Prescott.

"To Lorelei, keeper of the siren song." He finished his brandy-laced coffee and dropped the cup into the drink. As it splashed and began to sink to the bottom of the harbor, Paul swore he could hear the sounds of white water splashing over hidden shoals. Another sailor lured to the rocks, crashing into them head-on, going willingly, and not resisting.

* * * * *

"May I have this dance?"

Lorelei swung around, hoping, half-expecting to see Paul standing there,

360

hat in hand, that charming smile on his face. But it wasn't Paul who asked her to dance. It was Lee Piper.

"Of course, Captain," she smiled sweetly and took his arm. "I've been wanting to talk to you."

"I figured you might," Lee said. They reached the floor and began dancing slowly to the Ink Spots.

"You know about Paul and me, don't you?" she asked, but it wasn't a question. She knew he knew, and he knew she knew he knew. He smiled to himself.

"Something funny, Captain?" she asked, her eyebrows arched.

"He's not coming, Lorelei," Lee said firmly and flatly.

She looked around the room. It seemed all eyes were on them. What she didn't know was that one set of those eyes had been watching her for weeks, and had sent Admiral Prescott the anonymous note. Those eyes were watching them now with smug satisfaction.

"I didn't think he was," she said, a sadness creeping across her face. "Will you give him a message for me?" she asked, looking up into Captain Piper's eyes.

"Of course," he said.

"Tell him I thought about it, I really did."

"That's all?"

"Yes," she replied, her eyes tearing up.

"Okay, I'll tell him." The music stopped and they stood there for a moment, looking at each other. Lorelei reached up and gave Lee a kiss on the cheek, then turned and moved away.

The prying eyes watched the scene carefully, preparing another anonymous note to the admiral.

FIFTY FOUR

Pedro Almogordo was right about one thing: The engines were purring like they just arrived from the factory, and the evaporators were putting out fresh water in quantities unheard of in recent memory. The ship looked great inside and out, freshly painted and shined up. Captain Oliver smiled as he stood on the flying bridge, watching the deck crew secure the focsul for steaming. He was looking forward to this cruise. Three weeks on patrol would do the crew good, and he was looking forward to conducting the drill schedule. He would rid the men of any cobwebs they had gathered while in port.

The last time they were at sea, they rode out Typhoon Mabel. This time would be different, with good weather and calm seas in the forecast. And Palau was a beautiful part of the world, full of lush islands and water so clear sailors could see the bottom as deep as six fathoms.

Captain Oliver sat back in his steaming chair and relaxed. They had breached the breakwater and turned southwest. They would pass the Yap Islands, then the Palau Islands and make their first landing on Helen's Reef, the southernmost island in the Palau chain. They would then work their way back to Guam, stopping at several of the Palau Islands and Yap Islands before returning home. It promised to be a good cruise.

* * * * *

Jerry Snively had managed to mimeograph the drill schedule and informed the crew that the first drill would be conducted on the first night out, and it would be an anti-submarine warfare drill. The crew was ready. Many slept in their clothes or didn't go to sleep at all. They wanted to respond quickly to the drill to demonstrate their high level of efficiency.

Right on time, at twenty-two hundred, just after the watch had changed, Captain Oliver stepped onto the bridge and pulled the lever on the general quarters alarm.

"BONG-BONG-BONG-BONG," the GQ alarm blared loudly and sailors in every compartment hit the deck and rushed to their stations.

"Now hear this, now hear this! General quarters, general quarters! All hands man your anti-submarine warfare stations. This is not a drill." But of course it was a drill, the crew knew it and were ready.

"Every station manned and ready, Captain," Mr. MacDonald poked his head through the porthole from the bridge to the flying bridge.

The captain looked at his watch. That was unusually quick. Maybe the crew didn't gather as many cobwebs as he had imagined. It was almost as if they knew when the drill was scheduled. Maybe they did.

"Secure from general quarters," the captain said. "Pass the word to the crew. Your performance on this drill was excellent. Have a good night's sleep."

"Aye, sir." Mr. Mac saluted headed aft to pass the word.

The captain studied the duty schedule and saw that Mr. Barkman was the OOD on the mid-watch. He sent the messenger to bring the operations officer to the captain's cabin. When Mr. Barkman arrived, he and the captain spent several minutes together, and Lieutenant Barkman left smiling. The captain had left a wake-up call for 0200.

Just after 2:00 A.M. the captain arrived on the bridge and winked at Mr. Barkman. The OOD pulled the lever on the GQ alarm and the quiet night dissolved in a cacophonous blaring, rudely awakening the crew. "BONG-BONG-BONG-BONG!"

"Now hear this! Now hear this! This is not a drill! All hands man your battle stations!" "BONG-BONG-BONG-BONG!"

Shocked at the blaring alarm that invaded their sleep, the crew hurried to get up and dressed, and stumbled, swearing, to their battle stations. They fumbled with their life jackets and battle helmets. They scrambled up and down ladders, still half-asleep and irritable, confused by the early morning call to battle stations. When all stations were reported manned and ready, the captain looked at his watch. *Hmm, more than twice as long as the previous drill!*

"Looks like you were right, Cap'n," Mr. Barkman said, looking at his watch and grinning. "They must have a copy of the schedule."

"Not anymore, they don't," the captain replied. "Wait about a half-hour,

Jim, then secure from general quarters. Let them get back to sleep. They ought to be pretty well out of it before sunrise." The captain grinned at the OOD. "Then we'll run another drill."

"Aye, sir," Lieutenant Barkman beamed. The skipper was pretty sharp. If the crew thought they had put one over on him, they were wrong. In the next three weeks at sea, they would find out just how wrong they were.

* * * * *

Big Queen was pissed. Most First Class Boatswain's mates are pissed-off about ninety percent of the time, but Queen was the master of pissed-off. He had perfected it to an art form, and he wasn't shy about sharing it with people he supervised.

"You pussies blew it by two full minutes!" He raged at the tired, stumbling, sleep-deprived deck crew, painfully struggling to make their way back into the compartment, and to their bunks. They were worn out. One week into a three week cruise, and they had already endured twenty drills in seven days. With all the practice, Queen expected them to do well, perhaps break the record they had set on the first drill, when they had a copy of the schedule. Instead, they seemed to be getting slower. That pissed him off even more.

"What the hell'd you think when you joined the Navy?" he bellowed, making his charges shrink in shame and fear. "You think this is some dipshit fraternity where you get to guzzle beer and light farts?"

Queen adjusted his too-small hat on his head. It was twenty three hundred, only an hour before midnight, and even he felt these poor souls needed some sleep. He had heard a rumor about the purloined schedule. So had Chief Whipple, who expressed his dismay in rather strong terms, which still stung the big boatswain's mate when he thought about it. But the captain had made his point, right? He could back off now, right? Alfred Queen didn't believe that was going to happen.

Neither did the crew. They fell into their bunks exhausted, but unable to sleep. There was no telling when the next drill would be brought down upon them, and as tired as they were, sleep was impossible.

The captain had been unmerciful in calling the drills. They had secured from an anti-aircraft drill only to be forced into a man-overboard drill a few minutes later. No one knew what the captain had planned, so they tried to stay alert, forcing themselves to stay awake, afraid to fall asleep.

The captain knew this and refrained from drilling them for two days. This was unexpected, and made the crew even more paranoid. They were tired and strung out. They were being asked to perform at unreasonable levels when they were completely exhausted. Was this what the captain wanted?

Yes.

* * * * *

The arrival at Helen's Reef was a welcome break in routine for the sailors of the Haverfield. The crew welcomed the opportunity for an island landing and a respite from the never-ending drills.

Surrounded by miles of coral reef, much of it just below the surface of the water, tiny Helen Island perched like a sentry on white sand, looking like little more than a small clump of palm trees.

The three black inflatable rafts, powered by outboard motors, cruised slowly across the shallow reef toward the small island. A lookout lay across the bow of each raft and watched the coral closely, pointing to danger areas where the coral almost broke the surface. The reef was so shallow in some places, the bottoms of the rafts barely cleared it, and the coxswains had to pull the outboard screws up to avoid grinding them into the reef. R.J. relaxed in the lead boat, watching the colorful reef pass below them. He believed he could get out and walk to Helen Island across the shallow reef. He had landed on coral islands before, but nothing had prepared him for the spectacular beauty of Helen's Reef. Green sea turtles drifted along the coral among multi-colored fish. Some of the turtles broke the surface long enough to look curiously at the rafts, then dove back into the aqua water, propelled away by their powerful flippers.

Small, white clouds dotted the deep blue sky above the island, and the water changed color every few yards as the rafts made their way toward the knot of trees. Nearing the beach, the crews jumped into the water and guided the rafts onto the pristine sand. R.J. waded ashore and looked around. It was the most beautiful place he had ever seen. A soft breeze blew gently, cooling the crews and rustling the big palm leaves high up in the trees which swayed back and forth like dancers at a prom. Walking down the clean, white beach, R.J. noticed several big palm trees blown over by a recent typhoon, the big clumps of roots wrenched up and resting on the sand.

The landing crew made its way around the island, looking for signs of illegal fishing. Suddenly, thousands of white birds scrambled into the sky ahead of them, squawking and fluttering, swerving and diving, their wings beating the air with a sense of frightened urgency.

"What kind of birds are those?" R.J. asked.

"Terns," Mr. MacDonald explained. "We musta stumbled onto their rookery."

"Must be a million of 'em," Jefferson observed. He shaded his eyes against the sun, and watched the birds scattering around in the air.

"Look!" Sonny called, pointing down at the sand. The footprints of a large green sea turtle indented the sand. "He went this way!" Sonny pointed ahead and R.J. and Jefferson joined him, hurrying down the beach in pursuit of the turtle. They spotted him about fifty yards away, moving slowly, nonchalantly, toward some destination known only to the turtle. They caught up with him and he stopped in his tracks, pulling his head and legs into his protective shell. He was a big turtle, about four feet long and three feet wide. R.J. stepped up on his shell and posed while Mr. Mac took pictures. The turtle grew tired of his unwelcome passenger and poked his head out of his shell, straining his neck to see who or what was on his back. He began to move again, and R.J. jumped down and watched him. The big creature walked, unconcerned, to the water's edge and glided into the sea. He looked back once, seemingly aggravated by the interruption of his routine, then he ducked under the water, creating a small splash as he glided away.

"That turtle just gave me a dirty look," R.J. laughed.

"Why they call 'em green turtles?" Cotton asked, watching the big turtle swim away. "He ain't green. His shell is kinda brownish black."

"Must be a splib turtle," Jefferson mused.

Circumnavigating the entire island in less than half an hour, the landing party found no evidence of Japanese fishing boats, not even a single colored glass ball. They finished surveying the island and Mr. Mac ordered them back to the rafts.

"Man, I could stay here forever," R.J. said, looking around the island. "This is the coolest place I've ever seen."

"Okay, Robinson Crusoe," Mr. Mac grinned. "Let's get back to the ship."

There was no surf to overcome, and the crews walked the rafts away from the beach and jumped in as the water became deep enough. The outboard motors were pull-started and the rafts began the long, slow trip back to the ship. The Haverfield looked small, laying to well away from the reef, and it seemed to R.J. that it would take hours to get back. He sat in the raft and watched Helen Island become smaller and smaller as the rubber boats glided softly over the colorful reef. *I'm coming back here, someday,* he thought.

* * * * *

The Haverfield worked her way north, landing on two islands a day and conducting two drills per night until they finally reached Yap Island. The entire off-duty crew was allowed to go ashore to explore the village of Colonia and see the famous stone money of Yap, then on to Ulithi and the last island landing. By the time the ship returned to Guam, the crew was sunburned, sore and exhausted. The captain had worked them extremely hard, but they had become very efficient in all areas of ship's operations. They were glad to be home, and welcomed the sight of Apra Harbor. It was Monday, February 3rd. The crew had performed well, working closely together and getting along better than they ever had before. The division between white and black sailors seemed to be a thing of the past as the crew became closer and began developing a cohesive bond. That lasted only a week. Chief Twitchell had other ideas.

FIFTY SIX

Quentin Prescott was usually a direct man who was used to having his orders followed without question. He believed in going at a problem directly, a frontal assault, quick and decisive. The admiral was also very much in love with his wife, and truth be told, he felt a little intimidated by her beauty and the force of her personality. This inner conflict caused the admiral to delay confronting Lorelei when she first arrived. He tried to think of the best way to approach her. Should he jump right in and demand an explanation? Should he let her settle in before bringing it up? Unusually indecisive, Admiral Prescott put it off for a few weeks after Lorelei's arrival in Subic Bay. Then, becoming more like himself, he leaned across the dinner table one evening, in the middle of the salad, and said bluntly, "I'm aware of your affair on Guam, Lorrie."

Lorelei's eyes were on her salad, and she didn't look up. Blood rushed to her face and she felt short of breath. She quickly regained control and slowly set her fork down on her salad plate. She dabbed at the corners of her mouth with her napkin and dropped it back into her lap. Then she looked up at him, her eyes flashing anger, her cheeks flushed red.

"What in the world are you taking about, Quentin?"

He handed her the two anonymous notes he had received. She read them very quickly, frowned, and dropped them on the table. "Not signed," she said, contemptuously. "Do you know who sent them, Quentin?"

"No," he admitted. He stared down at the hand-written notes. "I don't recognize the handwriting." He looked into her eyes. "It says you were seen in Captain Piper's car with him."

She shook her head sadly, slowly, and sighed. "Quentin, I was in Lee Piper's car, but I wasn't with Lee Piper." She reached across the table and took his hand. "I was with Paul Oliver," she said, staring directly into his eyes. "Paul borrowed Lee's car to take me to the dinner party he arranged aboard his ship. Remember?" She was lying. A Navy sedan and driver had transported them to the Haverfield dinner. She had no way of knowing how many times the prying eyes had seen them together in Lee's car, so Lorelei included the dinner party as cover.

Quentin stared at her, eyebrows furrowed, a tight frown on his lips. "I don't know what to say," he murmured.

"Another time, Paul Oliver escorted me to a dinner party for newly arrived officers." She patted the admiral's hand. "He was always a perfect gentleman, Quentin," she assured him. "He's pretty much obsessed with his ship."

Admiral Prescott nodded absently, staring at nothing in the corner of the room. He had been wrong. *How stupid of him.* He let his jealousy and his pride get in the way of his good judgment. *Two anonymous notes?* He should have had more evidence than that. Now, he was neatly tied up and unable to do anything about it. He had falsely accused her of an affair with Lee Piper, and he had been wrong. He knew better now. The affair had been with Paul Oliver. That made a lot more sense, but even as certain as he was, Quentin Prescott was powerless now even to mention it. He smiled at his wife and took a large drink of his wine.

* * * * *

Betty called Gino on Thursday afternoon, just hours after the Raptor had left port for another training mission. Their husbands would be gone for four days, Betty told him, and the girls wanted to get together. They arranged to meet at the end of the pier, away from any lights or prying eyes.

R.J., Gino and Pea, in fresh white uniforms, piled into the trunk of the Impala and Carol hit the gas, pointing the big Chevy toward Naval housing. Inside the trunk, Gino sang softly, *'Will You Still Love Me Tomorrow,'* and Pea and R.J. kept the beat by tapping on the trunk lid.

"Quiet!" Betty whispered through the back seat. "It sounds like we're throwing a rod or something."

R.J. knew there was something wrong as soon as they got inside the darkened house, and Gino and Pea led Betty and Carol upstairs. Annie sat quietly on the couch, her legs crossed at the knee and her arms folded tightly against her chest. She was staring at the floor. *Uh oh,* R.J. thought as he sat next to her. He knew trouble was coming when her mood became this dark.

"What's wrong, babe?" he asked reluctantly, afraid she would tell him exactly what was wrong. It was somehow his fault, he knew that. He playfully put his whitehat on her head. She removed it and set it neatly on the coffee table.

"Nothing," she said firmly, still staring at the floor.

Okay, good, R.J. thought. *Let's go get a beer.* But he knew it wouldn't be that easy. He sat quietly next to her, waiting. He lit a cigarette and she took it from his mouth.

"Thanks," she said.

"My pleasure," he replied, lighting another cigarette.

"I'm so messed up," she whined suddenly. "I don't know what to do."

"C'mon," he nudged her. "It can't be that bad, what's wrong?"

She looked up at him with her sad face, tears welling up in her eyes. She bit her lip and looked back down at the floor. "It's that bad," she whispered.

He tried to keep the conversation light, so she wouldn't start crying. "So, what is it?" he teased. "You pregnant or something?"

She began sobbing.

"That's it?" he asked, astonished. "You're pregnant?"

"A little," she sobbed weakly.

"A little?" he shouted, jumping to his feet and stubbed his cigarette out in the ashtray. "You're either pregnant or you ain't!" He began pacing around the living room. "A little! How you gonna be a LITTLE pregnant?" He stopped pacing and looked down at her. "Hey," he said.

She lifted her head, sniffling, and looked up at him.

"Who's the father?"

She began sobbing again and dropped her head down. She blew her nose on a hanky and dabbed at her eyes.

He cupped her chin in his hand and gently pulled her head up until she was looking into his eyes. "Whose baby is it, Annie?"

She shook her head. "I don't know...I...I'm not sure." She began sobbing again.

"Well, how many candidates are there?" he shouted angrily.

She began sobbing loudly. "Just two, damn you!" she sobbed. "Just two!" She jumped up and ran into the bathroom, locking the door behind her. R.J. could hear her sobs through the door.

* * * * *

Chief Twitchell stood in the middle of the engine room, looking at the dozen or so sailors gathered around him. He was satisfied with these men, all white, all southern, all deeply prejudiced against black people. Maybe they weren't extremely bright, but they were loyal. It was time they got a chance to show it. He checked to see that both overhead hatches were being guarded by one of his men. He didn't want some moron stumbling in on this meeting.

"We gotta get organized," the chief said, walking among the men, who nodded agreement in unison. "These darkies are gettin' their black asses organized, for God knows what, and we gotta be organized too, so's we can meet whatever bullshit they got up their sleeves!" He stopped and leaned against the metal railing surrounding the engine room. "Keep a close eye on these nee-gros, and don't let 'em get away with anything." He poked his finger into his palm, making points. "If they're fuckin' off on the job, write them up. If three or more of them get together, make them break it up. Mosta youse are petty officers. Make the crow work for you."

"So, we harass them?" Crawford drawled, a stupid grin on his face.

The fat chief grinned, then began laughing, holding his jiggling round belly in his hands as if he were afraid it would work itself free and fall to the floor. "That's right, Crawford," he boomed. "We harass the shit out of 'em!"

When Mr. Almogordo opened the hatch to inspect the engine room, he was surprised at the hilarious laughter coming from the engineering space. The hatch watch had signaled the lieutenant's arrival and the laughter died as he made his way down the ladder.

"What's going on, chief?" he asked Twitchell.

"Just shootin' the breeze, sir," the fat chief replied. "We were just gettin' ready to break it up, anyway." He made his way to the ladder. "Goodnight, sir," he said as he climbed out of sight, followed by the rest of the men.

Mr. Almogordo stood staring at the hatch, wondering what this group was planning. He vowed to keep an eye on Chief Twitchell and his merry band of rednecks.

* * * * *

Gino came downstairs and found R.J. in the kitchen and Annie locked in the bathroom. *Another fight. Those two couldn't get along, so why did they bother?* He was glad Betty wasn't the needy type. *She just wanted to have a little fun, like me. Nothing serious. No drama, no fighting, just having a little fun.* He shook his head, disgusted at his friend, and returned upstairs to collect Pea.

Later, walking down the pier toward the ship, Gino looked sideways at his friend and shook his head slowly. *The dumb bastard had it bad, all right.*

Dumb shit.

"She's pregnant," R.J. blurted.

"What?" Pea asked, grabbing R.J. by the arm and spinning him around. "Pregnant?"

"Yeah, and she won't tell me who the father is."

"It's either you or Gary," Pea decided.

"She's all pissed off at me," R.J. said to no one in particular. "Said she don't wanna see me again."

"Good!" Gino said. "Let's find you another chick, one that won't drive you crazy."

"Yeah," Pea said enthusiastically. "One with some really big knockers."

R.J. grinned and shook his head sadly. "I wish I woulda gotten a picture from her," he said softly.

"Forget about her, R.J.," Pea said.

"I'm gonna concentrate on the third class test next week," R.J. said emphatically. "I don't have time for her bullshit."

"There you go!" Gino slapped him on the back and strutted off toward the ship.

R.J. lay in his bunk, staring at the pipes along the overhead. The third class test was next Wednesday, and Billy and Teresa were getting married on Friday, Valentine's Day, so he had enough on his mind to keep him busy. He decided he was glad he didn't have a picture of Annie to moon over. He glanced through the study materials again, but he knew he was as ready as he was ever going to be for the exam.

* * * * *

Paul Oliver sat at his desk in his cabin, reading and re-reading the note from Lorelei. She had arrived in Subic Bay without incident, and was immersed in running the new household. The admiral was fine, and the new house was much bigger than the one on Guam. *Why does she insist on telling me all this mundane crap?* he thought. He scanned through the mundane to the last paragraph:

> *I want you to know that I shall always love you, Paul. What we shared was more than good, it was wonderful, and I'll never forget it. You are the love of my life, and will always be the only man who could ever touch me as deeply as you did.*
>
> *I know we can't be together, but you will always be with me, here in my heart.*
>
> *Love,*
>
> *L'*

Paul had the urge, for the umpteenth time, to tear up the letter and throw it away, but he didn't. He folded it gently and returned it to its scented envelope. He dropped it into his top drawer and picked up his cap. He left the cabin and pulled the door shut behind him. He walked toward the flying bridge, packing tobacco into the bowl of his pipe. He would sit in the captain's chair and look out at the harbor while he enjoyed his pipe.

FIFTY SIX

R.J. leaned against a torpedo tube on the fantail, greeting the arrival of Monday morning. The weather had been perfect for over a month. The high humidity had subsided, and the entire crew was looking forward to the wedding on Friday. R.J. waited patiently for the sun to make its way to the top of the mountains and spill over, flooding the harbor with warm yellow light.

He forced thoughts of Annie from his mind and concentrated on the third class exam he would take in a couple of days. He thought he had the material down, but he still spent every spare moment studying the same things over and over again.

The sun finally made it down the mountain, reveille was called, and the sleepy ship began to stir. Down in the messdecks, several black sailors were gathered around the two rear booths, laughing loudly. Hawkins sat amidst them, and he appeared to be the subject of their hooting.

"Hawk, you a dumb shit, man," Jefferson was saying. "That old man, Liston, hell, he even older than you. How he gonna beat a strong, young black dude like my man, Cassius?"

"Liston gonna put a whuppin' on that loud-mouth," Hawkins objected. "You mark my words, boy, that old man ain't as old as you think!"

"Get yer money outta yer pocket, old man," Andy slapped a twenty dollar bill on the table. "Twenty say Cassius Clay gonna whup that big bear."

"You on!" Hawkins laid his twenty next to Andy's. "Sonny Liston been knockin' everybody out," he stated. "This whipper-snapper can't last with big Sonny."

"If the man say he gonna do somethin'," Rafer observed, "I gotta believe he gonna go and do it." He put a twenty down on the table. "Any other fool around here wanna bet on a fat, old washed-up lookin' muhfuh?"

A stubby white hand reached into the crowd and dropped another twenty on the table. Rafer looked over and saw Twitchell standing next to him.

"Yeah, I got your twenty," Twitchell sneered. "See, the difference in these two coons is simple," he explained, looking around at the black faces. "Sonny Liston is what you call a good nigger. Cassius Clay is what you call a jive-ass, always runnin' his big, black mouth." He nudged Jefferson in the ribs. "Kinda like you, Jefferson," he laughed.

The blacks who were sitting in the booths got to their feet and faced Twitchell. Several white sailors stepped up behind the fat chief and faced off with the blacks. The situation was getting tense when R.J. walked into the messdecks. *Uh oh,* he thought, looking at the two opposing groups around the rear booths.

"You know what, Chief?" Rafer said, picking up the money from the table and folding it in half. "You got yourself a bet, and I'm gonna let Hawkins hold the stakes, okay?" He handed the money to Hawkins without waiting for an answer and smiled at Chief Twitchell.

"You're covered," Twitchell said, backing up a little and looking at the men behind him. "Don't make me come after my money when your big mouth coon gets his ass whupped."

Rafer glared at the chief as he turned and left the messdecks, followed by his redneck entourage.

"Looks like he gotta clan of his own," Andy said, studying his brother's face.

Rafer nodded. "Yeah, we know all about the Klan, don't we, bro?"

* * * * *

R.J. sat in the rear booth of the messdecks and sweated over the third class Signalman's test. He knew the material, but he was nervous and having a hard time concentrating. Anselmi sat in a booth across the aisle from him, proctoring the test and keeping an eye on the time. R.J. had only an hour to finish the exam, and he had fidgeted away a quarter of that without marking a single answer.

"Hey Slick, you better bear down on that test," Anselmi declared, pointing at his wristwatch.

R.J. nodded and focused on the exam, pushing all other thoughts from his mind, including those of Annie. He had breezed through the Morse code portion up on the signal bridge, and did well on the semaphore; better, in fact, than he thought he would. The written part of the test was more difficult. He had to identify all the flags in the flag bag and several foreign country flags. He struggled through the international signals, but recovered and did very well on signal light nomenclature. He could do that part in his sleep. He had broken down and cleaned the signal lights at least once a week, lovingly lubricating the moving parts and polishing the reflector.

When he was finally finished, his head was swimming with test questions and possible answers and he honestly didn't have any idea how he had fared. He signed the exam booklet and gave it one more quick look before handing it over to Anselmi.

"Three minutes left," Anselmi observed, looking at his watch. "You cut that kinda close, Slick. How'd you do?"

"Hell, I don't know, Flags. I couldn't remember some of the foreign flags, and I got mixed up on a few things." R.J. chewed on a fingernail, frowning. "I think I blew it," he said quietly.

"Well, old buddy," Anselmi said, grinning. "You'll find out in ninety days. No need to worry about it now. Forget it until you get the results."

R.J. nodded and left the messdecks with the feeling that he had gotten his chance and he had blown it. *Screw it,* he thought, *I can take it again in six months.*

FIFTY SEVEN

Our Lady of Guadalupe Chapel was brightly decorated with crepe paper, bright flowers and dozens of white carnations made out of tissue. Decked out in dress whites, R.J. stood at the altar next to a very nervous Billy, and waited for Teresa and Mr. G to make their way down the aisle.

Gino and Pea served as ushers, and two of Teresa's friends were the brides-maids. Pea delighted in making faces at the bridesmaids, sending them into giggling fits. Gino elbowed Pea in the ribs.

"Ow!" Pea whispered. "What you do that for?"

"Shhh," Gino scolded. "Here they come."

The church organ began playing 'Here Comes the Bride' and all eyes turned to the rear of the chapel. Teresa and her father came down the aisle slowly, smiling at the guests along the way. Teresa wore a long, white dress with a high collar of lace decorating her neck. Her face was covered with a lace veil and she held a small bouquet of white flowers in her trembling hands. Mr. G wore his best suit, his only suit, actually, a white gabardine he had purchased years back, when he was a little thinner. The buttons on his vest were stretched across his belly, threatening to pop loose. Mrs. G said a quiet prayer and was glad she had taken the time to reinforce those buttons. He would be encouraged to take off the vest for the reception. There was no use taking any chances.

Mr. G beamed broadly as he led his daughter down the aisle. He was very proud of her, and he loved Billy as if he were his own son. Mr. G was a very happy man as he and Teresa reached the pulpit. He smiled happily and proudly, and tears of joy flowed down his cheeks.

When the priest asked, "Who giveth this woman to be married to this man?" Mr. G answered in a voice that was cracking with emotion, "Her mother and I do." He lifted Teresa's veil and kissed her cheek. He then turned to Billy and gave him a big hug. Then Mr. G hugged R.J. and Gino and Pea. When he began hugging the bridesmaids, the crowd giggled and Mrs. G gave him a look that said, "Sit down, you fool."

Billy's knees were shaking as he knelt in front of the altar with his bride. His hand shook as he placed the ring on her finger, and his voice wavered when he repeated the priest's words to love, honor and obey, in sickness and in health, for as long as they both shall live. He was perspir-ing during the entire ceremony and dabbed at his face and neck with a handkerchief limp with sweat.

Finally, it was over. The Havernauts stood at attention along the sides of the aisle, saluting, and Billy and Teresa made their way between them and out of the church. Billy breathed deeply outside, relieved that the cer-emony was over. He wiped his face again with the damp handkerchief and looked down at Teresa. She was looking up at him with a tender expres-sion, and his heart melted.

"I love you, Billy Lopez," she said.

"I love you, too, Teresa Lopez." He pulled her close and kissed her. "I'm sure glad that's over."

She laughed and hooked her arm in his. "They're coming out," she said. "Smile and act like you're happy."

"I am happy," he whispered in her ear. "And later tonight I'm gonna be even happier."

She playfully slapped him on the arm, blushing through her smile, as her parents came through the door and all four of them embraced warmly on the steps of the church.

The reception was held in the recreation center adjacent to the church. The tables were decorated with the same flowers, crepe paper and tissue carnations that had decorated the church, and a tall three-tier wedding cake sat on a table at the head of the room. Champagne punch bubbled from a fountain into a large glass bowl, and several guests lined up to fill their glasses. R.J., Gino, Pea and the rest of the Havernauts stood in a circle off to the side, passing a bottle of Jack Daniel's between them. Only Rafer and Andy declined to drink. A five member band played softly in the corner of the room.

Teresa and Billy arrived, greeted by a standing ovation and cheers from the Havernauts. The bride and groom smiled, waved and took their places at the head of the table. R.J. and Teresa's maid of honor, Gloria, prepared plates of food from the buffet and brought them to the newlyweds. That signaled the rest of the guests to line up at the buffet and the party began.

Mr. G and Teresa took center stage after dinner, dancing the father and daughter dance as the band played a soft rendition of the Chantels' 'Look in My Eyes.' They were joined by Billy and Mrs. G and the guests cheered. Mr. G led Teresa to Billy and they began dancing as Mr. and Mrs. G stood off to the side, arms around each other, smiling happily and wiping at tears. Billy and Teresa danced to their favorite song, 'I Only Have Eyes for You,' alone on the floor, gazing lovingly into each other's eyes. Soon they were joined by several other couples and the dance floor became crowded.

R.J. tapped Billy on the shoulder and Billy backed away, smiling. R.J. danced with Teresa, Pea danced with Teresa, Gino danced with Teresa, and all the Havernauts lined up to dance with the bride. R.J. and Billy watched, their arms draped across each other's shoulders.

"She's really beautiful, isn't she R.J.?" Billy asked proudly.

"Absolutely beautiful," R.J. answered. "You are a lucky man, Charming Billy."

"Yes, I am," Billy agreed, proudly watching his wife dancing with his shipmates.

"I mean you are a very lucky man," R.J. said, staring down at his shoes. "Most people don't get this lucky."

Billy turned to face him. "You'll find the right one, R.J." he said.

"Not me," R.J. said, a little high from the whiskey. "I ain't gonna fall in love with anyone."

Billy smiled charmingly and patted his friend on the back. "Don't give up on love, buddy," he said, and went to join his bride.

R.J. stood and watched Billy and Teresa dancing. They certainly looked happy. *Don't give up on love, huh?* he thought. *What happens when love gives up on you?* Annie's lovely face popped into his mind, but he shook it off and went looking for the bottle of Jack Daniel's.

Gino and the Deck Apes took the stage with the band and quickly collaborated on some songs. The guests stayed on the floor, dancing and singing along until Billy and Teresa changed their clothes, said their good-byes, and left for their honeymoon, which would be spent in an isolated cabin, high up in the hills. Mr. and Mrs. Gamboa stood on the steps of the rec center, arm in arm, smiling happily and waving at the departing newly-weds. Only two of Mr. G's vest buttons had survived the reception, but by then neither he nor Mrs. G seemed to notice.

The Havernauts piled into the New Pickup and the Bomb and made their way back to the base, singing raucously in the evening air. By the time they got back to the ship, they were exhausted and fell into their bunks. All agreed that it was one of the best times they had ever had. It would be their last good time together as a crew.

FIFTY EIGHT

During the week before the heavyweight championship fight, tensions among the crew grew steadily, with Chief Twitchell orchestrating several incidents of confrontation between whites and blacks. He was becoming more aggressive in his treatment of black sailors, insulting them flagrantly in front of other crew members and laughing when they became angry. Then one night an ugly incident occurred on the fantail after the movie was shown, and almost came to blows. Rafer, Andy and Jefferson, along with several other black sailors, arrived for the movie together and sat in a group on the deck in front of the screen. Snively was showing *"One Eyed Jacks."*

Twitchell sat on a torpedo tube toward the rear, and all through the movie, he heckled the blacks sitting in front.

"Don't you darkies know your place?" he called to them, grinning at his redneck friends. "You need to sit in the back, like in the buses down south!"

Encouraged by his grinning supporters, Twitchell kept needling the blacks all through the movie. "Where I come from, nee-groes ain't allowed to sit in a movie theatre with white people. We'd hang your black asses in Mississippi!"

The black sailors suffered Twitchell's diatribe in silence. When the movie ended, they stood together to leave.

"Better frisk those bastards," Twitchell yelled. "They probably stole something when we weren't looking!" This brought laughter from his friends.

"Why don't you shut your fat mouth, cracker?" a black voice called out. Twitchell strained to see who had said it, but the blacks were leaving together.

"Why don't you say that to my face, nigger?" Twitchell spat.

The group of blacks stopped and turned toward Chief Twitchell. They glanced at each other and started toward the group of rednecks, anger and frustration on their faces.

"C'mon, darkies," Twitchell prodded. "Come get your black asses kicked."

The two groups moved toward each other. R.J., Pea, Gino and a few others tried to calm them down by stepping between them.

"Get outta the way, R.J.!" Jefferson warned, his fists balled, his face seething in rage.

"Cool it!" R.J. insisted, holding his hands up, trying to stem the tide. It wasn't working, and R.J. was pushed aside. Just as the two groups were getting close enough to throw punches, the 1-MC blared, "Haverfield arriving!"

Captain Oliver came up the brow as Lee Piper drove away in his Ford Fairlane. He saluted the OOD and looked around at the men gathered on the fantail. He sensed the tension between the two groups, and it wasn't lost on him that one group was black, the other white.

"Movie over?" he asked no one in particular.

"Yes, sir," several voices answered.

The captain looked around at the faces of his men. "It's almost taps," he said quietly. "Better get some rest, men." He turned and walked slowly up the ladder toward his cabin.

With the tension broken, the two groups began breaking up and moving away, glaring at each other. R.J., Gino and Pea stood together on the fantail and watched the men depart for their compartments.

"What the hell just happened?" Pea asked.

"You mean what didn't happen?" Gino offered.

"This is bad," R.J. said, shaking his head.

"Yeah, and it's gonna get worse," Gino replied.

* * * * *

Armed Forces Radio broadcast the fight at 6:00 A.M. on Guam, and when the messdecks began filling early for breakfast, the tension between blacks and whites was palpable. Hawkins turned up the speakers as loud as possible and began serving the food as the introduction of the fighters began. The blacks gathered in the rear half of the messdecks, the whites forward, toward the galley.

Most everyone clearly expected Sonny Liston, the big heavyweight champion and ex-con, to easily dispatch the rash young challenger, but Cassius Clay had other ideas. He danced and jabbed through the first two rounds, making the champion look slow and lumbering. In the third round, Clay cut Liston over the eye with a combination and the blacks responded with cheers.

"Big ugly bear goin' down!" Andy yelled.

In the fifth round, Clay couldn't see, no one knew why, and he ran from Liston as the champ pursued him doggedly around the ring.

"The pretty boy is done!" Crawford announced. "It's only a matter of time!"

The problem with his vision cleared up, however, and in the sixth round Clay took over the fight, peppering Liston with lefts and rights. At the end of the round, Liston returned to his corner slowly, obviously tired.

Anxious for the seventh round to begin, the messdecks became silent between rounds. Trays of food, untouched, sat on the tables as all eyes and ears were on the radio. Suddenly, it was announced that Liston could not continue, and the fight ended with the champion sitting on his stool, and the challenger running hysterically around the ring.

For a few brief moments, the silence continued. Then, through the speakers came the strident voice of Cassius Clay, screaming into the microphone in the ring, "I shook up the world! I shook up the world!"

The rear of the messdecks erupted as black sailors jumped to their feet, their arms high in the air, cheering. The whites sat quietly, in stunned silence. Hawkins made a production of turning over the money stakes to the blacks and returned to his galley, grinning. He had bet on Liston, but this was just too good.

Chief Twitchell sat with his friends and seethed as the blacks pointed and laughed at the whites, chiding them with the result of the fight. The fat chief stood and threw a tray of food at the blacks, who ducked. Several more trays were thrown by the white sailors and a melee began, first with a food fight, eventually with punches being thrown.

"Let's get the hell outta here!" R.J. yelled at Pea and Gino. The three of them made their way forward through the starboard hatch just as Mr. MacDonald and Chief Whipple rushed into the messdecks.

"Attention on deck!" Chief Whipple roared. The messdecks became quiet as the sailors snapped to attention, expecting the captain. Mr. MacDonald strode in and looked around. The deck was littered with trays, food, coffee and whitehats. Several punches had been thrown, and some sailors, black and white, were sporting bruises and swollen lips. Somehow, Chief Twitchell and Crawford had slipped away during the commotion. Hawkins stood in his galley, surveying the mess, seemingly close to tears.

Mr. Mac stared into the faces of the combatants, disgusted at what he was witnessing. Shipmates punching each other over a boxing match? Obviously, it wasn't that simple. Chief Whipple stood leaning on the bulkhead, a scowl on his face, writing names down on a notepad. When he had recorded everyone's name, he nodded to Mr. MacDonald.

Mr. Mac could hardly contain his anger. "I want this messdecks squared away right now!" he demanded, teeth clenched. "Then I want every one of you to get your asses back to your compartments, and stay there until you hear from your department heads."

Sailors immediately began picking up the food and trays from the deck. Hawkins passed around mops and brooms and the deck was swabbed clean. Within minutes, the trays were deposited in the scullery, the food was cleaned from the deck, tables and bulkheads, and sailors were returning contritely to their compartments. Hawkins walked up and down the messdecks, nodding, satisfied that the mess had been cleaned up. He wiped his hands on his apron, sighed heavily, and returned to the galley to plan lunch.

Mr. MacDonald made individual reports to each department head and the executive officer. The exec reported to the captain and within fifteen minutes a meeting of all department heads was assembled in the wardroom. When the meeting broke up, the department heads left the wardroom with angry, set expressions on their faces. The captain had decided against putting the men on report, after being assured by his department heads that this was an isolated incident and would not recur. He wasn't so sure, and

to be on the safe side, he suspended all liberty, except for married personnel with dependents on the island, until further notice. The announcement
angered the men who were not involved in the altercation, and created a
sense of resentment toward the men who were involved. The gulf between
the two groups was widening.

* * * * *

"All this over a prize fight?" The exec sat across the wardroom table
from the captain. The department head meeting had concluded, and the
exec had stayed to talk with the captain.

"It goes a lot deeper than that, Ed," Captain Oliver replied. "There's an
old Chinese curse that goes, 'May you live in interesting times.' Well, we
are certainly living in interesting times." The captain lit his pipe with a
wooden match and leaned back in his chair, a thoughtful look on his face.

"I hate to think this is racially motivated," Mr. Martin said. "This crew
has been working so well together. After the last cruise, I have to tell you,
I was very proud of them. They performed terrifically, even with all the
drills we threw at them."

The captain nodded silently and puffed on his pipe. He looked up suddenly and smiled. "I think you just hit the proverbial nail on the proverbial
head, Ed," he grinned. "We need to get back to sea."

"We aren't due for a patrol until later next month," the exec said, but
the captain was lost in thought and didn't hear him.

"Ed, ask RM-1 Murray to come up here."

* * * * *

Big Queen paced the compartment, staring down the members of the
deck force who dared to meet his eyes. His trademark good-natured
needling was gone, and he fumed as he stalked between the bunks, looking
for the slightest infraction, and barking at the offending sailor when he
found one.

"Make up that rack, shit-for-brains," he growled at Jefferson. "Get that
laundry folded and stored away," he barked at Pea. "Trice up them damn
racks! Put that fuck book under your mattress," he ordered Gino, who
quickly shoved his Playboy magazine under his bunk. "You ladies wanna
act like high-schoolers, I'll treat you like high-schoolers!"

"We didn't start nothing,'" Andy complained. "We was just listenin' to
the fight."

Queen stopped pacing and turned to stare at Andy, who cringed a bit.
"Did I ask for your friggin' opinion?" the big boatswain's mate demanded.
"Don't matter what you was doin,' you still got this whole damn deck force
grounded."

Andy did the only right thing he could have done. He shut up. Rafer
stood silently, meeting Queen's gaze, his face impassive.

"No liberty until further notice," Queen bellowed. "Now get up on deck
and turn to!"

Pea almost pointed out that it wasn't 'turn-to' time yet, but thought better of it and followed the others up the ladder and onto the fantail. As they arrived on deck they saw Chief Twitchell standing on the 02 level, sipping coffee and grinning down at them.

"There's the asshole who started everything," Pea pointed out.

Rafer stood on the fantail staring up at Chief Twitchell. Andy came up next to him. "Don't let 'im start no more shit, bro," he said quietly. Rafer nodded slightly and turned to his brother.

"I feel like killin' that cracker," he seethed.

* * * * *

RM-1 Murray left the captain's cabin with the message he had been instructed to send to the new admiral at Naval headquarters, Guam. He read it quickly as he headed down the ladder to the radio shack. The captain was requesting gunnery exercises for the Haverfield, to be held west of Saipan. They would be joined by a target-towing sea-going tug and would conduct drills for three days and two nights. Night time gunnery exercises were unusual, but the captain thought his ship was ready for them. After the exercises, the ship would proceed to the Truk Islands and patrol for two weeks.

The captain knew that at sea, the crew would have little time to bicker among themselves. Underway, there was no time for anything but the ship. The ship was the priority, and individualism had no place in its operation. No matter what their differences were, at sea their entire beings had to be focused on the ship. Captain Oliver believed the bitter feelings would evaporate with the crew working together at sea. It almost worked, but the bitter feelings did not evaporate. They were merely pushed below the surface, where they simmered, and would eventually, predictably, rise back up.

* * * * *

"Surface action port!" Lieutenant Westerman barked into his sound-powered phone. The forward three-inch gun swiveled around and came to bear on the target, towed behind the USS Seneca, ATF 91, a sea-going tug. Walt Bixby sat in the forward gun mount and expertly moved the three-inch barrel to 'bulls-eye' the target.

"On target!" he called into his sound-powered phone, squinting as he lined up the sight.

"Fire!" Lieutenant Westerman commanded. "Fire at will!"

The gun cracked loudly as the three inch shell went flying toward the target. The shell splashed into the sea just beyond the target and the Seneca recorded a hit from the target's antenna system.

"He gets any closer," the captain said, looking through his binoculars at the white splash, "he's going to blow that target out of the water."

As if hc had heard the captain, Bixby's next shot hit the towed target direct and splintered it into pieces. Within seconds it broke loose from its cable and sank. A cheer rose up from the sailors on deck who were watching the gunnery exercises.

The captain turned, grinning, and looked at Mr. Westerman. "Hell of a shot, huh, Bill?" he asked.

"Yes sir!" Mr. Westerman replied proudly. "Bixby ought to join a carnival with that eye."

"Well, that's it for the gunnery exercises," the captain said, shrugging. "It's only the first day."

"There's always Bird Island," Lieutenant Westerman suggested, referring to the small island northwest of Saipan often used as a gunnery target.

Captain Oliver pondered the suggestion. "We might as well head there," he decided. "I want this ship to get some practice, and we can't do that if Bixby keeps sinking the targets." He stuck his head through the porthole and into the pilot house. "Mr. Martin?"

"Yes sir," the exec replied.

"Set a course for Bird Island."

"Aye, sir."

"Mr. Thompson?" The captain summoned the communications officer, who joined him on the flying bridge.

"Yes, sir?"

"Contact the powers that be on Guam and make sure no other surface craft is in the vicinity of Bird Island. Ask permission to proceed there and conduct gunnery exercises."

"Aye, sir."

"And Mr. Thompson." The captain was grinning.

"Yes sir?"

"Please signal the Seneca and offer my apologies for the abbreviated exercise."

"Yes, sir," Mr. Thompson replied with a grin of his own.

Before Mr. Thompson could pass on the order to the signal bridge, the Seneca's signal light was flashing.

"Got that, Slick?" Anselmi pointed toward the flashing light.

"I'm on it!" R.J. called and swung his light toward the Seneca, signaling 'go ahead.'

As the Seneca flashed the signal, R.J. read aloud, "Outstanding shot, who's the shooter, Wild Bill Hickock?" Anselmi and Mr. Thompson laughed.

"Send the captain's apologies," Mr. Thompson said. R.J. complied.

The Seneca began flashing again, and R.J. again read the signal aloud. "No problem, early liberty for us. Well done. See you in port."

R.J. acknowledged the signal and Mr. Thompson returned to the flying bridge to convey the message to the captain. The ship turned to the new course and steamed toward Bird Island. They would arrive just after dark.

FIFTY NINE

The Haverfield steamed southeast toward the Truk Islands, having spent two nights and one day pummeling Bird Island with three-inch shells. Bixby had proven to be an expert marksman and was enjoying celebrity status among the crew. The forward gun crew had scored twice the hits the aft crew had scored, and some good-natured ribbing naturally followed.

The ship was operating smoothly, all crew members functioning at peak efficiency. There was, however, a coolness between the black and white sailors, and even R.J. was being treated with indifference. The blacks did their jobs well, alongside the whites when on duty, but off duty they kept to themselves. The cohesiveness with which the crew had performed during the typhoon, the friendliness and camaraderie they had displayed during all the sea-going drills had all but evaporated under Twitchell's constant agitation.

Chief Twitchell rarely came out of the engine room, preferring to stay with his beloved machinery. He had not had a drink in several days. Mr. Almogordo had warned him that any on-board drinking would result in disciplinary action, and Chief Twitchell loved his gold hash marks as much, if not more, as he loved his scotch whiskey.

He busied himself with the maintenance of the machinery and seethed over what he called the 'niggerizing of the Navy.' During off-duty times, when he rarely came out of the engine room, he spent his time with like-minded rednecks among the crew, who sat around complaining about the blacks and feeding off each another's racism.

Rafer, clearly the leader among the blacks, preached separatism and urged his charges to avoid any unnecessary contact with non-blacks, whom he referred to as, 'Whiteys, Honkies and Chucks.' He lumped all whites into that category and made no exceptions, even for R.J., Gino and Pea.

The ship's officers perceived the widening gulf, but were unsure how to deal with it. Clearly, the racial landscape was changing in the states, and even thousands of miles away, on a Naval vessel at sea, the changes could not be denied; but the crew continued to function without any flare-ups, and so the officers opted to 'let sleeping dogs lie,' as long as there were no overt problems that threatened the harmony of the ship's operation.

The island landings during the patrol were conducted mechanically, devoid of the thrill and sense of adventure that had accompanied previous patrols. R.J. got to land on most of the islands, but didn't enjoy the landings as much as he had in the past. Perhaps he was becoming jaded, after so many island surveys, but his sense of unease over Rafer's attitude weighed heavily on his mind. He was relieved to see the last of the Truk Islands fade into the horizon as the Haverfield finished the patrol and headed for Apra Harbor and home, or at least home away from home. R.J.'s thoughts had been dominated recently with memories of Longmont and Denver. He had only five months left on his tour, and he was becoming sick of Guam, especially since his break-up with Annie.

He stood on the 02 level, staring aft over the fantail at Fayu Island, the last of the Truk Islands. It faded into the eastern horizon as the sun was fading into the western horizon. The ship seemed balanced precariously between the two points, just as he seemed balanced precariously between the Haverfield and home. He was engaged in these thoughts when he heard someone come up from behind him. He turned in the deepening dusk and was surprised to see Mr. MacDonald standing there.

"Good evening, Davis," the lieutenant said pleasantly.

"Good evening, sir," R.J. responded.

"This is one of my favorite times at sea," the lieutenant said, looking around at the darkening Pacific. "It reminds me of northern California, in the wine country, when the day's work is done and the grape vines are settling down for the night."

"I bet it's beautiful up there," R.J. replied.

"You're from Colorado, right?"

"Yes sir. My mother lives in Denver and my dad lives in Longmont."

"Divorced?"

"Yes, sir. A long time ago, when I was about eight."

"You like Denver or Longmont better?" The lieutenant was making pleasant small talk, but R.J. couldn't help but feel there was a deeper purpose for this little chat.

"I got friends in both places," R.J. replied, "but I really like Longmont. It's a small town, and really peaceful." He smiled wanly at the First Division commander. "Where I grew up in Denver was not always so peaceful," he said softly.

Mr. Mac nodded. R.J. figured sooner or later the lieutenant would get to the point.

"Not many black people in Longmont, I'll bet," he said finally.

"No, sir, not many," R.J. answered. He was curious about Mr. Mac's statement.

"I hear you grew up in a rough part of Denver," Mr. Mac said matter-of-factly. "I'm guessing that's why you seem to get along with everyone, including the black sailors aboard this ship."

R.J. nodded, saying nothing.

"I've seen you with Rafer and Andy Sample. You seem to be friends."

"Yes, sir," R.J. answered. He thought to himself, *at least we were friends.*

"Then, maybe you can tell me what's going on aboard this ship," Mr. Mac said firmly. "With the black versus white thing."

"I dunno, Mr. Mac," R.J. replied hesitantly.

"It's just you and me talking here, R.J.," Mr. MacDonald said, pulling himself up onto a vent. "No ranks. Not an officer talking with an enlisted man. Just you and me." He stared into R.J.'s eyes intently. "Talk to me."

"There's some racial conflict," R.J. started. "I don't know how to describe it, but..."

"But what?"

R.J. decided at that moment to level with the lieutenant. Mr. Mac had always been more than fair with him, and R.J. respected him as much as he respected anyone, including the captain and Chief Whipple. He laid it all out for him. He described the many problems with Chief Twitchell, the resentment felt by the black sailors, and Rafer's overreaction in withdrawing from all whites. He told Mr. Mac about the incidents involving Twitchell and his rednecks, including the near fight on the fantail and the near riot in the messdecks during the Clay/Liston fight. He held nothing back, including his opinion that Chief Twitchell was the main instigator of the trouble. He relayed the name-calling and humiliation the fat chief had heaped on the blacks for the past several months, and the deepening resentment the blacks were feeling. He offered the opinion that something bad was going to happen between the two groups if the situation did not improve.

Mr. MacDonald listened quietly, asking only a few questions, and nodded patiently as R.J. spoke. When he was finished, Mr. Mac hopped down from the vent and patted R.J. on the arm. "This conversation will remain between us," he said reassuringly. "I won't tell anyone we talked, but I will see to it that this information reaches the right people." He started to leave, then turned back to R.J. "I hear you took the third class exam," he said, smiling.

"Yes, sir," R.J. said proudly.

"You'll make a damn good petty officer," Mr. Mac said. "Good night, R.J."

"Good night, sir," R.J. replied. He watched thoughtfully as the lieutenant walked forward toward officer's country. *That was interesting,* he thought to himself. *Very interesting.*

His thoughts were interrupted by Pea who stormed up the ladder from the fantail. "Hey R.J.," the diminutive sailor called out. "We got a pinochle game going in the messdecks and we need a fourth. You game?"

"Sure," R.J. answered, turning toward his friend. "Let's go."

* * * * *

The Haverfield crew settled into a mind-numbing routine through the months of March and April. The blacks kept mostly to themselves, interacting with whites only when it was necessary, or at sea where there was no choice. The whites played pinochle or hearts with other whites, and the blacks played dominoes or acey-deucey with other blacks. There were no cross-overs in the respective games, though they often played next to each other in the mess decks. Rafer hardly spoke to R.J. anymore, except to say 'hello' in passing. It was obvious to R.J. and everyone aboard that Rafer had retreated into himself, seething with anger over what he perceived as the racist treatment of blacks in America. He kept current on the civil rights movement back home, and talked incessantly of black power and equal rights. But Rafer was not a revolutionary in the strictest sense of the word, because he was very much like his father, the Reverend Mordecai Sample, who believed in Dr. King's non-violent approach to the struggle. Rafer's anger urged him to react in kind to Twitchell, but he thought of his father and prayed for guidance. So, while other blacks openly advocated the violent overthrow of the government, Rafer fought back his anger and reasoned that change would only come from within the system, and only when blacks had become empowered. He cautioned the more outspoken blacks against railing against the system, but, instead, becoming more involved in the process. It would take time, he reasoned, but he urged them to believe that the struggle they were involved with today would reap benefits for future generations. That's what they were struggling for, he reminded them, the future.

In his heart, Rafer cultivated a bitter hatred of Chief Twitchell, and that hatred was fast coming to a head. Rafer saw Twitchell as the personification of the American racial struggle. Twitchell was the hooded horseman in Alabama, the vicious plantation owner in Mississippi, the axe handle-wielding bully intimidating black voters all across the south. Rafer became angrier every time he laid eyes on the fat chief. To force violent thoughts from his mind, Rafer prayed hard every day for the Lord to give him the wisdom to lead, and to take the sword from his hand.

Chief Twitchell continued his racist harangue at every opportunity. His group of rednecks had grown slowly, to almost twenty men. They got together every evening in the engine room and plotted ways in which to harass the blacks. Most of their actions were juvenile in nature, consisting of high school pranks such as grabbing a whitehat off a black sailor's head and throwing it into the harbor, or sneaking into the First Division compartment and putting garbage on the bunks of black sailors.

These types of actions, while petty and senseless, kept the tension high between the two groups, which was just what Chief Twitchell wanted. He knew if he constantly pushed Rafer and the other blacks, sooner or later something would happen that would result in a physical confrontation. He wanted a fight, so he could blame it on the blacks and get them sent to captain's mast. At every opportunity, the rednecks would get into the faces of the blacks and try to provoke them. Rafer preached restraint. Never throw the first punch, he told them, and always have a witness.

At the end of April, after returning to Guam from patrol, Chief Twitchell finally managed to push a black sailor too far. Timothy Jefferson was messenger of the watch when Chief Twitchell and two of his cronies returned to the ship from a night of drinking at the Mocombo Club. Crawford was the OOD, so Twitchell and his drinking buddies hung around the quarterdeck laughing and joking with Crawford.

Timothy Jefferson stumbled into the group on the quarterdeck after making his rounds of the ship. When he saw Twitchell and the others, he made an attempt to back away, but the fat chief spotted him and called him over.

"Lookey here," Twitchell said in a sing-song voice. "Ol' Crawford has got his own personal nigger." The other rednecks giggled.

"Don't use that word on me," Jefferson warned, glaring at the drunken chief.

"What word, boy?" the chief asked, grinning at Jefferson's discomfort. "You mean nigger?" He stood close to Jefferson, his face inches away, breathing heavily, his breath putrid with the stench of whiskey and cigars. "Well, that's what you is, boy. Your daddy was one and your momma was one, and you're one, too!"

"Don't talk about my mother, you cracker son of a bitch!" Jefferson exploded. Then he made a mistake. He put a hand on the chief's chest and pushed him away hard. "You stink, man. Get away from me!"

Chief Twitchell stumbled backwards and was kept from falling by his buddies. He scrambled to keep his feet under him, and straightened up, fixing his cap on his head. He took a step toward Jefferson, fists balled, ready to throw a punch. Crawford stepped between them.

"Cool it, Chief," Crawford said quietly and soothingly. "This man is on my watch."

Chief Twitchell seemed to relax. He grinned broadly at Jefferson. "You on report, nigger," he spat. "And I got witnesses here that saw you hit me."

"I didn't..." Jefferson began.

"Shut the fuck up, Jefferson," Crawford intervened. "You took a swing at a superior officer, and you're gonna pay for it." He glared at Jefferson contemptuously. "You are relieved from watch. Surrender your duty belt and nightstick and get your ass below."

"Screw you, Crawford," Jefferson retorted, taking off the duty belt and tossing it and the nightstick onto the desk. "And screw all you honky bastards." He walked across the fantail and down the aft ladder.

Chief Twitchell watched with amusement as Jefferson disappeared down the ladder. "I'll write this up in the morning and you witness it," he told Crawford, who nodded agreement. "I'm gonna get me some shut-eye." He smiled and nodded to his friends, then went through the port hatch toward the chief's quarters. He was quite pleased with himself.

* * * * *

Billy Lopez drove the New Pickup close to the brow and parked. Timothy Jefferson, accompanied by big Queen and Mr. MacDonald, strode down the brow and tossed his seabag into the truck's bed. He climbed into the cab and scooted over so Mr. MacDonald could sit shotgun. Queen climbed into the bed and braced himself against the side of the truck. He had ridden with Charming Billy several times, and knew what to expect.

Billy put the truck in gear and started down the pier. "Thirty days ain't nothin', Jefferson," he said reassuringly. "You'll be out in twenty-five. Just like a little vacation."

"Drive the truck, Chuck," Jefferson said bitterly.

Billy shrugged and sped up. He reached the end of the pier and turned right onto the road that would lead them up to the Marine brig.

Rafer, Andy and a few other blacks stood on the fantail and watched the truck make its way down the pier. Chief Twitchell, Crawford and a few others came up behind the blacks and watched the truck disappear.

"Well," Twitchell said, loud enough for the blacks to hear. "One nigger down, about thirty to go." He laughed loudly and slapped Crawford on the back. "At this rate, we should be a one hunnerd percent white crew in about a month." The rednecks moved away, laughing, leaving Rafer and his friends to stew.

"This ain't right," one of them said quietly. They all moved away except for Rafer and Andy, who stood near the lifeline, talking quietly. Rafer's face was set in a grim frown, and he felt himself sinking into a blinding rage. At that moment he realized that the peaceful, non-violent approach wouldn't work with people like Twitchell. There was only one way to deal with a pig like him. Even the Lord became angry every once in a while and smote someone who deserved it...

"What you thinking, bro?" Andy asked his brother.

"Only one thing's gonna make things right," Rafer said.

"Yeah, we gotta get rid of Twitchell."

"Oh, yes. We're gonna get rid of him, that I promise you, little brother."

"What you got in mind?" Andy asked, frowning at his brother.

Rafer looked up into Andy's eyes. "I'm gonna kill him," he said matter-of-factly.

SIXTY

Since he and Annie had broken up, R.J. spent almost all of his time aboard ship, only occasionally visiting the Mocombo Club. At R.J.'s insistence, Gino and Pea continued to see Betty and Carol when the Raptor was at sea. They told R.J. how unhappy Annie was. She missed him, but wouldn't call him because she was still mad at him. One other thing they related to him; Annie had suffered a miscarriage. For reasons R.J. couldn't quite understand he felt both relieved and saddened. But he shrugged it off and concentrated on his duties. Work, he discovered, kept his mind off her. Sometimes he went hours without thinking of her. Sooner or later, he believed, she would break down and call him. Then maybe they could talk.

He stood on the signal bridge and watched the Raptor come back into port. They had been gone for ten days, during which time R.J. seldom saw Gino or Pea in the evenings. He didn't mind. He was glad his friends could continue to enjoy themselves. They were doing it right, he decided. They weren't falling in love, they were just having some fun. It wasn't serious for Gino or Pea, and R.J. envied their casual attitude. Why did he always have to fall in love before he could fall into bed with a girl? Gino and Pea weren't miserable. Gino and Pea weren't in love.

R.J. wandered to the starboard wing bridge and watched as Timothy Jefferson climbed into the New Pickup, followed by Mr. Mac. It had been a year since he had taken that ride to the Marine brig himself. He marveled at the passing of time, a full year gone already, and wondered what Pinney, Bobby Jim and Beatty were doing at that moment.

Jefferson fell into Twitchell's trap just as he and Rafer had fallen into it. With Timothy Jefferson going to the brig, that made a total of five men who were sent there as a result of Chief Twitchell. Two of them had since transferred, and only one of them, R.J., had been white. One good thing, R.J. decided, was that once Twitchell was successful in getting someone sent to the brig, he lost interest in that man and began concentrating on another, new victim. Jefferson was going to do his time, but when he got out, Twitchell would, in all likelihood, leave him alone.

R.J. looked aft and saw Andy and Rafer talking quietly on the fantail, their heads close together, and wondered what they were talking about. *Probably Twitchell*, he decided.

* * * * *

"I would like to keep this between us, on the division level, if at all possible." Mr. Almogordo referred to the typewritten report on the table, marked 'confidential.'

Mr. MacDonald, the only other officer in the wardroom, nodded. "No problem, Pete. I think we can handle it on that level, but if anything untoward happens as a result of this conflict..." He let the words trail off. Pete Almogordo knew the stakes. Mr. Mac didn't have to tell him.

"I've had a conversation with Chief Twitchell about this," Mr. Almogordo said, picking up the report and weighing it in his hand. "Last summer I talked to him in my office. He promised he would avoid confrontations."

"He hasn't lived up to it, Pete," Mr. Mac replied, nodding toward the report. "His behavior is the stuff for a court martial."

"Whoa!" Mr. Almogordo protested, holding up his hand, palm out. "Mac, I need this man. He's the best engineer in the fleet. I know he's got some rough edges, but..."

"Rough edges?" Mr. Mac asked, picking up the report. "He's actively engaged in the harassment of blacks on board this ship. He's sent five of them to the brig already." Mr. Mac did not point out that one of those men was white.

"He's got a clean record, Mac," the engineering officer pleaded. "He hasn't actually attacked anyone physically, has he?"

MacDonald stared at the table, deep in thought. He had no evidence that Twitchell was involved in the mess decks incident. He never personally witnessed the Chief's behavior toward blacks, but he could sense the resentment aboard ship, and he could feel the growing gulf between black and white sailors. "No, I don't think he's actually attacked anyone, but, Pete..."

"Let's keep a lid on this, Mac," Mr. Almogordo said. "We'll watch the situation carefully, and if we get even a hint of a bigger problem, we'll take it to the exec and let him decide how to handle it." The engineer picked up the report and stacked the pages neatly. "It won't get out of hand, Mac. We'll see to that."

"Okay, Pete," MacDonald replied, sighing. "But please keep an eye on him, will you?"

"Yes, I will," Mr. Almogordo replied. He stood and shook the First Division commander's hand, and Mr. Mac left the wardroom.

Pete Almogordo sat alone at the green-covered table and leafed through the report Mr. MacDonald had prepared. It was quite an indictment of Chief Twitchell, he had to admit. Taken separately, each incident that had occurred had been minor in nature. Sure, the chief had pissed off some people, he was pretty rough around the edges, but when it came to the ship's machinery, Twitchell was the best.

The engineering officer remembered the nightly 'training' sessions in the engine room. He had been a little suspicious of those meetings, but he had assumed the men were getting together to gamble, which was not allowed on board ship. Could they really be plotting against blacks, as MacDonald had indicated? Was Chief Twitchell the head of some racist group like the Ku Klux Klan? Mr. Almogordo considered the idea to be preposterous, but he decided to keep a very close eye on Jaspar Twitchell. If Chief Twitchell *was* a racist and *was* organizing whites against blacks, Mr. Almogordo would personally drop him into the reassignment pool, minus his gold hash-marks, and to hell with the machinery. He folded the report in half, length-wise, and took it back to his quarters, where he slipped it under the mattress on his bunk.

* * * * *

Charming Billy Lopez had not spent many nights aboard ship since his marriage to Teresa Gamboa. On duty Friday night, he joined the group of sailors on the focsul to listen to the Deck Apes break in a few songs. With Timothy Jefferson in the brig, Pancho Cortez took over the baritone spot. He wasn't as good as Jefferson, but he sang the songs with enthusiasm. Billy was glad the singing group remained intact. The group was one of the few things everyone aboard ship agreed on, because the group was a source of pride for the crew, and for all their difficulties, the men aboard the Haverfield were still a crew. They gathered on the focsul every third night, when all four members were off duty, and always attracted an appreciative audience. The racial tension eased during these evenings on the focsul, though Rafer made it a point not to attend. Chief Twitchell and his rednecks did not attend either, preferring to meet in the engine room, plotting against the black sailors.

On duty as focsul watch, Billy sat on the capstain head and helped R.J. unhook barracuda and bonk them on the head with the nightstick. It was just after movie call and the fish were biting like crazy. R.J. pulled a dozen aboard in just a half hour, and, bucket full, decided to sit back and enjoy the music.

A breeze wafted across the focsul and stirred up the usually calm harbor water. It lapped gently against the ship, sounding like the happy splashes made by children playing in a swimming pool.

"Hey, Billy!" Sonny Metzner, petty officer of the watch, came up the port side of the focsul and interrupted the peaceful evening. "Phone call. It's Teresa, and she sounds like she's crying."

Billy handed the nightstick to R.J. and ran toward the fantail.

"What's wrong?" R.J. asked Sonny.

Sonny shrugged. "Dunno, she said she needed to speak to him and she was like crying, you know?"

"I'm gonna check on him," Pea announced and headed aft down the starboard side. The remaining sailors looked around at each other, concerned for Billy and Teresa. The Gamboa family was another special thing the Havernauts shared. They had a lot of affection for the Gamboas. They treated the Haverfield crew like family, and the Havernauts had adopted them as family, so, naturally, they were concerned.

"Yahoo!" Billy's happy yelp could be heard all over the ship. The men on the focsul looked at each other questioningly, wondering what was going on.

Billy came running up the port side and grabbed R.J. in a bear hug, holding him off the deck and shaking him.

"Damn it, Billy," R.J. protested. "Put me the hell down!"

Billy set R.J. down and beamed at him. "She's pregnant!" he hollered. "We're gonna have a baby!"

As the Havernauts gathered around Billy, slapping him on the back and congratulating him, Pea came up the starboard side, slightly out of breath.

"Did Billy come back up here?" he asked, exasperated. He spotted Billy surrounded by well-wishers. "Now, what the hell?" he wondered aloud.

"Teresa's pregnant!" Billy beamed proudly.

Pea's eyes grew large and round. "Well, don't look at me!" he protested, to the laughter of everyone on the focsul.

R.J. held up a hand for silence. "There's an old Navy tradition," he began, grinning at Billy. "When a man is about to become a father, it is traditional to throw his ass over the side!" R.J. began moving toward Billy, who was fast being surrounded by a grinning group of Havernauts.

"Wait a minute," Billy protested. "I never heard of that tradition."

The Havernauts lifted Billy up and carried him to the lifeline.

"Wait!" he yelped, "There's barracuda feeding in that water!"

"Bon voyage!" Pea yelled, and Billy went over the side and splashed into the harbor as the Havernauts looked down at him and applauded. Billy swam easily toward the pylons and pulled himself up on the wooden beam. He sat there for a moment, soaking wet, grinning happily. The Deck Apes serenaded him with 'I Only Have Eyes For You.'

Chief Risk, the evening's OOD, came up to the focsul during his customary rounds, just as Billy was swimming toward the pylons. The chief looked down and frowned at Billy splashing around in the harbor.

"What's going on up here?" he asked, still frowning.

"Billy just got the word," R.J. explained. "Teresa's pregnant. We were just celebrating."

Chief Risk looked around at the men, then back at Billy who was sitting on the pylons, wringing the water out of his whitehat. He seemed uninjured. In fact, he was grinning happily.

"Carry on," the chief said, smiling, and walked slowly down the starboard side.

"We're having a party tomorrow!" Billy yelled as he climbed up the pylons and made his way to a point where he could climb back aboard. "A cook-out at Mr. & Mrs. G's and you're all invited!"

Pea took the duty belt from Billy and relieved him as focsul watch so he could go below and change into a fresh uniform. When Billy returned to the focsul he was still grinning.

"Noon tomorrow," he instructed. "Be there at noon."

Later, lying in his bunk, staring up at the myriad of pipes and wires snaking along the overhead, R.J. wondered wistfully what it would be like to be married and have a baby. He thought of Annie and the baby she had lost. He wondered if it had been his. He fell into a fitful sleep and tossed around most of the night.

* * * * *

The party was a big success. Mr. and Mrs. Gamboa were delighted with the prospect of becoming grandparents, and they doted on Teresa and Billy.

Almost all of the Havernauts were there; the only ones missing were Rafer and Timothy Jefferson. Andy and a few black sailors showed up for the festivities, but Rafer wanted to be alone, saying he had plans to make.

Mr. Gamboa was the life of the party, as usual. He dressed in a brightly printed Hawaiian shirt and danced around the front yard like a drunken Indian around a bonfire. Mrs. Gamboa sat on the porch, rocking in her chair, a happy smile spread across her face.

Teresa looked beautiful. She glowed with young motherhood as she sat closely to Billy, her head on his shoulder, holding his hand in both of hers. Billy was the picture of a proud father-to-be. R.J. envied him his happiness, his contentment, and wondered if he would ever have the opportunity to feel the way Billy and Teresa felt that day.

Slowly, close to the end of the day, with Teresa tiring and Mrs. G clucking around her, the party-goers began to drift off, heading back to the ship or to downtown Agana.

Pea, Gino and R.J. climbed into the Bomb and headed down Highway One.

"Let's stop at Talagi's," Gino suggested. "It's too early to go back to the ship."

"Talagi's it is," Pea said, stepping on the gas and speeding up. "Maybe the girls will be there."

"The Raptor's in port, Pea," R.J. said absently.

"You never know," Pea said, winking at Gino. R.J. wondered if they were up to something.

Pea piloted the Bomb into Talagi's parking lot and screeched to a stop, swirling dust around the lone car-hop, a pretty, young Guamanian girl named Stella.

"Damn it, Peacock," she complained when Pea rolled down his window. "You make a big mess here!"

"You still love me, Stella?" Pea grinned up at her.

"Not no more!" she replied, brushing dust off her short skirt. She took orders for three Pepsis and stepped into the diner.

Gino spotted them first. The late afternoon sun was ebbing, its harsh glow streaking at an odd angle over the landscape, and the Chevy Impala, carrying Betty, Carol and Annie, had rolled silently into the gravel parking lot of Talagi's, so quietly that no one saw them at first. Gino happened to be sitting with his back to the drive-in, facing the parking lot and Highway One.

"Hey, fellas," Gino whispered, lowering his head and sipping at his Pepsi to hide his face. "Check it out."

Pea and R.J. turned to look. Pea beamed brightly. R.J. scowled.

"Okey dokey," Pea exclaimed, slurping down the last of his Pepsi and slamming the plastic cup unnecessarily hard on the table. "Here come my baby!" He pushed his whitehat back on his head and sauntered over to the driver's side of the Chevy, grinning lasciviously at Carol, who sat behind the wheel, giggling demurely at the approaching Pea. R.J. thought he was going to puke.

"You guys set this up?" R.J. asked suspiciously.

"Who, us?" Gino asked with false innocence.

"Man," R.J. sighed. "This ain't good."

"Just go fuckin' talk to her," Gino said as he approached the Impala and jumped into the back seat. Betty wrapped herself around him and Gino lay back, a silly grin on his face.

R.J. walked reluctantly over to the passenger side, where Annie sat, staring straight ahead, a pair of sunglasses on her face. She sipped slowly at a straw poking out of the top of a plastic Pepsi cup.

R.J. leaned against the door and smiled. "Howdy," he offered. She ignored him.

"Howdy," he said again.

She turned very slowly, agonizingly slowly, to face him. She deliberately lowered her sunglasses and looked up into his face. Her eyes fixed on him and he watched as the expression in those blue eyes evolved from irritation to what? *Amusement? That was like Annie. She could change moods like a chameleon changed color.*

"Howdy?" she asked, incredulously. "I don't see or hear from you in months, and all you have to say for yourself is, howdy?"

"You said you didn't ever want to see me again," he complained. "What was I supposed to do?"

"You're such an idiot," she said, slurping the last of her Pepsi and throwing the cup aside.

He stared down at her. *How was he an idiot? Didn't he do what she told him to do, get lost? What the hell was the problem?* He did it, he got lost, just like she told him to do. So, now what the hell was the problem? "Now I'm an idiot," he stammered.

"You don't know shit about women," she accused. "If you did, then you'd know..."

"Know what?" he demanded, frustrated. "What?"

"Oh, never mind," she said, obviously trying to conclude the conversation. She looked up at him over her sunglasses. "I lost the baby," she said flatly, then pushed the sunglasses up on her nose and stared ahead, through the windshield.

R.J. stepped back two paces. *What the hell was he supposed to say now? What do you say to a girlfriend who got pregnant, told you to fuck off, then lost the baby, and still was pissed off at you?*

"You wanna go for a walk with me?" he asked, clumsily.

"No." She took off the sunglasses and laid them down on the seat next to her. "But I will." She opened the door and swung her legs out.

R.J. held the door open for her and she moved next to him. He closed the door and put his arm around her waist. Annie snuggled close to him and laid her head on his shoulder. They walked away slowly, arm in arm, heads pressed together, whispering softly to each other.

"Isn't love wonderful?" Betty sighed as she watched R.J. and Annie walk away together.

"Sex is wonderful," Gino countered, idly squeezing one of Betty's boobs. "*Love* ain't nothin' but a pain in the ass."

R.J. led Annie to a picnic table toward the rear of Talagi's, partly obscured by trees and vegetation. They sat across from each other, holding hands, looking into each other's eyes.

"I'm not mad at you anymore," Annie said quietly. "I was, I was really mad, but I'm not anymore."

R.J. looked into her eyes and decided not to argue with her. "I know," he nodded.

"I can't explain it, R.J.," she said, frowning down at their intertwined hands. "When I knew I was pregnant I..." She began to cry, and tears ran down her cheeks. She fumbled into her jeans pocket for a hanky and dabbed at her eyes. R.J. sat quietly, not knowing what to say.

"There you are!" Pea appeared at the edge of the table and looked down at R.J. and Annie. "Wha's wrong?" he asked hesitantly.

"Nothing," Annie said, wiping her eyes.

"Well," Pea ventured. "We're goin' to the USO beach, you guys coming?" He started back toward the car and turned. "Well?" he asked impatiently.

"Yeah," R.J. answered, staring into Annie's eyes. "We're coming."

Dark had enveloped the island when the two cars pulled into the USO beach parking lot. R.J. looked to see if the Ford Fairlane was parked there. It was not. The beach was dark, no moon lighting the sky. The surf broke and crashed over the beach, reflecting a soft, phosphorous glow in the waves as they crested onto the sand.

Pea broke out two wool blankets he had stashed in the trunk of the Bomb and the three couples sat on them in a circle, smoking cigarettes and talking about not much of anything.

R.J. stared silently at Annie. She was beautiful. Her face was lit by the ember on her cigarette when she took a puff, and she idly flipped her blonde hair back over her ears with the tips of her fingers. It suddenly occurred to him that his heart was not racing like it always had in her presence. His feelings for her were still strong, but something had happened to him over the past few months. At first, after their breakup, he couldn't get her out of his mind. Then, slowly, almost imperceptibly, she began to fade from his thoughts. Some nights recently, he had not thought of her at all while he lay in his bunk staring up at the overhead, waiting for sleep to come.

"What are you thinking about, R.J.?" Her sweet voice broke into his thoughts.

"I'm thinking about you," he answered. "I'm always thinking about you."

"Aw, that's so sweet," Betty cooed. She looked up at Gino. "Don't you think that's sweet, Gino?"

"Yeah," he murmured. "Real sweet." He got up and pulled Betty to her feet. "Let's go for a walk in the surf," he said. They pulled off their shoes and socks and gamboled down the beach. Soon they were laughing and splashing around in the surf.

Pea and Carol got up and moved to the back seat of the Bomb. R.J. and Annie sat cross-legged, talking quietly and necking passionately. Up on Highway One, lights of passing cars streaked by, throwing just a little light on the beach as they passed.

"What are we gonna do?" Annie asked.

"About what?"

"About us."

"What do you want to do?" he asked.

"I don't know. What do you want to do?"

"I don't know," he said impatiently. "Why do we have to decide things now?"

"Your tour is going to be up in three months, and I'm scared I'll never see you again." She pouted, hoping it would have an effect on him. It did. It pissed him off.

"We haven't seen each other in quite a while," R.J. reminded her. "You broke up with me. I never did nothing to make you mad, but you got mad anyway."

"I'm not mad anymore, R.J. Please let's not fight."

He took her in his arms and together they fell back on the blanket, locked in a passionate embrace. They made love gently on the blanket while Gino and Betty frolicked in the surf and Pea and Carol tested the shock absorbers on the Bomb. When they were finished, R.J. lay back on the blanket and lit a cigarette for Annie, then one for himself. She snuggled next to him and sighed.

"That was wonderful," she said breathlessly. "I've missed you so much."

R.J. stared up at the star-filled sky and blew smoke slowly through his nose. *It had been wonderful,* he thought. *Just like it always was, but...*he sensed a change in his feelings toward her. It just wasn't the same. There seemed to be a cloud hanging over them, something he couldn't quite grasp, something obscure that made him hold back just a little. *Maybe it's because we haven't been together recently,* he thought. *Or maybe it's because I don't care as much as I used to.* He closed his eyes and breathed deeply, trying to sort it out in his mind. *Maybe it wasn't love. Maybe it never was love. Does love fade away like this?*

"R.J.," she whispered.

"Huh?"

"What're you thinking about?"

"Nothin.'"

"Will you tell me a poem?" she pleaded.

"Okay," he agreed. He took a deep breath.

"It was many and many a year ago
in a kingdom by the sea,
that a maiden there lived whom you may know
by the name of Annabel Lee.
And this maiden she lived with no other thought
Than to love and be loved by me..."

* * * * *

The Haverfield was scheduled to be in port for the next few weeks, and the captain had ordered the ship to be freshly painted. R.J. and Billy worked furiously to paint the signal bridge, lay down new non-skid on the deck and clean out the flag bags in preparation for painting. R.J. was airing out the flags from the port flag bag when Anselmi appeared on the signal bridge, a cup of coffee in his hand and a big grin on his face.

"That non-skid's still wet," R.J. warned. Anselmi stepped over the fresh non-skid and sat down on the rung of the flag bag. He was still grinning.

"You grinnin' like a Cheshire cat, Salami, what's going on?"

"Nothin' much," the second class signalman said, still grinning. "Oh, I forgot, there's this..." He reached into his back pocket and pulled out a sheet of paper. It was some sort of list.

"What's that?" R.J. asked.

"Oh, nothin' much," Anselmi grinned. "Just the promotion list." He studied the sheet of paper while R.J. held his breath. "It says here," Anselmi said, pointing to a spot on the list, "that someone named Davis, R.J. passed the third class signalman's exam."

R.J. grabbed the list out of Anselmi's hand and scanned it quickly. There it was, Davis, R.J. was now a third class signalman. He had his crow!

"Way to go, R.J.," Billy said, slapping R.J. on the back.

R.J. stood staring at the list, almost afraid to take his eyes off it. A year ago he had been in the brig and his future in the Navy had seemed to be limited. Now he had his crow, and he had worked hard for it. He got it because he wanted it so badly. R.J. felt at that moment that he could do anything.

Later that evening he came up on the focsul to listen to the Deck Apes and catch some barracuda. He knew what was coming, but he didn't mind at all when most of the Havernauts showed up, lifted him up over the lifeline and threw his ass into the drink.

As he swam to the pylons and pulled himself up, the Deck Apes began serenading him, looking down at him from the point of the bow:

"Duke, Duke, Duke, Duke of Earl, Duke Duke..."

R.J. sat on the pylons, soaking wet and tried to catch his breath. He had never been so happy in all his life. He felt vindicated, renewed, certain that he was on a fast track to success. He climbed up to the pier and walked, shoes squishing, to the low point on the ship, and climbed over the lifeline, joining his friends on the focsul.

SIXTY ONE

Rafer rarely came out of the shell he had built around himself. He hardly spoke to anyone, with the exception of Andy, unless he was touting the black power philosophy. Inside, he was seething with anger.

Rafer worshiped his father, and he tried hard to be just like him. But since his stint in the brig, listening to the militant Jeremy Washington rail against the peaceful approach, Rafer had begun to wonder if his father's way, if Doctor King's way, was really the best way. His anger at Chief Twitchell fueled his frustration.

His rage burned deeply, and drove him to want to try to correct the wrongs heaped on his people for generations. Always smoldering, ever deeper into his soul, the anger enveloped him, encompassed him, dominated him, in much the same way as the Lord's work encompassed and dominated his father.

Often, late at night, Rafer would get up and climb the aft ladder to the fantail, where he would stand at the stern and stare off across the harbor, focusing on some shadowy point in the distance. During these times his thoughts were dominated by one topic: how to kill Chief Twitchell and make it look like an accident. His father, Rafer knew, would never approve of such thoughts, let alone any violent acts. But his father was in Alabama, tending to his flock, and Rafer felt he had a flock of his own to tend to on the Haverfield.

He examined and rejected several scenarios where the chief would meet his untimely end. One thing Rafer was certain of. It was going to have to happen at sea. He would never be able to pull it off when the ship was in port. But at sea, late at night, with the ship darkened, many opportunities presented themselves. Rafer pondered them all, staring across the harbor. He had not yet decided on the exact plan of action, but he knew it had to happen. There was no other choice. With Twitchell out of the way, the other rednecks would back off. Rafer was sure of that. Twitchell was the key.

Andy's only concern was his brother. Rafer was the only thing Andy cared about deeply, besides his family back home, and he understood Rafer's feelings about Chief Twitchy, but Andy didn't agree that killing him would solve anything. He wanted to dissuade his brother from harming the chief, but he knew, when push came to shove, he would back Rafer to the end.

* * * * *

Jefferson returned from the brig late in the evening on the last Saturday in May. Most of the crew was ashore on liberty, and Jefferson smiled happily as RM-1 Murray, OOD, logged him in.

"So how's the brig, Jefferson?" Murray asked good-naturedly.

"Good chow," Jefferson replied.

"Lemme see your hands," Murray said. Jefferson showed his hands, palms up. "Looks like they worked you pretty good," Murray said, appraising the calluses on Jefferson' hands.

"Hard work," Jefferson agreed.

Murray cocked his head and looked bemused as he studied Jefferson's face. "You used to talk a lot more," he chided. "They brainwash you up there?"

Jefferson laughed. "Hey, man I'm just glad to be back with Momma Haverfield!"

"So, all that surly crap is gone?" Murray grinned at Jefferson.

Jefferson grinned back. It was true he felt different, better than he had when he had left for the brig. He was happy to get back to the ship, partly because he knew Twitchell would find someone else to occupy his crosshairs. "It's behind me," he said quietly.

Murray smiled and nodded slowly, searching Jefferson's face. "Stay away from him, man," he advised.

"That's jus' what I aim to do," Jefferson replied. He hefted his seabag onto his shoulder and made his way down the aft ladder to First Division's compartment.

Murray watched him go below and stood on the quarterdeck, deep in thought. Truth be told, Murray disliked Chief Twitchell almost as much as most of the crew. He didn't approve of the chief's bullying attitude, especially toward blacks. His thoughts were interrupted by the arrival of the first shuttle bus, depositing a small group of sailors on the pier. These were the early-birds. They either got drunk too early or they got broke too early, so they had no other choice but to return to the ship.

Murray greeted the early arrivals at the brow, arms wide, a big, welcoming smile on his face. "Welcome home to Momma Haverfield," he greeted warmly. And thus a tradition began. From that point on, the ship was often referred to as 'Momma,' or 'Momma Haverfield.'

* * * * *

Captain Oliver sorted through his mail, the official stuff first, the personal stuff to be saved until later. A soft knock on his cabin door interrupted him. "Come!" he called.

RM-3 Riley opened the door and removed his whitehat. "Morning, Cap'n," he said, handing him a clipboard holding several radio messages. Riley was grinning.

"What arc you so happy about, Riley?" the captain asked, amused.

"Last message, sir," Riley said, nodding toward the clipboard.

Paul Oliver flipped through the first few messages until he reached the last one. He read it quickly, glanced up at a smiling Riley, and read it again, slowly, going over in his mind the potential consequences to this particular message. He initialed all the messages and took his copies. "That'll be all," he said.

"Aye, sir." Riley left the cabin.

Captain Oliver sat back in his chair and read the message again. A feeling of dread, followed by a feeling of excitement, rippled through him. He got up with the message in his hand, put on his cap and walked the short distance down the passageway to the exec's cabin. He knocked, heard the call to enter, and opened the door.

"Oh, morning, Captain," Lieutenant Martin rose to his feet in front of his desk. He had several Navy manuals open on the desk, next to a pad of yellow, legal paper with several notes on it. "Some new regs to be reviewed and logged," he said, explaining the cluttered desk.

"We got some new orders, Ed," the captain said, waving the message slip in the air. "We're going to Subic Bay."

"Subic Bay?" The exec seemed caught off guard.

"Yes, Ed," the captain smiled goodnaturedly. "It's in the Philippines. We have a Naval base there. Surely you've heard of it?"

The exec grinned. "That's a good liberty port," he said, taking the message and reading through it. "Ten days' R&R! What'd we do right?"

"Apparently enough to rate some R&R," the captain replied. "I'm glad we got the painting done."

"Shall I pass the word to the crew?" Mr. Martin asked.

"Tell you what, Ed," the captain replied, handing the message slip to the exec. "Pin this on the board next to the plan of the day, and I guarantee this crew will know about it before noon chow."

The captain left the exec's cabin and headed to the signal bridge. R.J. and Billy were practicing semaphore together, and snapped to attention, saluting as the captain came up.

"As you were," the captain said. "Can you raise the Brister for me?"

"Yes sir!" R.J. replied and turned on the flashing light, aiming it at the Brister, signaling *dah-dit-dit, dah-dah-dit-dit-dit,* or D7, the Brister's abbreviated call sign. "Got 'er, Cap'n," R.J. announced as the Brister answered.

"Please ask Captain Piper to join me for lunch at the Officer's Club at twelve-hundred," the captain ordered. "And ask him to confirm."

R.J. sent the message and acknowledged the receipt from the Brister. "They're asking us to wait one," R.J. said.

"Very well," the captain agreed. He leaned back against the bulkhead and looked around the signal bridge. "You men have this place ship-shape," the captain said, smiling benevolently.

"Thank you, sir," Billy and R.J. said in unison.

"Congratulations on your crow, Davis," the captain said, pointing at R.J.'s left sleeve.

"Thank you, sir," R.J. said, smiling proudly. He stood a little taller.

"Light!" Billy called out.

R.J. spun the light around and answered the Brister. A short message was flashed back and R.J. receipted for it and signed off. He turned to the captain. "Captain Piper has confirmed, sir," he reported.

"Carry on," the captain said. He turned and left the signal bridge.

"You seem real chummy with the captain," Billy teased.

"Yeah, we're good buds," R.J. winked.

Paul Oliver sat down in his chair and stared at the surface of his desk, thinking about the upcoming trip to Subic Bay and the possibility that he might see Lorelei. Memories of her rushed into his mind. He could smell her fragrance, feel her nakedness, hear her voice, but for the life of him, he couldn't picture her face. He shook his head, frustrated, and returned to his mail. He would talk it over with his best friend at lunch. He knew that just talking about it to Lee Piper would make him feel better.

* * * * *

Early Monday morning, the 8th of June, the Haverfield set sail for Subic Bay, Philippines. In his customary seat on the flying bridge, Captain Oliver sipped a cup of black coffee and reviewed the departmental readiness reports. The ship was operating very smoothly, and Captain Oliver was quite happy with the crew's efficiency. He allowed himself to reminisce, remembering the shabby shape the ship was in when he first assumed command. This was a different ship, indeed. The engines were running at peak efficiency, thanks to Chief Risk and his engineers, the problem with the evaporators was apparently solved by Chief Twitchell, the crew performed their duties with a sense of teamwork and the ship looked like a U.S. Navy warship. The fresh paint, the shining brass, the proudly displayed green 'C' and white 'E' announced to the world that this was a proud and efficient vessel.

Beyond that, the crew performed in a crackerjack fashion during all drills, shaving valuable seconds off their response times. Captain Oliver believed his ship and crew were ready for anything. He welcomed the time at sea, with the ship and crew functioning so well, and he looked forward to conducting more drills on the way to Subic Bay.

He did not look forward, however, to what awaited him in Subic Bay. There would be no chance to avoid Lorelei. Paul Oliver had received a message from Admiral Quentin Prescott, advising him that a reception would be held on Saturday evening, the thirteenth, at the Naval base's Officer's Club. He would receive an official invitation upon arrival at Subic Bay. He did not want to see Lorelei again, but he knew it was inevitable and unavoidable. He looked through the windows of the flying bridge and gazed out at the open sea. If he closed his eyes and concentrated, he swore he could hear that siren song, beckoning him toward the shoals. He shook his head to rid himself of the image and concentrated on the readiness reports.

* * * * *

Rafer stood on the 02 level with Andy, watching Chief Twitchell and MM-1 Crawford talking and laughing on the fantail. The sea was becoming a little choppy, and the ship began rolling, just slightly at first, then more dramatically as the waves grew bigger. Sailors moved easily up and down the decks, walking bow-legged in complete rhythm with the movements of the ship.

Down on the fantail, MM-1 Crawford stood with his feet set apart and rode the ship expertly. Chief Twitchell, however, had trouble with the movement of the ship when he was on deck. Down below, in the small engine room, he had no problem adjusting to the rolling ship, but up on deck, his perception changed, and he held on to the lifeline while he stumbled to keep his balance.

"Dude ain't got no sea legs," Andy observed quietly.

"You right, bro," Rafer said, nodding and watching the fat chief struggle with his footing. "I used to think he was drunk all the time, but he can't handle being on deck. Weird." Rafer stared at Chief Twitchell and slowly nodded. An idea was forming in his mind, and he wanted to think it over before he said anything to Andy. There was a good possibility they could get rid of Twitchell and make it look like an accident. It would take luck, and timing, but Rafer was beginning to put together a plan. They would have to get Twitchell up on deck at night. Late at night when no one was around except the aft watch. Rafer decided to look at the duty schedule for the next four days to determine who was standing the aft watch and when. He began to get excited as the idea formed in his mind. Luck and timing, that's all it would take.

* * * * *

Lieutenant MacDonald pored over his notes at the wardroom table. He was delighted that the ship was headed for the Philippines. This would be the perfect opportunity to lecture on the Battle for Leyte Gulf, a battle he felt perfectly demonstrated the stupidity of the Japanese Navy and the pure, dumb luck of the American Navy. Leyte Gulf was another battle that should not have been won; another case of the Japanese Navy's making critical mistakes in the heat of battle.

Mr. Mac hummed 'Anchors Aweigh' happily as he sorted his notes. The crew was going to love this story. He reached for the sound-powered phone and connected to the ship's office.

"Snively speaking, sir," Jerry Snively stopped typing the plan of the day and answered the phone.

"Come up to the wardroom, will you, Snively?" Mr. Mac asked. "I have some mimeographing I need you to do."

"On my way, Mr. Mac," Snively answered.

Mr. MacDonald hung up the phone and returned to sorting his notes and humming 'Anchors Aweigh.' The ship would arrive in Subic Bay on Friday afternoon. Mr. MacDonald would give the lecture on Leyte Gulf Thursday night. He studied his notes and chuckled to himself. Bull Halsey had almost lost that battle for the Americans, but few people knew that. Not a big fan of Admiral Halsey, Mr. Mac was going to enjoy this lecture.

The word spread quickly through the crew about Mr. Mac's lecture, and the turnout was more than he expected. Mr. Mac's 'stories,' as they were called by the crew, were very popular, and discussion was lively and animated for several days after one of his lectures. A sense of history was one of the things the crew had in common. To understand what had happened in the World War II Navy gave them a sense of belonging, of continuity, of tradition. The fact that they were sailing in the very same waters where many of these battles had occurred was not lost on a single man. So, they came to hear Mr. Mac, black and white. They didn't sit together, and they rarely spoke to each other, still, they shared the same history, the same pride, and the same uniform. That night they shared the incredible story of the Battle for Leyte Gulf.

The new moon was but a thin outline in the sky and cast no light on the Pacific, but a bright sprinkling of stars dusted the heavens and painted the ship and crew with a soft glow, making it easy enough to see each other in the night. The sea was calm and the Haverfield rolled easily, first to port and then to starboard, the ship rolling as though with a soft, loving lullaby. Many of the men, having learned during other moonless nights, carried small flashlights with red lenses so they could read maps in the dark. No one thought of suggesting the lecture be moved below decks. Mr. Mac's stories had to be heard and appreciated on deck, with the historic Pacific listening in, sharing a story that must have sounded familiar, echoing down into the vast ocean's depths.

"Good evening, men," Mr. MacDonald greeted, popping up on the fantail through the aft porthole.

"Good evening, sir," several sailors replied as they gathered around the lieutenant, eagerly anticipating the evening's lecture.

Mr. MacDonald pulled himself up on a torpedo tube and wasted no time getting started. He passed out mimeographed sheets on which the map of the Philippine Islands was neatly sketched. "I know it's gonna be hard to see this map," MacDonald went on, "but share your lights as much as you can." He settled back on the torpedo tube. "Do you men remember General Douglas MacArthur's promise to the people of the Philippines, 'I shall return'?" Many nodded. "Do you remember seeing that picture of General MacArthur wading through the surf as he returned to the Philippines?" Again, many nodded. "Well, he walked ashore on the island of Leyte, right here, in Leyte Gulf." He pointed to his map and waited until the audience had located the island of Leyte. "If we hadn't won that battle when the Japs attacked, there's a good chance old Doug would have been stranded there, cut off from the American forces." Mr. Mac lit a small cigar, the flame splashed his face with a soft glow, and in that light, he looked like an older and wiser version of himself. A fleet Navy man, born to the sea.

"The battle for Leyte Gulf was the largest naval battle in history, and the last time a naval battle was fought in the traditional 'battle-line' style. Leyte Gulf actually consisted of four different naval battles over a period of three days." Mr. MacDonald looked at his notes. "Those four battles are the battle of the Sibuyan Sea, the battle of Surigoa Strait, the battle off Cape Engano, and the Battle off Samar." The lieutenant's cigar had gone out and he paused to re-light it. He looked around at the men, pleased to see rapt attention on their faces.

"The Battle for Leyte Gulf was the last hope of the Japanese Navy in World War Two," he began slowly. "In fact, it was the last hope for the Japanese Empire because they knew that losing the Philippines would doom them to defeat. So they assembled a great fleet of ships and developed a brilliant plan to secure the Philippines, and thus extend the war. Remember men, the allies were moving ever closer to the Japanese mainland, island by island, and the Japs were taking heavy losses."

Mr. Mac puffed his cigar and continued. "Admiral Kurita came up from Borneo with a massive fleet, intending to slip through the San Bernardino Straits and clobber the U. S. Seventh Fleet which was supporting MacArthur's landing force on Leyte. This attack would come from the northeast, after Kurita had come through the San Bernardino Straits and around the island of Samar. Admiral Nishimura also came up from Borneo and was joined up by Admiral Shima's force which had come in from Japan. These two forces planned on coming through the Surigao Strait, north of Mindanao, and attacking the Seventh Fleet from the south. To insure that Halsey's powerful Third Fleet, which was protecting the Seventh Fleet and the Leyte landing, would not ruin their plans, the Japs sent a decoy carrier force under Admiral Ozawa in a feint toward the Philippines from the north, hoping to draw Halsey away from protecting Leyte."

The first lieutenant paused and looked at his notes. "I'm going to concentrate on Admiral Kurita and his force, because therein lies, I believe, the proof of my assertion that American luck and Japanese blundering was the deciding factor in the naval war in the Pacific. And I kinda feel sorry for old Kurita. He had bad luck from the get-go. He was coming through the passage west of the island of Palawan believing he was undetected. Two American submarines spotted his force and attacked with torpedoes, sinking the Atago, Admiral Kurita's flagship." Mr. Mac took the cigar out of his teeth and chuckled. "Kurita found himself dumped in the drink as his flagship sank, and he had to be rescued by a destroyer. He transferred his flag to the battleship Yamato and continued toward the Sibuyan Sea. Can you imagine what he must have felt like, being pulled out of the water and delivered to the Yamato soaking wet?"

"Must have pissed him off royally," R.J. said. Everyone laughed.

"Old Kurita kept coming, though," Mr. Mac was clearly enjoying himself. "He made it to the Sibuyan Sea and toward the San Bernardino Straits, when aircraft from Halsey's third fleet attacked him continuously, all day, sinking several Jap ships until Kurita decided to turn west to get away from the American aircraft. When he turned west, Halsey took this to mean he was retreating. This was important, because the Jap carrier decoy force had been spotted to the north, and Halsey, on the bridge of the New Jersey, decided to pursue and destroy them.

"Meanwhile, Admiral Nishimura's fleet of two battleships, a heavy cruiser and several destroyers were entering the Surigao Strait to attack the seventh fleet from the south. If the plan had worked, the seventh fleet would have been destroyed, and MacArthur would be stranded on Leyte with no protection from the sea. He would have been a sitting duck.

"Unfortunately for the Japs, the Americans set a trap in the Surigao Strait. It started with PT boats harassing the Jap fleet as they crawled through the strait. When they emerged, they found they were facing several American battleships, waiting for them in battle line formation." Mr. Mac looked up at the sky and took a deep breath. "The American battleships were the West Virginia, the California, the Tennessee, the

Pennsylvania and the Mississippi. All but the Mississippi had been damaged in the Pearl Harbor attack. This battle was the last time naval forces squared off in 'battle-line' formation, with Nishimura's ships coming through the strait in a single file. The American destroyers jumped on them and sunk one battleship and two destroyers. The American battleships did the rest. Nishimura's force was all but destroyed. Admiral Shima, coming through the strait about an hour behind Nishimura, was faced with a terrible sight, Japanese ships on fire and sinking. He decided not to try and engage any American ships, and he reversed course, retreating back to where he came from."

Mr. Mac paused and looked around at the eager faces of the men. They were enjoying the story, he could tell. "Remember when Halsey missed the battle of Midway because he was in the hospital?" he asked, grinning. "Well, here he saw his final chance for that great surface battle he had always wanted. Because of his egotistical desire for glory, he took the Japanese carrier feint and, with his entire third fleet, headed north at flank speed to destroy the enemy's last significant carrier force." Mr. Mac shook his head as he watched the faces of the men. "Halsey didn't leave any ships to protect the landing force, leaving the seventh fleet do that job." Mr. Mac inspected the tip of his dead cigar and threw it over the side. He began unwrapping a fresh one.

"Now, let me tell you about the incredible heroism displayed in the Battle off Samar.

"As Halsey steamed north, Kurita and the main Japanese force steamed through the San Bernardino Strait and hurled themselves against the three elements of the seventh fleet which were left to protect MacArthur's landing. These elements, known as Taffy One, Two and Three, were made up mostly of escort aircraft carriers and small destroyer escorts, much like the Haverfield. These escort vessels were up against Kurita's massive fleet. Remember, after the battle of the Sibuyan Sea, Halsey believed Kurita was retreating, and pretty much put him out of his thoughts. The main elements of the seventh fleet were fighting the battle of Surigao Strait, leaving Taffy One, Two and Three as the only American force left to face Kurita."

The men were sitting quietly on the deck, listening intently as Mr. Mac described the battle. "When Kurita's forces began to appear on the horizon, the ships of Taffy One, Two and Three thought they were witnessing the defeat of the Japanese forces. Imagine their surprise when Kurita's battleships steamed straight for them with malice in their hearts."

Lieutenant MacDonald lit his cigar and puffed hard on it, creating a bright orange tip that reflected off his cupped hands. "The American escort force scattered, laying smoke screens and rushing away from the oncoming Kurita. Luckily, a rain squall helped to hide them and Kurita's force became scrambled all over the ocean in pursuit. Admiral Kinkaid, the commander of the Seventh Fleet, frantically signaled to Halsey to attack Kurita's forces. Kinkaid thought Halsey had left Task Force 34, a fleet of battleships and support vessels, behind to help protect MacArthur's landing.

"Now, Kurita had to hear the messages sent from Kinkaid to Halsey, and he had to believe Halsey was on his way back, after destroying the Jap carrier fleet off Cape Engano, and he would hit the Japanese from the north. Meanwhile, the American destroyer escorts and carriers continually harassed Kurita's forces with quick hit and run attacks. They did some damage, but they lost several ships in the process. They kept up the harassment, however, and managed to scatter Kurita's powerful fleet all over the place. Kurita, listening to the pleadings for Halsey to return, was convinced that Halsey and the powerful third fleet were rushing back to join the battle. Frustrated by the American escort vessels, and still stinging from Palawan Passage and the Sibuyan Sea battles, he decided to gather his forces and retreat back through the San Bernardino Strait. When Halsey finally returned, the next day, Kurita had withdrawn and all Halsey could do was order his aircraft to attack them as they retreated."

Mr. Mac rolled up his map and tapped it on his palm. "Those escort carriers and DE's should have been completely wiped out by Kurita's fleet. There was no way the Americans could have maintained the hit and run tactics indefinitely. If Kurita had known how far north Halsey was, he would have destroyed Taffy One, Two and Three, and turned his attention to the Leyte landing. That would have been a disaster. But an out-gunned, out-manned, out-numbered task force of American escort ships managed to hold on, in the face of almost certain destruction, until Kurita picked up his marbles and went home." Mr. Mac chuckled at the thought. "Poor old Kurita sure had a bad day, didn't he?"

The sailors chuckled and nodded with pride. Ships like the Haverfield had turned the tide in that battle. They looked at their maps, and at each other, sharing a special feeling of pride and history.

"Halsey was a prima-donna in my opinion," Mr. Mac said firmly. "While he was off looking for glory and Taffy One, Two and Three were locked in a desperate battle, Halsey received a message from Admiral Nimitz in Pearl Harbor. In those days, American messages were transmitted in code, with a meaningless phrase in front of the message, and a meaningless phrase behind the message. This was to confuse the Jap code breakers. The message Nimitz sent to Halsey said, 'TURKEY TROTS TO WATER GG WHERE IS, REPEAT, WHERE IS TASK FORCE THIRTY FOUR RR THE WORLD WONDERS.'

"The last three words of that message, 'THE WORLD WONDERS' was a meaningless phrase attached to the end of the message. But ol' Bull Halsey and his gigantic ego became insulted by what he thought was a reprimand. It pissed him off something awful, and he threw his cap to the deck on the bridge of the New Jersey, his flagship."

MacDonald shook his head slowly. "Halsey was a good admiral, but he let his ego determine his actions. He took a great risk by rushing north with his entire fleet, leaving McArthur's landing woefully underprotected. But, again, because of American luck and Japanese mistakes, we won the biggest naval battle in the history of the world."

Mr. Mac stood up straight and stretched. He looked around at the ship, the sea, the stars and the men. When he spoke his voice was soft, reverent.

"You men are part of the greatest Navy this earth has ever seen. You are the descendants of John Paul Jones, David Farragut, Oliver Hazard Perry, Chester Nimitz and all other American Naval heroes." He paused and blinked away tears. "Including James Wallace Haverfield."

The sailors' heads came up proudly and they stared at Mr. Mac.

"We've shared a lot of naval history together," he said quietly. "It is important that we learn the history of this great Navy, because we, you are charged with protecting this history and making significant contributions to it. We are all part of that history. We sail the same waters and feel the same salt spray as those World War II sailors did, and we must remember their sacrifices and honor their memory...every day." He adjusted his cap on his head and nodded to them. "Good night, men," he said as he left the fantail.

R.J. stood and lit a cigarette. He blew the smoke out of his nose and looked around the fantail. Everyone was lighting up and smoking quietly. No one said anything, but Pea walked up to R.J. and hugged him.

"What's that all about?" R.J. said, smiling down at his friend.

"I dunno," Pea replied, his voice choking. "I'm just...oh, hell. Goodnight."

R.J. smiled wanly as he watched Pea disappear down the hatch to First Division's compartment. He knew he could never put it into words, but he knew exactly how Pea felt. Taking a last look around at the beautiful Pacific, he tossed his cigarette butt into the drink and headed to the signal bridge.

SIXTY TWO

The Haverfield sailed into Subic Bay Friday afternoon, June 12th. The destroyer tender Piedmont was anchored a few miles from shore, and the Haverfield glided next to her and tied up to her port side. R.J. shifted colors and returned to the signal bridge. Anselmi was waiting for him in clean whites and shined shoes.

"Look around, Slick," Anselmi said, indicating the harbor with a sweep of his hand. "How many ships you see?"

R.J. looked around the harbor. Besides the Haverfield and the Piedmont, only a few ships rode their buoys in the bay. "About six," R.J. answered.

"Exactly!" Anselmi said with a grin. "Won't be much competition in Olongapo tonight."

R.J. had heard about Olongapo, the little town off Subic Bay. Its main commerce was the cluster of go-go bars lining the dirt streets. Anselmi had compared Olongapo to Tijuana with better looking girls. R.J. had no desire to visit Olongapo, but had given in to Gino and Pea's pleading to go ashore with them. Since Billy Lopez was becoming efficient at Morse code, and it was Friday evening, R.J. agreed to go, leaving Charming Billy to man the signal bridge. Being happily married with a baby on the way, Billy had no desire to visit Olongapo.

R.J. left Billy on the signal bridge and went below to change into dress whites. Gino and Pea had an hour's head start, and R.J. had agreed to meet them at the Honolulu bar in downtown Olongapo.

* * * * *

Captain Oliver sat in his cabin, reviewing and initialing departmental readiness reports. The trip from Guam had been smooth and effortless. The crew responded to the various drills with speed and efficiency, and the captain was satisfied with their performance. A hot, humid breeze blew into his cabin from the open porthole and Captain Oliver recognized the heavy, pungent aroma of the Philippines. He stood and put on his cap, intending to return to the flying bridge and look around at the bay. When he opened his door, Riley stood there, about to knock on the door. They stared at each other for an awkward moment, and the captain smiled.

"Riley, why are you sneaking up on me?"

"Sir?" Riley shuffled his feet nervously. "I didn't mean to..." His voice trailed off.

"It's okay, Riley," the captain assured him. Riley relaxed. "What have you got for me?" The captain took the clipboard from Riley and scanned the brief message. He looked up at Riley, then back down at the message, his head spinning, and he felt blood rushing to his face.

"The admiral is requesting confirmation, sir," Riley said sheepishly.

The captain initialed the message slip and pulled it off the clipboard. "Go ahead and confirm," the captain ordered. "That'll be all, Riley." The radioman nodded, saluted and returned to the radio shack.

Paul Oliver sat down at his desk, his cap still on, and re-read the message slip.

From: COMCRUDESPAC
To: Commanding Officer, USS Haverfield DER-393
Subj: Dinner reception

Your attendance is requested at a dinner reception at the officers' club, Subic Bay Naval Base at 1900 hours, Saturday, 13 June. Dress whites. Please confirm.

Quentin Prescott
COMCRUDESPAC

Paul Oliver stared at the message slip. The admiral had promised a formal invitation, and here it was in his hand. It irritated him somehow, and filled him with dread. *Your attendance is requested.* Admirals don't *request*, they order. Therefore, he was being *ordered* to attend the reception. A flood of memories rushed through his mind, memories of other dinners, of riding through the Guamanian hills with the top down, the musical sound of Lorelei Prescott's laugh, the feel of her naked body. He shook his head to clear it. He was exasperated that he couldn't picture her face.

R.J. waved away the street vendor trying to sell him monkey meat on a stick, and hurried up the dirt road toward the Honolulu Bar and Lounge. Gino and Pea had a good hour's head start on him, and he imagined both had pounded down several San Miguels in the interim.

"I will knock your big ass out!" R.J. heard the yelling before he reached the Honolulu and instantly recognized Pea's voice. "You big, dumb shore patrol puke!" Pea was being restrained by a very large black sailor wearing a shore patrol arm band and carrying a nightstick. He had Pea's arms pinned behind him and was struggling to keep the small sailor under control. Pea was not cooperating, wriggling and twisting, trying to break the big man's grip. As R.J. approached the scene, he noticed that the big shore patrolman was a second class signalman.

"Gino!" Pea yelled. Gino stood off to the side, Pea's whitehat in his hand, scowling, disgusted at the scene. "Gino! Get behind this fucker and whomp up on his head!"

"You gotta settle down, Pea," Gino advised. "Quit fightin' or you goin' to the brig."

R.J. nodded to the big signalman and looked directly at Pea. "Shut up, Peacock!" he yelled into Pea's face. Startled, Pea looked at R.J. questioningly. He was having trouble focusing both eyes. One seemed to look straight at R.J., but the other roamed around randomly in Pea's head, sometimes disappearing completely.

"Hey, Flags," R.J. greeted the big shore patrolman with what he hoped was a pleasant, friendly smile. "He's our shipmate." R.J. looked down at Pea disapprovingly. "Can we maybe just take him back to the ship?" R.J. smiled his most disarming smile.

"He outta control," the big shore patrolman had the kind of deep, bass voice R.J. expected. He held Pea's wrists with one hand and pulled the nightstick out of its scabbard with the other. "I oughta go upside his head."

"Lemme up you flag-raisin', Morse code-flashin', skivvy-wavin' sumbitch!" Pea struggled hopelessly. "Gimme one shot, that's all I ask. One shot. I'll put your skivvy-wavin' ass on the deck!"

"Ah'm getting' tired o'this." The shore patrolman lifted his nightstick and eyed Pea's skull.

"Whoa!" R.J. put out his hands and formed the letters A-S in semaphore. A-S was a code for "wait." The big signalman lowered his nightstick and put it back in its scabbard.

"I don' wanna take the little dude in," he explained. "But he be pissin' me off big time."

"What can we do to make it right, Flags?" R.J. used the affectionate nickname for signalmen again, and smiled disarmingly.

The big shore patrolman pondered for a moment. "He gotta say he sorry," he decided.

R.J. and Gino nodded agreement. "Pea," R.J. said soothingly at the still-struggling Peacock. "Tell the man you're sorry and we can go back to Momma."

Pea looked up with disgust on his face. "You panty-wavers stick together, huh?"

Gino had enough. He reached over and slapped Pea in the face with his own whitehat. "Shut the fuck up, Pea!" he yelled in his best Brooklynese. "Quit actin' like an asshole!"

Pea's mouth turned down in a sad frown. "I'm jus' havin' a little fun," he protested sorrowfully. He looked up sadly at the shore patrolman. "I'm sorry. I apologize. Please forgive me." He seemed sincere.

After a few moments the shore patrolman released his grip. "Okay, y'all need to get off my street," he cautioned. R.J. and Gino nodded and took possession of Pea. Gino placed the little sailor's hat on his head and they half-walked, half-dragged Pea down the street toward an awaiting jitney jeep.

"How the hell did he get so drunk?" R.J. asked.

Gino chuckled. "He hit the bar and had three shots of tequila and three beers in about fifteen minutes." He hefted Pea up to a standing position. "After that," Gino shook his head sadly, "it was jus' a matter of time."

"I get my hands on that big fuckin' skivvy-waver, I'm gonna knock him out!" Pea yelled as R.J. and Gino dragged him toward the pier and the waiting liberty boat.

Once on the boat, headed back to the ship, R.J. looked over at Gino and grinned. "So much for Olongapo," he said, looking askance at Pea who was slumped over on the wooden bench, snoring loudly.

"Tomorrow," Gino replied. "We'll come back tomorrow."

R.J. nodded and watched as the liberty boat approached the Piedmont. His first, quick impression of the Philippines was unfavorable. The streets of Olongapo were mostly dirt, with trash and debris scattered everywhere. Little Filipino children ran the streets almost naked, digging in trash bins and begging spare change from sailors. He smiled to himself. Olongapo was a lot like Tijuana. *That's it*, he thought. *Tijuana without the class.* He'd come back with Gino and Pea tomorrow, just to say he'd been there, but he decided to spend his time aboard ship, reading. He was working hard to memorize The Raven. It was a difficult poem, and R.J. kept a dictionary next to him as he read. He thought about writing a poem for Annie, but abandoned that, preferring to quote Poe to her. He didn't miss Annie as much as he had on previous trips. Were his feelings for her diminishing? He couldn't really tell. Their passion had cooled, that was certain. R.J. tried not to think of the future when it came to Annie. He had never thought they had much of a future. She was married, and didn't seem inclined to do anything about that. Maybe she was content with the way things were and didn't want any change. R.J. shook his head to clear away thoughts of her.

"You okay, m'man?" Gino asked.

"Yeah, just daydreaming," R.J replied.

"That love shit again?" Gino asked, shaking his head at R.J.

"For being young and dipt in folly, I fell in love with melancholy," R.J. quoted, grinning.

Gino shrugged. "Whatever," he murmured, looking down at the snoring Pea. "Good thing he ain't any bigger. We'd have a hell of a time carrying him up the ladder," he mused.

"Good thing he ain't big Queen," R.J. pondered. "He'd spend the night in this boat."

Gino chuckled agreement. The liberty boat pulled up alongside the Piedmont, and R.J. and Gino hefted Pea between them and dragged him up the ladder to the quarterdeck. The OOD looked at Pea and shook his head.

"That was a quick liberty," he said, nodding toward the semi-conscious Pea.

"He's little, but he packs a lotta shit into a short period of time," Gino explained.

The OOD of the Peidmont, a gregarious lieutenant j.g., smiled and nodded. "Well, tell him to pace himself," he said.

R.J. and Gino nodded and murmured, "Yessir," while they dragged Pea across the tender's deck to the Haverfield's quarterdeck. Chief Whipple had the duty as OOD.

"An early casualty?" he asked as they dragged Pea aboard.

"Naw, he got bored and fell asleep," R.J. quipped. Chief Whipple grunted. It was probably his way of chuckling.

"Well, make sure you toss him in his bunk face down," Chief Whipple cautioned. "Don't want him throwing up and drowning in his own puke."

"Roger that," R.J. agreed. Every sailor who ever sailed heard the stories about men coming back to the ship drunk, passing out on their backs and drowning in their own vomit. No one knew if it had ever actually happened, but the story had to have started somewhere.

The ship was quiet that Friday afternoon. Evening was settling on Subic Bay as the sun made its way slowly west. R.J. hung around on the fantail, looking around at the scenery, trying to figure out why so many sailors loved the Philippines. So far, there didn't seem there was a lot to love. It was hot and humid, and smelled like a garbage can. R.J. found himself missing Guam and the cooling evening breezes that swept away the humidity and brought a fresh, clean smell to the night air. He took another look around and went below to the compartment and climbed, fully clothed, into his bunk. He lay there a while, staring at the pipes and wires along the overhead until he fell asleep. Though it was just past sunset, he slept soundly the entire night. The next morning he awoke refreshed, realizing he had done no reading the night before.

* * * * *

Lester coxswained the captain's gig around the tender to the platform at the bottom of the ladder. He waited there for Captain Oliver to descend the ladder into the motor whaleboat. As Lester, designated coxswain of the motor whaleboat, was often heard to say, "This's a motor whaleboat until the captain needs it, then it's the captain's gig, and I'm the only boatswain's mate sumbitch aboard who's authorized to coxswain the captain's gig." Lester took the assignment seriously, believing it gave him bragging rights in the First Division compartment. Lester exercised those bragging rights often. Since Tanner left, Lester's star had risen a notch.

Captain Paul Oliver, decked out in gleaming dress whites, descended the ladder and stepped, sure-footed, into the boat. Lester saluted smartly and slowly backed the gig away from the tender, easily turning the bow toward the landing on the dock. The gig cut quickly and smoothly through the calm water of the bay, and Lester expertly guided the small boat. The captain sat forward, quietly watching the approaching landing. He tried to blank out the feelings and memories that swirled in his mind. Just another reception, he told himself, nothing to worry about. Deep down, he knew that was not the case.

The gig moved easily to the landing and Lester cut the motor and let the gig drift into place. He hurriedly tied up the motor whaleboat, fore and aft, and stood by, saluting as the captain stepped up onto the landing.

"Pick me up at twenty three hundred," Captain Oliver said, smoothing the creases on his trousers.

"I'll be here, Cap'n," Lester replied.

Captain Oliver walked up the pier toward the waiting car, its driver standing next to the open back door.

"Evening, sir," the driver greeted.

Paul Oliver nodded and slipped into the back seat. The driver closed the door and slid behind the wheel. "It'll only take fifteen minutes to get to the Officer's Club," he announced, starting the car.

Captain Oliver sat quietly in the back seat, watching the evening pass by the car windows. The scenery sped by quickly, like the thoughts in Paul Oliver's mind. It had been months since he last saw Lorelei, yet her image was still fresh in his mind, her scent still fresh in his nostrils. He dreaded seeing her again, almost as much as he looked forward to it. He concentrated on recalling her face, but couldn't quite complete the picture. He clearly saw her hair, heard her voice, felt her embrace, but he couldn't see her face.

The car pulled up to the officers' club and stopped at the entrance. Somehow, Paul Oliver had pictured a sweeping staircase leading up to a landing where Lorelei and Admiral Prescott would stand, greeting the guests. Instead, he stepped through double doors which led directly into the low-ceilinged bar. Colorful Japanese lanterns dotted the ceiling and a reception line was forming to the right. Captain Oliver joined it. As he approached, Admiral and Mrs. Prescott were exchanging pleasantries with a tall officer and his wife. The couple passed out of view and Paul Oliver suddenly found himself staring into the beautiful face of Lorelei Von Dulm Prescott. She beamed when she saw him, and he stood awkwardly staring at her. A bittersweet, familiar feeling rushed into his chest and he had a little trouble catching his breath. They stared at each other for what seemed like eons, eyes searching each others' faces.

"Well, hello Paul!" Admiral Prescott seemed genuinely happy to see him. He came forward, hand outstretched. Paul snapped out of his trance, took the hand and shook it.

"It's been a while, admiral," he said graciously.

"Too long, Paul," the admiral said, beaming. "I hear good things about the Haverfield."

"We're operating nicely, sir," Paul said, glancing quickly from the admiral to his wife. "I believe we are prepared for anything."

"Good," the admiral nodded, suddenly serious. "You're going to need to be prepared."

"Sir?" Captain Oliver said, somewhat surprised by the serious tone.

"Later," the admiral said. "We'll talk after dinner."

"Yes, please do," Lorelei said, taking the admiral's arm. "Let's enjoy the evening. You and your officers can talk later." She led the admiral toward the dining room, with Paul Oliver following close behind.

Dinner was pleasant enough, but Paul couldn't concentrate on his food. He kept stealing glances at Lorelei, who sat between her husband and Rear Admiral Pollock. She never met Paul's eyes, seemingly ignoring him throughout the meal, laughing her musical laugh and generally being the gracious hostess.

As dessert was being served, Admiral Prescott stood, smiling broadly, and tapped the side of his crystal water glass with his butter knife, sending a *ping-ping-ping* echoing through the room. "May I have your attention, please?" It was not a request. The room grew quiet very quickly as heads turned toward the admiral.

"One of the more pleasant duties an admiral has," he announced, still smiling, "is approving promotions for deserving officers, and tonight we have in attendance four officers who made the promotions list."

A scattering of applause rippled through the room as Admiral Prescott put on his reading glasses and unfolded a piece of paper. "When I call your name, please join me here," he instructed. He looked over his glasses and scanned the room. "New Lieutenant Commander Edwin Johnson," he announced to more applause. A young lieutenant stood, grinning, and made his way to the head table. Admiral Prescott shook his hand, offered congratulations, and Admiral Pollock handed him a small box containing the gold oak leaf collar pin of a lieutenant commander. Edwin Johnson acknowledged the applause and made his way, still grinning, back to his table to accept the congratulations of his dinner mates.

"New Commander D. Paul Oliver," the admiral announced.

Paul sat dumbly in his chair, not quite comprehending what was happening. In a daze, he stood and made his way to the head table, where he accepted a warm handshake and congratulations from Admiral Prescott. He stole a glance at Lorelei and saw that she was smiling sweetly at him.

Admiral Pollock handed him a box containing the silver oak leaf of a full commander, and Paul thanked him as he shook his hand.

"You deserve this, Paul," Admiral Pollock said. "You've done one hell of a fine job with your ship."

"Thank you, sir," Paul muttered. He returned to his table and to more congratulations. Two more officers were called up to receive new insignia, but Paul didn't hear their names. His head was swirling with hundreds of thoughts, all coming at once, and he was having trouble sorting them out.

The last newly promoted officer returned to his table, and the admiral smiled benevolently. "And now, if you don't mind, I'll see my officers in the map room." He turned and disappeared through the map room door, followed closely by the dozen officers in attendance. Admiral Pollock closed the door after the last officer and nodded to Admiral Prescott, who pulled down a large wall map. Paul was not surprised to recognize the now-familiar map of Southeast Asia.

"Gentlemen," COMCRUDESPAC began, "as you are undoubtedly aware, things are becoming very interesting in this part of the world." He paused to let his words sink in. "Recent reports indicate activity in this area," he pointed to the map, "in the Tonkin Gulf." He paced in front of the map, his hands folded behind his back. "Most of this activity consists of small craft, since the North Vietnamese have no navy to speak of. But even these small craft can cause problems with our ships patrolling the Gulf, if they decide to engage in quick hit and run harassment tactics." He pointed again at the Tonkin Gulf. "Our objective is to insure the security of this body of water, so that supplies, ammunition and other services can be safely delivered to our ground forces in South Viet Nam."

Newly promoted Edwin Johnson raised his hand. "Pardon me, sir."

"Yes?" Admiral Prescott acknowledged.

"I thought our forces in the south were there only in support of the South Vietnamese army."

"That is correct, Lieutenant Commander," Admiral Pollock stood in the rear of the room and fielded the question with a nod from Admiral Prescott. Heads turned toward him. "But recent developments encourage us to be prudent in our preparation. We believe," he continued in a serious tone, "that America's role in this conflict will be expanded soon, and, therefore, so will the role of the Navy."

The officers looked around at each other, none concealing surprise. This was a new development, they realized. An expanded role? What exactly did that mean for the U.S. Navy?

As if he had read their minds, Admiral Prescott once again took center stage. "What this means for us," he explained, "is a heightened state of alertness, and an imperative to maintain a high level of training. What I mean, gentlemen," he looked over his glasses and scanned the faces of his officers, "is that some of you, many of you, may receive orders to join the patrols in the Tonkin Gulf."

Paul Oliver raised his hand.

"Yes, Commander?"

"Sir, can we anticipate these orders anytime soon?"

The admiral nodded solemnly. "Anytime soon, Commander."

Thoughts of his ship surged into Paul's mind, and he mentally made a check list of things he wanted to make certain were completed. They would need more surface action training, their weapons had to be maintained and ready at all times, and the crew had to be made to understand the seriousness of the situation. This is where the drills, the training, the planning all paid off. He couldn't contain the excitement he felt about possible combat situations. He looked forward to it; he yearned to prove the worthiness of the Haverfield. As he looked around the room at the other officers, he realized they were feeling the same thing.

"We're going to break up now," Admiral Pollock announced suddenly. "I know you are anxious to inform your crews about the possibilities, so thank you for coming tonight and congratulations once again to our newly promoted colleagues."

The officers began filing out of the room and through the front door, each stopping to say goodnight to Mrs. Prescott. Paul hung back a bit, waiting for the crowd to clear, and offered his hand to Lorelei. She was not smiling.

"God speed, Commander," she said sadly, squeezing his hand.

"Thank you, ma'am," was all Paul could think of to say. He put on his cap and walked to his waiting car. Once inside the backseat he noticed a large, round hat box with a silver ribbon wrapped around it.

"What's this?" he asked the driver.

"Dunno, sir," he answered. "That lady up there put it in the back seat and told me to give it to you." He nodded toward the entrance to the club where Lorelei stood alone, staring at Paul through the back window. She lifted her hand in a slight wave and disappeared into the club. The driver started the car and began moving down the road. Paul opened the box and pulled out a shiny, new officer's cap with the gold 'scrambled eggs' on the brim. Only commanders and above could wear the gold on the brim of their hats. Paul noticed that the size was perfect, and as he lifted it to his head, a small envelope fell into his lap. He picked it up and held it to his nose. It was from her. He opened it and unfolded the small piece of notepaper. He recognized her handwriting immediately.

Commander,
I am so very proud of you. Please wear this cap and think of me often,
as I will be thinking often of you.
All my love,
Lorelei

Paul Oliver slowly fitted the cap on his head and lowered his eyes, hoping his driver didn't notice the tears in them.

"Back to the landing, sir?" the driver asked, looking at Paul in the rear view mirror.

"Yes," Commander Oliver answered, his voice breaking a bit. "I need to get home."

The car eased down the road and Commander Oliver looked back toward the empty doorway of the club. In his mind's eye he imagined the siren's rocks along the shore of the Rhine, and he felt drawn to them once again, compelled to be shipwrecked and lost in the beautiful, violet eyes of Lorelei Prescott.

SIXTY THREE

By Monday morning the entire crew had heard about the promotion of their skipper. It was further validation for the crew, and they each felt they had a small hand in it. The captain's programs had transformed the ship; the crew was trained to a sharp edge, and the green 'C' and white 'E' proclaimed the crew to be among the best. But the promotion was bestowed on their captain, well deserved in their opinion, and they were, to a man, genuinely pleased for him.

After quarters, R.J. and most of the deck force crowded onto the signal bridge, waiting for the captain to appear on the wing, as was his habit each morning. Riley joined them from the radio shack, and Snively was there, too. He was invited because he had slipped into the captain's quarters and retrieved the object they needed for this particular ceremony.

The captain came out on the wing to look around at the bay, and was a little surprised to see the group of sailors gathered on the signal bridge. They approached him cautiously, R.J. leading the way.

"Excuse me, sir," R.J. said tentatively.

The captain looked at the group suspiciously. "Don't you men have work to do?" he asked.

"Yes, sir, but..." R.J. began. Snively prodded him in the back. "Well, Captain," R.J. went on. "We want to congratulate you on your promotion to commander."

"Thank you," Captain Oliver said, a slight frown on his face as if he didn't know where this was headed.

"Well, sir," R.J. continued. "We have a little tradition we kinda follow when one of our own gets promoted."

The captain knew of the tradition, and he met the eyes of each man, making them wilt under his gaze.

"And?" he challenged.

"Well, sir," R.J. stammered. "Well, since we obviously can't ask you to go along with the tradition, we have an idea."

The captain looked at R.J. skeptically, one eyebrow raised, waiting to hear the idea.

Snively passed a small, paper-wrapped package to R.J. as the rest of the group shuffled their feet and looked nervous. R.J. opened the package and held the object up for the captain to view. It was Captain Oliver's old officer's cap, the one without the scrambled eggs.

"With your permission, sir?" R.J. asked.

The captain smiled, which made the group relax. "Very well, Davis," he said, amused. "Proceed."

The sailors began grinning, and R.J. held the cap in the air, and threw it like a Frisbee out into the bay. It landed flat on the water and floated gently as the men let out a cheer.

"Congratulations, Commander," R.J. announced, saluting. The rest of the group came to attention and saluted the captain. He returned the salute, took a last look at his old cap floating in the water, and returned to his cabin, smiling broadly.

"Well," Snively remarked, watching the cap float away. "It would have been a lot more fun throwing *him* over the side."

* * * * *

R.J. received the 'Dear John' letter the next day in the afternoon mail. It took some time for the mail to catch up to the ship, and R.J. looked at the postmark, Longmont, Colorado, and noticed it had been mailed two weeks earlier. It was from Renee, of course.

> Dear R.J.,
> I've fallen in love with someone else. I know you remember Chuck Phipps from Niwot. He's a really nice guy, and it just sort of happened. I wrote you quite a few letters and you hardly answered any of them. You're so far away, and I never hear from you, so I have to assume you aren't thinking of me.
> Chuck and I are going to get married September fifth and we both really hope you can come. Please wish us well, and please be happy for me.
> Renee

R.J. leaned against the port side flag bag and stared into the bay. This letter wasn't a surprise, really. As much as he cared about Renee, he had to admit he hadn't been very responsive to her letters. He didn't blame her, but in the back of his mind, he had always assumed that Renee and Longmont would be waiting for him when he returned. He imagined coming home and finding things unchanged, just the way he had left them. Had he received a 'Dear John' from Tonya it wouldn't have bothered him. They had never been very close, but he and Renee had spent some wonderful summer nights in Sunset Park, lying under the pine trees, talking about life and their future together. He thought of Chuck Phipps and smiled to himself. Chuck was a nice guy, and R.J. felt genuinely happy for them, as bittersweet as the feeling was.

Later that evening, the first symptoms of acute tonsillitis appeared. The illness sent him to bed for a week, where he would sleep fitfully, in a dreamlike haze, waking for brief periods of time. While awake he was weak and his head felt like it was stuffed with cotton. He would open his book on Edgar Allen Poe and study his poetry until he drifted back into the haze, often rolling around restlessly, his body fighting the infection and wracked in fever. He was hardly aware of the stinging penicillin shot he had to accept daily. He lost track of time and no longer recognized the difference between being awake and being asleep. The disturbing dreams, many intertwined with Poe's enigmatic poetry, seemed to occur whether or not he was asleep. It was during that time, in that haze, that he overheard something he shouldn't have. Thinking back on it later, he wasn't really sure he had actually heard it or imagined it, but after the terrible incident happened, he realized it had been real, and the feeling haunted him for the remainder of his life.

* * * * *

"But Psyche, uplifting her finger,
Said, "Sadly this star I mistrust,
Her pallor I strangely mistrust.
Oh, hasten, oh let us not linger,
Oh, fly! Let us fly! For we must..."

R.J. tossed in his bunk, only half conscious, muttering quietly to himself.

"I replied, "This is nothing but dreaming.
Let us on by this tremulous light!
Let us bathe in this crystalline light...
"Thus I pacified Psyche and kissed her,
And tempted her out of her gloom,
And conquered her scruples and gloom.
And we passed to the end of a vista,
But were stopped by the door of a tomb.
By the door of a legended tomb.
And I said, 'What is written, sweet sister,
On the door of this legended tomb?'
She replied..."

R.J. sat bolt upright, gasping for air. His heart pounded hard, he held one hand clutched to his chest and forced himself to calm down, to wake up. Sweat poured off his face, and he shuddered, suddenly cold. He rubbed his temples with the heels of his hands and mumbled, barely audible, *"Ulalume, Ulalume, tis the vault of thy lost Ulalume..."*

"R.J.! R.J.! Can you hear me, boy?" Pea's voice cut through his foggy thoughts. "You awake, or what?" Pea demanded.

R.J. shook his head, fighting off the headache, and squeezed his eyes shut hard. He opened them and stared into the concerned faces of Gino and Pea, who examined him as if he were a dissectible frog in a high school biology class.

Pea looked at him suspiciously. "What the hell you talkin' 'bout, boy? Yoola who?"

"No offense, dude," Gino offered, "but you look like shit."

R.J. dropped his head, groaning. "I feel worse than shit." He shook his head again, trying to gain some clarity. "Man, I keep having these bad dreams..." he began.

Pea looked over at Gino. "See? I told you he was nuts," he pointed a thumb at R.J. and circled his index finger around his temple.

Gino stepped close to R.J. and squinted at him. "You probably right, little fucker," he agreed. "He does look like a nut...at least the ones I seen in Brooklyn."

"What time is it?" R.J. pleaded.

"Time for some fuckin' chow!" Pea declared. He turned to Gino. "Can we fuckin' eat now? The boy ain't dying, but he is nuts like I said, so can we go to fuckin' chow now, or what?"

Gino stared at R.J. "You okay, m'man?"

"Yeah, yeah, you guys go to chow. I'll meet you down there."

"Okay," Gino said reluctantly. "See you down there." He and Pea left

R.J. alone, sitting on his bunk with his head in his hands.

"Hey, hey! The mummy walks!" Pea exclaimed. He and Gino were just finishing breakfast in the mess decks when R.J. came in, walking slowly and purposefully. The ship was on its way back to Guam, and the pitching and rolling had encouraged R.J. to leave his bunk. He was feeling better, but was a little weak, and he was still very pale. Being at sea was just the tonic he needed, he thought, and he was glad to be out of his rack.

"You still look a bit puny, m'man," Gino said, grinning at his friend. "You were in bed for a week!"

R.J. slid into the booth and declined the offer of coffee. "I feel like I might actually live," he said. "Man, I was sicker than a dog."

"That you were," Gino said. "We came by a few times to check on you, but you were so far out of it, you probably don't even remember."

R.J. shook his head. "No, I was pretty sick." He rubbed his temples. "I tell you, though, I had some weird dreams." He tried to focus on the memory that floated wisp-like just out of the reach of his mind. "I had a dream about Rafer and Andy..." He shook his head again, trying to clear it.

"What dream?" Pea demanded. "You havin' dreams about guys? Shit, boy, you ain't turnin' queer, are you?"

R.J. chuckled and rubbed his temples. "Naw, I ain't turnin' queer. I can't quite remember..." He shook his head again. "Never mind." He gave up trying to retrieve the memory.

"We'll be back on the Rock in a few days," Pea declared, rubbing his hands together. "We'll get with the chicks and have a little party."

"You missed a lot of action in Olongapo," Gino told him. "We had a helluva time with those little Flip bar girls."

"They was just about my size," Pea explained, grinning widely. "In fact, they was small enough, I took two of 'em!"

"He did," Gino agreed, corroborating the story. "I seen him when he done it."

R.J. nodded, but he wasn't listening to Gino or Pea. His mind was on Annie and the nagging dream he'd thought he had. Every time he got close to remembering the dream, it evaporated like Pea's cigarette smoke drifting up to the overhead. R.J. felt like his head was stuffed with marshmallows, and he shook it again, trying hard to clear it.

When he thought of Annie, he became curiously irritated, without understanding why thoughts of her would affect him that way. Earlier in their relationship he felt a thrill at the thought of her. Lately, especially after the miscarriage, his attitude toward her had changed. The change had come quickly and R.J. couldn't explain it.

"You okay, bud?" Pea asked, searching R.J.'s face. The little guy was obviously concerned about his friend.

"Yeah, I'm okay," R.J. answered, rubbing his temples. "All those penicillin shots made me goofy."

"Well, shake it off, Bud," Pea suggested. "We'll be home soon and you know what that means." Pea began grinding his hips in an obscene manner, leering lasciviously.

* * * * *

Twitchell came out on deck near midnight the night before the ship arrived back in Apra Harbor. The fat chief was drunk, mumbling to himself, staggering around and hanging on to the lifeline in an attempt to keep from falling down. He gulped fresh air greedily and struggled to control his legs, which felt like all the muscle tone had left them.

Andy and Rafer were making their way down the 02 level on their way to the First Division compartment when Rafer spotted the drunken chief staggering around the fantail.

"He's alone," Rafer said softly.

Andy nodded. "What you wanna do, bro?"

Rafer looked around. The moon was bright, throwing soft, pale light across the ship. No one was on deck. He looked over to where the aft lookout was stationed. It was Cotton, and he was standing inside the hatch on the 02 level, his back turned, talking with someone. Rafer calculated the distance between him and Andy and the staggering chief, and decided they could get rid of him quickly, before anyone took notice. As they started moving quietly down the port ladder to the fantail, the port hatch opened, throwing a slice of yellow light across the darkened fantail, and MM-1 Crawford came out on deck, a big cigar stuck in his teeth. Rafer and Andy froze on the ladder.

"Chief?" Crawford called out, blinking his eyes, trying to get used to the dim light. "Y'all out here?"

"Wha?" Chief Twitchell spun around and almost fell down. "Wha?" he demanded.

Crawford grabbed the chief by the upper arm to steady him and led him back toward the hatch. "Chief, you gonna fall over the side one these days, you ain't careful, y'hear?"

"I don' give a shit!" The chief yelled at the night sky. "Y'hear me? I don' give a shit!"

"Yeah, yeah, I hear ya," Crawford said soothingly, half-leading, half-dragging the chief toward the hatch. "Let's get y'ass below before you wind up in the drink."

"I don' give a shit!" the fat chief yelled as Crawford pulled him inside and closed the hatch.

Rafer and Andy stared at each other in the moonlight. "Damn!" Rafer swore softly. "We was this close." He held his thumb and index finger an inch apart. He noticed his hand was shaking and he dropped in quickly to his side.

Andy nodded solemnly. "He gonna get drunk and come up here again," he said quietly, biting on his lower lip. "He always do."

* * * * *

R.J. tossed around in his rack, more asleep than awake. The dream haunted him, pursued him with wisp-like images and words he couldn't quite understand. Someone was talking about Twitchell, something about his being in the drink, then laughter. Shrill laughter. R.J. sat up in his bunk, almost banging his head on the overhead pipes. He stared at his hands. They were covered with blood, and someone was cackling. He looked around and saw pale images of Rafer and Andy. They were pointing at his hands and laughing. R.J. tried to wipe the blood from his hands, but it wouldn't wipe off. He awoke in a start, sweating profusely, his heart pounding. He looked down at his hands. There was no blood on his hands, and the laughter had died away. R.J. shuddered involuntarily and lay back down, exhausted. He slept fitfully the rest of the night, for the dream had faded back into the recesses of his mind where it wouldn't bother him any longer. *At least not that night.*

SIXTY FOUR

"Shit," Pea exclaimed as the Haverfield passed the breakwater and began moving through the channel toward the inner Apra Harbor. It was just past noon on Friday. "I thought they was at sea!" He was standing on the focsul, leader line coiled in his hand, pointing toward the USS Raptor, which was tied up along the pier.

"R.J. told us they were getting underway today," Gino said, coming up next to Pea. He looked up at the signal bridge where R.J. stood, looking back at them. He pointed to the Raptor and shrugged, his hands palms up.

Pea and Gino stared at the minesweeper as the Haverfield cruised past, moving slowly toward her berth a hundred yards forward of the Raptor.

"Why ain't y'all at sea?" Pea grumbled to no one in particular as he hefted the leader line in his hand.

Captain Oliver watched as Pea swung his arm through the throw and the weighted end of the leader line sailed in a perfect arc and thudded onto the concrete pier. In a matter of minutes they were tied up, the colors were shifted and the deck force began washing down the ship with fresh water. Soon, the tarp was erected on the fantail and the quarterdeck was set up on the starboard side. Liberty call was announced and sailors in clean whites began lining up to go ashore.

R.J. stepped into the pilot house and began leafing through the ships' movements reports. The Raptor was delayed getting underway because of a problem with her number two engine. Apparently, it had been repaired and they were scheduled to put to sea the next morning. He smiled to himself and set out to find Pea and Gino.

* * * * *

Lieutenant Frank MacDonald sat in his cabin, re-reading the report he was writing. It was about Chief Twitchell and his behavior toward black sailors. Mr. MacDonald believed Twitchell was a big problem aboard ship, regardless of his talent for maintaining machinery. Through many anecdotal accounts from other officers and petty officers, Mr. Mac had begun to develop a pattern of behavior, which, he believed, proved that Chief Twitchell was not fit to be a chief petty officer in the United States Navy.

The only other officer who knew about this report was Lieutenant

Almogordo. The engineering officer had balked at the conclusions at first, but, after reading and re-reading the report, Mr. Almogordo had begun to take notice of Twitchell's behavior. After a few weeks, he drew the same conclusion MacDonald had drawn: Chief Twitchell was an unsettling force aboard the ship. They agreed to continue compiling information until they had an iron-clad case against the chief. They would then present it to the captain and request he have the machinist's mate transferred to another ship. Both agreed that court martialing Chief Twitchell would serve no purpose other than making the issue public, and neither officer wanted that. They knew the captain was very sensitive about shipboard harmony, and that he held Chief Twitchell in high regard because of his uncanny ability with machinery. Mr. Mac nodded to himself. They would need more time to put the report together. In the meantime, it was best to stay alert and observe the situation.

* * * * *

Gino and Pea talked R.J. into hitting the Mocombo Club, hoping that the next night, Saturday, they could meet up with the girls. R.J. went along only to please his friends. He was still a little weak from his bout with tonsillitis, and the massive doses of penicillin had left a nasty metallic taste in his mouth.

The Mocombo Club was not yet crowded, and the trio found a table situated between the bar and the bandstand. They sat down with cans of beer, relaxed, and watched the stream of sailors come through the front doors. R.J. sat up suddenly and stared at the door. Gino and Pea followed his gaze. Four sailors from the Raptor came in and found a table next to Gino, R.J. and Pea.

R.J. raised his beer can and called out, "Hey Raptor, thought you guys were supposed to be in the wind!"

The Raptor sailors waved and smiled. One of them, a tall, good-looking blond came over to the table and grinned down at the Haverfield sailors. "Only ship in the harbor spends more time at sea is you guys," he said affably.

"Why don't you guys join us?" Pea asked. He winked at Gino, who ignored him.

"Naw, can't," the big blond said, motioning toward his friends at the other table. "Gary's got problems with his ol' lady and we're tryin' to cheer him up." He smiled again. "Thanks, though."

R.J. looked at Pea and Gino and raised his eyebrows. He looked over at the other table. He saw the second class radioman's crow first, then he looked into the face of Gary Nelson, Annie's husband.

R.J. didn't know what he had expected, but Gary did not look anything like what R.J. thought he would look like. The radioman was about the same height as R.J., with dark, curly brown hair. He looked young to be a second class petty officer. He had a pleasant looking face, but his brow was furled and his mouth bent in a frown. He was clearly troubled. The tall blond returned to his table and said something to Gary, motioning toward the Haverfield trio. Gary smiled wanly, held up his glass of tequila in a salute, and took a sip. R.J., Gino and Pea saluted back with their beer cans.

"How 'bout that?" Gino said, a sardonic grin on his face. "Ironic, huh?"

"Hey," Pea leaned over and whispered, "let's call the girls." He grinned his mischievous grin at R.J. "At least we know where their hubbies are."

R.J. scowled. His friends obviously thought the situation was funny. Maybe it was a little peculiar, but R.J. failed to grasp the humor. Still, he couldn't help but overhear snatches of conversation from the Raptor's table. Most of the talking was done by Gary, and the main topic was Annie.

"...all the time, just bitching and complaining about being here," Gary was saying. "Always wants to go home. Never happy about anything."

"It's just marriage," his friend was saying. "It's just the shit you go through when you're married."

"She don't wanna be married to me," Gary complained. "Hell, we ain't even had sexual relations in months." His friends shook their heads slowly.

That's a funny way to put it, R.J. thought. *Sexual relations?*

"Wha's funny?" Pea asked, sipping his beer.

"You are, Peacock, my boy," R.J. said brightly, suddenly smiling and animated. "You are the funniest little dude I ever met, and I'm gonna buy you a beer." R.J. stood and patted Pea on the shoulder.

Gino raised his empty beer can and R.J. nodded as he headed for the bar.

"He seems to be feeling a little better," Gino mused, watching his friend make his way to the bar.

"Yeah, he does," Pea agreed. He motioned to the Raptor's table with his head. "This is weird," he whispered. "You think that's Betty's and Carol's ol' men?"

"Dunno," Gino replied. "Why don't you go ask 'em?" He laughed at the horrified look on Pea's face.

R.J. brought the beers back to the table and smiled to himself. *Sexual relations, that's funny*, he thought. *Hey honey, you wanna have sexual relations?* He laughed out loud and sat down.

Through small bits of conversation from the Raptor's table, R.J. pieced together the picture of Gary and Annie Nelson's marriage and life together. They had married young because they thought she was pregnant. *Interesting*, R.J. thought. She never liked the Navy and their problems started two years ago when he shipped over to make second class. Being transferred to Guam was the last straw for Annie. She hated Guam and everything about it. She wanted to go home. She cried constantly. Finally, about six months ago they quit having sexual relations. R.J. thought about it, doing the math in his head. So, the baby she lost wasn't Gary's. It was his. If there ever had been a baby...

R.J. began to see Annie in a different light. After the incident with the pregnancy, he had begun to mentally keep her at arm's length, not letting her get too close, physically or emotionally. Maybe he was trying to defend himself. Maybe he was just being a guy. Now he began to see her as Gary saw her, and he wasn't sure that was a good thing. He downed his beer and stood just as Tiny and his hogs took over the bandstand.

"I'm pretty tired, fellas," he said. "Think I'll grab a shuttle and go back to the ship."

Gino pulled Pea's arm over and looked at his watch. "It ain't even twenty-hunnerd," he complained.

"He been sick," Pea leaned forward and explained carefully, slurring his words slightly. "He jus' startin' to get back to normal." He patted Gino's arm paternally. "Don' worry 'bout him."

"That's true," R.J. agreed, a serious look on his face. "I'm just starting to think clearly."

He put on his whitehat and waved to his friends. As he stepped through the double doors into the evening air, he glanced back quickly at Gary and his Raptor friends. They were deep in conversation, his friends obviously trying to shore him up.

Annie and I have a lot to talk about, R.J. thought as he hopped aboard the shuttle bus. He rode back to the ship in silence. Very few sailors were returning this early and R.J. had the bus almost to himself. He sat all the way in the back so he could stretch out on the long back seat. He tilted his whitehat over his eyes and tried hard not to think of Annie. He was tired. Recently, thinking of her seemed to make him more tired.

Back aboard ship, R.J. undressed quickly and rolled up into his bunk. He stared up at the overhead pipes and filled his mind with thoughts of being at sea, the spray coming over the bow, the ship rolling comfortably, the sun warm on his face. His bunk felt comfortable and familiar and he squirmed around, molding his body to the mattress, establishing the perfect position for sleep. "*...and to sleep you must slumber in just such a bed,*" he muttered. He closed his eyes, fell asleep without a thought of Annie, and slept through the night. The dream stayed away and let him sleep.

* * * * *

The Raptor left port on Saturday morning. She was due back in two weeks, during which time the Haverfield was scheduled to remain in port for minor repairs. R.J. got the call at sixteen-hundred, just as he was leaving the signal bridge.

"Phone call, R.J.!" Pancho stood at the bottom of the ladder, motioning toward the quarterdeck with a hooked thumb. R.J. slid down the ladder without touching the rungs and led the way aft.

"She sounds nice," Pancho said, grinning broadly.

"It's probably my aunt," R.J. said.

Pancho laughed aloud and handed R.J. the receiver.

"Hello?" R.J. said into the mouthpiece.

"Hi R.J." Her voice sounded sweet. "Miss me?"

"Course I did, baby," R.J. drawled. "Tonight?"

"Yes, tonight. Betty's place, okay?"

"What time should we be there?"

"Well, we'll be there about ten," she said sweetly.

R.J. knew the shore patrol cut down on their rounds after twenty-two-hundred, and it was easier to sneak into Naval housing. "See you then," he answered, and hung up the phone.

"How's your aunt?" Pancho grinned as R.J. placed the receiver in its cradle.

"Mui bien, amigo," R.J. answered. "Mui bien."

* * * * *

R.J. and Annie lay naked on the couch, snuggling together. She put her head on his shoulder and sighed. "R.J., tell me a poem," she cooed, twirling the hair on his chest with her index finger.

"Stop that," he pushed her hand away.

"Tickle?" she giggled.

"It bugs me," he said, irritably.

She pulled herself up on one elbow and looked at him. "What's the matter?" she asked, frowning. "Why are you being such an ass?"

He stared at the ceiling and the bumping noises coming from the bedrooms upstairs. He didn't know what to say to her. He didn't know how to describe the feelings he had, and how they were changing faster than he could keep up with them.

"So now you don't wanna talk to me?" she sat up and swung her legs over his. She lit a cigarette and offered it to him. When he shook his head she took a deep drag and blew the smoke at his face. "Don't you want me anymore, R.J.?" she asked.

He looked at her in the dim light. "I met Gary last night," he said flatly, watching her face for a reaction.

"So that's what you're so glum about?"

"He seems like a nice guy."

"Do you wanna talk about Gary, R.J.?" She ran a hand through her blonde hair. "I thought you wanted to talk about you and me, you know, our future."

"Future," R.J. repeated the word as if trying it out on his lips. He frowned.

Annie felt a pang of panic in her gut. "Maybe this isn't the time to talk about it," she said softly. She got up and pulled on her panties and bra. R.J. watched distractedly. The sight of her in her underwear used to thrill him. It still did, just not as much. Annie went into the kitchen and put on a kettle to brew some tea. R.J. stayed where he was on the couch, naked, staring up at the ceiling.

* * * * *

"Guess what?" Charming Billy had the duty on the quarterdeck when R.J., Pea and Gino got back to the ship. It was zero-two-hundred and the ship was quiet except for the hissing and clanking of its machinery.

"Don't tell me!" Pea exclaimed. "Teresa's pregnant?"

Billy grinned. "Yep, she sure is. Seriously, though, guess what?"

"Billy," Gino said wearily. "Will you please stop fuckin' with us?"

"We're getting underway first thing Monday morning," Billy explained, pleased that he possessed, and could pass on, this information.

"Oh, shit!" Pea snapped and threw his whitehat down hard on the deck. "We just got back, man." He pleaded to Billy as if Billy could change things just because he had passed on the bad news. "C'mon, Billy, we just got back in the saddle, y'know?"

"I'm only the messenger," Billy protested. "You wanna complain, you go see the captain."

"Where we goin?" R.J. asked.

"Gunnery practice," Billy said, once again pleased he could enlighten his friends. "Back here next Friday," he smiled at Pea who smiled back. "Then back out the following Monday." He frowned at Pea who frowned back. "That's gonna be the routine for the next three weeks."

"What the hell is going on?" R.J. asked. "Something must be up."

"Dunno," Billy replied. "Snively told me about it at the movie tonight. He just finished typing up the plans for the next three weeks. Gunnery exercises and more gunnery exercises." Billy shrugged.

"Man, I just got back in the saddle," Pea whined weakly. "I'd much rather be with Carol than at sea."

R.J. stared at his friends absently. *I think I'd rather be at sea just now,* he thought.

* * * * *

Annie's reaction to the gunnery exercises was not pleasant. "What am I supposed to do?" she cried over the phone. "I'm tired of being alone!" She hung up, leaving R.J. standing on the quarterdeck, staring dumbly at the receiver. He hung up, shook his head and headed for the signal bridge. They were getting underway right after breakfast the next morning, and he wanted to make sure everything was lashed down and secured.

* * * * *

Everyone agreed that Bixby was the best shot they had ever seen with a three-inch gun. The forward gun mount consistently scored in the high nineties all throughout the three day gunnery exercises, and the Haverfield returned to Apra Harbor on Friday, July third with a proud and tired crew.

Gino and Pea were anxious to contact the girls. Pea called Carol and set up a meeting at the USO beach for Saturday night at twenty-two-hundred.

"Why not at Betty's place?" Gino asked.

"Some deck ape got caught up in Naval housing last night," Pea explained what Carol had told him. "The S.P.'s are all over the place." He shrugged. "It's the beach or nowhere."

"Okay, the beach," Gino agreed.

R.J. just nodded. The beach would be fine. He wanted to talk things out with Annie and he thought the beach would be the most pleasant place for it. *Yes,* he thought, *Annie would come around.* He just needed to talk to her.

He was wrong, of course.

SIXTY FIVE

"Pete? You got a minute?" Mr. MacDonald stuck his head into Mr. Almogordo's engineering office. The engineer was poring over some electrical schematics and looked up, irritated at the interruption. He smiled when he saw it was First Division's lieutenant.

"Come in, Mac," the engineer greeted him warmly. "Sit down." He offered a chair and looked curiously at the file folder MacDonald held in his hand. It looked like the report they were preparing on Twitchell. "What you got, Mac?" Mr. Almogordo asked, nodding at the file.

"We may have a problem brewing," MacDonald explained. "We may be able to stop an ugly incident." Mr. Mac opened the file and handed the message slip to the engineering officer. It was a teletype news release. Pete Almogordo read the release, looked up at Mac, and read it again.

"You think this might set him off?" he asked.

MacDonald nodded. "It fits his pattern. Remember the Clay-Liston fight? Remember the march on Washington last year?" Mr. Mac nodded slowly, pointing to the news release. "That's gonna set him off, Pete."

Mr. Almogordo picked up the news release again and scanned it. He nodded. He was sure Mac was right. Chief Twitchell was not going to like it when he learned that President Lyndon Johnson had just signed into law the Civil Rights Act of 1964.

* * * * *

The tide was coming in fast, a little more than an hour before high tide. R.J. and Annie walked barefoot in the rising surf. The water felt good crashing into their ankles, and Annie jumped and hopped around through the foam, giggling and kicking water into the air, her blue jeans rolled up to her knees. To R.J., she looked like a little girl on her way home from school, happy, carefree. That was just like Annie. One day she could be deeply depressed, and the next day she could frolic around in the surf, laughing like a little girl. She seemed beautiful to R.J. that night. He mentally shook off his angst and joined in the surf-frolicking. They had a lot to talk about, but they could talk later.

"I don't wanna talk about it, R.J." Annie sat up on the blanket and wrapped her arms around her knees.

"You wanna talk about the future?" he asked. She nodded. "Then you gotta talk about Gary."

"I don't want to talk about him, R.J.," she pleaded. "Can't we just enjoy the night, enjoy being together?" She sat cross-legged on the blanket and took his hands in hers. "I know we need to talk," she said, staring into his eyes. "But right now, I just wanna..." she looked helplessly around the beach. "You understand, don't you, R.J.?"

"Sure," he said, and he meant it. Though he knew they had to talk it out, he wanted as much as she did to delay the conversation as long as possible. So, he gave in to the moment, to the night and to the crashing surf, and buried his face in Annie's hair. She snuggled next to him and patted his head lovingly.

"That's nice," she whispered. "That's very nice."

* * * * *

When R.J., Gino and Pea returned to the ship at zero-one-thirty the harbor was quiet. There had been a Fourth of July celebration on base, and a fireworks display for dependent children in the harbor, along with a parade of sail boats, but the harbor was quiet at that time in the morning.

Chief Lyons had the deck and nodded to the trio as they saluted him and stepped down from the brow. They had just come aboard when the telephone rang and Chief Lyons answered it. He listened intently, frowned, and said, "Yes sir, will do, sir." He hung up the phone and looked around the fantail. "Where's Andy?" he asked.

"Right here, Chief," Andy came out of the shadows wearing the white duty belt and billy-club of the messenger of the watch. No one had seen him back there.

"Go wake up Mr. Almogordo," Lyons said. "Tell him we got an emergency."

Andy looked at the chief blankly.

"Now, Sample!" the chief barked, and Andy took off for the engineering officer's quarters.

Chief Lyons looked over at R.J., Gino and Pea. "Why don't you men go below and hit the sack?" he said gently. He looked around nervously, and the trio moved back into the shadows under the tarpaulin. They knew something was up and they wanted to see what it was.

Mr. Almogordo arrived on the quarterdeck just as the shore patrol paddy wagon was screeching to a stop at the foot of the brow. The converted panel truck was rocking violently to the left and right, and inside, where the prisoners rode, someone was pounding loudly on the interior and a deep, grumbling voice was yelling, but it was too muffled to clearly understand.

Chief Lyons spoke quickly and quietly to Mr. Almogordo, who nodded, frowning. They stood at the head of the brow, watching as a grizzled chief warrant officer, an SP armband around his bicep and a clipboard in his hand, walked wearily up the brow to the Haverfield quarterdeck. He saluted Chief Lyons and the engineering lieutenant.

"Permission to come aboard, sir." It didn't sound like a request. The name tag on his shirt read, HATFIELD.

"Granted," Lyons said. He nodded toward the shore patrol wagon. "What's going on?" he asked.

The warrant officer looked back at the wagon. Two large, muscular shore patrolmen climbed out of the cab and stood next to the rear door. They were both black and they were scowling at the truck's back door. The pounding and grumbling from inside continued. "Well, sir," he said, taking off his cap and scratching furiously at a bald spot on his head. "We got wunna yourn handcuffed in the backa that truck. He drunk, he disorderly, and if you ask me," he leaned over the lifeline and spit tobacco juice into the harbor, "he in a big pile o'shit." He wiped his mouth on his sleeve, handed the clipboard to Mr. Almogordo who read it, shook his head and handed it to Chief Lyons. R.J. strained as much as he could to get a glimpse of the paperwork without revealing his concealed position. He couldn't see anything.

"Assault and battery?" Chief Lyons blurted out, reading the report. "Who'd he assault?"

Hatfield chuckled. "Well, sir," he drawled, "now that there would be a intrastin' story." He accepted Lyon's signature on the report, gave him a copy, and turned to the shore patrolmen at the truck. "Bring 'im aboard, boys," he called out.

The noise from inside the wagon stopped when one of the SP's unlocked and unbarred the back door. The other SP pulled the door open slowly, and they both stood back, billy clubs in hand eyeing the paddy wagon's inhabitant. The truck began to sway slightly, as the prisoner inside made his way toward the rear door and moved slowly, one step at a time, down the back stairs until he reached solid ground. His hands were cuffed behind his back, and as he turned slowly, the light hit his bloated face.

"Twitchy!" Pea gasped. Mr. Almogordo and Chief Lyons turned and looked at Pea, R.J. and Gino. Lyons scowled, but the trio stayed where they were.

The two black shore patrolmen held the snarling chief by his arms and marched him up the brow toward the quarterdeck. All the way up the brow Chief Twitchell kept up a running diatribe aimed at the black SP's.

"You black bastards! You think you takin' over but you ain't, you god-damn niggers! I don't give a shit about your black asses, and I don't give a shit about your nigger president!" He stopped when he saw Mr. Almogordo standing spread-legged at the head of the brow, arms folded across his chest, a disgusted scowl on his face.

The noise had filtered down into First Division's compartment and Jefferson came up on deck to see what was going on. He took one look and scurried back down to the compartment where he woke up all the blacks. Soon, the fantail was populated by curious sailors of all colors. Chief Lyons frowned. He didn't like the feel of this.

"Can you find your bunk by yourself, Chief?" the engineering officer asked between clenched teeth. "Or do you need some help?"

Twitchell looked around, bleary-eyed at the sailors gathered there, watching him. He couldn't see clearly, but he knew they were all black. Niggers always stuck together, that's why they're here. He stepped forward and stared at one face, trying to bring into focus. When the face became clear to him, he backed up, snarling. He was looking into the angry face of Rafer Sample. In his alcohol-infested mind, Chief Twitchell associated all his recent problems on this one face, this one nigger, this Rafer Sample. He stared hard at Rafer, noting every curve, every scar, every blemish on that face. This was a face he would remember forever. Maybe he couldn't keep the darkies from taking over back in the states, but he could stop one nigger. One single nigger. If every good white man in the world would do that, there wouldn't be no racial problems. The solution was so obvious, Twitchell almost broke out laughing, but he kept his outside emotions in check. All anyone saw was a sneering grin that didn't last too long. No one could tell from his face that he had decided what he had to do. "I can find my way, sir," he said sheepishly.

"Very well," Mr. Almogordo said. He turned to the crowd on the fantail. "You men go below," he ordered. "Get back to bed. There's nothing to see up here."

Slowly, the crowd dispersed. Chief Twitchell lumbered to the chief's quarters and fell into his bunk. He was suddenly very sober, thinking about his plan. He would tell no one, not even Crawford or the others. So far they had been going about it all wrong. How do you kill a snake? You cut off its head. It was laughingly simple, really. He had to get rid of Rafer Sample. How to do that short of killing him was the problem. *Killing him? Hmm.* The chief fell into a fitful sleep.

* * * * *

Monday morning the Haverfield got underway for more gunnery exercises with the crew gossiping about Chief Twitchell and the reason behind all the gunnery practice. They were certain of only one thing: Chief Twitchell had gotten into some kind of trouble at the base enlisted men's club and some people on base were yelling for his head. That was all Snively could glean from the few reports which weren't sealed. Snively would read the contents of an open envelope, but would never try to open one that had been sealed. It was beneath his sense of standards.

Twitchell kept to himself. He wasn't drinking or plotting with other rednecks, preferring to stay below, next to his beloved machinery. The captain had received a complete written report (sealed) from the base shore patrol office, and was required to reply in person as soon as the Haverfield returned to port. Meanwhile, Chief Twitchell was keeping a low profile.

Mr. Almogordo had questioned Chief Twitchell closely over a period of three days. He had the chief write out, in his own words, exactly what happened the night of July fourth. The engineering officer read the chief's version, grimaced at the spelling and grammar, and put it in the file, uncorrected. He delivered the file to the exec, who read it and took it personally to the captain.

"He's a bigot, Captain," the exec said after the captain had finished reading the file, which included the report prepared by Mr. Almogordo and Mr. MacDonald. "I wish we could get rid of him."

The captain sighed and set Twitchell's file on his desk. He leaned back in his chair, and put his hands behind his head. "Look at his file closely, Ed," the captain said. "We didn't see the pattern, because he had a spotless record, but take a close look." He picked up the file, flipped through a few pages and handed the file, open, to the exec. "See, right there." Captain Oliver pointed to the last four duty stations Chief Twitchell had been assigned to. "No longer than eighteen months at any post. And every C.O.

gives him a glowing report, almost sounding relieved that he's gone. I'll tell you what I'd like to know, Ed." The captain shook his head. "I'd like to know how a man like that kept those gold stripes this long."

"Just lucky, I guess," the exec replied. "He's always kept one step ahead of Javert." Lieutenant Martin chuckled at his own clever reference.

"It's going to have to stop here, Ed." The captain looked serious. The exec sat up in his chair.

"Shouldn't we just transfer him, sir? I mean, glowing recommendation and all?" The exec's grin faded when he noticed the captain was not amused.

"We need to compile a complete file, including his service record, these reports, and statements from individuals involved with Chief Twitchell." The captain was on his feet, pacing. "I want you to head this up, Ed." He stopped to look at his executive officer. "I want all the dirty laundry included. We don't gloss over anything, understood?"

The exec nodded and got up, putting on his cap. "I'll get on it right away," he said. "In the meantime, about Twitchell..."

The captain sat back down in his chair. "He's confined to quarters until we get back. Make certain he understands that he is gliding on very thin ice and should keep out of my sight."

The exec saluted and stepped into the passageway, pulling the door shut behind him. He hefted the paperwork in his hand, looked back at the captain's door, nodded and headed to the wardroom, where he expected to find Mr. Almogordo, and if he was lucky, Mr. MacDonald.

Captain Oliver sat at his desk, reviewing the numbers on the week's gunnery exercises. Even the aft gun-mount was shooting well. Not like Bixby in the forward mount, of course. That lad was in a world of his own. The captain wondered how the young gunner's mate would do in a real battle, with real targets that shot back. *Only time and circumstance will tell,* he thought. *Time and circumstance.* He pondered the thought for a moment, then shook his head and went back to the reports. One more week of this and he believed his crew would be ready for a patrol under combat conditions. He both dreaded and looked forward eagerly to that time and those circumstances.

* * * * *

As expected, the Raptor was in port when the Haverfield returned on Friday after their second week of blowing up towed targets. The USS Seneca, the sea-going tug responsible for the targets finally got smart and brought along three, not just one towed target. Bixby sank two of them, but the third survived to get shot at another day. Before the weekend was over, a bet had been made by Haverfield sailors that Bixby would sink all three targets the next week. The Seneca sailors jumped at the bet, and over a hundred dollars was wagered. Snively locked the wager in a cabinet.

R.J. stayed aboard all weekend, helped Billy polish brass and air the flags, one flag bag at a time. With the Raptor in port, he couldn't see Annie, and the ship was going out again on Monday, anyway, so he stayed aboard.

He wanted to write a letter to Renee, and he had been composing one since before he got sick. He wanted to finish it, mail it and get it out of his mind.

He sat on the signal bridge on the deck, legs folded, and wrote the letter that had been rattling around in his head:

Dear Renee,

I understand. Don't feel bad and don't think I do. Chuck is a very good guy, and I am truly happy for both of you.

I probably should have been more attentive, or maybe answered your letters more often, but what's done is done. I want you to be happy.

I'm probably going to be transferred next month when my 18 months are up, so I would like to come to your wedding, if the invitation still stands.

Good luck and give my regards to Chuck. He's a lucky guy.

R.J.

He looked it over, nodded, satisfied and put it in the envelope. He slipped the envelope into the ship's post office outbox. One less thing to worry about.

Late that night he sat up out of a sound sleep, startled, and looked down at his hands. They were covered with blood. He looked up, expecting to see Rafer and Andy laughing at him, but this time it was Twitchell's face, also covered with blood, laughing and pointing at him. He shook himself awake and rolled out of his bunk, landing heavily on the floor. His heart was pounding, he was sweating, and he was gasping for air. He looked down at his hands. No blood. He rubbed them together and climbed back into his bunk. He was exhausted. His heart slowed eventually and he began breathing easily. He nodded off to sleep and dreamt of Helen's Reef and big, lumbering green sea turtles waddling across pristine, white sand.

* * * * *

Bixby sank the third target on the second day out. The Haverfield sailors cheered and split up the earnings even as the blown up parts of the target were sinking to the bottom. The Seneca sailors shook their heads in wonder at the forward gunner who was such a good shot. Towed targets are outfitted with sensitive radio-transmitting equipment which can record a 'hit' on the target, even though the actual projectile only comes close. The logic held that in a surface action, a real target would be much larger than a towed target.

Captain Oliver was especially pleased with Bixby, although he wouldn't show it outwardly, because the captain knew how hard it was to actually hit a target that small from a few thousand yards away. He also knew how small PT boats were. They were the threats the Haverfield might be facing, and the captain was glad he had such an accurate gunner. He reached for the sound-powered phones and rang up the bridge. Mr. MacDonald was the OOD and the captain asked to speak to him.

"Yes, sir?" MacDonald's voice came on the phone.

"Set a course for Bird Island, Mac," the captain ordered. "We're fresh out of targets."

"Aye, sir," MacDonald hung up the receiver and grinned. He looked down at his chart and made some calculations. "Come right to zero-one-five," he ordered.

"Zero-one-five, aye," Sonny Metzner turned the helm to starboard, settling the ship on course.

"Might as well blow up some rocks," MacDonald said. Everyone on the bridge smiled.

After three weeks, the gunnery exercises had been concluded with a "Well done," officially issued from the new admiral. Captain Paul Oliver was pleased with the performance of his ship, but was worried about the meeting he had to attend upon returning to port. One week earlier, he had delivered his own report, compiled by the exec, to the admiral's office for review. They would decide what course of action to take. He sat at his desk and once again reviewed the report on Chief Jaspar Twitchell.

Combined with eyewitness accounts of Twitchell's behavior at the E.M. club on the fourth, the report done by MacDonald and Almogordo, and Twitchell's own meandering, self-justifying account of the events, Captain Oliver believed the report meant he would soon be losing a good engineer. It was obvious Twitchell had a problem with blacks, a big problem. He had gone from table to table at the enlisted men's club, insulting, in the most obnoxious manner, every black face there, regardless of age or gender. He had spat into the faces of black women and called them niggers. He punched two blacks who came to the women's aid and it took four men to hold him down until the shore patrol could get there. When he saw the S.P.'s were black, he went into a rage, kicking and screaming at them while they cuffed him and struggled to get him into the paddy wagon. The captain closed the file and put it away. It was out of his hands now.

* * * * *

The Raptor was still there. Tied port-side to the pier, the mine sweeper was undergoing a new paint job. Sailors poured over her like ants, painting, scraping, sanding. It looked to R.J. like they were almost done. The little minesweeper looked good sporting all that fresh paint. R.J. checked the ships' movements reports again. The Raptor was not scheduled to get underway for two more weeks. *Great,* he thought. *We're both gonna be in port at the same time. We won't be seeing much of the girls.* It didn't bother him as much as it bothered Pea and Gino. R.J. was coming to the realization that there was no future with Annie. The only thing they had in common was the sex. Without that, they probably wouldn't be together. When they weren't having sex, they were arguing about something. She said she wanted to talk about things, but she didn't want to talk about Gary. He felt like they were moving in two different directions. Why did it have to be so complicated?

"Hey Slick!" Anselmi came around the corner and spotted R.J. staring into the harbor. They had tied up and R.J. hadn't shifted colors yet. "Shift colors!" Anselmi yelled at him and pointed to the ensign still flying from the main mast. R.J. hurried down and untied the lanyard and brought the flag in, carefully folding it in a triangular shape.

"Sorry 'bout that, Salami," he said sheepishly.

Anselmi grinned, shook his head and slid down the ladder to the 02 level.

R.J. stored the flag and took a quick look around the signal bridge. Not much cleaning to do. Billy could handle it. He went below to the compartment and rolled up into his bunk. He folded his hands behind his head and stared up at the overhead, determined to figure out what to do about Annie. He fell asleep at once, as if his mind was tired of thinking about her.

* * * * *

Captain Oliver returned to the ship on Monday, having attended the meeting on base about Chief Twitchell. The blacks from the enlisted men's club had declined to file charges. They just wanted to forget the entire affair. Captain Oliver had listened, surprised at what the chief of staff was telling him. It seemed they wanted nothing to do with what they perceived as an isolated disciplinary problem. They suggested he take it up with his officers aboard ship and work out the problem at that level. Captain Oliver had been stunned. With all the evidence presented to them, the base command staff had decided to throw the problem back into his lap. They had many more important things on their mind, the chief of staff had explained, and this minor racial conflict was to be concluded by the Haverfield command. After all, it was the Haverfield's problem. The chief of staff cited Chief Twitchell's exemplary service record, and dismissed the report as a 'personality conflict.' The chief of staff was sympathetic, though, and to ease the situation he cut orders for the Haverfield to get underway for two weeks' R&R in Yokosuka. Paul Oliver was appreciative of the gesture, but doubted it would go very far in diffusing what he considered to be a ticking time bomb aboard his ship.

"Haverfield arriving!" Captain Oliver stepped quickly up the brow, saluted the flag and returned the salute of Chief Risk, the OOD.

"Find Mr. Almogordo and Mr. MacDonald and ask them to join me in the wardroom," he instructed.

"Aye, sir," Chief Risk sent the messenger to find the officers. He tried to read the captain's face and discover a clue to the fate of Chief Twitchell. The whole ship knew what was going on, and most of the crew believed Twitchell would be transferred or court martialed.

"I thought you'd be here, Ed." The captain stepped into the wardroom and removed his cap. The exec stood up from where he was studying operational reports and drinking coffee. The captain waved him down and sat across from him, pouring a cup of coffee from a silver pot.

MacDonald and Almogordo entered the wardroom. The captain motioned to a couple of chairs and they sat down. Captain Oliver handed headquarters' written response to all three officers and waited while they read it. He watched surprised expressions appear on each of their faces. They looked up at him and he nodded.

"That's about it, men," he said. "The Navy wants us to handle it as a disciplinary problem."

"All due respect, sir," Pedro Almogordo said, "I don't think the command staff takes this stuff seriously." He tapped his finger down hard on headquarters' response.

"Go on, Pete," the captain urged.

"I think this is more than just a disciplinary problem. At least it has the potential to become more," Lieutenant Almogordo continued. "The chief of staff may see this as an isolated incident. I see it...we see it...," he nodded to Mr. Mac and the exec, "as symptomatic of a changing society."

"How so, Pete?" The captain knew what the engineering officer meant, but he wanted him to vocalize it, as if by saying it aloud, a simple solution would present itself.

"We've been out here in the Pacific, and though we get news reports of the civil rights movement back home, we feel isolated from it, perhaps even exempt from it. But the black sailors on this ship, and everywhere in the Navy, for that matter, are embracing this 'equal rights' thing with a passion."

"It hasn't become a problem yet, Pete," the exec said gently.

"It's a time bomb, sir," Mr. Mac cut in. "There's a lot of resistance back home to the civil rights issue. Some of it is becoming quite contentious. I've been reading the reports on the riot in Harlem this weekend. You know what caused it?" The other three officers shook their heads. "A white policeman shot a fifteen year old black kid. The Congress for Racial Equality organized a peaceful protest and it turned into a full scale riot. It started two days ago, and it's just now winding down." He took out a folded, teletype news message and set it on the table. "I've been monitoring the racial situation in the states, primarily because of the trouble we're having here."

"But this problem is truly isolated, Mac," the exec said, playing the devil's advocate. "We've got a problem with only one man aboard this ship."

MacDonald and Almogordo exchanged a look. "Sir," the engineering officer began, "it goes a lot deeper than that. We've seen groups of sailors isolating themselves from others, on both sides of the color line. There's a real resentment building, and I think we need to get a handle on it."

"I agree with Pete, sir," Mr. Mac added. "We need to find a solution, and quick, especially with what's going on in Southeast Asia. We're going to need a crew working together, not at odds with each other."

The captain nodded slowly, flipping through the pages of the report. "Perhaps the best solution is the one you came up with, Ed." The captain nodded to the exec.

"You were opposed to that solution, Captain," the exec reminded him.

"Yes, I was. However, that was before I was stonewalled by the command staff." He frowned down at the report. "I hate to make this someone else's problem, but..."

"You mean transfer him?" Mr. Mac said hopefully, glancing at Mr. Almogordo who nodded enthusiastically, eyebrows upraised.

"You would be losing one of your best engineers, Pete," the captain cautioned.

"We're in good shape, skipper," Pete replied. "All the hard work has been done, and our power plant is running like a clock." He nodded to himself. This was perhaps the best possible solution.

"Ed," the captain interrupted the exec's thoughts, and he looked up.

"Sir?"

"There's a list of open billets in the fleet. Find it, and let's locate an appropriate duty station for Chief Twitchell."

"Are you going to take any other actions, Cap'n?" Mr. Mac asked.

"Like what, Mac?"

"Captain's mast?"

Captain Oliver pondered for a few moments. "No," he said finally. "Let him keep his gold hash marks, but I will put a letter of reprimand in his jacket."

"It'll be the first one he's ever got, sir," the exec pointed out. "He's going to be unhappy about it."

"Bring him to my cabin tomorrow morning at zero nine-hundred. All of you be here. We'll call it an informal mast, the reprimand being the worst of it. We'll impress upon him how lucky he is not to be busted. That ought to shut him up." The captain smiled at his guests and stood, indicating the meeting was over. "By the way," he said as they started to leave. "The chief of staff is rewarding us for our outstanding gunnery exercises." He handed the order for Yokosuka R&R to the exec. The other two officers read it over the exec's shoulder, and all three grinned broadly.

"Pass the word to the crew and tell them I want to see a squared away ship by the time we leave on Thursday morning. And Ed," the captain looked at the exec with a serious expression. "Find that billet for the chief."

"Aye, sir." The exec and the three officers left the captain's cabin.

Commander Paul Oliver sat down in his swivel chair and pondered the situation with Twitchell and the conclusion they had inevitably come to for solving the dilemma. He didn't like passing on a problem to some other commanding officer, but with the command staff taking the stance they had, it was painfully obvious to Paul Oliver that they had bigger fish to fry in Viet Nam. They were sweeping this problem under the rug, and Captain Oliver was certain it would not remain there. Forces were building back home, and the civil rights movement was gaining momentum. The president had signed legislation guaranteeing civil rights. Bigotry and resentment between the races had to be addressed at some time, hopefully in the near future. It was just like the Navy to ignore a problem until it became a crisis. It was nearly impossible to get fast decisions from a huge bureaucracy like the US Navy, and, even once the decision was made, it was nearly impossible to move that big organization quickly. Captain Oliver decided it was the nature of the beast. At least he could get rid of a problem on board the Haverfield. Chief Twitchell would become someone else's problem. Paul Oliver shook his head and walked out on the wing bridge, putting on the new commander's cap Lorelei had given him. Lorelei and their affair seemed to have happened years ago, rather than months ago. He could still smell her fragrance, and it still irritated him that he could never picture her face.

SIXTY SIX

The crew was ecstatic that they were going back to Japan. After three weeks of intensive gunnery training, they were tired and ready for a break. The weather was hot and humid on Guam, rarely cooling off even at night. Summer was pounding down hard on the Pacific islands in the trust territory. Word of the Harlem riot spread quickly throughout the ship, and many blacks welcomed the news. 'Burn, baby, burn' became a catch-phrase with black sailors, which caused a great deal of resentment from the southern whites aboard ship. Chief Twitchell, however, stayed under the radar. He was still stinging from his 'informal' Captain's mast, and he was infuriated about the Harlem riot. "Stupid porch-monkeys," he said quietly to MM-1 Crawford. "They get pissed off and what do they do? They burn down their own neighborhood. We should buy them all a five gallon can of gasoline and a book of matches and let 'em burn, baby, burn all they fuckin' want."

When R.J. heard about the Japan trip he had mixed feelings. He needed to get together with Annie and talk things out. The more he thought of it, the more he felt there was not much to salvage, but he did care for her, for whatever that was worth, and he wanted more than anything to clear the air. The problem was the Raptor was still in port, and there was a good chance he wouldn't see Annie until they returned from Japan. That was three weeks away. He was deep in thought when a light flashed from the Raptor. R.J. turned on the signal light and swung it around, pointing it at the minesweeper. He signaled 'go ahead,' and the Raptor began flashing. Their signal bridge was out of red bunting and the base didn't have any to spare. Could the Haverfield spare some? R.J. answered that they could, indeed, let the Raptor have some red bunting. The Raptor's signalman thanked him and added that they were going to need the red bunting for Bravo flags. They were leaving the next day for a three month deployment to the Tonkin Gulf to sweep mines.

'God speed,' R.J. sent back and turned off the light. He would get to see Annie before they left after all. His feelings were still mixed. He looked forward to seeing her, and he dreaded seeing her. He decided that was the way of love. It was never perfect, and sometimes it was downright horrid.

* * * * *

Annie buttoned up her blouse and pouted at R.J. He had not reacted the way she'd anticipated, and that pissed her off. Instead of trying to reassure her, he got up and walked down to the breaking surf, taking the bottle of Jack Daniel's with him. There, he gazed out at the inky ocean and spread his arms wide, throwing his head back. He smiled and drank in the warmth of the night sky. Then he drank in some of the Jack Daniel's. It was an Edgar Allan Poe kind of a night, he decided. Annie was right about one thing: he was a dreamer.

Annie composed herself and looked to Gino for support. "What is it with him?" she asked, pointing at R.J. who had taken off his shoes and was wandering in the surf. "I just told him I loved him. Is he some kinda weirdo?"

"Yeah," Gino replied. "He's known as a nut aboard our ship." He fondled Betty's left breast and added solemnly, "Some of us think he's queer." Annie and Betty giggled.

"You're some friend," Annie scolded.

"I'm just messin' with ya." Gino grinned. "What did you say to him to make him walk away?"

"You mean besides 'I love you?' I told him he was a dreamer." She pouted her lips and watched R.J. splashing in the foaming waves. "I meant it in a good way, but somehow it made him mad."

R.J. walked along the shore, barefoot, and stared up at the bright blanket of stars that twinkled down on the secluded and lonely beach. He came to a stop halfway up the beach and turned to face his friends. "Hey!" he called to them. They looked at him curiously. He took a long pull on the whiskey, and held an index finger in the air. "Listen to this," he said, and began reciting:

> "Take this kiss upon the brow,
> and in parting from you now,
> thus much let me avow:
> You are not wrong who deem
> that all my days have been a dream.
> "Yet if hope has flown away,
> in a night or in a day;
> in a vision, or in none—
> Is it therefore the less gone?
> All that we see or seem
> is but a dream within a dream."

R.J. picked up a fistful of sand and held it in the air. He let the sand slip through his fingers, and it filtered slowly down into the surf.

> "I stand amidst the roar
> of a surf-tormented shore,
> and I hold within my hand
> grains of the golden sand."

He watched the sand trickle through his fingers and fall into the foaming surf.

> "How few, yet how they creep
> through my fingers to the deep,
> while I weep, while I weep."

He opened his hand and the rest of the sand fell out and washed away in the swirling water.

> "Oh, God can I not grasp them
> with a tighter clasp?
> Oh God, can I not save one

from the pitiless wave?
Is all that we see or seem
but a dream within a dream?"

R.J. stared at the night sky, asking and re-asking his cosmic question.

"Is all that we see or seem
but a dream within a dream?"

The whiskey had made him philosophical. He stared up at the stars, expecting some sort of answer or revelation. The answer came, instead, in the form of Annie, who slid up behind him and wrapped her arms around his waist. She held him close, murmuring promises of a cosmic nature of her own. R.J. thought about it for a moment, a brief moment, and decided that the answer he sought was not forthcoming from the heavens, as he had hoped. "Yeah," he muttered quietly to himself. "Just a dream within a dream." And so he abandoned his philosophical question and gave himself up to the moment. He led Annie by the hand up the beach to where Gino and Betty sat on the blanket.

R.J. plopped down with them and passed the bottle to Gino, who took a big gulp and grimaced as the whiskey went burning down his throat. He looked questioningly at his friend.

"What's that poem all about, man? I mean, you sure know some spooky shit."

R.J. lay back on the blanket and put his hands behind his head. He looked up at the stars and smiled. "I think it's about the passing of time," he said softly. "The sands of time, you know?"

"How do you think up this shit?' Gino asked, handing the bottle back and lying on his back next to R.J.

"I didn't think it up. Poe did."

"You guys wanna be alone, or what?" Betty demanded. She turned to Annie. "Let's go swimming."

"Might as well," Annie agreed, frowning at R.J. and Gino. "These guys are off in a world all their own." She stood and unbuttoned her blouse, removed it and threw it down on the blanket. Next came her jeans and she threw them over R.J.'s face. Betty had stripped off her clothes and together they ran into the surf wearing only panties and bras. R.J. tossed Annie's jeans aside and he and Gino lay on the blanket staring at the starry sky, pondering the passing of time. Pea and Carol had taken the Bomb for a ride in the hills, and so far, there was no sign of them.

"We're on our way to Yokosuka tomorrow, m'man," Gino observed, drinking down the last of the whiskey.

"Yeah," R.J. said, eyes closed. "Been a while since we were there."

Gino sat up and looked at his friend. R.J. lay on the blanket, hands behind his head, gazing up at the sky. "You and Annie are having some problems, huh?"

"We been having problems since we met," R.J. said, picking up the whiskey bottle and shaking it, examining it. "We outta booze?"

"Yeah. So what you gonna do?"

"About what?"

"About Annie."

"What you gonna do about Betty?"

"That's different."

"Different how?" R.J. asked. He sat up and watched Betty and Annie squealing and frolicking in the surf. "How's it different?"

Gino took a deep breath. "'Cause me and Betty both know this is just a fling," he said. "Temporary, y'know?"

"So?" R.J. studied his friend.

"So, you and Annie...you're into each other. You and her are in love." Gino lay back on the blanket, looking up at the night sky, trying to understand what special things R.J. saw up there. "And don't tell me you ain't."

"I dunno, Gino," R.J. said sadly. "She's married, man. Deep down I know this whole thing is temporary, but I don't think she realizes that."

"Then maybe you oughtta tell her, m'man." Gino motioned to the girls. "Why you gotta fall in love, anyway?" he asked. "And why you gotta make things so sad?"

"That's just the way it happens," he said, frowning at his friend. "It's like the man explained in his poem." He closed his eyes and recited softly:

"For being young and dipt in folly,
I fell in love with melancholy,
And used to lay my earthly rest,
And quiet all away in jest.
I could not love except where Death
Was mingling his with beauty's breath,
Or Hymen, Time and Destiny
Were stalking between her and me."

Gino shook his head and lay back on the blanket. "You need to tell her," he said firmly. "Don't make her think something's gonna happen if it ain't."

R.J. thought about it for a moment. "Yeah, I guess you're right," he said. He stood and brushed the sand from his trousers. He walked slowly toward the girls who were laughing and splashing each other in the foaming surf.

Annie came up to meet him. Her hair was wet and her erect nipples poked through her bra. Her wet panties clung to her body, starkly outlining the triangle between her thighs. She looked beautiful and R.J. told her so. She kissed him gently and they walked down the beach while Betty ran up to Gino and shook her hair over him, sprinkling water on him. Gino reached up and pulled her down next to him. They giggled and rolled around on the blanket.

The conversation turned serious as R.J. and Annie walked down the beach hand in hand. "You're going away tomorrow," she said sadly. "Are you gonna miss me?"

"Of course."

"When you get back we probably need to talk," she said, glancing sideways at him.

"'Bout what?"

"About us, R.J.," she said impatiently. "About your plans, you know, for the future."

"My future's all mapped out," R.J. said.

"What?"

"I made a plan when I was fourteen," he explained. "I know what I'm gonna do with my life."

"Oh, you do?" she pouted and let go of his hand. She turned to face him, somehow knowing whatever plan he had in mind did not include her.

"Yeah, I do." He stared down at her. "I'm gonna make my life mean something. I ain't always gonna be some dumb shit from North Denver." He said it a little more bitterly than he intended. He looked up at the stars and took a deep breath. "I'm not going back to Denver," he said softly. "I'm gonna settle in California, go to school, and write a novel." He did not include the other goal: marrying the girl of his dreams.

She backed away from him, her arms folded defensively across her chest. "Where does your little plan leave me, R.J.?" she said coolly, glaring at him. "You're going to be transferred in a couple of months and we've never even talked about this."

"Annie..." he started.

"Don't 'Annie' me!" she said sharply. "Gary's gone for three months and you're going away, too. What about me? I'm gonna be all alone on this stupid, stinky island! How come I don't count in your plans?"

"Annie, you're married. Have you forgotten about that?"

"Almost," she whispered, staring down at the sand. "Almost."

"Look," he said reassuringly, moving closer to her. "We're going to Japan tomorrow and we'll be back in a couple of weeks and we'll work everything out, okay? I promise." He crossed his heart with his finger and grinned at her. She pouted back, staring down at the sand, moving it around with her toes.

He put his arms around her and lifted her chin, staring into her eyes. "I'm crazy about you, Annie. But you need to decide what you're gonna do about Gary."

"I know," she said impatiently. "I know. I'll see you when you get back." She pulled away and strode toward the spot where Gino and Betty lay giggling and writhing around on the blanket.

"Where you going?" R.J. called after her but did not try to catch her. He stood on the beach and watched her gather up her things and stalk off toward the car. Gino and Betty exchanged several good-by kisses before she hurried to catch up with Annie. There was still no sign of Pea and Carol.

As the Chevy Impala pulled out of the parking lot, the Bomb came pulling in, a grinning Pea at the wheel. He pulled up next to the exiting Impala and leered at Betty. He was alone in the car.

"Where's Carol?" Betty demanded.

Pea looked down at his lap and smiled. Carol's head came popping up and she blushed when she saw Betty and Annie. "Oh, hi," she said.

"We're leaving," Annie said flatly.

Pea and Carol exchanged a look that said, *"What, again?"* Carol kissed him hard on the mouth and bounced out of the Oldsmobile. She rushed around to the passenger side of the Impala and climbed into the back seat.

Betty pulled up onto Highway One and the cat-eye taillights slowly disappeared over a hill.

R.J. came up as the Chevy left. Gino turned to him. "You get anything straightened out?" he asked.

"We're gonna talk about it when we get back from Japan," he replied, shrugging his shoulders. "Let's split." He climbed into the back seat of the Bomb and Pea pulled onto the highway.

"We are going to Yokosuka!" Pea yelled out the window. "Man, I can't wait to get there." He floored the Olds and was soon roaring down Highway One at seventy miles per hour, yelling out the window, "Yokosuka, here we come!" He waved to a group of older Guamanians and called to them, his fist in the air. "Banzai! Banzai! Banzai!" The group looked at each other, back at the speeding Oldsmobile and shrugged.

SIXTY SEVEN

Unable to sleep, R.J. joined the mid watch when duty section III assumed control of the dark, quiet ship. The full moon was high and bright in the sky. R.J. climbed to the 04 level and stood amidships, holding onto the rail, his steaming hat folded and tucked into his hip pocket, head held back, the soft wind blowing gently on his face. The ship cut swiftly through a calm, dusky sea. The port and starboard watches ignored him, choosing to stand their watches in silence. Yokosuka was only a few days away, and R.J. looked forward to the visit. He wanted to climb the steps of the signal tower and show Carruthers and Chief Williams his third class crow. He sighed happily, breathed in the fresh salt air, and gazed up in awe at the full moon, huge and glowing in the night sky.

Large clouds were gathering, but they didn't look like harbingers of a storm. They puffed and clustered in the sky, drifting toward the moon which drifted toward them, almost involuntarily, seemingly mesmerized by one another.

R.J loved watching the moon drift in and out of cloud formations. It was like poetry. The moon fell behind a dark cloud, fading slowly until the only remaining light reflected off the inside of the cloud and bounced back, further brightening the moon.

Then, just before the moon broke away from the cloud and moved into full view, the edges of the cloud would glow in the soft, bright image it reflected, an image that was, actually, but a reflection itself. R.J. felt a profound sense of belonging, to the moon, to the sky and to the sea.

R.J. sighed. Everything seemed so simple, so basic out here. The Pacific recognized no individual, no ego. It just was, and seemed to pride itself in its aloofness and its superiority. No one escaped mother Pacific for long. She took you physically, or she took you emotionally, but she always prevailed. And her willing accomplice, her eager partner, was the bright and brilliant full moon.

The dark cloud surrendered its hostage slowly, hesitantly, aware that as the moon moved on, the cloud would return to being just a cloud, its rich glow diminished to a dark shadow in the vast sky. A cloud once again, a moon once again. The cycle concluded, to be repeated and concluded again.

The moon followed the course it had followed since before time began, lumbering forward predictably in the night sky, its course and destination pre-ordained eons ago, undeterred by the aimless, shiftless clouds it encountered, unaware of the admiring eyes of insignificant beings inhabiting the planet a quarter million miles beneath its orbit.

The pale moonlight bathed the ship in a soft glow, throwing curious shadows across the decks. The bow cut cleanly through the sea, creating white wakes to port and starboard, which caught the moonlight and reflected phosphorus blue-green before disappearing along the sides of the ship, only to be reborn at the point of the bow. Another cycle concluded, to be repeated and concluded again. And again.

R.J. breathed deeply, completely comfortable and at peace. *That's why they call it the Pacific,* he thought, *for peace.* It seemed to him that his personal troubles faded into insignificance at times like this, at sea. There was no better medicine, no better escape than being at sea. If only he could remain out here, away from the problems, away from Annie and the confrontation he knew was coming. It was unavoidable, inevitable he knew, but tonight, for a little while at least, he could be at peace with the Pacific. Out here, steaming on the warm, blue ocean, painful thoughts of Annie faded into mere annoyances, feelings he could deal with easily. He tucked them away, forced them into his subconscious where they would lay dormant until he returned to Guam and to the conflict that awaited him there. He would deal with Annie then.

He had no way of knowing he would never see her again.

PART FOUR:

THE HAVERFIELD
INCIDENT

SIXTY EIGHT

Yokosuka, Japan
July 27, 1964
0800 Local Time

"Hey, Chief!" SM-1 Carruthers stood on the outside catwalk of the signal tower and held a pair of binoculars to his eyes with one hand and gestured to Chief Signalman Joe Williams with the other. The chief stuck a cigar in his teeth and pulled himself up from behind his desk. He chewed on the cigar as he joined Carruthers on the outside catwalk. "Look who's back in town," Carruthers grinned, handing the binoculars to Chief Williams.

The chief raised the glasses and smiled. DER 393, proudly sporting the white E and green C, cruised toward her berth. "Yeah, I saw them on the schedule of ships' movements yesterday." He handed the glasses back to Carruthers and moved to one of the signal lights. "Better watch out for him, Pete," the chief warned, firing up the light and swinging it toward the harbor. "He's probably after your job."

"He can have it, chief," Carruthers said seriously. "That's where I want to be." He pointed down the harbor toward the USS Kitty Hawk, resting regally at her berth. "I swear, chief, she's the most beautiful aircraft carrier I ever seen. Ever."

"I know, Pete. We all know. You remind us daily every time she's in port." The chief spat out a piece of tobacco and made a face. He pointed the light down the harbor and began signaling.

"Light!" Anselmi called. "Tower!" He pointed toward the top of the mountain. A signal light flashed brightly and insistently.

"I got it!" R.J. was already at the light. *Been expecting you*, he thought. He flashed the go ahead, then left the light open. *Hope it's you, Chief Williams*, he thought to himself, grinning.

Chief Williams asked if R.J. Davis, SMSN was on the light. R.J. flashed back a negative. Chief Williams asked who was sending. R.J. replied, Davis, R.J. SM3.

"So Slick made third class?" Carruthers stood behind the chief, reading the code over his shoulder.

"Looks like it," the chief agreed, signaling congratulations to R.J. "The kid's a natural, Pete."

"Yep, that he is."

Chief Williams signaled an invitation for R.J. to visit the tower, and R.J. replied he would be there at 1000 the next morning, then signed off.

R.J. smiled to himself and turned off his light. He leaned forward, his hands apart against the railing, and breathed in the heavy morning air. The harbor still smelled like fish and garbage to R.J. It was a warm and humid morning by the time the Haverfield slipped into her berth, tying up to the outboard destroyer alongside the tender, Dixie. R.J. had shifted colors and pulled the canvas covers over the flag bags. Now, he looked around the signal bridge, making certain nothing was out of place or needed repair. The brass was turning green, but that was Billy's job now. He nodded, satisfied, went back to leaning and looking around the harbor. A light mist swirled around, hugging the surface of the water. Several ships were in port, which meant the Alley would be crowded with sailors. R.J. didn't feel like going to the Alley the first night in town. He decided to wait a few days, and so he didn't hesitate when Anselmi asked him to stand by his watch.

First Division scurried about, washing down the ship and stowing away all gear. Within minutes the canvas awning had been erected on the fantail, and the quarterdeck set up. The captain ordered immediate liberty for all off-duty personnel, and several sailors lined up quickly to be first down the brow.

Gino and Pea joined R.J. on the signal bridge once the ship was secured. They both belonged to the on-duty section, and wouldn't be able to go on liberty until the next day.

"Man, we put that awning up so fast," Pea exclaimed, flipping open his Zippo lighter and lighting his cigarette, all in one motion. "People just standin' around in awe, gawkin', y'know?" He grinned mischievously and blew smoke up in the air.

"You goin' ashore, R.J.?" Gino asked.

"Naw, standing by for Anselmi," he replied.

"Hey!" Pea exclaimed, pointing down at the pier. "There goes Riley. Hey, Riley!" he yelled down to the third class radioman. Riley looked up as he hurried toward the main gate, shielding his eyes with his hand, and waved. "Leave some chicks for us!" Pea shouted. Riley gave a thumbs-up and grabbed his rear end with both hands, squeezing it and pointing it at Pea before scurrying through the gate toward the taxi cab stand.

"That's a funny dude," Pea said, watching Riley climb into a cab.

"*You* a funny dude," Gino countered, pulling Pea's whitehat over his eyes. "And you a *little* dude, too."

"Damn right," Pea countered, pushing his hat back. "I may be little but I got a real cute way of climbin' on'n off." He grinned broadly at Gino. "C'mon, we gotta get back to work or Big Queenie's gonna nail our butts."

"See you later," R.J. said absently as his friends stormed down the ladder to the 02 level. He waited until Billy got there, gave him instructions to shine all the brass, took delight in Billy's reaction when he looked around at all the brass he had to shine, and slid down the ladder headed to the messdecks. He wanted to see if Hawkins had a fresh urn of coffee going.

* * * * *

R.J. took his time climbing the steps to the signal tower on Tuesday morning. He was in no hurry. The ship would be in port for two weeks and he could afford to do things in his own good time. He reached the top, took a deep breath, and pushed open the door to the tower. Three signalmen were out on the catwalk on flashing lights, sending and taking a steady stream of traffic from the crowded harbor. Chief Williams sat behind his desk in his office, chewing on a cigar and poring over message slips. Carruthers stood next to the chief, collecting the slips as the chief signed them.

R.J. tapped on the door. Chief Williams and Carruthers looked up and smiled warmly. "Well, well, look who's here!" the chief exclaimed. He got up and came around the desk, shaking R.J.'s hand warmly. "E-4!" the chief grinned, pointing to R.J.'s third-class crow.

"Congratulations, Slick," Carruthers said warmly, pumping R.J.'s hand. "You're on your way to chief."

"Not me, Flags," R.J. said, holding up four fingers. "Four and no more, remember?"

"That's what Carruthers said," the chief slapped the first-class signalman on the back. "And guess what? He's taking the chief's test next month."

"That's great!" R.J. said, and he meant it.

"So, that's gonna leave an opening here in the tower," Chief Williams announced, pointing his cigar at R.J. "You can be first class in three years."

"Not me, Chief," R.J. replied, shaking his head. "I'm a fleet sailor, it's in my blood."

"So, what can we do for you, Slick?" Carruthers asked. "You okay on blue bunting?"

"Just came up to say hello," R.J. answered. "I was hoping you'd show me those new carbon-arc babies." R.J. pointed out to the catapult where two large, carbon-arc signal lights were mounted on each side.

"C'mon out." Carruthers led the way, and they walked out onto the catapult. The view of the harbor was beautiful, with so many gray Navy ships tied up to piers or anchored out. R.J. looked around. He could see every ship in port.

"Where's the Haverfield?" he asked, looking around and trying to get his bearings.

Carruthers had a pair of binoculars to his eyes and he scanned the harbor. When he located the Haverfield he stopped and looked again, re-focusing the glasses. "Uh oh," he said softly.

"Uh oh, what?" R.J. asked.

Carruthers pointed toward the Haverfield and handed the glasses to R.J. "You're a signalman," Carruthers said. "You know what that flag hoist is." He shook his head slowly.

R.J. focused on the ship, and the two-flag hoist flying from the outside lanyard. It was the signal for all personnel to return to the ship. "Oh shit," R.J. said, peering through the glasses. "Personnel recall."

The chief had joined them on the catapult. "Something's up," he said, pointing to the ships along the piers. Seven ships in all were flying the recall signal.

Carruthers watched the Kitty Hawk raise the recall signal and turned to R.J. "You better take off, Slick," he warned, pointing at the big aircraft carrier. "Something's up all right, and it looks like whatever it is, you're gonna have air support."

R.J. looked around the tower quickly and headed for the stairs. "Catch you next time," he called over his shoulder as he stepped through the outside door.

Carruthers and Chief Williams stood staring at the closed door through which R.J. had rushed. "Viet Nam," the chief said through his stogie. "Shit's heatin' up over there." He took the cigar out of his mouth, made a face and threw it toward a small metal trashcan. It made a loud, wet *thunk* as it landed in the bottom of the empty can. The chief grunted at the sound. *Like an exclamation point,* he thought idly, pulling the wrapper off a fresh cigar. *Now, what the hell was the code for that?*

*   *   *   *   *

Task Force Foxtrot assembled under the shadow of Mount Fuji a few miles southeast of Tokyo Bay. The Kitty Hawk, under Captain H. D. "Skip" O'Neal, became the flagship with Captain O'Neal assuming command as commodore of the task force. Joining the aircraft carrier were a guided missile frigate, a cruiser, an oiler and three escort vessels, the Haverfield taking position to the rear to "...protect the carrier's ass-end," was the way Chief Whipple explained it. An urgent report of a PT boat build up and increased activity in the Tonkin Gulf had concerned COMCRUDESPAC. Aware of supply line vulnerability, Admiral Prescott dispatched Task Force Foxtrot to monitor the situation, and if necessary, intervene.

R.J. loved steaming with a task force. He spent almost every waking hour on the signal bridge, watching the Kitty Hawk for signals. During the day, course and speed changes were signaled by flag hoist. The Kitty Hawk's signal bridge would run up a flag hoist and wait for all ships in the convoy to respond. When each ship had duplicated the hoist, the flag ship's signalmen would jerk the lanyard down fast, bringing the flags quickly to the deck. That was the signal to execute the maneuver, and when it worked to perfection, as it usually did, all ships turned to the new course together with precision. R.J. loved watching the communications work and the ships execute the commands. It made him feel like a fleet sailor.

Sailing with a task force made everyone aboard feel like a fleet sailor, and the Haverfield crew performed exceptionally well. Spirits and morale were high, and some of the frosty feelings between blacks and whites began to thaw. For his part, Chief Twitchell kept to himself, rarely going up on deck. Since the captain had suspended his liberty privileges, before leaving Japan, he'd had an engineering petty officer smuggle aboard four bottles of scotch. The angry chief kept busy working to drain them. By the time the ship arrived on station, Chief Twitchell had only one bottle left. In his drunken stupor, he imagined himself attacking Rafer Sample and pummeling him with punches until he was dead. The chief loved the fantasy, and ran it through his mind over and over again. The scotch helped to encourage the fantasy, so that sometimes, when he was very drunk, he would awaken and believe he had actually done it.

On Monday, August third, the task force arrived southwest of the Chinese island of Hainan, after having negotiated the Luzon Strait north of the Philippines. The Kitty Hawk took up station outside the Gulf of Tonkin, along with most of her support vessels. The Haverfield and the destroyer

Parker were ordered to enter the gulf and take up patrol positions off the coast of Viet Nam near Dong Hoi.

R.J. thought the first night on station was spooky. There was no moon to speak of, the water in the gulf was smooth, and only a slight breeze blew to cool the ship as she patrolled at eight knots. Tensions were increased because of the reports of North Vietnamese PT boats attacking the USS Maddox the previous night as the destroyer patrolled off the coast of Thanh Hoa. There were some anxious moments when radar contacts reported two surface vessels headed toward the Haverfield, but upon closer inspection they turned out to be a couple of fishing junks on their way back home after a long day at sea. After that, the night became routine and R.J. hit the rack for some sleep. He promised Anselmi he would stand the mid-watch; he was looking forward to it, and he wanted to get some rest.

It seemed he had just fallen asleep when he had the dream again. He awoke, half-conscious, imagining Andy Sample was pointing at him and laughing. "R.J.," he kept laughing, "R.J., wake up!" R.J. started awake and realized it wasn't a dream. Andy Sample had the mid-watch, too, and was waking R.J. for his watch.

Andy was laughing. "Man, you musta been dreamin' somethin' cause you kept axin' me to get the blood off." Andy looked at R.J. curiously as R.J. pulled on his dungarees and tucked in his shirt. "What do that mean, get the blood off?"

"Maybe I thought you were on your period," R.J. replied impatiently. "Where's Rafer?"

"He got the aft lookout," Andy explained, chuckling at R.J.'s joke.

R.J. nodded. "Let's go topside." Andy was still laughing as they made their way through the ship's passageways to the bridge.

The bridge was dark and quiet, the red interior lights and the green lights coming off the radar screen and gyro-compass all the illumination needed. It took a few minutes for R.J. and Andy to adjust to the low light. Andy relieved the lee-helmsman and R.J. went aft to the signal bridge and relieved Charming Billy.

R.J. leaned against the port side railing and watched the Vietnamese coast. There was a clear demarcation point between South Vietnam and North Vietnam. When he looked south, he could see the many lights of the towns along the coast. When he looked north, all he saw was darkness. In his understanding, that was what the fight was all about: the darkness of the north attempting to overwhelm the light of the south. That was how he understood the global threat of communism: darkness trying to extinguish the light. It seemed simple to him, but he knew, even from his limited life experience that it could not be that simple. Nothing was that simple.

Occasionally, through the dark night, radar contacts were called out, investigated suspiciously, and dismissed when they revealed themselves to be fishing junks. Tensions were high on the bridge. Everyone had in mind the attack on the Maddox, and the usual leisurely pace during the mid-watch became a frenetic alertness.

R.J. stayed on the signal bridge except when he wanted to refill his coffee cup, which he did with regularity, though the caffeine was making him jittery. He slipped into the pilot house quietly when he wanted more coffee and he couldn't help but notice the silence. Usually during the mid-watch, the officers and sailors kept each other awake by telling stories or challenging each other with trivia questions. This night it was very quiet, and the silence was deafening.

When Anselmi came up to relieve him, R.J. had nothing to report, but he pointed out to Anselmi the difference between the lighted south and the darkened north. Anselmi didn't seem interested in the phenomenon, and merely grunted, "Gonna get me some coffee," and wandered into the pilot house.

It was 0400 and the morning watch was taking over the ship. Mr. MacDonald took over as OOD, and Lieutenant (j.g.) Anton was the Junior Officer of the Deck. Cotton stood peering into the radar screen, and Sonny had the helm. The lee-helmsman was a very sleepy Timothy Jefferson, who slumped over the lee-helm and groaned.

"Jefferson!" Mr. Mac's face appeared at the porthole leading to the flying bridge. "Wake up, sailor! You're on watch, let's look lively in there!"

"Aye, sir." Jefferson stood up straight and put his hands on the lee-helm levers.

R.J. chuckled at the sight and made his way down the aft ladder to the 02 level. He was headed to the fantail to witness the arrival of morning. He looked forward to that special time between the end of the mid-watch and reveille, when he could hang out on the fantail and watch the transformation of dark to dawn.

Thinking back on it later, R.J. realized he had had foreknowledge of the incident. The foggy memory, which tried so hard to break, dreamlike, through his sub-conscious, had forewarned him weeks before. He felt a sadness he hadn't felt before the dream started. Something was trying to tell him something. It was a little nagging feeling in the back of his mind, like the Raven tap-tap-tapping at the chamber window. He expected something to happen, he didn't know what, but the nagging warned him to expect something. Still, he was unprepared for the onslaught of feelings and emotions that engulfed him that terrible August morning, especially when he thought he might have been able to stop it from happening. When it was over, he realized that the sequence of events could not have been avoided, and the plans Rafer and Chief Twitchell had for each other were destined to play out in an unexpected way.

It began when three North Vietnamese PT boats attacked the Haverfield in the Tonkin Gulf just before dawn on Tuesday morning, August fourth, and it concluded with a surprising inquiry at Pearl Harbor some weeks later.

* * * * *

Rafer and Andy had finished the mid-watch and were hanging around the fantail, too tired to try to sleep the last two hours before reveille. R.J. was too keyed up to sleep, probably from all the coffee, and wandered aft to the fantail to greet the dawn, as was his custom. He waved to Rafer and Andy, who waved back from their position near the portside depth charge rack. R.J. stayed aft on the starboard side, giving the Sample brothers plenty of space.

The pre-dawn air was fresh and cool that morning, but R.J. knew that in a few short hours, the sun would hammer down on the gulf, and bring with it the suffocating humidity of Southeast Asia. These quiet moments before dawn, an hour before reveille, were the best part of the day in those tropical climes. R.J. breathed in the sweet-smelling air and closed his eyes, completely at peace. He didn't notice Chief Twitchell stagger out on deck from the port hatch.

"Whatta you fuckin' niggers doin' on my fuckin' fantail?" The voice was slurred, weighted from a night of drinking, but R.J. knew who it was. He turned to see the drunken chief stagger about, unsure of his footing, holding on desperately to the lifeline.

"Oh, crap," R.J. muttered.

* * * * *

"Sir, I've got three surface contacts coming this way." Cotton looked up from the radar scope. The Haverfield was just finishing her northern turn, and the coast was once again to port.

"Fishing junks?" Mr. MacDonald asked.

"I dunno, sir. They're steaming in formation and headed this way."

Mr. Mac took off his cap and looked at the radar screen. "Three small surface craft bearing zero-three-zero, approximately four miles away," he murmured. "They're moving like fishing junks." He stood up and put his cap back on. "Keep an eye on 'em, Cotton," he instructed. Cotton nodded and stared, fixated, at the radar scope.

Mr. Mac stepped out on the starboard wing bridge and called up to Pancho and Pea, the lookouts on the 04 level. "Keep a sharp eye up there! We have radar contacts off the starboard bow!" He pointed to the northeast.

"Aye, aye, sir," came the wind-muffled reply. The lookouts trained their binoculars at the horizon. Nothing visible.

* * * * *

Chief Twitchell held on to the lifeline with one hand and pointed at the Sample brothers with the other, swaying back and forth against the movement of the ship. He was in a drunken rage, brought on by his resentment over the rebuke he had received from the captain. His rage was further fueled by the full bottle of scotch he had downed during the night. "Fuckin' darkies! Get yer asses outta my Navy!"

Rafer and Andy stood up and began moving toward the drunken chief, circling him, stalking him like a couple of lions on a hunt. Rafer was looking around the fantail, making certain there were no witnesses. He had forgotten about R.J.

"C'mon nigger!" Twitchell focused his attention on Rafer. "Why don' you start a riot now, you black sumbitch!" He moved away from the life-line and Rafer circled in behind him, positioning himself almost exactly where the chief had stood braced against the lifeline. Rafer glared at the chief, who weaved back and forth on the deck. Rafer's adrenaline was high, and he concentrated on the drunken chief. Now was the time. This might be the best chance they had.

"Andy!" R.J. yelled at Andy Sample's back. Andy turned, startled to see R.J. standing there.

"Go below, R.J.," he said in a deep, gruff voice. Rafer was watching Twitchell and did not hear the exchange. His anger blurred his peripheral vision and roared in his ears so all he saw or heard was Chief Twitchell.

"Don't do it, Andy," R.J. warned. He watched the scene unfold, almost in slow motion, and he suddenly realized what the dream was all about. He knew exactly what was going to happen, and a helpless feeling of *déjà vu* engulfed him. He tried to call out to Andy again, but his voice was strange-ly gone. He felt he was back in the dream, drifting involuntarily with an unyielding tide, incapable of interfering, powerless to protest.

* * * * *

"The contacts are picking up speed, sir!" Cotton announced. "They're coming straight at us." He looked up from the scope and added quietly, "I don't think they're fishing boats."

"Contact!" Pancho stood on the starboard side of the 04 level and point-ed to the northeast, off the bow. "Three small boats!"

Mr. Mac came out on the starboard wing and trained his binoculars on the contacts. "Those aren't fishing junks," he declared.

"They're slowing down now, sir," Cotton announced.

* * * * *

Chief Twitchell turned to look behind him and spotted Andy circling around to his rear. He looked at Rafer, then at Andy, and he seemed to straighten up and catch his balance. All of a sudden he appeared sober and he stared at Rafer with a strange, determined look in his eye, as though he had made a decision. His bloated face and bloodshot eyes took on a pitiful, sorrowful appearance, and Rafer suddenly saw Twitchell for what he was—a pathetic drunken fool. He was surprised that he felt pity for the chief, and he backed up a bit, uncertain of what he was going to do.

Rafer was standing with his back to the lifeline when Chief Twitchell charged him, head down, swearing, throwing wild round-house punches with both hands.

* * * * *

"Torpedoes in the water!" Cotton yelled at the radar screen. "Three tor-pedoes bearing zero-two-five!"

Mr. Mac took command at once and scurried around the bridge shout-ing orders. "All ahead flank! Right standard rudder! Come right to course zero-two-five! Sound general quarters!" He ran to the starboard wing and spotted the torpedo wakes, still far away, but headed straight for them. He stepped back into the pilot house and met the eyes of the crew. "Goddam PT boats," he said, smiling. "They don't have any idea who they're messin' with." The comment brought nervous grins to the faces of the bridge crew.

* * * * *

Rafer was startled, surprised by the chief's angry charge, and instinctively stepped aside just as Twitchell reached him. The fat chief stumbled into the lifeline and tumbled over the side, splashing loudly into the water, just as the screws surged up to flank speed and the ship's stern swung quickly to port.

R.J. and Andy ran to the lifeline and looked over the side. They watched in horror as the stern moved into Twitchell, sucking him under the keel and into the speeding screws. The stern of the ship shuddered violently as Jaspar Twitchell was hit by the twin propellers. R.J. and the Sample brothers hurried to the fantail and looked over the stern. A large red stain billowed up and bubbled on the surface. The screws stopped shuddering and returned to turning flank speed. R.J. held his head over the side and threw up for the first time ever aboard ship. He turned to look at the Sample brothers. They were staring blankly back at him. The morning had become light with the pre-dawn, and the red stain dissipated in the ship's churning, white wake, blending itself in with the sea. R.J. leaned over the stern and threw up again.

"BONG! BONG! BONG! BONG! General quarters, general quarters, all hands man your battle stations! General quarters! This is not a drill!"

* * * * *

"What the hell was that?" MacDonald demanded as the ship shuddered and convulsed beneath him.

The captain came up on the bridge as battle stations were being manned. "Did we hit something, Mac?" he asked calmly. The captain was always cool, always calm. His presence made the bridge crew feel proud and confident. They concentrated intently on their jobs.

The sound-powered phone *whooped* shrilly and MacDonald snatched the receiver. "Bridge!" he snapped curtly.

"Bridge, this is engineering." It was Pedro Almogordo.

"What happened, Pete?" Mr. Mac asked, holding the receiver with one hand and watching the wakes of the torpedoes through his binoculars with the other.

"I think we hit a big fish with our screws," the engineer said. "Maybe a tuna or a school of smaller fish."

"Any damage, Pete?"

"Not that I can tell. The screws are turning just fine."

Mr. MacDonald hung up the receiver without answering and turned to the captain. "Engineering thinks we ran over a school of fish," he reported curtly. "No damage." The captain nodded and concentrated on the torpedo wakes.

"I'll take the conn, Mac," he said calmly, as if he were ordering lunch.

"Captain's got the conn!" Mr. Mac announced, and stepped back into the pilot house where he could monitor the radar screen.

* * * * *

"We gotta go!" R.J. insisted. "G.Q.!"

Andy nodded and took hold of Rafer's arm. The big man seemed to be in shock. His face had a depth of sadness R.J. had never seen before, and he seemed to slump as if he were being slowly deflated.

"C'mon, bro," Andy said gently, and began to lead Rafer away. Rafer turned once and looked aft at the ship's wake. His eyes seemed empty and terribly sad. He looked at R.J. with a look of deep pain and started to say something, his mouth moving, but no sound came out. Finally, he let Andy lead him away.

R.J. ran as fast as he could to the signal bridge. He put on his battle helmet and joined Anselmi on the starboard side, where he was watching the torpedo wakes bearing down on the speeding ship. Crashing headlong at flank speed, the Haverfield was closing the gap very quickly.

* * * * *

"Come left to zero-two-zero," the captain ordered, adjusting the course to the course of the torpedoes. The ship moved slowly and slightly to port, its bow aimed directly at the torpedoes. "We're going to split these fish so they pass down both sides of the ship," he explained to Mr. Mac, who nodded.

"They're moving away, sir!" Cotton yelled from the radar scope.

The captain trained his binoculars on the three small PT boats. "Wait till they get a taste of the three-inch gun," he said calmly. "Mac."

"Yes sir?"

"Ring up the forward gun mount and tell them the enemy PT boats are escaping."

"Aye, sir," Mr. Mac passed the information to Bixby in the forward gun. The lieutenant chuckled at the reply. "Bixby said, 'for how much?' sir."

The captain grinned. "Tell him to fire at will."

Mr. Mac passed on the order and the forward gun mount swung around, pointing at the fleeing boats. Two of the on-coming torpedoes passed harmlessly down the starboard side, and the third passed down the port side. The aft lookout was warned to keep an eye on them.

Bixby's first shot was fifty yards ahead of the lead boat. The second shot was splashed fifty yards behind, and the third shot hit the lead PT boat amidships, exploding the fuel in a huge billow of fire. Several seconds later, splintered pieces of the boat rained down, splashing sporadically across the water. A cheer rose up from the Haverfield bridge crew.

"Belay that!" MacDonald barked. "This ain't a goddam basketball game!"

The second PT boat was hit astern and was drifting, on fire and dead in the water. Its crew abandoned it and floated around in the debris, holding on to anything they could find.

The third PT boat attempted to zig-zag its course to throw off Bixby's aim, but the gunner's mate timed the maneuver perfectly and blew the boat out of the water. Later, when Mr. MacDonald told the story, as he was often fond of doing, he would say, "... Bixby got the last PT boat just after it had zigged, but before it could zag."

The captain stepped into the pilot house, cool and calm. "All ahead slow," he commanded. "Tell all department heads to report readiness." He knew the ship had not been damaged, but he worried about morale and the internal workings of the machinery. They had pushed the old girl pretty hard, and she had responded like a debutante. "Maintain this course and look for survivors," he said. "And take your time." He left the bridge and returned to his cabin, where he began writing the report COMCRUDESPAC would soon be insisting on.

The ship slowed and all department heads called in readiness to the bridge. There was no damage, externally or internally. Pedro Almogordo called in to report on engineering. MacDonald took the call on the bridge.

"We're in good shape down here, Mac," the engineer reported. "Everything is running smoothly. No apparent damage to the screws, so whatever we hit was pretty soft. Only one thing," he said slowly.

"What's that, Pete?"

"I can't locate Chief Twitchell. He's not up there, is he?"

* * * * *

"We have to go tell them what happened," R.J. pleaded with Rafer and Andy on the 02 level after general quarters had been secured. It was past 0800 and duty section II had taken over the watch. "We gotta tell 'em how he slipped and fell over the side."

Rafer shook his head slowly. "I kilt that man," he said sadly.

"No you didn't!" R.J. insisted. "I was there. It was an accident."

Rafer looked up at R.J. and said chillingly, "I wanted that man dead. I planned to make that man dead. *I prayed to God* that he would die, and he died. I kilt him, R.J., plain and simple."

Andy shook his head slowly. "Bro, that man attacked you and all you did was step outta his way."

"It was an accident, Rafer," R.J. insisted. "Maybe you wanted him dead, hell, we all did, but you didn't kill him." He stepped back and glared at the Sample brothers. "I'm going to report this to Mr. Mac. You coming?"

Andy took Rafer's arm and together the three of them made their way to the quarters of First Division's lieutenant. They spent ten minutes with Mr. Mac, with R.J. doing most of the talking. Mr. MacDonald swore them to silence and dismissed them. He took a deep breath and headed for Pedro Almogordo's quarters. After ten minutes with the engineering officer, they both headed for the executive officer's cabin. Soon, all three were knocking on the captain's door.

After a brief meeting, the captain and the three officers rushed into the pilot house and looked at the chart. It wouldn't take long to get back to the location where Twitchell went over the side. Maybe they didn't run over him with the screws. Maybe he was floating out there, waiting to be picked up. On the other hand, several survivors of the PT boats had been spotted in the water, and the Haverfield was moving to rescue them. The captain decided to leave the survivors to their fate and head back to look for his overboard sailor. His decision was eased when the radio blared a message from the Parker.

"Little Brother, this is Sister, do you require assistance?" The Parker used the task force code names assigned by Commodore O'Neal.

The captain looked over at the exec. "Do we require assistance, Ed?" he asked

Lieutenant Martin shook his head. "No sir, unless they would be kind enough to see to those survivors."

The captain picked up the microphone. "Sister, this is Little Brother, over."

"Come in Little Brother," the voice crackled.

"No assistance required. I repeat, no assistance required. Request you pick up survivors. We have a man overboard to deal with."

"Will do, Little Brother." A pause, then the radio crackled again. "That was one hell of a shooting display, Little Brother. We watched on the radar scope. Who you got on that forward gun, Annie Oakley?"

The captain smiled sadly. He was proud of Bixby and the rest of the crew for the way they performed in their first surface action. He was delighted that all the drills, all the training, all the hard work had paid off. But he was missing a crew member, and was anxious to get back and look for him. He turned to the helmsman. "Come about to course one-niner-zero," he ordered. "All ahead flank." The ship came left and picked up speed, returning to search for Chief Machinists Mate Jaspar Twitchell.

The sun was shimmering, plump in the early morning sky when the Haverfield reached the location where Chief Twitchell had gone overboard. A large, frantic flock of seagulls hovered over the spot, but dispersed when the ship came upon the scene. R.J. stood on the signal bridge with a pair of binoculars trained on the water. He could see nothing. The remains of Twitchell had either sunk or been picked over by the gulls. *Or both.* R.J. shuddered and continued to scan the ocean.

"I got something in the water!" R.J. looked up at the 04 level where Pea was pointing to a spot off the starboard beam. Several pairs of binoculars swung around and focused on an object in the water.

The ship slowed and came to a stop. Jaspar Twitchell's chief's cap float-ed gently on top of the waves, rising and falling with the movement of the sea. A grappling hook was thrown into the water and the cap was retrieved. The ship searched for another hour before it became obvious there would be no other remains discovered, and the captain ordered the ship to resume patrol. He returned to his cabin, motioning for Mr. Mac, Mr. Almogordo and the exec to join him.

"Alright, gentlemen," the captain said, easing down in his chair. "Let's go over it again, slowly, please."

The other officers looked to Mr. MacDonald. He sighed and began, referring to his hastily-scrawled notes. "Just before dawn R.J. Davis and the Sample brothers were relaxing on the fantail, having just finished the midwatch. Twitchell came out on deck, obviously drunk, staggering about, and when he saw the Sample brothers he made some unkind racial comments. They didn't respond and Twitchell started toward them, but staggered and fell against the lifeline. He lost his balance and went overboard just as we speeded up and turned to meet the enemy PT boats. He got sucked under the keel and into the screws. Neither Davis nor the Sample brothers were close enough to him to prevent it. They rushed to their battle stations and after the attack was over, they came to me and told me what had happened. So many things were happening so quickly, they didn't have a chance to declare 'man overboard.'"

Mr. Almogordo and the exec nodded solemnly. The captain stared at his desk for a moment, took a deep breath and let it out slowly. "Gentlemen," he said finally. "What I'm about to propose may seem dishonest to you, but please hear me out."

SIXTY NINE

Rafer sat on his bunk and chewed his thumbnail reflectively. Andy sat with him quietly, staring down at his hands. The word got around in a hurry, and everyone in First Division had heard about what happened. At least they'd heard the official version of what happened, but most of them imagined a different scenario, especially the black sailors, who looked admiringly at Rafer every chance they got. No one approached him, however. They all saw the look on his face, the sadness in his eyes and slump in his shoulders. All his hate had evaporated, leaving a sad, empty feeling in his soul like an emotional hangover. He hadn't pushed Twitchell over the side, but he wanted to...he had wanted him dead. His guilt overwhelmed him, and he couldn't get the picture out of his mind of Twitchell foundering around in the water just before he got sucked into the spinning screws. And the blood... He was silent and depressed, and wouldn't talk to anyone except Andy. The Havernauts gave him a wide berth.

Gino had the watch as messenger, and he came into the compartment looking around. He spotted the Sample brothers and approached them.

"You guys are wanted in the wardroom," he said flatly.

"Wha for?" Andy asked, looking up. Rafer continued to contemplate his thumbnail.

"I dunno, Andy," Gino said gently. "Mr. Mac told me to come and get you. He's in the wardroom waiting for you." Gino waited for a moment. "You comin'?"

"Yeah, we comin'," Andy replied. He stood, waiting for his brother. Gino returned to the bridge.

Andy and Rafer walked slowly toward the wardroom, heads together, talking quietly. "They know," Rafer said softly.

"Know what?" Andy asked.

"They know I kilt him," Rafer said, looking into his brother's eyes.

"You din't kill nobody," Andy insisted. "Don't go in there tellin' the man you guilty of anything." He stopped and took hold of his brother's arm. "Understand me, Rafer? You didn't do nothin' and you ain't admitting to nothin'. Right?"

Rafer nodded sadly. "I hope God will forgive me," he whispered.

They reached the wardroom, removed their whitehats and knocked on the door.

"Enter!" came the order from inside.

Rafer and Andy stepped into the wardroom. Mr. Mac, Mr. Almogordo and the exec sat at the table, some papers spread before them. They looked unhappy, and Rafer feared the worst. On the other side of the table, facing the officers, sat R.J. He exchanged nervous glances with the Sample brothers before they sat down on either side of him.

"This is an unofficial inquiry into what happened this morning," Mr. Mac began. "You are not going to be sworn in or questioned separately. We want you each to tell the story in your own words, just as you told it to me earlier, understand?"

The three sailors nodded. Andy looked at Mr. Mac intently. Rafer chewed his thumbnail, and R.J. stared down at the table.

"Who's going to start?" the exec asked. The Sample brothers looked to R.J.

"I'll start," R.J. said resignedly. He told the same story he had told earlier. Chief Twitchell was drunk and staggering around, like he always did when he was drinking. He yelled names at Rafer and Andy, who ignored him. The chief was weaving unsteadily and as he stumbled to the lifeline to hold on, the ship picked up speed and he somersaulted over the side and into the drink. As he fell, the ship turned to starboard, the stern sweeping to port, and Chief Twitchell was sucked under and hit the speeding screws. R.J. and the Samples had no chance to alert the bridge to 'man overboard.' R.J. concluded by saying, "General Quarters went down and we rushed to our stations. After the PT boat attack and general quarters was secured, we went to see Mr. Mac to tell him about Twitchell...I mean Chief Twitchell." He did not mention the horrible sound of Chief Twitchell hitting the screws, or the sight of the billowing red bloodstain that churned to the surface, making him vomit. He squeezed his eyes shut, trying to force the memory from his mind. He found he suddenly had a headache, and he rubbed his temples with both hands.

"Is that how it happened?" The exec looked at Rafer and Andy.

"Yessir," Andy answered without hesitation. Rafer sat quietly, chewing on his thumbnail.

"Rafer?" Mr. Mac asked. "Is that what happened?"

Rafer looked up at him with a look of pain in his eyes. He lowered his head and stared down at his hands.

For a brief moment, R.J. was sure Rafer was going to blurt out that he had killed Chief Twitchell, and R.J. held his breath, waiting for Rafer to reply. After what seemed like several minutes, Rafer looked up again.

"Yessir, that's how it happened," he said softly.

"I didn't hear you," the exec said, leaning toward Rafer.

Rafer cleared his throat. "Yessir," he said more loudly. "That's what happened, sir."

The three officers glanced at each other and leaned back in their chairs. Mr. Almogordo stacked the papers neatly on the table. Mr. MacDonald squirmed in his seat.

The three sailors sat quietly, tense and uncomfortable in their chairs. An underlying tension filled the wardroom, as if the officers were about to question the sailors' version of events. It was obvious they weren't happy with the story. R.J. felt the blood rush to his face, which made the headache worse.

"I want to ask you men a question," the exec said slowly, looking from one sailor to the next, searching their faces. *What was he looking for?* R.J. thought.

The exec continued. "I am well aware of the problems many on board this ship had with Chief Twitchell. He was not an easy man." The exec glanced again at Mr. Mac and Mr. Almogordo, and continued. "But do you men think that any good would be done by besmirching the man's excellent service record?"

The heads of all three sailors snapped up at once. They stared at the exec, trying to fathom what it was he was getting at.

"I believe this was a tragic accident," the exec went on. "And we are going to have to file an official report of the incident with COM-CRUDESPAC. Before we do, I want you to think about what this would mean to Chief Twitchell's record. I guess what I'm trying to ask you is, do you think it serves any useful purpose to report that the chief was drunk and stumbling around?"

R.J. stared at the desk and the paperwork stacked there, trying to sort things out in his mind. These officers weren't challenging the sailors' story. They were trying to get the three sailors to omit the fact that Chief Twitchell was a drunk, and his drinking led to his death. R.J. looked at Rafer to his right and Andy to his left. They were both staring at R.J., a look of disbelief on their faces.

"No, sir," R.J. said finally. "I don't see any reason to report that he was drunk."

The exec looked at Andy and Rafer. "What about you two?" he asked.

"No, sir," Andy quickly agreed. "We don't wanna hurt nobody's reputation."

Rafer swallowed hard and looked up into the exec's eyes. "Sir, I don't..." his voice trailed off. R.J. held his breath.

"You don't what?" the exec asked.

"I don't think we should speak ill of the dead," Rafer said flatly.

"Very well." The exec seemed satisfied. "Mr. MacDonald and Mr. Almogordo will write up your statements for the report. I appreciate your sensitivity in this matter, and I assure you, it will not be forgotten." He stood, and the others stood with him. "You are dismissed," the exec said firmly. "And please don't discuss this incident with anyone else."

R.J. and the Sample brothers left the wardroom and went out on deck. They stood by the motor whaleboat and R.J. lit a cigarette. The Samples didn't smoke, but he offered them one anyway, which they declined.

"They don't want anyone to know what a drunken asshole Twitchy was," R.J. said, exhaling smoke. "It's bad for the reputation of the ship."

Rafer nodded. "Let's not speak ill of the dead," he said softly, staring off into the sea. "If that's the way they wants it, that's the way it'll be."

Andy nodded slowly in agreement. "Only thing that matters is a man died," he added solemnly. "I'm okay with not telling the truth about the man, for the sake of the ship, I mean."

The Sample brothers headed aft and R.J. leaned against the motor whaleboat davits and smoked. The headache was getting worse, so he went below to sick bay to see Doc Gysler about some aspirin.

* * * * *

Captain Oliver read the report while drinking coffee at his desk. He was satisfied. It was cut and dried, only reporting the facts as the three witnesses had told them, and no mention was made of the drinking problem. The captain did not want to answer a lot of embarrassing questions about Twitchell's drinking. The ship had been through a lot of changes in the past year and a half, and the captain was not about to let anyone or anything cloud what had been accomplished. It was necessary to the morale of the crew, and the reputation they had worked so hard to build, to bring this situation to a quick conclusion. Tomorrow, they would hold services for Jaspar Twitchell, and the crew would assemble to pay their respects to a dead shipmate. Then they would return to the task at hand: patrolling the Tonkin Gulf.

It occurred to Captain Oliver that the death of Chief Twitchell solved many problems. He no longer had to worry about 'dumping' the chief on someone else, nor did he have to worry so much about racial division on his ship. With Twitchell gone, he suspected tensions would ease. Properly handled, he knew, tomorrow's service could write *finis* to the saga of Chief Twitchell. Captain Oliver was looking forward to bringing the incident to an end. He sighed, closed the report and summoned RM-1 Murray to his cabin. He would have the radioman transmit the report under a confidential heading to COMCRUDESPAC where he believed it would be read, understood, and filed away, never again to see the light of day.

Unfortunately, it did not happen that way.

* * * * *

All off-duty crew members assembled on the fantail in dress whites for the memorial service to Chief Twitchell. Crawford and a couple of other engineers put Twitchell's cap and dress uniform in a weighted bag and stood by to drop it overboard.

When the captain arrived, Mr. MacDonald barked, "Attention on deck!" and everyone snapped to attention. A small podium was set up near the aft gun mount, and Captain Oliver stepped up and unfolded a piece of paper which held his notes on the mariner's prayer he had selected for the eulogy. The sun beat down on the gulf, the water was smooth and the ship glided gently and silently, maintaining its patrol course.

"At ease. We are gathered here this morning," Captain Oliver began, "to lay to rest a fallen comrade." He looked over the attentive faces of the crew and continued. "Chief Jaspar Twitchell was an important member of this crew. His hard work and devotion to our engine room is one of the main reasons this ship runs as smoothly as she does. We are indebted to him for that.

"Every ship's crew must act in concert with one another. Every ship's crew must operate as a team, developing a synergy that makes the whole much more than just the sum of its parts. In every crew there is dissention and disagreements, but we are US Navy sailors, and as such, we must put aside our petty bickering and concentrate on the good of the ship. This crew has done an admirable job at that, and I am proud of you.

"It is not easy to lose a valuable crew member. It is not easy for some of us to lose a good friend, especially to a tragic accident such as this. But we honor our fallen shipmate, bury our dead and forge ahead, made stronger for the experience."

Captain Oliver looked at MM-1 Crawford and nodded. Crawford and another engineman lifted the weighted bag, held it poised over the lifeline and waited for the captain's signal.

"Please join me in prayer," the captain said softly. The heads of the crew lowered and some crossed themselves. "Lord God, by the power of your word you stilled the chaos of the primeval seas. You made the raging waters of the Flood subside, and calmed the storm on the Sea of Galilee. As we commit the earthly remains of our brother, Jaspar, to the deep, grant him peace and tranquility until that day when he and all who believe in you will be raised to the glory of new life promised in the waters of baptism. We ask this through Christ our Lord. Amen."

"Amen," the crew echoed. The bag was dropped and it fell splashing into the water where it floated briefly, and sank out of sight.

The captain turned to Mr. MacDonald. "You may dismiss the crew."

"TEN-HUT! Dis-MISSED!" Mr. Mac ordered, and the crew began to drift away. R.J. stole a sideways look at Rafer, and was surprised to see tears streaming down the big man's face. When he spotted R.J. looking at him, he turned away.

The captain returned to his cabin, relieved that the ceremony, and hopefully the entire incident, was over. He found RM-3 Riley waiting for him in the passageway.

Riley saluted. "Priority message just came in, Cap'n," the radioman said, handing the clipboard to Captain Oliver. The captain receipted for the message and stepped into his cabin. He took off his cap, loosened his tie and sat at his desk. The message was from COMCRUDESPAC, Admiral Prescott in Subic Bay. As he read it, a feeling of dread came over him.

From: COMCRUDESPAC
To: COMMANDING OFFICER
USS HAVERFIELD

USS PARKER WILL RELIEVE YOU ON PATROL.
HAVERFIELD WILL PROCEED IMMEDIATELY TO SUBIC BAY
NAVAL BASE.
REPORT TO STAFF HEADQUARTERS UPON ARRIVAL.
NO LIBERTY WILL BE GRANTED TO HAVERFIELD CREW.
ACKNOWLEDGMENT REQUESTED.

Paul Oliver read the message again. He shook his head slowly, his mouth set in a tight line. *So much for ending the incident*, he thought, and picked up the phone to call his exec.

SEVENTY

Rumors flew throughout the ship about the orders to Subic Bay: Chief Twitchell had been thrown over the side by R.J. and the Sample brothers. Rafer and the chief got into a fight and Rafer threw him overboard. The chief was drinking and depressed and committed suicide. Most aboard ship believed the story that Twitchell had stumbled and fell over the side, since they all had seen him stumbling around the deck. It was obvious there would be questions asked, but the only people alive who really knew what happened were R.J. and the Sample brothers.

"Twitchy hated Rafer," Pea observed. Gino and R.J. sat across the table from him in the messdecks. "In fact," the little sailor mused, picking at his teeth, "Twitchy hated everybody."

"I wouldn't blame Rafer if he threw that asshole over the side," Gino stated. He and Pea looked at R.J. curiously. R.J. said nothing.

"C'mon R.J.," Pea pleaded. "We your buddies. Tell us what happened."

"How 'bout it, partner?" Gino asked.

R.J. shook his head. "I can't talk about it, fellas," he replied. R.J. had a good idea why they were going to Subic Bay. He believed there would be an inquiry, and he was worried about testifying under oath. More accurately, he was worried about what Rafer would say under oath, considering the big man's current state of mind. Andy was a rock, and R.J. felt confident that Andy would stick to the story. The more he thought about it, the more holes R.J. imagined in the story.

"R.J.?" Pea reached across the table and shook R.J.'s arm. "You with us, ol' buddy?"

R.J. started and shook off the daydream. All he said to his friends was, "It was an accident."

* * * * *

"While I haven't been so informed," the captain was talking with Mr. MacDonald, Mr. Almogordo and the exec in the wardroom, "we have to proceed on the assumption there will be an official inquiry conducted at Subic Bay." The other officers nodded. Whenever a death occurred aboard a U.S. Navy ship an inquiry was held. "So, I want to make sure we're on the same page." Captain Oliver leafed through the report, which contained the signed statements of R.J. and the Sample brothers. "Mac, I want you to talk to these three men again, make sure they aren't forgetting anything. When we get to Subic I want their testimony to be consistent." The other officers nodded and left the wardroom.

What really bothered Captain Oliver was the unknown. It was unknown how the command staff would view the accidental death of Chief Twitchell. Accidents aboard ship did happen, even with a well-trained crew, but losing a crew member in that manner could not bode well for the ship, and by definition, its commanding officer. There was the possibility that an inquiry would discover that Chief Twitchell had a drinking problem. There was that report, given to command weeks before, that itemized the many confrontations Twitchell had had with blacks. While the report didn't come right out and say so, it hinted at a problem deeper than simple racism, if racism could be considered simple. The captain knew he was ultimately responsible for everything that happened aboard his ship. If the inquiry went bad, and they discovered how Twitchell's drinking had been covered up, only one man would be held responsible and accountable. That man would be Commander D. Paul Oliver.

* * * * *

The three-day trip to Subic Bay was uneventful. The crew went about their duties in a businesslike manner. The captain had not ordered any underway drills, so the atmosphere was relaxed. The night before they arrived in the Philippines, something curious happened. R.J. was hanging around the signal bridge, leaning as usual on the railing. Just after the watch changed at 2000, he thought he heard someone come up the aft ladder. He was surprised to see MM-1 Crawford step up next to him and look around at the sea.

"So, this is how the black-shoe Navy lives, huh?" he commented.

R.J. looked at Crawford questioningly and nodded. "Not like the engine room, huh Charlie?"

Crawford snorted. "No, not like the engine room a'tall." He took a deep breath of salt air.

They stood there looking out at the Pacific, saying nothing. Finally, Crawford cleared his throat and R.J. took it as a signal that the engineer had something on his mind.

"I spoke to Mr. Almogordo," Crawford said softly. R.J. held his breath. "Since me and Twitchell were kinda, you know, close, Mr. Almogordo told me about the report." He let his words hang in the air. R.J. fidgeted. After several moments, Crawford turned and faced R.J. "Y'all are doin' a good thing, R.J.," he said, his hand extended. R.J. took it. "I know Chief Twitchell was hard on y'all, bein' as mad as he always was. It would be easy for y'all to bad-mouth him, if you know what I mean." R.J. knew what he meant. "Anyways," Crawford continued. "I jus' wanted y'all to know that we was wrong about y'all. I guess some of us jus' got carried away because the Chief was so pissed." He shuffled his feet and stood up straight. "Y'know, bein' attacked changes things," he said softly. "This whole crew did real good, y'know? It kinda makes you think that maybe we do a helluva lot better when we together."

"You need to tell that to Rafer and the rest of the brothers," R.J. said. "They probably need to hear that."

"You right." Crawford replied, nodding. "I'll think about it." He grinned his down-home grin and left the signal bridge. R.J. stood at the railing, staring at the horizon and frowning to himself. He didn't believe that Crawford and the rest of the rednecks would suddenly stop their harassment of Rafer and his group, but he hoped it was true. Just talking to R.J. was a big step for Crawford. The PT boat attack had subtly changed the attitude of the crew. Their collective pride was overcoming their differences. They had been tested, and they had performed exceptionally well. There was a great deal to be proud about. Still, R.J. was worried about the inquiry. He hoped it would be over quickly, and the Haverfield could return to patrolling the Gulf. As with most of the crew, R.J. believed they were doing something important in the Tonkin Gulf, something they were trained to do, something they were meant to do. It was a heck of a lot more exciting and meaningful than chasing Jap fishermen out of the Trust Territory.

Rafer was still depressed. Andy had convinced his brother to stick to the story they had told the Haverfield officers, leaving out the fact that Twitchell was drunk, and not to volunteer any further information. In his heart, Rafer knew he was responsible for the chief's death because he had wanted it so badly, and he had prayed for it. He wrote a long letter to their father, the Reverend Mordecai Sample, telling him everything that happened, how Rafer felt responsible, and asking for guidance. Writing the letter had been a sort of catharsis for Rafer. He no longer felt it was his and Andy's burden alone. Their father was a wise and gentle man who had always listened to their problems and helped them find their own solutions. Rafer felt comfortable knowing his father was now working on this problem, and they would hear from him soon. In the meantime, Rafer carried his bible with him wherever he went and spent many hours studying its passages.

Without Twitchell to inflame them, the rednecks left the black sailors alone. Crawford convinced them the ship was the main focus of the entire crew. They put aside their hard feelings and while they didn't become friends overnight, the two groups achieved a peaceful accord, based on leaving each other alone. It seemed to be working.

* * * * *

The Haverfield tied up next to the tender Piedmont, anchored in Subic Bay, on Sunday afternoon, August ninth. The crew was unhappy about no liberty, and complained bitterly to each other, but they were to discover that it made no difference. They wouldn't be in the Philippines long.

Captain Oliver returned from his meeting with Admiral Prescott's chief of staff, Admiral Pollock. Admiral Prescott was in Pearl Harbor for a strategy meeting with CINCPACFLT. He and Lorelei would return in a week, and Admiral Pollock was tasked with handling the Haverfield Incident.

Admiral Pollock and Paul Oliver had always been on friendly terms, and the two of them had a drink together while Bill Pollock explained the situation. The Haverfield was being re-fueled and re-supplied for the trip to Pearl Harbor. When Captain Oliver expressed surprise, Bill Pollock opened his desk drawer and produced a copy of the report Paul had submitted to the command staff on Guam.

"Lots of explosive stuff in there, Paul," the admiral said.

"I didn't think anyone paid any attention to it," Paul replied. "I was told it was a minor disciplinary problem."

"Well, Paul," Admiral Pollock explained, somewhat stiffly, "that was before someone died." He leafed through the report. "Chief Twitchell's death demands a whole different perspective here. In its typical manner, the Navy under-reacted to *this* report, and now..."

"They're going to over-react to the accident," Captain Oliver finished the thought for him.

Bill Pollock nodded and sipped his scotch. He reached back into his drawer and pulled out the report Captain Oliver had filed on the Twitchell death. "The Navy didn't read enough into the last report," he explained patiently. "Now they're reading more than necessary into this report." He laid the report next to the first one. "In juxtaposition, these two reports say an awful lot, Paul." He paused and sipped his scotch again. "Mostly, I think the Navy is concerned about what they don't say."

"Sir?"

"It's hard to believe that a twenty-year Navy man would just stumble and fall over the side," the admiral said, leafing through the last report. "Are you sure he didn't have a little help, Paul?"

"What are you implying, sir," Captain Oliver asked defensively, "that my men would lie about this thing?"

"Not at all, Paul," the admiral held both hands up, palms out. "CINCPACFLT wants to conduct an investigation and a hearing in Pearl Harbor. Want to know what I think?" He sipped his scotch again and studied Captain Oliver over the rim of his glass.

"Yes, sir," Paul said. "Please."

"I think your first report was read and dismissed as a problem best handled within your own command. They didn't want to address the issue of racism. But, now, with the death of the man who obviously perpetuated the problem, they think they might have screwed up, and they want to cover their stern, so to speak." He smiled at Paul and leaned back in his chair. "Just ride it out like you would any storm at sea, Paul. It'll be over in a few weeks. The Navy will accept the plausible explanation your men testified to, and you'll be back on the line before you know it. In the meantime, you get to spend a little time in Hawaii."

Paul Oliver drained his scotch and stood. "I hope you're right, sir," he said. "I still think sending us back to Pearl is a little bit of overkill. We could easily conduct the inquiry here in Subic."

"It's the Navy way, Paul." The admiral stood and came around the desk. "Just roll with the punches."

"When do we leave for Pearl, Admiral?"

"As soon as you're fueled and re-supplied. Probably tomorrow morning."

Captain Oliver sighed. "They're certainly in a hurry," he commented.

"Roll with the punches, Paul," the admiral said, putting his arm around the captain and walking him to the door.

Paul shook the admiral's hand. "Thank you, sir. I appreciate the good thoughts."

"Good luck," the admiral said. "Try not to worry." He closed the door after Paul and returned to his desk to pour another scotch. He looked at the two reports on his desk, snorted through his nose and swept them into the desk drawer. Rear Admiral Pollock had deliberately failed to inform Captain Oliver that he would have a passenger aboard the Haverfield for the trip to Pearl Harbor.

SEVENTY ONE

"Cap'n?" Chief Whipple frowned as he spoke into the mouthpiece. "This is Whipple on the quarterdeck."

"What is it, Chief?"

"We got a Warrant Officer Deavers here asking to see you, sir." Whipple kept a wary eye on the visitor as he spoke to the captain. "He's got orders from COMCRUDESPAC," Whipple almost whispered into the mouthpiece.

"Are they in order?" The captain's tone was suspicious.

"Yessir," Whipple responded, nodding his head, though the captain couldn't see him. "Seem to be, anyway."

"Very well, Chief. Have the messenger escort the visitor to my cabin. What is his name, again?"

Chief Whipple squinted down at the orders. "Deavers, William C., Warrant Officer," he read.

"Carry on, Chief." Captain Oliver wrote the name on his notepad and stared at it, as if he could divine some clue as to the visitor's purpose.

Whipple hung up the phone and eyed Deavers skeptically. Out of the side of his mouth he addressed Cotton who was messenger of the watch. "Take this gentleman to the captain's cabin, will ya, Cotton?"

"Thanks, Chief," Warrant Officer Deavers said, smiling pleasantly. Whipple estimated he was in his early forties, about retirement age for most. He was tall, slim and strolled more than walked. His gait reminded Whipple of John Wayne. The chief shrugged and opened the ship's log to record Deavers' arrival.

"Enter," the captain called.

Cotton swung open the door and stood back. Warrant Officer Deavers strolled in and took off his cap. He smiled broadly and handed his orders to Captain Oliver. "Delighted to meet you, Captain," he said brightly. "It's good to be aboard. I'm looking forward to steaming with you."

Captain Oliver raised one eyebrow and motioned his visitor to a side chair. Deavers sat, still smiling. "That'll be all," the captain said to Cotton, who closed the door and returned to the quarterdeck. The captain pulled the sealing tape off the envelope and pulled out Deavers' orders. *Oh, great,* he thought.

"I'm here to compile facts for the inquiry," Deavers said. His smile seemed permanent. "Because of the unfortunate accident which resulted in the death of a US Navy chief petty officer." He was still smiling, but his tone had hardened just a bit, and his eyes grew colder, or maybe Captain Oliver imagined they had.

Paul Oliver nodded as he read the orders. When he had finished, he looked up at Deavers and slipped the paperwork back into the envelope.

"You're an investigator." It wasn't a question.

Deavers smiled warmly again. "Actually," he said, affably, a bit too affably for Captain Oliver's tastes, "I'm a *criminal* investigator." He let that sink in for a moment. "But don't fret, Captain. I'm here to gather information only. To tell you the truth, I personally don't think it was anything but an accident, judging from your report, but you know the Navy. They like to be thorough." He sat back and smiled pleasantly, folding his hands in his lap.

The captain stared at him for a moment, mulling over everything the warrant officer had said. "Mr. Deavers..." he began.

"Just Deavers, Captain. Everyone just calls me Deavers." He chuckled, then added, "Like beavers."

"Deavers," the captain said slowly, "my officers have already conducted an investigation and interviewed the witnesses at length. Why does COM-CRUDESPAC think another investigation, covering the same ground, would serve any useful purpose?"

Deavers stared blankly at Paul Oliver as if he thought the captain was a little dense. "Just being thorough," he said flatly, as if he required no further discussion on the matter. "When can I meet Lieutenants MacDonald and Almogordo and your exec, Ed Martin?" He smiled pleasantly again and looked down at his hands. "Ed and I served together on the Oriskany a few years back." He stared at his hands for a few moments, lost in some memory, then looked up quickly and smiled.

"I'll arrange it immediately," the captain said.

"No rush, Captain. We can wait until we're underway, if you like." Deavers stood and picked up his cap. "I left my gear on the quarterdeck. Where do I bunk?"

Captain Oliver billeted Deavers with Ensign Rodney Thompson. Cotton brought up Deavers' suitcase and set it inside the door. He began to leave when Deavers called to him. "Wait a minute, sailor. I want to talk to you." Cotton thus became the first man aboard to be 'interviewed' by Warrant Officer Deavers.

Cotton stepped inside the small compartment and removed his whitehat, revealing his shock of white hair. "Yessir?" he asked guardedly.

"What's your name, sailor?" Deavers was smiling.

"Christopher Haynes, sir," Cotton replied. "But everyone just calls me Cotton."

"And why is that?" Deavers said, still smiling.

"Well..."

"I'm joking with you, Cotton," Deavers said affably. "I can see why they call you Cotton."

Cotton squirmed uncomfortably and shifted his feet.

"How long you been aboard the Haverfield, Cotton?"

"Almost two years, sir."

"How do you like duty on this ship?"

"I like it very much, sir," Cotton said, brightening. "It's...I mean, *she* is a good ship, sir."

"That's what I hear around COMCRUDESPAC," Deavers said thoughtfully. The smile was gone and he stepped up close to Cotton. "What do you think happened to Chief Twitchell, Cotton, I mean, you must have known the man?" He stared into Cotton's bright blue eyes. "What did you think of Chief Twitchell?"

"I dunno, sir," Cotton mumbled. He was shifting his feet and wringing his whitehat in his hands.

"I hear he was disliked by the crew. That true?" The affability had returned.

"I guess so, sir," Cotton was squirming uncomfortably. "I... I gotta get back to the quarterdeck," he mumbled.

Deavers stared at him for a moment. He seemed to enjoy Cotton's discomfort. "Okay, Cotton," he said. "We'll talk later." He lifted the suitcase up onto the bunk and began unbuckling the straps. Cotton slipped out the door and hurried to the quarterdeck, where he would report the entire conversation to a very interested Chief Whipple. As soon as the watch was relieved, Chief Whipple went below to First Division's compartment and had a long confab with Big Queen.

* * * * *

"He's a big pain in the ass, Captain." The exec sat on the captain's bunk and sipped coffee. "We had a case on the Oriskany where one Marine was beat up pretty badly by several other Marines. Nobody would say anything, even the victim. They sent Deavers aboard to investigate. They billeted him with me. I was a J.G. then." Lieutenant Ed Martin sipped his coffee and shook his head. "The guy comes on real friendly at first," he said. "He likes to interview people a little bit at a time over a long period. It really throws them off balance."

"But he's good?" the captain asked.

"He's very thorough," the exec replied. "It took him five days, but he uncovered what happened with the Marines."

"Well, what happened?" The captain's curiosity was piqued.

"A couple of Marines caught this guy stealing wallets when everyone was asleep. They decided to handle it on the squad level. This one corporal gave the thief a choice. Get put on report for theft, in which case he would be a disgrace to the corps, or take punishment from the squad." The exec sipped his coffee and set the cup down on the desk. "The guy chose punishment and they beat the shit out of him. Apparently they got carried away, and the corporal had to put a stop to it. The victim spent two weeks in sick bay. Anyway, Deavers comes aboard and worms it out of them. He likes puzzles, that's what he told me, and he sees every investigation as a puzzle, to be put together piece by piece."

* * * * *

The Haverfield got underway at 0800 on Monday, August tenth with one extra passenger. Word soon spread through the crew about the mysterious and enigmatic Mr. Deavers and some of the questions he was asking. He tried to make it seem he was just making conversation, then, without warning, he'd stare into his subject's eyes and ask a benign question in a very serious tone. 'What's for chow today?' 'How many kids in your family?' 'Would you prefer sea duty or shore duty?'

As the days passed, and the ship settled into its steaming routine, Mr. Deavers picked up the pace with the crew, asking more pointed questions about Chief Twitchell and his attitudes toward the crew members, especially the blacks. He seemed keenly interested in Twitchell's racial attitudes, so much so that he was making the crew uneasy with his insistent questioning.

"He still ain't talked to me," R.J. said. He was playing pinochle in the mess decks with Pea, Gino and Charming Billy. "In fact," he said, taking a trick with a trump. "He ain't talked to Rafer or Andy, either."

Pea put his cards down flat on the table and looked up at R.J. "Ain't nobody here but me, Gino and Billy." He looked around the messdecks conspiratorially. "So tell us what happened to Twitchy. He really fall overboard or..."

"Or did he have help?" Gino finished the question.

R.J. stared at his friends. Billy was looking down at his cards, pretending to be disinterested. "Okay," R.J. said, with a note of impatience. "For the last time, he came up on deck, stumbling around like he always did, the guy had no sea legs, and fell over the lifeline just as the ship made that quick turn to starboard."

Pea and Gino stared unbelieving at their friend. Billy concentrated on his cards. "You gonna stick to that story?" Gino asked.

"Even with us?" Pea asked.

"That's it, fellas. That's what happened." R.J. picked up his cards and looked around the table. "Whose lead is it?"

They had been at sea four days before Deavers got around to talking to Mr. MacDonald, Mr. Almogordo and the exec. Deavers had indicated to the captain that he wanted to meet with the three officers as soon as possible, and the captain had relayed that to them, as Deavers knew he would. The investigator wanted to create some anticipation, some tension in the officers' minds, expecting them to be a little off-balance when he finally interviewed them. He had some success with those tactics when dealing with the enlisted men, but the officers saw through him right away, mainly because Mr. Martin told them what they could expect.

"Ed, it's good to see you again," Deavers stood and held out his hand. The exec smiled grimly and shook it. Deavers had his paperwork spread out in front of him on the green-covered wardroom table, and had stood when the exec, Mac and Pete entered. "I want to apologize for not getting together with you sooner," Deavers explained as the officers sat at the table. "I wanted to talk with the crew first, and well, you know the old saying: *tempus fugit.*" He smiled warmly.

"But you haven't talked with the crew yet," Mr. MacDonald stated irritably. He folded his hands on the table in front of him and glared at the investigator. "The only three witnesses to the incident have yet to be...what do you call it, interviewed?" Mr. Mac hoped he was properly conveying his contempt for Deavers' methods. The exec and Pedro Almogordo stared impassively at the investigator.

Navy Warrant Officers are not commissioned in the traditional manner. They are made officers by a warrant issued by the Secretary of the Navy, usually as a reward for more than fifteen years of loyal service. The warrant is also a personnel-retention tool, used to keep good people in the service.

The warrant officer is painfully aware of how the rest of the Navy views him. Officers consider him to be no more than a high-ranked enlisted man. Enlisted sailors see him as no more than a low-ranked officer. It is a fine distinction, but an important one. As a result, most warrant officers are a little defensive.

"They will be my last interviews, Lieutenant," Mr. Deavers' smile was neither warm nor affable. "And I'll talk to them in my own good time." Mac and Deavers played 'stare-down' until the exec broke it up.

"Let's concentrate on the task at hand, gentlemen," Ed Martin said. He was both firm and soothing. "You have some questions, don't you, Deavers?"

The warm and affable smile returned. "Why, yes," he said warmly. "Yes, I do." He shuffled through his paperwork and selected a single, typed page. "Mr. MacDonald," he began, looking up from the paper. "Why do you think Halsey took the bait and followed the Jap feint to the north instead of covering MacArthur's ass at Leyte Gulf?" He stared, smirking at MacDonald.

MacDonald's jaw tightened, and his eyes flashed anger. He did not like this man, Deavers. Mr. Mac took a slow breath and forced his face to look impassive. "Shingles," he said matter-of-factly. Mr. Mac sat back in his chair, folded his arms, and studied Warrant Officer Deavers.

Deavers seemed amused. "Shingles?" he asked, eyebrows raised.

Mr. Mac took a deep, impatient breath and looked at Deavers as if he were a slow student in the fifth grade. "Halsey missed the greatest carrier battle in history," he explained slowly. "He was in the hospital in Pearl Harbor with a case of shingles when the battle of Midway took place."

"And?" Deavers asked sarcastically.

"And," MacDonald went on, "he wanted to win a big battle, his carriers against the Japs' carriers. That's why he took the chance he took off Cape Engano. For his own glory."

The exec and Pedro Almogordo watched the exchange, their heads pivoting from Deavers to MacDonald as if they were watching a tennis match.

Deavers nodded slowly, seeming to understand. "Well, let me ask you this," he said thoughtfully, looking into Mr. Mac's eyes. "When exactly did you first hear about the death of Chief Machinists Mate Jaspar Twitchell?"

* * * * *

Deavers leaned against the bulkhead on the starboard side of the 02 level, seemingly inspecting the motor whaleboat. He smoked a cigarette and pondered his earlier conversation with the three officers. His gut told him they were hiding something, but he couldn't move them off their original story. Maybe they weren't hiding something. Maybe he was reading too much into the situation. Maybe he was getting too old for this shit. Recently, he had begun to think just that: he was too old for this. He had been tempted to put in his papers several times over the past couple of years. He had twenty two years in. Maybe it was time. He scoffed aloud and threw the cigarette over the side. Tomorrow he would interview the three witnesses. They must be anxious by now, he figured, he'd let them stew long enough. He sent instructions to the three sailors to meet him in the wardroom at 08:30, after breakfast. Tonight he would re-read Chief Twitchell's personnel file and the two reports submitted by Captain Oliver. The personnel file was a bit of a mystery in and of itself. The chief had glowing reports from every commanding officer and engineering officer he ever served with, but he never spent more than two years at any duty station. Deavers felt confident the personnel file held the key to the man, and subsequently the incident. He just had to study it harder.

* * * * *

R.J. fidgeted nervously in the chair. He didn't like being the last to be interviewed. The Sample brothers had each spent about twenty minutes with the investigator, and when they came out, they avoided R.J.'s eyes. The investigator, Deavers, was sitting across the wardroom table, leafing through a file folder. He apparently found what he was looking for, as he pulled out a piece of paper and closed the file. He looked up slowly and smiled at R.J.

"How are you this morning, sailor?" he asked affably.

"Fine, sir," R.J. replied guardedly.

"You've been aboard about...let's see," he leafed through the file again and pulled out another piece of paper. "Eighteen months, that right?"

"Yes, sir." Had it really been a year and a half since he first stepped onto the decks of the Haverfield? To R.J. it seemed like years, so much had happened.

"You like this ship?"

"Yes, sir, I do."

"You know, everyone I talk to says he likes this ship. This must be a special sort of vessel." He smiled and cocked his head, impatient for R.J. to answer.

"I think she is...sir."

"Was Chief Twitchell hard to get along with, R.J.?"

R.J. was uncomfortable with Deavers' addressing him as if he were a friend, and fidgeted around in his chair.

"Well?" Deavers was smiling, his head cocked, eyebrows raised.

"He could be tough, sir."

"Like the time he got you sent to the brig?" Deavers looked up from the file and pointed down at some papers. "Says here he wrote you up for insubordination."

R.J. fidgeted uncomfortably.

"He also caused two of your friends to get brig time," Deavers shuffled through some more papers. "Let's see, Sample, Rafer and Jefferson, Timothy." He closed the file and looked up at R.J. He was not smiling. "Sounds a little hard to get along with to me, sailor."

R.J. shrugged.

Deavers decided to lighten up. "What did you learn during your tour in the brig?"

"You mean besides how to chop boonies, sir?" R.J. decided to lighten up, too.

A flash of anger appeared, then disappeared in Deavers' eyes. He laughed out loud. "I hear you get pretty good at it, after a while."

"Yes, sir," R.J. grinned. He did not trust this man.

"So Twitchell just stumbled and fell over the side, huh?" He was smiling again, and his eyebrows were raised, but his eyes had gone cold. His voice had lowered an octave, and seemed to mock R.J. with the question.

"That's what I saw," R.J. answered, deliberately leaving off the 'sir.'

"That's pretty much what Rafer and Andy told me," Deavers said. "But, I gotta tell you, R.J.," he sat back in his chair and laced his hands behind his head. "Something ain't right here." He rocked slowly back and forth, watching R.J. closely.

R.J. looked up and met Deavers' gaze.

"We're missing an element, here, R.J.," Deavers explained, staring intently into R.J.'s eyes. "What I mean is, part of the story has been cut off. Amputated. It leaves one waiting for the other shoe to drop, if you know what I mean."

R.J. had an idea what he meant. He shrugged.

"It's all a big puzzle, R.J. My job is to put the pieces together so it shows a picture." Deavers leaned forward in his chair and folded his hands on the table. "It's like this: Chief Twitchell came out on deck, stumbled around and fell overboard. See what I mean? Something is missing." He frowned at R.J.'s blank expression. "*Why* did he stumble, *why* did he come out on deck, *what* did he say to any of you, if anything? *If* he didn't stumble and fall over by himself...I'm just saying *if*, here. That would mean someone helped him over the side, and that would mean he was murdered and the only three witnesses to that event keep telling the same story, over and over, as if it had been rehearsed." He leaned back in his chair again and stared at R.J.

R.J. fidgeted and shrugged.

"So tell me, sailor," Deavers said crossly. "Did you and the Sample brothers rehearse your statements?"

* * * * *

R.J. thought he had been with Deavers for about an hour, but the investigator stuck to his schedule of twenty minutes per interview. He knew he was getting nowhere. The officers and the witnesses were all telling the same story. Was it the truth, or were they all in on some sort of conspiracy? Deavers didn't believe in conspiracies. Most of the crimes he investigated were very simple and quickly solved. Besides, four officers, including the CO and exec, colluding with three enlisted men? It was unheard of.

Deavers sat at the wardroom table after R.J. had left, fingering the file and mulling over the just-concluded interview. Just more of the same story. They all tell the same story. Deavers pulled out Twitchell's personnel file. Something in that file was bugging him, but he couldn't figure out what it was. He decided to review the chief's past duty stations again, and was doing so when he spotted it. He smiled to himself, thinking he now had a chance to find out more about Jaspar Twitchell, and maybe discover the missing piece to his puzzle. He closed the file and headed to the radio shack.

* * * * *

"He asked me to transmit a confidential message to someone aboard the Long Beach." RM-1 Murray stood in the captain's cabin, nervously rubbing his hands together.

"So?" the captain asked. "Did you send it?"

"Well, no sir...I mean, he's not authorized to send traffic, is he?"

The captain frowned and thought about it for a moment. "Send whatever he wants, Murray," he said finally. "Tell him I authorized the traffic. Be sure and give me a copy of the message and any reply."

"Aye, sir." Murray left the cabin and headed back to the radio shack, shaking his head. He didn't like Deavers. He considered the man to be sneaky and underhanded, and he was upsetting the balance of the ship. Maybe the investigator knew Murray would clear the message with the captain, maybe he didn't. Either way, Murray didn't care. It was his job to keep the captain informed of all traffic coming in and going out of the radio shack, and he was going to do his job, regardless of what that *warrant officer* wanted.

Murray sat at his speed key and read over Deavers' message again, wondering what the investigator was up to. He shrugged and began sending code very rapidly and skillfully, his fingers lightly tickling the key.

* * * * *

The Haverfield steamed easily at twenty knots toward Pearl Harbor. Her crew performed their jobs quietly, subdued, acutely aware of the presence of an intruder aboard. No drills were held and shipboard routine took over. Duty sections rotated smoothly and the days and nights passed uneventfully, almost tediously as the ship steamed eastward. Two days out of Pearl Harbor the moon began to bloom, nearing fullness, and lighted the path home for the small DER from Guam. Many on board had not been in the United States for two years or more. Hawaii wasn't the mainland, but it sure as hell was a state of the union, therefore home, and the crew looked forward eagerly to their arrival.

Most of the crew had not and would not be interviewed by investigator Deavers, and those who had kept silent, so the crew engaged in speculation and conjecture at every opportunity. The closer they got to Hawaii, the wilder the speculation became.

"I know the Navy, man." Jefferson was sitting on his bunk, offering his theories to anyone who would listen. "They just playin' with my boys. That investigator is gonna make 'em feel real comfy, then BAM! The Navy's gonna hang these guys, you watch and see."

No one took him seriously, but Pea, lying on his side in his bunk, stared, frowning at Jefferson. "Hell, they ain't gonna hang 'em!" he protested angrily. "They didn't do nothing wrong."

"They didn't do shit!" Gino piped in. "This investigator guy's just on board to make everyone nervous. They can't do shit to those dudes." Gino chewed on the inside of his lip, scowling down at the deck. "They can't do shit to 'em," he whispered softly, as if he were trying to convince himself.

* * * * *

R.J. leaned against the starboard flag-bag and basked in the light of the full moon. It was close to midnight, and Billy would take the mid-watch, but R.J. wasn't sleepy. He didn't want to lie in his bunk and stare at the overhead, so he stayed on the signal bridge and watched the moon bathe the blue Pacific in a soft, almost twilight glow. As beautiful as the Pacific was in the trust territory, it seemed even more beautiful as the ship drew closer to the Hawaiian Islands.

It had been eighteen months since R.J. was last in Hawaii, but he had never been to Pearl Harbor. He had flown in on that big MATS jet and had only a short stop-over before he flew another big jet to Guam. He was looking forward to seeing Pearl Harbor. He was looking forward to sailing past the Arizona memorial, the resting place of Mr. Haverfield, and saluting, paying respects to his ship's namesake and the shipmates who forever lay with him.

Pearl Harbor represented even more to R.J. It meant the ending, finally, of the investigation, the inquiry and the tension associated with the Twitchell incident. For better or worse, good or bad, it would finally be behind him and maybe he could relax. Maybe he could sleep again. Maybe he could get rid of the headaches.

Andy seemed oblivious. He seldom allowed his feelings to show anyway, but now his face was a mask of nonexpression. He went about his business as if didn't have a care in the world.

Rafer was a different story. He couldn't get the notion out of his mind that he was responsible for Twitchell's death. His expression ranged from sadness to despair, and he spent all his off-duty time in his bunk, reading his bible. The other Havernauts let him be. He wished he had heard from his father. Maybe his father had written and the letter would catch up to him in Pearl.

R.J. worried about Rafer, and he worried about Andy, too. It didn't seem natural that Andy could take all this in stride. R.J. worried that Andy would let it pile up until it exploded. Who knew what would happen then?

"Hey, R.J.!" Someone whispered to him from the aft ladder. R.J. looked up, listening intently. Was that the wind? He chuckled. ...*tis the wind and nothing more.*

"R.J.! Hey, R.J.!"

R.J. walked to the aft ladder, peering into the dim light, trying to make out who was calling him. "Riley?" he asked, surprised. "That you?"

"Yeah, c'mere!" the voice urged.

R.J. came down the ladder and joined Riley in the dark shadows on the 02 level. "What the hell..."

"Shhh!" Riley clutched R.J.'s arm. "Quiet, will ya?" He looked around anxiously and whispered, "I got something you should see."

* * * * *

Captain Oliver sat in his chair on the flying bridge, sipping black coffee and contemplating the unpredictability of the future. He had spent the evening alone, eating dinner in his cabin while he read the message Deavers had sent to the Long Beach, and the subsequent reply from the cruiser. It seemed Deavers and a Lieutenant (j.g.) Drummond on the Long Beach had served together a few years earlier in Subic Bay. The USS Long Beach was Twitchell's last duty station, and he had served on board the cruiser with Drummond.

Deavers had asked Drummond for a frank appraisal and evaluation of Chief Twitchell, including the reason for his transfer, especially considering the high recommendation from the engineering officer. Drummond accommodated him, beginning his reply with,"...you wanted me to be frank. You asked for it. Please keep this response confidential."

Captain Oliver sighed as he recalled the message from Drummond. All Deavers really had to do was read the reports again and add two and two. It was becoming obvious to Paul Oliver that Twitchell's problem with alcohol was not going to remain a secret for long. What to do about it? Should he cauterize the situation by sitting down with Deavers and explaining to him why they covered up Twitchell's drinking? The ultimate responsibility for the conduct of his ship and crew rested on the shoulders of Commander David Paul Oliver, USN. He accepted that responsibility, and decided he *would* speak with Deavers, as soon as they tied up in Pearl

Harbor. It was not a conversation he looked forward to, but he knew it was his duty.

* * * * *

"Hurry!" Riley whispered. R.J. held the radioman's red flashlight in one hand and the message clipboard in the other. He read Deavers' message to Drummond. He read Drummond's reply twice. He clicked off the light and handed it and the clipboard back to Riley. "Thanks," he muttered.

"What's it mean, R.J.?" Riley whispered.

"I dunno, man," R.J. replied. He went up the ladder and left Riley standing on the 02 level.

R.J. thought about the situation for several hours, sitting on the flag-bag, drinking coffee. Considering Drummond's reply, it was only a matter of time before the whole thing unraveled. He decided to talk with Rafer and Andy, then to Deavers, first thing in the morning. He didn't get any sleep that night, but come morning he was relaxed and alert for his meeting with the investigator.

"I kind of expected you, sailor," Deavers smiled affably as R.J. stepped in and removed his whitehat. "Have a seat." The investigator gestured toward a chair and R.J. sat. Deavers had Drummond's message on the desk in front of him.

R.J. sat, leaning forward with his elbows on his knees. He kneaded his whitehat and waited anxiously.

"I want you to read something," Deavers smiled. "If you haven't read it already." He stared at R.J., obviously enjoying himself. He was sure R.J. had read the message, and that was why he showed up this morning. "You're kind of a leader on this ship, aren't you R.J.?"

R.J. read the message and handed it back to Deavers, ignoring the question. "That message says Chief Twitchell was an abusive drunk who couldn't get along with coloreds," R.J. recited the message almost verbatim. "He was a great engineer, but an embarrassment to the command. The engineering officer had a long, angry talk with him and transferred him to Haverfield because that was the most undesirable duty station he could think of."

Deavers stared into R.J.'s eyes, smiling broadly. "What did you have for breakfast this morning?" he asked in his affable manner.

"Chief Twitchell drank a lot," R.J. said softly but firmly. "He had no sea legs when he was sober..."

"He was drunk that morning, wasn't he?" Deavers demanded, leaning forward and glaring at R.J. "Staggering drunk, right?"

R.J. nodded.

"Did you inform any of the officers of that fact?"

R.J. shook his head.

"So you and the Sample brothers decided not to..."

"It was my idea," R.J. interrupted. "All mine."

"May I ask why?" Deavers leaned back in his chair and looked curiously at R.J. He was no more than a kid, really, but he seemed older, more experienced. He was a leader, without a doubt. Deavers had seen the way R.J.'s friends deferred to him. "I mean, look at this message and these two reports," he shuffled a pile of papers in front of him. "This is a man who is a drunk and a mean son of a bitch. He hates blacks and abuses them every chance he gets. He's done it wherever he's been, so there's a good probability that he did it aboard this ship. Am I wrong?"

R.J. shook his head.

"Then, again, may I ask why? Why cover up for a bastard like that?"

"He was a shipmate," R.J. said, trying not to sound sappy. "We got a proud ship here, Mr. Deavers. The captain and officers treat us well, and we got pride as a crew. You understand, don't you?"

Deavers understood. "I have to write this up, Davis," he said, shaking his head sadly. "You boys made a false report to your superiors. You opened them up for scrutiny and criticism."

"Nobody got hurt," R.J. said stubbornly.

"Nobody but Chief Twitchell," Deavers reminded him sarcastically.

"His record wasn't hurt, sir."

Deavers nodded thoughtfully at R.J. "Don't share this conversation with anyone, sailor," he ordered. "You are dismissed."

R.J. felt a burden lift from his shoulders. He walked out into the sunshine and caught refreshing salt spray as it flew off the bow. Hawaii's offshore winds whipped the ocean, creating creamy whitecaps atop deep blue waves. Oahu was in sight, and the ship's activity was pumped up to an urgent level. They wanted to make a good impression coming into Pearl Harbor. They would pass by Ford Island and the famed 'Battleship Row' where the Arizona lay in residency for all time.

Deavers sat at his desk, thoughtfully drumming his fingers on the stacked reports. He was tired, not just physically, but mentally and emotionally as well. He never slept more than a couple of hours at a time, and when he did sleep, it was the fitful, tossing around kind of sleep that never left him feeling rested. From his first step aboard the Haverfield, he had felt something was being hushed up. Being the suspicious investigator he was, with years of experience under his belt, he naturally expected the worst. Now he knew the truth, he had the missing element, and it did not make him feel triumphant, or happy, or satisfied. It puzzled him more than anything. Those three young sailors had conspired to protect one of their shipmates. But the shipmate in question was an abusive drunk. What would make men want to cover for a man like that? *Why* they did it wasn't as important as the fact that they did it. He looked at his watch. Three hours before the ship docks. He wanted to see Captain Oliver, but he decided to put together the first draft of his report before he met with the captain. Besides, he needed a shave.

He got to work on the report, typing furiously. He was almost finished with his draft when a knock came at the door.

"Enter!"

The door opened and Rafer Sample stuck his head in. He was the messenger of the watch. "Sir? The captain would like to see you as soon as we tie up," Rafer said quietly and began to leave.

"Hold up, sailor," Deavers called to him. "Come in here for a moment."

Rafer stepped into the cabin, looking around nervously. "Yes sir?"

"You're a very religious man, aren't you, Rafer?" Deavers asked gently, leaning forward with his forearms on the desk.

"Yes, sir," Rafer said. "I pray every day."

"Do you pray for Chief Twitchell, Rafer?" Deavers' voice was low and controlled.

Rafer looked into Deavers' eyes, and a spark of recognition passed between them. "I pray for Chief Twitchell every day, sir," Rafer said softly. "I pray for the salvation of his immortal soul."

"Thank you," Deavers smiled gently. "You may tell the captain I will report to him as soon as we are docked."

Rafer closed the door and exhaled. Deavers made him nervous. Rafer was sure Deavers could see right through him. Maybe they shouldn't have okayed R.J.'s plan to talk to the investigator and explain why they said what they said, leaving out the officers, of course. Rafer was sure Deavers held him responsible for Twitchell's death. He said a quick prayer and returned to the bridge.

Deavers stood over the small sink and filled it with hot water. He soaked a washcloth and held it hot against his face, softening his beard. He looked into the mirror above the sink and examined his face. A lot of lines and wrinkles, but the eyes were bright and intelligent looking. Overall he would have to say mature, if not distinguished.

He lathered his face and began shaving in quick, straight strokes. He stopped and stared into the mirror. *Could everything really be that simple?* he mused. *Did a few guys independently decide to protect the reputation of a chief petty officer even though by all reports he was an asshole? Did that really make sense?* He thought of the last several days aboard the Haverfield and how impressed he had been with the operation of the ship. At first he thought the crew banded together to shut him out because he was an interloper, but the investigator began to realize, through observing them on and off duty, that they were a proud crew, and it wasn't just their jobs that brought them pride. He pulled the skin tight on his left cheek and resumed shaving, running his hand behind his razor to make sure the shave was close. His reflection stared back at him defiantly. "What are you looking at?" Deavers asked his image. "I know what you're thinking and the answer is no!" He went back to shaving. His strokes were quicker, more urgent, and he nicked himself behind his ear. "Shit!" He threw the razor into the sink and picked up the wash cloth, dabbing at his ear. "See what you made me do, dammit?" he shouted at his reflection. He leaned over the sink and started laughing. He looked up at his image in the mirror and they both laughed. He splashed cold water on his face, satisfied with the closeness of the shave, and applied a styptic pencil to the cut behind his ear. That stung like hell! He stared at his reflection and thought about his conversations with the Sample brothers and R.J. Davis. *These were good kids who were doing what they thought was right*, the reflection seemed to say. "On the other hand, someone dies, you don't submit a false report," Deavers countered. *But look why they did it,* the reflection argued, *not to damage anyone, but to protect the reputation of a shipmate.*

Deavers splashed after shave on his face and winced at the sting. His reflection winced back at him. "Screw it!" the investigator spat at his image. He walked over to the desk and picked up the draft of his report. He leafed through it briefly and tore it up, dropping the shredded pieces into the waste basket. "Screw it," he repeated. He sat down heavily in the chair and began writing a new report. "I hope you're damn well happy!" he yelled over his shoulder in the direction of the bathroom mirror.

* * * * *

Paradise! R.J. stood on the starboard wing, watching the mouth to Pearl Harbor open in anticipation of another welcome visitor. He watched, awed at the beauty of the Hawaiian Islands. The mountains were much higher than on Guam, and the vegetation seemed greener, lusher. It sure was a lot bigger than Guam! He smiled to himself, admiring the dark green mountains, whose proud peaks reached up into the clouds. *That mountain on Guam,* he thought, *what the hell was the name of that mountain?* He promised himself he would find out as soon as he got back.

They hit the breakwater and the ship slowed, moving gently down the channel toward their berth. As the ship made its way toward Ford Island, all available personnel lined the side for the salute to the Arizona. R.J. stood on the port side of the signal bridge, looking up the channel toward Battleship Row. When the announcement, "Attention to port!" was made he stood at attention, and when the order, "Hand Salute" was announced, he and the crew of the Haverfield paid their respects to the fabled battleship and all the honored men who had died with her...one in particular.

* * * * *

"I don't know if I'm following you, Deavers." Captain Oliver skimmed through the investigator's hastily written report. "Your conclusion is what, exactly?"

"My report concludes that the death of Chief Machinists Mate Jaspar Twitchell was an unfortunate and unavoidable accident. There is no evidence of any wrongdoing or foul play." He smiled at the captain. "I predict the bosses will read my report and conclude that there is no reason for a board of inquiry." He sat down without being invited and crossed his legs. "The reason I'm closing the book on this incident is because I don't care to besmirch or blemish the reputations of some good men." He stared blankly at Captain Oliver. "Or a good ship," he added.

Captain Oliver's face reddened. He stared at the investigator but said nothing.

"I have to inform you, off the record, of course, that the three witnesses to the chief's death rehearsed their testimony and conspired to leave out what could have been important information."

Captain Oliver was growing weary of the pussy-footing. "Deavers," he

477

snapped, holding up a hand. "Just tell me what you're talking about."

Deavers nodded wearily. "All the reports on Twitchell say he was a bad customer, an abusive drunk. He was a racist who antagonized blacks wherever he ran into them. All in all, he was a pretty big prick. But," he held a hand up to stop the captain from interrupting. "Nobody mentions it aboard the Haverfield. I found that strange, so I looked into it. I'm sure you saw the message from the Long Beach." The captain nodded. "Well, the witnesses finally confessed to me that they decided to keep Twitchell's drinking to themselves, because, as Rafer Sample said, 'we don' wanna speak ill of the dead.'"

The captain stared at Deavers and nodded thoughtfully.

Deavers went on. "He was drunk, Captain," he said impatiently. "The chief was drunk and stumbling around back there. He might have seen the Sample brothers, but probably not R.J. He might even have yelled something at them as he staggered around the deck. It would be in character, considering his reputation. Anyway, he's staggering, the ship is rolling, he loses his balance, tumbles over the side just as the ship increases speed and turns to starboard." He looked pleased at his summation. "Bad accident. No fault and no blame to place except with Twitchell. I agree with these three men. There is no reason to bring up the fact that he was drunk. Doesn't change anything but a man's reputation. They took it upon themselves to keep it quiet for the sake of the ship." Deavers stood and held out his hand. "It's been a pleasure being aboard, Captain. I'm very much impressed with your crew."

"Thank you," the captain said, shaking the investigator's hand. "I'm glad to be rid of you." He smiled affably at Deavers, who smiled affably back.

Deavers saluted the OOD on the quarterdeck and the flag on the stern before stepping down the brow to the pier. A black Navy car sat on the pier and Deavers crawled into the back seat. He leaned over the seat and said something to the driver, who nodded and put the car into gear.

The car made its way down the pier toward the Navy base where Deavers had a small office in a small office building, tucked back in a small corner of the base. He sat back against the seat and watched the landscape of Pearl Harbor slide past his window. He had closed the book on the Haverfield incident but doubts lingered in the recesses of his mind. Letting his imagination go wild, he saw Andy Sample throwing the chief overboard. *Andy was a big, strong man, both physically and mentally. Deavers could imagine Andy doing it. Rafer? No, Rafer was too spiritual, too religious. If he had done it, he would surely have confessed just to get right with God. No, Rafer wasn't capable of killing Chief Twitchell or anyone else, for that matter.*

That left R.J. Deavers smiled. R.J. wasn't the type to physically attack someone. He was too friendly, too easy going. He was a thinker and if R.J. wanted to kill someone, he would have thought up some clever way of doing it and making it look like an accident. Deavers grinned to himself. *That's just what we got*, he thought, chuckling. *God, did R.J. pull this off as a well-thought out murder?* He shook his head quickly and decided to stop thinking about it. Instead, he thought about the decision he had made. He was tired, he no longer liked his job, and he had more years in than he wanted to think about. He closed his eyes, put his head back and thought of the next morning, when he would go into Captain Peterson's office and put in his retirement papers. It was time to get out and go fishing. Before the car reached his office, Deavers was sleeping soundly in the back seat.

SEVENTY TWO

"I listened, I agreed, I thanked them and I left," Captain Oliver explained. The exec, MacDonald and Almogordo were gathered around the wardroom table. The captain was describing his meeting with the officers who would have comprised a board of inquiry. Thankfully, the inquiry was unnecessary, thanks to Deavers' report.

"But Deavers knew about Twitchell?" the exec asked.

Captain Oliver nodded. "I wouldn't be surprised if they all knew it," he replied. "It just didn't come up as an issue."

"How about that Deavers?" MacDonald said, shaking his head. "Who woulda figured he'd turn out to be a good guy?"

"Maybe he always was," the exec mused, staring into his coffee cup.

"Please inform our three witnesses, I'm sure they'll welcome the good news," the captain said. "And tell them I'm proud of them."

* * * * *

R.J. enjoyed tidying up the signal bridge. He fussed around, wiping and dusting, arranging and rearranging the flag bags. Three days had gone by since Deavers' report was submitted. The entire Twitchell affair was behind him now, and he felt as if he'd been freed from jail. The headaches were fading, retreating into the back of his head. They didn't hurt when they were in the background, but sometimes, usually in the middle of the night, they would creep up into his forehead and awaken him with blinding pain. When they faded back, they sat right behind his ear, dormant but potentially painful, ready to strike. R.J. called it the 'Raven' period. He knew the specter was there, watching over him, awaiting its chance. Like Poe's Raven it seemed benign, but actually was not. When the pain came forward, R.J. called it the 'Demon.' He was thankful the Demon was subsiding. *A little more time*, R.J. thought. *In time it will go away completely.*

Billy Lopez, messenger of the afternoon watch, came sprinting up the ladder from the 02 level to the signal bridge. He seemed out of breath and came to a screeching halt in front of R.J., who was polishing the mirror on the starboard signal light. R.J. looked up, startled, and smiled when he saw Billy. *Guy walks like he drives*, R.J. thought with affection.

"What's happening, Billy?" he asked, cleaning the last of the smudge off the mirror.

"You got your orders, R.J.," Billy said, holding out a message slip and smiling charmingly. "You got thirty days' leave and then you report to the USS Prairie in Dago! You're leaving tomorrow before we get underway!"

R.J. took the message slip and stared at it, frowning. His mind was still trying to process what Billy said, and it took him a while to connect the two. The Prairie! A destroyer tender...hell...*the* destroyer tender! Home ported in San Diego. R.J. grinned at his friend. "I always liked them Prairie Burgers," he said. "You gonna miss me, Billy?"

Billy got a strange look on his face and R.J. thought the charming one might actually cry. Instead, he handed the message slip to R.J. and put his arms around him in a warm embrace. "This ship ain't gonna be the same without you, R.J.," he said sincerely. "I'm gonna miss you, Teresa's gonna miss you, the Gamboas are gonna miss you and..." he began to tear up. "The baby's gonna miss you, too," he managed to say before he choked up.

R.J. returned the hug. "You gotta do something for me, Billy." R.J. looked into his friend's eyes. "I'm gonna write a letter to Mr. and Mrs. G and I want you to deliver it. Okay, Billy?"

Charming Billy wiped a tear from his eye and managed a mangled smile. "Okay, R.J.," he said. "I promise I'll deliver it to them and I'll send you a picture as soon as the baby's born." Billy left the signal bridge and returned to the quarterdeck.

R.J. looked out at Ford Island and Pearl Harbor and thought of the appointment he and his friends had there in the morning. The ship was due to get underway at noon, again to the Tonkin Gulf, and R.J. and his friends had something they had to do before putting to sea. Now, his friends would be going back to Southeast Asia without him, and he felt a deep sadness. All the training, all the teamwork, all the troubles they had been through together, and, now, when it counted, they would carry on without him. It pained him deeply to think such thoughts. He had to tell his friends about his transfer sometime, but he wanted to put it off as long as he could.

After evening chow, R.J. decided to tell Gino and Pea about the transfer. He didn't want to wait until morning, when they had a mission to accomplish. He didn't want to detract from that. Their morning mission was extremely important; nothing must interfere with that. They had made a pact. They'd made a promise to someone who had died almost a quarter century before.

Pea started crying. They had gathered on the focsul to watch the harbor and talk. Gino and Pea were the first ones R.J. told, and the little guy broke into tears.

"I thought you was a tough guy," R.J. kidded him.

"Yeah," Gino said, snaking his arm around Pea's shoulder and squeezing him affectionately. "I guess all this time you just been a fag at heart, huh?"

"Fugh yue," Pea sobbed. "Ah'm gohne mish 'im!" He blew his nose on his handkerchief and stuffed it into his back pocket.

"I'm sorry you're goin' buddy," Gino said, giving R.J. a hug. "But you're goin' back to the *world*, my man. Back to the fuckin' world!"

"I think I'd rather be with Momma Haverfield a little longer," R.J. replied sadly. "I mean, this is so sudden, I never had a chance to be short."

"Well, you short now," Pea wiped his eyes. "You only got a wake-up and you gone." He started crying again and gave Gino the finger when he laughed at him. "Fugh yue!" he sobbed.

"Let's hit the beach and get shit-faced!" Gino suggested. "We got some celebrating to do!"

"Okay," R.J. agreed. "But remember our mission tomorrow."

Gino and Pea both nodded solemnly.

That evening, before they left on liberty, R.J. sat down and wrote a letter to the Gamboas for Billy to deliver.

> *Dear Mr. and Mrs. Gamboa,*
>
> *I always thought I would have a chance to say goodbye to you in person, but the Navy doesn't always check with us before they transfer us. Anyway, I wanted you to know how welcome you made us all feel in your home. You truly were the parents away from home that all of us needed, and I know all my shipmates agree with me when I say we love you like our own family.*
>
> *No matter how old I get, no matter what happens in my life, I will always cherish those times we shared on Saturdays, working on the trailer and discussing the world. I will never forget your love and your kindness.*
>
> *When I write my book I promise to send you the first copy.*
>
> *Please take care of yourselves, and remember I love you. And that goes for Bobby, too.*
>
> *R.J.*

Satisfied, R.J. wiped tears from his eyes, put the letter in an envelope and handed it over to Charming Billy.

*　*　*　*　*

"Man, I wish I were going with you, Paul," Lieutenant Commander Bill Wilson said. Captain Oliver sat with two old friends, academy classmates, sipping after dinner drinks, smoking and catching up at the Officer's Club.

"Me, too." Ken Summers, a thin commander with a cigarette constantly hanging from his mouth joined in. "But, we'll be there in a few months." He put out his cigarette and lit another. "Unless you've got it won by then."

Bill Wilson nodded. "This crap ain't a proper war," he complained. "Hell, put enough force in country and sweep the little yellow bastards away. This ain't a war, fellas. This ain't even a Korea. It's more like a small regional conflict."

"I'm not so sure," Paul said, lighting his pipe. "They fought off the French in a protracted guerrilla war that had to cost that country a lot of money and men. If we aren't careful, we can get stuck there just like we did in Korea."

"All the more reason to just overpower the North Vietnamese. Hell, we got enough firepower to wipe out half the world, we ain't gonna take crap off some little communist bastard like Ho Chi Minh."

Paul had stopped listening. He caught an image in the mirror behind the bar and he turned in his seat, looking past the dance floor. Lorelei Prescott and another woman had arrived and were talking to an officer near the door.

She seemed to be listening intently to the officer, and she glanced briefly over his shoulder, spotting Paul sitting with his friends. She looked quickly back at the officer. Her smile had broadened, and her eyes kept darting toward Paul. Eventually, she pried herself away and came walking straight to Paul's table. All three officers rose as she approached, and Paul took her offered hand.

"Commander Oliver, it is good to see you again," she said graciously, nodding to his table companions. Paul introduced her to his friends and held out a chair which she settled into. "I can only stay a second," she cooed. Those violet eyes reached out for him, drawing him in...

"We were just leaving," Bill said. He stood and held out his hand to Lorelei and then to Paul. "Good luck, buddy. Take care over there, you hear?"

"And leave some for the rest of us," Ken said, shaking his friend's hand. "God speed." They picked up their caps at the door and stepped out onto the driveway.

"Nice looking lady," Ken Summers said.

"Admiral Prescott's wife," Bill Wilson replied.

Ken Summers looked at his friend and raised his eyebrows.

Bill Wilson shrugged. "There were rumors, but I never paid any attention to them."

"He does have good taste," Ken said, looking up and down the drive. "Think we can get a cab? Let's go downtown."

* * * * *

"I thought you were in Subic." Paul sipped his drink and looked into those violet eyes.

"I was, but now I'm here." She sounded tart, impatient, and looked around the room. "It's a little crowded in here." She turned and concentrated her attention on Captain Oliver. "How have you been, Paul?"

"Good. We saw a little action in the Tonkin Gulf," he said, brightening.

"I heard," she said, holding a cigarette to her lips and waiting for him to light it.

"We lost a crew member in an accident." He lit her cigarette with a kitchen match and shook it out, dropping it into the ashtray.

"I heard that too," she inhaled and blew smoke out slowly. "I hear all the rumors."

"Rumors?" he asked.

"Yes, Paul," she leaned forward, giving him a view of her lovely bosom. "You're a big hero around CINCPACFLT." She was annoyed that he continued to look directly into her eyes. She shifted her weight slightly, bringing her breasts into better focus.

"What do you mean, Lorelei?" he asked guardedly. "I am no hero, I promise you that."

"I know all and see all, just like a carnival fortune teller," she chirped. She tossed her head, throwing her hair back. "Will you please order me a drink?"

Paul signaled to a waiter and ordered a vodka gimlet, up, just the way she liked them. "What rumors have you heard?" he asked.

"Let's go somewhere else," she said, looking around, annoyed.

"Where?"

"I dunno. My place?"

Paul studied Lorelei's face. This was not the woman he remembered, the vibrant, energetic, lovely woman who charmed everyone while on the arm of Admiral Prescott. She had hardened in a short period of time.

"Lorelei," he said softly. "What's wrong?"

"Not here," she said, looking into his eyes. "I have a car. Let's go for a ride in the hills, like we used to do on Guam." She smiled brightly and stood. "Will you get my wrap for me?" she asked, handing him a ticket. "I checked it when I came in." She gulped down her gimlet and set the glass on the table.

They drove along the coast until they found a quiet beach with a small parking lot. Lorelei pulled in and parked close to the sand. "It reminds me of the USO beach on Guam," she said. She turned off the engine and the lights and leaned back against the door. She kicked off her shoes and put her stocking feet in Paul's lap. "Quentin and I aren't getting along." She said it matter-of-factly, as if Paul already knew it. "That's why I stayed here while he rushed back to his beloved command."

"What did you mean, I'm a hero?" Paul massaged her feet absently and stared straight ahead, through the windshield, ignoring her comment about Admiral Prescott. "What have you heard?"

"Everyone heard about your crew, how loyal they are to you, what a great job you've done with your ship, how you're on a fast-track to flag rank, you know, stuff like that." She pulled her feet back and sat up straight. "The official report is one thing, Paul, but the facts are often very different." She produced another cigarette and he pushed in the lighter on the dashboard. "It's just a rumor, but word is that a few members of your crew covered up a chief petty officer's drinking problem to protect his reputation. And that was the same chief petty officer who died...accidentally."

Paul shook his head slowly. "And you really think the Navy would overlook something like that?"

"The Navy is proud of your ship, Paul. Your crew is very loyal and very efficient. The Navy needs ships like yours. Especially now." She made it sound sarcastic.

"So, you know where I'm going?"

"Oh, hell, Paul." She puffed at her cigarette and blew blue smoke out the window. "Everyone knows where you're going."

"So why aren't you in the Philippines," he asked.

"Don't want to be," she said flatly.

"Why?"

"I don't want to talk about it." She turned in her seat and stared at the ocean.

"Sure you do," he said patiently, taking her hand. "What is it, Lorelei?"

"I'm miserable, that's what it is!" She was crying suddenly. She scooted over in the seat, laying her head on his shoulder. "I thought I could do anything," she sobbed. "I thought I was invincible."

He handed her a handkerchief and she dabbed at her eyes. "You want to talk about it?" he asked gently.

"I lost you, Paul."

Paul Oliver felt himself tighten up. He looked around the parking lot, afraid to hear more.

"I blew it and I know it, and now I'm miserable." She looked up at his face. "I'm sorry, Paul."

"I don't know what to say." His thoughts returned to his ship. "I'm getting underway in the morning." He stared down at her tear-stained face, and all he could think about was his ship.

"Can we have tonight, Paul?"

He looked deeply into her violet eyes and listened for the sounds of water crashing over rocks, but he heard nothing. The siren song was silenced, the danger of the shoals disappeared. Paul felt he had safely navigated around the danger, had resisted the siren call, and had emerged undamaged, his ship intact. "No," he said simply.

PART FIVE:

DEPARTURE

SEVENTY THREE

Pearl Harbor, Hawaii
August, 1964

It was a mission, not a sightseeing trip. They took the shuttle bus from the pier toward the Arizona memorial, all five of them unusually silent on the ride. R.J. had procured a pint of Jack Daniel's and kept it hidden down the front of his trousers, tucked in neatly behind his shiny brass belt buckle. They took a water taxi out to where the Arizona rested.

Climbing out of the water taxi, they walked together to the observation platform built over the dead hulk of the battleship, and stared through the large, glassless windows down into the water of Pearl Harbor. The rusted stack of the battleship pierced the surface of the water, and even after twenty-three years, oil still leaked from the sunken Arizona, a lonely and sorrowful sight, bubbling up from the dead battleship as if to say, "Don't forget us. Don't *ever* forget."

R.J. opened the bottle and held it up over the railing. "To James Wallace Haverfield," he said solemnly. "May God bless his soul." He took a long pull on the bottle and handed it over to Rafer, who took it, looked down at the water and drank his first ever shot of whiskey. "James Wallace Haverfield," he saluted. "May God rest his soul."

It was Andy's turn next. He took the bottle and gulped down a big drink. "To James Wallace Haverfield," he said, coughing a little. "God rest his soul." Without looking, he handed the bottle to Gino.

"James Wallace Haverfield," Gino toasted, holding the bottle in the air. "May God bless him." He handed the bottle to Pea.

Tears streamed down Pea's face as he took the bottle and gazed down into the water. He sobbed slightly, then shook his head as if trying to shake off the emotion. He raised the bottle without looking at it, his gaze fixed on the murky water of the harbor where the oil bubbled up and sat, the sun reflecting a glimmering rainbow of colors off the oil-stained surface. "To James Wallace Haverfield," he proclaimed, a little louder than necessary. "God bless him." He took a long drink and swallowed it down, grimacing at the burning in his throat.

The Haverfield sailors stared down into the water at the still visible top of the Arizona's stack and tried to imagine the terror and fear of December seventh, nineteen forty-one. Their thoughts were interrupted by a self-conscious cough behind them. They turned in unison and saw Lieutenant MacDonald standing a few feet behind them. He stood back hesitantly, almost shyly, searching their faces.

Pea stepped toward Mr. MacDonald and held out the bottle to him. "Sir," he asked quietly. "Will you join us?"

Mr. MacDonald stepped forward to the railing and took the bottle from Pea. He raised it in the air. "James Wallace Haverfield," he announced in a strong voice. "God bless his soul." He drank the remaining whiskey in the bottle and looked around at his Havernauts, who smiled and nodded to him. The lieutenant nodded back and slowly dropped the bottle into the water where it bobbed and floated for a bit until it filled with water and sank, joining the crew of the Arizona on the bottom.

"They came in right over Palikea Peak," Mr. Mac said, suddenly breaking the silence and pointing toward the high hills to the west. "Those were the torpedo planes. The dive bombers came from that direction, over the village of Ewa." He pointed again, this time to the southwest. "It wasn't zero-eight-hundred yet, and most of the ships' crews were still asleep. The Japs had developed a new, shallow water torpedo and they were anxious to try it out." He looked back down at the water and the sleeping battleship below. "The Arizona was hit just after eight A.M., but not from a torpedo. Some people say a bomb dropped down her stack, but Navy engineers think the bomb went through her deck and into an ammunition magazine. Anyway, she sank in about nine minutes." He shook his head sadly. "Mr. Haverfield and most of his shipmates never had a chance. The ship sank so quickly that those who were still alive were trapped below decks." He took a deep breath and let it out slowly. "Nobody knows how long they lived down there."

"Jesus," Gino whispered and crossed himself.

"The Oklahoma took several torpedoes and sank," Mr. Mac continued, pointing toward Ford Island. "The California and the West Virginia sank at the pier, and the Utah flipped over, capsizing with her crew also trapped below." Mr. Mac took off his hat and ran his hands through his hair. "The Maryland, the Utah, the Tennessee were heavily damaged. The Nevada almost got out to sea, but got nailed by several bombs and was deliberately run aground by her crew. They didn't want her to sink inside the harbor mouth, where the ship could block the entrance.

"All told, after two waves of bombers and torpedo planes, the attack was over. The battleship fleet was destroyed, left burning and sinking. Thank God Bull Halsey had the foresight to keep his carrier forces at sea. You fellows know the rest."

The group of sailors nodded, recalling the story of the Pearl Harbor attack. After a few awkward moments, they climbed into the water taxi and sat quietly, most of them staring down at the deck. R.J. sat in the stern, looking back at the Arizona memorial. He would probably see it again. The Prairie was sure to visit Pearl Harbor, but he knew it wouldn't be the same. The moment he had shared with his friends and Mr. Mac had been truly special. He was grateful that his first visit to the monument was with men he liked and respected, hell, even loved. They had experienced a great deal of life together; many shared episodes, both good and bad. Now they were separating. Rafer and Andy were headed to Pensacola, R.J. to the Prairie, Pea and Gino back to the Haverfield, along with Mr. Mac.

They climbed out of the water taxi and caught a shuttle. They rode in silence as the bus made its way around the base, making its stops, toward the Haverfield's berth.

The shuttle arrived at the pier, and Gino, Pea and Mr. Mac got off. R.J. followed.

"Hold up!" Andy Sample instructed the shuttle driver. He and Rafer got off the bus and shook hands silently with Mr. Mac, Gino and Pea. Andy grabbed R.J. in a bear hug and crushed him. "Gonna miss you, white boy!" He laughed. R.J. struggled to catch his breath.

Rafer came up to R.J. and looked into his eyes. R.J. could almost feel the pain he saw on his friend's face. Rafer nodded slowly, smiled slightly, and put his arms around R.J., patting him firmly on the back.

"You a good man, R.J.," he said quietly. "You got a good heart."

"It was an accident, Rafer," R.J. whispered.

Rafer looked over at the harbor and sighed as he stared intently at the water. Without looking at R.J. he said in a quiet, peaceful voice, "It's somethin' I have to carry. It's my burden, and I'll carry it for the rest of my life." Rafer looked up and stared, transfixed, at the high, green volcanic mountains. "I got a letter from my daddy, and I feel better. I know what my destiny is. Like Doctor King said '...mine eyes have seen the glory...'" He looked back at R.J. and it seemed the pain was gone from his eyes. It was replaced by an inner confidence inspired with hope. His voice trailed off and he managed a weak smile. "I'm gonna make up for it, R.J.," he said. His face looked peaceful as he said it, as if he had made an important decision and, by doing so, felt a lifting of the burden. He continued the small smile. "Don't forget the struggle, R.J.," he said quietly. "You gotta write that book, so's everybody knows what happened and why. Nobody can tell the story 'cept you."

Rafer jumped onto the shuttle bus. "You ever find y'self in Alabama, you c'mon by, hear?" Andy joined him and the shuttle jerked away, the driver grinding the gears like Charming Billy.

R.J. watched the shuttle pull away and rubbed the back of his neck. His headache was in the Raven period, and R.J. hoped the Demon wouldn't slip its way through. "I'll write the story, Rafer," he mumbled, rubbing at his temples with the heels of his hands.

He shook off the headache and followed Pea and Gino down the dock toward the ship. Pea turned around, pretending to be surprised R.J. was following behind them.

"Where you goin', flag-fag?" Pea teased him.

"I'm goin' to see you girls off," R.J. teased back.

"You're just hopin' the captain changed his mind and you're not leaving," Gino laughed. "You already homesick for the Haverbucket."

R.J. laughed, but he had to admit Gino was not far off.

Gino's face became serious. "You gonna write to her?" he asked.

"Naw, just let it lay," R.J. answered, looking out into the harbor. "She'll get back to her life with Gary, and I..." he let the thought drift off and they walked down the pier in silence.

"We're going to miss you, Davis," Mr. Mac said when they reached the foot of the brow. "Momma Haverfield won't seem the same without you."

"I wish I were going with you, sir," R.J. replied. "It's like you guys are going off to war and I'm stuck ashore."

MacDonald chuckled. "It's just a patrol in the South China Sea," he said reassuringly. "If we have trouble, it's gonna be from little P.T. boats, and you know what we do to them." He smiled and his eyes twinkled. "Besides, this little affair is going to be over in a few months. Most people have never heard of Viet Nam, and probably never will."

"Lyndon Johnson is making it sound like another police action," R.J. said. "Some people are already saying it's gonna be another Korea, or worse."

Mr. MacDonald scoffed. "Not this time, lad," he said, shaking his head. "Like I said, it'll be over quickly. We learned our lesson in Korea, you can mark my words."

R.J. offered his hand. "I'm gonna miss your stories, Mr. Mac," he grinned. "You taught us a lot about history...our history."

"You take care of yourself, sailor," Mr. Mac said, taking R.J.'s hand and shaking it. "Remember to always take *forward* steps."

"Aye, aye, sir." R.J. saluted, and Mr. MacDonald returned the salute, then turned and walked up the brow.

Pea and Gino each hugged R.J. and walked up the brow to the quarter-deck. They were just in time. As soon as they were aboard, the 1-MC began blaring. "Now hear this, set the special sea and anchor detail! Make all preparations for getting underway!" Pea and Gino ran below to change into their dungarees as the crew began to single up lines. When they returned to the fantail they waved to R.J. one last time and rushed to their stations.

Up on the signal bridge, Billy was waving his arms, indicating he had a message. R.J. signaled 'K' and Billy began sending semaphore. "So long, buddy," it said. "Keep in touch."

R.J. held his arms straight out from his sides in the signal for the letter, 'R,' receipting for the message. He was going to miss Billy.

Up on the 02 level, Lester leaned against the lifeline, sipping coffee. He caught R.J.'s eye and slowly lifted his middle finger in the air, his face expressionless. R.J. grinned and returned the salute. Lester laughed.

The Haverfield's engines began turning, the screws churning up the water under the stern, and R.J. shuddered at the sound. *Forget it*, a voice in his head whispered. *It was an accident!*

"Hey, queer-bait!" Big Queen was standing near the stern, eating ice cream out of a paper cup with a plastic spoon. The spoon looked ridiculously small in the big man's massive fist, and R.J. marveled at how he could shovel the ice cream into his mouth so fast with such a little spoon. Chief Whipple stood next to Queen with a bemused look on his face.

"You got transferred, didn't you, skivvy waver?" Queen roared, grinning widely. Ice cream leaked out of the spaces between his big teeth. "You on leave now, right?"

"That's right, Queenie," R.J. called back.

"So get yer lily-white ass outta here, shitbird!" Queen grinned and waved his spoon in the air. R.J. waved back. Chief Whipple stood there, watching R.J. and nodding his head slowly. A smile crept onto his face and he seemed pleased. R.J. shook his head. In all the time he was on the Haverfield, he'd never seen Chief Whipple smile. No one had. It wasn't much of a smile, the man having so little experience, and it looked like it hurt.

The ship cast off and began backing away from the pier. The captain pointed her bow toward the channel and the Haverfield turned slowly, moving smoothly away down the harbor toward the breakwater.

R.J. stood on the pilings and watched the ship, *his* ship, sail away without him, and he felt a heavy sadness clutch his heart. His home for a year and a half *was* disappearing over the horizon with his good friends aboard. It felt like a dream, one which would soon be over, and then he'd wake up to find it was just a dream. A dream within a dream.

The ship moved away slowly, showing him her backside on which was lettered, *HAVERFIELD*. He watched her fade and become smaller until he could no longer read the name on the stern. "Oh, well," he muttered. "Back to reality."

He started to turn and leave when he realized he was not alone on the pier. A fresh-faced young seaman apprentice, looking like he just got off the bus from boot camp, stood near R.J., watching him watch the Haverfield sail away.

"That musta been your ship," the young sailor said, smiling sheepishly. "I mean, the way you looked when you saw it leavin'."

R.J. gave the kid a dirty look. "Fuck you, Wog," he said dismissively. Then he turned and took his first step, a forward step to be sure, toward Longmont, Colorado. He had a wedding to attend.

THE END

EPILOGUE:

(VIEW OF THE DEMON)

Laguna Hills, California
January, 2003

R.J. snapped open his cell phone and punched in the number. His heart jumped as the connection was made and the phone rang on the other end. He was tempted to hang up, hoping no one would answer. On the seventh ring the phone picked up and a deep voice answered, "Hullo?"

R.J. couldn't determine the age of the person answering the phone, so he asked, "Is Rafer there?"

A long pause ensued. Then, "He ain't here rat now." The voice spoke to someone else in the room, then came back on the line. "I can take a message, if y'like."

"Is Andy there?" R.J. asked.

"This here's Andy," the voice answered, sounding deep and confident, just like R.J. remembered Andy Sample sounding.

"Andy, this is R.J. Davis."

A long pause, then, "You probly lookin' for my daddy," the voice said. "He ain't here, but he be back in a minute."

"You Andy, Junior?" R.J. asked.

"Yessir," the voice answered. "You wanna talk to my daddy?"

"I want to talk to Rafer, Junior," R.J said.

Another long pause. "Who callin'?"

"Like I said, this is R.J. Davis. Rafer Junior wrote to me asking me to call."

More off-line conversations, then. "Hol' on. He comin'." The phone was set down with a loud clump. Then a bright-sounding voice came on the line.

"This is Rafer. You Mr. R.J.?" It sounded so much like Rafer Sample, R.J. almost dropped the phone.

"I got your letter," was all R.J. could manage to say.

"Yessir," the voice said. There were hurried conversations going on in the background, but R.J. couldn't make out what was being said.

"I appreciate you called," Rafer Junior said. "I been wantin' to talk to you." His voice was tired, resigned, full of emotion. "My daddy died," he said softly.

"What can I do for you?" R.J. asked, dreading the answer he knew would come.

"Tell me," Rafer Junior said. "Tell me what happened on that ship."

R.J. took a deep breath and tried to get his heart to slow down. Then he told him. He told him everything, leaving nothing out. He told him about Chief Twitchell and his hatred of blacks. He told him about the Havernauts and the ship and the officers. He recalled stories about Yokosuka and the Philippines and patrolling the Trust Territory. He told Rafer Junior his father was a hero. Rafer had stood up to racism when many thought it was no big deal, and he did so with pride and honor.

R.J. told him all about that dark August morning in the Tonkin Gulf. He shared details he thought he had forgotten. In the retelling, it came back to him in amazing clarity. He recalled every scene, every movement. He could see the sky and the water of the Gulf, he could smell the salt air, and hear Chief Twitchell roaring drunkenly. He described how the chief rushed toward Rafer and how Rafer had stepped aside...

"It was an accident," R.J. repeated wearily. "A stupid accident." The headache began to whisper to him; he winced and rubbed the bridge of his nose.

"My daddy never would talk about it," Rafer Junior said. "But he tol' me somethin' had happened that changed his life and brought him to the Lord. It was why he did the Lord's work. He used to tell me that."

"The Lord's work?"

"Yessir. My daddy is...was the minister of our church. He took over when his daddy died."

R.J. smiled to himself and nodded. "I can see him doing that," he said softly into the phone. "Who takes over now?"

"I do, sir. It's my time."

They talked for an hour, and R.J. answered every question the young man had. He felt the tension come out of Rafer Junior's voice. He relaxed, and R.J. thought he sounded very much like Rafer. He seemed to be comfortable with R.J., and peppered him with questions about his father, his uncle Andy, and the Haverfield and its crew. He seemed to relish the stories, and R.J. realized it was because he had never heard them before. Neither Rafer nor Andy had told him much of anything. As the conversation wore down, R.J. began to feel drawn and empty, like he had nothing more to give. The headache moved behind his ear and he felt heavy, burdened, as if Rafer Junior's burden had somehow been transferred to him.

"I'm glad you called, Mr. R.J.," Rafer Junior said respectfully. "My uncle Andy is here. You wanna talk to him?"

"I'd like to say hello."

Andy Sample came on the phone. "R.J.! How you doin', boy?" Same booming voice, full of laughter.

"Good, big guy. How're you?"

"I tell you, I may be gettin' old, but I'm still a damn sight better'n a wet night in Atlanta!"

R.J. chuckled. Same old Andy. "I'm sorry about Rafer," he said softly.

Andy's voice grew softer, too. "He died happy, R.J. He died just as he always wanted. He was finally at peace with himself, and finally felt right with the world. He took over our daddy's church, you know?"

"Rafer Junior told me."

"His whole life was the church," Andy's voice wavered just a bit. "He was the kindest man I ever knew next to my daddy." This time his voice broke.

"Andy?"

"Yeah?" The voice was back, strong.

"How come you guys never told Rafer Junior about what happened?"

Andy paused, and R.J. thought for a moment he had lost the connection. In a quiet voice Andy said, "Rafer always said you had to be the one to tell the story."

Rafer said...

"What?" R.J. asked hoarsely. "Me?"

"Rafer talked about you all the time," Andy's voice became serious. "He said of all the people on that ship, you was the one with the honest heart. He say if anybody was gonna make a true difference in this world it would be R.J." Andy sniffled and coughed self-consciously. "He believed in the struggle, y'know? He dedicated his life to it. Even after all the politics and bullshit took over, he believed in the movement. He used to get so tired of a long day...sometimes he come home all sad and draggin, y'know?"

Yeah, I know.

"He used to tell me all the time how R.J. was gonna do some important work. Gonna write some important book, somethin' like that. He said when the time come for Junior to know, then R.J. have to be the one to tell it 'cause he can tell it better than anyone."

R.J. said nothing, his mind suddenly caught up in so many memories, all bombarding his thoughts at once. *Rafer was the one with the honest heart. Rafer went home to face his heritage, and his destiny...He walked the walk.*

"So, you write that book, white boy?" Andy's laughing voice returned.

"Not yet," R.J. admitted. *But Rafer would have written it, because he said he would.*

"Well, send me a copy when you do, hear? Nice talkin' to you, R.J."

"You, too Andy."

I never went back home to face myself. I ran away and stayed away. I never saw a black face staring at me in the mirror. I passed for white because my skin was white. In Denver I would have been a nigger, but here I'm just another white face.

R.J. snapped the cell phone shut and slid out of the booth, making his way slowly, painfully to the restroom. He locked the door and stood in front of the big mirror above the sink, spread his hands on the counter and leaned forward, staring into his reflection. The cocky young sailor of forty years ago had disappeared, to be replaced with the tired old man who stared back at him. Dark circles hung under his eyes. His face was splotched with tiny red veins, put there from years of too much bourbon. Lines creased his cheeks and sagging jowls were forming on his jaw. His once dark, full hair was thinning and becoming gray. His eyes, still blue, were dull and life-less. The raven's shadow floated over him, bringing with it the dreaded headache, and he became despondent. Andy's words echoed in his mind. "You write that book, white boy?"

So many high youthful ideals, so many grand plans to change the face of the world. Rafer did all he said he would do and I...I...

He shook his head sadly and whispered, "Nevermore." He stared at the reflection for a long time, and then he began to weep. He hung his head and wept sadly, forlornly. He wept for Rafer and Andy, for Rafer Junior and for all the young sailors of the Haverfield. He even wept for Chief Twitchell. But mostly he wept for himself, for lost promise, for broken dreams and for forty long years rendered into dust by the inevitable grinding march of time. His tears flowed freely and splashed down into the porcelain sink, and he sobbed aloud, but because there was no one there to hear him, he made no sound.

ACKNOWLEDGMENTS

Special thanks to Debbie Hall of Hallway Productions, Las Vegas, Nevada for her expert editing job, and for all her encouragement, kind words and hard work.

Warmest thanks to my sisters who read the manuscript and commented on it: Terri Borchert and Nancy Martin of Denver, Colorado, and my daughter, Margaret Bristol of Lawrenceville, Georgia.

Thanks especially to my buddies who read the manuscript for me: Tom Jolicoeur of Newport Beach, California, Roger Lamb of Las Vegas, Nevada, Tom McCarthy of Wildomar, California, Tom "Bones" Lyons of Lake Havasu City, AZ and Mike Metzner of Laguna Niguel, California.

Heartfelt thanks to my dear friend, David Paul Oliver for lending his name to the captain of the Haverfield, and for all his encouragement and friendship over the past thirty five years.

And every day, with every breath I take, I thank God for Therese!

MUSIC CREDITS

"Sincerely"
The Moonglows
Music & Lyrics by
Harvey Fuqua &
Alan Freed
1954

"Do You Love Me?"
The Contours
Music & Lyrics by
Berry Gordy
1962

"The Man Who Shot Liberty Valance"
Gene Pitney
Music by Burt Bacharach
Lyrics by Hal David
1962

"Let's Dance"
Chris Montez
Music & Lyrics by Jim Lee
1962

"I Need Your Lovin'"
Don Gardner & Dee Dee Ford
Music & Lyrics by Don Gardner,
Bobby Robinson, James McDougal &
Clarence Lewis
1962

"Blue Moon"
The Marcels
Music by Richard Rogers
Lyrics by Lorenz Hart
1961

"Daddy's Home"
Shep & The Limelights
Music & Lyrics by
William Miller & James Shepard
1961

"Duke of Earl"
Gene Chandler
Music & Lyrics by Earl Edwards,
 Bernie Williams and Eugene Dixon
1962

"I Left My Heart in San Francisco"
Tony Bennett
Music by George Cory Jr.
Lyrics by Douglass Cross
1954

"You Really Got a Hold on Me"
Smokey Robinson & the Miracles
Music & Lyrics by William Robinson
1962

"Tear Drops"
Lee Andrews & the Hearts
Music & Lyrics by Edwin Charles,
Helen Stanley, Roy Calhoun &
Barry Golder
1957

"The Battle of New Orleans"
Johnny Preston
Music & Lyrics by Jimmy Driftwood
1960

"Just One Look"
Doris Troy
Music & Lyrics by Doris Payne &
Gregory Carroll
1963

"That'll Be the Day"
Buddy Holly & The Crickets
Music & Lyrics by Jerry Allison,.
Buddy Holly and Norman Petty
1957

"A Thousand Miles Away"
The Heartbeats
Music & Lyrics by James Shepard &
William H. Miller
1956

"Goodnight My Love"
Jesse Belvin
Music & Lyrics by George Motola &
John Marasalco
1956

"(I'll Remember) In the Still of the Night"
The Five Satins
Music & Lyrics by Fred Parish
1956

"Why Do Fools Fall in Love"
Frankie Lymon & The Teenagers
Music & Lyrics by F. Lymon & G. Goldner
1956